# The Words of the Pitcher

## Kei Swanson

RED SLIPPER

Red Slipper is an imprint of
Genesis Press, Inc.
315 Third Avenue North
Columbus, Mississippi 39701

Copyright © 2000 by Kei Swanson

The Words of the Pitcher

**ISBN 1-58571-014-8**

Manufactured in the United States of America

FIRST EDITION

This novel is dedicated to
My ever supportive
Husband, Tom,
And
My son,
Robert

*Enjoy the game*

# The Words of the Pitcher

*K. Sawamura*

# Chapter One

"Claire?" Dr. Carl Ramstein called at door of the shadowy office. He could see movement inside the room, but not a person.

He heard a thump followed by, "Wha...?"

"Claire."

The professor stepped farther into the room. He saw only a desk and adjacent computer station with its printer, monitor, and CPU. All across the desk was the clutter of knowledge. Claire Ferris's research work was evident everywhere...books, papers...print-outs, scribblings on scraps, lists on note cards...pens, pencils. A lamp shone over the landscape of academia.

Dr. Ramstein spotted Claire as she crawled from the kneehole of the desk. Her oval face, with its clear complexion, had a red flush over her cheeks in evidence of pain and disgust at having hit her head. In an instant, tears pooled and ebbed in her gray-green eyes as she blinked at the professor.

Claire rubbed her crown and rose from the floor.

"Hello, sir."

"Are you all right?" He came to the front of Claire's desk. "What were you doing down there?"

"I'm fine," Claire spat. Ramstein didn't know if she was angry at him or the desk. "I was looking up some stuff in Turnbull's Book of the Samurai. I spread it out on the floor since..." She waved her hand over her desk.

"You're certainly persistent, young lady. I've never had a doctoral candidate so eager to finish her dissertation."

"I don't have anything else to do, sir." Claire flopped into her chair. She pushed long bangs from her eyes and flipped waist-long hair over her shoulders.

"Oh? Shouldn't you be out socializing with some young man? It's Friday night."

"I don't...do that much." Claire picked up a pair of black, large-framed glasses and put them on her face as if to shield herself from Dr. Ramstein's personal attack. "Why were you looking for me?"

"What do you know about baseball?"

"I know where Jacobs Field is."

"That's a start. Don't you follow the Tribe?" He used the nickname of the Cleveland Chiefs major league baseball team.

"As a native Clevelander, I'm sorry to confess that I don't." Claire eased back in the chair. The professor noticed the bare feet she pulled up under her. She wore a T-shirt, sweat pants, and a hooded sweat shirt jacket, all navy blue.

"Well, you're about to learn a whole lot. The front office called and asked me to recommend someone to interpret for them."

"Dr. Ramstein, I'm not a Spanish linguist!" Claire blurted out. She removed her reading glasses and placed them on her desk.

"Yes, I know. And I can't fault you for assuming I meant translating for one of the Puerto Rican players. This is in your area of expertise. They've signed a new player, a free agent from Nagasaki, and are having a problem with his lack of English. I recommended you for the job."

"Dr. Ramstein," Claire began her defense.

"No." He held up his hand to silence her. "Claire, you can't get out of this. You need something else in your life besides hiding in this room and translating archaic Japanese text. Your dissertation isn't due for two years. You are over three-fourths finished, while still doing all the other work you do as my assistant. This is a great opportunity. You'll go to

2

the appointment, talk to the manager and player, and, if it all works out, interpret and teach him English."

"I don't want to be a teacher! At least, not yet. I want to translate books of old Japan, Heian era, like The Tale of Genji."

"Claire, I doubt if Genji needs another translation since the definitive ones have already been done by Waley and Morris."

"I agree, but there are other books I want to tackle."

"They're not going anywhere. You can't realistically hope to start on them until you finish the doctoral program. If by chance you can, you'll still have access to your research via all this new technology while you're away. I'll get you a laptop for your birthday."

"You're too generous." Claire smiled at her faculty advisor's joke.

Ramstein returned the gesture, touched by the beauty of the girl.

"Only if you'll promise to go to Jacobs Field, the general manager's office, Monday at ten." Dr. Ramstein stood. He gave her a scrap of paper and straightened his rumpled suit coat.

"If you insist," Claire gave in.

"I insist."

Two hours after her conversation with Dr. Ramstein, Claire entered her small apartment. She couldn't figure out why he thought it was necessary she get out in the world. Yet, it was the same conversation she had every Sunday with her mother.

"Why don't you have a boyfriend?"

"Why don't you go out?"

"Don't you have any friends?"

She had friends. All students at Case Western Reserve University, all doctoral candidates, all linguists. They went to movies, the fitness center and had dinner out. And spent hours studying. Who cared if they weren't men? Claire didn't, but it didn't mean she wasn't shopping for a man. She just hadn't seen any she wanted. And there was Jason to fall back on.

Claire ran her bath water. She poured a generous portion of bubble bath into the fast torrent while she fumed at the attitude of the more mature adults in her world. Back in her bedroom, Claire undressed beneath the stare of the picture on the wall opposite the foot of her black, wrought-iron double bed. It was a large canvas reproduction of a samurai astride a rearing black horse, a work of Kuniyoshi's...a gift from her parents on her recent twenty-sixth birthday.

Claire eased into the tub. She allowed the steaming bath to remove the chill of a Cleveland February. Soapy water covered her full breasts and, when she sank in deeper, the bubbles lapped her chin. Her long hair floated in the water as she closed her eyes, soothing heat and water relaxing her muscles and mind.

Dr. Ramstein's words echoed in the recesses of her head until, at last, she concluded he was right. She had buried herself so deeply in prehistoric and feudal Japanese research that she was now unable to relate to the world she lived in. Working as this baseball player's interpreter and teacher would be a challenge. Then again, he might not want her for the job. Or, she wouldn't be able to stand him. It might prove to be a very interesting Monday morning, even if she just returned to her office and computer after the meeting.

Saturday, Claire shopped at Beachwood Place Mall for an outfit to wear to the interview for a job she didn't want. It took until late afternoon to put the outfit together. Since it was a baseball office, she settled on black Dockers, a white oxford cloth shirt beneath a crew neck cotton sweater of gray. Black Hush Puppy oxfords with gray socks completed the ensemble.

Sunday, she begged off the customary dinner with her parents. She didn't want to share the news of Ramstein's recommendation with them, afraid they would not approve. On the other hand, she was sure her father would be pleased. But her mother would protest because her little girl would be amid sweaty jocks.

Claire passed the afternoon in her quiet apartment. Located on the fourth floor at the front of a building erected in the 1930s, it consisted of two rooms, a living-dining area with a tiny kitchen hidden behind a half wall and a bedroom a little wider and longer than her bed. The bathroom, with a deep, footed, cast-iron tub, was in the corner. Sparse furniture filled in the rooms. As frugal as Claire chose to live, no one would guess that her father was a leading doctor at Rainbow Babies and Children's Hospital or that her mother was the heiress of one of the founding families of the city. Her father bankrolled her studies even though she had earned numerous grants through her studies of the Japanese language. She counted herself fortunate to be able to pursue a subject that would seem, at most, to be a hobby. Because her father provided her a considerable allowance, she would never have to worry about whether or not her degree would feed her.

"Oh, God!" Claire threw herself on the couch, face into the pillows. She was comfortable. Why couldn't people see that? Why had Ramstein done this to her? She didn't want to think about how her life might change come Monday.

# Chapter Two

Monday came after a night of fretful sleep. Claire rose and looked out the window and saw a light sprinkling of snow had fallen on Surry Road in the night. Shivering, she turned up the heat then bathed and dressed with the usual haste of those who lived in the North and were accustomed to the cold winters.

Better eat. My stomach will start complaining if I don't give it something.

She toasted a Biali bagel, one of the dozen she, along with hundreds of people from Cleveland Heights, bought every Sunday. It was tradition. As a child, she had gone to Biali's bakery with her father. Now, alone, she would read the front page of the Sunday Plain Dealer while she waited in line.

"Blagh!"

This morning, the crispy bagel held no reward. She stuffed the second half in her purse and gathered her things to leave.

At Jacobs Field, the new home of the Cleveland Chiefs, Claire found a parking place in the lot across the street and walked to the impressive stadium. The majority of the people of Cleveland felt the destruction of the old ballpark with its caricature of Chief Wahoo, the red-faced, feather-wearing Native American mascot of the Chiefs, was a desecration. This white and steel structure was designed to reflect the industrial nature of the city and was pretty impressive. Time had not yet covered the structure with the soot and grime of industry.

Claire entered the adjacent building reserved for the corporate workings of the team and took the elevator to the top floor. When the doors whispered open seconds later, Claire took a deep breath and entered the deep carpeted world of executive baseball. Crossing the hall to the office, she opened the glass door.

"May I help you?" The receptionist looked up from her calendar.

"I'm Claire Ferris. I have an appointment at ten with Mr. Jamison." Claire stood as straight as she could with a confidence she didn't really feel.

"Go right in. Mr. Jamison and Mr. Horsch are waiting to see you."

"Thank you." Claire walked past the desk, hesitated, took another deep breath, then opened the door.

"Ms. Ferris?" An older man with receding white hair dressed in a black three-piece suit rose from behind his desk and extended his hand. A younger man also stood from the seat he had in front of Jamison's desk.

"Yes." Claire stepped forward to take the offered hand. "Good morning."

"I'm Charles Jamison, CEO of the Chiefs, and this is David Horsch, team manager."

"Ms. Ferris," Horsch shook her hand.

"Please, have a seat." Jamison nodded toward a chair near Horsch. "Would you like coffee, tea, a soda?" he offered once they all were seated.

"No, thank you." Claire clenched her hands together in her lap and worked to keep her voice even.

"I suppose Dr. Ramstein has told you what we need?" Jamison began.

"A little," Claire admitted.

"I'll try to expand. We need a top-notch interpreter for the rookie we signed from Japan. He speaks very little English and, to date, we have been unable to provide an interpreter he approves of."

"Might I ask why he didn't approve of the others?" Claire wanted to know what she was in for.

"The first came with him from Japan. I really can't say why he didn't like him." Horsch sat forward to prop his arm on Jamison's desk. "The translator told us he said his words were not being translated correctly. It seems someone else was telling him what the quotes attributed to him were."

"Japan's divided into numerous districts known as prefectures. Was he from the same one as your pitcher?"

"I have no idea. And his name's Kentaro Ikuta," Horsch spoke again.

"Well, there're different dialects in different prefectures," Claire explained. "The changes are subtle, but they are different and someone from one prefecture could have difficulty translating correctly the words of someone from a different district."

"Hmm." Jamison muttered. "We never thought of that. Since the guy came with Ikuta, we assumed he'd hired him. What was it with the other guy?" He looked at Horsch with question marks in his eyes. "The one from LA?"

"Phillips. Ikuta said something about his not being qualified to speak his level of Japanese." Horsch shook his head and settled back into the chair. "I'm completely lost as to what he means."

"Japan's always had several layers of language. Until the Tokagawa shoguns lost their power and the samurai fell from grace, the upper echelon of Japanese society spoke a different language from that of the farmers and peasants. If Ikuta-san is from the caste of samurai, even so far removed in years, he could have been reared with an attitude of superiority."

"I'll say he's got an attitude of superiority!" Horsch commented with a dry chuckle.

"There could be many reasons for his attitude." Claire was bewildered. They had just signed this man to play and already formed a negative opinion of his attitude. "His speech could be the more formal form that many interpreters do not study." Claire stopped. She hoped her next statement did not sound as if she were bragging. "I can speak most levels of Japanese."

"That's the reason we contacted Case's language department," Jamison said. "Dr. Ramstein agreed you were the best choice for the task." The baseball team's owner took a packet of papers from a file folder. "We've drawn up a contract. Look it over and see what you think. It's pretty standard, but we can negotiate. You'll be required to accompany Ikuta any time he will need to speak."

"Which could be twenty hours a day, seven days a week." Claire was looking at the papers. It was all legalese, a language she didn't speak. She could, however, translate the six digit figure in the area of salary. "I'd like to have my attorney look this over." She didn't tell him she didn't have an attorney.

"Sure. Also, you'll start giving him English lessons as soon as you can set it up. You'll attend all games, home and away, pre- and post-season. Naturally, you will be attending spring training starting next month."

"Spring training? In Florida?" Claire forgot the paper.

"Of course. I don't think Ikuta can have a working knowledge of English by then, no matter how smart he is." Horsch smiled at the young woman. "He's been in the States a month, and his English hasn't improved at all."

"Ms. Ferris," Jamison cut into Horsch's thoughts about the pitcher and his ability to communicate. "Ikuta will need you to speak, especially in Florida. He's the first Japanese national to be signed to an American major league ball club in thirty years."

The phone at Jamison's elbow rang and Horsch moved to answer it. He spoke in the background while the team's owner talked to Claire.

"The media will be all over him and we need him to put his best foot forward. You are here to insure that."

"Oh." Claire kept her eyes on the contract. "How long?"

"How long what?"

"Will I be needed?"

"Depends on how long it takes Ikuta to learn English. Or at least become comfortable with it. He doesn't have to be able to read a scientific paper, but..."

"You'll get to meet him now," Horsch declared and hung the phone up. "That was Steve Martella, the pitching coach. Ikuta's coming up from the locker room. We've already told Phillips we're going to make a change. He'll stay on until you make your decision."

"I'm not sure if I'm the one you want." Claire studied the contract, unsure of what she looked at or for.

"Well, we'll see," Jamison commented.

At the pause, a knock sounded and the door opened.

"Good morning, Mr. Phillips, Mr. Ikuta," Jamison greeted.

Claire turned in her chair and looked toward the doorway at the men stepping across the threshold. The first was a tall Caucasian man with light brown hair, wearing a dapper gray suit and a swaggering attitude.

I wonder what Horsch thinks of his attitude.

Behind him was a man who, for an instant, made Claire's heart tremble.

This was Kentaro Ikuta. He stood a head taller than Phillips.

The post-war diet changes in Japan must be making for an increase in height of the inhabitants of the "Land of the

Gods," Claire thought as she surveyed his tall, six feet plus frame. The sheen of his thick, raven black hair rivaled that of a crow's wing. Long, it brushed his wide shoulders three inches below the collar of the white cotton shirt which stretched over his broad chest. A jacket of navy blue and gray slacks completed his attire in an effective *GQ* style.

Ikuta studied Claire from a lean face with wide oblong eyes above high cheekbones. His nose was long, flaring slightly over full lips that Claire did not think knew how to smile. Though his face was blank, she could tell his dark, oblong eyes took in everything.

# Chapter Three

"Ms. Ferris, this is Kentaro Ikuta and his interpreter, Jack Phillips," Jamison said by way of introductions.

"Former translator," Phillips corrected as he stepped to Claire. "How do you do? You must be the rookie brought in from the farm team." She flinched at his snide remark.

"Fine." Claire shook his hand. All the while she considered how to greet Ikuta. If she held her hand out, she might seem presumptuous. If she bowed to him when he had not bowed to her first, he might be offended.

"*Ohayo gozaimasu, Ikuta-san.*" Claire greeted the pitcher with words instead of actions.

"*Konnichi wa.*" Ikuta made a slight noise through his nose and held out his hand. Claire accepted it. The slender hand had a roughness to it from pitching a baseball; the fingers were long and well-sculptured.

Claire chanced a closer look into Ikuta's eyes. She could see an attitude, but she wasn't sure it was one of superiority. While she didn't read people well, she didn't sense Ikuta felt superior.

"Jack, will you please tell Ikuta Ms. Ferris is to be his new interpreter?" Jamison asked.

"Sure." Phillips turned to face the Japanese man. The pitcher inclined his head toward the other man and listened, concentrating on each syllable. A frown formed on his face.

"Yes." Ikuta added the strange nasal sound to his word to his response.

"*Sumimasen.* Excuse me," Claire broke in. She almost winced at Phillips' translation of the CEO's words. Phillips used much of modern slang in his translating. No wonder Ikuta was not pleased with his work. When she spoke, Claire used the most precise, most elite Japanese she knew. *"Ikuta-san*, these gentlemen feel I might be better able to interpret your words with more accuracy. I wish to do so only if you are pleased."

Claire watched as Ikuta thought about what she had said. She felt uneasy as the pitcher took another look at her.

*"Ferris-san*, I will have to see how well you perform before I can say whether I am pleased. Now, I must attend practice." Ikuta left the room without warning. Phillips followed.

Claire stood stunned. He had almost rejected her help.

"Well, Ms. Ferris?" Jamison asked. "What did he say?"

"He must listen to me for a while." Claire watched the door through which Ikuta had passed, her thoughts preoccupied. "Mr. Jamison," she asked, swiftly facing the team CEO, "is Phillips still translating for him?"

"Until you accept the job."

"Then let me sign right now!" Claire reached for the pen in the holder on Jamison's desk and signed her name to the contract. *"Ikuta-san* needs all the help he can get."

"Very good." Jamison took the signed document and put it in the file at his elbow.

"How will I know when Ikuta needs me?" Claire remained standing.

"I'll get the message to him through Phillips that you've taken the job. You'll need to carry this beeper." He handed her a small, square, black device. "That way, any one of us can notify you of the need for your services. We'll give him the number. Then he'll call you to set up a time he wants to study English."

"Oh." A feeling of uneasiness was heavy on her as Claire studied the beeper. She realized she had committed herself to this project. "I guess I'll go home and wait."

Claire gathered her purse as the phone on the desk rang. She'd have to wait until Jamison was free to tell him good-bye.

"Ms. Ferris," he replaced the receiver, "a reporter from the *Plain Dealer*'s here and..."

"You need me to translate," Claire finished. Her heart pounded, and she hoped the men in the room didn't hear it or the fear in her voice. She had told them she could do this, but could she? Her best Japanese involved reading and writing. Could her talent also be verbal?

"Yes."

"All right then." She tried to sound enthusiastic.

"Ms. Ferris, do you realize much of your time will be spent in the locker room?" Horsch asked.

"Uh, well, I hadn't thought about it." Claire gulped, this time in response to Horsch's question. The locker room meant sweaty, naked men. Oh, boy. "I suppose if Hannah Storm can do it after basketball games, I can too!" She tried to laugh. "But, Mr. Jamison," Claire paused a beat, "I don't know anything about baseball!"

"You're about to learn, young lady. Let's go." Jamison came from around the desk and with a gentle, father-like hand at her back, guided Claire toward the locker room many stories below the executive offices.

The locker room was quiet, occupied by fewer than ten men. Claire had met only two of them in the last fifteen minutes. Relieved they were all clothed, she followed Jamison and Horsch farther into the room.

"Gentlemen," Horsch spoke to the group. "Good morning."

There were mumbles in reply. Claire noticed Ikuta standing off to the side near the lockers. Phillips was just as aloof, even farther away. Taking the initiative, Claire approached Ikuta.

"*Ikuta-san*, I have accepted the position and hope you will find my services satisfactory. Jamison-san has asked me to help you with an interview with a newspaper reporter. Is there anything you wish me to know before we start?" Claire had no idea what she needed to know about the pitcher or where to start to interpret for someone.

"No." Ikuta repeated the nasal sound that seemed to come naturally to his speech. Claire hadn't decided whether the noise was one of surprise, disgust, disbelief, or annoyance.

Claire's attention was caught by the men who moved nearer her and Ikuta.

"Charles Penticoff," Horsch addressed the reporter from the Cleveland newspaper, "this is Kentaro Ikuta, our newest rookie. Just signed him from the Yokohama Bay Stars. You have his stats on the player roster."

"I want to ask a few things not related to baseball. You know, human interest things so the fans can relate to him as a person." The reporter readied his tape recorder.

Claire was panicked, aware her words would be the ones on the tape, not Ikuta's. It would be her voice which changed his words to English on the tape.

"This is Claire Ferris, Ikuta's new interpreter. Claire," Horsch led Penticoff to Claire and Ikuta and addressed her, "this is Charles Penticoff, sports writer for the *Plain Dealer*."

"Nice to meet you, Mr. Penticoff." Claire realized she was in the world of men when she experienced his firm handshake. She would have to get used to this. "*Ikuta-san*'s ready if you are." Her subject stood with his arms crossed on his chest, looking bland and uninterested. She introduced the writer to him. Ikuta merely nodded his response. The thick hair swayed slightly. Claire took a position at his side, behind him at his right shoulder.

"First," Penticoff began, "where in Japan is Mr. Ikuta from?"

Claire translated and awaited for Ikuta's answer.

"*Ikuta-san* was born in a small city outside Nagasaki."

"Any brothers or sisters?"

Claire spoke to the pitcher.

"*Hai*," Ikuta answered.

"Yes," Claire echoed.

They continued with the interview. The man asked what Claire thought to be irrelevant questions, personal ones she felt Ikuta was not comfortable with, judging from his mono-syllabic responses.

Before Claire realized it, her first press conference was over as Penticoff expressed his thanks then moved off with the executives. Claire was alone with Ikuta since Phillips had disappeared long before the interview was finished.

"Are these the questions they usually ask?" Claire questioned him.

"Of late, yes. At the press conference, after my contract was signed, the questions were more about baseball," Ikuta responded. It was the longest, most direct statement since they had met in Jamison's office. This gave Claire the confidence to initiate a conversation.

"*Ikuta-san*, I assume our arrangement will be the same as you had with Phillips-san. I have a beeper and here is my card." Claire rifled through her purse. She pushed the half bagel aside until she found her billfold and removed a small white business card. "My home and office number are there. Call me when you are ready to set up English lessons and, of course, if you need my help."

Ikuta took the card then, in typical Japanese business etiquette involving business cards, carefully examined it before putting it in his pocket.

"I will speak with you later." Ikuta handed his own card to Claire. Then, he performed the business-like bow so automatic to his being. The inclination of his upper body was to Claire and no other. The sentiment of sharing something "special" with Ikuta that the men didn't evaporated quickly when he left her so abruptly she stood bewildered.

Looking around, Claire found no one to direct her to the door. The locker room was large, an open space with walls formed by cubicle-like lockers which wound around toward the secluded showers. She knew she'd taken a wrong turn when she stumbled upon Ikuta.

The Japanese pitcher stood with his back to her, half-undressed. Claire studied the broad muscular expanse of golden flesh before her. The skin covering well-defined cords of muscles shifted like water with his arm movements as he pulled off the white cotton T-shirt. His long hair ruffled a moment before it fell to cover his neck.

"Excuse me," she blurted out in English then repeated, "*Sumimasen.*"

Ikuta turned. He stood, his T-shirt wadded in his hands before his midriff, unconcerned that he was bare-chested. Claire was surprised to see an inch long gold cross dangling from a chain around his neck then realized she had fallen into the trap of stereotyping Ikuta as a Buddhist. Thoughts about his religion flew out the window though, as she noticed his slacks were unbuttoned, the fly half-zipped.

"I seemed to have made a wrong turn," Claire said easily in conversational Japanese. She hoped he didn't see the deep flush she felt covering her face.

"I will show you." Ikuta moved past her to guide her to the doorway. Claire followed. Her eyes watched the broad back she had studied before. A closer inspection showed a flawless, rich, tan surface which looked like satin. It was all Claire could do not to reach out and touch him. Just the thought of doing so made her feel hot in the cool locker room.

When Ikuta came to a halt, Claire almost collided with him, faintly disappointed that she was able to catch herself. They were at the front of the locker room, the doorway evident.

"I must have turned wrong here."

"It is easy to do."

*"Domo arigato."* Claire started to move to the door.

*"Sayonara."* Ikuta departed back into the bowels of the locker room.

Claire pushed open the door and exited into a quiet corridor. She leaned against the wall and breathed a sigh of relief. What had she promised to do?

# Chapter Four

Claire relaxed once she was back at Case Western surrounded by her books and papers. She retrieved the half bagel from her purse and, with cafe mocha from Arabica, she sat at her desk with her feet propped up, sipping and chewing, safe within her cocoon.

"So?" Dr. Ramstein approached. His arrival in her office reminded Claire she had shaken up the crystal snow-globe of her life and the glitter was falling, their exact alignment yet to form.

"I'm *Ikuta-san*'s new interpreter!" Claire announced with false bravado. "Despite my misgivings." She dropped her feet to the floor.

"You'll do wonderfully. Your usage of Japanese is perfect, almost without accent, and you'll love the traveling."

"They must've told you more than you told me." Claire threw away the last bite of bagel and took a long swallow of her lukewarm coffee.

"Well, they did expand some," Dr. Ramstein evaded. "May I sit?"

"Sure."

He settled into the uncomfortable chair.

"What else happened? Did you meet Ikuta?"

"Yes, and I'm inclined to agree with Mr. Horsch. He has a huge attitude."

"Claire, you of all people should understand his attitude. His culture and social upbringing all formed a personality which we might find so different from ours that we assign the label of attitude to it."

"Yes, of course, but he seems…I don't know…cold. It's as if he has some sort of wall between him and everyone else."

"Put yourself in his place. Far from home, with no family or friends, a new country. You don't know the language. It must be very hard on him."

"I see your point," Claire conceded.

"Add to that the immense pride of a man, especially a Japanese man, and you, Claire, have a couple of big problems."

"I have big problems?"

"When you interpret, you must develop a rapport with your client. You must be able to read his mood to tell the exact sense of the words he wishes to be used. You know from your choice of study, Japanese has harsh and nice words. If you don't know he's in a foul mood, you run the risk of using the wrong English." The professor grinned at her. "And, you're a woman…"

"Oh, please! I doubt my femininity has anything to do with his demeanor. I see what you mean, though," Claire stated. "The manager thinks *Ikuta-san* has an attitude but, now that I've met him, I think he's shy. How can I learn all that since he's so quiet."

"You will." Ramstein began to stand. "Just give it time. And remember, no matter how many centuries have passed, deep within this baseball player, there's a samurai. I must go. Class." He walked out.

Claire pondered her big problem, the one of not offending the essence of the samurai in *Ikuta-san*.

Kentaro Ikuta arrived at his apartment, finished with his practice. During the pitching session, neither he nor his coach spoke one word of Japanese or English. After he stepped across the threshold and closed the door, he slipped off his loafers and placed them into a small cubbyhole shelf. He then walked sock-footed into the foyer.

"Kentaro?" A female voice called from the inner room. "Is that you?"

"*Hai*." He came to the room where a young woman sat on the sofa. "Who else were you expecting, *Taka-chan*?" He addressed her with the affectionate form of her name. It was a comfort to be speaking Japanese without it being translated.

"Nobody." She stood and came to stand near him. "How was practice?"

"It was all right." Kentaro moved past her to the kitchen where he got a small bottle of apple juice from the refrigerator.

"You must have left the stadium in a hurry," she said from the doorway.

"Why is that, Takahiko?" He opened the bottle and drank a small amount.

"Because you neglected to dry your hair. Come into the bathroom so I can do it." Takahiko led the way with Kentaro behind her.

"What is bothering you, big brother?" she asked once he was seated before the large mirror in a chair in the middle of the bathroom. She ruffled his hair with a towel. Kentaro's only vice was a preoccupation with his hair. Something must be wrong for him to have failed to do more than run a comb through it after his shower. He spent long periods of time working at the long silky strands. "You usually dry it before you come home."

"They have hired a new interpreter," Kentaro announced, the words preceded by his nasal sound.

"Oh." From behind him, Takahiko watched Kentaro's eyes reflected in the mirror as she combed the thick hair. She switched the blow dryer on and aimed the hot air at his head.

"What do you mean by oh?" Kentaro's eyes widened in inquiry.

In the mirror, Takahiko saw very much a face like her own, the eyes and lips alike. As many of the inhabitants of Japan's southernmost island of Kyushu, their features reflected the influence of Manchu blood from an invasion lost before recorded history. Their faces were more linear than round with prominent cheekbones, lips defined and supple, eyes not angled sharply but open with soft curves revealing dark brown eyes. Takahiko transferred her gaze from her brother's face in the mirror to his hair.

"Something is bothering you about this interpreter." Takahiko waved the hot air at the side of his head.

"There is no way I can decline her services."

"Her? Oh." This time the sound was one of understanding. She styled the hair around the thick bristled brush and fanned it with the dryer.

"Again with the 'oh.' What do you mean?"

"What do you mean there is no way to decline her services? Why do you wish to avoid being able to speak with people? They are trying to help you." Takahiko moved to the opposite side. Kentaro took the opportunity to drink some of his juice before his sister resumed brushing his hair.

"I understand their effort but…I am not comfortable speaking with or without an interpreter. I wish you were available to translate for me. I trust you to know what I wish to say with my words. I have always felt closer to you than any one else."

"My translating would not be a very good idea, Taro. And I have school," she explained.

"Your translation of the newspaper articles and television interviews has helped me see how people can manipulate my words. That is why I have the predicament of a third translator. It also makes it easy to avoid the media."

"You should be nice to the American press. You do not wish to have problems with them as you did in Japan. Besides, learn English!" Takahiko admonished. "It should not be so difficult for you. We studied it in school."

"Not so easy, little sister. I have not studied anything in years."

"You just do not want to." Takahiko tapped his head with the brush in a playful gesture. "Big brother, I know what your heart feels about your dreams. Here you are, playing baseball in the American major league where you have wanted to be since I was a baby." Takahiko worked to coax the natural wave on the back of his hair to straighten out. "Only if you are able to speak will you be able to enjoy the experience."

"I suppose you are right."

"Tell me about her."

"Who?" Kentaro was drinking juice again.

"Your new interpreter." She rapped his head with the brush not as gently as before. "Is she *gaijin*?" Takahiko used the Japanese word for a foreigner, indicating Caucasian.

"*Hai*."

"So. Tell me more." Takahiko sensed she would have to drag all the details out of her brother since that was the way he was when something bothered him, either in a good way or bad.

"Not much to tell. I did not pay much attention to her. She's young, about twenty-five I guess. She has creamy skin and blushes easily. Her eyes are a deep green with a strange golden glint in them. Her mouth is small and she has a habit of licking her lips when she is nervous. And she has the usual long nose with a soft tilt to it."

"And you did not pay attention to her," Takahiko scoffed.

"I remember some things easier than others. She is tall. Taller than you. The top of her head comes to my chin."

"You suppose it would," Takahiko speculated, "if you put your arms around her." She turned off the blow dryer and put it down, but ran the brush and her fingers through his luxuriant hair.

"I do not know what you are talking about, little sister." Takahiko watched Kentaro. He hid his embarrassment by finishing the juice in the bottle.

"Yes, you do. I have seen the magazines in your room when you were in high school and the ones Saburo has now." Takahiko let the silken fibers of his hair fall through her fingers. "Your hair is much like those *bishomen* comic books. Is that where you got the idea to let it grow?"

Before speaking, Kentaro made a noise in his throat which reminded Takahiko of a harmless growl, so she knew she'd irritated him.

"You are too nosy for your own good. You will recall that *bishomen*, the delicate androgynous young heroes of Japanese *anime*, are usually in girls' comics and are homosexual."

"I do not suppose you could be accused of that, huh, big brother?"

"Are you finished?"

"Uh oh. I am about to see the infamous Kentaro temper," Takahiko proclaimed. She knew it was not her place to comment on his liaisons with the opposite sex, nor did he like to be reminded of it. She put the brush down so she could admire her work of organizing the unruly hair. "Yes, I am through."

"Thank you." Kentaro stood. He ran a hand through his hair from brow to crown, rearranging the style his sister had fixed with such care. He walked out of the bathroom.

"Is she blonde?" Takahiko asked when she returned to the living room.

"What?" Kentaro lay on the couch, the television remote in his hand. "Who?"

"The girl who interprets for you now. You described everything but her hair. Is she blonde?"

"Why?" Kentaro flipped through the thirty-four channels cable television provided. ESPN was the channel where he stopped, but he paid no attention to the basketball scores.

"Are you going to get to 'when,' 'where,' and 'how' next? I am the one who is a journalism student." Takahiko sat on the floor, her legs folded up under her.

Kentaro looked at his sister lying on the carpet five feet away from him. She read a newspaper spread out in front of her. Her comprehension of English was excellent, and she wanted to be a reporter for an American newspaper or even CNN.

"Her hair is dark brown and comes down to her waist with bangs like yours. What does it matter?" He moved to sit up on the edge of the couch. Why was his sister questioning him about Claire Ferris?

"I was just wondering if you would be attracted to her."

"I did not know that was what an interpreter was for."

"She is a woman, is she not? Some of your girlfriends in Japan were blonde. If you listened to the media, they would have you to believe Japanese men like blonde, Caucasian women."

His sound was explosive in response to his sister's observation.

"Do they not have courses in propaganda at the University?"

"Yes. I have studied how people manipulate the press. What about Hana?" She mentioned the latest of her brother's conquests.

"It was her choice to dye her hair." It had been a year since he had seen Hana, a baseball groupie he had dated for about three months. "I did not ask her to."

"Well, you know Father and Mother are planning for you to marry Katsuko."

"There has never been anything formally arranged. Besides, she is more your friend. She has been around the house since you were both two years old. It would be like marrying my sister." Kentaro smiled at his sister who giggled.

Takahiko came to kneel in front of Kentaro. She leaned against his knees to reach forward and encircle his neck with her arms.

"When are you going to Florida?"

"End of the month." Kentaro returned her hug.

"I will be leaving a week from Friday."

"I will miss you. I appreciate all the work you have done to make this apartment livable."

"You are going to be alone when I leave. Maybe your interpreter can keep you company," Takahiko giggled.

"Enough." Kentaro pushed her away playfully and Takahiko took advantage of the movement to fall over backwards, shrieking in laughter. "Sisters!" Kentaro left her to her fits of hilarious glee.

"I am going out for a walk," Kentaro announced to Takahiko ten minutes later.

"I will wait dinner until you return."

"You do not need to."

Kentaro was out the apartment door. Their mother had sent Takahiko to Ohio to take care of her older brother in the same manner as his mother would, had she not had a husband and another child to care for in Japan. He was grateful to Takahiko, but would be happy when she returned to school.

Passing the security guard standing behind his desk in the foyer of the building, Kentaro walked left. The Chiefs had directed him to live in the upscale, well secured Bratnael Place and he enjoyed walking around the area along the shores of Lake Erie. Snow covered the grassy areas, but the pavement and sidewalks were clear. He recalled the infrequent snowfalls in Nagasaki, but never was the city this still, nor was his hometown this open and spacious.

Hunching down into his heavy overcoat, Kentaro pressed his hands into his pockets. After Takahiko left he would be alone. America's vastness was unsettling to him. He wasn't sure how he would be able to deal with it, along with the other pressures in his life.

The only other person with whom he could easily communicate was his agent, Michael Sangyo, who was in Los Angeles at the moment, not due home in Cleveland until Monday. Kentaro turned, shoved his hands deeper into his pockets, and walked back to his apartment.

# Chapter Five

"Keep those knees high, girls!" As she kept up with the other women working out to the blaring rock and roll music, Claire wished the anorexic aerobics instructor would pass out. Forty-five minutes into the hour workout, Claire dripped sweat like a furnace stoker in July. She hoped she would last until they got to the floor work and that she wouldn't be tempted to take a nap instead of doing sit-ups.

At last, the music stopped and the women dragged their tired bodies to the showers. Claire wiped her neck and chest with a towel, then took her pulse at the base of her throat.

"Claire!" Andrea Borchert approached her. She made the same calculations as Claire. "I haven't seen you in weeks. Is everything all right?"

"Yeah." Claire finished drying and joined Andrea to walk toward the showers. "I've been busy with...work."

"I'm having problems with my stuff, too. Want to join me at the juice bar?"

"Sure."

The two women showered and dressed, then went to the second floor to the fitness center snack bar. There the physical fitness addicts could find treats designed not to damage the benefits achieved in the workouts they had completed.

"So," Andrea said as she drank the concoction known as a fruit smoothy. They sat at a small table near the railing. It overlooked the weight equipment and the muscle-bound people using them. "What's new?"

"Oh, not much." Claire took a drink of the cold, thick fruit juice. Her conscience pricked her because she did have something to tell. She was embarrassed. What would Andrea think about her working for a baseball team? Would she laugh at her? Could she stand the humiliation? "Andrea, I have a job." It was a blurt that surprised even Claire. "I'm interpreting for the Cleveland Chiefs."

"You're what?" Andrea sputtered. "You don't have to work."

"Thanks, Andy." Claire flinched, her feelings a little hurt by her friend's sarcastic comment, but Andrea had stated the truth and probably meant nothing by the remark. "Dr. Ramstein sort of forced it on me."

"Oh, for your dissertation."

"No. For my socialization into civilization."

"What in the world are you talking about?"

"Ramstein told the Chiefs I would be the perfect person to translate for the pitcher they brought from Japan."

"I've heard of him. My father was so excited about the announcement. He's supposed to be the new 'wunderkind' of baseball. He wanted to play in the American major leagues so badly, he retired from Japanese baseball at the age of twenty-six to get around the laws they have regarding free agency and changing teams."

"You know a lot about baseball, and I don't know anything!"

"I'll tutor you," Andrea offered.

"I'll hold you to it. Anyway, I did an interview, signed a contract, and haven't heard from them since. I even have this beeper I wear around in case they need me." Claire fingered the small black square clipped on her jeans. "That was ten days ago."

"Spring training doesn't start until week after next. Maybe they don't need you until then." Andrea finished her juice. "Does this mean you're going to Florida?"

"I guess so. He has to talk to people there, too!"

"This is so exciting."

"I'm not so sure." Claire shrugged. "I have to go." Now that she had told Andrea the secret of her employment, she felt free. Maybe she could enjoy the experience.

"I'll walk you to the parking lot."

They were almost to the garage when Claire's beeper chimed. Unused to such noise, she jumped, shouted and clutched at her waist.

"Oh, my goodness!"

"Who is it?" Andrea was as excited as Claire.

"I guess it's the Chiefs. No one else has the number." Claire fumbled with the beeper. "How does Daddy work these things?"

"Could be a wrong number."

"Maybe. Oh, here."

"Here yourself. Use my phone." Andrea handed her the cellular from her purse.

"Thanks." Claire punched in the number as they continued to walk toward the cars. "This is Claire Ferris. I was paged. This is so cool," she said in an aside to Andrea. "I sound like my father."

Andrea stood beside Claire's Mustang, tapping her foot and teeming with impatience as Claire listened to the phone.

"Well?" she asked.

"They're checking." Claire informed her. "Probably a mistake. Maybe *Ikuta-san* has decided he doesn't want me so they're looking for someone else. That's why...oh, yes, I'm still here." Claire's attention was back to the phone. "I'll be there right away." She pushed a button, folded the phone up and gave it back to Andrea.

"Well?"

"I have to go to Jacobs Field. Personnel needs me to sign papers," Claire informed her.

"Oh."

"Don't sound so disappointed." Claire punched the remote to unlock her car then opened the door. "I'll let you know if anything exciting happens."

"Just you do that!" Andrea moved to her own car several spaces down.

Claire started the engine, then backed her black Mustang convertible out into the lane to head downtown to the stadium. Maybe she should tell her parents now.

"Just need your signature on some paperwork, Ms. Ferris," Arthur Ostervich told Claire as she sat across from him in his office.

"Sure." Claire didn't know what else to say. Somewhere inside her, she had to admit she was disappointed her page was for something so banal as paperwork. She didn't want to admit she was disheartened it wasn't Ikuta who needed her.

"Insurance forms, payroll forms, W-2s." Ostervich doled out the forms over his desk. "When they are away, the team'll put you up in a hotel and you'll have an expense account. There's also a matter of an identification card. You'll need to go down the hall to have a picture taken."

"All right." Claire took the forms to read and sign one by one before handing them back across the desk.

"That's all." Ostervich stacked the forms with the preciseness of an accountant and returned them to a file folder. "Here's the spring training schedule of practice and games." He offered her a packet of papers. "Flight arrangements will be forthcoming by messenger. We're just getting things together for the players and management."

"I see." Claire looked at the papers. "Thanks."

Claire left his office. When she flipped through the schedule of events for spring training, she noticed her name followed Kentaro Ikuta's every time he was listed.

"*Ferris-san.*" Claire was surprised to hear his voice from behind her.

"Hello, *Ikuta-san.*" She stayed with English, sure that most people knew the greeting words in some languages if it wasn't some obscure dialect.

"*Genki desu ka*?" Kentaro asked.

"*Watashi wa genki na.* Thank you. And you?" Claire accommodated his language. She tried to stuff the schedule into the soft-sided briefcase while she fought with her purse swinging in the way.

"I am taking my sister to the airport."

"I did not know your family was here."

Ikuta seemed to hesitate between going and staying. "Just Takahiko." Kentaro moved on down the hallway without farewell.

Claire watched him go, her mouth agape. How rude! She didn't think she'd ever had someone not at least say "Bye"!

As she left the stadium, a tall man dressed in the traditional uniform of a preppy businessman—blue with a red tie and sports coat over khaki slacks—approached Claire. His blonde hair was freshly styled and neat, longish yet above his collar in a conservative manner.

"Claire Ferris! What in the world are you doing here?" He greeted Claire with an embrace and kiss.

"Hi, Jason." Claire ducked her face. She was uncomfortable in his embrace, but didn't move.

"What are you doing at the Jake? You can't be buying tickets, you hate baseball!" Jason's arm was over her shoulders to hold her at his side as they walked toward the doors.

"I don't hate it, I just...don't know much about it."
Claire was glad her paperwork was in her briefcase. The last
thing she wanted was for Jason to see it. She managed to
escape his grip. "I have business here."

"You? Business?" Jason's laugh echoed off the steel and
concrete.

"And just what are you doing here?" Claire turned the
discussion to him.

"Business." His blue eyes hinted of a secret.

"Well, I have to go." Claire hurried away from him
toward the sidewalk.

"I'll call you!" Jason shouted at her as he held the door
open.

"Sure." Claire waved without turning to face him. "I
won't be answering," she said to herself.

She felt dirty from Jason's touch. How could she have
ever dated him?

"Mother and Daddy," Claire announced at Sunday dinner. "I
have a job." She sat opposite her mother with her father at
the head of the table. The meal had been served, blessed, but
not started.

"A job? Claire!" Claudia gave her daughter a bewildered
look.

"Yes. I'm working for the Cleveland Chiefs." Claire
waited for the explosion.

"Wonderful." Dr. Ferris attacked the chicken instead of
her as Claire expected.

"How can you work for the Chiefs? What can you do?"

"Claudia, she's probably in the front office," her father
answered for her. "Aren't you, sweet pea? Can't expect you

to be the pitching coach, can we?" Dr. Ferris laughed at his own joke.

"Since you mentioned it, Daddy, in a way, I am." Claire hadn't thought much about it, but her father was close to the truth. She'd be relaying the pitching coach's instructions to Ikuta. "I'm the interpreter for the Japanese pitcher. Dr. Ramstein thinks it'll be good for me."

"I do, too," Claudia told Claire.

"I'm going to Florida, I think, first of the week. They're sending my information by messenger." Surprised at how well her parents were taking the news, Claire decided it was safe to eat.

"Florida. Wonderful. We'll go shopping tomorrow."

"Mother, I don't need clothes." Claire despised shopping and her mother lived for it.

"Of course you do. You'll need summer things."

"This boy's supposed to be the answer to the Chiefs' pitching woes," Dr. Ferris said thoughtfully. "Will you be traveling to all games?"

"Yes. I'm on call twenty-four hours a day. I've already helped with one interview for a reporter from the *Plain Dealer*."

"I skimmed that article," he replied. "Didn't see your name."

"I'm not sure you would. I'll also teach him English. If he learns quickly, I'll be out of a job." Claire worked at the vegetables on her plate and took a bite of the potatoes.

"Surely the paper would mention you. We'll keep an eye on the articles from now on," Claudia promised. "What'll happen to your school work?"

Now more excited about the job and traveling to Florida, Claire went on to answer the questions, allowing herself to see the adventure.

# The Words of the Pitcher

Monday, Claire relented and went shopping with her mother, who was more excited about the excursion than Claire. By lunch, Claire had two swimsuits, several shorts, T-shirts, sandals, three spring dresses, and shoes to match. After noon, they bought luggage, stationery, and books to entertain Claire in her spare time.

Exhausted when she got home, Claire collapsed on the sofa. She had just flipped on the television when the messenger rang the doorbell. As she read her scheduled departure for spring training in Winter Park, Florida, Tuesday morning at seven, a knot formed in her stomach.

# Chapter Six

The sun was still asleep Tuesday when Claire arrived at Hopkins International Airport. She found her way to the VIP lounge through the quiet terminal. There, a crowd of team members, the coaching staff, and family members huddled together to wait. Claire was sorry she had talked Claudia out of coming with her since she was the only one alone, or so she thought, until she saw Kentaro Ikuta in a corner, reading. Claire decided, since she was his interpreter, she should be with him. With a deep breath, she crossed the room.

"*Konnichi wa, Ikuta-san.*"

"*Ferris-san.*" Ikuta looked up, then went back to his book.

"May I sit with you?" Claire was annoyed, but tried to be nice. She had to work with this man. Didn't he see pleasantness would make things easier? Then again, maybe he thought he was being nice.

"As you wish."

Silently, they sat side by side. Claire read the newspaper, Kentaro, his book. Just when Claire thought they'd never be called to board the plane, a flight attendant came by and asked for team credentials. Finally, Claire thought, she was going to do her job.

"She wishes to see your team papers," Claire told Ikuta in Japanese.

"Thank you. However, I could figure that much out without help." Ikuta gave the woman the card and papers which she read and returned.

"I am sorry," Claire demurred, rebuffed. She proffered her own materials to the attendant.

"We will be boarding in ten minutes," the attendant told them as she handed the paperwork back.

"*Ikuta-san*, perhaps we can work out some sort of signal so I will know when to translate or not?"

"You will know." Ikuta didn't raise his eyes from the book.

Claire began to get anxious from more than Ikuta's attitude. She looked around, swinging her foot, and unable to keep her hands still. Until now she'd put off thoughts of flying.

"Do you have to go to the bathroom?" Kentaro asked.

"No! Why?" Claire's cheeks instantly burned at his question.

"You are acting like a little girl who does." Ikuta's eyes were back on the Japanese characters on the page of his book.

"I am not comfortable with flying. Actually, it's the takeoffs and landings I'm not comfortable with. In between, I am fine."

Ikuta made an untranslatable noise.

When the intercom crackled and asked the team to board, Claire stood and reached for her carry-on bag, but Kentaro picked it up. Was he going to become chivalrous? They moved toward the gate with the others. As the wives and girlfriends spoke good-byes, Claire felt conspicuous, as if she needed to explain why she was getting on a plane full of men while they stayed behind.

Ikuta, accustomed to women walking behind him, led her to their seats toward the back of the plane. There, he allowed Claire to take possession of her bag to put where she wished. By the time she had stowed it in the overheard compartment, he had settled into the aisle seat and she found it necessary to climb over his knees to get to her window seat. It was awkward having to touch him to keep her balance. At the same time, Claire felt a jolt rush through her, leaving her hot and flushed when she sat down.

The flight attendants began offering refreshments after everyone was aboard and seated.

"Would you like something to drink?" an attendant asked in the direction of Ikuta and Claire.

Claire didn't rush to translate until Kentaro looked at her. His eyes evidenced his incomprehension. She told him what the woman said and he gave Claire his response.

"He would like two bourbons and a Coke. I'd like a plain Coke." Little early to be drinking, she thought.

The plane taxied down the runaway as the drinks were served. Claire gripped the armrest, ashamed of her fear. She concentrated on Kentaro. He opened the two tiny bottles of Jack Daniels and poured the contents into the small cup of cola and ice.

"Here." He handed Claire the drink. "This will help your nerves."

Claire took it, not sure of this sudden concern for her. He reached across to her fold-down table and took her untouched Coke for himself. Claire sipped the strong alcohol-laced Coke. By the time the plane leveled off, she was drowsy without a care.

Kentaro Ikuta, oblivious to the chatter of his fellow players, watched Claire nod off. When her head fell toward the window, he put one of the small airline pillows between it and the bulkhead. He wondered if she normally drank. Perhaps he had miscalculated with the alcohol in his desire to help her. Trying to be someone's benefactor often backfired on him.

As the plane reached an altitude above the clouds, soft sunlight bathed Claire's face, forcing a deep red-gold hue from her hair. Her nose, long, straight, and narrow, threw a shadow on her round cheeks. The pliable lips of her small mouth formed into a smile in her inebriated sleep. Kentaro hoped she sobered before the team management saw her. He'd be forced to take the blame should someone fault her.

Claire stirred and took a deep breath, which caused Kentaro to lower his gaze. Her round breasts lay beneath the smooth oxford shirt and her waist was slender. Long legs stretched out in the cramped space between seat rows.

Kentaro dragged his gaze away and tried to concentrate on his book.

*"Ferris-san."* Kentaro nudged the young woman.

She didn't respond.

*"Ferris-san."*

When Claire continued to sleep, Kentaro shook her with more vigor.

"Claire." He finally used her given name.

"What?" she responded at last.

"We have arrived in Florida. At the airport in Winter Park." He studied her, then asked, "Are you all right?"

*"Hai."* Claire rubbed her face with both hands. "Or, I will be. I do not know whether I want to thank you or kill you."

"Perhaps we should leave it alone then." Kentaro felt the need to distance himself from Claire, uncomfortable with the responses beginning to develop.

When the seatbelt light went out, Kentaro stood and stepped into the aisle. He reached up and retrieved both his and Claire's carry-ons.

"Come," he ordered Claire, and she dutifully followed. "If someone should ask, I will tell them you were suddenly taken ill."

"You should. It is your fault," Claire muttered as she walked in front of Kentaro. They didn't worry about someone overhearing their plan because they were speaking Japanese. "My head is pounding."

The emerging baseball team was met by the press and subjected to the bright lights and loud roar of questions. Luckily for Claire, the pitchers and catchers were not allowed to remain exposed long and no direct questions were directed at Ikuta. The group finally moved to a chartered bus for transportation from the terminal.

Claire sat next to Kentaro in the same relative position as on the plane. As the vibrations of the bus lulled her back to sleep, her head lolled onto his shoulder.

Kentaro felt the movement against him and looked to his left. Claire's head lay on his shoulder, her hair brushed his neck. Her closed eyes had thick black semicircles of lashes fanned out on her cheeks.

Kentaro's body reacted to the softness at his side as Claire sighed and snuggled against him. The arrival at the hotel eliminated time for further thoughts about her.

Claire heard a bell far away in a mist. It came and went, like a foghorn on a lighthouse, as she burrowed deeper into the warmth of her bed. The sound continued and she woke, wondering where the noise was coming from. Then she knew. The phone.

"Hello?" She sat up in bed, her feet drawn up underneath her, sleep still in her brain.

"Ms. Ferris?" a man's voice asked from the other end.

"Yes." Claire tugged the hem of the T-shirt she wore for a nightgown out from under her hips so it no longer pulled at the neck.

"This is Steve Martella of the Chiefs pitching staff."

"Oh." Claire looked toward the clock. Six-thirty.

"You're supposed to be down here at the field."

"I must have overslept. I'll be right there."

"See you then."

"Oh, Mr. Martella?"

"Yes?"

"Where are you?"

While she unwrapped the muffin she had picked up on her way out of the hotel, Claire gave the taxi driver the name of the baseball complex. She sat in the back of the vehicle, balancing a paper cup of coffee, unsure why they needed her at the beginning of practice. Wouldn't Ikuta know what they wanted? After all, it was baseball!

Claire exited the taxi at the field and followed the security guard through the fence. On the diamond stood the men she had shared a plane ride with, the pitchers and catchers lined up as neatly as soldiers. The Florida sun rose, slowly dissipating the low temperatures.

"Ms. Ferris." A well-kept young man lifted his baseball cap to reveal close-cut hair as he ran up to her. "Steve Martella," he introduced himself. "We need you to stand next to Ikuta so you can relay the instructions the coach gives."

"Okay." Claire followed him to Ikuta who stood at the edge of the formation. She spoke to him. "I will give you a running interpretation of what they are saying."

Kentaro made the guttural noise he always did. Claire had decided the sound must be the one books about feudal Japan referred to as a sound used to indicate a general response from a samurai.

Claire's eyes, hidden behind sunglasses, watched Kentaro as they stood waiting for the first moves of the coaches. Like the rest of the team, he wore loose cotton shorts over tight lycra shorts and a T-shirt beneath a short sleeve sweatshirt. His lengthy hair was tied back with a ponytail fastener and a bandanna was rolled and wrapped around his forehead. Long, straight, muscular legs ended with heavy high-top Reeboks. The morning sunlight glinted off the cross exposed outside the sweatshirt when he moved.

Claire was called into service as the coaches began the workout. As she translated calisthenics instructions to Kentaro, she felt so silly as a bystander that she decided to go through the same exercises.

"You are not doing that correctly," Kentaro announced when they were doing push-ups. He spoke the form of Japanese used between men and women of a close relationship. Did he intend to presume such about them?

"Who cares? I am only doing this because of you!" Claire panted. Her hands were planted in the grass and her knees dug into the ground as she held her body at an angle.

There was that noise again from Kentaro.

"Straighten your back and arms." He came to kneel beside her so he could push one hand against the small of her back and the other grasp her biceps.

Until Kentaro touched her, Claire wasn't having problems with the exercise. The instant he placed his palm next to her skin, she didn't think she could do a rep if her life depended on it. His touch sent a shock of electricity coursing though her body, to a spot Claire wasn't sure she knew existed until that moment. The pounding of her heart and the shortness of her breath were not the result of her exertion.

"Why are you not doing your own?" She had to get his hands off her before the two of them did something not meant to be done on a baseball field.

"Do not be concerned about me, *Ferris-san*." He released her and moved to his position.

# The Words of the Pitcher

Push-ups over, the group began to run laps around the outer perimeters of the baseball field. Claire kept up with Kentaro, who was one of the leaders of the group. After ten laps, they broke up to work on the components of their position on the team.

Claire was busy as she followed Kentaro from drill to drill. She translated the coaches' instructions on how to pitch, how to stand, how to throw a runner out on first. By evening, everything hurt—body and mind; arm; leg; and tongue. She was so tired of speaking Japanese!

She spent an hour in the tub, ordered room service, and went to bed.

By the time a week had passed, Claire had become adept at the exercises. The practice was so routine she wasn't needed to translate, but she continued to work out. She shopped for exercise clothes, not tight leotards such as she wore at the gym at home, but shorts and tops easy to move in. A freak cold snap brought this choice of clothing into question.

# Chapter Seven

As she took the field with the pitchers and catchers, now joined by the rest of the team, Claire wore only a T-shirt and bike shorts layered beneath a pair of sweat shorts over them. She shivered, rubbing her arms with her hands.

"Are you cold, *Ferris-san*?" Kentaro asked, his own hands shoved into the pockets of his team issued warm-up sweat suit.

"Yes," Claire snapped, not sure why she was angry with him.

"Here." He unzipped the hooded sweatshirt, slipped it off his shoulders, then draped it around Claire.

"*Arigato*." Claire pushed her arms into the sleeves. The warmth of Kentaro's body clung to the fibers and she huddled into the cozy cocoon. It was then Kentaro's eyes caught hers.

As she stood beneath his stare, a strange need rose in her and a hot rush moved through parts of her. What was it about the way his dark brown eyes looked at her that made her feel so funny? Though she couldn't stand to break away, she had to for fear of what might happen next.

"It is stupid to come dressed so in this weather." Kentaro broke the spell.

"I did not realize it was so cold," Claire retorted. Her voice rose with her irritation. "I promise not to keep it long."

"It is quite all right. I have another." Kentaro left her standing in left field.

Claire could have killed him! Why did he do that? Every time it looked as if he had done something nice, he managed to make it unpleasant. She began to wish spring training was over.

After the team practiced several weeks, they started playing exhibition games. Ikuta didn't play until the third game, one against the Boston Red Sox. His performance was remarkable. The Chiefs won the game with Ikuta credited with the win. She could tell he felt it was not indicative of his ability. Afterwards, he faced the press. Claire stood at his side, behind his right shoulder.

"Mr. Ikuta, how different do you find the pitching styles of the American major leagues versus the Japanese teams?" a reporter posed the first question.

Claire repeated the inquiry into his ear in hushed tones. Ikuta replied in like manner as if it were only the two of them in intimate conversation.

"It is not easy to compare American and Japanese styles as they are both subtly different. I have only my style of pitching and hope it will be adequate for the needs of major league play." Kentaro's words were spoken by Claire.

She looked at Kentaro to see if his face would tell her if she had correctly interpreted his words. His knowledge of English was enough to know the gist of her translation. The sound he made was that of satisfaction. Claire smiled at him. Her first hurdle was completed.

"I wish I had a work-out partner," Martella commented to Claire as she stood at homeplate. The team was busy with individual training areas. The coaching staff treated her as if she were an extension of Ikuta.

"What do you mean by that?" She dried sweat from her neck and chest with a towel. Spring training was half over and the heat of Florida was just beginning.

"I was teasing, Ms. Ferris. You're pretty good at all this fitness stuff."

"Claire," she said. "I usually go to the fitness center at Case. I must admit this is a little harder."

"You're in pretty good shape for all the talking you two do out there."

"We're usually fighting about one thing or another." Claire shook her head in agitation.

"Lovers' quarrels?"

"Puleezee! He doesn't even like me!" Claire looked toward Kentaro ten feet away on the pitcher's mound. She saw the scowl on his face, as if it were painful for him to watch her talk with Martella.

"Coulda fooled me. But you know guys," Martella philosophized.

"No, I don't. What do you mean?"

"We show our affection in different ways." Changing the subject, he asked, "Have you started English classes for Ikuta?"

"I mentioned it once, after the first week here, and he put me off. I don't think he wants to learn."

"He'll have to sooner or later. The press isn't patient enough to keep dealing with your translating all the time."

Claire began to walk toward the clubhouse. Steve walked with her.

"Maybe if he got married and his wife spoke perfect English, he wouldn't need an interpreter."

"Sure. The Chiefs can buy him a wife!" Claire laughed and moved farther away from Martella.

"Maybe we already have," he said, just loud enough for her to hear.

46

As Kentaro took his schooling in pitching for the Chiefs, Claire sat in the dugout. She was required to be nearby in case they needed her translating talent, and to pass the time, she read. At intervals, she looked up over her reading glasses from the pages. Every time, Kentaro seemed to be staring back at her from the pitcher's mound. It got on her nerves. Then again, she liked it.

"*Ferris-san.*" Ikuta came into the dugout. His cleated shoes made a clatter on the concrete, and he barely missed hitting her with the leather glove he threw onto the bench.

"*Ikuta-san.*" Claire had gotten used to his outbursts. She would wait it out. He'd tell her what he wanted, given time.

Kentaro sat next to her to unlace his shoes. When they were loose, he slipped his feet out. Claire looked down at his long, narrow feet. Why was he taking his shoes off in the dugout?

"What are you doing?" She took off her glasses and laid her book aside.

"Sitting here. What does it look like? Would you please get me some Gatorade?"

"What am I? Your *jochu*?" Claire complained about being his maid, but stood and went to the plastic cooler filled with iced Gatorade. She put a paper cup under the spigot and pushed the button to release the green fluid.

"What were you and Martella-san talking about?" Kentaro asked across the expanse of the dugout walkway. They carried out their conversation in Japanese, Kentaro seemed reluctant to be drawn into any speech in English.

"What?" Claire returned and handed him the cup. She reclaimed her seat beside him.

"You and Martella-san. What did you two have to talk about?" He took a long drink of the sports drink.

"The fact that you are not studying English."

Kentaro made the noise Claire was getting used to hearing. She didn't always know what it meant, but it always happened in response to something she said or did.

"We have to start working on it."

Kentaro's noise was his only response.

"Have it your way."

Claire repositioned her glasses on her nose. She stuck her bare legs and feet into the sun and went back to her book. As she noticed his eyes surreptitiously cast her way, she enjoyed the feel of Kentaro's looking at her long limbs covered with a rich tan after so many days in the Florida sun.

"*Ikuta-san*," Claire called across the field as she made her way to the mound. "I have to tell you something."

"Is it about English classes?" Kentaro completed his wind-up and released the ball to the catcher squatting behind home plate. The ball smacked into the leather mitt.

"No. I am not talking to you about English ever again. The coach wanted me to remind you that the team is going to Disney World tomorrow."

"Why would a group of grown men go to Disney World?" Kentaro reached his mitt out to the left to catch the ball the catcher threw to him. The other player ignored their conversation in Japanese.

"Some of their families are here, but it is a media event. Surely you have figured out that just about everything you do is press-related." Claire watched Kentaro raise both his hands over his head, turn his body almost completely around before spinning forward and hurling the ball back to the catcher. "You and I have to go. The Chiefs want to show how you have assimilated American culture. I think it will be fun."

"You are a child then, *Ferris-san*?" Kentaro's eyes studied hers.

"No, but Disney World does have a part called EPCOT and it is more for adults. I was hoping we might have a good time. I guess I was wrong!" Claire fled the mound area, afraid Kentaro might see the hurt in her eyes, or the tears.

She heard him make his noise as she left.

Probably means good riddance!

The players and their families assembled early the next morning to board buses to Orlando and Disney World. Children, excited and rambunctious, ran up and down the aisles, restrained, after a time, by their already-exasperated mothers. Claire sat beside Kentaro who had not even said good morning, but had greeted her with a nod and what Claire had come to call his 'samurai noise.' They both pretended to be reading.

The buses disgorged their passengers at the park amid hundreds of other families. Claire and Kentaro remained at the back of the group as they made their way through the gates. It was hard not to noticed the minicams and photojournalists who hovered around the entrance, their attention on the baseball players.

"Are you not interested in this at all?" Claire broke down and asked Kentaro.

"I might find something of interest. Why do you not guide me." Kentaro's face seemed to soften just a little.

"Very well. I have not been here since I was twelve." Claire found she was excited about introducing Kentaro to the experience of Disney and Mickey Mouse, although she was not much of a Mouse fan. She unfolded the map of the park they had been given. "Let's start with Cinderella's Castle."

"Very well." Kentaro waved his hand before her as if to invite her to lead. Claire moved and a group of photographers followed.

"We seem to have lost the rest of the team," Kentaro noted four hours later. They ate ice cream at a sidewalk cafe on Main Street and watched the boisterous parade move in front of them.

"So it seems. And the paparazzi, too." Claire looked around. She brought the ice cream mound on the sugar cone to her mouth. Kentaro watched as the pink tip of her tongue moved to wrap around and remove a portion of the cold treat. There was something very erotic in the simple movement, and he decided he would do better to watch the Disney characters in the parade instead.

"I think we should move on." Claire stood, her hips against the plastic chair. "Unless you are interested in this?" She waved her hand toward the almost finished parade.

"No, but..." He cleared his throat. Standing would not be the best move at this moment so he had to find a way to get out of it. "I have a blister. Can we just sit here a while longer?" Unable to keep from watching Claire, he could only hope she finished the ice cream soon.

"Okay." Claire slid down the back of the chair to return to her seat. No one in the area paid any attention to the couple speaking a foreign language so common was non-English in the amusement park.

Kentaro continued to watch her, spellbound by her face. Her hair was loose. Tendrils blew about her head in the gentle breeze as she tried to keep it out of her ice cream and subsequently her mouth. Her eyes were shielded by sunglasses, but he could see their outline behind the not-so-dark lenses. A gentle patina of sweat covered her bare shoulders and upper chest revealed by the tank top she wore. Kentaro watched her absentmindedly rub the cloth into that space between the gentle swells. A tiny rivulet must have tickled as it ran between her breasts. Their slight movement stirred Kentaro.

"Are you not going to eat your ice cream?" Claire indicated the small bowl of chocolate mush in front of Kentaro.

"I am not hungry." For food.

"Oh." Claire put the last bite of cone in her mouth, then said, "I have to go wash the sticky off. Be right back." She left him alone at the table.

Thank goodness. Kentaro worked to put his body back to sleep. This was not the first time Claire had caused such a response, just the first time it had lasted so long or been so intense.

"Want to go over to EPCOT?" Claire was back at his side. "They have little kiosks from countries around the world where you can see things from that country. I know Japan has one."

"Very well." Kentaro stood, relieved to find his jeans fitting appropriately over his groin.


"This is very nice," Kentaro commented when, three hours later, they stood in front of the exhibit from Japan in the international area of EPCOT. They had taken their time to sightsee as they walked to the area. With Kentaro behind, Claire entered the small kiosk. She wound her way through the stacks of T-shirts with Japanese designs and words, figurines of geisha, fishermen, Buddhist and Shinto gods, as well as the obligatory samurai swords for sale.

"Oh, my! This is gorgeous!" Claire stood before a mannequin dressed in an elegant kimono of thick lilac silk embroidered with designs of hibiscus and iris with butterflies. "It is beautiful." Claire never questioned the ease in which her conversational Japanese was coming to her.

"You are interested in buying kimono?" Kentaro joined her.

"Well,...they are very expensive. And I have no idea how to wear one. I understand even young women in Japan have to take courses in how to wear a kimono."

"Yes, many do, but it is a talent you could learn. Why do you not see what the price is?"

"All right." Claire moved around the model to look for a price tag. "I can not find it," she stated after a few minutes.

"Surely it is somewhere." Kentaro joined in the search, circling the opposite way. "I would suppose it is for sale since it is displayed so openly."

"No, nothing. Oh!" The cry of surprise escaped Claire's lips as she came around the mannequin.

Kentaro responded with his noise when they collided. He reached out to take hold of her arms and Claire held him in the same manner. For long seconds Claire, so close to Kentaro's body, looked up into his eyes. More than anything, Kentaro wanted to embrace her, to pull her against his chest. Instead, he released her. Claire's hand, for an instant on his body at the spot where his heart pounded, pushed until she was away from him.

"Sorry," they both muttered. They turned to look at other things of Japan in the shop, but in reality saw nothing.

# Chapter Eight

The trip back to Winter Park was made in a reserved silence, Claire and Kentaro each in their own thoughts. After the kimono incident, they had returned to the bus without stopping to enjoy any more of the sights or refreshments. The only pause had been when Claire detoured into a restroom.

Inside the public bathroom, crowded with children and mothers, Claire washed her hands. She pushed her sunglasses up onto her head and splashed cool water on her face. As she raised from the lavatory bowl, she caught a glimpse of her face in the mirror. Sunburn stained the bridge of her nose, her cheeks, forehead, and chin. She swept her bangs from her brow, fluffing them with her fingers. Avoiding her eyes, she pulled the shades back down to her nose. The green of her eyes was more intense today, and they had a light, a sparkle, she never noticed before. Where did it come from? She dried her hands, then left the sanctuary of the busy restroom.

Kentaro, forced to wait for her on a bench, watched the visitors pass him by. Other men with the same bored look on their faces loitered around, waiting for their women and children. Kentaro's thoughts drifted, or to be more exact, rushed back to Claire. Her nearness at the Japanese kiosk was so overpowering he had been unable to savor the event. Now, on the bench with strangers, he could dwell on every minute detail.

The skin on her arms and hands was smooth and soft. Her eyes were bright, a sparkle in the green sea accentuated by golden motes as they looked into his. Her luxuriously long hair, held back by two barrettes at either side, swung so gently as she moved to step away from him. Her lips, moist and pink, begged to be kissed. He regretted he hadn't. If only he had put his arms around her slender shoulders, she would have been unable to escape, and he could have kissed her. That was all lost now. He knew he would not let a second chance pass without his acting on the impulse to show Claire his desire for her.

Kentaro stood as she approached. He appeared, for a moment, to be about to speak, but instead silently led her on their way.

Once aboard the bus, the huge wheels turning over the highway in the dark night, they continued their silence. The sun had sapped the morning's energy from the group and many were asleep. It was all Claire could do to keep her eyes open. She knew that if she did nod off, her head would find its way to Kentaro's shoulder and she did not want that.

Or did she?

Kentaro's thoughts followed the same path. He wished she would drop into a nap so she would nestle into his side. The thought of her so soft and warm next to him renewed the desires he had only hours before vowed to avoid. Every nerve in his body screamed with lust.

Women had never been a problem for Kentaro. Without emotional cost, he had taken advantage of every baseball groupie and everything they had offered him. But now, in a short period of time, this woman assigned to change his Japanese to English, to become his "words," had caused him to assess his life.

Never had he encountered a female who would stand up to him or allow him to do any task for himself. Women adored him as a professional athlete or wanted to mother him. They never saw the man beneath the persona. Now, at twenty-eight years of age, he wanted a woman to share the most personal things of his life, one he could love with all his heart, one who would love him in the same way.

As she sat beside him, Kentaro allowed his eyes to feast on the view of Claire's breasts, their curves exposed by the tank top. Her long, slender legs were bare; her hips covered with shorts. She had kicked off her tennis shoes, and he could see the outline of Disney World grime on her ankles where the shoes had ended. Could Claire Ferris be the woman his heart searched for? Would she be the one to share his life? Could his heart survive a brief collision with her? Would he dare to find out?

"What are you staring at?" Claire broke into his thoughts.

"Nothing." Kentaro wrenched his stare from her bodice. He squirmed in his seat to ease the pressure of the tightness in his jeans.

"I do not believe you." Claire looked out the window into the darkness.

Kentaro responded with the usual sound.

Claire was relieved Kentaro did not voice his thoughts because she was afraid of what he was thinking. What if he thought about her in a sexual way? How would she deal with that? She was drawn back to him.

He stared down the aisle, so she was able to study his lean, angled face. His bronzed skin was pulled over high cheekbones. Beneath his straight, long nose, an occasional flicker of his tongue escaped his full, soft lips. His long, thick hair hung down his neck, unbound, to cover his shoulders. The forelock, longish between haircuts, was suspended over his forehead to tease the angled fold of his sloe eyes.

The knit shirt stretched over his broad chest so tight she could see the musculature it covered. Tight jeans encased his narrow hips and straight legs ended in high top shoes.

For the first time since the incident at the kimono mannequin, Claire allowed her thoughts and body to react instead of suppressing the desires. Her breath was tight in her chest and a burning began in her deepest parts. What if Kentaro was a man in her life, not a job? What would she do? What should she do? Would he reject her if she blurted out her desires? Could she bear to have these new hungers go unfulfilled?

There were too many questions and feelings to deal with in this short night. Claire turned her head from Kentaro. She didn't dare to hope he felt anything toward her but his usual aloofness.

*"Ikuta-san,"* Claire confronted the pitcher in the hallway of the clubhouse, "we are going to start your English lessons today."

*"Wakaru masen?"* Kentaro looked down at her. It had been three days since the Disney World trip, and the two had not spoken more than the necessary translation words. "What do you mean?"

"I was hired to translate and teach you English. Up until now you have put me off, but we have to start. You are doing your job as a pitcher, allow me to do mine."

"I do not wish to...," Kentaro sputtered his protest. He could not help noticing the flush on Claire's face or be touched by the way it caused a deep rosy hue to cover her cheeks. Nevertheless, she was telling him what to do. No woman had ever done this.

"Stop. You cannot refuse. Now, there is a room two doors down from the locker room where I have set up a classroom. Practice is over at three. We will start at five. Be there." Claire left him standing alone in the hall.

At five, Claire sat alone in the room she had fashioned into a classroom. There was a small table with two chairs. On it, books, papers, and pens lay awaiting a pupil. A chalkboard stood along the wall with scribblings Claire had started. She looked at her watch: quarter past five. Kentaro had had plenty of time to shower and join her. Maybe her ultimatum wasn't going to work.

*"Ferris-san?"*

"Here," Claire replied to Kentaro's call in the hall.

"I must have misunderstood you." He entered the room and faced Claire. "I thought you said the other direction."

"I thought I was quite clear. The second room after the locker room. Did I rush you?" She nodded her head toward his shirt that hung unbuttoned from his torso. A wash of passion rose as she looked at the chest muscled with hard pecs and stomach displaying the washboard effect so sought after by bodybuilders. His long black hair was damp and clung to his head.

"I...I...was delayed." Kentaro buttoned his shirt. Claire was sorry she had mentioned it when his magnificent body was covered. "Shall we begin?"

"Yes. Please sit."

The daily classes started with simple phrases and moved toward the more difficult grammar and verb usage. Kentaro had studied the basics of English in Japanese schools, so it was not impossible for Claire to tap into the knowledge he had hidden deep within his brain. The lessons continued until the last week of March when the ball team began to pack up to return to Cleveland for the opening of the regular season.

# Chapter Nine

Hopkins International Airport loomed large as the plane dropped to land. Claire, beside Kentaro as she had been for eight weeks, was more confused than ever. She didn't want the trip to end; nevertheless, she was eager to get home. Although she would be free of Kentaro's constant presence, she would miss their private quasi-companionship. While she had not put a name to her personal feelings, had even able to push them aside in their last days together, Claire knew she was attracted to Kentaro in the most intimate way.

"The snow has started to melt." Kentaro looked across her to the view out the window.

"It has. Spring should be here soon." Claire began to gather her belongings. On this trip, she had lulled her nerves with a glass of white wine instead of the strong bourbon.

"Do you need a ride from the airport, *Ferris-san*?"

"Suddenly concerned with my arrangements, *Ikuta-san*?"

He made the guttural noise and turned away from her. Claire was sorry she had been so sharp tongued. Why had she done that?

"I have a friend coming to pick me up. *Domo arigato*." She tried to restart the conversation.

It didn't work. Kentaro was quiet after he had made his samurai sound to indicate he had heard her. A palpable icy chill emanated from him. It was equal to standing at the corner of Lake Shore and 9th where the Canadian wind crossed Lake Erie to blow through the downtown corridor and freeze anything in its path.

They deplaned into a crowded airport lined with Cleveland Chiefs fans waving pennants, flags, and hats as the team passed by them. Claire huddled at Ikuta's back as they moved away from the gate, conscious of the small round buttocks clad in tight jeans as she bumped into him by accident.

The fans called out to the players, but few responded with more than waves and smiles. Claire noticed Ikuta ducked his eyes while waving his hand.

"You will not have to speak, *Ikuta-san*," Claire sought to reassure him. "The front office has agreed to let me know in advance about all your interviews."

"That was not my concern, *Ferris-san*. I was not prepared for such a greeting."

"Japanese fans must be quiet," she commented. She'd made her way to his side.

"They are a little more reserved." The ice thawed.

They arrived at the area where their personal luggage sat. Kentaro helped Claire collect hers, and they found themselves faced with farewells.

"Do you see your friend?" Kentaro asked.

"*Iye*. Andy is going to meet me at the curb." Claire noticed Kentaro shifted from foot to foot as she did. It was as if they were strangers, the casualness of Florida at an end. "I suppose I will wait for your call or that of the office."

"I would assume so." He wouldn't meet her eyes.

"Can we give you a ride?" Claire strove not to end the trip.

"I do not wish to impose. I will get a taxi. Good day, *Ferris-san*." Kentaro took the action to break the interlude and walked away from her.

"Hello, Claire!" Jason Stewart approached Claire as she stood on the sidewalk.

Oh, God! Claire, watching Kentaro at the nearby taxi stand, saw him turn to look at her in response to Jason's loud voice.

"Hi, Jason." She endured his disturbing kiss and hug with the arm that did not leave her shoulders all the more uncomfortable because she knew Kentaro watched them.

"Getting in from Florida? Aren't you a little old for spring break?"

"I was visiting friends," Claire lied and shrugged his arm off. "I have to go. Bye."

"I'll call!" Jason's usual remark was shouted to her back.

Kentaro Ikuta arrived at his empty apartment and went through the usual arrival rituals of homecoming. The apartment had been tended to by a housekeeping firm employed by the Chiefs management so it appeared as if someone had just left the living room. Kentaro was unsettled by the vast space of his dwelling. Born in a country so filled with people who existed in such close quarters they sought their whole lives for a privacy he found here in America, he felt guilty. Still, he realized his discomfort wasn't wholly because of this fact. He was moved to telephone his family.

"May I speak with Takahiko?" Kentaro asked after he spoke with his parents.

"Taro?" His sister was on the phone now. "It is wonderful to hear your voice! How was spring training?"

"It was training, Taka. How is your schooling?" Kentaro needed to ask his sister about his feelings, but could not. Early in life, he had been trained to keep a front between himself and others to avoid causing discomfort. To voice his quandary, even to Takahiko who shared so many of his secrets, would be a violation of all his social standards.

"Taro, you did not call to ask about school. I can tell by your voice something is wrong. Would you tell me?"

"It is not important." He made light of his confusion.

"Very well. How are your English classes? As difficult as when we were in public school? Do you wish to speak English? Has your interpreter made you fluent yet?"

"No. Hmmgh. I never wish to speak English and you are aware of that. I do not see why it is so important for me to be able to speak English." Kentaro was sorry he had called.

"Ah ha. I have found the nerve of your problem. What is happening with your interpreter?"

"Nothing is happening with *Ferris-san*," Kentaro spat. His words hinted at hostility.

"Big brother, you are lying to me."

"What should be 'going on' as you put it? She does her job and I do mine. Besides, she has many boyfriends."

"I saw a news report of you at Disney World and she was with you. It looked as if you were having a good time."

"It was...interesting." Kentaro's thoughts brightened as he came to a decision. "Takahiko, I have something I want you to do for me."

"Well, well, well, look at you!" Andrea greeted Claire as she slipped into the passenger seat of the BMW. "All tanned and lean. Looks like you worked out as hard as the team!"

"I did get in a good deal of exercise." Claire avoided looking at her friend while she settled her things in the car.

"Did you have a good time?" Andrea shifted gears and began to pull from the parking area.

"It was fun."

"And how's Mr. Baseball-san?"

"Andy!" Claire faced her friend. "That's not funny. And it was all right."

"I think you're a little defensive there, Claire. You're blushing." Andrea was quiet for a minute, concentrating on the traffic leaving the airport parking lot. "Jason Stewart called me. He wanted to know where you where," she said after merging to the highway.

"Our mothers must have had lunch together." Claire paid attention to the window again and not Andrea. "I ran into him at the airport. Did you tell him where I was?"

"No. Didn't think you wanted me to."

"He must have found out from someone because he knew I was coming from Florida."

"I don't know why you don't like Jason. He's nice."

"You go out with him then. I happen to find him boring and plain. He has no ambition. In fact, he's a slug."

"Claire! I've never heard you talk about someone like that."

Claire didn't respond. In light of the emotions emerging for Kentaro Ikuta, she knew she felt nothing for Jason. She became aware of how uncomfortable she was with her long-time friend.

"I called your mom like you asked, and she said she'd see about your apartment." Andrea interrupted Claire's thoughts about the men.

"Thanks. I didn't want to talk to her. You know, I did-n't really want to come home," Claire laughed.

"I wouldn't want to come back from Florida either," Andrea agreed as she pulled to the curb before Claire's apart-ment building. "Here we are."

"Uh-huh," Claire nodded. She didn't want to tell her friend the relationship with Kentaro was what she didn't want to leave.

"Thanks, Andy. I'll see you at the gym tomorrow."

Claire exited the car. They exchanged waves and Claire stood on the curb watching as Andrea pulled away.

Maneuvering her luggage into the building and home, Claire sensed the rooms had never before seemed so quiet.

She dumped her things in the middle of her bed, and while putting them away, decided to call Kentaro. She told herself it was to touch bases about resuming classes. Would he think her forward?

Come on, Claire! You're calling about work, not a date!

She would not admit to herself she wanted to hear his voice.

*"Ikuta-san?"* Claire spoke when the Japanese baseball player answered his phone with the traditional *'Moshi-moshi'*.

*"Ferris-san."*

"I...I hope I am not disturbing you." Claire twirled her hair with the hand not holding the receiver.

"I was unpacking, but it can wait. How may I help you?"

"We did not set up a time for class."

"You are correct. We did not."

Claire hesitated. Did she detect a warm note in his voice as they spoke about the lessons he hated so?

"I...when...I was wondering what you thought would be a good time? The season opens next Saturday and you have practice every day until then..." Claire rambled in her nervousness. What if he said he didn't want to meet her for lessons? But he had to. The team managers wanted him able to speak soon. Still, he could be unfriendly during the lessons, and she couldn't face his coldness.

"I think we should continue with the schedule we had in Florida. After practice. You will be at the field during the day." It was a statement.

"Definitely."

"I will see you then."

"Very well."

"Is that all you wanted, *Ferris-san?*"

"I...yes,...that is all."

64

# The Words of the Pitcher

"I am glad you called to remind me. I will study your lessons this evening."

"I just realized we had not...," Claire didn't want to hang up and she sensed Kentaro didn't either. What else could she say to keep him on the line?

"English teaching is your job so it is only right you should attend to the details of it. Just as my task is to pitch well. I can only think about what I need to do to that end, planning when and how to practice. I will put myself in your hands in regard to English."

"Thank you. It is nice to have you co-operating with me."

"Why should I hinder you? As I said, it is only your job. I must respect that."

"Well..." They were back to that uncomfortable silence.

"Yes?"

"Oh...nothing. I suppose I should let you get back to unpacking."

At the other end of the line, Claire heard what she had wanted to hear, making her feel warm inside, just as she wanted.

Kentaro's samurai noise.

"*Oyasumi nasai, Ikuta-san.*"

"Sleep well, *Ferris-san*," he returned.

# Chapter Ten

Jacobs Field was packed on opening day of the baseball season. Claire stood in the hallway behind the dugout, waiting for the team. She wore what she had decided would be her uniform, khaki Dockers and red oxford cloth shirt. Her hair hung straight and she wore a Chiefs baseball cap.

She didn't know if she was nervous because of the game, the interviews that would occur after the game, or the anticipation of meeting Kentaro. Everyday, as she approached the stadium to be with him during practice, she found her heart beating a mile a minute, her breath short. All this disappeared when she joined him on the field. And he had begun to smile when they first met everyday. That smile caused the heat to rise to her face and made her feel comfortable inside. That feeling was what she waited for this afternoon.

"*Ferris-san*." Kentaro startled her as he always did. He had a way of coming up behind her without a sound. "*Konnichi wa*."

"Hello." Claire whirled around, excited at his arrival. Her anxiety disappeared, and she felt a contentment settle over her. "Are you ready for the game?"

"I have to be." Kentaro was in uniform. The knit material hugged every bulge and curve of his body. "I am a little apprehensive about starting."

"Oh?" This was a rare display. Claire fell in step with him as he made his way to the dugout.

"I have dreamed of pitching in an American major league game since I was a child. Now, I am here."

"You will do great. I watched you practice earlier today," Claire encouraged.

"I was unaware you were there." Kentaro looked at her, surprise written in his eyes. "Were we to meet?"

"No. There was no official reason for it." Claire blushed, flustered at being caught showing up when unexpected, afraid he'd think the wrong things, or, perhaps, the right things.

They came to the doorway of the home team dugout behind third base, guarded by two security guards.

"Afternoon," the one on the right spoke.

The guard at the left reached to open the door for Ikuta. Claire started to follow him in.

"Excuse me, miss, but you'll have to wait in the office down the hallway."

"*Ferris-san*?" Kentaro called to her when she didn't come after him.

"They say I have to stay in an office down the hall. I guess they will come get me if they need to talk to you on the mound or something."

"You must be in the dugout," Kentaro demanded.

"Mr. Ikuta says he needs me in the dugout," Claire translated to the guards, who exchanged baffled looks.

"Only players and coaches are allowed there."

Claire explained it to Kentaro who came out to stand in the hallway with her. He refused to remain in the dugout without her.

"I'll have to talk to management," one guard announced and left to find an executive.

"We'll be right here," Claire said.

Claire and Kentaro waited in the hallway, shifting their weight, neither looking at the other. People moved around them going on their own personal journeys and pre-game business.

"I had meant to ask before," Kentaro broke the embarrassed silence as they waited the return of the guard, "was that your young man who picked you up at the airport?"

"Uh? Oh, no, no," Claire stammered her answer, caught off guard. "He is a family friend."

The guard returned with one of the pitching coaches, cutting off any further discussion of Jason.

"Problem, Ms. Ferris?" Steve Martella asked.

"*Ikuta-san* refuses to be in the dugout without me. The guard says only players and coaches."

"Looks like you'll have to become a coach then, Claire. You're now the official English coach of the Cleveland Chiefs." Steve chucked her on the shoulder in the manner she had seen him do with the players. "Now, get in there and get ready for the game!"

"Thank you." Claire turned to tell Kentaro what Steve had said and noted the scowl on his face. "Martella-san says I am now a coach, so I can come into the dugout." Unable to stand the look on his face, she asked, "What is wrong now?"

"What did he call you?" Kentaro growled.

"Claire. It is my first name."

Kentaro responded with his noise as he returned to the dugout. Claire followed.

Emerging from the interior of the stadium, Claire was momentarily blinded by the sun which had decided to shine on Cleveland in a rare early spring appearance. The audio system blared with rock music as the crowd filled the seats. Kentaro removed his jacket and handed it to Claire, who folded it over her arm. As she viewed the fans, she pulled her arms across her stomach in hopes the butterflies flying around inside her would be quelled.

Claire watched Kentaro, the reason she was even at Jacobs Field, leave the dugout to take his place in the bull pen and begin his warm-up. Ramon Vasquez caught for him as the two were scheduled to start for the Chiefs. Kentaro's body moved with a fluid grace each time he released the ball. He pitched with intensity and his face was hard.

Kentaro's well-fitted uniform stretched over his wide chest, small buttocks, and firm thighs. The short sleeves looked as though they cut into his biceps. His hair was confined by his cap and a band at the nape. On occasion, he would remove the cap and, with the back of his hand, wipe his brow, giving Claire a brief glimpse of his loose forelock.

Claire didn't know what to do with herself as she looked around the male-dominated area. A long bench lined the front of the concrete room. A rack filled with bats covered the front corner. A television was mounted high in the wall, and a ten-gallon jug of Gatorade sat iced and ready for the players. With near reverence, Claire hung Kentaro's jacket on a pegboard for jackets.

"Well, Coach," Steve teased her, "just find a seat, preferably near Ikuta. He'll probably sit at the back like he did during exhibition. After the game, we'll meet with the press. During these media events, we'd like for you to stand in front of Ikuta. Since you are so small, he hides you from view."

"I can't stand in front of him. It would be offensive to him," Claire explained.

"I don't understand. What does it matter where you stand?"

"You have mentioned *Ikuta-san* has an attitude. Or at least, Mr. Horsch did. Anyway, he acts the way he does because of the society he grew up in and, for a woman to be standing in front of him, doing business, is insulting. Besides, no one needs to see me. Just hear his words from me."

"Whatever, Coach. You know your job, I know mine. Enjoy the game. Oh, someone sent you some flowers." Steve handed her a bouquet of roses wrapped in green florist paper. "Your English student?" He winked at her.

"I don't think so. Thanks." Claire took the flowers without looking at the card. They were probably from her parents. The Ferrises were so excited about her job, her father had arranged for his partner to take calls so he and Claudia could attend the game and take Claire out to dinner afterwards.

"If you say so." Steve shrugged and went out onto the field.

Claire would have enjoyed standing at the front of the dugout where she had the best view of Kentaro, but she didn't want to draw attention to herself. So, she took a seat at the end of the bench away from the team. She placed the roses to her left.

Claire watched Kentaro pitch to Vasquez. The public address system made announcements which the team and coaches ignored. Curious, she picked up the small white envelope accompanying the roses. Lifting the flap, she pulled the card from inside, then stuffed it back quickly. Had she really hoped they were from him? It wasn't disappointment she felt. It was anger.

As the game was about to start, Claire forgot the flowers. Kentaro returned to the dugout. He looked toward Claire.

"Flowers, *Ferris-san*?" he commented.

"Yeah." Claire glanced at the roses. She tucked the envelope further inside the green florist paper.

"Who from?"

"A friend." Claire dismissed the gift.

"Where is my jacket?"

His team mates ignored the couple as they chattered on in Japanese.

"I hung it over there." Claire pointed to the pegboard.

"You were to keep it for me." Kentaro went to retrieve the garment, but not without issuing his sound to signify his attitude.

"I am not your wardrobe mistress." He was seriously mistaken if he thought her to be his attendant! A grown man didn't need a mother to keep up with his things.

The team mustered as the crowd watched the mayor of Cleveland throw out the first pitch. The Chiefs team and coaching staff then moved out to line up along the third base to homeplate foul line as their opponents did the same along first and homeplate. Kentaro, the starting pitcher, stood at the end nearest the dugout.

Claire joined the others in the dugout for the singing of "The Star Spangled Banner." When the cry of "Play ball!" rose from the over-eager crowd, the teams trotted back into their respective dugouts. The coaches gave last minute instructions as the players removed jackets and applied the serious gear of baseball. At Ikuta's side whispering the Japanese translation of Martella's coaching to him, Claire found herself once more in possession of Kentaro's jacket. With the Chiefs in the outfield first, Kentaro went to the mound.

Eagerly listening, Claire felt goosebumps as the game announcer began to read the starting lineup. Claire's heart was in her throat as he finished with the name of the home team's starting pitcher, afraid the Chiefs would change their plans.

"And, as starting pitcher for the Cleveland Chiefs, playing in his first American major league ball game, from Nagasaki, Japan, KENTARO IKUTA!" the announcer intoned in a deep baritone with echoing effect.

Claire applauded as loudly as anyone in the stadium, then was embarrassed to find herself the only one in the dugout to pay attention to the announcements. She sank into her seat, hugging Kentaro's jacket to her as protection. Anxiety seized Claire as Kentaro went into his wind-up, stretched his tall slim body out, and delivered his first pitch.

A strike. She released her held breath.

He struck three batters out and came to sit at Claire's side. After he took the jacket from her, he draped it over his right shoulder and arm. They sat silently. Kentaro, into his game mind-set, barely acknowledged the young woman at his side.

For nine innings, Claire watched Kentaro pitch, a lump in her throat each time he almost walked a batter. He threw 136 pitches, allowing only two hits and no walks and no runs.

It must be good as excited as everyone is.

Then Claire was called to meet the sports reporters at Kentaro's side. Her enthusiasm evaporated.

# Chapter Eleven

"Great game, men. Great game." Horsch greeted players as they entered the dugout, slapping them on the back or shaking their hand. "Everyone hit the showers! Let's go, let's go!" He clapped his hands after the last player exited the dugout.

Claire followed Ikuta and the rest of the team into the hallway. She hesitated as the men approached the locker room. She wasn't sure she wanted to repeat the incident of the first day.

"Claire," Steve Martella spoke. He guided her down the hallway to a room filled with media. "After Ikuta showers, you and he will go here and answer questions." He looked her up and down with a bewildered look on his face. "Is that what you're wearing?"

"Well, yes." Claire moved Ikuta's jacket which she somehow continued to hold to her side and looked down at her slacks and shirt.

"This goes." Martella pulled the cap off her head, freeing her long hair. "But wear the jacket." He took the garment and put it on her. "Much better." Martella disappeared into the showers before Claire could explain it was not her jacket to wear.

Kentaro approached Claire in the hall.

"Are you nervous, *Ferris-san*?"

"Do I look nervous?" They made their way toward the room set aside for press conferences.

Kentaro looked down at Claire with an expression that surprised her. It was a smile almost loving in appearance.

"Yes."

"I will endeavor not to."

"You look quite pleasing, Claire. Especially in my jacket." Kentaro entered the room.

Claire was left with her mouth agape. She had never heard Kentaro speak her name, except for the time on the plane which was a mere hint of it. It was as if his tongue caressed her when he spoke. Her face aglow with emotion, she hurried to regain her composure and catch up with him.

Taking her seat at a long conference table lined with microphones, Claire adjusted the chair behind Ikuta who faced the numerous mini-cams and reporters. Martella, Horsch, and Jamison were down the table from her left. She ruffled her bangs and shook her hair back over her shoulders.

"...the game's outcome was what we expected. Ikuta is going to prove his worth to the team," Jamison spoke first. "Now, I turn you over to our winning pitcher, Kentaro Ikuta."

"Ikuta?" a reporter asked.

"Ikuta!" another shouted to the pitcher.

"Over here, Ikuta!" still one more called out.

Cameras flashed. Tiny red lights on the minicams on the shoulders of the cameramen glowed to indicate they were rolling.

Claire could see Kentaro becoming rattled as everyone called out at once. She touched his hand below the table. Kentaro didn't look toward her. He didn't move his hand either.

"Mr. Ikuta," the ESPN reporter seemed to dominate the reporters. "Did you do as well as you expected?"

Claire whispered the Japanese words into Kentaro's ear and listened as he spoke in response.

"I was pleased with my performance, yes. I was not as nervous as I expected I would be, this being my first

American major league game." Claire concentrated on her words in hopes of getting the exact translation of his Japanese.

And so it continued. Claire, in an easy pattern of interpretation, gave a running translation to Kentaro. Soon enough, Horsch and Jamison took over the questions and Kentaro was free to depart.

As she made her way out the door, Claire saw Jason Stewart. He stood against the wall at the back. In his hands were the roses, the ones he had sent her and she had dropped into the trash can in the dugout. Claire continued out of the room.

"Are you going home now, *Ferris-san*?" Kentaro asked on their way out of the stadium. He seemed at a loss of what to do or where to go.

What happened to 'Claire'?

"My parents are waiting to take me out to dinner. Would you like to join us? They are celebrating my job. We could celebrate your win."

"I would enjoy that, Claire." Kentaro smiled as he emphasized her name.

"They should be over at the players' gate." Claire directed him, content and feeling special, yet she dipped her face so he would not see it.

Walking toward the gate, Claire realized Kentaro's mood swings probably had nothing to do with her, only his relief at having done well. During their time in Florida, he had hinted at his concern with his performance. From what she saw this afternoon, he had nothing to worry about. Then again, she still didn't know anything about baseball.

"Mom, Dad," Claire greeted her parents who stood on the sidewalk outside the stadium, "I'd like you to meet Kentaro Ikuta. *Ikuta-san*," she said in Japanese, "my parents, Dr. Robert and Claudia Ferris."

"Nice to meet you. You pitched a great game." Dr. Ferris shook the pitcher's hand.

"*Ohayo gozimus, sensei.*" Kentaro added a slight bow of his head to Dr. Ferris.

"How are you?" Claudia asked in what Claire called her mother's 'junior league' voice, the one where she seemed to speak through her nose.

Kentaro greeted Claire's mother.

"*Ikuta-san* is going to join us for dinner, if it's okay?"

"Surely," Dr. Ferris replied. "The car's over in that lot." He pointed toward the tall parking garage across the street. "Why don't I go get it and pick you up here? Mr. Ikuta seems to have his hands full."

Claire turned to see Kentaro busily signing autographs for the young fans who hung around the gate to meet the players as they left the stadium. He had learned this practice in no time and didn't need Claire since it took no actual speech to accomplish.

"That would be grand, Robert." Claudia waved her husband away. "So, Claire, how'd the game go for you? We saw you down in the dugout." Claudia took her daughter's arm, pulling her close to her side.

Claire tried to resist, but knew it was impossible. She caught sight of Kentaro, who was trying to keep his mind on the baseballs being thrust his way for his signature. She could swear she saw a smirk on his face after her mother said, "You looked so cute in your little hat and jacket!"

"Mother!"

As if to derail Claudia, Claire extracted her arm from her grasp and removed the garment.

# The Words of the Pitcher

"*Ikuta-san*, here is your jacket. Mother, this is *Ikuta-san*'s.*" It was not as difficult to switch between English and Japanese as she had thought it would be.

"Oh?" Claudia's eyes widened.

"Mother, I just happened to have it." Claire, cheeks reddened, knew that, in her mother's day, the exchanging of 'varsity sweaters or jackets' made the couple an item. Just what she needed! Claudia would be thinking of her as romantically involved with Kentaro.

"Here's Daddy." Claire watched her father's Mercedes slow at the curb.

Claire sat with Kentaro in the backseat. She was nervous about the dinner, afraid her mother would say something awful as mothers were known to do at times without even being aware of it. Would it be ethical if she neglected to translate certain things? What would it hurt if she didn't tell Kentaro everything that was said? She decided she would have to wait to see what was said before she made a judgment.

"How did the press conference go?" Dr. Ferris asked over his shoulder as he drove along the street congested with fans returning home.

"It went fine. Easy actually." Claire glanced at Kentaro, who looked expectant. "Father asked about the press conference. I said it was easy. Was it so for you?"

"I found your words correct. Your father is a doctor? What sort?"

"Pediatrics with a specialty in oncology. What does your father do?"

"He is an accountant. My mother takes care of him, my sister, and brother."

"Mother stays home also. She keeps busy with her clubs and charities. She helps with the Rainbow Babies and Children's Hospital Auxiliary here in Cleveland."

# Kei Swanson

They lapsed into silence.  Claire pondered Kentaro's
meaning of his mother 'taking care' of his father.  Finally,
she felt compelled to ask.

"*Ikuta-san*, is your father ill?"

"No.  Why do you ask?"

"You said your mother 'takes care' of him."

"I also said she took care of my siblings.  Perhaps 'takes
care' is the wrong phrase."

"Maybe.  I understand your words mean 'tending to,'"
she explained.

"That is more correct.  She tends to the house and family.  Her duty is to care for my father's needs."

"Do you require the same duty of a wife?"

"Why do you ask?"  Kentaro's question caused Claire to
flush.

"No reason."  Claire turned her attention to the scenery
flashing by as the car made its way to the restaurant.


"This is Sterle's," Claire told Kentaro.  "We come here for
almost all celebrations.  It is a long-standing establishment in
Cleveland."

Kentaro responded with his sound...softer than usual.

It was busy inside the restaurant, loud as always.  The
oomph band played while couples crowded the small dance
floor.  The hostess led them to a table away from the band-
stand, which provided a clear view of the dancers.

"Do you like German food?" Claudia asked the young
man through her daughter.

"I do not believe I have ever had it, unless you count hot
dogs at the stadium," Ikuta answered.

"That does not count," Claire responded after the translation to her mother.  "I think you will enjoy the wiener
schnitzel.  It is a beef dish of a fried, breaded cutlet.  They
also serve a very nice chicken noodle soup."

78

"I will allow you to take care of me, Claire." Kentaro's eyes twinkled with a hint of mischievousness.

"You may be in big trouble!" Claire laughed. She noticed that her parents watched their exchange with amused bewilderment. The waitress poured everyone a glass of wine.

Dr. Ferris directed personal conversational questions to Kentaro, which Claire interpreted back and forth. After ordering the meal, Claire's parents excused themselves to take advantage of the dancing. Claire and Kentaro occupied themselves with wine and conversation.

"They do this every time," Claire stated as if embarrassed. She emptied her glass.

"And you do not?" Kentaro poured them both a second serving of the Moselle wine.

"I dance with Father occasionally, sort of an obligatory dance. I am not very good at doing the polka. But he and mother really enjoy it and execute it well."

"They appear to." Kentaro watched the couple. He sipped from his glass while Claire watched him.

His face was soft, almost vulnerable, which led her to wonder about his thoughts. Did he regret he did not have family nearby to share his accomplishment? He could share with her, but who was she? An interpreter, only his 'words.' She was surprised at the disappointment which flooded her body as she realized she was no more important to Kentaro than his teammates.

Food arrived as Robert and Claudia returned to the table, out of breath from dancing.

"I'd like to make a toast." Dr. Ferris lifted his glass of wine and announced, "Claire, you interpret."

"Father wants to propose a toast."

Kentaro picked up his glass, as did Claire and her mother.

"To Kentaro Ikuta, who has successfully pitched his first American league game, and my lovely daughter, Claire, who has triumphantly translated for him at a press conference. Congratulations. Cheers!"

They clinked glasses as Claire changed the toast to Japanese. Kentaro and Claire added their "*banzai*" a beat too late, causing them both to break into laughter. The wine had loosened Kentaro's formal attitude. His laugh was warm and rich.

"Did you enjoy the soup?" Claire asked Kentaro.

"It was very good." Kentaro had finished the soup and was halfway through the schnitzel. "What is this called again?"

"Schnitzel or wiener schnitzel. Steve Martella commented on your healthy appetite. He said your agent did all the talking and you all the eating at the dinner when you and your agent met with the managers."

"You are saying I eat a lot, *Ferris-san*?"

"No. I was just...repeating what Martella-san said." Claire was aware of her blush. Why did she fall into his traps so easily?

"Claire, what are you two talking about?" Claudia asked.

"Nothing important, Mother." Claire's tone was harsh, her exasperation at Kentaro directed at her mother.

Silence crept over the table even while the band continued to play. The diners finished and sat over coffee.

"Claire, have you heard from Andy lately?" Claudia opened the conversation with what she thought was an innocent question.

"Yes. A week ago." Claire noticed Kentaro's eyes dart toward her as though he knew what her mother asked and was affected by it.

"Are you two planning on getting together?" Claudia quizzed.

Kentaro made his usual noise, and Claire realized he could understand them.

"Mother, I don't think we should continue this here."

"Oh, Claire, he doesn't understand what we're saying," Claudia said in a hushed tone.

"I think you'd be surprised." Claire looked at Kentaro, who flashed a knowing grin. "You are beginning to understand more English, are you not?" she asked him.

"You can never tell." He drank from his coffee cup, keeping his eyes averted from her.

"So, since you talked to Andy, how about Jason? His mother and I had lunch a couple of weeks ago. He's recently returned to join his father's firm." Claudia stirred her almost empty coffee cup.

"Mother, please stop," Claire said through gritted teeth. "I don't want to talk about Jason tonight!"

"My word, Claire. You'd think I asked you to give away state secrets or something! I doubt Mr. Ikuta cares if you have a boyfriend."

"Jason is not my boyfriend," Claire insisted.

"Now, Claudia," Robert Ferris cut into the conversation, "I agree with Claire. Let's drop the subject."

"Well, I never!" Claudia pouted.

"It's fine, dear." Dr. Ferris patted his wife's hand.

"Excuse me, *Ferris-san*," Kentaro spoke up. "I must be going. The game and the wine have taken away all the energy I had."

"Do you want us to give you a ride?" Claire started to rise, surprised at the suddenness of Ikuta's announcement and his icy manner.

"I will get a taxi." Kentaro stood. "Please tell your parents I have enjoyed their company and look forward to seeing them again."

Claire spoke to her parents, then answered, "They said they are glad to meet you and hope to do it again. Do you want me to call the taxi?"

"I can do things on my own, Claire. I survived in Cleveland one and a half months before you became my keeper!"

As Claire watched Kentaro disappear through the doorway, she experienced an overwhelming dizzying sensation. Blood roared in her ears and her stomach convulsed. The meal she had just consumed threatened to return.

"Claire. Are you all right? Did he say something to upset you?" Claudia questioned.

"No, no. I never thought I was...Oh, never mind, Mother." Claire sighed. The evening had been so pleasant and suddenly the spell was over. What could she do to make sure such pleasant interludes with Kentaro never ended?

# Chapter Twelve

Claire woke late Sunday morning. She lay beneath the covers, her pillow clutched to her chest. The spring sun streamed over her through the window. It was nice not to have to get up, be able to enjoy waking at her own pace. It gave her the opportunity to remember the telephone call she received after her parents dropped her off from Sterle's.

Claire had just walked into the apartment and closed the door an instant before the phone rang.

"*Ferris-san*?"

"Yes, *Ikuta-san*. What is wrong?"

"Must something be wrong? I wanted to assure you I could arrive home without incident."

"I did not doubt you could." Claire found herself becoming irritated with him. She fell onto her couch. "I was being polite."

"You are always so polite, *Ferris-san*. Do not think I do not notice it."

"I wonder sometimes what you do notice. Are we going to continue our English lessons this week?"

"If you wish. Who is Andy?"

"What? Andy who?" Now she knew that he did notice.

"The Andy your mother was asking about and who gave you a ride home from the airport."

"A friend. Someone I grew up with." Dread filled Claire's being. Would he mention Jason next? Didn't he hear her mother asking about him, too? Hadn't he seen the offensive, spoiled rich kid at the airport, also?

Kentaro's sound was loud in her ear.

"Are you concerned or something?" Claire pulled the couch pillow close to her chest, giving her something to snug-

gle against. When Kentaro replied with his samurai noise, a
warm ease filled the space made as she felt the irritation flow
out of her.

"What would I be concerned about? I merely called to
allow you to sleep well, knowing I was safely home. The
team would probably blame you if I was lost in Cleveland."

"Yeah, right." Claire laughed. "I am glad you called. I
would have worried."

There was a pleasant quietness, and Claire pictured
Kentaro in his apartment, the phone held to the side of his
face, his lips as close to the mouthpiece as hers, almost a long
distance kiss.

"Sleep well, Claire."

"You, too, Kentaro." She spoke to a dead line. She did-
n't think he had heard her speak his name.


When Claire remembered it was the day after her first baseball game, she dressed in a flash in jeans and sweat shirt,
pulled her hair back into a ponytail and was out the door.
Ten minutes later she stood in line at Biali's, the Sunday
*Plain Dealer* in her hand. Skipping past the front page, she
found the sports section. There he was in full color: Kentaro
Ikuta hurling his famous fork ball from the mound. The
headline read:

CHIEFS' TSUNAMI BLOWS OVER RANGERS

Down the page, beneath the fold, was a picture of the
press conference, all the men at the long table with her at
Kentaro's side. Claire read the article and paid close attention to the quotes attributed to Kentaro.

She made her purchase of hot bagels and hurried home,
glowing with pride, until she read the sports section further.
Seated at the small table with a warm bagel, cream cheese and

strawberries, and a cup of hot tea within reach, Claire spread the paper out and very carefully studied the article.

In a separate feature column, a reporter questioned Kentaro's inability to speak English without a translator and what that said about his respect for the American sport. The article, while not directly attacking Ikuta, was contrived to put questions in the reader's mind.

Claire stared out the window and thought about the article. Everyone was entitled to an opinion, but this was only opening day. If the reporter was hateful now, how much worse would it get further into the season? Claire made up her mind to have Kentaro speaking English before the All-Star break. And maybe, given time and sterling performances, Kentaro's obvious and genuine love for American baseball would win the reporter over.

The third week of the season the Chiefs faced the Toronto Blue Jays. Claire, in the dugout behind first base, watched Kentaro pitch in the fifth inning. The Chiefs led by four. As the last batter struck out and the infield players ran into the shelter, a cold breeze blew in across the field.

The weather wasn't the only thing chilly. Kentaro had treated her with indifference since the night out with her parents. He spoke to her about baseball or not at all. Her hurt, if that was what it was, had evolved into resentment.

Kentaro sat beside her in the back of the dugout.

"Are you cold, *Ferris-san*?"

"If I were, I would not tell you." Claire tried not to shiver.

Kentaro made his familiar noise.

"You would think your friend, Andy-san, would buy you a jacket." Kentaro put his pitching arm into the sleeve of his own jacket.

"Why would she buy me a coat?" Claire's face wrinkled in confusion.

"She? I thought..." He did not finish.

"So that is why you have been so angry with me!" Claire laughed. The revelation that he thought Andy was a man explained much about his behavior. Her resentment evaporated. "You thought Andrea was a guy! You are jealous!"

"I think you should be quiet, *Ferris-san*, so I might concentrate." He made his noise again, harsher than before.

Claire was silent as ordered.

At the completion of the inning, Kentaro stood to return to the mound. Claire kept her eyes forward, refusing to speak first. Let him be the one to break the silence.

"Here, Claire." Kentaro slung his jacket toward her. "I do not wish you to catch cold."

"Thank you." Claire smiled softly in answer to his concern for her health.

"I can not allow you to be unable to be my words." Kentaro left Claire astonished. He didn't care about her, only that she be able to speak! She dropped the jacket on the seat he'd vacated. It could snow and she would not wear it!

"Mr. Ikuta," a reporter from *The New York Times* addressed him at the press conference after the game, "during the first half, you seemed to have trouble focusing, but in the sixth, you settled in and put the game away quickly. Any comments on the reasons?"

# The Words of the Pitcher

Claire translated and waited. Kentaro took a longer time than usual to form his answer. And his gaze held hers with a curious set to his eyes.

"I was having a problem with control earlier, especially with my fast ball. I had a talk with one of the coaches and was able to straighten it out."

Claire wondered if she translated correctly. He hadn't talked to Steve or any of the other coaches after the fifth. Did he mean his talk with her? Was their relationship significant enough to upset his pitching?

After the media finished their rehash of the game and left the players free, Claire accompanied Kentaro to the Toronto hotel where the team was lodged.

"*Ikuta-san*," Claire spoke to the pitcher outside the door to his room, "did I understand what you said? You did not talk to the coaches after the inning."

"Did not Martella-san make you a coach?"

"Was it," Claire gulped, not sure she wanted the answer to her question, "because you found out Andy was Andrea? A girlfriend?"

"I do not know what you mean." Kentaro shook his hair back. The gesture reminded Claire of a stallion shaking his mane in anger. His back was straighter, his bearing stern.

"Never mind." She smiled, satisfied with the friendship forming. "Never mind."

Claire left him in the hall and went to her room.

Once again in Cleveland, the Chiefs played an afternoon game in bright sunshine. Claire was glad she had changed from her usual slacks to khaki shorts and sandals when she was called out to the mound to speak for Ikuta. She had learned to forget the cameras she knew would be focused on her with the group at mid-field.

The catcher stood on the mound with Ikuta, Martella, and Claire. All four people were intent on Ikuta's hand, specifically, the second finger of the right hand. His pitching hand.

"Oh, man, that's gotta hurt," the catcher observed.

"Does your finger hurt?" Claire changed his words. "I can not see how it does not."

Kentaro had, without thinking, caught a line drive ball with his bare hand in order to protect his body. At the cost of his finger, he'd made the throw resulting in an out. The nail was split almost to the back cuticle, blood seeping from the nail bed. Claire could not resist reaching out and holding the injured hand.

"Yes, *Ferris-san*, it is very painful." Kentaro let her continue to hold his hand.

"This is not good, not good at all! Ask him if he can still pitch," Steve ordered harshly.

"Can you pitch?"

"*Iye.*" Kentaro hung his head.

"He says no." Claire caressed the injury as she dabbed at the blood dripping from his finger.

"Very well," Steve announced. "To the showers. Let's get Russell."

The group moved off the mound. Ikuta and Claire went through the dugout and up the tunnel to the showers. The others continued with the game.

"Do you wish me to help you with your hand?" Claire asked at the door to the locker room.

"I can manage." Kentaro looked down at her. "Thank you for your attention."

"You are welcome. I do not see how you will be able to shower. It looks very painful. I wish..." She couldn't finish, couldn't tell him how she wished she could take his pain unto herself.

"What is most hurtful is I will not be able to pitch until it heals. And with the location, it will not heal quickly."

"Hmmm." Claire thought while she looked down at her own manicured nails. "I think I know what we can do. You go shower and meet me at our classroom. I am going to call my father, and I will be able to tell you something then."

"Very well, *Sensei*." Kentaro smiled as he gave her the title of 'doctor' which could be translated 'teacher.'

Claire rushed down the hallway as Kentaro disappeared into the locker room. Using her cellular phone, she called her father and he agreed to her plan. By the time Claire finished the arrangements, Kentaro stood in the room.

"Oh, that was quick," Claire said. She closed the phone and put it in her shorts pocket, then with gentle fingers took his hand. Kentaro had fashioned a crude bandage around it. She looked up into his face with quizzical eyes. "Do you trust me?"

"Why should I not? I have trusted you to be truthful in your translations for me," he responded with a look of curiosity.

"Then come on." She took his wrist preparatory to leading him away. He did not move, but cleared his throat instead.

"Claire, I need for you to do something...embarrassing."

"Yesss?" Claire looked up into his face.

"Can you button my jeans? I was unable to."

"You want me to...?" Claire noticed how the red flush crept from his chest up his throat to his face and was sure he saw the same on hers. She released her hold. "Sure."

Claire's eyes went down to the waist of his jeans. She hadn't noticed before that his belt was hanging unsecured. Kentaro had managed to tuck his shirt in so she would not touch his skin in any fashion. With all due care, she slipped her fingers into the band behind the button and guided the button through the hole. She could tell Kentaro held his breath so she could fasten it with the least amount of movement of her fingers against his abdomen.

"There." She pulled the zipper up further in the fly, then fastened his belt. Claire stepped back. She tried not to let on that she detected the manly ridge filling his jeans

"No. Not at all." Kentaro's samurai sound was strangled.

Claire then knew he knew she had seen.

"Now, where are we going?" he asked.

"Just follow me." She turned and exited the room, her own body responding to Kentaro's.

# Chapter Thirteen

"A nail salon?" Kentaro asked as Claire parked her Mustang at the curb.

"Yes. My manicurist can fix the nail so it will be strong enough not to break repeatedly, allowing it to heal," Claire explained. They had both relaxed, the sexual tension ebbing away. "It will be clear and thin. No one will be able to tell unless they examine your hand closely."

"*Ferris-san...*" Kentaro hesitated.

"Did you not say you trusted me? Get out of the car." Claire opened her door and left him alone. She stood on the sidewalk until Kentaro moved to join her.

"I do not know about this." Kentaro shook his head, his loose hair swinging about his neck and shoulders. He had been unable to bind it with his hurt finger.

"My father said it would be perfect." Claire took hold of his arm and pulled him along. "It will not hurt your nail, just your pride. Now, come on."

When Kentaro followed as Claire ordered, she released his arm.

"Patsy, this is Kentaro Ikuta," Claire introduced the pitcher to her manicurist, slipping easily from English to Japanese. "*Ikuta-san*, this is Patsy."

"Hi." Patsy greeted. "I'm all ready. I got things fixed just like you said, Claire. Don't be shy, honey," Patsy addressed Kentaro. "Lots of guys come get their nails done. Even the straight ones." Patsy showed him the way to her station while Claire translated her words.

Kentaro made his sound in response.

Once seated, his long, slender finger in Patsy's trained hands, Kentaro relaxed a bit. Claire watched with rapt attention.

Patsy removed the bandage. "Oh, this is nasty. How'd you do this, honey?" she asked.

"During a baseball game," Claire answered without bringing Kentaro into the conversation. "He pitches for the Chiefs."

"Really? My guy's a big fan, but, to tell the truth, I don't care much for baseball. Just football." Patsy cleaned his nail. She wiped away the blood that seeped again. "I'll trim this up a little, then put a tip over it, then an overlay. That's what we want, right, Claire?"

"Yes." Claire felt derelict about not translating, but Patsy's words weren't important to Kentaro. She glanced at him as Patsy worked.

"So, Claire, how're things? Seen Jason lately? He was here thirty minutes ago," Patsy chatted as she worked on Ikuta's finger nail. "Looking good."

"You're as bad as my mother." Claire saw Kentaro studying her face, baffled. "Are you all right, *Ikuta-san*?"

"What are you two talking about?" he asked in Japanese.

"Girl stuff. She is going to trim your nail and fix it."

"Very well."

Standing behind Kentaro as he watched what Patsy did, Claire looked at his hair. He had managed to comb it, but she was sure he was annoyed because it was unbound. He was always so careful to have it confined. Without thought, she reached into her purse and took out a comb and one of her many ponytail holders cluttering the bottom of it. Behind Kentaro, beginning to work on his hair, she could feel him relax. The silky strands slid with ease through her fingers. Claire wrapped the elastic around the thick bundle then continued to caress the ponytail with her fingers, reluctant to stop.

Thirty minutes later, the nail was repaired and almost indistinguishable from the others.

"How does it feel, honey?" Patsy asked.

"Does it hurt?" Claire came around to Kentaro's side. Her hand pushed his bangs off his forehead, a last languishing touch of his hair.

"No. But it feels strange." Kentaro studied his hand.

"You will get used to it. Patsy says it will fall off in about two weeks. If you need it replaced, she will do it. Any other questions?" Claire asked.

"Anything special I have to do?"

"No." Claire turned to the manicurist. "Patsy, send a bill to the Chiefs' management."

"Okay, but I did it because we're friends." Patsy cleaned her station.

"I appreciate that, but get paid anyway." Claire stood. "We'll see you later."


"Claire! What a surprise!" When Claire and Kentaro left the nail salon, they found Jason leaning against the hood of her car.

"Hi, Jason." Claire tried to move past him to the car, but he took hold of her arm.

Kentaro watched detachedly.

"Where're you rushing off to, Claire? She's always trying to escape me," Jason addressed Ikuta. "I just don't understand it." Jason shook his head in mock disbelief.

"He doesn't either." Claire jerked her arm out of Jason's vise-like grasp. "He doesn't speak English."

"Yeah, I keep reading about that in the paper. You'd think if someone wanted to play our sports, in our country, and take our money, they'd learn to speak our language."

Jason looked at Claire, but his loud words were directed to Ikuta.

"Look, Jason," Claire faced him, her face hot and flushed. "*Ikuta-san* is working very hard to learn English! It is not an easy language. You should try learning Japanese! It's even harder. Now, please leave me alone."

Claire marched to the car.

"*Ikuta-san*, we need to go," she spoke to Kentaro. She could not read his face well enough to know what he thought about the encounter with Jason. As she put the key in the ignition, Jason leaned into the window.

"I don't know what your problem is, Claire," he said. "You never treated me this way before."

"You were never such an idiot before!" Claire started the car and backed out, nearly running over Jason's feet.

"You'll be sorry, Claire!" he shouted.

"I apologize for my former friend," Claire said. They were stopped at a red light, and she had time to get her thoughts together. Kentaro hadn't said anything since getting into the car.

"Do not be concerned," he responded. "This man is a friend?"

"I have known Jason since we were kids. Our mothers were college friends. We took dancing class together when we were six. Then it seemed only natural that we be paired for things like recitals and cotillions. He was my designated date for everything—junior high school dances, proms, my debutante ball. It was easy to ask him because of the connection between our families," Claire explained dispassionately. "I never realized what an idiot he was."

"You are growing up, Claire-san." Kentaro reached and took her hand from the wheel. "Friendships of youth are often grown out of."

Claire liked the feel of her hand in Kentaro's, the sense of callused roughness from his years of baseball. A warmth spread from her hand to center at a place between her breasts. Her chest tightened. "I guess you are right." Claire was forced to retrieve her hand to shift gears. And breathe.

"Do you think you can play tomorrow?" Claire felt more comfortable with such questions.

"I am not scheduled until Friday." Kentaro's hand rested over hers on the gear shift.

"Maybe it will be healed by then." Claire found a pleasantness in his touch. "Want me to drive you home?"

"If it is not out of your way."

"I do not know where you live, so I would not know." Claire merged into the traffic.

"You will need to go back the other direction." Kentaro laughed.

"Figures."

After Claire dropped him off, Kentaro entered his apartment. He was thankful to Claire for getting his nail fixed, even in the unorthodox manner she had accomplished it. It was nice to be with her outside the stadium.

He went to the kitchen and put on the kettle for instant ramen. He had made a steady diet of the noodles so common in Japan. To indulge in the American male habit of channel surfing, he found his comfortable spot on the couch with the bowl in one hand and the eating sticks in the other. The artificial nail did not hinder his use of *hashi*.

Bored by the television programs, he slurped the noodles and pondered the two people he could call to get together with. Michael Sangyo was out of town. That left Claire.

Would it be ethical for him to call and ask her to go somewhere with him? He'd felt betrayed by his body when she'd buttoned his pants and was ashamed when Claire noticed. But she'd seemed to enjoy the time in the car to and from the manicurist's. Holding her hand had opened his feelings for her. And he remembered the touch of her fingers in his hair. Had electricity rushed through her body as it had through his?

Why hadn't he asked her to go to dinner before she dropped him off? It would have been justified in return for helping with his injury. But there was that man she so adamantly denied liking. He'd found that women did that when they really cared for a man. Was Jason Stewart a rival? What was he thinking! A rival! For what? Claire Ferris was his interpreter and no more, he told himself. No, he'd go to a movie alone. He didn't think his ego could accept rejection should Claire refuse him.

"That was very good, *Ikuta-san.*" Claire praised Kentaro's translation of a paragraph she had selected from a magazine to give him experience with vernacular English. They sat in a study room at the Case Western Reserve library, isolated from those who needed silence to study. "Now. We will try something a little more difficult." She flipped through the magazine.

Kentaro lounged back in the chair with a comfortable but bored attitude. Face toward the glass wall behind Claire, he picked at the injured finger where the artificial nail had fallen off the day before.

"We are about to have company," he announced.

"Oh? Who?" Claire turned in her chair to peer over her shoulder. She didn't recognize the Japanese man who opened the door to their cubicle.

"Am I interrupting?" he asked in polite Japanese. Claire noticed a bit of a Southern Californian accent. She wondered if Kentaro noticed an accent in her Japanese.

"No. Welcome, Sangyo-san. *Ferris-san*, this is my agent, Michael Sangyo. I left him a message I would be here." Kentaro made introductions. "Sangyo-san, Claire Ferris."

"Good to meet you, Ms. Ferris." Sangyo held out a hand for her to shake.

"Nice to meet you." She noticed they were speaking English. As simple as the conversation was, Kentaro wasn't left out. "I understand you and the Tsunami have made a good deal of progress in the last month. Kentaro will be speaking English better than you and I in no time." Sangyo sat at the table. "Would it bother you if Kentaro and I took a moment to discuss baseball business? We won't take long."

"Sure. I will leave you men to your work." Claire changed to Japanese for Kentaro's benefit, then began to leave. Sangyo was obviously an American. Claire based this on the way he used English.

"It will not be long," Michael assured her, making the language switch also.

Claire left the study room. She returned thirty minutes later with books she'd plucked from the shelves.

Claire poked her head into the room and noticed an open briefcase and papers in front of Kentaro. "Am I too soon?"

"No, no. We've finished. Come on in." Sangyo replaced the papers and closed the case. "Kentaro, remember we have reservations for dinner tonight to celebrate your twenty-ninth birthday." He stood. "Why do you not join us, Ms. Ferris? My wife, Audrey, will be with us."

"Thank you. I would be happy to." An evening out, even a business dinner, would be a change. Had Sangyo said it was Kentaro's birthday? Perhaps she should pick up a present. "Where are we dining?"

"Otani's. We have reservations at seven."

"Very well, I will meet you there. Now, if you will excuse us, we have studying to do." Claire reclaimed her seat.

"Do not cheat, Kentaro. I do not think your teacher would be very lenient," Sangyo chuckled as he left.

A concerned look crossed Kentaro's face as he studied a paper Michael had left with him.

"Is something wrong?" she asked.

"Sangyo-san was showing me some articles in the newspaper in which a reporter wrote that my not speaking English is a bad thing. He said I am being disrespectful to the American baseball fans because of my lack of English."

"Oh?" Claire raised her eyebrows.

"The writer seems to think I am not speaking English because I do not want to. Do you think that is the reason, *Ferris-san*?" Kentaro's eyes pleaded for her reassurance.

"Well," Claire worked on her response, hoping to phrase a diplomatic one, "I think you have a desire to speak the most perfect English possible before speaking without me."

When Kentaro made his noise, Claire didn't know whether she had insulted him or pleased him. He fixed his eyes on the papers in front of him.

"Mother," Claire called down the staircase to Claudia. "Where did you put that black, after five dress? The one you wanted me to wear to the banquet for the pediatric fellows?"

"It's in the cedar closet in your room. What do you need it for? You said it was embarrassing." Claudia came up the stairs to the hall where her daughter scurried about in her underwear. "Do you have a date?"

"Not really. I have had an invitation to join Ikuta and his agent and wife for Kentaro's birthday dinner." Claire started away. "We're going to Otani's."

"Why are you dressing here?" Claudia watched Claire enter the room which had been hers growing up.

"It was nearer than my apartment after I went shopping." Claire located the dress and took it from the plastic garment bag. "You know I always keep extra clothes here."

"I don't think you'll ever move out completely," Claudia stated. "You'll need your hair done. Oh, and some jewelry. I know you don't have anything to go with that dress."

Claudia disappeared into her bedroom, still talking, eager to help her daughter prepare for her special evening.

At seven o'clock, Claire had yet to appear at Otani's. Kentaro looked at his watch. Sangyo's invitation for Claire to join them was not something he would have thought of, but he was pleased Sangyo had done it. Now, it looked as if she wasn't coming. He felt disappointed.

Over the past weeks, he had come to enjoy his English lessons only because of Claire. He often found himself staring at her when she wasn't aware of it instead of concentrating on translations. He had especially come to like the way she licked her lips when intent on her work. The tip of her pink tongue moved over the supple full lips in an erotic way he was sure Claire didn't recognize or plan.

"Looks as if she has stood us up," Sangyo spoke from Kentaro's side. They stood inside the foyer of the trendy Japanese restaurant waiting for their reservation.

"Oh, do not worry," Audrey Sangyo commented. "She is just being fashionably late."

Kentaro made a noise, his attention back on his watch. Sangyo and his wife, fourth generation Japanese-Americans, were much more comfortable in this situation than he was. If he had had anything else to do with his time, he might have begged off from this dinner. Maybe he could develop a headache and leave if Claire didn't arrive.

"They have our table ready." Audrey brought Kentaro's attention back to the matter at hand. The trio followed the maitre d' to their table.

"So, Kentaro," Audrey broke the silence after they were seated, beverages ordered, "tell me about your young lady."

"She is not mine except as an interpreter and English teacher." Kentaro fidgeted in his chair, regretting that he had taken the place that put his back to the doorway.

"Oh, I thought...Michael said you and she were involved. Michael, look what you have done!" Audrey administered a playful slap to her husband's arm. "You have made me embarrass him!"

"No, Audrey, we are not involved," Kentaro stated, intent on the oversized menu. He had known Michael and Audrey since he had turned professional and Michael had become his agent. They were friends as well as business partners, which was why Audrey felt comfortable enough to tease him.

"From what I saw, I would say you are," Michael defended himself. "Maybe you just do not know it."

"I think I would know it," Kentaro countered.

# The Words of the Pitcher

"Oh, boy." Michael looked over Kentaro's head. "I bet you will want to be involved once you see what is headed this way. Look."

# Chapter Fourteen

Kentaro turned in his seat to look in the direction Michael indicated. Suddenly, he recognized the vision crossing the room. Time crawled as Claire made her way to their table. She looked more like a supermodel than an English teacher.

Kentaro's eyes started at her head, the long brown hair now swept up into a roll with tendrils falling casually down around her ears and slender neck. Bangs ruffled over her forehead. Passing over her face, radiant with excitement and pleasure, he took in the bare shoulders and throat, ivory and smooth, exposed by the black slip of a dress tightly covering her body. The low-cut bodice followed the heart-shaped curves of her breasts; the soft tops rounded up out of a neckline dipping into a deep cleavage.

From her bust, the dress followed the inward wave of her waist to fan ever so delicately over narrow hips and encase the slender thighs in a tight hug. The garment ended four inches above her knees, allowing long, silk-wrapped legs freedom to move. On her feet she wore plain, steep heels with a tiny black strap around her ankles.

Gradually, in slow motion, Kentaro rose to join Michael, also out of his chair. Kentaro's breath was tight in his chest and a hot surge filled his body.

"I am so sorry I am late!" Claire announced out of breath. "I had the worst time getting ready."

"It was well worth the wait, Ms. Ferris," Michael announced.

"Yes." Kentaro found his voice after a slight cough to remove the lump clogging his throat. He held Claire's chair for her.

"Thank you."

As she slid into the chair, Kentaro discovered the dress was backless, the front supported only by her breasts. He fought the urge to press his face against the smooth expanse of skin revealed to the small of her back. Instead, he leaned forward as he pushed the seat beneath her and whispered, "You are very beautiful, Claire."

"Thank you again," she whispered in return. A crimson blush covered her throat and face.

Kentaro took his chair, unable to keep his eyes off the beauty at his right. He found himself desperate to possess Claire. He wanted to take her in his arms and make love to her here, on this table, at this very moment! More than anything else, he wanted to assuage a passion he had never felt for a woman. His manhood, usually unruly but controllable, threatened to burst from his trousers. It was all he could do not to take Claire and relieve the rising pressure.

"These oafs are so unmannered," Audrey laughed. "We'll never meet if we leave it up to them! I'm Audrey Sangyo."

"Hello. Claire Ferris." The two women joined hands loosely across the table as the men continued to gape at Claire.

"I'm glad to meet you. Michael was telling me about you. You're Kentaro's interpreter and teacher, I understand?"

"Yes. Perhaps we should speak only Japanese since I don't think my lessons have helped Kentaro much." Claire turned to her student.

"We can, but I don't think that's the reason they're so tongue-tied. Where did you find that dress?"

"My mother selected it for me for a banquet in honor of my father, but I was too embarrassed to wear it!" Claire laughed, her words spoken in the language Kentaro would understand.

*103*

"It is lovely," Audrey commented.

"I dare say you are what makes the dress," Kentaro replied.

"I have a present for you." Claire handed a large gift bag to Kentaro. He could see she was embarrassed by his remark about her body and dress. "I hope I am not too presumptuous. I did not know when, or if, you were receiving them."

"No, not at all." Kentaro forced his eyes from the exotically erotic Claire to reach inside the bag. He removed a moderate-sized carton. Inside it he found a glass box encasing a samurai doll six inches tall and in the extended fighting stance. The warrior pointed a sword in front of him and flew a koi-shaped kite from a pole strapped to his back.

"I understand boys receive such dolls for the Hine Matsuri. I hope you like it and do not have one."

"I suppose you have learned of the doll festival through your studies." Kentaro examined the warrior doll closely. "It is perfect, Claire. As perfect as you are. *Domo arigato*."

"It looks very old," Michael stated.

"The gentleman at the store said it was, but you know how those dealers are. They tell you anything just to get you to buy it."

Kentaro watched Claire take a sip of water with supple, ruby red lips. Though he and Michael had *sake* in small flasks with tiny cups, Kentaro had taken only one cup, so intoxicated was he by Claire.

"I would believe him." Kentaro put the antique doll back into the box. Claire had given him a very rare doll for which she probably paid a large sum.

"Do you like sushi, Claire?" Audrey picked up the menu.

"I think I do. I have had only the common, more bland sort because I have never had anyone knowledgeable enough to order it properly."

"Then we must educate you!" Michael joined his wife to decide what to order for their meal.

Kentaro continued to watch Claire, intrigued by the enchantress beside him. He desired more to feast on her body than on food.

"This has been the most wonderful evening," Audrey Sangyo announced as the foursome sat over tea. "I hate to see it end."

"It has been fun." Claire glanced at Kentaro who had not taken his eyes off her for very long all evening.

"I know! We should go dancing. Oh, Michael, could we?" Audrey once more held her husband's biceps. "It has been ever so long and we must allow Kentaro to show Claire off."

"What do you say, Kentaro? It is your birthday party."

"If Claire wishes to…" Kentaro's eyes captured hers.

"I do not know about the showing off part, but I would enjoy dancing." Claire's heart trembled at the thought of being held in Kentaro's arms, close to his body. Dare she admit she hoped for it?

"Claire, did you drive yourself?" Michael asked.

"I took a taxi." Claire hadn't wanted to be concerned with driving this night.

"Then by all means, let's go." Michael waved for the check and they were off to a ballroom across town.

"I am sorry that I do not dance very well, *Ferris-san*," Kentaro announced as they were seated at a small table near the dance floor. Drinks had been served and the Sangyos had departed to dance.

"If you remember, I said before I did not either." Claire looked at her hands in her lap. Now that they were here, he was not going to dance with her! Not hold her as she had allowed herself to hope!

"You have since admitted that you took dancing lessons as a child." Kentaro smiled at her. "I wish to see if you learned anything, Claire."

Claire's heart redoubled its pace as Kentaro stood and held his hand out to her. She gingerly placed her fingers in his palm.

Kentaro led her to the crowded floor. It was a slow song, just begun, and the couple stepped, inept and uncertain, into each other's embrace. As Claire looked up into Kentaro's face, the other dancers disappeared. His eyes were on her. A smile on his lips and a crinkle at the corner of his eyes endeared him to her heart. She moved closer to his chest without thought, feeling the rough material of his suit coat against her bare shoulder as his embrace tightened. His hand stroked the small of her back with a delicate touch as they moved to the rhythm of the music.

Kentaro's arms constricted to draw Claire even closer. She came, nestling against him. She felt his soft lips on her hair.

"Claire," he whispered, his cheek next to her hair.

"Yes?"

He did not answer, just made a peaceful version of his samurai noise. Claire responded by cuddling nearer.

"You two looked good out there," Audrey said when they all returned to the table.

"Audrey, leave them alone," Michael instructed. "You are such a manipulator."

"I was having a nice time. Too bad the song ended." Claire sipped her Coke.

Silent, Kentaro fixed his attention on his glass of water.

"There will be another one, Claire," Michael and Audrey laughed. "This is a ballroom!"

"I do not think it will be the same," Claire replied quietly and grinned as Kentaro uttered his noise.

Music swelled, fast paced and frantic. The Sangyos were off.

"Do you...?" Claire questioned.

"Do you...?"

"No."

"Then we shall sit." Kentaro took Claire's hand in his as they watched the dancers. The spell of their last dance lingered in their thoughts.

Claire scrutinized Kentaro's slender fingers entwined with hers, imagining them moving over her body, touching places no man had ever explored. Her thoughts provoked her woman's body to respond as if he actually caressed her. Claire bowed her head, her eyes closed, trying to shut off the erotic images. Her face was flushed, and her body burned with the desire for such touches.

"Claire?" Kentaro's voice drifted to her. He held her hand with a firmer grasp in response to hers.

"Yes?" She could not afford to raise her eyes to his, so afraid he would see her lust in them.

"Are you all right?" Kentaro's crooked finger touched her chin to pull her face up so he could see her eyes. "Are you crying?"

"No, no."

"Then...?" Kentaro's chocolate brown eyes searched her face for an answer.

"I am...overwhelmed with all of this." Her voice dropped to a whisper.

Kentaro's hand again took hers, but gently.

"I know how you feel." His stroke on the back of her hand sent quivers of electricity up her arm.

Some ten minutes went by before the orchestra played a slow song and Claire was again in Kentaro's arms. The spell had never been interrupted. The song drifted along and she melted into the cocoon of his embrace. Her mind wandered to being next to him forever. What would the end of the evening bring? Would they part, easily returning to the position of teacher and student?

Claire didn't want to think about tomorrow. She didn't want to remember she was his interpreter and he, more or less, her employer. But the thought refused to disappear. She was suddenly awash in panic.

"I...I...I have to go." Claire put her hands on his chest and pushed away. "This is...No...!"

"Claire?" Kentaro watched as she fled to the table. He followed, a step behind her as she grabbed her purse and was out the door.

"Claire!" She was in a taxi and gone.

All too aware she left him confused and dazed, Claire could not explain her actions. She didn't know herself.

# Chapter Fifteen

"What happened, Kentaro? Did you step on Claire's foot one time too many?" Audrey Sangyo sat down and took a long sip of her drink. She pushed her short hair back out of her face.

"I can not say," Kentaro replied, a quizzical tone to his voice. "She fled without explanation. Just some confused sputtering."

"Uh huh," Audrey nodded her head. "Michael is right. She cares for you."

Kentaro made his harsh sound.

"Do not get huffy with me! I am a woman, so I know what I am talking about. And, face it, you are her boss. What could she hope you would do? What will you do?"

"I do not know. However, I think I am talking to the wrong person. Thank you for your counsel and this lovely evening." Kentaro rose. "I will talk to you later."

"Let me know where to send the wedding present!" Audrey called. Kentaro heard her laughter as he made his way to the doorway. He responded with his huffing sound.

"Claire! What in the world?" Andrea opened her apartment door to find Claire standing in the hallway, her hair disheveled and her face tear-stained. "Come in, come in. What happened to you?"

"I went dancing," Claire announced as if telling her friend what she had for lunch. But the statement did not coincide with her appearance. "Do you have something I could change into? I couldn't go home."

# Kei Swanson

"Yeah, sure. Come on. What's going on? Did someone hurt you? Did you get mugged?" Andrea led Claire into her bedroom.

"Just give me a minute." Claire plucked tissues from a box on her friend's dresser and blew her nose loudly. "I'll tell you everything in a minute."

"Here." Andrea handed her a pair of shorts and a T-shirt. "I'll wait…"

"No! Stay with me!"

"Claire, you're scaring me. What's happened?" Andrea sat on the bed.

"It's okay. Really. I'm just upset."

Claire worked at getting out of the dress which had affected Kentaro so strongly. Her fingers wouldn't work and Andrea helped her.

"I went out to eat with Ken…*Ikuta-san*, his agent, and his agent's wife. It's his birthday. Then we went dancing."

Claire threw the dress across the room and yanked her hose off. She pulled the athletic clothes on quickly.

"Can you help me with this?"

She ran her fingers through her hair to feel for the pins which had held the upswept tresses in place and had not fallen when the hairdo began to collapse.

"Sit down." Andrea changed places with Claire. "Keep talking."

"It was so nice. We talked and laughed. I learned more about him and his childhood. Anyway, he kept looking at me with a kind of…desire in his eyes. It was so wonderful to be looked at like that. I…never had anyone so…interested in me!"

Claire took a moment to dab a tissue at her wet eyes.

"Then, his agent's wife suggested we go dancing. Ken…*Ikuta-san* once said he couldn't dance, but we went anyway." She sobbed.

*110*

# The Words of the Pitcher

Claire paused, a wistful look in her eyes as she remembered the slow dancing in Kentaro's arms. It all came back to her, the touch, the smell, the movements.

"Go on." Andrea had Claire's hair in her hands now as she worked a brush through it to put it in a ponytail.

"Well, we danced a slow dance. It was so nice to be in his arms."

Claire's own arms hugged her torso. She closed her eyes as if still on the dance floor as she told Andrea about the episode.

"His body's so firm and hard. He smelled so beautiful. His heart was pounding as fast as mine was! Andy, I thought I was going to die right there, and I would have been so happy. But I realized," Claire's eyes flew open and the terror she had felt before filled them, "I can't mean anything to him! He can't possibly want me. I'm just his...interpreter...or, as he calls me, his 'words'!" Claire's tears flowed unhindered down her face as she stared at her friend.

"Oh, Claire, of course he can." Andrea enfolded Claire in her arms.

Claire sobbed, the anguish rolling out of her in loud waves. "He's my boss!" She pushed away and dabbed at her face with fresh tissues Andrea handed her.

"People fall in love at work all the time." Andrea walked toward the living room. "Let's get some coffee."

Claire followed, saying, "I don't know what to do, Andy!"

"Tell him how you feel. You'll never know if he cares for you unless you tell him. Give him a chance to let you know what he feels. Your job is words. Use them to your advantage, Claire! You're intelligent. I think you can find the words in either language. You just need the courage to use them."

The women sat on opposite ends of the couch, each with a warm mug of Irish coffee. Claire had her feet tucked beneath her. The thick, rich, creamy coffee with its strong dose of Irish whiskey calmed Claire's nerves.

"Andy, what if...?" Claire took a sip.

"If what? He rejects you? Or he keeps you?!"

"Keeps me. What happens then?"

"You are such a baby, Claire! Haven't you ever... been in love?"

"I don't think so. I've never felt the way I do now. I've always had Jason. You know, the old designated date. Safe and comfortable. I certainly have never had sex, if that was your first thought."

"It was." Andrea giggled along with Claire. "Seriously, I know how you feel. We've all gone through that first love thing. Maybe I haven't felt as much as you say you feel, but I know what it's like to be vulnerable. You don't want to get hurt by putting yourself on the line with a guy. You just have to do it. Take that leap of faith and see where it gets you. You can never tell."

"Can I stay here tonight? I don't want to go home to an empty apartment."

"Ever thought of going to his?"

"Yes. But, I can't. Not now. Maybe later."

"Very well. Let's crash."

Confused and bewildered, Kentaro let himself into his apartment. The red light flashed on his answering machine and he rushed to punch the message button. It wasn't Claire and he understood enough to know the messages were from reporters with inquiries about interviews. Dejected and worried about her safety, he went to his bedroom. There he placed the samurai doll on his chest of drawers. He then sagged onto the edge of his bed, his head in his hands.

What was he going to do? His feelings for Claire were different from anything he'd ever felt. Yet he didn't know how to express this love. In Japan, he would know what to do, but here in the States, customs, rules, and women were so different.

Claire was so innocent and naive. And, for some reason, scared of him. Kentaro didn't know why she had run away, what she had said no to. Was it because he was Japanese? Because he was a sports star? A million other reasons flooded his brain. None of his questions would have an answer until he talked with Claire.

He picked up the phone at the bedside table and punched in her number. Anxious to hear her tender voice, he held the receiver to his ear. It rang twenty times before he gave up. She either was not there or would not answer.

Now, he worried for her safety. He left his apartment to find her.

"Ikuta, I don't know how much of this you'll understand," Steve Martella spoke before the evening game against Anaheim. The players were getting ready for the game. "but I have to tell you Claire called in sick. She'll be out for the week. Hopefully, she'll meet us in Baltimore next Tuesday. Do you understand?"

"Yes." Kentaro understood. Claire did not wish to see him. He moved into the dugout, glad he was not scheduled to start since his mind was occupied with Claire. He had come away from her apartment last night without finding her and now, a day later, he was no closer to an answer for her behavior than he was then. At least now he knew she was safe, even if sick, an excuse he doubted.

∽

"Claire?" Andrea shouted down the hallway of the large and empty university building.

"In here!" Claire called, angry to have been found at her office. She had hoped to elude her friend and her persistent nagging about Kentaro. If she went home, Andrea couldn't bother her as easily as she did. But, if she was home, he would find her. At least, it took Andrea longer.

"Ah, ha!" Andrea confronted Claire. "What are you doing?"

"Studying." Claire reached to turn the television set off, but Andrea's hand was quicker.

"What have we here?" She turned the screen to her so she could view it from her side of Claire's desk. "Baseball?"

"Okay. You caught me. Big deal!" Claire turned the set back and readjusted her feet under her.

"And you're eating ramen noodles?" Andrea came to Claire's side of the desk. She took a seat on the edge of the heavy mahogany desk between Claire's chair and the television.

"I eat ramen all the time." Claire brought a spoonful of noodles to her mouth, intent on the screen. "Hush."

"Oh! I forgot he's pitching. Forgive me." Andrea feigned humility.

"Damn!" Claire erupted in response to the batter's hitting Kentaro's pitch. Some noodles sloshed on the floor. "That's the fourth hit! And he's walked three."

"He's got 'Claire fever.' Here. Give me some of that." Andrea took the cup of noodles from Claire who was preoccupied with watching the television screen.

"That can't be! He's got to do better." Claire leaned over and mopped the rug with less than thorough results. She righted her position to see the screen. Kentaro performed his wind-up and released his fast pitch. The player connected with the hard ball.

"Damn it! Oh, no." Claire was on the edge of her chair. "Steve's going to take him out of the game."

"Go help him."

"Huh? How can I help him? He's at the Jake and I'm here."

"Go down there and help him. Tell him how you feel."

"That won't help." Claire sagged into the chair as the game went to commercial. She couldn't face Kentaro, ashamed of her actions and afraid of what might happen if she told him anything.

"Yes it will." Andrea continued to eat Claire's noodles. "Go!"

"I can't!" Claire agonized through two more batters. "Oh, no!" Claire bemoaned. She hid her face in her hands.

"Look at him, Claire." Andrea pointed with her spoon to the image on the television. "The guy's in agony."

Claire raised her head to look at the close-up the camera showed of the Japanese pitcher. Kentaro's eyes were strained beneath their exotic folds. She tried not to see the tense, aching look in his eyes or the hard line of his lips. Had she hurt him? It raised her hopes for something she knew she could not afford to let happen.

"No!" She shouted at the television as the camera pulled back to show the entire pitcher's mound. The catcher and pitching coach joined Kentaro.

"What's happening?"

"Oh, God, Steve's throwing him out!" Claire fell forward over her tucked-up legs, her forehead against her shin. "That's never happened to him." Her voice was muffled.

"Claire," Andrea whined, "you have to help him.  Go, now!"  Andrea ordered.

Claire looked at her friend for ten seconds, then ran out of the office.

# Chapter Sixteen

Claire made it to Jacobs Field before the ninth inning. She flashed her team credentials at the gate and cruised through the turnstiles. Her only thought was to get to Kentaro.

Ousted from the game, he would retreat to the locker room long enough to shower and change. From there, she had no idea were he would go. She was only sure he would not remain at the Jake to have his humiliation rubbed into his injured ego. It had to be such a wound to his self-esteem and she was the one who caused it. It was a mistake she was going to mend.

Claire confronted a guard at the door to the Chiefs locker room. She held her ID up and charged through the doorway when he stepped aside.

"*Ikuta-san!*" Claire called into the deep steamy room. She walked with hesitancy through the wide area of the locker room.

"Ikuta!" She did not encounter anyone as she made her way further in. "Kentaro!"

"*Koko de, Ferris-san.*"

Claire hurried to the area his voice came from. The closer she came, the more determined she was. There he stood before the shower stall. The water ran, steam billowing out into the area. It was now or never. A low bench ran toward him and, on impulse, Claire stepped up on it and marched down to him.

"*Ferris-san*, I thought you were sick," Ikuta spoke. His face was puzzled and his eyes searched her face. "I am so glad you are well. I came by your apartment that night. You did not answer. You did not pick up the phone. I was so concerned for you." Words rushed out of him as if a dam had been broken.

"Kentaro, *shizuka ni*," Claire ordered his silence.

"I was even more worried when Martella-san said you would be out because you were ill. I hope it was nothing serious." Kentaro continued as if unable to stop himself.

Claire reached out to clutch the edges of the jersey that hung open over his broad chest. She surprised herself by yanking him to her so she could put her lips firmly on his. Kentaro responded by putting his arms around her. He pulled Claire tight against his body.

His lips, supple and soft, moved against hers. Claire's mouth opened to accept his tongue's advances. She savored the sticky sweet taste of Gatorade that lingered on it and returned his kiss with equal passion. As though she had to hold him secure to prevent his escaping, she held the jersey tightly.

Kentaro's hands moved over her back; one rubbed the small of it. His breath was hot and ragged against her cheek. The wide, damp chest heaved against her breasts. A tingle began between her legs and moistness escaped in response to the hard ridge against her pelvis. Her legs threatened to buckle.

Her hands caressed the smooth, velvety skin of his back. Mischievously, while intent on his mouth, she reached beneath the jersey and her hands rounded the shoulders to push the shirt off. She then tugged the tight baseball pants down over his firm buttocks. Kentaro's hand slid beneath her T-shirt and found her bra-less breast. He caressed the soft mound with his callused fingers, rolling the nipple.

She moved herself against Kentaro's hard thigh that he had wedged between her legs and gnawed hungrily at his lips.

"No," Claire panted. "I cannot...I do not want it to be this way."

"How else...?" Kentaro's mouth was at her neck, his lips caressing her ear as he spoke. His hands cupped her buttocks.

"Not in the locker room. Take your shower."

Claire wiggled away. She slipped off the bench to stand on the tile floor. The separation between them allowed her complete view of Kentaro's nude, powerful form. His abdomen was flat, muscles pulling taut from hip bone to groin. Her breath caught in her throat as her eyes took in the view of his manhood, rampant and full, extending from the jet-black hair between his thighs.

Taking time only to step out of his uniform pants, Kentaro picked Claire up and stood her on the bench. He helped her pull her T-shirt over her head and kissed her while his fingers worked at the elastic of her shorts. When he moved his mouth to her breasts, Claire sighed as he took her nipple between his eager lips. With unsurprising tenderness, his long gentle fingers moved lower and teased apart the wet opening of her secret place.

The clink of cleats on the tile flooring and the sound of voices penetrated their passion.

"Oh, God!" Claire whispered, taking Kentaro's head in her hands. "Stop. The game is over."

Quickly, Kentaro swept Claire into his arms and took her into the shower stall next to the one he had readied for his own use. Claire found her back against the shower wall with Kentaro's hot body pressed against her front. His hands continued the maddening caresses for a brief instant before he stepped outside the closed canvas shower curtain.

Claire breathed heavily from both passion and the fear of being caught naked in the player's shower. She had to find a way to escape without being seen.

Almost in answer, Kentaro's hand thrust her clothing at her from outside the curtain. Claire took the shorts and T-shirt. She doubted Kentaro had meant to give her the Chiefs jersey which she found tangled with her clothes.

Dressing hurriedly, Claire pulled the jersey on over the T-shirt. She stuck her head out of the curtain to check the area for occupants. It was vacant. Kentaro was in the stall which had been his destination until she interrupted him.

Claire slipped into the locker room, passing through the room filled with players. In the distraction of the team's conversation and preparations to leave the stadium, she was unnoticed.

"Hey, Coach," Steve Martella greeted Claire in the hallway. "How you feeling? You look a little feverish."

"I'm fine, thanks," Claire replied.

"Ah, you know that jersey belongs to the team," he said, a laugh in his voice.

"Not today." Claire continued down the hall.

"Oh, Coach," Steve called to her.

"Yes?" Claire faced him.

"There's a press conference in one hour. Since you're well, you need to be there."

"Okay."

If she was to meet the press, Claire realized she needed better clothing.

Claire returned to a pressroom jammed with reporters and cameramen, as well as many of Ikuta's team-mates and coaches. Not since the first day he had pitched had she seen so many people. Something important was about to be announced.

"Do you have your own locker room, *Ferris-san*?" Kentaro asked as he came to her side, noting her usual khaki shorts and cotton shirt. Nothing about his behavior hinted at their feverish interlude.

"*Iye.*" She enjoyed their conversations in Japanese when they were with others. It was like being in a secret club. "I went shopping at Tower Cities Mall," she answered. "Martella-san caught me in the hall and told me about the press conference. What is going on?"

"I believe it has to do with the Baseball Hall of Fame." Kentaro glanced around the room. "Shall we go take our seats?"

Claire followed Kentaro to the spot they often occupied at the long conference table. She nervously settled in next to him. While she listened to Jamison and Horsch talk to the press, Claire caught sight of Jason standing at the back of the reporters. What was he doing here?

"We would like to announce that, along with many other honors bestowed upon our newest pitcher, Kentaro Ikuta is to be honored at Cooperstown with the enshrinement of memorabilia from his first no-hitter pitched last week in Seattle," Horsch announced.

When the crowd responded with applause and cheers, Claire noted that Kentaro was fighting not to react to the praise.

"This is wonderful, Kentaro," she told him, again in their secret conversation. "Is this not too soon for you to be in the Hall of Fame?"

"It is only an honor they do me, not an election into it. I understand there is other memorabilia exhibited there. The greatest honor is that you are here to share it with me, Claire." Kentaro's deep eyes held hers, his fingers brushing against her thigh beneath the table. Now she was the one fighting not to have her face turn beet red.

"What is your response, Mr. Ikuta?" the ESPN reporter shouted to remind the couple to translate their words.

# Kei Swanson

"Mr. Ikuta was telling me how he feels this to be a great honor." Claire did not bother to repeat the question to Kentaro and was not about to add his last sentence.

After the press conference, Kentaro walked with Claire along the Cleveland Museum of Fine Arts lagoon, a favorite place of couples. The water rippled toward the shore with languid waves while a large group of ducks, white domestic as well as wild mallards, floated on the surface. An occasional swan swam with them, its head held high on a regally curved neck. Children tossed bread pieces to the waterfowl, and fish stirred the surface to catch their share of crumbs. Claire watched the children, and Kentaro watched her.

"Do you wish to purchase something to feed the ducks?" Kentaro asked.

"I think I will pass. Thanks anyway." Neither wanted to broach the subject of what had happened in the locker room. "Do you miss your family? Regret being here alone?"

"I am not alone. Not any more." Kentaro's hand brushed Claire's. "I have you."

Claire's face dipped as she allowed him to take her hand.

Though Kentaro sought to catch her eyes, Claire kept her face down. He wondered why she was afraid to look at him. His heart skipped several beats as it increased its pace and his palms sweated as they had the day he started in the exhibition baseball game during the summer Olympics. That day he had conquered his nerves by himself.

"I think I will get some popcorn for the ducks," Claire remarked abruptly. Before Kentaro could speak or pull a dollar from his pocket to give her, Claire walked to the vendor. He waited by the lagoon's edge.

When she returned, he spoke with solemnity. "Claire, what are we going to do about this afternoon in the locker room?"

"I do not know." Claire squatted beside the water and tossed popcorn on the surface for ducks and fish.

"Do you wish to proceed? Or forget it ever happened?" Kentaro stood behind her, his hands on her shoulders. "Please tell me what you wish."

Claire leaned back against his legs, her hand coming up to caress his arm.

"I have never felt like that before."

"Never?" Kentaro moved to squat at Claire's side and took her hand in his. "Are you telling me...?"

"I am trying...not to tell you." Claire's face dropped again, embarrassed by the confession. "You figure it out."

"Oh." Kentaro's noise was one of understanding. "Do you wish...?" They were into a conversation of omission.

"Oh, God, yes!" Claire's eyes shone into his momentarily, then dropped to fix on the ducks. "More than anything, I want you..."

Kentaro's finger under her chin raised her face up to him so he could study her eyes.

"...to be the first. And the only one, Kentaro." Now her look appealed to him.

"Then you shall have it, Claire." Kentaro moved to kiss her, his actions soft and gentle. "I, too, desire only you."

"It is...not just what we want. Have you thought any further about what the media will say? The coaches? It could change things." Claire's eyes were full of questions Kentaro could not answer. "Already the press is complaining about your lack of English. They are asking why you do not use it more since we are studying. I understand how Japanese is more comfortable for you when you and I talk. I even enjoy it, but the media does not understand."

"It is none of their business. You are correct that it is easier for me. It allows me to tell you things I do not wish any other to know. As for the press being concerned with us being involved with each other, Sangyo-san will deal with them. You do have a point that we should be discreet."

"And go slow," Claire said. They stood up, Kentaro's arm around Claire's waist. "I want the first time...to be special."

"It will be." He kissed her forehead. "Now. Give me some of that." He reached into the carton of popcorn. "These ducks are trying to eat my shoe laces."

Kentaro lay in bed, his body tired from baseball and his mind full of questions. All he really knew was that he missed Claire. For two weeks nothing had transpired between them because both were involved in their work. He practiced and Claire worked on her doctorate.

He stared across the room to the warrior doll on the dresser. It made him remember the box from Japan he'd received the day before.

He'd removed the brown paper and tape to unwrap the three-foot long, two-foot wide, and five-inch deep box. At the white box engraved with the *kana* of a leading department store in Kyoto, he'd hesitated. A trusting and co-operative sister, Takahiko had made the purchase and mailed it to him weeks before. Now, he wondered if he'd made a mistake by asking her to. Before he could face the contents of the box, he had to take a step forward in his relationship with his interpreter. Sighing, he slid the unopened white box from under the bed.

# Chapter Seventeen

"*Ferris-san*," Kentaro spoke into the phone after Claire answered. "I was wondering if you would like to go to the movies tonight."

"That would be fun," Claire replied. "I'll pick you up."
"Very well," Kentaro responded in English. "Is seven all right with you?"

"Are we going to try to speak English now?"

"If I feel like it, yes," Kentaro answered, reverting to Japanese.

"You're getting better at this than I think, aren't you?"

Kentaro could mentally picture Claire grinning at him.

"Maybe." Kentaro gave a grin of his own, aware she couldn't see it. He hoped she would feel it as he felt hers.

"Then seven it is."

Kentaro heard Claire hang up with a soft click. As he released the receiver, he found it coated with sweat from his hand.

Claire arrived at the apartment on time.

"What theater are we going to?" Claire asked once Kentaro was settled in the passenger seat of her Mustang. She pulled out into traffic.

"The one on Lee Road. Cedar Lee theater. They are showing Kurasawa-sama's picture, *Throne of Blood*. Have you seen it?" Kentaro buckled the seat belt and settled comfortably into the bucket seat.

"Toshiro Mifune is a Macbeth-like *daimyo*?" Claire asked, echoing his choice of languages, Japanese. She'd noticed a slight nervousness to Kentaro's voice.

"That is right." Silent, he stared into the black night.

"Yes. A long time ago," she answered.

"It has been a long period since we were together," Kentaro commented. Claire sensed he alluded to their locker-room lust. She was present for press conferences, but conspicuous in her absence from the dugout or showers. "I have missed being with you." His hand found its way to Claire's thigh.

"I...," she choked. Her concentration on driving could not divert the awakening sensations spreading through her body.

"You do not have to say it." His hand left her leg. "I am sure your family would not be happy with such a liaison." Kentaro's face turned to the window.

"My family does not get a vote in my love life. No one does!" What was he trying to say? Or not say? Maybe her confession had scared him. This Japanese inscrutability was wearing a little thin.

"They would probably vote for Jason-san." Kentaro spoke into the dark glass.

"I do not want to talk about my family or Jason!"

"Very well." Kentaro followed the words with his sound, his attention riveted outside.

Claire nosed the Mustang into the parking lot behind the Lee Road movie house. They walked in silence to the theater. Inside the lobby, Claire moved in front of Kentaro to approach the ticket booth.

"*Ferris-san*," Kentaro's voice was soft. "I'll attend to the admission."

Claire stepped to the side so he could precede her. She watched protectively while Kentaro purchased tickets. As a teacher, she was as relieved as if he had passed a final exam when he returned with tickets.

"Any trouble?" she asked.

"Why? Should I have? Do you think I do not emerge from my cocoon except when *Ferris-san* is at my side?" Kentaro waved his hand forward to indicate she should pass before him into the theater. "I warned you once not to think you are my keeper." There was a sly twinkle to his eyes.

"And I will remind you that I said then I did not want the job!"

Claire walked down the aisle to midway seats in the dark, empty theater. She sat, face forward, her feelings mixed. Why did he do this all the time? One minute he was sweet and warm, the next cold and harsh. Perhaps, as Dr. Ramstein had said at the very beginning of this adventure, there was a disgruntled samurai inside him. Claire took a deep breath.

Claire and Kentaro watched the images on the screen, the subtitles wasted on them.

"Would you like a drink?" Kentaro's breath teased her face and ear so near was he. It sent shivers down her spine.

"Sure." Claire's eyes followed Kentaro as he shuffled along the seats, then she returned them to Toshiro Mifune once he disappeared through the doorway.

Before long, Kentaro rejoined her.

"I selected a cola since you did not specify," Kentaro said as he handed her the cup and took his seat. "I noticed you drank it at games."

"Great." Claire sipped and then set the cup in the holder at her left. "Want to know what you missed?"

"I have seen it before."

"Oh." Claire snuggled further down in her seat, her shoulder nearer Kentaro's side than before. Her fingers crept

# Kei Swanson

to his thigh, the tips beginning to play over the hard muscle beneath the denim jeans. Kentaro did not move away. In fact, he seemed to settle closer.

Keeping eyes straight forward, Claire rubbed her hand on his leg, inching ever closer to his groin. Her foot slipped out of her flats to play with his, the bare toes stroking the skin of his ankle above his sock.

Kentaro performed the age-old—and highly cliched—movement of feigned stretching as an excuse to place his arm across the back of her chair. His arm found its way to her shoulders, then his hand to her full breast. The movie did not deter their petting.

When the lights came up, they responded as if they were teenagers in the Ferris' living room and the doctor had flipped on the lights. Kentaro retracted his arm and Claire sat up straight in her seat, her face away from him.

"Did you enjoy the movie?" Kentaro did not rush to move as Claire did.

"It was...fun." Claire looked at him with mischief in her eyes.

"A movie about feudal warfare, fun?" Kentaro questioned from his seat.

"I was not talking about the movie...actually. Are you going to stay here?" Claire reached a hand out to him.

"I suppose not." Now that the tightness of his jeans had eased, Kentaro took the small hand. When her touch reawakened his body, Kentaro forced himself to think of the bloody scenes of the movie instead of how delicious her fingers would feel on that unruly part of him. He led her through the aisle and out of the theater.

"Where do you wish to eat?" Claire asked as they reached the car. Kentaro was still at her side, her hand in his.

"You choose."

128

# The Words of the Pitcher

At the driver's side with Claire, Kentaro pushed her against the Mustang, crushed her lips with his mouth. Claire sighed into his mouth as she accepted his tongue and embraced him. The kiss was short and savage, both assuaged momentarily. Kentaro broke it off and, without a word, went to the other side of the car.

Nor did they speak as Claire drove toward a small pub and grill in the neighborhood. Once seated in a booth, Claire and Kentaro held hands across the table.

"We have to talk about business for a moment," Claire said, broaching a subject she knew Kentaro didn't want to address.

"What is it?"

"You need to speak English more often."

"Why? We are doing well with the arrangement we have," Kentaro countered.

"Yes, we are. You understand more English now and it would benefit you greatly if you showed it."

"For what purpose?"

"Kentaro, what do you think the team management thinks about my ability?"

"You translate very well."

"But my other job is to teach you English. If you do not show you are learning, they may fire me."

"And if I do learn to speak well enough by myself, they will relieve you of your position anyway."

"I will always be there in case you are at a loss for words. At least, until the end of the season." Claire touched his cheek.

"But what of the rest of my career? What if I should request your services further?" Kentaro took the hand from his face.

"I will always be around, somewhere, to help you. Just a phone call away."

"Am I nothing more to you than someone whose words you translate?"

"*Iye.*" Claire answered no quickly. "We are friends, but that doesn't get you out of speaking English. You would not dare allow any of the pitching staff to not do their job. Martella-san would be equally remiss if he let you get away with being lazy. It is laziness that we speak Japanese when we are together."

"What if someone overheard us using English? Would that not put more pressure on both of us?"

"You are stubborn, Kentaro Ikuta! For every issue I raise, you have another. I give up!" Claire threw her hands up in surrender.

"Very well." Kentaro crossed his arms over his wide chest and leaned back against the wooden panel behind him. "What do you suggest to eat?"

"I do not know." Claire studied the menu to avoid facing Kentaro. Just looking at him increased her desire.

"How about a hamburger?"

"That'll be fine." His words were English.

"Was that so hard?"

"You are correct. I need to practice," he said in his native tongue. "My teacher is very taxing."

The waitress took the order from Claire. She disappeared and reappeared with the drinks Claire had ordered, beer for them both. They each took sips while an easy silence settled over them.

To Claire, Kentaro's eyes, deep and solemn, looked as if he worried about the world's problems.

He broke the silence. "You said you had seen the movie before. Why did you agree to see it again?"

"I am a Kurasawa fan. I can see his work over and over again." Claire took a long swallow of her beer. She hoped the icy brew would wash the heat from her face. "I have not seen *Throne of Blood* in years. Why the cross-examination? You have seen it before also."

Claire couldn't fathom why he was asking such questions. Couldn't he allow her to enjoy his presence? She would go to an abhorrent boxing match if Kentaro was with her.

"You have studied Kurasawa in addition to your language studies?" Kentaro played with the sweating mug of beer, having only tasted it.

"I saw *The Magnificent Seven* when I was ten and was fascinated with it. So, Daddy took me to see the original, *The Seven Samurai*, at a film festival. I was hooked. What bothered me the most was this rich language I could not understand. I knew there was more to the story than the subtitles indicated. So, I began to take Japanese lessons privately and then continued in high school. Once I graduated, I knew I wanted to pursue a career translating Japanese texts." Claire paused to take a long drink.

"And now, here you sit, translating, not the great historical works of Nihon, but the words of a baseball player."

"I admit I was not thrilled to be offered the job." Claire would never have confessed to Kentaro that she had not wanted to work for him if she were not a little fuzzy in her thinking from the beer.

Before Kentaro could comment, a man intruded.

"Claire Ferris! As I live and breathe!" Jason Stewart called out across the crowded pub. "How you doing?" He slid into the booth at Claire's side and took her into a sideways embrace, placing a sloppy kiss on her cheek.

"Fine, Jason, fine." Claire made to squirm away from him, but he held her fast in his embrace. She saw a flash of anger in Kentaro's eyes, which he mastered while making his snorting noise. "Stop. I don't think you met my friend the other day, Jason. The one you insulted. This is Kentaro Ikuta, pitcher for the Chiefs. *Ikuta-san*, this is Jason

Stewart." She made the introductions in the appropriate languages.

Neither man spoke to the other. Each nodded curtly like two bulls in a pasture with a lone cow. Claire took another swallow of her beer, but Kentaro continued the glass ballet with his.

"I was wondering where you were keeping yourself, Claire," Jason rambled on. "I'm really sorry about the way I acted the other day. Boy! Was I outta line or what? I tried to call and apologize but kept getting your machine."

"That's fine, Jason. I've been out of town." Claire drank again.

"So your mother says. Traveling with a baseball team. Boy, how to ruin a reputation, Clairy!" Jason signaled for the waitress to bring him the drink she carried. "Thanks, sweetie." He took the glass and napkin from the tray. "I ordered at the bar," he explained to Claire.

"I'm not traveling around! It's my job." Claire suspected Jason had already had a few too many drinks while at the bar.

"What's your job? Team tramp?" Jason's guffaw filled the pub.

"Jason, you're rude. Please leave."

"What've you got planned for tonight? Want to join me? I've got some friends and their girls and we're all going down to the Flats." He took a long drink of the brown liquor in his glass. The Flats was an area downtown on the shores of Lake Erie lined with restaurants, bars, and clubs.

"Jason, I'm with a friend. Will you go away?" Claire growled.

Kentaro continued his silent observation.

"Okay, then. I see you're still at work. I have a cousin's wedding next weekend. You can go then and make it up to me."

Claire saw Kentaro's eyes look up into hers and she knew he understood not only the last of Jason's words, but, she suspected, the whole conversation.

"Jason, I have to be out of town with the Chiefs. We have a game in New York," Claire explained. "Then I have to go to the Baseball Hall of Fame. You should know that, you were at the press conference."

"Oh, man!" Jason took his arms from around Claire. He didn't comment on the press conference. "I was planning on it, Clairy!!"

"Don't call me that. I'm not someone you should count on. I have a life, Jason." Claire moved to the corner of the booth. "And you're not in it."

Kentaro continued to watch the drama playing out before him. He lifted the beer glass to his lips, eyeing Jason over the rim.

"Claire, come on! You can't let me down." Jason pouted.

"Excuse me, but I believe *Ferris-san* has indicated she has other plans," Kentaro spoke up. His words came forth clearly.

"What? Who're you to tell me what Claire wants?" Jason turned his selfishness on Kentaro.

"Claire has told you what she wants. Have you not, *Ferris-san*?" Kentaro's face was stern, reminding Claire of Mifune's in the movie they had just seen.

"Yes. Jason, go away. You've had too much to drink and I don't want you around me." Claire pushed Jason away.

"I guess ole Jase can take a hint! I'm outta here." The young man staggered to his feet and disappeared into a group of his friends at the bar.

"I am so sorry, *Ikuta-san*." Claire felt her embarrassment on her face. She finished the dregs of her beer.

"It is not you who should apologize. That young man is the one who should excuse his presumptuousness." Kentaro eased back against the wooden booth.

"Well, that will never happen so I will say it for him."

"No!" Kentaro slapped his open hand down hard on the table top and came up from his lounging position. "The only words you will speak for another are mine!"

"Oh?" Claire's eyes widened at his outburst. "Very well, but if you keep speaking English, I will not have a reason to speak your words."

Kentaro's countenance told her that perhaps he was afraid she spoke the truth.

The waitress arrived with their meals and cut short the conversation. Claire noted the server's strange looks toward Kentaro and herself.

"You'll have to forgive my friend. He's acting crazy," she explained to the woman. "*Baka* if you don't understand English," she directed at Kentaro in Japanese.

"I'm not crazy. Excuse my outburst." Kentaro apologized to the waitress and then aimed his attention at his food. He appeared embarrassed by his explosion.

The server walked away without comment.

"I did not mind." Claire reached out and stroked the long hair curtaining his face. "I like that in my men."

"Your men?" Kentaro lifted his eyes to look into Claire's. "Now you are alluding to your past."

"Well, my man." Claire regretted her words, but they were the truth. "Oh, hush and eat!" Claire withdrew her hand.

As she ate, Claire glanced at Kentaro who seemed more interested in his food than her. But, then, she caught his eyes studying her when he thought she was unaware. When Kentaro's leg rubbed against hers under the table, the shock spread through her. Heat moved over her, from head to toe, making her feel it necessary to drop her gaze to her plate.

Kentaro watched Claire across the narrow table as she dipped a long, limp french fry in catsup. Had she meant him when she said 'my man'?

He had planned, after the kiss in the theater parking lot, to make advances in that direction later tonight. Jason's arrival had poured cold water on his designs. If Claire wanted him, Kentaro, why did she tolerate Jason? Kentaro could not share her with any one, particularly as dishonorable a man as Jason.

As he contemplated the connection between his 'words' and the other man, Kentaro's hope deflated. Even if Jason was not her choice, there was no chance for him to build a relationship with Claire. He was not Caucasian or American. No matter what she said, Claire's family would never approve of him without the round eyes and blonde hair Jason possessed. He could not entertain thoughts of making love to Claire tonight or any other night.

"Are you finished with your food?" Claire pushed her own plate aside and wiped her mouth with the paper napkin.

"I will be in a minute." Kentaro put the last bite of his hamburger into his mouth.

Claire watched, anticipating a lust-filled night. At the same time, she feared the coming events. What could she give a worldly man like Kentaro? He would probably find her lacking compared with the women he must have known in his career as a professional player. She did not want to disappoint him but she would.

"It is getting late," Claire said as they exited the pub.

"Yes, it is." Kentaro's voice lacked the life she was so accustomed to. His hands were pushed into his jeans' front pockets, his shoulders rolled forward and his head down.

"Is something bothering you, Kentaro?" Claire touched his arm softly.

"No...I was...," Kentaro cleared his throat. He raised his shoulders and straightened his back. "I suppose I am tired."

"Then you will be glad to get home to bed." Claire did not think of her words.

"I doubt it," Kentaro mumbled.

Claire drove toward Kentaro's apartment, going down Surrey Road past her own building.

"I...live in that building," she pointed out. Did she hope he would suggest a visit to her home?

"It is a nice place," Kentaro commented. "I have passed it often during my walks."

"You should stop by sometime." Claire continued down the road.

"Maybe I will."

The awkward silence crept over them.

"Have you ever been to the Baseball Hall of Fame?" she asked.

"No. You?"

"No. It should be fun, out of town without a game to play. No hotel roommates or curfew." If they could not consummate their love tonight, Claire'd give him something to think about in regard to Cooperstown. She pulled into the parking lot behind Kentaro's building and kept the engine running. If she turned it off, she might seem brash.

"I will be forced to make a speech longer than the interviews." Kentaro unbuckled his seat belt but made no move to get out of the car.

"Are you concerned?" Claire waited and hoped for an invitation.

"A little. Sangyo-san has helped me. He says I should give you a copy so you can become familiar with it."

"Do you wish me to come up with you and get it?" A lump rose in her throat as she held her breath for his answer.

Kentaro made his customary sound before speaking.

"I will bring it to you at the stadium." Kentaro opened the door. "I have enjoyed our evening."

"I have too." Claire could not look at him.

"*Claire-chan*," Kentaro whispered. "Look at me."

Claire slowly faced him. Kentaro leaned toward her, his lips brushing hers lightly.

"Good night," he said softly in English.

"'Night," Claire responded, no breath left in her body.

As she watched Kentaro walk to the door, silent tears rolled down her cheeks at the lost chance for him to make love to her, and her to him. Would she ever have a chance again?

# Chapter Eighteen

"I have to go to the ladies' room," Claire whispered into Kentaro's ear. They were at a banquet at the Baseball Hall of Fame in Cooperstown honoring the Japanese pitcher by placing into exhibit the ball and ticket stubs from his first no hitter. Kentaro nodded his head in acknowledgment. "I will be right back."

Claire felt safe in leaving him alone since all the talking had been done, and the board members, team representatives, and media were enjoying dessert and coffee. She walked discreetly away from the table and out of the room.

She had been very meticulous in her dressing for the evening. The dress she wore was strapless like the black dress she'd worn to Otani's, but not as form-fitting. While the bodice was close to her body, the light crepe handkerchief skirt was full. The whole garment was as red as the sun on the flag of Japan. Her hair was upswept casually. Claire hoped Kentaro made some kind of romantic move since they were unencumbered by a baseball team while out of town. She had even gone, to her gynecologist for a prescription which she had started taking the very night she had it filled in anticipation of making love with Kentaro. She contemplated this on the way to the ladies' room.

The restrooms were located two halls away from the banquet room. Being one of the few women in the building, Claire didn't pass anyone and her heels clicked on the hard floor. Eerily, she thought she heard an echoing step to her own. She paused once to look behind to see if someone were actually there.

The hall was vacant. When she continued, the heavier footsteps resumed and she increased her rapid pace. With relief , she entered the sanctuary of the ladies' room and locked the door behind her.

"Claire."

A familiar voice greeted her as she exited the bathroom.

"Jason?" Claire turned to face him. "What are you doing here?" She had no idea he was in Cooperstown or why he would be at a baseball function. He didn't even like Kentaro. Why attend a banquet in his honor?

"Yep, it's me. Good ole Jase." His slurred words revealed he was drunk. "Just me, your old buddy, your pal. Someone you can throw away whenever you want."

As Jason approached Claire, he seemed to stumble forward and caught himself by draping his arm over her shoulder and around her neck. She struggled to stand up under the weight of his body and momentum of his fall. In stepping backward to keep her balance, she found herself against the wall. Jason pressed his body against her.

"Claire." Jason's free hand stroked her face. His breath was heavy with alcohol.

"Jason, let me go. You're drunk."

Claire tried to push him away but he began to kiss her, his tongue deeply invading her mouth. Claire shook her head and worked her mouth out of his reach, but Jason caught her wrist and held it over her head against the wall. He did not fail to notice that the position pulled a breast out of the strapless bodice.

"Such a beautiful body." He dropped his head to kiss the exposed nipple.

"Please, stop this." This is Jason! We grew up together she told herself. He wouldn't possible hurt me. Could he? "You're being silly."

"You're mine. Remember that! You are MINE!"

Jason seized her other wrist and raised her arms over her head. He imprisoned both wrists in one hand and with the other worked his way to the hem of her skirt.

"Jason, don't do this!" Claire struggled to free herself, trying to knee him in the groin, but he was too close.

"Never. I want you, Claire." Jason pulled savagely at the elastic of her panty hose.

"You're hurting me," Claire whimpered.

"I told you, he can't have you! I'll have you one way or another."

She felt his teeth bite into her flesh. "Please don't!" Claire cried, hurting and really scared.

"I don't want to hurt you, Clairy, just to love you." Finally, Jason managed to rip the panty hose from her hips and his hand now moved between her legs.

Jason's fingers dug deeper. Claire gasped from pain that stabbed through her lower abdomen. All at once she heard a welcomed voice.

"Let her go," Kentaro Ikuta ordered with quiet authority.

"Go away, Jap, and leave us alone!" Jason shouted over his shoulder. "I don't need your help."

"I asked you to stop. You are hurting her."

Behind Jason, Claire could see Kentaro coming nearer.

"Oh, I forgot. You don't speakee the English. Why don't you translate what I said, Clairy? Tell this yellow bastard to get the hell away and let you be loved by a real man." Jason's fingers probed deeper.

"She doesn't need to translate for me. I understand exactly what you're doing. Now let her go." Kentaro's voice remained calm but stern.

The look in Jason's eyes thoroughly frightened Claire. Then he struck her furiously across the face, smearing her cheek with her own blood.

Claire screamed. Through teary eyes, she saw Kentaro moving toward Jason with a raised baseball bat. She supposed it was the one she'd seen a photographer handing him in the pre-meal photo shoot, but she really didn't care where it came from.

"Kentaro, don't!" she shouted. "Jason, let me go now!" she demanded.

Jason stared at her, then at the ball player, and released her. Claire pulled her dress up over her bare breasts. She mutely watched Jason approach Kentaro in a fighting stance.

"You wanna fight me, Jap? Well, drop that bat and come on!"

"I don't wish to fight anyone. Leave us alone and I won't have to hurt you," Kentaro advised.

"No, man, you're gonna leave us so we can get back to our business."

Claire slumped down the wall and tried to gather her wits. She couldn't allow Kentaro to use the bat on Jason and commit a felony. Jason, with his family's money and position, would be seen as the injured party.

"Stop." Claire struggled to her feet and fearfully moved between the men. With all her heart she wanted Kentaro to beat Jason to death, but she said, "Kentaro, please lower the bat." She spoke in precise Japanese then changed to English for Jason. "Jason, leave and no one will ever know this happened."

"You don't have to speak Japanese, Claire. This demon must know what you're saying," Kentaro instructed. He held the wooden bat over his left shoulder.

"Very well. Jason, I told him to put the bat down. Now, you must leave."

Jason looked at her, his face a hard, cold mask.

"Not without you!" Jason spat. "You're mine, Claire! I'll have you!"

Claire moved to stand as close as she could to Kentaro. His arm shifted her behind him. Claire huddled at Kentaro's back. Though she wanted to sag against him in surrender, wanted to let him handle the situation, she couldn't. He didn't see the danger to himself.

"Kentaro, please put it down. Jason, tell him you'll leave." She was still protected at Kentaro's back.

"Hell, no!" Jason's hands clenched into fists. "I'm not gonna leave without you. Then I'll do exactly what I want!" Jason's feet moved. He came toward Kentaro fixed on capturing Claire.

Claire felt Kentaro's muscles tense in his right shoulder.

"Kentaro, no," she whispered. She couldn't let him do this.

"Need a woman to protect you, Jap?" Jason spat.

"I need no one to protect me from idiots," Kentaro returned. "Will you leave or must I use this?"

"Big man with a weapon," Jason countered. "Can't you do without one?"

"I can, but it'll be quicker for you if I swing."

At that moment, Kentaro's arm moved the ash rod to cut through the air. Claire felt the power in the swing and heard the violent swish. She collapsed and put her hands over her ears, afraid of the sound of the bat connecting with Jason's head.

It never came.

Claire looked up to see Jason as he fled down the corridor. Kentaro dropped the bat. It clattered to the floor and rolled to the wall. He knelt down and pulled her to his chest. Claire held her face against Kentaro and sobbed. Her tears and the blood stained his white shirt.

Kentaro pushed her from him when she had quieted enough to listen to him.

*142*

"He hurt you, Claire." It was a statement. "Let me look."

He studied her face. Pushing the disarrayed bangs from her forehead, his hand came to rest on her right, undamaged cheek. There was a deep bruise over her left cheek which caused her eye to begin to swell. Trickles of blood ran from her eyebrow, the corner of her mouth and the bite wound on her right shoulder. Kentaro pulled a small packet of tissues from his coat pocket and began to dab at the wounds. Once the bleeding stopped, he brushed his lips ever so tenderly against the battered mouth. His hand cupped her jaw.

"Oh, Kentaro," Claire sank against him again.

"Ssssh." Kentaro helped her to stand. "Go in there." He propelled her toward the ladies' room.

Once inside, Kentaro directed her into the handicapped stall because it was the largest. Claire, limp as a rag, allowed him to remove the torn panty hose. His hands were soothing on her legs, the unintentional caresses of a lover. Kentaro moved her to sit on the toilet to facilitate his removal of her shoes and hose.

"Claire."

She couldn't answer.

"Your dress was so pretty, Claire. I am sorry I did not tell you so before."

She knew he was saying words, but she couldn't understand them.

"Claire." Kneeling in front of her, Kentaro put his hands on her arms. He gazed into her face. "You must go to the hospital."

"No," she whispered, shaking her head.

"Yes." Kentaro's voice was insistent.

"I can't." It was all so clear now. She clutched his arms. "Don't you see? If I go to the hospital, they'll make me report this to the police, and I can't do that because then you'd be involved. Oh, God! Where's the bat? You've got to go get it. Don't let anyone else find it. Kentaro, we can't let anyone know about this. The press'll have a field day. Jason'll tell everyone you started it and you tried to...rape me and he'll come out the hero and...," Claire's words were rapid-fire English, slurred and confused, her train of thought convoluted.

"Claire, hush." Kentaro's hand caressed her cheek, a finger on her lips.

"No, we can't. You have to leave. Go. Let me take care of things. No one can know. They'll blame you and you...only love me!" Claire's sobs erupted. Her hands covered her face and she fell forward over her legs.

Kentaro's hands rubbed her back in consolation.

"I do love you, *Claire-chan*," Kentaro murmured, his face bent close to her head. "Still, you have to go to the hospital."

"No."

"Claire, you are bleeding," he insisted. "It comes from..." Kentaro couldn't finish the sentence.

Claire raised her face to him. Horror filled her eyes.

"You've been injured. I'm taking you to a hospital. I'm going to tell the limo driver to move the car to the back." Kentaro stood as Claire sat upright. He removed his dinner jacket. "I'll come back in just a minute." He draped the jacket around her shoulders. "Wait for me."

Claire nodded, unable to argue with him.

"Kentaro," she breathed his name as he was about to step out of the stall.

He hesitated and turned back to her.

"Yes?" His eyes spoke to hers.

"Nothing." She stared at him, afraid of what might happen when he left her alone.

"I'll be right back." Kentaro leaned over and kissed the top of her head.

"Please hurry." Claire put her arms in the sleeves of the too-large coat. She rubbed her cheek against the cloth. It smelled of Kentaro. She held the coat around herself, cloaked in its protection and warmth.

# Chapter Nineteen

Claire made no sound as she wiped at her tears. Lying on the exam table, she could see the top of the doctor's head between her sheet-draped knees. She pulled several more tissues out of the box sitting on her chest.

"You can sit up now, miss. The nurse will dress that shoulder," the doctor spoke.

The nurse at her side helped her sit up.

In the crowded waiting room, Kentaro Ikuta stood beside a window looking out at the dark parking lot, oblivious to those around him. A ten-year-old boy had recognized him from baseball and started to ask for his signature. But Kentaro put up the traditional emotional wall necessary to isolate himself from others and the boy's mother intervened. He could not wall away the horror of Jason's assault on Claire.

His Claire.

Kentaro regretted he had not left the banquet sooner to look for her. What damage had Jason perpetrated on Claire that he was not aware of? Could she be injured emotionally, unable to trust a man, ever? The injuries to her face and blood on her thigh were enough for Kentaro to hope something terrible happened to the crude man.

"Mr. Ikuta?" the receptionist called. "They'd like you back in the exam room."

Kentaro turned and walked back into the interior of the emergency room, afraid something more dreadful had happened to Claire. Terror welled up in his chest. A nurse pointed toward the room where he could find her.

"She'll be fine. The doctor wants to talk to her, but she wants you with her," she explained.

Relief washed through him. Kentaro found Claire sitting on the examination table in a paper gown that hid very little of her slender body. He stepped to her side and, like a drowning person, she reached out to clutch his hand.

Kentaro pulled her to him. She laid her head on his chest. He felt the thick gauze dressing on her shoulder.

"It will be all right," he spoke into her hair. His heart was breaking. He wished Jason had not retreated and he had been allowed to use the bat on his head.

Claire was subdued and quiet.

"I was explaining Ms. Ferris's condition but..." the doctor commented.

"Please, go on."

"She has severe abrasions and bruising to her vulva and vagina. The bleeding's from a hymeneal tear typical of a wedding night injury and will subside in time. It's the shoulder wound I'm most concerned about. Human bites can be worse than an animal's. I've given her a shot of penicillin and script for an antibiotic. Plus, the nurse is going to give you a sleeping pill to give her once you get her home. That's what she needs most. Rest."

"Thank you, *sensei*. I'll take care of her."

The doctor left the room and the nurse came to take Kentaro's place.

"Let me help you get dressed, sweetie."

"I'll help her." Kentaro excused the nurse.

"Okay. I'll get her meds."

"You should sleep, little one." Kentaro came to sit next to Claire, careful not to jostle her. He had put her to bed at the hotel and given her the medicine.

"Thank you for taking care of me." Claire returned the soft words. Her hand reached out to touch the long hair against his neck and shoulder.

"You are welcome." Kentaro gently took her hand from his hair and laid it on the bed, then straightened the sheets around her. "*Oyasumi*."

"I thought I should call and tell you what happened, Sangyo-san." Kentaro used the phone in his hotel room. He had left Claire asleep and would return to her room as soon as he finished business. "I am sure it will be in the papers as soon as he is arrested."

"This is not going to be good. I will get busy on the PR end of things. Are you sure there will be an arrest?"

"Yes, Claire identified him for the police."

"Man, I wish you had called me first."

"My first concern is Claire."

"You would do well to remember your career, too. Look, I am sorry for what happened, but I could have handled the press better had I known first. Take care of her, *Kentaro-san*, and I will call you later."

"Kentaro?" Claire whimpered several hours later.

"I am here." Kentaro sat at her bedside. He put his book down, retracted his sock-covered feet from where they were propped up on her bed, and leaned forward. His hand stroked the hair off her face. "What is it, *Claire-chan*?" The endearment, a term not used freely, was the closest thing his language had to a pet-name.

"Hold me."

Kentaro carefully arranged himself to half-sit on the bed with Claire's head resting against his torso.

"When are you leaving?" Her hand drew circles on Kentaro's abdomen. He wore only a pair of sweat pants. "The team has a game scheduled for tomorrow."

"I do not pitch until Tuesday." When he felt pressure growing in his lower body from her stroking, he took hold of her hand and held it still. "I called and told Martella-san and Sangyo-san about...the incident, so they could contend with the media. Martella-san said I could stay and take care of you. That is, if you wish."

"I am glad you are here with me." She grasped his hand tighter. "I want you to take care of me."

"It may be difficult for me. As an eldest son, I have always been the one cared for." Kentaro smiled at his joke and brushed his lips across the crown of her head.

Claire sighed. She slept while Kentaro balanced his book on his leg and continued to read.

"Oh, Claire! My poor baby!" Claudia exclaimed as Claire came through the door of her family's residence. She rushed to enfold Claire in her arms.

"Mother, you're always so melodramatic." Claire submitted to her mother's embrace and kiss. "See why I did not want them to come?" she murmured in Japanese to Kentaro who stood at her side, her hand in his.

"I'm glad to have you home, sweetheart." Dr. Ferris came to greet the group in the foyer. He kissed Claire's cheek. "How's your shoulder?" He attempted to peek at her wound hidden by her clothing.

"Always the doctor, huh, Daddy?" Claire moved her father's hand away from the neck of her shirt. She wondered if she was going to regret giving the emergency room doctor permission to give her father the medical information. "Let me get settled and you can do your thing."

"I can take a hint. Hello, Kentaro." Dr. Ferris shook the young Asian's hand firmly, with the other hand on Kentaro's shoulder. "Thank you so much for taking care of our little girl."

*"Do itashimashite."*

"Because Claire's used your language around here since she was a teen-ager, I know you just said it was nothing. It's a lot to me, young man." Dr. Ferris moved toward the library, hopeful Kentaro would follow. "Come with me while Claudia gets our girl settled."

"Mother will probably make me get in bed," Claire told Kentaro in Japanese. "Go. They are treating you as if you are a member of the family."

"Not a bad family to be a member of," Kentaro commented. "How much Japanese do they understand?"

"Just a little. Now, go on." Claire pushed him away with a playful shove. "Daddy doesn't bite..." Claire followed her mother up the staircase to take up temporary residence in her old bedroom. "At least not often." Her giggles floated down to Kentaro's ears.

"I want to get your opinion about something," Dr. Ferris started once the men were settled in chairs in front of his desk. He had poured them each a liberal glass of bourbon.

"I'll try to help you in any manner I'm able." Kentaro sipped the drink.

"Do you think Claire's up to hearing any more about this mess?" It was Dr. Ferris' turn to drink.

"She's very strong, sir. I know she would wish to know whatever she needs to hear."

"Well, I'm going to take the coward's way out. You two seemed to have gotten so close, I'm going to let you tell her."

"Very well, sir. What will I be telling her?"

"Jason was arrested and bailed-out. He pled guilty and is now out on probation." Dr. Ferris' voice rose and his face turned bright red in his rage. "I honestly wish you'd finished the job."

"I can understand your feelings, sir. I wish I had also."

"We're all thankful she had you to take care of her."

I'd like to take care of her for the rest of her life, Kentaro thought, but said, "I'll tell her, sir." He finished his drink and stood.

"I'm going up with you and check on that wound." Dr. Ferris drained his glass and joined Kentaro.

While Dr. Ferris examined Claire, Kentaro excused himself.

"Okay, sweet pea, let's have a look." Her father took on his doctor persona.

Claire, propped by several pillows, sat up in bed and shrugged her shoulder out of the gown. A small bloody area stained the gauze dressing taped there. Dr. Ferris, as attentive as if he were caring for one of his terminally ill children, removed the soiled dressing. To better inspect the inflamed tissue, he put on his half-framed reading glasses. Small areas of infection were evident in the clearly defined teeth marks. With a touch developed over decades of treating toddlers, he felt the area and noted the warmth.

"You're taking antibiotics?"

"Yes, doctor."

"It's got a nasty infection in just two days. I may have to drain it."

"Please don't!" Claire held her hand over the open wound, not touching her sore shoulder, in a defensive posture not unlike those of his usual patients.

"I'm just thinking out loud." Dr. Ferris patted her leg and removed his glasses. "I'll clean and dress it. Where'd your mother put the stuff?"

"In the bathroom," Claire directed. "Do you think out loud at the hospital at your patient's bedside? I don't think so!" Claire huffed.

"You're fortunate, Claire." He began to cleanse the wound with hydrogen peroxide. "It could've been much worse."

"It's bad enough, Daddy." Her eyes filled with tears.

"You're lucky Kentaro was there." Dr. Ferris applied antibiotic ointment.

"I think he would've killed him." Claire's eyes were now clear and bright with the thought of Kentaro's rescue.

"Probably should have. I don't understand what happened with Jason," her father mumbled while he applied tape to secure the gauze. "Anything you want to tell me about Kentaro?"

"Just that I love him," she spoke in confidence to her father, unable to fully admit her feelings until this moment.

"Oh." Dr. Ferris pulled Claire's gown sleeve up over her shoulder.

"Something wrong with that, Daddy?"

"No, not at all. You've been my little girl for a long time. I'm not ready to share my baby with another man." He kissed her forehead. "How do you feel about baseball now?" He grinned at her.

"Daddy!"

"Get some rest, sweet pea." Dr. Ferris stood. "Kentaro's outside."

"Tell him to come in." Claire slipped further down under the comforter.

"Sure thing."

Kentaro found Claire neatly tucked into bed in the very femininely decorated room. Stuffed animals, pink ruffles, and pillows were everywhere. A jewelry box, an antique Japanese-style lacquered music box, and a lacquered tray with perfume and trinkets sat on the heavy wooden dresser. Picture frames with photographs of a little girl, a teen-ager, and a debutante were there also. Kentaro glanced at them, delighted to see Claire at those ages. They hinted of the adult woman she had grown into.

"How does it feel to be a child again, *Claire-chan*?" He sat on the edge of the bed facing her.

"Weird." Claire's fingers found their way to Kentaro's loose hair. The silken locks were smooth and comforting on her skin. "I am not tired, but Mother seemed to think I should go to bed, so I humored her."

"It is the only thing she knows to do with you."

"You keep putting me to bed, also." Claire smiled, an impish sparkle to her eyes.

"Enough of that talk. Rest, little one." Kentaro took her hand from his hair and held it in his.

"Lie down with me."

"*Claire-chan*," he scolded.

"Not in bed with me. Here." Claire scooted over toward the middle of the bed and slapped the vacated spot. "On top of the covers."

Kentaro moved to sit at her side with his arm around her shoulders. Claire snuggled next to him.

"This is nice."

Kentaro replied with his gentle samurai sound.

"What did Daddy tell you? Was it about Jason?"

"Yes." Kentaro's cheek rested on her head. "Do you want to know now or later?"

"Now." Claire buried her face in his chest as if hiding from the words Kentaro was about to speak.

"He did admit his guilt, but, in doing so, his punishment is probation."

Claire's hand, lying motionless on his chest, now bunched his shirt when it clenched into a tight fist.

"It is not fair," Claire spoke into Kentaro's body. "He deserves more." Tears began to flow despite her attempt not to cry. "He took something special from me."

"He did not take your life, *Claire-chan*." Kentaro, not cognizant of her meaning, moved his cheek gently against her hair.

"He took the one thing I wanted to give to you." Claire's words were very soft, almost inaudible.

"He did not take your heart. That is what is important to me." Kentaro held her closer. His hand tightened on her arm, careful not to hurt her wound. "I gave you mine the first day I met you."

"What happened to the tough samurai?" Claire gazed up at him, her eyes bright with tears and adoration.

"You have tamed the warrior. Now, go to sleep."

"Only if you stay with me." Claire rested her chin on his chest to study him.

"Very well. Sleep, little one." Kentaro kissed her forehead and she closed her eyes to sleep, the energy drained from her. Kentaro napped with her.

Claire spent ten days enjoying being coddled by her parents. Flowers and get-well cards came from all over. The Chiefs sent a large spray of pink roses; Kentaro's two dozen were red. The Baseball Hall of Fame sent a bouquet of spring flowers. The sportswriters and networks also offered floral gifts and baskets of fruit. Fans of Ikuta, as well as the team members, sent single blossoms, cards, candy, and small toys. The toys she sent to her father's office to be given to sick children. She donated the boxes of chocolates, fruit baskets, and most of the flowers to the nurses' station on the pediatric ward at Rainbow Babies and Children's Hospital.

Her bruises disappeared and her shoulder healed. Dr. Ferris wasn't called on to do anything further to the wound except nightly dressing changes. Claire kept up with the Chiefs via television, radio, and the newspaper. The features reporter upset her everyday with his column. The man continued to question Kentaro's lack of English. Why was he so venomous, she wondered.

Her greatest fear was the reporter would reveal details of her attack at Cooperstown. The fans thus far knew only that the interpreter for Mr. Ikuta had had an 'accident.'

Claire would have to hold her breath and hope the shoe didn't fall. What would happen if it did?

# Chapter Twenty

"Well, well, well! Look who's decided to return to work!" Steve Martella greeted Claire as she entered the dugout.

"I couldn't let you guys have fun without me!"

"How are you really, Claire?" Steve came close enough to whisper. He appraised her usual game outfit of khaki, red oxford shirt, and the Chiefs team jacket. "You look good."

"I'm great. Really. I'm fine. What bothers me most is the press!"

"Yeah, they're riding Ikuta hard. Without you in the last games, he hasn't talked at all. I must confess, Claire, I don't understand why Ikuta doesn't do better."

"He does, but he's self-conscious about it. When he goes alone to the press conference for the first time, he wants to be able to speak perfectly. During the two weeks I was out, we worked whenever the team was in town. Now, with me on the road, too, we'll really get busy. It won't be much longer." Claire took her seat, Steve alongside her. "You know, though, I'd have thought there'd have been more about...Cooperstown. Kentaro was with me the whole time until he brought me home."

"I expected more, too," Steve confessed. "You never know with the press. It may show up later."

"After so long, perhaps they've forgotten about it."

"I hope you have, at least a little bit."

"I'm fine, Steve. But I'm tired of people walking on eggshells around me. I wasn't seriously hurt and my psyche's not destroyed. Now, are we going to win this game or what?"

"Your boy's gonna do it for us, Coach." He chucked her arm and stood up.

Claire sat drinking in the excitement, thrilled to be back amid the athletes. Familiar habits took hold. She felt at ease amid the sounds of the crowd, the blaring of the PA system, the chatter of the players, and the clink of their cleats on the concrete. It was a comfortable feeling, like the one she had previously enjoyed only in her office at Case Western.

When Claire arrived, Kentaro had already started the second inning, so she sat alone until the other team struck out. She handed him his jacket and an ice pack as he entered the dugout. Kentaro cupped the pack around his elbow before he draped the jacket over his arm in the night-chilled air.

"Good evening, *Ferris-san*." He took his place at her side. "How are you?"

"Well, thank you." Claire picked a sunflower seed out of the cup she held and put the salty bit into her mouth.

"I thought you hated those."

Claire put the hull into another cup.

"An acquired taste. I used to think it was a disgusting habit the guys had, especially when they got bored and started flicking them at each other."

"I did not know they did that."

"You are too preoccupied during games." Claire ate more sunflower seeds. "How have you been since class this afternoon?"

"It has not been that long, *Claire-chan*," Kentaro spoke softly. The corners of his mouth hinted at a grin.

"Behave." Claire took a seed and placed it on her thumb in front of her index finger. "Or I'll have to punish you."

"You wouldn't dare," Kentaro challenged in English.

"Watch."

Instantly, they were into a sunflower seed fight. Claire launched her missile toward Kentaro. He dodged, returning upright to reach into the cup Claire held. She held the cup out of his reach to prevent him from arming himself. Kentaro managed to obtain ammunition and spilled some of Claire's supply. He moved down a seat or two while he set up his retaliatory shot. He launched it off kilter and Claire was free to keep up a rapid barrage. Kentaro found himself covered with the seeds as he evaded them by leaning as far away from her as he could. Claire kept coming, laughing hysterically.

"I surrender!" Kentaro admitted as he hid behind his arms.

"See? There's something I can do better than you!" Claire laughed. It was nice to be back in the dugout with him.

Kentaro's participation in her seed war surprised Claire. He was usually so serious about baseball and himself, that for him to react frivolously was a new side to his character. Maybe, as he became more comfortable with her, he was relaxing his defenses. No matter the reason, she liked it.

The Chiefs had won a three-game home stand against the New York Yankees. Kentaro and Claire, along with others, exited the stadium through the players' gate to find a swarm of fans. The guards were unsuccessful in keeping the fans back. Young boys, teenagers, men and an occasional female, all crowded about the team, pushing baseballs, cards, jerseys and eight-by-ten glossies into their hands to be signed with broad-pointed, felt-tipped markers.

Claire wedged herself in front of Kentaro as a shield since he was the target for most of the autograph seekers. She was soon separated, lost amid the bodies crowding the sidewalk.

"*Ikuta-san!*" She was afraid he would be overwhelmed by the barrage of English thrown at him.

"Over here, *Ferris-san!*"

The crush surged toward the shy pitcher, pulling Claire with it. She struggled through the wave of bodies to at last reach his side.

"Are you all right?" Kentaro continued to sign the Japanese character of his name.

"Just a little winded." She noticed a large number of women and girls encircling Kentaro. He could probably have any one of these women, she thought, jealousy invading her heart. Without thinking, she put her hands on his biceps as if to mark him as hers. "How are you doing at understanding their questions?"

"I need only to write." Kentaro smiled down at her.

"Are you sure some people have not asked you anything?" She eyed the women who didn't disappear after Kentaro wrote his name for them.

"Well, I have understood some, but I have not felt the need to answer. And I do not think I wish for you to translate any of their suggestions."

"I get your point. I will leave you with your women." Claire took her hands off his arm and stepped to the corner a distance away.

After fifteen minutes of indulging their public, the team made their way further down the sidewalk toward their cars. The crowd thinned, but Claire saw women hovering about. Kentaro was the last to be released. In silence, they walked to Claire's Mustang.

Once in the car, Claire chanced an occasional glance at Kentaro as she drove. The broad shoulders were evident beneath the knit shirt he wore tucked into tight jeans. Often when she stood behind him for some media coverage, she had the urge to step up against him, to put her face against the expanse between his shoulder blades, her arms around his waist, and feel his buttocks next to her hips. She never did and at times, as now, she felt her desire awaken.

"Do you wish to have a late dinner, *Claire-chan*?" Kentaro asked as she drove.

"Love to, but are you up to it?" Claire forgot all about the jealousy as he stroked her name with the affectionate term. "You did just play a game." Claire reached a hand to touch his neck under the pretense of moving a stray hair.

"I merely pitched the last inning." Kentaro shifted his torso to put his shoulder nearer Claire's.

"Do you want me to go somewhere now?" She positioned her shoulder so it brushed his.

"No. Come to my apartment. I have to make a phone call home. It is Saburo's birthday. I must also shower," Kentaro explained.

"Why did you not shower at the stadium?"

She turned onto Kentaro's street.

"I did not work up much of a sweat. Nor did I wish to be away from you that long. Besides, locker room showers are not as much fun as they were once."

Kentaro opened the door to his apartment and stepped aside to allow Claire to enter ahead of him.

"This is nice," she commented, following Kentaro's lead in removing her shoes.

"My sister arranged it for me," Kentaro explained. "I will make my call using the phone in the bedroom."

Claire noticed the subtle Japanese touches to the furnishings. A Satsuma vase sat in a corner nook with an understated and beautiful arrangement of silk flowers.

"Would you like something to drink?" Kentaro offered.

"No." Claire turned from the flowers. "I'll wait here."

"Very well. I will not be long." Kentaro went into his bedroom, closing the door quietly.

Claire didn't sit on the couch, but walked around the room and looked at his possessions. Much of the furniture was

# The Words of the Pitcher

non-descript, colors which blended with each other. The pictures on the walls were artwork of the masters in Japan. She was impressed with the work and stood before each one as if she were at a museum. Yet, she was distracted.

Her attention turned to the closed bedroom door. Behind it, Kentaro was going about his preparations for their dinner. She walked to it. Listening, she could not hear him talking. What would happen if she opened the door? Did she dare?

Claire's fingers touched the cold metal doorknob. If she opened the door, she would be invading his privacy.

Her hand turned the knob and the door moved open. Kentaro was not in sight.

"Kentaro?" she called, cautious not to startle him. She walked to the bedroom and saw the warrior doll on the dresser, prominently across from his bed. "Kentaro."

He did not answer. She could see where he'd sat on the bed to use the phone. His watch and the gold cross on its chain lay next to the telephone on the bedside table. On the floor, she followed a trail of clothes. Socks marched one after the other to the end of the bed. There, shirt and T-shirt lay piled together. Jeans and underwear were heaped together halfway to the bathroom. When she heard the shower running, Claire shuddered with a wave of desire.

Her hands went to her buttons.

# Chapter Twenty-one

Claire pulled back the shower curtain. Kentaro stood with his back to her beneath the flood of water, his hands rinsing the shampoo from his hair. Claire watched as the suds cascaded over his wide, well-muscled torso to his narrow waist, then over his small buttocks and down his slender, long legs to disappear into the drain.

"*Taro-chan.*" Claire used his boy-name and he turned, wiping water out of his eyes. She caught sight of his body, his slightly erect member.

Claire stood before him, naked and bare, vulnerable physically and mentally.

"Claire? What...?"

"Mind if I join you?"

Claire didn't wait for him to answer. Stepping into the shower, she went into Kentaro's open arms. Water sprayed from behind him to wet her body. She looked up into his dark, angled eyes as his arms encircled her.

"I do not mind at all," he answered. Claire felt him become firmer as he touched her body.

Kentaro bent his head to cover her mouth with his own. Very gently, his tongue slipped between her parted lips to taste the sweet cavern of her mouth. Claire's heart flipped and her chest heaved in response to the heat of his body next to hers. Her hand caressed the smooth, wet skin of his back and then teased between the hard mounds of his hips.

Kentaro moaned.

His hands were busy. One cupped her breast, rolling the nipple firmly. The other held her buttocks; gentle fingers kneaded the firm muscle. As Claire's curious hand took hold of the hard cylinder of his manhood, Kentaro moaned again.

Her inexperienced fingers wrapped the hard flesh. Her own body ached for attention and she brought the tip of him to the edge of her forested lips.

Kentaro interrupted her. Careful not to slip in the wet shower, he moved her backwards until Claire felt the cold tile on her back. Thus supported, Kentaro could caress her fully.

Kentaro kissed her lips, eyes, cheeks and neck. His tongue was like velvet on her skin. He made his way to her breasts, his mouth giving each round orb its special attention. Fire raced from her nipples to the secret spot between her legs. If not for the support of the wall and Kentaro's body, she would have slipped to the floor. Claire was afraid her legs would buckle for sure when his fingers probed the tender folds, seeking the firm spot hidden by soft curls.

With practiced skill, Kentaro stroked that erotic spot. A long finger circled the opening of her sex. The hot moisture increased its flow. Claire twisted her fingers in the long ebony strands of his hair as Kentaro's lips kissed a trail down her body.

Kentaro now knelt, his face at her groin. Claire, her eyes on him, continued to hold his raven hair. His hands worked to spread her thighs farther apart. His fingers opened the nether lips and his tongue touched her with the softness of a feather. Claire gasped and clenched his hair in tight bunches.

His probing tongue worked at the rigid button of pleasure. Claire sighed and writhed against him.

He stopped.

"Oh, God, please don't quit!" Claire pleaded.

"I can...not love you in this position," Kentaro panted.

In a flash, Claire understood. It repeated the position in which Jason assaulted her. Kentaro's strong arms lifted her up and he stepped toward the bedroom. Claire held his neck, aware of his maleness moving against her hips as he walked.

Claire shivered as she lay on the soft bed where Kentaro placed her. She saw him standing over her, his maleness rampant, his eyes feasting on her.

His chest heaving, Kentaro wanted to plunge into Claire's fiery, wet chamber with his own eager flesh. He forced himself to take his time and enjoy the view of Claire laid out before him. Her eyes, soft with passion, begged him to continue. The firm breasts stood up from her chest, the pink tips puckered. Below her ribs, her stomach concaved to emphasize her hips. The brown nest of soft curls parted slightly to expose her.

He saw her shiver.

"Are you cold, *Ferris-san*?" It had been a question he asked before that usually led to verbal sparring.

"No." Claire shook her head and, opening her arms, invited him to return to her. "Come."

Kentaro rubbed her feet and ankles. His fingers played along her calves and thighs. When he finally returned to the spot where he had left off, he knew she desired him. His lips replaced the stroking fingers in caressing her.

Claire's breathing changed to moans as she neared the peak of her passion. Before she could erupt, Kentaro lay over her, his hard extension poised at the opening of her body. He moved forward with an agonizing deliberate pace to become soaked in her moisture.

"Claire," he spoke her name. He concentrated on her eyes and held his position. "Should I?"

"Yes, oh, yes, Taro, please!" Claire clutched him to her. His chest pressed against her breasts.

Kentaro rocked, surrounded by the moist cavern of Claire's body. He felt her shudder as he ground his pelvis harder and in response to the pain heard her utter a sound that changed to a sultry growl low in her throat. Claire's feet massaged his lower back and buttocks. He worked faster, desiring to control the flood he had restrained for so long. The heat of her furnace threatened to consume him. At length, Kentaro pushed farther into Claire and released the torrent residing deep within. His body shook and, if not for his mouth buried against her tender neck, his groan would have been heard throughout the building.

Kentaro and Claire lay entwined, heaving and dripping with perspiration, and spent.

Claire woke to find a sheet draped over her. She lay cross-wise in Kentaro's big bed in the same place he had placed her. A pillow was beneath her head. Still nude, she held the sheet around her and sat up. She was alone.

"Kentaro?" A frightened feeling came over her. What if he had left her? Used and abandoned her?

"I am here." The Japanese baseball player stepped from the bathroom. He toweled his long hair and had another towel wrapped around his hips.

Claire held her arms out to him, relieved he had not disappeared. The sheet fell down to reveal her breasts.

"Come back here. I am not finished."

Kentaro obliged, coming to lie on his side near her.

"I have created a monster." He grinned at her.

"Just call me Godzilla!" Claire laughed. She pulled the towel off his body and pushed him onto his back. "And I am going to conquer Tokyo!"

Claire straddled his hips. She leaned forward to kiss him with a hunger as passionate as before and restarted the fire of lust.

"Are you asleep?" Claire purred from Kentaro's side. She snuggled closer to his bare skin. Her lips nibbled at him.

"I am not." Kentaro's hand rubbed her arm stretched across his chest.

"Are we still going to dinner?"

"Are you hungry, Godzilla? You have eaten all of Tokyo," he teased.

"Yes!" Claire pretended to bite his ribcage.

"Very well." Kentaro wiggled out of her clutch. He reached to the bedside table and checked his watch. They had spent hours engaged in lovemaking and no part of either body had not been caressed. "It is too late to go anywhere. I will order a pizza while you shower."

"I do not want to get up!" Claire complained.

Kentaro sat up on the side of the bed. Claire tenderly touched the scratches she had inflicted on his back.

"If you wish to eat, you will shower."

"Can I borrow a T-shirt? For a nightgown?" Claire knelt behind him and pressed her body against his back as she reached over him to pick up his necklace from the table. "I suppose I am staying..." She fastened the chain around his neck, then leaned further on him. Her arms draped around his neck and her fingers teased his chest. "I am not sure of the etiquette here."

"Of course you are staying." Kentaro paused, his face crestfallen. He stroked her arms. "Unless you want to leave."

"I should be here. Mothra might show up and Godzilla will be needed to save Nagasaki." Claire reached down to take his sleeping manhood in her hand.

"*Claire-chan*, you were asking about food." Kentaro took her hand off him. He kissed her forearm then disengaged her from his neck. "Go shower, Godzilla."

"Arrgh," Claire grumbled as she moved off the bed, taking the sheet with her. Kentaro was speaking into the phone, a silly grin on his face as she passed him.

Claire felt the results of their passion as she stood beneath the hot water. The washcloth she brought from between her thighs evidenced bleeding, which made her wonder if Jason's assault had really destroyed her maidenhead or Kentaro's love had done it. She decided she would hold Kentaro responsible.

She stepped out of the shower and began to towel off. She found Kentaro's plain white T-shirt hanging on the bathroom doorknob where he had placed it.

Using Kentaro's comb to straighten the tangles of her long wet hair, Claire walked into the living room. The baseball player's T-shirt hung down to mid-thigh on her slender body. Kentaro, sitting on the couch, was overcome by her natural beauty and once more he found his body stirring awake.

"I hope I ordered what would please you." He brought his thoughts to something more benign, indicating the square, flat box on the coffee table.

Claire sat at the end of the couch, her knees close to her chin. Glimpsing a flash of her panties covering the treasure between her thighs didn't help his lusty thoughts. When she pulled the tail of the T-shirt over her knees, he cleared his throat.

"I am sure whatever you ordered will be fine. I am starving!" Claire lifted the cardboard box lid and found a pizza with everything.

Kentaro sat watching her for long minutes.

"What? Do I have sauce on my face?" She wiped at her lips and cheeks with the paper napkin.

"I was enjoying the view."

Claire flushed a bright crimson and ducked her face. Kentaro began to eat, not wanting to say anything more to embarrass her.

"So what do we do now, *Claire-chan*?" he asked when he had finished. Claire wasn't through eating. She appeared to be set on consuming everything edible in the box.

"Oh." Claire removed the triangle of pizza slice from her mouth before her teeth could close in on it and placed it in the box. Her feet dropped to the floor. "You do not have to marry me or anything. Just because it was...the first...I'll go home."

Claire stood and started to the bedroom where her clothes were.

"Claire!" Kentaro jumped up and raced to her. He took hold of her arm. She stopped, her back to him. "What do you mean?"

"I mean, it's all right. I knew what I was doing. I'm a big girl. We can say it was something that just happened. It doesn't mean anything. I'll be fine."

Kentaro heard the tears in her voice and knew she couldn't face him.

"But I wouldn't. You're not something that happened. You're someone I love." Kentaro responded to her English with his own. He forced her to turn toward him, both hands on her shoulders.

Kentaro suffered the long silence as Claire studied his face. The deep stare told him she wondered if he told the truth. Or said what she wanted to hear. He smiled so she would see the sincerity of his heart on his face and in his eyes.

"Oh, Taro! I love you so much!" She flung her arms around his neck. Kentaro held her up off the floor with strong arms around her.

"Are you through eating, Godzilla?" he whispered.

"Only room enough for Nagasaki as dessert, why?" Claire raised her head and stared at him.

"Because we have other things to do."

Continuing to support her, Kentaro took Claire back to bed.

The phone rang to interrupt Kentaro's drowsy thoughts of Claire. She had awakened him as she got out of the bed, leaving him in the twilight between waking and slumber. He reached out to lift the receiver to his ear.

"Where the hell's Claire?" Steve Martella shouted when Kentaro had greeted him.

"I don't know. Am I her keeper? Last night she said something about shopping today. Why?" Kentaro lied. He could hear the shower running and knew Claire was there.

"Look. I don't care that she spent the night with you, but the paparazzi have camped out at the gate to your building. The security guard called me about them. And there's a big article about you two in today's paper."

Kentaro saw the sunlight shining into the room. They had slept very little, only toward dawn, and it was now mid-morning.

"Martella-san, I don't know what you mean," he feigned innocence.

"Tell her to avoid the gate. Find some way to get out and stay away from you!"

"When I see her, I'll tell her."

"Whatever!" Steve hung up.

"Who was that?" Claire came out from the bathroom. She wore her skirt and shirt from the night before.

"Martella. He says to avoid the front gate. It seems photographers think you are in here."

"Not me. Just Godzilla." Claire pulled her hair into a ponytail as Kentaro got out of bed. "Go shower. I'll fix breakfast and we'll figure something out."

"I have it all planned out," Claire announced the moment Kentaro stepped into the breakfast nook. She handed him a cup of coffee which he accepted as he sat down at the round table set with breakfast. "Didn't you tell me that your friends from Japan who live in New York are visiting Cleveland?"

"Yes. Abe Hiro and his wife." Kentaro lifted his fork to taste the food on his plate.

"You should go visit such an old friend." Claire spooned oatmeal into her mouth as she spoke. After she swallowed she elaborated. "That way, the photographers will follow you over there. I can sneak out and go home. Alone."

Kentaro ate his food as he thought about Claire's plan.

"Why must I visit Abe-san?" He buttered his toast.

"Well, you could go anywhere. I just thought you would enjoy visiting an old friend. And, the team leaves for Kansas City this afternoon." Claire put her empty bowl back on the table. "I'll take that." She took the toast wedge from him after he finished applying grape jelly. "You've already had three pieces."

"By all means," Kentaro relinquished the toast. "Left by myself without anything to do, I could finish my own food." He grinned at Claire, who put the last bite of toast in her mouth with a contemptuous push of her finger. "I will call and see if Abe-san is free."

Kentaro, finished with his meal, made the phone call.

"He's delighted I called," Kentaro said as he returned to the room.

Claire came to embrace him, her arms around his waist.

"Do you feel comfortable speaking English?"

"I'll speak English only for you." Kentaro kissed her. "Now I must pack."

"Do you want me to help?"

"I can do it."

Claire left him in the bedroom packing.

"I am ready," Kentaro announced five minutes later when he returned to Claire with a small overnight bag. "I wish last night would never end."

"I feel the same." Claire stood near him. "We'll have to be cool to each other in public. It'll be hard but that'll make the time we do spend together all the better."

"I hope so. Or else this deception will be for nothing." Kentaro moved to the door. "I'll meet you at the airport."

"I'll be there." Claire raised on her tiptoes to kiss him, her arms around his waist. "I'll be the one with the satisfied smile."

"You're very special to me, Claire." Kentaro hugged her with one arm.

"Go away." Claire stepped back and pushed him toward the door. "The sooner we get this adventure started, the sooner it'll be over."

Kentaro left the apartment, followed by the photographers as planned. Claire settled to wait an hour before trying to sneak to her apartment. She hoped this worked.

# Chapter Twenty-two

Kentaro took a taxi to his school friend's hotel, happy to have an excuse to visit. Hiro and Hatsu had attended high school with him in Nagasaki and Hiro Abe had been in his college classes. They had lost touch when the Abes emigrated to New York.

"I am glad to see you, *Ikuta-san*," Abe said. He and Kentaro sat in the hotel restaurant having tea. Hatsu had visited briefly then disappeared. "It has been a long time."

"It has. How are your parents?" Kentaro sampled the tea. It was tasteless. He didn't know if it was because he'd developed a taste for coffee or Americans' way with tea. In the eight months he had been in the States, he had become very Americanized.

"They are well. My father continues to help with the inn, even though my eldest brother is actually now owner. In fact, I received a letter last week mentioning you."

"Really?" Kentaro's eyes narrowed in surprise as he looked at his friend across the table.

"They always ask about your playing, but this letter was personal. It seems as though your parents and the Ashinos were at the inn to celebrate the making of your marriage contract."

"My *omiai*?" Kentaro followed the words with his snorting sound. He noticed the smirk on Abe's face. Was he telling the truth? "What do you mean, *Hiro-san*?"

"My father says your father was hosting a dinner at the inn after he had settled the contract." Abe Hiro sipped his tea.

"I have not heard of this." Kentaro's spirits dropped rapidly. Just when he had opened his heart to Claire, he would have to shut her out. Custom and duty would force him to keep his father's promises, unless he could talk his father into breaking the contract. He would worry about that once he found out for sure the contract was made.

"I understood all through school that Katsuko Ashino was to be your wife," Abe stated.

"That was supposed, but," Kentaro admitted "never formalized."

"Looks like they have done it now."

"So it would seem." Kentaro pushed his cold tea away, uninterested in it. "I will have to ask my father."

Hopkins International Airport was crowded and busy, but Kentaro didn't notice the people as he made his way from the curb to the VIP lounge. He wanted to clear his mind, to forget Katsuko, as he had managed to do for years, but Hiro Abe's words repeated themselves in his brain. Kentaro knew why his father was so eager to make the *omiai*. Kentaro's father and hers were business associates, so a marriage would be a bond of their professional relationship. It would also be monetarily beneficial for Katsuko's family to have a major league baseball player with a multimillion dollar contract as son-in-law. Kentaro would receive only a sycophant wife in the deal.

He wanted to be with Claire only, but his conscience reminded him that to continue with Claire would be unfair under the circumstances. However, his father had not actually informed him of the contract, he rationalized. Until he knew for certain, he would proceed as his heart and body directed him.

Claire sat in a corner seat, waiting for him. He greeted her in his customary manner and took the seat next to her.

"How were your friends?" She used their customary Japanese in public. Her hand brushed his for longer than necessary as she adjusted her purse between them.

"They are fine." Kentaro pulled a book out of his pocket and they settled into the usual traveling mood except for the occasional secretive smile or touch. Soon the team was allowed to board.

"This is cozier," Claire said when they took their seats. She snuggled closer to him, her hand on his thigh.

"Yes it is." Kentaro bowed his head closer to hers. "I missed you," he whispered.

"Me, too," Claire replied. "But we have to stop this."

"You started it." Kentaro sat up straight.

"That is not all I started." Claire grinned devilishly at him. They felt safe with the love words since they were spoken in Japanese.

"Are you going to take credit now? I thought I was the monster maker." Kentaro chuckled beneath his samurai sound.

"I think we are both to blame."

The Cleveland Chiefs were scheduled to play Boston after Kansas City. Kentaro and Claire checked into the hotel, each going to their separate rooms only to meet in Claire's room for an afternoon frolic. Sneaking around made the sex all the better. It added a dangerous element to it. They met later for a public dinner at an elegant restaurant. The media was evident, snapping pictures of any baseball player, but concerned chiefly with the Japanese pitcher and his interpreter.

Kentaro started the baseball game the next evening, his energy level lowered by the exercise Claire had put him through. It was a nice tiredness and he managed to perform well. The Chiefs' lead was so great, Kentaro left the game in the fifth inning to allow a fellow pitcher to have a work-out.

After the afternoon game the next week in Cleveland, Claire waited for the team and press to assemble in the media room. Steve Martella had hinted to her something was to be announced. She had no idea what it was, but the room had an air of anticipation. There were reporters she had never seen packed into the small area before the conference table. The number of minicams seemed to have doubled.

"Good to see you, Ms. Ferris. How are you feeling?" a man greeted her as she hovered by the table lined with micro-phones.

"Hello?" Unable to place him since she'd met so many reporters over the months with Kentaro. They usually were very brief introductions, quickly forgotten. "Pardon me, do I know you?"

"Richard Schaeffer, syndicated sports columnist, based here in Cleveland." He extended his hand for her to shake.

"Oh?" Claire registered the name as the reporter who was so vocal about Kentaro's lack of English. She'd expect-ed some older man, possibly one from the World War II era. Schaeffer was about thirty, very GQ in his looks and attitude. "May I help you with something?" She didn't try to defrost the ice in her tone and she didn't accept his hand.

"Not unless you can explain what Ikuta's learning dis-ability is." Schaeffer withdrew his hand.

"He doesn't have one, and personally, I can't understand your assassination of his character," Claire defended.

"I feel, and I'm speaking for many Chiefs fans here, if we pay a player as much as Ikuta's being paid, he should speak our language. He has had the time and the teacher."

"You never make any complaints about the Hispanic players," Claire countered.

"They learn quickly. Ikuta hasn't spoke one word."

"Oh, please! He has!" Claire tried to remember if Kentaro had said anything during press conferences when she was absent.

"I don't remember anything but your voice saying his words. You, Ms. Ferris, are the words of the pitcher."

Claire was cut off from further defense of Kentaro by the arrival of the team and management.

"Excuse me. I have a job to do."

"I bet. Can't have Ikuta speaking unless his words are there. Is that all you do for him, Ms. Ferris?" His remark was made loud enough for the room to hear. It seemed to Claire as if every reporter turned toward her.

Embarrassed, Claire could only glare at him from her place at the conference table. With disgust, she took note of the smirk on his face.

"What is wrong, *Ferris-san*?" Kentaro asked.

"Nothing." Claire was aware of Kentaro's slipping back to the less familiar form of address. She missed the closeness she felt when he called her Claire. He was near enough for her to smell the soap from the locker room and his cologne.

"Ms. Ferris?" a voice filtered through her distracted thoughts.

"Yes?" She came out of her fog.

"Mr. Armstrong asked Mr. Ikuta about his change up in the second. Would you please translate?" Horsch asked.

"Certainly." Claire whispered the Japanese translation and gave Ikuta's answer in English.

Horsch took the floor again.

"We'd now like to make the announcement which most of you have come to hear. Our rookie, Kentaro Ikuta, will be the starting pitcher for the American League in the All-Star game in Los Angeles two weeks from now."

The crowd responded with applause, whistles, and male hurrahs. Claire saw Kentaro's face begin to color. She reached to take his hand beneath the table.

"This is a very great honor, *Ferris-san*," he whispered to her. "No Japanese national has ever played in the All-Star game, much less started."

"I know." Claire returned. "You deserve it,"

"I am pleased you are here to share the honor with me." Kentaro increased the pressure of his hand on hers.

"I am, too." Claire felt a flush rising to her cheeks.

"Ms. Ferris?" the NBC sportscaster asked. "Would you please share with us what Mr. Ikuta said?"

"*Ikuta-san* says this is a great honor, one he never expected," Claire paraphrased, the first time she'd ever done so. Her thoughts began to run toward Los Angeles. The All-Star game was surrounded with tradition and events. It would be a busy time for them.

"This is so exciting!" Claire and Kentaro sat at an out-of-the-way table at Sterle's about to enjoy a quiet meal. She had suggested it since it was the traditional celebration place for the Ferrises. "Are you not excited?"

"Yes I am." Kentaro sipped his wine.

"You have been moody since before the Kansas City trip. Is something wrong?" Japanese had returned as their primary language.

"No, not wrong. Just confused." Kentaro sighed. "It is nothing, *Claire-chan*. It will work out."

"What will?" Claire leaned forward, her fingers entwined with his.

"Patience, Claire. What are you going to choose for me tonight that you will eat half of?" Kentaro changed the subject.

Claire retracted her hand.

"I do not always eat half your food!"

"Yes, you do. Now, what are we going to eat?"

"I do not know." Claire pretended to study the menu, resigned to his silence. She decided on what she wanted and laid the menu down to looked at Kentaro. "I think I will take you home to feed you."

"What do you mean?"

"I mean," Claire lowered her voice and leaned in to speak to him, "this is my parents' celebration place. We could go to my apartment and celebrate in our own way."

"You are suggesting?" Kentaro bent his head toward hers.

"Are you accepting?" Claire tilted her head so their foreheads touched.

"Very well, Godzilla." Kentaro sat back, put his napkin on the table, and waved for the check.

"I liked your idea, *Claire-chan*."

"I thought you might." Claire lay atop him beneath a sheet. The window air conditioning unit worked well enough to cool them in the summer heat after they had finished a wild and frenzied episode of lovemaking.

"You have a great love for samurai, *gaijin*." Kentaro called her the Japanese word for 'foreigner.' He had an uncomfortable awareness of her Caucasian-ness lately. Hiro's announcement of his marriage contract, yet to be confirmed, was a sword over his head. It didn't allow him to enjoy Claire as he wanted. Though unfair to her, here he was in her bed. "I am afraid I am not like him." He pointed to the mounted warrior in the picture on the wall at the foot of Claire's bed. "He probably never knew love unless it was for another samurai." Kentaro laughed. "I am not as brave as he was either."

"Oh I do not know." Claire toyed with the gold cross. She arranged it over his smooth chest. "I think you are. You rescued me from Jason without thought to your safety or reputation."

"I did slink off to *Hiro-san*'s to avoid a confrontation with the press."

"Yes, but you were told to. He," she pointed to the samurai painting, "always followed orders without question."

"Or he killed himself. I know I could not do that." Kentaro pushed the tresses of Claire's long hair back over her shoulder. His hand stroked her cheek.

"I do not want you to be able to do that." Claire kissed his chest. "You are very brave, samurai. You chose to play baseball when it would have been easier to follow in your father's footsteps. Then you came all the way over here to Ohio. Until I came along, you were unable to speak to people. It must have been hard for you."

"You do not know...what is it?...the half of it?" he questioned his translation.

"No." Claire eyed him with a mischievous twinkle. "I know the whole of it. Now that it is filled with you, I realize now how cold my bed was." Her hand on him caused him to grow.

"You are never satisfied." Kentaro reached his hand to the back of her neck and pulled her down until her lips met his.

"I just found a new toy." Claire returned his hungry kiss.

∞

"Things will be very busy up to and through the All-Star game," Kentaro said as he dressed.

"I know." Claire lay watching him tuck his shirt into his jeans. She hugged her pillow to her chest.

"Practice, games and more practice." Kentaro sat on the bed to pull on his shoes.

"I have been around baseball enough to know what you have to do to prepare for such a game." Claire stroked his hair while Kentaro tied his shoes. "I have some work to do at the University, too."

"You may not see much of me."

"I have seen a lot tonight." Claire continued to play with his hair.

"Claire, I want you to understand it is…nothing personal." Kentaro put his arm around her as she lay on her stomach in her bed. He kissed her bare shoulder.

"Of course. Now, nothing personal, but go home so I can sleep." Claire threw the handful of hair up into the air and watched it fall, featherlike, over his shoulders.

"You are cruel, *gaijin*." Another gentle kiss to her shoulder and Kentaro was gone.

Out in the hallway, as he walked away, Kentaro was overcome with the sadness, aware he might not be able to be with Claire again.

# Chapter Twenty-three

By the time he arrived home from Claire's, Kentaro had convinced himself there was a way he could talk his stubborn father out of the contract. All his arguments flew out the window, when he found a message to call his sister at any time regardless of the time difference.

"*Taka-chan*, is everything all right?" he asked when his sister took the phone from their mother.

"For me, yes. I am calling to warn you."

"Warn me? About what?" Kentaro couldn't think of any reason he would be in danger.

"The Chiefs' management has arranged for us to be in Los Angeles for the All-Star game," Takahiko paused.

"I would like that. I have missed you, little sister," Kentaro said. Claire was the only person other than the Sangyos whom he could talk to intimately. He would not admit to himself he might be homesick.

"Katsuko is coming, too."

"Is that the warning part?"

"Well, yes, but not just her coming. Father has made the contract."

Kentaro uttered his noise.

"So I have heard from Hiro Abe. He was in Cleveland last week and I had tea with him and Hatsu-san." Kentaro told his sister of his meeting with their family friend.

"*Taro-chan*, they will hold you to it," Takahiko warned.

"I understand, little sister. More than you know, I understand. I will deal with it. Thank you."

"I do not deserve thanks. It is not a good thing."

"I thought you liked Katsuko?"

"I do. As you said before, she has always been around. She is my best friend. She should be your sister, not your wife. But, things have changed since you left to play baseball."

"Yes. They certainly have. Good bye, *Taka-chan.*"

Kentaro didn't see Claire for the next week, kept busy by his practice and game schedule. Claire, true to her word, was at CWRU doing work on her doctorate that couldn't wait until the season was over. There was a relief to her absence, but a terrible hole in his heart. This would be how he felt when he was married to Katsuko. The second week, Kentaro flew to Los Angeles to spend time with his family, practice for the All Star Game, and try to confront his father.

He left without calling Claire. He couldn't face telling her about the *omiai*.

"Steve!" Claire called down the hallway of the corporate offices of the Chiefs at Jacobs Field. She hadn't been to the stadium for days since he didn't need her during training. "Do you have a minute?"

"Sure, Coach, what's up?" Steve stopped walking to allow Claire to catch up with him.

"Isn't the All-Star Game this Tuesday?"

"Yes." They walked toward the elevator.

"In Los Angeles?"

"What's your point?" Steve pushed the button to bring the elevator car.

"I haven't gotten my tickets or itinerary."

"You won't be needed." The elevator opened and the two stepped in. "Where to?"

"Wherever you're going. Why won't I be needed? The press is all over *Ikuta-san*'s starting. He'll have to talk to the media." Claire was worried. What was going on?

"He will, but his agent will be there and will translate for us." The elevator stopped and the door opened. "Here we are." Steve let Claire step out ahead of him. "Look, Claire." The pitching coach looked like a small boy caught with his hands in the cookie jar. "I have to be honest with you. That reporter keeps fueling the fires of anti-Ikuta sentiments. The fans love Ikuta, but if the reporter keeps writing editorials about his lack of English, they might turn on us. The PR department thinks it would be better if someone else translates for him every now and then. I don't suppose you've seen today's article or you wouldn't be so calm."

"What'd it say?" Claire held her lips in a tight line. What could this reporter possibly be writing now? He had already said some of the most awful things about Kentaro.

"He's implying that Ikuta is not learning English because he is romantically involved with you." Steve's look made Claire cringe. "There's a picture of him in a hotel corridor in Kansas City. They stop short of saying he was in your room."

"That's not so!" she protested. "He's working very hard. He understands much more than he did and it won't be long before he can face the press. And that picture was after he had seen me safely to my hotel room after dinner as a gentleman should!"

"Well, I don't really care what you two are up to as long as you're doing it in English." Steve strained not to laugh.

"Nothing's going on!" Claire angrily retorted, her face reddened by embarrassment as well as her lie.

"Claire, I don't care. Take the week off. I think Ikuta's planning to visit with his family. They are here for the game."

"Are you telling me not to be with *Ikuta-san* unless it has to do with teaching?"

"I can't tell you what to do, Coach. And the front office hasn't issued any kind of order. You're a fully grown woman. Do what you have to. Is that all?"

"Yeah, sure." Claire was lost in her own thoughts.

What would she do if the front office fired her because of these rumors? What did it matter if they were involved as long as he learned to speak English? And who should care that they were sexually involved? Claire's face felt hot as she thought about it.

Kentaro Ikuta watched the crowd of people moving through Customs from the international gate at LAX. He caught sight of his mother first. The small woman carried two bags almost as big as she was. His father, taller by one and a half heads, followed, a bag in each hand also.

Behind were the two girls. Kentaro had difficulty discerning who was who...sister or betrothed. Both girls wore their long black hair straight over black leather jackets and Levi's with white T-shirts tucked in snug. Kentaro had sent the jeans as gifts to the girls. They looked to be clones instead of two individuals. And, he realized, very young looking. Takahiko was only two years younger than he and Katsuko was about her age. Why did he feel so much older?

"You look skinny, *Taro-chan*," Miyoko Ikuta commented as she met her son.

"Mother," Kentaro welcomed and admonished in one word. He had met his family with the traditional bow and now herded them toward the parking garage. His greetings to his sister and Katsuko, the young girl designated to become his wife, were perfunctory.

"She is right," Shigeki Ikuta supported his wife's observation. "We named you Taro because you were such a round baby."

"I have not been chubby since I was three," Kentaro countered. His parents were proud of the fat, healthy infant he had been. He wished they would be as proud of the man he was now. "Were is Saburo?"

"He did not wish to come," Miyoko answered, a note of sadness in her voice.

"Probably just as well. He has never liked baseball," Kentaro replied. Katsuko stood very near his side and looked at him from veiled eyes. It made Kentaro uncomfortable. "Was your flight pleasant?"

"Long," Takahiko answered. "I think we all need a nap."

"Once I get you all settled at the hotel, you will be free to do just that." Kentaro felt a sudden relief at knowing he would have a legitimate excuse to be free of his family. He was also saddened by the feeling. Had he changed so much in such a short time that he had grown away from them?

"Are we sharing your hotel room?" his father asked.

"No, Father," Kentaro answered. "I have to share a hotel room with another player. I thought you might feel more comfortable alone. The girls have their own rooms also."

"We live in three rooms at home," Shigeki stated.

"Father," Miyoko chimed in. "a young man needs his privacy." She apparently hadn't listened to Kentaro's explanation.

"Man? What man?" Shigeki continued to argue with his wife. "He is my son. He is no man. And privacy? What privacy will he need from his family?"

"I have made arrangements for you." Kentaro felt as if he were ten years old again under the berating of his father. "Now come this way." Kentaro pointed to the exit. Until this moment, he hadn't realized how long this visit was actually going to be.

"Where is your interpreter?" Katsuko asked when she and Kentaro were in the hotel. Takahiko was there also but his parents had disappeared. All three felt relieved. Their father had grumbled about things all during the cab ride. Miyoko excused her husband because of fatigue, but Kentaro knew it was the old man's nature.

"Why do I need an interpreter here? I do not see anyone speaking English!" Kentaro wondered how long he had to stay before he could politely depart.

"I thought she might come with you," Katsuko replied.

"Katsu wants to meet Claire," Takahiko said.

"No one will be meeting *Ferris-san*. Sangyo-san is translating for me while we are here. I have to leave now. I will be back this afternoon." Kentaro left the two girls.

Back in his hotel room, Kentaro telephoned Michael.

"I had forgotten what my father was like," he reflected.

"You just have to go with it. At least, for a while," Michael counseled.

"I tell them they must stay in a hotel without me because of the rules of the league. But they don't hear. My father thinks it is because I have become too much an American. My father complains and reminds me that our house in

# The Words of the Pitcher

Nagasaki is small. Admonished me because I have become accustomed to having space."

"You say that as if it were a bad thing."

"When you are reared in tight quarters, you tend to feel guilty if you have a larger space. To become used to it is almost a sin." Kentaro tried to laugh but sobered. "They have brought Katsuko with them. Takahiko says my father has made the marriage contract."

"So, that's what this is about. Have you told Claire?"

"Not exactly."

"You have to tell her. It is not fair to lead her on."

"I do not think I can. I do not wish to be blamed for hurting her."

"It is going to hurt whenever you do it and you will be the one to take the blame. The sooner you tell her, the better."

"I suppose I will tell her the next time I see her."

"Look, I have to run so, if you want to confess anything else, you will have to do it tomorrow."

"No. That is all."

Kentaro was left to wallow in his own culpability, miserable in his anguish.

# Chapter Twenty-four

Claire unlocked the door to her apartment. She struggled with the McDonald's bag and soda cup as her phone rang and she rushed to answer it. Maybe it was Kentaro.

"Hello?" Claire sprawled over the couch and hastily placed the fast food on the coffee table.

"*Moshi-moshi.*" As she heard the traditional Japanese telephone greeting, Claire's heart rose to her throat. But was it Kentaro? The voice didn't sound right. "This is *Ferris-san*?"

"Yes. Who is this?" Claire knew this was not Kentaro. It was a woman.

"I am Takahiko Ikuta. Taro is my brother."

"It is nice to hear from you. What can I do for you?" Claire moved to sit more comfortably on the couch.

"I wish to ask that you come to Los Angeles."

"Oh? I thought Sangyo-san was translating."

"He has been and will continue if my brother's coaches have anything to say, but I think Kentaro wishes for you to be here with him."

"Excuse me, Takahiko-san, I do not understand. Why would Kentaro want me to come, but not call me himself."

"Kentaro is a stubborn man. Surely you are aware men rarely say what they want. It is up to us to see that their desires are tended to. Taro needs you, Claire. Could you please come?"

Claire could hear the pleading in the voice of Kentaro's younger sister. What was she to do? Kentaro had not said he wanted her to be with him. He had left before the All-Star break without a good-bye. What right did he have to expect her to rush out at his command even if it was through his sister?

"I do not think I want to make sure his needs are tended to, Takahiko-san. Perhaps he should tend to mine."

"I understand how you feel, being a liberated woman and all. I may have used the wrong word."

"I think it was the right one. *Kentaro-san* used it in describing your parents' relationship. If he wants me to tend to him, as you say, why does he not ask me? Takahiko, does Kentaro know you have called me?"

"No. I risk making him angry because he will not admit he wishes to see you. But I know he does. Please come."

"I will have to think about it. Where can I reach you?" Claire found a pencil and scribbled a number on the McDonald's bag.

"Thank you, *Ferris-san*. Good-bye." Takahiko cut the connection off.

Claire sat thinking about what to do while she munched on cold french fries and sipped diluted Coke. Her heart told her to bolt to the airport. Her brain said to call Kentaro and ask him what he wanted. Was Takahiko right? Did men have this flaw that prevented them from knowing what they wanted or acting on those desires?

Claire moved to her bedroom to pack.

Takahiko stood at the gate waiting for Claire Ferris to deplane. She hoped she would recognize her. During the broadcast of the Chiefs games on the Japanese television stations, she had seen the young American girl who translated for her brother. Then there was Kentaro's description of her. His words, when he did say something, glowed, if you knew where to look between the lines.

A dark-haired woman approached her.

"*Ikuta-san*?"

"*Ferris-san*, hello."  Takahiko recognized Claire easily. Kentaro's tender words were justified.

"Did Kentaro come with you?"

"I did not tell him you were coming.  This way.  We can get a taxi."

"He does not know...?  Are you sure that was wise? What if I am upsetting his plans about something?"

"You will not.  Taro has made very few plans.  We tell him what we want to do and then he goes places with us, but he is not really there mentally.  I could tell something was bothering him, no matter how he tried to cover it."

"Has he said...anything?  About me?"

The two women sat in the back of the taxi and Takahiko told the driver where to take them.

"He speaks only generally about you, mostly your work, but I can read him well.  He and I have been very close since we were small.  Saburo, our younger brother, is five years below me."

"I know he is excited about the game.  But I am not certain about surprising him.  I have never gotten the impression Kentaro likes surprises very well."

"There are certain ones he finds pleasant."  Takahiko smiled.  "I remember how he acted the first day you met.  I knew sparks were about to fly between you and my brother."

"Oh?"  Claire whispered to herself.  Sparks were the least of their problems.  It was the  bonfire that had erupted that threatened to consume them.  "I think I will meet him in the dugout at the game tonight.  If that is all right with you?"

"Very well.  At least he will know you are here to share his performance."

# The Words of the Pitcher

Claire nervously entered Dodger Stadium. The arriving crowds filled the arena with sounds now second nature to her. She began to think Takahiko was wrong in her plan. What if her appearance upset him, either good or bad, just before the game? Would she cause him to pitch poorly?

As Claire walked through the hallways, she passed the locker rooms and offices resembling those at the Jake. Her identification credentials hung from the chain around her neck and kept people from questioning her presence. At the American League locker room, Claire paused and talked to the guard.

"Has Kentaro Ikuta arrived yet? I'm Claire Ferris, his interpreter."

"He's checked in, but after suiting out, he went out onto the field," the man answered.

"Thank you. I'll look for him there." Claire went toward the dugout.

Claire didn't want to interrupt his meditation, well aware of how Kentaro worked on his game demeanor. It was a ritualistic habit he had maintained since spring training. She was certain it was something he had done with every game for all of his life.

The guard at the dugout looked at her credentials for moments longer than she was accustomed to. It was all she could do not to charge past him.

"You're an 'English coach'?" the man read.

"Otherwise known as interpreter."

"There's already a guy in there who's an interpreter."

"Well," Claire hesitated, "now, he has two. Excuse me." She entered the dugout and the guard didn't stop her.

"Michael," she greeted Kentaro's agent who stood at the back of the dugout. There were no other people present.

"Claire! Am I glad to see you." Michael held out his hand for her to shake. "This interpreting gig stinks!"

"I don't know." Claire laughed. "It has its benefits. How's he doing?" She turned her attention to the field.

"Been out there on the mound for about fifteen minutes. Just standing there."

"He's reading the diamond," Claire explained. She took a seat on the back row.

"Does he know you're here?" Michael Sangyo sat beside her.

"No. His sister called and suggested I come out. I was hesitant but..."

"You don't have to explain." Michael patted her arm. "Maybe we'll all go out to dinner again. You didn't finish the last evening out."

"Don't remind me. I was so rude. I'm sorry."

"It's okay. Don't apologize."

"The team didn't want me to come translate for him," Claire blurted out. "The PR people are afraid of the negative editorials some sportswriter is doing."

"I've been reading them." Michael cleared his throat. "I'm not too worried. Kentaro's English is getting better so it won't be long until he goes before the press and everything'll be all right. Don't worry, Claire. My job is to take care of him."

But are you going to take care of me? she wondered.

Claire watched Kentaro as he pitched an imaginary ball to an invisible catcher. He then walked the baseline, looking at the ground and sky, and around the stadium at the seats filling with fans. She could almost read what was on his mind.

Here I am at the major league All-Star game and I am starting.

It was a heavy responsibility for a rookie, especially one from Japan. Claire wished she could carry some of the load for him.

"Michael," Kentaro came into the dugout, "after the game, they will probably want to set up a press conference like the ones...Claire? What...?" He approached her at the back of the dugout.

Claire stood to greet him and Kentaro enfolded her in his arms.

"I have missed you," he whispered into her hair.

"Me, too!" Claire returned his hug. She deeply inhaled the musky scent of him...a mixture of perspiration and cologne so unique to Kentaro.

"When did you arrive?" Kentaro stepped out of the embrace as others players began to arrive in the dugout.

"This morning." Claire moved away from him.

"Now that Claire is here, you will not have to put up with my lousy interpreting!" Michael said.

"Your interpreting is not too bad, but, I am accustomed to Claire's being my 'words.' She is better at understanding what I mean."

Kentaro had not stopped staring into Claire's eyes and she studied him in return, as if they were the only two people in the world.

"I will wait in the pressroom until after the game."

"Very well." The pitcher and his 'words' did not know when the agent left.

Kentaro Ikuta, the first rookie player from Japan to play in the American major leagues, started the All-Star game with a rousing no-hitter first three innings. Claire watched, enthralled at the manner in which he pitched, so calm and precise. Each hurl of the ball was calculated to cross the plate at exactly the right moment and at the perfect speed. And each one did. At the conclusion of the inning, Ikuta returned to the dugout. He took his seat with Claire, his right arm draped with his jacket to keep it warm, even in the muggy California heat. As was usual, he did not speak with Claire, but his free hand brushed hers at intervals.

"Kentaro," she whispered before he left the dugout for the fourth inning, "I am going to the press box with Michael. I think it would be better that way. These players are not used to me and, if you need me, I can come."

"Claire." Kentaro stared at her as if he would never see her again. "I saw the paper this morning."

"It does not mean anything. Now, go finish this game so we can go to my hotel." Claire squeezed his arm and left.

From the railing, Claire watched the game conclude with the American League winning. She walked to the team exit and awaited Kentaro and Michael.

"You know, Claire, you really earn your money," Michael said as he, Kentaro and Claire walked to the parking lot of Dodger's Stadium.

"Thanks. Sometimes my brain gets fuzzy with both languages." Claire took a seat beside Kentaro in the backseat of the car. "And sometimes I go home and my tongue hurts."

Claire noticed a smirk on Kentaro's lips. She hit his thigh, a motion designed to remove his tacky thoughts. He took her hand and squeezed it.

"Should I drop you off at your parents' hotel?" Michael asked over his shoulder.

"No," Claire answered for them. "Mine."

"Yours?"

"Watch the road," Kentaro admonished.

"What do I tell the folks?" Michael looked forward, but still asked questions. "Don't you have a curfew?" He began to speak English in hopes of getting Kentaro to do the same.

"Michael, we're not teenagers!" Claire laughed.

"I will worry about them," Kentaro answered in English. "And the curfew is lifted after the game is played."

"You know best."

Michael drove in silence. Claire could see him glance from time to time into the rearview mirror to see what they were doing. Kentaro was nodding off, his head on Claire's shoulder, lulled by the motion of the car and tired from the game and its excitement. Just to give Michael something to see, she caressed his cheek and winked at the agent.

The press had not discovered Claire's presence in Los Angeles and Michael managed to elude any that might be following Kentaro. He dropped the couple at the curb in front of the hotel where Claire had reserved a room. They walked through the lobby unaccosted.

Kentaro was wide awake now, and Claire could see his eagerness as he unlocked the door. He pushed the door open and held it for her. She entered and, when he had closed the door and turned around, jumped into his embrace. She crossed her ankles at his back to keep from falling although she doubted Kentaro would allow her to since his arms felt like steel bands around her.

"*Claire-chan.*"

"I can feel how much you missed me!" Claire laughed as her hand slid between their bodies to touch his groin.

"Claire," Kentaro's voice admonished.

"Oh, hush." Claire covered his mouth, her tongue seeking his.

Kentaro returned her enthusiastic kiss while he walked to the bed. Feeling the furniture on his shins, he turned and sat down with Claire on his lap. His hands pulled her shirt up and over her head, taking her bra with it. Claire worked at taking his shirt off as his hands covered her breasts. She splayed her fingers out over his firm male breasts and felt his nipples harden beneath her palms.

Claire slid down his legs to kneel on the floor before him. Her hands reached up to unbutton his jeans. Kentaro lifted his hips so they would clear as Claire drew the jeans and briefs down. When she took the semi-erect flesh between her lips, the golden rod expanded to its full distended length. After enjoying her hot, wet laving for as long as he could stand them, Kentaro took her arm.

"Come."

"Aw," Claire whined. She came up to lie over his chest.

"This'll prove more exciting for both of us."

Kentaro lifted Claire into his arms and rolled them over. Naked and sweating, Kentaro pulled her shorts and panties off. His hands placed behind her knees, he spread her thighs wider and put his mouth on the moist secret spot. Claire was filled with fire blazing from the center of Kentaro's touches. She was almost at the peak of excitement when he placed himself for entrance. He pushed her knees toward her shoulders to open her further and allow him to penetrate her completely.

Her passion increased as Kentaro ground his hips into hers, moving forward and back with increasing speed and power. Claire's arms encircled his shoulders to hold him closer and her mouth sought his. She covered him with kisses, tasting her juices on his lips. Unable to contain her desires, a deep, warm groan escaped. Kentaro responded with the same sound, his pelvis held next to hers.

"*Taro-chan*," she sighed into the deep silk of his hair. "I love you so much."

# The Words of the Pitcher

Kentaro moved off her body and her legs settled to the bed. Some creative writhing enabled him to pull the covers from beneath them to cover their naked bodies. He held her in his embrace as they drifted into a sensual exhaustion, their passions satisfied. They moved only when the sun awakened them.

Claire stretched languidly and turned over to find Kentaro facing her, sleeping contentedly. When she brushed his hair off his face, he woke.

"Good morning, *Taro-chan*."

"Good morning to you." Kentaro took her hand and held it. "How are you?"

"Perfect. What do you think made last night so wonderful?" Claire asked. "The sneaking around or the fact that we have not...in a while?" She retrieved her hand and combed his hair with her fingers, the strands falling like water over the pillow. "Or the fact we love each other so much?"

Kentaro didn't respond with words, instead making his usual noise. She pushed his feathery forelock back off his brow.

"We need to speak English," she announced without preamble.

"All right." Kentaro moved to sit on the side of the bed, his back to her. "Why?"

"Because they're going to force you to. And I know you can." Now she pulled the sides of the lengthy hair back to his neck.

Kentaro responded with his nasal burst.

Claire came up onto her knees beside Kentaro.

"Get dressed, Claire." He moved away from her. He reclaimed his clothes before going into the bathroom.

"Oookay." Claire got off the bed and started to dress.

Kentaro emerged from the bathroom and, without a word, walked to the wet bar in the corner of the room. He knew what he had to do, but it didn't make it any easier. The lovemaking, which he hadn't planned but didn't regret, made it even harder. He hadn't spoken a word, yet his heart ached with the thought of what he had to say. Could he put it off? No, it would only make it worse.

# Chapter Twenty-five

"What's wrong?" Claire came out of the bathroom to find Kentaro drinking a glass of orange juice. He leaned against the bar, his shirt open to expose his chest. His jeans, low-cut and unzipped, threatened to reveal the soft curls covering his groin. Claire stroked the area over his briefs with her fingertips.

"Please don't." Kentaro captured her hand.

"Did I say something?"

"No."

"Do something?"

"No."

Claire freed her hand to touch the gold cross lying over his heart on the wide expanse of his bronze chest.

"You never explained why you wear this."

"Why does anyone wear such a symbol?"

"Kentaro." Claire became exasperated with his attitude.

"My great-grandmother was from one of the samurai families first to accept Christianity before the Meiji restoration." Kentaro took her hand again in his, this time in a warmer gesture. "She put it on my grandfather when he was six and sent out of Nagasaki to be away from the bombing of the war. She died in the atomic blast. He passed it to my father, who gave it to me."

"For your son."

"Tradition. It's like patience, something we Japanese have perfected." He turned and placed the glass on the bar. "I don't seem to be abiding by the tenets of any traditions which I have been taught."

"Feeling guilty about us?" Claire took her hand back. Kentaro responded only with his nasal flaring which Claire couldn't translate.

She left him to go to the tiny refrigerator for some juice of her own.

"So." Claire could not understand his coldness and aloofness. His mood had changed so since the night before. He spoke in riddles she couldn't follow. What was the reason? Maybe she had stepped out of line with her remark. She changed to a topic they both were comfortable with. "Are you looking forward to the game with Denver? You have a three-game stand against Tampa Bay after that."

"I've never pitched at Coors Stadium. I hear it's a challenge with its high altitude." Kentaro's words were lifeless, showing no interest even in baseball. Claire didn't know what to think. There was an ominousness about his demeanor.

"You should do all right." Claire took a small bottle of cranberry juice and followed Kentaro, who sat on the couch. He finished tying his shoes and began buttoning his shirt.

"When will I see you again?" Claire tried not to hold her breath in anticipation of his answer.

"Claire, I'll be busy for a while." He stood and after tucking his shirt in and zipping his jeans, began to fidget. It was something she had never seen Kentaro do. "My family's still here."

"Takahiko said they would be leaving this afternoon. Your game in Denver is tomorrow. We can get together between." There it was. Just as she feared. Was he ending their relationship? His answer would tell her.

"Ah, *Claire-chan.*" Kentaro did face her and now she was sorry. His face was flat, without expression. "I don't think that would be a good idea. I must concentrate...on the games. I can't be distracted." Now his English was perfect.

"I understand." Claire sagged onto the couch. She knew what he meant with the same surety that she knew she loved him. Baseball was his life. It was as important to him as he was to her. No matter how much she loved him, she would not get in the way of the dreams he'd had since childhood. "I want to be with you." She tried to bolster her spirits and push him to say something definite.

"Claire." Kentaro stared at her with a strange yet soft cast to his own eyes. "I think we might have made a mistake."

"Excuse me? A mistake?" She was stunned and anger rose. "That's not what you said that night in your apartment."

"I can't say I don't have feelings for you." Kentaro spoke as if the words were full of glass. "I can honestly say in a way...I love you."

"Only in a sexual way?" Claire countered with hard words.

Kentaro uttered his sound sharply. "Do not put words in my mouth." He had his own anger now. "You of all people should understand how different we are. We each have learned customs so opposite, the other calls them strange. You and I both know there are some traditions we can't change to fit our desires." His anger evaporated into resignation. He moved toward the door.

"You're scaring me. What aren't you saying?" Claire came to her knees on the couch. She felt dizzy. "Kentaro, I'm also familiar with the Japanese way of telling a person something without telling them. The attempt to spare another's feelings."

"I must go now," he whispered. His hand was on the door knob. As slow as he turned it, Claire could hear the tumblers rolling. "In fact, I can't see you again. I'm sorry."

"Kentaro, I don't understand." She stood up in front of the couch. "Kentaro?"

He didn't turn. Claire could see his shoulders move in a way which caused her to think his body had a mind of its own and wanted to return to her. She realized he had mastered the insubordinate muscles when she heard a faint expression of his samurai noise before his back disappeared and the door slammed.

"What...?" Claire sagged down onto the couch.

She couldn't believe him. He had waltzed in, swept her into bed, and made incredible love to her. He had allowed her to sleep in his arms, content and warm, then, this morning, left her cold and empty! And yet, he didn't tell her what was going on! Was he out of her life? Was it truly baseball he was eliminating her for? Or was there another woman? Claire had too many questions and no answers.

First, she was bewildered, then heartbroken. Tears rose and fell down her cheeks in a flood, burning hot tracks as they went. So, quickly as it had all started, it was over.

And so was the crying. She needed to pack and catch a plane home.

As he stood outside the door to her hotel room, Kentaro heard Claire's tears. His hand was still on the knob, his back against the door, his head thrown back onto it. He closed his tear-moist eyes, unable to shut his ears to her pain or stop the chastisement of his own conscience. His heart urged him to turn around and go to her, to tell her he was sorry and forget everything he'd said. Reason told him he couldn't. In his own good time, Shigeki Ikuta would tell him he had committed his son to Katsuko. Until he was able to convince his father, or Katsuko's, to release him from his contract, he could not wholly be Claire's. Although to be with her was the greatest desire since he'd made the decision to play baseball, he realized the sooner he took himself out of Claire Ferris's life, the easier it would be for her.

Kentaro pushed himself erect and began to walk down the hallway with the steps of a man going to his execution. He would have gone more happily to his death than away from Claire.

Kentaro stood at the international gate and watched the JAL plane leave with his parents, sister, and his now official fiancée aboard. Never had he felt so much relief. Or shame. When Shigeki had dropped the bomb of the marriage contract, he had not mentioned Claire. Never challenged Shigeki.

It had happened this morning, the same morning he had broken the heart of the woman he loved. The scene of his father's speech was clear in Kentaro's mind...alongside the scene with Claire.

He had left Claire's hotel to join his family in their large suite for breakfast. After the meal, the women obediently disappeared.

"I have settled an arrangement with Katsuko-san's father," Shigeki spoke.

"What do you mean?" Kentaro feigned innocence. He deliberately stirred more sugar than usual into his coffee.

"You are betrothed to Katsuko-san. When you return home, the contract will be sealed." Shigeki lit a cigarette from the butt of one he had been smoking.

"Why did you not ask me before doing something so personal?" Kentaro turned the cup around and around on the saucer.

"Why should you be consulted? You are aware your opinion does not matter." He made the sound through his nose similar to that of Kentaro yet deeper because of his age and years of smoking.

"Just like that I am to submissively marry Katsuko-san?" Kentaro put the cup to his lips and tasted the syrupy brown liquid.

"Of course. As did I and your grandfather before me." Shigeki's face was hard, a mask Kentaro was familiar with. "There will be no further discussion."

"Yes, sir." Kentaro submitted. He had cut off romantic ties to Claire. Now his father had spoken. All the pieces were in place, arranged without his input and against his will and without thought to his heart.

Kentaro left the JAL gate to enter the VIP lounge and wait for his flight to Denver.

Claire flew home to Cleveland in a daze. Like an automaton, she unpacked and then flipped through mail. After she paid the few bills she had, she went to bed. Sleep didn't come until late in the night. Staring up into the darkness, Claire sensed the samurai looking down at her from his picture on the wall. She could hear the silent horseman laughing as he said, 'I told you so.' Her heart ached with the tears she refused to shed. Even if Kentaro was out of her arms and bed, she had to work with him. Now she was pleased with the management's idea of someone else translating for him. Let Michael put up with his arrogance and snorting noises.

Claire rose in the early morning, tired though she'd been in bed twelve hours. She'd fill the time away from home at her office at CWRU.

∞

"Claire?" Dr. Ramstein called at the doorway to Claire's office at CWRU.

"Yes, sir?" Claire looked up over the rim of the reading glasses sliding off her nose. It was three days since she had left Kentaro in Los Angeles. Three days since he'd walked out of her life.

"I heard you were here." He entered the room. "Shouldn't you be at a baseball game?"

"The team wants someone else to translate for a change. Bad press lately." Claire would not share her heartbreak with her mentor. "If you remember, I didn't want the job anyway."

"But you found something you liked about it."

"I should've kept to translating." Claire pretended interest in something on the paper in front of her.

"Things with the reporter will die down. They always find something else to write about. I'm sure you're doing a good job."

"I know I am. Kentaro can speak English. He just doesn't want to."

"Why?"

"That's a good question, but it doesn't have anything to do with me. At least, not any more."

"Well, maybe you'll find out the truth eventually." Ramstein turned to the papers in his hand. "Could you translate these articles?"

"Sure." Claire took them and glanced at the Japanese characters running over the pages.

"I'll see you later this afternoon and pick them up. They're uncomplicated."

"Unlike my life," she thought out loud.

∞

"Why aren't you at the game?" Andrea asked Claire. The two women were at the Pub on Lee Road having dinner and watching the Chiefs play the Blue Devils for the second game of their three-game stand.

"Management wants a different translator for a while." Claire cut up the chicken breast in her salad. "And Kentaro wants a new girl friend." She said it matter-of-factly and put a bite of food in her mouth.

"Excuse me?" Andrea dropped her fork. "Mr. Baseball-san has dumped you?"

"I guess that's what he did. He says he can't have a relationship with me. So, how's school?" Claire worked a large lettuce leaf into her mouth. If she kept her mouth full of food she wouldn't have to speak.

Andrea began eating also. She was onto Claire's trick and waited until her friend swallowed before she spoke, "You can't mean that?"

"Yes." Claire eyed the game on the television over the bar while she used a napkin to wipe her face.

"You're taking it well."

"How else can you take it? I can't make him want me," Claire said.

"I don't know what to do with you, Claire. He's a jerk! Just like Jason!"

"No he's not!" Claire shouted, slapping her hand down on the wooden table. She felt as if she had lived this before, recalling how Kentaro had hit the table in the same manner. In a lower voice, she said, "Jason tried to rape me! Kentaro may have led me on and broken my heart, but that's different."

A great commotion erupted at the bar in response to something happening in the game.

Claire turned to the screen.

"What's going on?"

"Claire, you've turned into a real baseball groupie." Andrea tried to get her attention. "What about...?"

"Not now, Andrea." Claire waved her off. "Something's wrong." She got out of her chair and walked to the bar. "What happened?" she asked the men she wedged between at the bar.

"The pitcher's collapsed," one of them said. "He's unconscious."

"Oh, my God!" Claire's hand went to her mouth while she kept an eye on the screen.

"It's unclear to us right now exactly what has happened to Cleveland Chiefs pitcher Kentaro Ikuta," the sportscaster was saying. "Moments ago, just before releasing the pitch, he collapsed without warning. The coaching staff and medical team are now at the mound. It seems he is still unconscious."

Claire didn't hear anymore of the prattle as she watched Steve Martella at Kentaro's side and a stretcher being rolled out to the mound.

The television network went to a commercial.

"Audrey," Claire said into the phone. Her mind raced and she had to remind herself to breathe. "I'm so glad you're home! What happened? How can I get in touch with Michael? I can't find out anything!"

"Claire, slow down. Michael's waiting for you to call. Here's his beeper number." Audrey called off the digits and Claire wrote them down.

"How's Kentaro? What happened to him?"

"Call Michael. He'll tell you."

Claire hung up and dialed Michael's beeper. It was forever before he called her back.

"He's out of danger." Michael answered her questions but not in detail.

"I'm flying there now," Claire announced.

"Figured you would. I'll meet you at the airport and fill you in then."

∞

"Michael," Claire greeted the agent at the airport. "I have to see him."

"I'm not sure that's what he wants," Michael hedged.

"Did he tell you?"

Michael and Claire rushed out of the airport.

"He tells me everything."

"I don't care what he wants. I have to see him." Claire was determined.

"I'll get you there." Michael smiled at the young woman's adoration and concern. He didn't care what Kentaro said, he knew he would want to see Claire.

"Michael, I want to know exactly what happened to him? Do the doctors know?" Claire asked as they rode toward the hospital.

"He had a ruptured appendix. His fever was 104. I don't know how he played with that pain," Michael answered. "Your father's a doctor, isn't he? You probably understand more than I do."

"My father's a pediatric oncologist. I don't know anything about surgery," Claire admitted. "Will he be out for the season?"

"We just want him awake and breathing, Claire. We'll worry about baseball after that."

At the hospital, Michael took Claire to the intensive care unit, then went alone to the nurse's station. He spoke to one of the nurses and came back to Claire.

"I told her you were his fiancée," he said.

"What?"

"Just go with it. They won't let you see him otherwise. Just don't look at the nurses. Anyone might be a baseball fan. Don't want them to recognize you as his 'words,' as he calls you." Michael held her elbow and guided her to Kentaro.

Claire followed Michael to a glass-walled room. The windows were obscured by closed miniblinds. She stepped through the doorway and found the cubicle filled with the bed and equipment. Monitors were everywhere, hooked up to Kentaro. Though used to hospital settings, Claire's heart was in her throat as she approached Kentaro. He lay on the white sheets, pale and lifeless, with closed eyes. The long black eyelashes made dark smudges beneath his eyes. His thick mane of raven hair was brushed back on the pillow. Oxygen tubing ran beneath his nose. EKG leads were pasted to his broad chest and the gown was opened from the shoulders to free the wires. The stark, crisp sheet was taut over his lower body and legs. IV lines and a blood pressure cuff wrapped around his arms. Several bottles of different medicines dripped into one line. Another tube snaked out from beneath the sheet and Claire didn't speculate where it led.

"Has he wakened yet?" Claire whispered to Michael.

"At times. He seems out of it much of the time. Maybe your voice will help him stay awake. I'll be outside." Michael left her alone with Kentaro, sliding the door closed behind him.

"Kentaro?" Claire whispered. She looked up at the heart monitor. The blips moved along in an orderly fashion. She put her hand on his forehead, stroking his hair back. His skin was hot. "Taro, it's me, Claire. Please wake up."

Kentaro didn't move. Claire continued to caress his hair. Her hand touched his cheek and jaw, prickly with beard. She let her finger trace his lips, dry from the bottled oxygen and fever. Finding a washcloth, she wet the cloth with cold water and dabbed his lips, then bathed his face. It made Claire feel as if she were doing something.

"Kentaro, I know you do not want me here, but I am sorry, you are stuck with me," Claire spoke as if he were awake. She used Japanese, reasoning that his brain would more readily accept Japanese. "I'm going to stay here. In fact, if you want me to go away, you have to wake up and tell me."

Claire picked up his hand, the one with nothing taped to it, and moved her fingertips over his long slender fingers. The hand was quiet. Except for the warmth it held, she would have thought him dead. She caressed the back of his hand. Easy to trace the veins on it and the blood that pulsed through them. She raised the hand to her cheek, pretending Kentaro was making the move on his own.

"I...I do not...wish you...to leave...Claire." Kentaro's tongue sounded as if it were stuck to the roof of his mouth. Claire laid his hand on the bed at his side and wiped his mouth with a wetter cloth.

"You sure go to great lengths to get my attention." Claire tried to laugh even though she wanted to cry.

"It was not attention I wanted." Kentaro's eyes searched for hers. He appeared to have trouble focusing.

Claire watched his face. His eyes were tired and sorrowful when they found hers. She wiped his cheeks. Did she see tears in his eyes?

"Why are you crying, *Claire-chan*? Am I dying?" Kentaro tried to smile at her.

"Please do not talk that way." The tears rolled down her face and she wiped ineffectually at them. "How do you feel?"

"Very tired."

"Then sleep." Claire put her hand against his face. "I will not go anywhere. Michael told the nurses I was your fiancée."

"Did he also tell them your name was Katsuko Ashino?" Unable to remain alert, Kentaro dropped back into his sleep.

Claire sat in a chair beside Kentaro's bed and held his hand in hers. What had he meant about a different name? She decided she wouldn't worry about asking him until he was well. An hour later, the nurses remembered she was there.

"You'll have to leave," the nurse said when she came to take readings of the monitors. "Visiting hours are posted in the waiting room."

"I'm staying," Claire asserted. "I'll stay out of your way."

"I'm sorry but our policy is that only close family may stay. Are you his wife?"

"Are you saying I can't be his wife?" Claire questioned. The nurse's judging appraisal did not escape Claire's notice. Was it because she was Caucasian? Claire guessed she was not one of the nurses Michael had told his story to. "I'm...his fiancée." She continued Michael's simple lie.

"Oh. I didn't know. Well, I guess you can stay. Dr. Appleton will probably want to talk to you."

"Okay." Claire stood and moved closer to the bedside. She neatly tucked the sheet around Kentaro's athletic body. "Is she gone?" Kentaro spoke softly, with his eyes closed. "Yes. What are you doing? Playing possum?" Claire smiled at him when his eyes batted open.

"What is that? Playing opossum?" His voice seemed a little stronger, his eyes a bit brighter.

"Pretending to be asleep. Are you feeling better?"

"Some. But what strength I have must be used to hurt you. I must tell you to leave." Kentaro's voice was stern. "I told you before there is no future for us. You have to believe me. I didn't want to hurt you." He switched to English. "I love you very much, *Claire-chan*, but I can't have you."

"You have me, Kentaro, all of me." Claire sat on the bed facing him. "Are you worried that you are Japanese and I'm...not?"

"That's the least of my problems." Kentaro took a ragged breath.

"Does your abdomen hurt?" Claire put a hand over the lower right side of his abdomen.

"Somewhat. Claire, listen to me. You've studied our ways, tradition, customs, honor. They're all uniting against us to make me hurt you. I don't want to but I must. I can see no other way."

"Kentaro," Claire straightened her shoulders and braced herself, "you left me before with veiled words and excuses. You can't do it again. Tell me exactly what's keeping you from me. And tell me now." She squeezed his hand firmly.

"I am...betrothed to Katsuko Ashino." Kentaro watched her raptly. She seemed bewildered. "Claire, I know now why the men of my country take mistresses so easily. Forced into marriage with women we do not know does not insure we love them. Everyone says love comes, in time, but I will never love Katsuko the way I love you. I will take her to bed, have children, but I will not enjoy it."

Kentaro took a breath, resting for a moment while Claire's tears rolled copiously down her cheeks. His next words were again Japanese.

"Husbands of Japan find love in the arms of the 'other woman.' I can not ask you to stoop to that level, a position you would abhor, even if I swear my devout love to only you."

"No, I could not," Claire murmured.

"I hate myself for your pain, *Claire-chan*. Yet it is better for you to hurt now and get it over with. I will ache the rest of my life. Every time I make love to Katsuko, I will remember your touch, the thrill of your body. You will recover. Katsuko will be a friction to rub open the wound of my heart, never allowing it to heal."

"Kentaro..." Claire tried to speak, but she couldn't find words.

"Claire..." Kentaro gasped her name. His hand on hers became tighter. Claire noticed a grayness to his lips.

"Kentaro, are you all right?" She was frightened as her tears continued to flow. "Taro!"

She watched hopelessly as his head lolled away from her and his eyes fluttered close. His chest rose in great, rapid gasps, then began to slow. Monitors began to bleep and scream. Nurses rushed into the small room and Claire was forced away as they worked over Kentaro's body.

Something caught her eye on the small table in the corner. His necklace. Claire's fingers closed around it unseen as a nurse steered her out of the room. Blinded by the tears of pain, anger, hurt, and fear, the gold cross clutched to her chest, she made her way to the waiting room where Michael sat.

Claire collapsed in the agent's arms. She sobbed harder as Michael held her.

# Chapter Twenty-six

"Come now, Claire." Michael guided her to a chair. "His condition's not fatal. Or at least, that's what the doctors told me."

"I don't know. But it's my fault." Claire wiped her tears away and blew her nose on the tissues Michael handed her from the box kept in the ICU waiting room for such purposes. "He was talking to me, getting upset, and he passed out. The nurses all rushed in and pushed me out."

"What was he saying that upset him?"

"I think you know." Claire ducked her face. "You said he told you everything."

"Ah," Michael uttered. "Katsuko."

"Yes," Claire whispered. She held the gold chain tightly in her fist.

"Kentaro should never have started this with you. He knew better." Michael stood and paced a few steps away from Claire. "But," he turned and faced her, "your arrival at Otani's on his birthday didn't help matters much." Michael laughed and smiled. He hoped to remind Claire of the pleasant evening. Then, again, perhaps the young woman didn't need to be reminded of such outings.

"Maybe I was wrong." Claire looked up at Michael. "Maybe I read his signals incorrectly. I was the one who initiated everything. I kissed him first. I went to him in his shower...," Claire paused, her cheeks aflame with embarrassment. "I'm sure he told you about that, too."

Red-faced, Michael nodded.

"Telling me to leave him is the only thing he did without my prompting." Claire laid her head on the back of the couch.

"Claire," Michael sat beside Claire, "he welcomed every advance. He's too stupid or shy to do it himself. He could've said no." He watched the tears well up in Claire's eyes. "It wasn't his idea to leave you. He wants to be with you."

"Oh, yeah, right." Claire raised her head.

"Give him some credit. When he left Nagasaki, he wasn't betrothed. But, as I understand it, the Ashinos have been watching the broadcasts of the games and press conferences afterwards. They pushed for an official betrothal because they noticed something between you two."

"An *omiai*, an arranged marriage in this day and age. How stereotypical." Claire fell into Michael's outstretched arms, her head on his chest.

"Oh, it's a big industry now. Video dating and match-makers on the Internet." Michael laughed. Then he turned serious. "Ever since he was a child, Kentaro's been pulled by so many non-traditional things. Not only did he not want to be a salary man, he wanted to play a professional sport. Not content with Japanese professional baseball, he set his sights on the American major leagues. He's achieved all he desired, but at a price. He turned his back on much of his heritage. He doesn't feel he can turn a blind eye to...this. From all your studies of Japan, you must know traditions die hard." Michael handed Claire a wad of tissues. "Even so far removed from Japan as Audrey and I are, we feel the traditions of our great-grandparents. Our parents would've been happy to pick our partners."

"He could've been honest with me." Claire laid her head on Michael's shoulder and he stroked her hair out of her face. Claire wiped her nose. "He never said anything remotely suggesting someone else was in the picture."

"Kentaro's never taken Katsuko seriously. I don't think he thought they'd hold him to marrying her. He used to laugh about her and the suggestion. Then he met you. And all memory of Katsuko flew out of his mind. Especially when you walked into Otani's in that little black dress. He fell in love with you, Claire."

She sat upright.

"Why are you telling me this?"

"I'm not really sure," Michael sighed. "I want you to understand it's not been easy for him. He loves you. No matter what happens with him and Katsuko, she'll never have his heart."

"But she'll have him." Claire stared at the agent. "Michael, what should I do?"

"What did Kentaro tell you to do?"

"Leave." Claire was back to whispering. "And forget about him."

Michael took a deep breathe and Claire knew his words would not be what she wanted to hear.

"Then I'd suggest you do exactly that." He held her hand tightly. "I'll keep you posted on anything you need to know. You have my number. Call whenever." He winked at Claire, shaking their clasped hands. "Do you want to go to the airport now or a hotel?"

"The airport. But can we wait until we find out how he is now?"

"Sure."


They sat in their own thoughts until a doctor came and asked to speak with Mr. Ikuta's fiancée.

"Since Katsuko is not here, I will be her," Claire spoke to Michael in Japanese. "I'm Claire Ferris," she addressed the doctor.

Claire and Michael approached the doctor.

"Mr. Ikuta's condition's weakened by a number of things. The ruptured appendix was the worst event. He neglected the symptoms for too long. Then the strenuous practice for the All Star Game, the game itself, and all the other Chiefs' scheduled games," he began his impersonal account of Kentaro's condition. "Added to that, he came down here in our heat and humidity. We've cleaned the area surgically, stopped any bleeding, and started him on antibiotics. Until the infection subsides, he'll be in serious condition. His fever also caused his electrolytes to get out of balance."

"Will he be able to finish the season?" Claire noticed a messenger arrive and hand Michael a large envelope.

"We'll have to see. I think a three or four week post recovery will be enough," the doctor answered. "Now, if you don't have any further questions?"

"No. Thank you."

The doctor left the room and Claire turned her attention to Michael. He read through the contents of the envelope.

"Claire, we have another problem. This is from the Chiefs. They want you to be in the corporate offices tomorrow afternoon."

"Why?" Claire sat at his side again.

"I have no idea. This," he handed her a sheaf of faxed newspaper articles, "is probably the reason."

Claire perused the articles. Different newspapers, tabloids, and even a prominent entertainment magazine, had pictures and columns about her and Kentaro. Images of them together in innocent situations which could be looked on as romantic interludes accompanied the news items. The words told the readers what to make of the pictures.

"Oh, my." Claire sighed.

"My sentiments exactly," Michael agreed. "Did you see the one which mentions Katsuko? The press found out sooner than you did."

"That's not funny, Michael. I'm not a homewrecker as they allege. I didn't know." Claire looked at him with serious eyes. "Don't let Kentaro see these."

"I won't." Michael was putting the articles back into the envelope.

"Please take me to the airport."

# Chapter Twenty-seven

Claire had a foreboding feeling as she arrived at Jacobs Field. When she entered the conference room on the top floor and was confronted by five men, her uneasiness increased. She knew Jamison, Horsch, Martella, Ostervich from personnel, and Michael Sangyo. She was surprised to see Kentaro's agent. He hadn't mentioned coming to Cleveland last night when he called to give her a health update on Kentaro. The missing name was supplied quickly when they were introduced. Raymond Callaman, publicity department.

"Glad you could make it, Ms. Ferris," Jamison greeted her. He repeated his ritual of offering her something to drink, which she declined. She sat between Michael and Steve, supposing she was aligning herself with friends.

"Why am I here, sir?" She was unable to tolerate the anxiety. "If this concerns *Ikuta-san*, perhaps we should wait until he's well."

"You're correct. It does involve Mr. Ikuta, but more directly, you," Callaman spoke. He pulled a section of newspaper from the pile of papers in front of him. "Mr. Sangyo says he showed you these yesterday."

"He did. What of it?"

"I'd like to read from Schaeffer's column today. And I quote, 'This reporter must ask the same question today as he has raised every day since the All Star break. Why is Claire Ferris still translating for the Chiefs' prima donna pitcher, Kentaro Ikuta? After six months of personal tutoring, Ms. Ferris has yet to prove she has succeeded in teaching this high-priced player anything. Previous columns have laid the blame on Ikuta. However, after some reflection and actually speaking with the illustrious linguist from CWRU, as well as other recent revelations, this reporter has decided he is searching for answers in the wrong direction. Is it that Ikuta doesn't want to speak English? Or does he like having the pretty Ms. Ferris around? The Chiefs management is paying a big price for this service. And won't the team owners pass this cost on to the ticket buyer who is already saddled with the escalating price of going to the ball park?' End quote.

"What do you have to say, Ms. Ferris?" Callaman replaced the newspaper and stared at Claire.

"I don't really understand what he's trying to say," Claire stuttered. "*Ikuta-san* has a better knowledge of English now than the day I first started with him. As for him not addressing the press, you'll have to ask him about it. I can't make him speak to reporters."

"I don't find that a reasonable answer," Callaman stated. "We have a PR problem here, Ms. Ferris. A big one." He waved a stack of paper about an inch thick at her. "These are letters from fans who are now becoming embroiled in Schaeffer's brouhaha. Fans who buy tickets. Who spend money on team gear, much of which is printed with Ikuta's name and jersey number. Who spend well-earned, blue collar money on beer and hot dogs at the Jake. We're responsible to them and are charged with making them happy. If they don't come to the game, we don't make money to pay Ikuta's millions or your salary, Ms. Ferris."

"Why are you attacking me? I'm doing exactly what you hired me to do." Claire's face was hot and she knew it was red. She became mad because these men would think she was weak.

"How do we know exactly what you're doing? He's not speaking English to anyone!" Callaman exclaimed.

"Talk to him!" Claire countered. She saw what was happening here. This stranger was the enemy. When were her 'friends' coming to her aid? "He'll translate anything you want."

"I want him in front of the press speaking to them, answering their questions. I want the fans to know the man they gave millions of their dollars to in a four-year contract is respectful enough of them to learn to speak their language. All they feel now is insulted. As for Schaeffer's aspersion that we are paying you to be his girlfriend, what do you have to say about it?"

"I don't think that is any of your business," Claire said.

"I agree with Ms. Ferris." Michael Sangyo came into the conversation. "Knowing Mr. Ikuta as I do, I feel I can say that his relationship with her has no bearing on his reluctance to speak to the press in English. I understand his reluctance to speak a language he isn't comfortable with, leaving himself open to ridicule by the media. As a Japanese national, Mr. Ikuta's a very proud man. As an aside, he is betrothed to a woman in Japan."

"Please," Callaman scoffed. "It's been six months! Surely he has a working knowledge by now!"

"I think we should attend to the business at hand." Ostervich cut off any argument. "Ms. Ferris, we feel, due to this negative press, that your services are no longer needed."

"You're firing me?" Claire's breath tightened in her chest.

"This is your severance pay, a bonus, and letter of reference." Ostervich avoided answering Claire's question and held out a brown envelope to Claire who didn't take it.

"I can't believe you're doing this to *Ikuta-san* while he's in the hospital. Is this how you repay him for risking his life to win a baseball game for you? You're going to make him face the press without an interpreter?"

"I'll be there." Michael spoke softly as if embarrassed about his part in this betrayal of both Claire and Kentaro.

"Has any one told *Ikuta-san* these plans?"

"He's not strong enough for business just now," Michael commented. "And, he's going to Japan as soon as he's stable."

"What?" Claire gasped.

"He wants to recuperate in Japan," Michael went on to explain. Ostervich laid down the envelope and pushed it across the smooth table to Claire. Michael picked it up and placed it in front of her. "He should be gone by the end of the week."

"I still can't understand," she commented while she stared at the envelope. If she picked it up, it would be final. Her last tie to Kentaro broken.

"And, Ms. Ferris, we ask that you have no contact with Mr. Ikuta, once he's back in the game. Like you said, we don't want any disruption of his concentration," Martella said.

"Now you're saying I can't talk to him? If I'm not his interpreter, I'm not his friend?"

None of the men would speak, but Claire understood clearly what they were doing. They were embarrassed by the proceedings and concerned only with the bottom line. The players were money-makers first, baseball players second, and men last. If her presence cut into profits even slightly, she had to go.

"I see," she muttered out loud. "It's been a pleasure." Claire stood. "Good day, gentleman." She left the room.

"Claire, wait up!" Michael called as she fled down the concession corridor of the stadium. She passed the boarded-up hot dog and beer stands. "Claire!"

Claire slowed but didn't stop. She turned into the concrete tunnel which led to the seats.

"Claire, come on! Stop!" Michael followed her.

He discovered her leaning against the cold, rough wall just short of the bright sunshine of the ball field. She stared at the pitcher's mound, a familiar sight.

"Will you tell him?" Claire didn't turn to Michael, not wanting him to see the tears.

"When he's well enough. How are you?"

"When he first told me about Katsuko, I thought I wouldn't be able to be with him, even professionally. Then I decided that it would be the only way I could be with him. Even that's taken away from me now." Claire turned. "What am I going to do?"

"I don't know."

"Has anyone thought of Kentaro? What about his feelings?" Claire pleaded his case. "You'll be there to translate for him, but it won't be the same. We...we...we had a rapport."

"Claire, you and I both know Kentaro was using language as a way to keep you at his side. He knows the minute he can face the reporters without you, you're released. And what if you disappeared from his life? This was the only way he could be with you."

"And now, he's told me to go away so he can marry his arranged bride and the Chiefs have co-operated by firing me. How convenient." Claire passed him to leave the corridor.

"Claire, here. This is yours." Michael held out the envelope.

"I don't want it," Claire paused to tell him, her back to him.

"Take it anyway. They'll just mail it if you don't." Michael put the envelope into her hand. When she turned to take it, his own two held her hand for brief seconds.

Claire pulled her hand and the envelope back and disappeared.

Claire fled to CWRU and her office to isolate herself from the real world as was her custom before becoming involved in the exciting world of baseball. She hid for a week before Dr. Ramstein summoned her.

"You wanted to see me, sir?" Claire entered her mentor's office. The room was as cluttered as hers.

"Sorry to hear about your termination," the older professor said, but his attention was on his paper-strewn desk.

"Thank you, but it's fine. I can get back to work."

"That's what I wanted to see you about." He found what he looked for. "I want you to go to the University of Tokyo and give my paper on the changes of the Japanese language in the last one hundred years."

"You're kidding, aren't you?" Claire couldn't believe he was sending her to Japan. Of all the places in the world, she least wanted to be there right now.

"You did do most of the research, and I have mistakenly overbooked myself." Dr. Ramstein handed her the proper folders. "You leave next week. Enjoy the vacation."

"Yeah, right." Claire left the office. She wondered what trouble she could get into in the "Land of the Rising Sun."

# Chapter Twenty-eight

"Dr. Ramstein's at it again," Claire said as she and Andrea ran down the tree-lined street. Sweat poured off their lithe bodies. "He's sending me to give a paper in Tokyo."

"Is that old man blind-siding you?" Andrea panted. "I'm gonna die!"

"No you're not. Just put one foot in front of the other," Claire advised. They approached the hill both of them dreaded. "He has some conflict in scheduling. His secretary's always doing that," Claire panted.

They didn't speak again for five minutes as they tackled the hill.

"So are you going?" Andrea huffed. Their pace was faster coming down the hill.

"Can I refuse? He's my advisor."

"Isn't he in Nagasaki?" Claire realized Andrea echoed her thought about Kentaro.

"I'm hoping he stays there! I'll be in Tokyo."

Claire arrived in Tokyo, her spirits no brighter. She had been to Japan three times before, venturing into the north twice and the south once. She avoided giving any thought to stepping on Kyushu, much less in Nagasaki. The first evening, she holed up in her hotel suite, but her love of Japan lured her out the next day.

She wandered the Ginza and explored the shops further back from the thoroughfare which were often overlooked by tourists. A textiler's storefront caught her eye and she went inside. There, she found samples of the fabric with the intricate weaving necessary for a kimono. Under the eye of a small elderly woman, she studied the dyes and textures for a while.

"How much is this?" Claire asked the woman when she found a kimono she liked in the layers of garments on a shelf.

When the woman answered her, Claire felt her jaw drop. The dollar exchange made the kimono cost fifty thousand dollars.

"What makes it so...expensive?" she asked.

"The style of weave. We get them from a textiler in Kyoto where the weavers of the Nishijin-ori style settled after the Onin Wars."

"Oh."

Claire left the store with a small square of silk woven in the style she had admired. She thought she'd have it framed.

She ate lunch at a noodle shop and started to return to her room, but found herself in a movie theater, watching an obscure Kurasawa movie. Not until she exited the dark theater and people began to stare at her, did she realize she was crying. It was time to go into hiding again.

"*Ferris-san?*" a soft female voice came at Claire from the crowd.

"Yes?" Claire had finished Dr. Ramstein's speech and answered questions posed to her for another hour afterwards. Her feet hurt, she had a headache, and she wanted only to go back the hotel. And home.

"It is you, *Ferris-san!*" Takahiko came out of the crowd to greet her.

"Takahiko-san! What are you doing here?" Claire failed to stop and consider that Kentaro might be nearby. She bowed respectfully to his sister as Takahiko bowed to her.

"I am going to school here. Post-graduate work like you," Takahiko said. "I read about the lecture and decided to come hear it. I thought a *Sensei* Ramstein was to give it?"

"His secretary has a habit of overbooking him."

Claire and Takahiko began to walk from the lecture hall. The humid and hot Tokyo weather did not prevent people from clogging the sidewalks.

"Would you like to join me for tea?" Takahiko suggested. "I would like to return your hospitality."

"I would love to."

"So. Tell me about America," Takahiko started. The women had found the nearest tea house and were settled with tea and a tray of manju, pastries Claire savored when in Japan.

"You have only been away for a month. Nothing has changed." Claire laughed and sipped her tea.

"But things have changed, *Ferris-san*."

"Why do you not call me Claire? I do not call you *Ikuta-san*." Claire was sorry she'd accepted the tea invitation from Takahiko. She didn't want to talk about Kentaro and his predicament. Yet something inside her refused to let go. Refused to hate him or wish him ill. She wanted him and there was always hope for his return until he took that final step.

"Habit. Taro calls you that." Takahiko's hand flew to her mouth as if to catch the words escaping her lips. "I am sorry."

"Do not be. I..." Claire's face was toward the window. "I have...gotten over...him." She hoped Takahiko wouldn't be able to read the lie on her face. Would she ever forget Kentaro Ikuta, a man of bronze skin, raven hair, and exotic eyes?

"You have not, Claire-san. And he will never get over you. I would like to help you win him back."

"He does not want me, Takahiko. He sent me away."

"Because he sees no other way. You must show him that different path. Give him a reason to make the difficult journey. And if you will allow me, I will help you." Takahiko took Claire's hand in hers. "Will you?"

Claire looked deeply into the young Japanese woman's eyes, so like Kentaro's. Her heart ached to see him again, to be held by him, to be kissed by the lips so like the ones she saw before her now.

"Oh, yes, Takahiko, yes. Please."

"Then we must go. I can make better tea than this!" Takahiko threw some yen on the table and they left.

"How is he?" Claire asked as they took a taxi to wherever Takahiko was taking her.

"He is well. He is here in Tokyo visiting me before he returns to baseball," Takahiko explained. "He leaves for Cleveland next week."

"He would die without baseball," Claire said.

"He will die with it, if you are not with him. We have to stop at my apartment, and then we must go to your hotel room."

"What are you up to?"

"It is a secret."

When he entered the Tokyo Hilton, Kentaro was still reeling from Takahiko's message. And he didn't know why he had responded. Yes, he did. He had no will power when it came to the American woman. He needed to see Claire, wanted to be with her, and away from the sniveling Katsuko. The glass enclosed elevator rose to the eighth floor. He walked down the corridor and knocked at the door. It was opened by Takahiko.

"She is in other room," Takahiko announced without preamble and passed her brother as she went out the door and down the hall.

Kentaro was taken off guard, but entered Claire's suite.

"Claire?"

"I'm coming."

When she appeared, Kentaro paused in mid-motion of sitting, mesmerized by the sight of his interpreter standing before him. Slowly straightening his knees and standing as much as his growing erection would allow. "You're beautiful," he whispered, unable to take his eyes off Claire.

She wore the kimono he had asked Takahiko to send to him so many months ago when he was just beginning to feel his love for her. He didn't stop to wonder what it was doing here in Japan when he'd left it in Cleveland.

"I don't know if *Taka-chan* and I got it put on right," Claire disparaged, looking down at the garment.

"You've done very well." Kentaro came to take her hands his. He held her arms out from her sides to allow the wide kimono sleeves to drape to their full depth.

The elaborate kimono clothed her as if she were meant to wear it. Of the weaving style used in Nishijin-ori silk, it had the color of a ripe apricot. A plain under-kimono of white silk showed at the neck and where the garment overlapped around Claire's body. Her slender height allowed the material to cascade smoothly, to expose in detail the splayed fans decorated with apricot blossoms, small white and silver chrysanthemums, and pink and white primroses, all framed within and from behind with young tender green bamboo. The flowers were outlined in embroidery using the subtlest gold threads. A wide obi of a deep rich burnt orange circled her waist.

Her hair remained untouched. The dark, thick brown river hung to mid-back, held by two tortoise shell combs at her temples. Her bangs were fluffed over her brow. On impulse, Kentaro placed his lips on her cool forehead as if kissing a delicate cherry blossom.

Kentaro released her hands and moved his own to lie on her shoulders. He looked into her face, her greenish-gray eyes returning his gaze. Her lips were moist and inviting. He laid his mouth softly on them then embraced her. When her arms encircled him, the kimono sleeves wrapped him in familiarity. The well-known feel of silk on his cheek reassured him.

Kentaro extended his arms to push Claire away so he could look at her again.

"It's perfect for you, *Claire-chan*."

"I don't know," Claire scoffed.

"Sssh." Kentaro turned Claire around and his hands went to the knot Takahiko had so expertly tied. "If you don't think it fits you, you don't have to wear it much longer." He undid the obi and unwrapped the tiny waist. He let the lengthy sash flow ribbon-like to the floor. Moving her to face him, he put his fingers inside the edge of the kimono to open the dress.

"Can you put it back on me? Without Takahiko-san, I don't…"

"Hush." Kentaro brushed his lips over hers to silence her words. He wanted to savor the undressing of the package before him.

Beneath the kimono, Claire was nude, but Kentaro did not expose her. He let the edges fall so a mere hint of the soft breasts was revealed. His cross dangled between her breasts from the gold chain around her neck. His hands slid to her buttocks, to cup the rounded flesh in each palm.

Claire sighed as Kentaro put his lips to hers. His tongue greeted hers gently, then became more ardent as his hands came up to push the kimono off her shoulders. It whispered as it pooled around her feet. Kentaro continued the gentle exploration of her supple body until both were too excited to restrain themselves.

It took very little coaxing to bring Claire down onto the floor where the silken kimono made a bed for Kentaro to continue his pleasantly agonizing caresses after he practically tore his own clothing off. His skilled hands, followed by his mouth, explored Claire's body from foot to head and back. Claire could do little but enjoy the attention. Ultimately, he placed his rock hard erection at her portal and escape into the deep, soaked refuge. They both climaxed and then lay draped in the traditional silken garment.

"Do you think we ruined it?" Claire asked after they both had relaxed and their erratic, heavy breathing had subsided.

"It can be cleaned," Kentaro answered. He pulled her closer, their bodies entwined.

Claire was silent, and Kentaro pondered what had just occurred. Being with Claire returned the desire to begin his life again. Until he'd seen her, he even had thought of sitting out the rest of the baseball season. Now, he knew completely what he had to do and what he wanted. Claire.

"Kentaro, is this just a 'Wham, bam, thank you, ma'am'? Are you going to tell me to leave again?"

"I will never ever tell you to leave again." Kentaro rubbed his face in her hair.

"Then what are you going to do? You said..."

"Claire." His words were so close her hair moved with his breath. "I'm truly sorry for all I've done to you. Can you forgive me? I was crazy to think I could live without you."

"Kentaro, don't you think I've just forgiven the hell out of you?" Claire laughed. "What are we going to do?" Claire lay across Kentaro's chest.

"I'll figure something out. Patience." Kentaro caressed her arm and played with the gold chain. "I was wondering where I had lost this."

"Want it back?" Claire studied his face. His eyes sparkled. His skin, taunt over high cheekbones and square jaw, was covered with a hint of beard, his upper lip the darkest with a black shadow.

"Would you give it back to me?"

"No." Claire kissed him.

"Then keep it, but you have to promise to give it to our son." Kentaro gazed deeply into her green eyes.

"Of course. But you have to get rid of..."

"Ssh."

# Chapter Twenty-nine

"What are you doing in Tokyo anyway?" Claire asked as she and Kentaro walked through the part of the Imperial Garden open to the public. They used English now as they had Japanese in the States, to isolate themselves from those around them. Claire was pleased that the language she had taught Kentaro came so easily to his tongue.

"My parents' home was too restrictive so I came to see Takahiko. I'm returning to Cleveland in two days." Kentaro was bold enough to hold her hand as they walked. "When do you leave?"

"Tomorrow. Are we going to talk about Katsuko?"

"I wish we didn't have to, but we must. I have refused to sign the contract. That doesn't mean I'm not still bound to her. I have time to come up with a reason."

"You have a reason. Me." Claire announced.

"Perhaps I should have said, an honorable reason."

"Oh, I'm not honorable?" Claire gave him an elfish look. She stopped walking to stand beneath a cherry tree.

"You're honorable." Kentaro let go of her hand and walked halfway across the footbridge over the Imperial pond. He stood looking down at the water and the ducks swimming there. "I'm not."

"Yes, you are, honorable samurai." Claire came to his side, a hand on his back and the other on his arm. "If you weren't you would not tell anything. You would either marry her and have me as your mistress, if I would co-operate, or you would just forget all about the *omiai*. You're concerned with her honor, not yours."

"I suppose you're right, *Claire-chan.*" Kentaro turned and embraced her as he leaned against the railing. "I'm also concerned with yours."

"Don't worry about me." Claire put her arms around his neck. "I want to be with you. I don't care how."

"You would care eventually. Now, go home and think kind thoughts of me." Kentaro hazarded a brief public kiss.

"Always." They began walking again. "Did Michael tell you what happened with the Chiefs?"

"He said you had been dismissed." Kentaro snorted after speaking.

"Are you all right with that?" Claire had a comfortable sensation as she heard his sound.

"No, but..."

"I've come to understand why they did it, but you know what?"

"I only know I love you." Kentaro smiled at her. "What do you know?"

"One of the last articles in the paper that I read talked about Cooperstown. Except it asked why you would be waving a baseball bat at—I quote—'an unknown person'—unquote. It never named Jason and made you the aggressor. And never mentioned me or what Jason did to me."

"That's interesting."

"It is, isn't it? I think I'll see what I can find out, since I have so much time on my hands now."

"That will give you something to do to keep you out of trouble."

"I stay in trouble. Ever since I met you." Claire wrapped her arms around Kentaro's upper arm. "Now. Do you know where we can get some great sushi in this town?"

"Do I?" Kentaro smiled at her. "Just let me show you, *gaijin.*"

# The Words of the Pitcher

∞

Kentaro came to the language department of Case Western Reserve University, anxious to see Claire. He had been in Cleveland for three weeks, joining the team as if nothing had kept him away. But Claire was absent from the stadium, and he had seen her only twice. Because of her banishment, they met at Michael and Audrey's house. None of their dates were long enough or personal enough for either of them.

He longed for the time when he could stay with her, hold her through the night, and publicly depart in the morning without regard to who saw. So much he wanted and needed, so much he was denied.

When she had called him to meet her at her office, she explained how she thought the visit would go unnoticed since he could be seeing any number of people in the huge building. When he found her office on the fourth floor, he had a feeling of deja vu, as if he had crossed through a doorway into Japan. The room was full of items familiar to him, but out of place in America. A full suit of samurai armor clothed a mannequin in a corner. The faceless warrior stared out from the helmet.

"I've found out who is behind all this bad press," Claire told Kentaro after they spoke hellos.

"Really?" Kentaro stood beside her desk, flipping through one of the numerous research books in the clutter. A piece of paper bookmarked a page concerning marriage. His eyes glanced at the words. The information made him uncomfortable and he closed the book. "You're aware my relationship with the press has never been very good."

"The Japanese press is different. But I know why this Schaeffer guy's doing this." Claire found the paper she had scribbled on at the library. "Here. Look at this." She handed it to him.

235

He read the paper while sitting in the chair in front of her desk. Claire stood beside him.

"See?" She draped her arm across his shoulders as she sat on the arm of the chair and pointed to several items. "Every time Jason talked to me, and I made him mad, a negative article about you appeared."

Kentaro snorted at the information. His back stiffened in response to Claire's arm.

"I asked my mother about it. She found out from Jason's mother that Jason and Schaeffer were roommates at Penn State where they both went to graduate school."

"What are you planning to do with this information?" Kentaro handed Claire the paper.

"I want to go to the Chiefs and tell them it's not our fault." Claire sank down onto the edge of the desk, facing Kentaro, close enough their knees touched. "And I think we should tell the press about our relationship."

"I don't think that would be the best thing to do right now," Kentaro hedged. He stood and walked to stand behind the chair, his hands on the back. "I don't think they care what's going on with us personally."

"Excuse me? They fired me as your interpreter and do not want me anywhere near you! If we come out in the open with our relationship, they can't object. The press doesn't like secrets. They can't hold it over our heads if we go public."

"They can and will." Kentaro's knuckles whitened as he held the chair. "I think we should leave things as they are for now. We can see what develops after the season is over."

"You want to let them get away with it?"

"They're not getting away with anything," Kentaro said. "They're management. They can do what they want with us. We're employees. Especially you."

"Me? Just an employee? Is that all I am to you? An employee?"

"No, of course not. You're very special to me. But I have to be concerned with my career. I have to concentrate on the game right now. Can you understand that? I don't want anything to happen now that will interfere with my pitching."

"I understand how important your career is." She dropped her head dejectedly and crossed her arms on her chest. "I thought I was important, too."

Kentaro stepped around the chair and reached out to put his arm around Claire's waist and pull her from the desk to him. He held her to his chest. Her arms reluctantly embraced him.

"*Claire-chan*, you'll never know how important you are to me. I'll never be able to tell or show you."

"I would if you'd go to the press with me," Claire suggested.

"No. I can't. It'll pass and perhaps afterwards we can find a way for ourselves." Kentaro squeezed her, then pushed her away. "Remember, Katsuko-san is still betrothed to me. But I can't deal with it now."

"Why not?" Claire demanded.

"*Ferris-san*, you sit here, surrounded by Japan," Kentaro waved his hand at the books and paraphernalia which lined the walls of the small office, "and do not see. Of all the things which define a person of Japan, it's patience. We have refined it to an art. Try to develop your own, *Claire-chan*, and wait. Good things come to him who waits. Is that not what they say?"

"Yes." Kentaro could see Claire relax. "I'll wait. I don't know how patiently, but I'll do as you ask."

"Thank you. It makes my path easier. Now," Kentaro again pulled her to him, "kiss me and then I must leave."

Claire turned her face eagerly to him and Kentaro placed his lips on hers. Claire's hands pressed his shoulder blades and Kentaro felt her firm breasts against his chest.

"I must go," he repeated when he released her mouth.

"Oh," Claire sighed. She laid her head on his chest.

Kentaro settled into the embrace, his chin resting on the top of her head. He recalled the conversation with Takahiko when he had first met Claire about how she would fit under his chin. It warmed him to remember it. "I have practice."

"I'm sorry." Claire stepped away from him. "I forgot you had a job to do."

"Just be patient," he repeated.

"Easy for you to say."

Claire settled back at her work after Kentaro left the office.

Kentaro walked to the car he had decided to lease so he wouldn't have to rely on Michael, Claire, or public transportation since his face had finally become well-known. He felt confused as well as guilty over the situation with Claire. Every fiber of his being wanted her yet could he ever have her? Although he'd refused to sign the betrothal contract, he was still expected to marry Katsuko. His father had refused to release him from the obligation.

Now, Claire was pushing him to tell the world about their relationship. She couldn't understand how it would compromise any hopes he had to destroy the *omiai*.

There had to be some way to make it up to her. He drove away from the parking lot, an idea brewing, his face set as purposefully as a samurai going into battle.

# Chapter Thirty

Kentaro entered the newspaper office building, his face a warrior's mask.

"I'm Kentaro Ikuta. I'd like to see Mr. Schaeffer," he said to the columnist's secretary.

"Just a moment." She picked up the phone, punched a few buttons, and spoke. "Mr. Schaeffer, Mr. Ikuta would like to meet with you."

She listened.

"Yes, sir." She replaced the phone. "You may go in." She waved a hand toward the closed door.

"Thank you."

Kentaro entered the office, a determined set to his jaw and shoulders.

"Aren't we supposed to clear all interviews with the Chiefs' press office so they can arrange a translator?" Schaeffer went on the attack immediately. He did not stand to greet Ikuta.

"This is personal," Kentaro responded. "I wish to discover what I must do to stop this censure of Ms. Ferris."

"So you do speak English. And well."

"Yes, thanks to her hard work. Now, what do we need to do to stop this assault on her character?"

"Well," Schaeffer leaned back in his chair, stretching his long body out, "I don't know."

"I've recently learned where you've gleaned your information about Ms. Ferris and me," Kentaro continued. "I'd appreciate it if you'd limit your concern to baseball and myself. Ms. Ferris has very little to do with baseball."

"But yourself? Isn't she...? How do I say this?"

"You need not look far for a word to describe Ms. Ferris. I don't feel I need to defend our relationship."

"But didn't you attack a guy who was just talking to her at the Baseball Hall of Fame?"

"Your informant, who happens to be the one you accuse me of attacking, has misinformed you. It was he who was assaulting Ms. Ferris. I merely suggested he stop."

"By using a baseball bat?" Schaeffer sat up and leaned forward to rest his elbows on his desk.

"I was holding it after I'd finished having pictures taken for the Hall of Fame," Kentaro continued.

"And it just happened to swing toward his head?" Schaeffer challenged.

"How would he know where it was aimed? His back was to me as he ran down the hall." Kentaro would not be shaken in his persistence to stop Schaeffer and his denigration of Claire.

"Are you calling him a coward?" Schaeffer eased back in his chair.

"I didn't call him anything. You did." Kentaro refused to add fuel to Schaeffer's ravaging fire of words. "Again, I ask what I must do to have you stop this libel of Ms. Ferris?"

"You like the role of White Knight, don't you?" Schaeffer continued to answer question with question.

"I can see you don't care what you say or do." Kentaro decided this was useless. "I'll not take up any more of your time." Kentaro moved to the door. "Oh, by the way. I plan to have a press conference after each game from now on. I'll make sure you're barred from them."

Kentaro left the office.

The baseball season was rapidly coming to a close. Claire, so unfamiliar with the game at the first of the year, was now enthralled with it. At the same time she placed a large bowl of popcorn and a can of Coke on the coffee table, she punched the POWER button on the television remote. The commercial on provided time to make a bathroom run. Out of some ridiculous habit, she ran a comb through her bangs after washing her hands. Her hair was pulled up in a pony-tail and swung down her back. She adjusted her shorts and Kentaro's jersey. His gold chain was around her neck.

When she sat on the floor before the couch, cross-legged with the bowl on her lap, the announcer was beginning his discussion of previous games. He thoroughly dissected Kentaro's pitching the first time he faced the Oakland A's along with his relief in another. Although he had started weakly against the A's, he had steadily improved.

"He'll do great!" Claire shouted at the screen, bored and bothered by the sportscaster's ramblings to fill time.

At length, the game started. The Chiefs were up first, Kentaro on the mound. He stood straight, the glove and ball held together close to his chest. He turned his back to the plate, twisting his upper body to bring his left leg up, the knee almost in his arm pit.

He paused.

In the movement, Kentaro had brought his right hand to his shoulder. With a reverse, swift motion, he whirled and threw the ball as hard as he could over the home plate.

"Strike one!" the umpire shouted.

Claire exhaled. Absently, she placed popcorn in her mouth.

Kentaro repeated his unorthodox style of pitching eight more times and three batters were up and down. A shut-out for the first inning. Claire watched intently as the camera panned the field, coming to settle on Kentaro as he trotted to the dugout. A ballboy handed him the jacket as she had so often. Kentaro took the jacket mutely, going to sit at the back of the dugout, his face a hard stare. No one approached him and the announcer, in his comments, was concerned about this.

"In his whole season, Ikuta has yet to join in any conversation with his teammates during a game. And they have come to respect his privacy. It must be noted, however," the slick-haired reporter continued, "that when his interpreter, Claire Ferris, accompanied him in the dugout during the games, they were often observed carrying on very animated conversations. In Japanese, of course. When Ikuta becomes more fluent in English, will he talk with his teammates during games? It is something we will have to wait to see."

"Oh, puleeze," Claire moaned to herself aloud. "I didn't talk to him that much! He doesn't like to talk to anyone during games. Just start the next inning."

At the bottom of the second inning, Kentaro took up his position. Robotically, he repeated his moves, pitching and retiring two batters. The third got a hit, making it to third base. Then his pitching began to go south. Each pitch wobbled and failed to deceive the batter. Soon, the Oakland ball club had three runs ahead of the Chiefs.

"Not again," Claire moaned. She remembered the day she sat watching as Steve approached the mound to pull Kentaro from the game.

Kentaro left the game to boos from his fans. Regardless, he waved his cap and disappeared into the dugout.

Claire muted the television and put her popcorn and soda in the kitchen, no longer interested.

Kentaro stepped into the dugout and accepted his jacket and the ice pack from the ball girl. He looked at the teenager's fresh face with her mid-length hair bound by a ponytail topped with a Chiefs' cap. He thought of Claire. That was his problem. Too much reminded him of her. In the away games, he did not feel her absence as he did here at Jacobs Field. He sat watching his team play, his hand holding the ice to his elbow. The chair on his right was empty. Claire's chair. He shook his head.

Baseball should be his primary concern. Never had he had such a casual feeling about baseball. During the Olympics, he had had his share of distractions. Nothing changed for him before or after. Claire had destroyed his game.

No. Claire hadn't. His heart had done him in. He had to find a way to remedy the problem.

"Not doing so well, huh?" Steve Martella sat down beside him.

"I want Claire back," Kentaro stated, startled at his bluntness.

"I don't know about that," Steve stammered. He leaned forward with his elbows on his knees. "Management says it's not good press. They've worked hard to get Cleveland to accept a foreign player. No offense."

"I don't care. I need her here with me." Kentaro's mind raced. If management allowed Claire to return to her position, he would need to face the highest hurdle. Could he tell his determined father that he wanted Claire for his wife? Would his father stand for such a defiance? "I've put a stop to articles by the reporter. Have you noticed any more critical reports?"

"No. I haven't." Steve glanced at Kentaro. "Your English is getting better. Claire has done a great job."

"Yes, she has.  But I still need her to help with more difficult conversations."

"Okay.  Let me talk with them.  I'll see what we can do."

"Just remind them that they wish to win the Series."

"I get your point."  Steve started to return to the field to coach the relief pitcher.  "We have to get into the play-offs first."

"If Claire's here, you can count on it."

# Chapter Thirty-one

"What are you doing?" Andrea asked her friend as she stood in Claire's office. Claire appeared to be standing on her head behind a body form wearing a full set of samurai armor.

"I'm trying to figure out if I translated this article on samurai clothing correctly. Or if, in a pique of spite, I'm translating Japanese badly." Claire righted her posture and came to the front of the mannequin. "I find it fascinating that anyone would care what kind of underwear a feudal warrior wore. Especially a current article. Oh, well." She tossed her pad and pen on her desk.

"When did you get back? How was Tokyo? Anything interesting happen?" Andrea asked.

"I've been back a month." Claire sat behind the desk, her attention on the computer screen.

"I've been away so I missed your return." Andrea perched on the front of Claire's desk. "So, answer the questions."

"It went fine. I ran into Takahiko, Kentaro's sister." Claire shuffled some papers. Did she dare expose herself to her friend?

"And?"

"And what?" Claire's eyes focused over her glasses on Andrea. She loved making Andy sweat! "She called Kentaro to come to meet me at my hotel room," Claire gloated.

"You didn't!" Andrea's mouth dropped, satisfying Claire with the reaction.

"We did. He promises to dump Katsuko."

"His fiancée? Her name doesn't work."

"What?" Claire crinkled her nose at her friend.

"Katsuko and Kentaro. Too many Ks. Claire and Kentaro, that works better. The C is softer that a K," Andrea explained. "So, he says he's going to break up with her. Has he?"

"Not yet. I'm afraid I don't know if he's telling me the truth." It was a hard admission for Claire. She wanted with all her heart to believe Kentaro but actions spoke louder than words.

"Your samurai might have clay feet," Andrea observed smugly. "Claire, I'm going to say something that's not going to make me very popular with you."

"You're my friend, Andy. You can say anything."

"OK." Andrea took a deep breath. "You know I've been used and dumped by the best of them, so I speak from experience. Have you ever thought that maybe Mr. Baseball-san might be using you?"

"I don't think so. Why would he use me? In what way?"

"Think about it. You speak his language fluently and you understand his culture. Maybe it's easy to be with you because of that."

"Andrea," Claire started.

"No. It's easy to sleep with you since he can be comfortable. It's like being home but being here."

Claire gave Andrea a look of contempt, but it dissolved quickly.

"I don't want to believe that," Claire confessed. "I believe he loves me."

"I know and neither do I. I want you and your samurai to walk into the sunset happy and together. But, I want you to have your eyes open when you take that walk."

"I'll think about it." Claire threw her papers on the desk and sat back.

"Relax, Claire. Maybe he's just slow. How long has it been?"

"A month and a half since we were together in Tokyo."

"And how long has he been Japanese?"

"I don't understand what you're getting at."

"It's going to be hard for him to change, Claire." Andrea sobered considerably. "When you're in love, you want to believe it's a two way street and everything he says is true." Andrea's manner changed abruptly. "Now, I really came to see if you wanted to go to lunch or the gym?"

"How about the gym and dinner?" Claire put her glasses on and sat forward to better see the characters on the screen.

"You're on. See you at four." Andrea left Claire to her work.

But Claire couldn't work with Andrea's remarks haunting her. She glanced around the room, slowly taking in all the material of Japan that surrounded her.

Could Andrea be right? Was she drawn to Kentaro because of his face and heritage? Or was it the man beneath the facade? She wanted to love him because of him. It wouldn't be fair to either of them if her love was based on her infatuation with the past. She stood and removed a book from the very top shelf.

Seated at her desk, she opened the book to colorful plates of erotic pictures drawn in the sixteenth century. Claire didn't see Kentaro's face superimposed over any of the samurai illustrated in the midst of sexual escapades. The pictures didn't define a samurai or his ways of affection. Only the flesh and blood of Kentaro Ikuta could show her those.

Claire had her answer.

"Andrea, how'd you like to go to a baseball game or two or three?" Claire stood in the steamy shower after they had completed the aerobics class and weight workout.

"Claire," Andrea's head poked into Claire's stall. "What are you planning?"

"The Chiefs don't want me in the Jake, but they didn't say anything about Yankee Stadium." Claire worked the shampoo into a frothy lather on her head. "I talked Daddy into using his connections to get me tickets to the three out of town games. When they get back to Cleveland, I'll have to watch television."

"Are you sure you want to do this to yourself?" Andrea asked from the shower stall next to Claire's.

"I'll be in the stands, not the dugout or pressroom." Claire was toweling off. "He'll never know I'm anywhere near. Now, wanna go?"

"Sure. Are the seats any good?" Andrea joined Claire at the benches to dress.

Wearing an outfit designed to camouflage herself, but with Kentaro's Chiefs jacket and cap, Claire sat with Andrea in the first few rows behind the first base line at Yankee Stadium. Binoculars helped her to closely study Kentaro as he warmed up in the bull pen. Watching him, she decided he had dropped a few pounds. His face looked drawn. Probably from stress. He didn't have the same intense look she had noticed when Andrea diagnosed him as having 'Claire fever.'

"So how's the boy look?" Andrea asked. "Want some peanuts?"

"His control's good." Claire put the binoculars down and reached into the bag. "I think he'll do all right."

"And you?"

Claire glared at her friend while drinking from her plastic cup of beer.

"OK. More nuts?" Andrea giggled and stomped her feet on the concrete floor. She was ahead of Claire on her consumption of alcohol. "I crack myself up!"

"You're the one who's nuts!" Claire joined in her laughter.

Claire settled into the game, carefully assessing each play as if she were an experienced baseball fan. Kentaro, not aware of her presence, pitched flawlessly for two innings. When he retired to the dugout, Claire was overwhelmed with the desire to be down there with him, to share their language and the jokes special to them. To know he was literally sitting beneath her in the visitor's dugout gave her a tremendous rush.

"What are you smiling about?" Andrea slurped the foam off a fresh beer.

"He's beneath me," Claire stated complacently.

"Excuse me? What are you talking about?"

"Kentaro's in the dugout, under these seats." Claire pointed down at the concrete beneath their feet. She hugged herself in satisfaction.

"Oh. Strange observance, Claire." Andrea drank her beer.

The PA announcer, finding himself with a game delay because of a pitcher-coach conference, began to tell the crowd about the important people in the stands.

"And in the stands, as a special treat for Cleveland Chiefs pitcher, Kentaro Ikuta, we have his fiancée all the way from Japan, Katsuko Ashino." A picture of Kentaro from the team lineup flashed on the scoreboard.

"Oh my God!" Claire rose from her seat. "I can't believe it! Come on, Andy, let's go." Claire moved down the aisle toward the exit. "Come on!"

"I'm coming." Gathering their things hastily, Andrea hurried to follow Claire up the steps to leave the stands.

Claire slowed only when she was among the crowds around the concession stands. Andrea was at her side.

"I can't believe they said that!" Claire looked up to the ceiling to prevent the tears from falling. "It can't be true."

"Why else would they say it? Doesn't he tell the PR department that stuff?" Andrea asked.

"No. PR tells the stadium people what they want announced." Claire's face was wet with tears. "He didn't say anything about her coming to the States. All he said is a lie. It hurts, Andy."

"I know." Andrea hugged her friend. "God, when it comes to guys, you're such a rookie. Let's go to the hotel and get drunk."

"Great idea." Claire tried to smile through the tears in her eyes.

"Want the last beer?" Andrea waved the bottle over Claire's head as she lay on the bed. Claire was on her back, her head hanging off the foot of the bed. They were in their room at the hotel, two six packs killed between them. Claire reached for the brown bottle. "Are we going to the second game?"

"Hell, no." Claire rolled over on her stomach and twisted off the cap. "It's over between us! When I get home, his stuff goes back. Never again will Kentaro Ikuta darken my door!"

"You go, girl! This is your party. I'm just along for the ride." Andrea sipped her own brew. She sat on the floor, leaning against the foot of the bed, a few inches from Claire. "We could scalp the tickets for great money."

"Why don't we give the tickets away?" Claire turned the bottle up to her mouth. "The busboy in the cafe would like them."

"Whatever."

"Let's stay here as planned." She wiped the dribble from her bottom lip. "The plane leaves Sunday night. I don't want Daddy saying I told you so."

"Boy, do I know that feeling!" Andrea agreed. "I gotta go to bed." She crawled toward the bathroom. "We're not going to be in any condition to go anywhere tomorrow."

"You're so right." Claire tossed the empty bottle into the wastebasket. "I don't think I'll ever watch baseball again."

"You can always follow football," Andrea called from the bathroom where she changed into her gown and brushed her teeth.

"Naw. I'm through with sports. Period." Claire put on her own gown she had pulled from her suitcase.

"You don't have to blame every professional athlete, Claire." Andrea came from the bathroom. "Claire?"

Claire was sound asleep. In the dim light of the bedside lamp, Andrea saw the gold cross on her friend's throat.

"Your guy won both games," Andrea whispered as they flew back to Cleveland. "He got the Chiefs into the play-offs."

"Shssh. My head hurts." Claire rested her head against the headrest, her eyes closed. Her headache helped her forget her fear of flying. "Two days and I'm still hung over."

"If you were concerned about sobering up, maybe you should have stopped drinking," Andrea commented. "Aren't you a little bit excited for them? For him?"

"No." Claire turned her head and to look directly at Andrea. "I don't want to talk about it."

# Chapter Thirty-two

"Don't look now, but I think you may have to talk about it," Andrea warned as they walked from the baggage carousel after retrieving their bags at the Cleveland airport.

"Huh?" Claire looked around. "Why?"

"Mr. Baseball-san's over there." Andrea pointed in the direction of the exit, inclining her head to speak into Claire's ear.

"Then we go the other way." Claire charged to the opposite egress.

"*Ferris-san*," Kentaro called before the women could escape. "How are you?" He used English.

"I'm fine," Claire spat over her shoulder, afraid to turn around. She felt Andrea disappear.

"It's good to see you." Kentaro came to face her.

Claire looked into his face despite herself. The dark, angled eyes watched her soulfully as if his best friend had died. Claire knew it was exactly how she felt.

"I'm not going to get into this with you here, in public. Tell Katsuko I said she wins. You're hers."

She was not going to let him see her pain. Turning, she rejoined Andrea, who stood far away from them by the exit waiting to leave. This was hopeless. Why did he even bother speaking to her? There was nothing either of them could do. It was finished.

"Kentaro, this came for you." Miyoko entered the living room carrying a brown paper wrapped box.

"I will take it," Kentaro said and did just that.

"What do you think it is?" his mother quizzed. "Something from a baseball fan?"

"It is personal." A hopeless dread clutched his heart as he recognized Claire's precise handwriting. He knew without opening the carton what it contained. He cursed his family.

Kentaro went to his bedroom.

An hour later he was in the fitness room at Jacobs Field with Michael Sangyo. They had the place to themselves.

"Claire returned my gifts," he stated flatly, the first words either man had spoken since they had begun working out fifteen minutes before. As usual with Michael, they spoke Japanese.

"That why you called?" Michael was spotting for Kentaro who was bench pressing two hundred pounds. It was not much of a challenge so he kept raising and lowering the bar.

"Did you tell the PR office about Katsuko? That she was in New York?" Kentaro huffed as he pushed the bar up toward Michael who stood over his head his hands following the bar.

"I would not do something like that unless you told me to. I am your agent. I want good things for you."

"My parents showed up with her and Takahiko just before I left for the game. I had no warning." Kentaro continued the up and down movements of the bar. Michael could see his arms tiring. The bar was unsteady. "How do you deal with your parents?"

"You just do, man." Michael caught the weight bar and took it from Kentaro. "My turn."

The men exchanged places, Kentaro spotting and Michael lying on the bench. Kentaro removed half the weight before Michael attempted to lift it out of the rack.

"Do you know if the television network carried the announcement on the air?" Kentaro asked.

"They were at commercial. I was up in the booth."

"I saw her at the airport and she told me to tell Katsuko that she had won. How did Claire know it?"

"She was at the game." Michael struggled with a tenth rep. "You did not know that?"

"No. But, now that you mention it, I did think I saw her in the crowd when I entered the dugout." Kentaro took the bar from Michael. "I thought I was seeing things, just wishing she were there."

"It was our Claire. Her father called and asked for tickets." Michael sat up on the bench and watched Kentaro move to the leg press machine.

"I can imagine what she thought when she heard the announcement." Kentaro lay on his back, the weight resting on the soles of his feet, his knees bent to almost touch his chest. "I guess she means it this time." He pushed the weight up the tracks, his legs extended powerfully.

"It is time you developed some balls, buddy," Michael resorted to English to express himself in the manner he wished. "You've let Claire and your parents run this show for months. If you want her, you're going to have to take her. You're going to have to stand up to your old man and tell him exactly what you want."

Kentaro snorted, using the explosion of air to help push the weights up again and indicate he understood his friend's words perfectly. The metal slammed hard and a ringing filled the fitness room. Over and over, the long legs extended and slammed the weights home. He grunted and groaned with exertion until he couldn't straighten his legs one more time. He rolled from under the weight apparatus until he lay on his back on the floor.

"You're right," Kentaro continued in English. "Claire and Takahiko have more balls that I have. Did you know Takahiko set me up with Claire in Tokyo when she was there? She gave her the kimono I bought her and helped her put it on. It was the most beautiful sight I ever saw. And I couldn't wait to take it off her."

"This may be more than I want to know. I know Takahiko had asked Audrey to express mail the box to her. She didn't tell her what was in it, just where to find it in your apartment. Audrey picked it up when she went to get the items you asked to be sent. Your sister seemed to know you hadn't given it to her."

"Why did she request the kimono?" Kentaro stared at his friend who again seated on the bench. "She didn't know Claire was coming."

"Beats me. Maybe she hoped if she gave it to you while you were there, you might remember why you asked for it in the first place. Do you remember?"

"I wanted to honor Claire with something she would never be able to give herself. To repay her for the Hana Matsuri doll." Kentaro paused, then said, "Something from my heart."

"Then make sure she knows that. The ball's in your court." Michael played with the towel around his neck.

"Wrong sport." Kentaro grinned at his agent.

"You know what I mean!" Michael snapped a towel at Kentaro's thigh. "Are you through or are you going to put me through more torture?"

"To the showers." Kentaro stood up and led Michael to the locker room. "I have things to do."

The Ikutas planned to remain in Cleveland until the end of the season. Kentaro couldn't understand why they stayed. His father was disgruntled most of the time, and they didn't attend many of the games. Though he wished they'd leave, he couldn't bring himself to order them away. Much to his father's dismay, he did rent an apartment for them.

Kentaro was unable to find either the courage or the time to confront his father. And he couldn't approach Claire until the matter of Katsuko was resolved. So he practiced, played his games, and hid in his bedroom since he couldn't get his family to stay at their apartment except for sleeping.

"I suppose you think you have done a good thing, coming all this way to play a game, but I do not see it, Taro." Kentaro's father muttered to anyone who would listen, but directed his speech to his son. "Your team did not win. At least in Japan, your team endeavored not to lose."

"I am aware of that, Father." Kentaro kept his eyes forward. The family was in the living room of Kentaro's apartment. His mother had made tea which Shigeki had complained about before drinking any of it.

"Then I do not understand why you would wish to do this? They took you out of the game." Shigeki slurped the hot tea loudly. "You obviously do poorly."

"I...must go out." Kentaro stood, claustrophobic. "Feel free to remain. I may not be back until late."

"We must have permission to stay in our son's house?" Shigeki challenged.

"Father," Miyoko put a quieting hand on her husband's arm.

He went back to his tea.

# The Words of the Pitcher

"May I accompany you, Kentaro?" Katsuko came to stand beside him at the door. She helped him into his jacket.

"I do not think so." Katsuko had been taking over more and more of the tasks usually attended to by his mother and, often, Takahiko. It was as if she tried to worm her way into his life without his noticing. He had to stop her before she succeeded.

Katsuko went back to her room as Kentaro left the apartment. Before the elevator arrived, Takahiko trotted down the hall.

"Would you mind me?" she asked.

"I do not know where I am going."

"I do not care." They entered the elevator and left the building.

"Why do you treat Katsu-chan so badly?" Takahiko asked as they walked down the quiet, night-cloaked street.

"I did not realize I was," he prevaricated, knowing full well he was not courteous to the woman designated to be his wife. His hands were stuffed deeply into his jacket pockets, yet he held his head high.

"Well, actually, it is no worse than how Father treats Mother." They spoke Japanese between themselves.

"I was unaware of treating her in any way. I have made sure she has had a pleasant visit, seeing all the sights of Cleveland."

"All well and good, but you have not been with us. Your mind is somewhere else."

"You are correct, little sister." Kentaro led her into Arabica. "Would you care for coffee and maybe a dessert?"

"I would die for a piece of chocolate cheesecake! I missed it when I went back to Tokyo."

Once seated with coffee and cheesecake, she returned the conversation to her brother's treatment of his betrothed.

"Katsuko is not where your mind is." Takahiko put a delicate bite of cheesecake into her mouth as if wanting to savor every morsel.

"And where would you think it is?" Kentaro stirred the sugar and cream into his coffee.

"Claire."

Kentaro's response was his usual nasal snort. He sipped his coffee to avoid his sister's seeing eyes.

"I am right, am I not? You miss her."

"Just as you have missed cheesecake," Kentaro admitted. He folded his long fingers around the white coffee mug, his shoulders hunched over the table. "I do not know what to do about this whole mess."

"I am not sure I can be much help." Takahiko was halfway through with her cheesecake. "I should have talked them out of this trip."

"They would not have listened to you." Kentaro again lifted his mug to his lips.

"It has not been a good year for them. You moved here. Did Mother tell you about Saburo?"

"No. I have not even talked to him since his birthday." Kentaro toyed with the coffee mug, staring out the plate glass window. The sun had disappeared in the time he and his sister had walked and talked. Night was covering the city.

"He moved out of the house and now lives with his girlfriend in Osaka. Father forbids us to speak of him."

"That makes my obedience more priceless. If I defy his wishes with Katsuko, then he will have had two sons abandon him. You will be under more pressure to succeed in pleasing him."

"I have already failed that. Going to university was all right, but studying journalism was not. He does not think my writing is good.  Just like your pitching."  Takahiko worked at mashing the crumbs of cheesecake on the plate onto the back of the fork.

"We are sorry children, *Taka-chan*."

"We are children of the twenty-first century.  We rebel at being held to the traditions of the fifteenth century."

"Interesting argument.  Are you finished or are you going to lick the plate?"  Kentaro smiled at his sister.

"I am finished!"  She dropped the fork with a loud clink.

When Kentaro and Takahiko returned home, the Ikutas left for their apartment.  Kentaro showered and crawled into bed, depleted mentally and physically.  Unable to sleep, he lay in the dark, his hands under his head, and stared at the ceiling. He wondered what Claire was doing.  What she thought about his poor showing in the last game.  His father could berate him all he wished, but only Claire's opinion counted.  His discussion with Michael came to mind.  Michael was right.

Kentaro put his feet on the floor and reached for his jeans.

# Chapter Thirty-three

As Kentaro entered his parents' apartment, he steadied himself for his father's sure-to-come barrage. He knew his parents would be awake as it was not very late. He used his key, the one his mother insisted he keep in case of emergency, to let himself in.

"*Konban wa, Kentaro-san*," Katsuko greeted him in almost old world style. "I am pleased you are here."

Kentaro brushed past her, not surprised to find his betrothed opening his door for him. He found his father watching television. "Good evening, Father."

"Oh, the great baseball player," Shigeki responded from the chair in front of the television.

"Are you watching the sports news, Father?" Kentaro walked to the kitchen and poured himself a liberal portion of Scotch. He noted the level on the bottle was considerably lower than the day before when he had been in the apartment. His father had a large thirst for the favorite whiskey of his contemporaries, Johnny Walker Black, being the most expensive and eagerly sought Scotch in Japan these days. His father would be very well oiled by now. He was tempted to join him, but decided one of them needed a clear head, so he set his drink aside. "I did not think you were interested since you refused to come to the game."

"I watched," his father snorted his reply.

"Were you planning to stay up a while?" Kentaro sat on the couch near Shigeki's chair. "I have something I would like to talk with you about."

"Hmmgh." Shigeki made a noise similar to the one his son affected.

"Takahiko," Kentaro called to his sister.

"Yes?" She came in the room.

"Would you keep Katsuko and Mother occupied?" Kentaro asked. He didn't want to be interrupted in this most delicate of discussions.

"Sure." Takahiko agreed. "How long?" she asked *sotto voce*.

"An hour should decide my fate," Kentaro murmured to his sister.

"You are brave, big brother." Takahiko returned to the back rooms where her friend and mother were.

"What do you wish to talk about, Taro?" Shigeki turned off the television.

"Have you ever," Kentaro gulped, "not done what was expected of you?"

"Hmmm." Shigeki lit another of his many cigarettes. "I could have. Why?" He did not commit himself to admitting his disobedience.

"I am sorry but I will not marry Katsuko." Kentaro blurted it out as if taking a dose of foul tasting medicine.

"You must."

"You are the one who put the contract in motion." Kentaro found it easier to argue now that he had made his first statement. "I did not ask for such."

"It is not for you to decide. Such arrangements must be made by the clearer heads of the older generations," Shigeki argued.

"It may have been for generations prior, but times have changed and so have traditions. So have people."

"Things have not changed that much. Marriages are still arranged by parents."

"Many of my peers have chosen who they married. I wish to do so also." Kentaro searched his memory for the names of schoolmates who had departed from tradition. He couldn't come up with any and hoped his father would not press the point.

"This generation," Shigeki shook his head. "I should have seen this coming. First baseball, then you come to America. Should I expect this American woman to be mentioned next?"

His father's eyes were hard behind the veil of smoke. For the first time, Kentaro noticed how old and drained his father looked. He wished he could take his challenge back, but he couldn't. He wouldn't. He was of age and could make his own decisions. That this news hurt his father was not his fault.

"You have always turned away from your heritage," Shigeki continued. "Do you actually wish to be American?"

"I do not wish to be an American," Kentaro protested.

"Of course you do. You have made a career playing the American pastime, baseball. You eat everything they serve without question, enjoying it. You live in Ohio, only planning short visits to Nagasaki. Admit it, Taro, you wish to be American." Shigeki paused to take a drag from his cigarette.

"I do not wish to be an American. I only wish to have Claire as my wife." Kentaro did not want to think his father was right.

"Then she will make you more of an American," Shigeki pointed out.

"I do not want Claire because she is American. Have you never loved a woman, Father?"

"I suppose I have." Shigeki hung his head and his son knew he had hit a nerve. "There was a girl I fell in love with during the war. But, I was the obedient son and returned home and married the woman your grandfather chose for me years before. Your mother. No matter how customs change, filial obligation will never disappear."

"I have fulfilled my filial obligation many times over." Kentaro felt the heat rising to his face. So many times he'd done what was expected of him, without question. "Do you mean to tell me that, because of ancient obligation to the Son of Heaven, you would pat Saburo on the back and encourage him to step into a Zero strapped with dynamite to ram into a U. S. carrier? Would you sell Takahiko to a geisha broker to pay for our family's debts because it was the custom and her duty to provide for her family?"

"Of course not. Times were different then." He drank deeply from his glass of Scotch. "Our ancestors had difficulty accepting the changes of Meiji and his restorations, but they did not foresee the greater change power hungry militarists would force upon them. Now, so long after the war, we are reaping what was sown."

"I apologize for my actions. It is not out of disrespect that I refuse Katsuko." Kentaro strove to make himself feel better about his defiance.

"I am aware of that. Despite this rebellious nature you have, you are a good son, Taro." Shigeki looked at him as he drew deeply on his finishing cigarette. "I can not allow you to break my word. When you finish this season, you will return to Japan and fulfill your obligation. There will be no further discussion about it."

Shigeki stood laboriously to walk to the bar. Kentaro watched him refill his glass and walk to the back bedroom.

Kentaro sat, dejectedly staring at the bottle of Scotch, trying to find a way to convince his father that marrying Katsuko would be a disaster. And it came to him. Marriage arrangements were made in the past based on what the two families could get in the deal. Money or property was the goal. And woe to the party who did not comply, as he or she would be thrust into abject poverty because of it.

With all the benefits his family had reaped because of his position in professional baseball, Kentaro felt he'd performed his filial obligation. He realized the course he could take to remove his marital obligation to Katsuko. With a more determined set, he went to the room where Takahiko and Katsuko played a game.

He broke into their giggling conversation, "Katsuko-san, may I speak with you?"

"Certainly." Katsuko folded her hands in her lap.

"I will go watch television with Father." Takahiko rushed out of the room.

"What do you wish to talk about, *Kentaro-san*?" Katsuko faced him, innocence written on her round face.

"Our *omiai*." Kentaro closed the bedroom door.

Who...? Claire heard the thunderous pounding at her door. She kicked her feet out from under the quilt and got out of bed, causing her book to fall to the floor. She pulled on a pair of sweatpants over the T-shirt she wore as a nightgown.

"I'm coming!" she called to the person at her door. "Is the building on fire?" She jerked the door open. "Oh, it's you."

She slammed the door and walked away.

"Claire," the door opened and her caller spoke her name. "May I come in?"

"I don't know." Claire sat on the couch, her back to the door. She heard it click and lock, then felt the presence of a body in the room. "What do you want?" She wouldn't even concede to speaking Japanese with him. Let him struggle to make himself understood in English.

"I don't know how to make coffee," Kentaro Ikuta confessed. Claire heard something heavy being set on the table but she didn't turn.

"Do I look like Juan Valdez?" Claire would not allow herself to look at him. If she did, her resolve would collapse. "What do you want?" she repeated.

Kentaro did not speak for long minutes. She knew he was standing near her. If she turned she would probably catch him looking down at her.

"I asked you what you wanted," Claire said through gritted teeth. Her hands balled into fists. She wouldn't look at him, knowing his eyes would cause her to melt.

"*Claire-chan*," Kentaro's voice was soft and open, "I want you."

"No you don't!" She bounded from the couch to confront him. "You don't want me! If you did, she'd be history! You wouldn't keep popping into my life for a quick jump into bed. My heart can stand only so much. I won't let you do this to me anymore. Not this time!"

Hot and angry tears rolled down her face and dripped off her chin. Though her fists were at her side, she wanted to pound Kentaro's chest with them. Through the blur of her tears, she saw his face. The soulful puppy eyes pleaded with hers. His mouth was set in a boyish pout.

"Claire, I never meant to hurt you." He stepped toward her. "I'm sorry."

"No! Stay away from me." Claire backed away. "Leave me alone. You have her! What do you need me for?"

"I love you, not her," Kentaro answered. "I'll do whatever you ask. Say the word and I'll leave."

Claire glared at Kentaro. Every inch of her heart said 'stay' but her mind tried to force 'leave' to her lips. She uttered a strange and garbled sound

"Kentaro," she managed after a gulp of air. "I want you to..."

"Say it, Claire. Say the word."

Kentaro stepped closer to her. He was so near, all she had to do was fall into his arms. She wouldn't give him the satisfaction.

"English! Japanese!" Kentaro shouted, his hand on her arm. "Either one, I'll understand. Just say it!"

Dumbfounded, Claire's eyes searched his. The tears fell in great waves of hurt.

"I... can't!" she wailed. She jerked her arm free and fled to the kitchen.

Claire stood alone, trembling. Her muscles spasmed as she sobbed, her face hidden in a cup towel. Over the half-wall separating the kitchen from the living room of her small apartment, she knew Kentaro could see her, but she wouldn't give him the satisfaction of hearing her cry.

Emotions collided within her. Her heart burdened with so much confusion threatened to explode. She wanted him to stay and to go. To be there in the morning for the rest of her life. To disappear from her life. Finally able to dam back her tears, she dried her face and took a deep breath. She stopped shaking.

He wanted coffee. She'd give him coffee.

Filling the glass pot, she turned to the coffee machine on the counter. Her back to Kentaro, she felt the heat of his body. Claire had a surge of desire. She needed to climb into his arms and lie next to his chest for comfort. No. He had deliberately broken her heart. He had ripped it out and stomped on it. He'd done it three times before; she would not allow him to do it a fourth time. He would find no sort of comfort here.

Claire scooped coffee grounds into the paper lined basket and set the machine to brewing.

Kentaro was nearer.

"Claire." His words were so close, his breath was on her hair. "Are you finished with your fit?"

Afraid to move, Claire sighed, scared she would rush into his arms. The desire was so strong it hurt.

"I have something for you." Kentaro's arms snaked around her waist.

Claire forgot all the anger. The only place she wanted to be was in his embrace. "Other than this?" Claire pushed her hips back into his pelvis. The swell of his manhood was evident.

"Yes."

Extending his arm, Kentaro opened his palm for Claire to see. He held a small rolled scroll tied with a red ribbon. Claire picked it up and slipped the ribbon off. The unrolled paper exposed small characters of Japanese *kana*, filling the rectangle lengthwise. As she worked at translating the words, Kentaro's cheek, rough with beard, caressed her neck, his face hidden in the hair at her neck.

Claire relaxed in his embrace. "Is this what I think it is?"

"It is my turn to be the teacher. What does your translation tell you it is?" Kentaro's lips moved next to her neck as he spoke.

"A dissolution of your *omiai*." Claire told him. "Signed by Katsuko."

"That's exactly what it is. I have signed it also." Kentaro kissed her cheek. "You win. I'm yours, if you'll have me."

For a moment, her arms held his arms around her midriff, the scroll crushed in her hand. Then Claire turned in his embrace and began to kiss his eager lips.

"I do want you, Kentaro! Oh, God, do I!" Claire's words were mixed with sighs but they were understood.

# Chapter Thirty-four

Lovemaking had been long and slow, resulting in a burst of emotion and fire. The couple lingered in a passionate embrace, the ultimate release complete, yet they continued with the stroking caresses and kissing of foreplay. When their heart beats returned to normal, Kentaro left the warm bed. Claire lay listening to him make noises in the other parts of the apartment. He returned to lift her out of the bed and carry her into the bathroom. There, with lighted candles all around, he placed her in a warm bubble bath and stepped in behind her. On the wooden stool at the tub's side sat a flask and two small cups.

"*Sake*," he explained, "to celebrate our own *omiai*." He handed Claire a cup of the stout rice wine and picked up his own. "*Banzai*," he said gently.

"*Banzai*," Claire repeated and they drank.

Claire sat back into Kentaro, thankful for the old large tub, so deep and sturdy. As they sipped *sake*, Kentaro's long fingers ran the length of Claire's body. Her eyes half-closed in satisfaction. He tormented her by drizzling warm water over her breasts and shoulders. She snuggled further back to him, her face beside his.

"I want you at the opening of the World Series," he announced. It seemed as though English had become their primary language. "I want you back at your job. Martella-san is working to arrange that. The first game's in Denver."

"I watched the play-offs." Claire held her cup out for Kentaro to pour more *sake*. "They didn't play you much."

"They didn't need me. I need you." Kentaro nuzzled her neck. "Can I count on you?"

"Only if I'm the only woman in your life. Other than your mother and Takahiko."

"You put some hard demands on a samurai."

"Really?" Claire wiggled her bottom against his growing passion. "Is that what you mean?"

Kentaro snorted and Claire turned to face him. His hands smoothed over her lower back to stroke her buttocks and pull her closer to his midsection. She sighed, mewing like a kitten as he kissed her. His tongue glided over her throat and the firm breasts she offered him as she wrapped her legs around his waist. Beneath the soapy water, Kentaro guided his throbbing hardness up into her. Soon water flooded over the side as they rocked with feverish energy.

"Tickets to the game will be at the desk of the hotel for you in Denver," Kentaro said over breakfast the next morning.

"What about the Chiefs? They don't want me there." Claire ravenously ate the scrambled eggs and bacon she had prepared for them.

"I don't care what they want. I want you there. Be there." Kentaro pointed his fork at her.

"Oh, forceful samurai." Claire feigned fear as she smiled at him.

"No. Lovesick samurai." Kentaro returned her smile. "I'll meet you after the game. Now, I have to go." He took the last bite of his food. "I have to take some people to the airport."

"Anybody I know?" Claire asked.

"You've only met one of them." Kentaro returned to the table after placing his dishes in the sink. He kissed the top of Claire's head. "I'll leave you the rest of the *sake*." He put his hand on the paper-wrapped wine bottle resting on the counter.

"Oh, thank you. I'm not a very good drinker."

"You don't look like you're hung over."

"Maybe I just can't drink beer." Claire put her empty plate in the sink. "I must be a *sake* drinker."

"You didn't have that much then." Kentaro hugged her. "Meet you in Denver."

"I'll be there."

They exchanged a lingering kiss and then Kentaro left her apartment.

❦

Claire entered Coors Stadium sanctioned by at least one member of the Chiefs. Although the ticket to the first game of the World Series was next to a very heavy, sweaty man, she didn't care. Kentaro was back in her life and she couldn't see anything beyond that.

For eight innings, Kentaro's pitching was precise and accurate. The Colorado Rockies did not get a single hit. The announcer worsened the pressure by pointing out how hard it was to pitch a no-hitter, especially in this stadium with its altitude. As Kentaro performed his windup, Claire sat, tense. He didn't bat an eyelash as he methodically pitched three more times for the final out.

It was over. Kentaro was carried off the field on the shoulders of his jubilant teammates. Though Claire jumped up and down, screaming and shrieking, she didn't miss Kentaro's smile when he looked her way. As the team disappeared into the dugout, Claire eased back into her seat. Dying to rush out and tell him how wonderful he was, she couldn't because she was banished from the shower room.

Claire picked up her purse and merged with the crowd leaving the stadium.

∽

A delicate arrangement of two roses awaited Claire in her room...in Kentaro's hand.

"How did you get in here?" She took the flowers and put them beneath her nose.

"I told the desk clerk I wanted the key to my sister's room." Kentaro sat in the chair next to the bed.

"Aren't you the sneaky one?"

"At times." Kentaro brushed his hand sensuously against Claire's thigh as she stood before him. Claire took the hand and kissed his fingers.

"Do you want to get something to eat?" Kentaro offered.

"I'm full of popcorn." Claire sat down on the edge of the bed. "And the thrill of your no-hitter!"

"Then let's go for a walk." Kentaro stood. Their hands separated.

"But the paparazzi? How can we get past them?"

"You'll think of a way."

∽

Kentaro and Claire moved through the busy lobby unnoticed. They huddled together looking to all the world like the lovers they truly were. Chiefs baseball caps covered their hair, the bills pulled low over their faces. Claire wore jeans topped with a suede jacket and Kentaro's form was hidden by his long, woolen, black overcoat. As they clung to one another, their heads close, they escaped out the rear entrance.

"Success," Claire announced as they came to the corner of the block where their hotel sat.

"My hat's off to you."

"Here let me." Claire plucked the cap from Kentaro's head. Freed from the cap, the luxuriant mass of midnight cascaded over his shoulders. Her fingers ran through it, flouncing it away from his head. "There. Much better."

"I'm glad you like it." Kentaro reset the cap on his head.

They resumed their walk. Claire was warmed by the feel of his fingers laced with hers. A simple gesture done so publicly became greater. They spoke little, each content with the solitude. A wind cold and crisp with the hint of snow blew through Denver's quiet streets. A full moon illuminated the night. At the corner of a street, Kentaro guided Claire into a convenience store. There, they purchased hot chocolate for Claire and, for Kentaro, a bottle of water. They resumed their walk, coming back to the hotel over an hour later.

"I'll see you in Cleveland," Kentaro said as Claire recaptured his hair beneath the cap.

"It'll be an eternity." She snuggled against his chest, her arms beneath his heavy coat.

"Yes, it'll seem so." Kentaro held her.

"*Oyasumi.*"

"Good night."

The lovers parted. They didn't wish to risk being caught a second time. It would tempt fate too greatly.

The Chiefs won the second game of the Series, then returned to Cleveland for the next two games. Four hours after she arrived home, Claire had a visitor at her apartment.

"Hello, Steve," she greeted the pitching coach. "Come in."

"I'm surprised you'd see me." Steve Martella entered and sat on the couch.

"Things have a way of changing. I'm about to have coffee. Want some?"

"Yes, thank you, if it's not too much trouble." He waited until Claire returned to the room. "I came to apologize."

Claire set a cup of coffee in front of him on the table and took her seat across from him. "Lots of that going around." Claire sipped her coffee and waited.

"I should've said something...that day. But I couldn't." Steve held his cup with both hands, his back relaxed into the couch.

"Steve, I know you felt you had to do what was best for the team and the bottom line. I was concerned about Kentaro."

"I had your concern, too. I was afraid it would upset his form and it has, to some degree. That's why I went to bat for you."

"Kentaro told me you were trying to get me back to translate," Claire admitted. "Even if I don't get to, everything's worked out."

"I noticed." Steve grinned at her. "You two fooled everyone in the hotel the other night."

"But not you?"

"Nope. Clever idea of hiding Kentaro's hair, a stroke of genius. Most of the media recognize him by it alone."

"Well." Claire shrugged her shoulders. She fingered the gold chain around her neck with the inch-long gold cross. Although she had returned it to him in her anger, Kentaro had left it under the pillow for her to find when she went to bed after their secret walk in Denver.

"Down to business. I spoke with Jamison and Horsch and they've agreed. They're more concerned with the World Series now than anything else, so they barely noticed my bringing it up." Steve reached into his pocket. "Here're your credentials back."

Claire took the envelope, a familiar feel to it.

"I'm rehired?"

"Not actually. You'll be in the dugout and at press conferences in case Kentaro has a problem. He's agreed to speak with the press himself. In fact, he has already. You did a great job."

"Kentaro's the one who's worked hard," Claire commented.

"Will you be there?"

"Do you have a doubt that I won't?"

# Chapter Thirty-five

Kentaro Ikuta entered Jacobs Field to practice for the sixth game of the World Series. His spirits were high, more excited for the start of a game than he had been in some time. Everything was falling into place. He was playing in the American baseball league, actually becoming a star in professional ball as he had been in Japan. He didn't pursue that thought, uncomfortable with the egotistical leaning. He would rather think about Claire. She was with him now, as close to him as anyone in his life.

His good spirits were dashed by the presence of Jason Stewart in the spacious lobby of Jacobs Field. "I would speak with you," Kentaro snarled at the young man.

"I don't want to talk with you," Jason retorted as he moved away.

"Come." Kentaro read fear and panic on his face. He put his hand on the young man's arm and steered Jason to the men's room.

The power of his touch, although gentle, did not allow Jason to do anything but what Kentaro wished. Once inside, Kentaro released him and turned his back to Jason to lock the door. When he faced Jason again, he was met by the man's fist. It struck him across the left side of his face. As his head whipped to the right, Kentaro felt the cut of Jason's university ring across his cheekbone, As he brought his face back forward, he saw the movement of Jason's right arm. Without thought, Kentaro clasped Jason's wrist and whirled him around, his face hard against the wall and his body crushed by Kentaro's as the baseball player yanked Jason's arm up toward the middle of his back.

"Perhaps I should manhandle you as you did her," Kentaro growled his suggestion. "But it would not be the same. Listen closely. You have no need to be here, so you'll leave and cease your harassment of Claire. If you must attack someone," Kentaro pulled his arm harder, "make it me. Do you understand?"

"Yes," Jason choked.

Kentaro released him and stepped back a few inches. "Also, don't think you can get much sympathy from anyone about this. I believe you threw the first punch. I'm sure your probation officer will be fascinated with the information. It's my guess you would not survive well in prison."

Kentaro watched as Jason sagged on weak knees. "What are you waiting for?" Kentaro snarled. He unlocked the door, then moved back toward the row of sinks. "Go."

Jason straightened his suit coat and the knot of his tie. He tried to look confident as he ran trembling fingers through his hair. Kentaro tried not to smile as he noticed Jason's halting steps and the tremors in the hand that reached for the door.

Kentaro idled in the restroom to give Jason time to escape the stadium. He washed his hands, then dabbed at the bleeding cut on his face with a wet paper towel. A dark bruise was rising. He would manage to have some sort of baseball injury to give him an alibi for it.

Claire resumed her place in the dugout for the sixth game of the World Series. She was greeted by Kentaro's teammates as if it were a family reunion.

"Not going very well," Claire stated. The Chiefs had lost the third and fourth games, and won the fifth, making the Series three to two.

"No, not at all." Kentaro was at her side, not scheduled to play. His jacket was on, firmly zipped.

"Steve," Claire spoke to the pitching coach who stood nearby, "why aren't you playing Kentaro?"

"Can't. If this goes to a seventh, we'll really need him then," Steve explained. "I'm not sure he'd be much help today. You should have seen him take that hit while fielding fly balls." Turning to Kentaro, he said, "I don't even know why you were out there doing that."

"That's nasty, Kentaro." Claire turned and put her fingers on the bruised, cut cheek with a tender touch. They had yet to dress the injury. Kentaro cut her off each time she tried.

"It is not as bad as it looks." Kentaro tried to move out of her reach. The ball he had put his face beneath looked worse than it was, but it connected enough to give him an viable story.

"Enjoy sitting this one out." Steve walked toward the opening of the dugout. "You'll be on the spot next game." He left Claire and Kentaro alone.

"I wish this were over," Claire lamented. She slid down in her seat.

"You do not like losing, *Claire-chan*?" Kentaro addressed her Japanese even though they spoke English more often now.

"No." Her arms were tight across her chest. "I really want this to be over so we get on with us."

"Patience." Kentaro's hand on her thigh increased its affectionate pressure.

"*Shizuka ni nara.*" Claire grinned at him and took his hand in hers.

The game ended thirty minutes later, and a dejected Chiefs team moved to the locker room.

"I'll meet you in our classroom," Kentaro said as he and Claire stood in the hallway outside the showers.

"I'll wait patiently." Claire left the hallway.

"No you won't," she heard Kentaro comment.

"Shall we risk a dinner at Sterle's?" Kentaro asked as he and Claire walked to the parking lot. "I don't think the press cares about us anymore."

"I guess we could." Claire noticed they now spoke English more often in private, reserving Japanese for the stadium, as if they didn't want anyone else in their world. She opened the door of her Mustang. "What is this?"

"Why do you not open it?" Kentaro was sitting in the passenger seat but a large white box blocked her seat.

Claire tore at the carton and found her kimono.

"Oh, Taro," she sighed. She sagged limply into her seat. "I'm sorry."

"Forget it, *Claire-chan*." Kentaro put his hand at the back of her neck. "I wanted you to have it. It's yours no matter what happens between us."

"But it's so expensive." Claire protested.

"You're worth it." With pressure on her neck, Kentaro pulled her to him for a kiss. "Now, I'm hungry."

Claire put the kimono in the back seat and started the car.

"How do you think the game in Denver will be?" Claire asked Kentaro over their dinner at Sterle's.

"It'll be fine. We don't need to talk about it. This night's for us. We're celebrating being out of the media spotlight."

"I don't understand what happened," Claire admitted. "Schaeffer stopped writing about us so abruptly."

"Don't question karma." Kentaro sipped his wine.

"Now you're the inscrutable samurai." Claire eyed him. "You had something to do with it, didn't you?"

Kentaro made his noise and shrugged his shoulders.

"You did!" Claire began speculating. "He hit you!"

"No, he didn't hit me." Kentaro again snorted.

"But someone did, didn't they?" Claire continued. "I don't believe you got hit by a baseball. You're a pitcher, for goodness *sake*!"

"I did get hit with a ball."

"Kentaro," she strung out his name accusingly.

"After Jason hit me," Kentaro admitted.

"Jason? He hit you? When, where?"

Kentaro filled her in on the occurrence quickly.

"Such a brave samurai." Claire reached across the table and stroked his wounded cheek. "I love you so much."

"And I love you also." Kentaro took her hand.

"Then win the next game for me."

"I will do my best. A tied Series is very stressful. Especially in their stadium."

# Chapter Thirty-six

It had come down to the seventh game of the World Series at Coors Stadium. Coaches and players were tense, all anxious about the outcome. Before the night was over, careers would be made or broken; million dollar contracts written or torn up; bonuses inked or erased.

In the locker room, the Cleveland Chiefs suited out. Kentaro sat on the bench, his torso bare, taking off his shoes and socks. He stood, unzipped his jeans and absently rolled them down his slender hips, thinking about his pitching game. Mentally, as he dressed in the snug uniform, he worked his way through wind-up to release of the ball. He could almost hear the ball as it thudded into the catcher's mitt.

"How's it going?" Steve Martella came up behind him.

"All right," Kentaro answered. He tucked the jersey into his pants. "And you?"

"Just fine. You know you're starting, right?" Steve leaned against the locker next to Kentaro's.

"Yes." Kentaro fastened the web belt around his waist.

"Seen Claire?" Steve pretended to read the lineup on the clipboard he carried.

"She's in the dugout." Kentaro pulled his lengthy hair back and wrapped a band around it at the nape.

"She's a great kid. Anything happening in that direction?" He still pretended.

"You might say so." Kentaro adjusted his cap over his head. "I'll let you know."

"Be sure to. You know, she's become like a kid sister to a lot of us." Steve and Kentaro began to walk toward the field.

Claire's stomach ached and her nerves were on edge. She couldn't do anything to help the Chiefs win this game, and it rattled her. She sat at the front of the dugout, leaning forward with her hands under her thighs, her feet swinging wildly. Out on the field along the baseline, Kentaro warmed up with the catcher. The loud and lively crowd screamed for the Rockies and against the Chiefs. Banners around the outfield proclaimed their support. Kentaro's shutout of their team in the last visit here was prominently on their minds.

Claire stood up and paced the front of the dugout.

"You act as if you're playing," Steve greeted her.

"I'm scared," Claire admitted.

"Why? You've done your job perfectly. I'm the one responsible for his pitching."

"I don't want him to fail. I don't want any of them to."

"He'll do fine, 'Mother,'" Steve teased.

Claire sat down again.

Game opening rituals began. "The Star-Spangled Banner," sung by a favorite pop star, was followed by the ceremonial first pitch. Then the teams took the field. The Chiefs were batting first. This left Kentaro with Claire.

"Martella-san tells me you are nervous as a cat." He changed back to Japanese for dugout talk with Claire.

"I am crawling out of my skin!" Claire laughed. "How do you stay so calm?"

"Who says I am calm? I am inscrutable." Kentaro grinned in her direction.

"You make me sick!" Claire sagged back against the chair, her legs extended in front of her.

"Pati..."

"Don't even think it!" Claire silenced him. "I'm as patient as I'm going to get. Now get out there and put this inning away."

"Yes, ma'am." Kentaro joined his teammates in changing places with the offense.

Both teams were hitless for the first three innings, then the Chiefs scored two runs. Kentaro's pitching was not flawless, but the runners never made it into home. In the fourth, he began to throw poorly. Steve approached him on the mound.

"You okay?" he asked. The catcher joined them.

Kentaro took his cap off and wiped his forehead.

"I'll be fine."

"I'll take your word for it. Finish this inning, but if you're still having trouble, I'm pulling you." The coach and the catcher went back to their places.

"Are you going to pull him?" Claire asked Steve as he stood at the mouth of the concrete room.

"Sit down, Claire, this is my business."

Claire sat, trying not to be offended at Steve's remark, but she understood. This was not her business and the outcome of the game was extremely important.

Kentaro responded positively to Steve's words. He brought the inning to a close by putting the ball over the plate with precision for the next two batters.     He was his usual quiet self as he took his seat beside Claire who had moved to the back of the dugout. She gave him a cup of Gatorade, their game customs moving as if never interrupted. She didn't say anything to him, comfortable with his silence.

The sixth inning showed improved pitching, Kentaro's control perfect. He threw the runner out at first and allowed only two hits.   The seventh and eight innings continued uneventfully. The offensive side of the team kept up their end, making four runs, which put the Chiefs in the lead.

# The Words of the Pitcher

It came down to the ninth inning.

Kentaro stood on the mound with a stoic persona as he faced the third batter at the bottom of the ninth. No one watching could realize he felt his heart pound against his hand as he held the ball in his glove close to his chest. He took a deep breath, hoping to still the thumping organ. It didn't help. He focused his eyes on the batter who stood ready, the wooden bat held over his shoulder. It was time to move.

Kentaro turned his back to home plate, avoiding the view of the dugout because he was so conscious of Claire's being. He didn't know whether the pressure of the game was causing him to sweat or the knowledge she was watching his every move. He could smell the oil from the leather glove held under his chin. Another deep breath and he whirled and hurled the ball with all the expertise of his years of training.

The batter moved. The bat swung with intense power toward the spherical object hurling his way.

"Steerike two!" the umpire shouted.

Kentaro allowed himself a simple, quiet smile while he looked down at the ground, kicking the rubber of the pitcher's mound. Vasquez returned the ball and Kentaro started the procedure again.

"Ball three!" the umpire announced with this pitch.

It was a full count, two strikes, three balls. A runner on second. The score seven to six. Now the pressure increased. Kentaro sighed.

The whirl of his pitching style came automatically and Kentaro found his body extended toward the plate, his right arm coming back to his body. He watched the batter connect with the ball. It moved back toward him on the mound, falling from a high arc. He responded with instinctive training. He moved up and under the ball as it dropped from the zenith. It plopped into his glove with a resounding thud.

The second out. Only one to go. Kentaro returned to the mound and steadied his nerves for the last out of the final game of the World Series and the end of his first season of American major league baseball. So much of his life had changed in the brief season. Traditions fallen or cast aside, changed by baseball and Claire Ferris. He felt an anxiety he rarely experienced begin to brew inside him. A glance to the dugout gave him a tightness in his stomach. Claire sat on the edge of her seat, chewing a finger. He forced himself to think of the game.

Kentaro pitched the first ball and the batter swung. A strike. As he began to throw a second ball, a movement at second base caught his eye—the runner was trying to steal third. Instead of releasing the ball toward home plate, Kentaro let fly in the direction of the third baseman who tagged the runner out.

The Cleveland Chiefs had won the World Series.

In the dugout, Claire shouted, jumped out of her seat, and grabbed the bat girl standing next to her. She released her when she heard the prepubescent's scream so like her own. Claire wrapped her arms around her midriff to keep from acting in a manner Kentaro would not appreciate, although the very thing she wanted to do was to rush out onto the diamond and grab him. She watched as his teammates did what she wanted to.

The players remaining in the dugout exploded onto the field to join the group celebrating with their pitcher. In the middle of the field, Kentaro was hoisted onto the jubilant shoulders of his teammates and carried toward the dugout. Claire was surprised to see a grin spreading over his face. Behind her, she heard the popping of champagne corks and then felt the spray on her face as the effervescent spew of wine filled the small concrete room.

The players arrived, careful to deposit Kentaro on the ground before his head collided with the roof of the dugout. Now the champagne poured like a waterfall into paper cups and over the heads of the Chiefs' players. Some players even shook the large bottles of wine to cause the geysers. Claire came in for her own share of dousing when Kentaro neared her.

"You did it!" Claire surpressed the urge to grab him. He would not want such a display of emotion.

"We did it!" Kentaro did grab her.

"You were so great!" Claire held on to his neck and restrained herself from kissing him.

"I couldn't have done it without you, *Claire-chan*." Kentaro lowered her to the floor.

"Great game, guys! Great game!" Steve Martella shouted toward the players, who were celebrating uproariously. Claire didn't think anyone heard him. "Kentaro, your play was perfect! The pop-up catch was outstanding. Maybe that practice of catching flies was worth the casualty of your face!"

"Well, I suppose." Kentaro ducked his head, embarrassed both by the praise and the secret knowledge of why he was out catching fly balls in the first place.

"All right! World champions! Yeah! Let's hit the showers, the press awaits." Steve left Kentaro and Claire to herd his players along to the next stage of the World Series.

"Do you want me to meet you in the pressroom?" Claire stood at Kentaro's side, her arm around his waist, his over her shoulders.

"Yes, but only as an observer." Kentaro kissed her head and moved away.

"Very well." Claire walked with him to the locker room, entering the family area while he went to shower.

"Ms. Ferris?" one of the security guards spoke her name.

"Yes?" Claire turned her face to him.

"Coach Martella sent me to get you. The team's meeting the press in the locker room. They want you there."

Claire joined the team inside the showers.

She had a flash of memory. Nine months ago, this world of men, locker rooms, and ball players had scared her. Now, it was second nature to be surrounded by the sweat and testosterone. She moved unabashedly through crowds of male bodies in many stages of dress. The press was everywhere as she made her way toward Kentaro. Many of the team, like Kentaro, had not yet showered and the room reeked of male bodies and the sparkling wine.

She found Kentaro standing before his locker, his jersey unbuttoned. It hung open to expose his hard-muscled chest, so like the first day when she had seen him changing clothes for practice. His hair was still bound, but tendrils escaped to fall over his forehead. Claire was very aware of the moment his exotic dark eyes caught hers. She smiled as his hand extended toward her through the mass of bodies.

"Please, make way for *Ferris-san*. This is her day also," he said. The television reporters parted and the minicams trained on her as she came to Kentaro's side.

"Are you here to interpret, Ms. Ferris?" the ABC network sportscaster asked.

"No. I'm here as..." Claire looked at Kentaro whose gaze was on her, full of his love. "As a friend." His hand, dangling at his side close to hers, now closed around her fingers.

Claire felt at home as the reporters went to work, asking Kentaro more questions. The questions were familiarly redundant.

How did it feel to pitch the winning game?

Did he have any plans when he started the game?

What were his plans now?

At this question, Kentaro cleared his throat and his eyes searched Claire's face.

"My plans are to return to Nagasaki and marry my 'words.'"

"Excuse me? Marry your 'words'? What do you mean?" the ESPN sportscaster asked. All the reporters had a confused look on their faces. "Ms. Ferris, can you interpret what he said?"

Claire, too, was bewildered. She had stopped listening to the questions and answers until Kentaro had said the word 'marry.'

"I'm...not sure what...*Ikuta-san* means," she stammered. She slipped back into Japanese. "Is this a marriage proposal, samurai?"

In front of all the reporters, the reserved pitcher turned to Claire and put his arms around her. Still speaking their shared language, he said, "Yes. I love you. And want you with me. Always. Not speaking my words. Being my wife."

Claire rose on her tiptoes to kiss him, the act filmed and broadcast to the world.

"I accept. I love you so much." His body, so close to hers, was familiar with its after-game smells.

"Ms. Ferris? Remember us?" The ESPN reporter pressed for information, although the press corps surely knew what had transpired.

Claire turned her face to the press.

"This is my last act as interpreter." The reporters laughed along with Claire. "*Ikuta-san* has asked me to marry him and I have accepted."

The locker room crowd of reporters, film crews, coaches, management, and his fellow baseball players responded with shouts and applause. Then the media remembered the real reason they were assembled. They again directed questions to Kentaro about his pitching. Claire drifted to the background to watch.

With great pride, she observed her student speaking the words she had worked so hard to teach him. Kentaro didn't need her for translations. He needed her as his partner, his lover, his wife. She realized she would no longer be the 'words of the pitcher.' She was now the 'heart of the pitcher.'

## ONLY ONE OF THEM COULD RULE
## FORTUNE INTERNATIONAL . . .

### CHRISTINA FORTUNE

Twenty years ago the pretty young heiress disappeared and was presumed dead. Now a woman who says she's Christina has surfaced, hoping to claim the power and privilege that was Christina's birthright. She faces the Fortunes with an astounding knowledge of Christina's life—every memory, every tragedy. And she wears a priceless heirloom that reaches to the core of the Fortune family's darkest secrets.

### RICHARD FORTUNE

His niece Christina was the only obstacle to his taking complete control of Fortune International. Now the raw power that has eluded him for so long is almost in his hands. He simply has to prove this arrogant woman a fraud—or stop her any way he can.

### ROSS McKENNA

The handsome, ruthless CEO of Fortune International, he faced Christina as an adversary, searching for the missing link to prove her an impostor. But as passion sparked between them, he found himself wanting her—and wanting to believe in her—against all reason.

### KATHERINE FORTUNE

Christina's grandmother made a public ceremony of welcoming her granddaughter home again. But behind closed doors the indomitable matriarch would show her true colors—and prove she'd stop at nothing to protect the family fortune.

### *FORTUNE'S CHILD*

Bantam Books by
Pamela Simpson

PARTNERS IN TIME

FORTUNE'S CHILD

# *Fortune's Child*

## PAMELA
## SIMPSON

**BANTAM BOOKS**

NEW YORK · TORONTO · LONDON · SYDNEY · AUCKLAND

FORTUNE'S CHILD

A Bantam Fanfare Book / May 1992

ISBN 0-553-29424-5

Published simultaneously in the United States and Canada

PRINTED IN THE UNITED STATES OF AMERICA

OPM   0   9   8   7   6   5   4   3   2   1

# Chapter 1

September 18, 1990
San Francisco

*S*omeday I'll come back. I'll find out who did this to me,
and I'll make him pay.

The words, scrawled in the diary of a fifteen-year-old girl,
were as crystal clear in the woman's memory as if she were
looking at them now. As she stood on the sidewalk, staring up
at the stark, impressive facade of the massive Fortune Tower
building, she thought, It's taken twenty years, and I've waited
until the last day, the last hour, the last minute, but I'm finally
here. And I'm going to keep that promise.

She was filled with a sense of urgency so razor sharp, she
could barely control the excitement racing through her. She
had been waiting for this moment, preparing for it, for her entire adult life. Now that it had come, she was both frightened
and exhilarated. She had no idea what would happen when
she walked into that building. She knew only that at last, for
better or for worse, the past would be laid to rest.

But despite her determination to get on with it, she was reluctant to enter the massive building that was so intimidating.
Fortune Tower, Embarcadero Center, in the heart of San
Francisco, rose thirty-six stories into the crystal clear morning
sky, a huge, dark monolith dwarfing the pale granite and con-

crete buildings that surrounded it. It stood invincible like the public image of the powerful family whose name it bore.

As the woman thought of that family, her face was transformed by an expression of determination that emphasized her prominent cheekbones, large, dark brown eyes, and a full mouth that curved upward slightly at the corners. That mouth would get her in trouble one day, she had been warned when she was thirteen. And it had.

She forced herself to walk toward the huge doors, passing a flower kiosk in the center of the plaza in front of the building. Bouquets of roses, carnations, chrysanthemums, and baby's breath filled dozens of containers. The vendor extended a red rose to her, but she shook her head and continued walking toward the building. It loomed over her in the bright morning light, the sun reflecting off the bronzed glass windows.

*It was dark that other night, the sky void of any moon or stars . . .*

A faint, tangy breeze off the bay stirred a wisp of fine, chestnut hair against her cheek.

*There was no breeze that night. It was achingly cold and completely still, except for the ominous sound of footsteps closing in on them . . .*

The sidewalk was filled with dressed-for-success executives on their way to meetings, uniformed messengers, and the assorted odd street people that big cities like San Francisco were known for.

*There wasn't anyone to help them . . .*

The laughter of two passing girls surrounded her, then faded as they disappeared into the crowd.

*She heard only the haunting wail of sirens that cut through the cold darkness . . .*

Her gloved fingers locked around the handle of her eelskin attaché case as she passed the huge sculpture of an anchor and reached the bronzed glass doors of Fortune Tower.

She saw her image in the glass door, a tall, slender figure in a conservative, dove gray suit. As she swung the door open, an exact duplicate was reflected against the bronzed windows—dual images, reminding her of two fifteen-year-old girls who bore such a striking resemblance to one another.

*"You have to live for both of us."*

The urgent words reverberated in her mind. Even after all these years she hadn't forgotten the sound of them, spoken in a tremulous whisper. The door closed behind her, but the words remained fixed in her mind as she walked to the wall of brass-doored elevators.

Despite the fear that made her mouth go dry, she stepped into the elevator. She had promises to keep.

The elevator doors whispered open on the eighteenth floor. Plush pewter-colored carpet muffled her footsteps as she crossed the foyer toward the receptionist's desk to the right. She knew from reading a private detective's detailed report that the executive offices and the boardroom were down the hall to the left. She smiled coolly at the receptionist, and in one fluid movement sidestepped the young woman.

"May I help you?" the receptionist called after her, hurriedly coming out from behind her desk.

The large teak double doors to the boardroom were at the end of the hallway. With measured steps the woman crossed the black-marbled entry. For just a moment her hand hesitated on the brass door handle, as a wave of nervousness washed over her.

Brass and teak. They were hallmarks of the company's history in the shipping business, a history that went back over one hundred fifty years to the time of multi-sailed schooners and clipper ships. But today those doors signified something else—they were doors to the past.

From beyond the doors she heard a muffled exchange of voices.

The receptionist's irritated voice sounded behind her. "You can't go in there. They're having a board meeting."

The woman took a deep breath and swallowed against the sudden tightness in her throat. Just as the receptionist reached her, she pushed down on the door handle with cool determination and stepped into the boardroom.

The contemporary conference table, mahogany inlaid with black jade from the Orient, filled the center of the room. At the head of the table a massive mahogany and leather chair was occupied by the president of the company, Richard Fortune. A dozen leather and brass Gunlocke chairs rimmed the table's jagged perimeter. In six of them sat the members of the Fortune family who composed the board of directors. Ross McKenna, Chief Executive Officer, sat in the seventh.

As she entered the boardroom with the frantic receptionist hot on her heels, everyone looked up in surprise.

"I'm sorry, Mr. Fortune," the receptionist apologized. "Miss, you'll have to leave. This is a private meeting—"

"For members of the board," the woman finished, using every ounce of self-control she possessed to keep her fear from showing. She turned back to the assembled board. "I understand the meeting is to begin at ten o'clock. It's exactly that time now."

They were all amazed at her cool presumption. Everyone except Ross McKenna, whose expression of surprise had quickly turned to thoughtfulness. His eyes narrowed as he watched her with faintly amused curiosity. He was the only one who sat back in his chair, seemingly relaxed. But she knew that his air of calm must be deceptive. He had to be as confused as the others at this unexpected interruption. He was just better at hiding his confusion.

"Oh, for heaven's sake, get rid of her so we can get on with this!" a sleekly dressed, middle-aged woman—the only woman at the table—muttered to the receptionist.

Richard Fortune glared at her. "This is a closed meeting. Miss Bennett, escort her outside."

"That won't be necessary, Miss Bennett," the woman said as she laid her attaché case down on the conference table.

Then she turned back to the circle of people.

"My name is Christina Grant Fortune. Today is my thirty-fifth birthday, and I've come to claim my inheritance."

# Chapter 2

Complete silence engulfed the boardroom.

Christina had imagined this moment a thousand times, wondering what their reactions would be—surprise, outrage, furious shouts of denial. Now she saw expression ranging from disbelief to irritation to outright anger.

Sharp, feminine laughter broke the momentary silence. "I suppose we should have known there'd be at least one more person claiming to be Christina at the eleventh hour," Diana Fortune said, rising from her chair.

She crossed to the far wall, where glass panels reflected the images of the people at the table. At a light touch one of the panels receded, exposing a fully stocked bar. She poured herself a drink. "But you're too late, my dear." She raised her glass as if to toast her. "Although I will admit you've got a bit more style than the others."

She was just about to drink when Richard spoke in a sharp tone that betrayed his annoyance. "Sit down, Diana. At least wait until after lunch to begin the cocktail hour."

Uncle Richard. My primary adversary, Christina thought. Everything about him was perfect—the conservatively tailored suit he wore with ease, his gray-flecked brown hair with not a strand out of place, the deeply tanned skin that suggested tennis or perhaps the family passion for sailing, and the buffed sheen of manicured nails.

The name, the social position, the money, he had it all—except for the power. That had eluded him all his adult life. Until today. Once Christina's shares in the company were distributed among the rest of the family, Richard would finally be in a position to take full control of Fortune International. Of all the family, he had the most to lose if her claim was successful.

Diana Chandler slammed her glass down on the exposed marble bar. She gave her brother a sullen look, but said nothing as she returned to her chair.

Aunt Diana. Christina had always thought her so beautiful. Now in her early fifties, she was still a strikingly attractive woman, her pale blond hair swept back into a sleek chignon secured at the nape of her slender neck. The severe hairstyle was meant to be sophisticated in its simplicity. But it revealed far too much—the taut gleam of skin that had been chemically peeled to recapture a youthful luster, the slight puffiness that suggested collagen injections to eliminate unwanted lines. Hers was a beauty that had been scraped, sliced, and tucked.

Uncle Brian sat quietly beside his wife. He wasn't sixty yet, but looked years older. An engineer with Fortune International, he'd married the boss's daughter, sired three sons to continue the dynasty, and sat on the board of directors. But it was a token position. Diana controlled their shares in Fortune International, just as she controlled their lives.

Their eldest son, Steven, was the heir apparent, for Richard had no children. Christina was surprised at how little Steven had changed over the years. Tall and handsome in an almost too-pretty, male-model way, he had thick, golden brown hair and his mother's ice blue eyes.

He had been supremely confident at eighteen. An all-around athlete, he was always the strongest, the fastest, the best at any sport. After graduating from Stanford, the college that every member of the Fortune family attended, he'd taken his place in the company, secure in the knowledge that one day he would run it. Just last year he had been appointed vice president in charge of operations in Hong Kong.

The charm that he could show when he felt like it wasn't evident now, as he spoke to Christina. "Get out, before we have you thrown out."

"You haven't changed, Steven. You always did like to give orders," Christina remarked. Aware that she'd caught him momentarily off guard, she took advantage of his discomfiture. "You insisted on being the captain when we took the sloop out on the Bay. Remember when your overconfidence caused us to capsize?"

She knew the effect that last remark would have, and she smiled inwardly at his stunned expression.

"My God," murmured Jason Chandler, "I'd completely forgotten about that." He stared at her with dark, intense eyes. Younger than Steven, he took after his father in his short, slight build and dark hair and eyes. After the death of her parents, Jason had been the only person in the world Christina had loved and trusted.

She smiled tentatively at Jason. They had once been extremely close, but they'd quarreled bitterly the last night they'd been together, twenty years earlier. Now his expression was cautious.

He went on, "We must have struggled for an hour to right that damn thing."

She nodded, taking up the story. "We probably would have all drowned if the Coast Guard hadn't come along when they did."

"This is incredible! No one else knew about that."

"I was hoping you'd remember, Jase," she said softly, calling him by the familiar nickname.

"Remember?" Diana was incredulous as she came out of her chair. "How can he remember a complete stranger? My God, you *are* good. But not good enough. You'd better leave before we call the police. You have no idea who you're dealing with, Miss . . . whoever the hell you are. But I assure you, you are *not* Christina Fortune. She's dead."

Christina recoiled. She'd expected them to deny her claim, but she wasn't prepared for the venom in Diana's voice.

"I'm sorry to disappoint you, but as you can see, I'm very much alive."

Andrew, Diana's youngest son, spoke for the first time. "This changes everything." His gaze met hers briefly, then slid away, making it impossible to tell whether he believed her or not.

He was two years younger than Christina. Like Jason, he had his father's dark eyes, and like his father, he seemed to wear a constantly troubled expression. He rose to leave. "Obviously we won't be concluding any business today." His gaze swept across the table. "I'll leave you to deal with this unexpected turn of events. I have to get back to the shelter."

"Sit down," Diana ordered her son. "Those disgusting street people you insist on working with can damn well wait. This is far more important."

Seeing his face redden with embarrassment and an impotent anger, Christina ached for him. Andrew was always so shy and sensitive when he was younger. Now he fixed his downcast gaze on the annual report in front of him, his emotions carefully closed away.

The only one who appeared to take her announcement in stride was Ross McKenna. He sat there, one ankle casually crossed over his knee, his expression enigmatic. He had been brought into the company ten years earlier by Katherine Fortune, Christina's grandmother. As executrix of Christina's estate, she controlled the shares Christina had inherited from her father. Therefore she controlled Fortune International, at least until Christina's thirty-fifth birthday. If Christina didn't return to claim her inheritance by then, the shares were to be divided between Richard and Diana.

Katherine ran the company with an iron hand and an innate understanding of Pacific trade learned from her husband, Alexander. In recent years, as age and poor health took their toll, she was forced to rely more and more on Ross. But she refused to relinquish control of the company to her second son, Richard.

Katherine knew exactly what she was doing when she hired Ross. According to *Forbes*, he was ranked one of the ten most-respected—some said feared—businessmen in the world. He and Richard were constantly at odds, but as long as Katherine had control, Ross won every battle. Now, with the

stock distribution from the trust, Richard would have control
of the company because Diana always voted her shares with
his. It was common knowledge that his first act would be to
remove Ross McKenna.

Christina knew that her claim would change everything for
everyone—including Ross. If her claim was upheld, *she*—not
Ross or Richard—would control the company.

She had seen photographs of him and was prepared for the
fact that he was darkly good-looking. She had dismissed him
as being almost too handsome, with his angular features, precisely cut black hair, strong chin, and firm, full mouth. But in
person he had an aura of ruthless masculinity that was distinctly unsettling.

His suit hinted at the finest tailors in Hong Kong. Not the
ones that crowded tourist row, but the others found on some
side street only the locals knew about, where the tailor's name
was hand-stitched in Chinese inside the left jacket cuff. The
fabric was flawless, the cut and fit perfect. The jacket was left
casually unbuttoned, but that, too, was deceptive. There was
nothing casual about the man. She sensed that the refined
clothes, the relaxed manner, the careful scrutiny were all deceptive.

His mouth curved into a slight frown at one corner—the
only indication he was the least affected by all this—and his
dark blue eyes narrowed thoughtfully. His was a hard, perhaps even unforgiving, face. She'd been concerned about
fighting Richard. Now she realized this man might be an even
tougher adversary.

Steven abruptly rose from his chair. "I've had enough of
this." He started toward Christina, but his uncle restrained
him with a hand at his arm.

Richard stared at her down the length of the conference table. "As of this morning, all claims to Christina's estate are
invalid."

Christina took a deep breath. Her fingers clenched around
the handle of the attaché case. She'd rehearsed this countless
times, and reassured herself it would be simple—just walk in,
say what she had to say, and then leave. Now she struggled

to maintain her composure as she snapped open the latches on the eelskin case.

"My attorney obtained an injunction in superior court late yesterday afternoon, blocking distribution of the trust and formally establishing my claim."

Taking a manila portfolio out of the case, she tossed it onto the center of the conference table. "There are copies of the documents. You'll find everything is in order." Her dark gaze swept the boardroom and the faces of those seated around the table. "The other information in the folder should answer all your questions. My attorney's name is on the cover letter." She snapped the attaché case closed. "I can be reached at the Hyatt Regency."

Her gaze went to Jason, the only person in this room who had felt genuine affection for the young Christina Fortune. She saw confusion, pain, and a tenuous hopefulness in his expression. Was he remembering that last night? The bitter argument? The words that came too easily and could never be taken back? Was it possible that Jason could have been responsible for what happened afterward?

Or was it one of the others?

A tide of profound emotion flooded through her, like the reopening of an old wound that refused ever to heal completely. The fear and feelings of degradation that she'd buried deep resurfaced with ugly images she'd never been completely able to block from memory, no matter how desperately she tried.

Suddenly she felt that she couldn't stand there one more moment. She turned, quickly walked past the startled receptionist, and closed the door behind her.

In the elevator she shivered with a fear she hadn't allowed herself to show in the boardroom. Alone in the elevator she collapsed against the back wall and closed her eyes. Relief poured through her. After all the years of trying to run away from the past, followed by more years of attempting to come to terms with it, she had finally done it. She had begun a process that was as necessary as it was frightening.

A few moments later she stepped out into the brilliant San Francisco sunlight. She simply stood there for a while, letting it warm her. The brightness chased terrifying memories back into the past once more.

"Who the hell is she?" Steven angrily demanded.

Diana furiously ground out her cigarette. "Mother must be behind this!" Ignoring Richard's earlier order, she headed back to the bar. She quickly downed a strong drink, then poured another. "She told us she was too ill to attend the meeting, but that was just a trick! I knew she'd pull something like this. She'll never give up control."

Jason looked wistful. "But . . . she looks so much like Christina. There was something about her eyes."

"She's an imposter," Richard declared, "just like all the others."

Andrew rose from his chair. "I'm leaving. I'm sure you'll let me know when you've dealt with her."

Diana didn't try to stop him this time.

Looking up from the open portfolio that lay before him, Ross spoke for the first time. "I don't think it will be quite that easy."

"What is that supposed to mean?" Diana demanded as she returned to her seat, drink in hand.

Ross closed the portfolio. "Katherine doesn't know anything about this," he stated flatly. "She would have told me. And I assure you, the court would never have granted that injunction if they didn't believe there was some merit to her claim."

"That's ridiculous!" Diana slammed her glass down on the table. Scotch sloshed over the rim, puddling on the black jade surface. "Christina is *dead*. If my mother had accepted that fact years ago, we wouldn't have had to go through the parade of frauds who've tried to steal Christina's inheritance."

"Christina's death was never proved," Ross reminded her. "Her body was never found."

"The police found her clothes and identification in that rundown motel in Tucson. She ran away for God-knows-what reason, got mixed up with the wrong people, and got herself killed. It happens all the time to rebellious teenagers. The authorities were satisfied that's what happened."

"It doesn't matter what the authorities believed. Katherine *never* believed it."

"Of course not. She refused to believe the truth when my brother and his wife drowned in that sailing accident. She didn't accept it until their bodies were found days later. Then it started all over again when Christina disappeared."

The Scotch was starting to take effect, making her less cautious than was wise. "We've had to live with that for the past twenty years. And now, this woman appears out of nowhere and expects all of us to believe she's Christina?"

She pounded her fist on the table. "I'll be damned if I'll wait another twenty years, or however long it takes for Mother to finally accept the truth or . . . die!"

"That's enough!" Richard cut her off.

"It's not enough!" She turned on her brother. "You said this meeting was merely a formality, the final step to settle the inheritance once and for all." Her voice shook with anger. "What are you going to do about this woman?"

"She has an injunction. Legally, we can't distribute the trust as we'd planned. It will take a few days to straighten this out." His glance took in everyone at the table. "I'll take care of it, just as I took care of the others. The threat of arrest for fraud, or a few thousand dollars, should send her on her way."

Ross said quietly, "I don't agree."

"What do you mean?"

Ross gestured toward the portfolio that he'd quickly skimmed through. "She's *not* like the others. She knows we'll attempt to disprove her claim, and she's supplied an impressive amount of information about her background."

"That will make it easier for us." Richard's tone was impatient. When he wanted something, he didn't like waiting to get it, and he'd waited twenty years for control of Fortune International.

Ross glanced down at the small card attached to the portfolio. It was a courtesy business card the Hyatt made available to its guests, embossed with the hotel name, address, and telephone number. She had written in her name, *Christina G. Fortune*. Rising, he tucked the portfolio under his arm, and turned to leave. At the door, where only moments before the young woman claiming to be Christina Fortune had stood and confronted them, he paused briefly.

"I suspect her price may be higher than you're willing to pay."

It was late afternoon when she finally returned to the Hyatt Regency. The lobby was enormous, filled with full-size potted trees, abstract bronze sculptures, and a central fountain with water splashing softly over marble tile.

Exclusive shops lined both sides of the lobby on the ground floor. At one end of the lobby, hotel guests dined in a perfect reproduction of an outdoor garden. A fashion show was under way in the central pavilion, and at the far end wedding guests waited in a reception line beside an intricate ice sculpture of two swans.

Those famous elevators that looked like gilded glass bird cages swooped silently down from the towering floors above, delivering guests to the lobby, and taking others back to their rooms or to the exclusive rooftop restaurant with its breathtaking skyline view of San Francisco.

The hotel was abuzz with activity and hundreds of guests. Christina had chosen it for just those reasons. She preferred the anonymity that could be found in a large hotel, where it was easy to go unnoticed in a crowd.

She collected her messages at the desk. There were only two, discreetly tucked inside envelopes. She slipped them inside her jacket pocket, intending to read them when she got to her room.

From the Fortune building she'd immediately gone to an appointment with the attorney she'd hired to obtain the injunction. He was naturally curious about the results of the board meeting. Especially since she had insisted on delivering copies of the injunction to the board of Fortune International herself, rather than following the usual procedure of having them delivered by an officer of the court.

In their meeting he advised her what to expect next—the usual affidavits and forms that would be counterfiled to temporarily block her claim. This maneuver would gain time to prove her claim invalid. He also warned her that Richard Fortune would undoubtedly hire an investigator to check out the information she had supplied in her portfolio.

She felt only a momentary twinge of uneasiness. She'd expected all of this, prepared herself for it. Still, she couldn't help feeling profoundly uneasy at the thought that she had handed her life over to people who would sift through every detail of the past twenty years, looking for the tiniest flaw or inconsistency that could discredit her.

Now she felt the strain from the emotionally charged board meeting, followed by the lengthy meeting with her attorney. As she crossed the lobby, all she wanted to do was to go up to her room and relax in a hot bath. Maybe that would ease her jangled nerves.

She didn't see him at first. Then he rose from a nearby table in the garden restaurant, and she stopped abruptly. The fear she'd felt only a moment earlier was sharper now. She hadn't left the danger behind in that imposing boardroom—it had followed her. She felt like an animal being stalked and cornered.

When he was certain that she had seen him, Richard Fortune deliberately waited for her to come to him, rather than taking those last few steps himself.

Power. Once again she was reminded of it. Even now he stood apart from the guests having a late lunch at the restaurant. Here was an arrogant, ruthless man who wouldn't give in without a bloody fight to the finish.

Christina had no choice but to face him. She walked toward him slowly, trying hard to conceal the old fear that tightened her throat and stomach. Somehow he was even more intimidating here, facing her alone, than he had been when he was surrounded by the other board members.

"Hello," she said, her tone neutral.

"I thought we should talk."

She slipped into a chair, and he took the one across the table, putting as much distance as possible between them. She returned the unwavering scrutiny of that cool gaze, determined not to flinch. But inside she trembled.

After a moment he began, "You realize, of course, that this

claim of yours will be quickly dismissed. You can't possibly hope to achieve anything with it."

"The court seems to believe there is some validity to it."

"You are *not* Christina Fortune."

"Are you certain of that?" she shot back.

"Absolutely certain. If my niece was alive, she would have come back long before now."

That was the critical issue, the one she had known would be thrown at her the moment she appeared. She had practiced her answer, and she gave it with an ease that belied her inner nervousness. "I had no desire to return. I came back now only because if I didn't, I would forfeit my inheritance."

His narrow mouth curved in an ironic smile. "Of course, the inheritance. Christina's shares of the company are worth millions. That money has attracted several impostors. You're simply the latest."

Before she could argue, he asked tersely, "How much?"

She was confused. "I don't understand."

"Ten thousand should be sufficient to send you packing."

She stared at him. She hadn't expected bribery.

When she didn't speak, he went on, "Twenty thousand?" He gave her an appraising look. "I suppose, considering all the effort you've put into this, you think it should be more. All right, fifty thousand. That should reimburse you for all your expenses, and the cost of the flight back to wherever it is you came from."

She said nothing. Misunderstanding her silence, he said, "Don't try to get any more. That's my final offer. Take it and quietly disappear. Or I'll charge you with fraud and you'll end up in jail, with *nothing*."

Reaching into his inside jacket pocket, he withdrew a pen and checkbook. Flipping open the leather cover, he said, "I'll make it out to cash, since I'm sure you won't give me your real name."

Christina stood abruptly, jarring the table. "Is this how you got rid of the others?"

"Sometimes. Occasionally the threat of legal action was enough." He went on, his tone scathing, "People like you always have their price."

"I won't take one penny from you—except what's rightfully mine."

Richard rose from his chair. "You'll be exposed as just another fraud. In the end you'll lose everything."

The memory of another loss, so profound, it was nearly physical, washed through her. "I've already lost everything that's important," she answered with far more truth than he could ever know.

Or did he know?

Did he know what happened that night twenty years ago?

Was *he* the one?

The sudden suspicion sharpened the fear, and it was all she could do to stand her ground when all she wanted to do was to turn and run. She forced herself to walk—not run—away from him.

"You're a fraud!" he called after her. "I'm going to prove it! And then I'm going to destroy you!"

She stopped and slowly turned around, meeting his cold, hard gaze. "Someone already tried that, twenty years ago. He didn't succeed, and neither will you."

# Chapter 3

Christina closed the door of her suite on the fourteenth floor of the central tower. The housekeeping staff had drawn the heavy drapes across the windows, and the room was dark.

Something about the sudden darkness and the outlines of furniture looming in vague shapes made her hesitate. She shivered, although she wasn't cold. She often experienced that same sensation first thing in the morning when her senses hadn't yet cleared from sleep and her bedroom was hidden in deep shadows. Or returning home late at night to find she'd forgotten to leave on a light. Or those rare occasions when the power went off, and every light with it.

She was afraid of the dark. It brought back memories of a darkened alley twenty years ago. Sometimes the memories became so intense, so real, that it seemed if she took a step forward in the darkness, she would find herself back in that alley.

Now she kicked off her high-heeled shoes and forced herself to cross the carpet in stocking feet. Seizing the drapes, she drew them back. Late afternoon sunlight poured in through the glass panels, and she immediately felt better. But a lingering edginess from her meeting with Richard drove her out onto the terrace, where she could bask in a panoramic view of the city and the Bay.

She had known he would be her toughest adversary. After all, he had the most to lose. She had steeled herself for her confrontation with him, assuring herself she was prepared for it. But when it happened, she was even more nervous than she had expected to be. When he turned up so unexpectedly at the hotel, it was all she could do to maintain a semblance of composure.

He'd made it clear that he would do whatever it took to deny her claim. Would that ruthlessness extend to physically removing her? she wondered. She told herself she was over-reacting. Once he realized that he couldn't disprove her claim, he would accept her. After all, this was a matter of family.

But it was a family member who had played such a violent role twenty years earlier. Could it have been Richard? Could his lifelong jealousy of his brother, Michael, have driven him to such an act?

She couldn't bear to think of it any longer. Instead, she concentrated on the spectacular view. At this point in the late afternoon, time seemed suspended between day and night. The sun slipped westward, creating shadows in the concrete and steel canyons of the streets below. Out across the Bay fingers of mist stole across the water, wrapped around the support columns of the Golden Gate Bridge, and shrouded the Marin coastline.

She closed her eyes and breathed in the cool air from the brisk breeze fourteen stories up. Heights never bothered her. Instead, she found them exhilarating. She felt as if she were standing on top of the world and looking down on everything else. The sensation of being above it all, in control, was a reassuring one.

The sky was salmon pink one minute, as the Pacific Ocean swallowed the molten sun, soft lavender the next. She'd lived in Boston the last several years, when she wasn't traveling on business, and she loved almost everything about that city—the seasons, the sense of history, the lush, green terrain. But nowhere else on earth had sunsets like California.

She lingered, savoring the fading beauty of the sky above, as lights began to wink to life across the city. Soon it would be dark, and San Francisco would glisten like a jeweled crown jutting out at the tip of the peninsula. The ugly confrontation with Richard faded from her mind, and she told herself everything would be all right. She had the kind of strength that comes from surviving the very worst, and emerging from it tougher and more resilient. And she'd prepared for this battle for years. She could handle whatever obstacles Richard presented. He was driven by a lust for power, but she was driven by something even more profound. Some people might call it revenge, but she preferred to think of it as justice.

The breeze took on a damp chill, and she stepped back into her suite. Slipping off her gray suede jacket, she draped it carelessly across the back of the couch. In the bedroom she removed gold earrings, a small black onyx and gold ring that she always wore, and a bracelet watch, placing them on the dresser. She slipped off the rest of her clothes and draped them across the bed.

Wearing only a white lace and silk teddy, she returned to the sitting room, and selected a drink from the honor bar—a small bottle of Grand Cru Pouilly Fume. The wine soothed her ragged senses as she turned on the television and heard the newscaster with the local affiliate begin the six o'clock broadcast.

Opening the messages she'd picked up at the front desk, she saw that the first one was from her attorney, asking her to call him in the morning. She laid it aside. The second message read simply: *Top of the Hyatt. Seven o'clock. Ross McKenna.*

The edginess she'd brought back to her room with her sharpened to irritation. She'd already had one confrontation that afternoon, and wasn't sure she could handle another. Most women would have been intrigued by an invitation from such a disturbingly attractive man. But Christina knew there was only one reason he wanted to see her.

If only half of what she knew about him was true, he could be extremely tenacious when he wanted something. There was no telephone number where she could reach him, an omission she was fairly certain was deliberate. This way she couldn't decline his invitation.

*Power.* Once more she was reminded of it, just as she had been with Richard. There were those who had it, and those who were manipulated by it. The Fortune family, and Ross McKenna, were among those who had it. They meant to manipulate her, but she wasn't about to let that happen. She'd waited too long, worked too hard, and come too far to let their power intimidate her.

She picked up the phone and dialed the telephone number for Fortune International.

"I'm sorry," the service answered, "everyone has gone home for the evening. I can take a message for you."

"I need to get a message to Mr. McKenna."

"Mr. McKenna left several hours ago."

"Is there another number where he can be reached?"

"He didn't leave a number."

Christina muttered a terse good-bye and slammed the phone down. "Damn!"

The anger built, raw along every nerve ending. She closed her eyes and massaged back the pain that throbbed at her right temple. The board meeting, the long meeting afterward with her attorney, and the confrontation with Richard had all taken their toll. She wasn't ready for another confrontation. She needed time to relax, to think over everything that had happened that day, and to contemplate her next move.

She picked up the phone again, called the restaurant, and left a message. "When Mr. McKenna arrives, would you please tell him I won't be able to join him this evening."

With that taken care of, she called room service and ordered dinner. Then she went into the bathroom, slipped out of the teddy, and relaxed in the marble bath filled with hot water.

It would be an hour before room service delivered her dinner. In the meantime she leaned back against the angled end of the tub and closed everything out of her mind, letting the heat ease the knotted tension from her muscles. Through the open door she heard the newscaster announcing the local news. He began a new story.

". . . Police report that a teenage girl was found stabbed to death near the Oakland waterfront late last night—"

Suddenly it all came back. Even after all these years, the memory was terrifying in its intensity . . .

"Come on! Hurry! This way!"

Two fifteen-year-old girls raced into the dark alley, one pulling the other by the hand. The stench of rotting garbage filled the alley—discarded trash caught at their running feet. The darkness smelled of terror.

He was close behind them now. They could hear the sound of his feet pounding the wet pavement, coming closer.

"Hurry!"

She'd thought this would be a shortcut from the deserted industrial streets of this part of the city to a busier street where crowds of people would provide safety. Now she wasn't so sure.

"I can't," the other girl whimpered, her breathing ragged, dragging back on her friend's hand.

"It'll be all right." Inwardly terrified, she didn't dare let her fear show. She had to be strong for both of them.

The two girls looked so much alike, they might have been sisters, both dark-haired and dark-eyed, with delicate features that promised real beauty. Yet despite their startling physical resemblance, there was a clear-cut difference between them. The girl leading the way was visibly the stronger of the two. Her friend was more fragile, and ready to surrender to her terror.

They cut down another alley. A dead end. She whirled around to lead her friend back, then stopped short. A tall, powerfully built man blocked the entrance to the alley.

"Don't move, you little bitches!" he ordered. His voice was low and threatening. "You're comin' with me."

"No!" she shouted as she slowly backed away from him, pushing her friend behind her, hoping desperately that someone would hear them. The hand clinging to hers stiffened, and she heard a low whimper of fear.

"I said, you're comin' with me!" he repeated, his eyes hard, his mouth thinned in anger. Both his hands were extended in front of him. As he slowly came toward them, a sliver of light glinted off the steel blade of the knife he held in one hand. Without warning he lunged at them.

The first girl tried to push him away, but he grabbed her arm, twisting it painfully. She fought him, screaming at her friend to run. They couldn't give in to him. Dying in this stinking alley was better than what he intended for them.

Her friend clung to her, terrified of their attacker but even more terrified to let go. In the scuffle a gold chain with an intricately carved jade pendant fell to the ground.

Suddenly the knife slashed through the air. A long, drawn-out scream of pain echoed in the darkness, a body crumpled onto the pavement, blood pumping into a dark pool beneath her.

The chilling wail of an approaching siren filled the air. As their attacker fled, the girl knelt beside her friend, who lay bleeding and unconscious on the cold concrete. Through the tears streaming down her face, she noticed the golden gleam of the necklace and slipped it into her pocket.

Later she sat in the emergency room of the hospital, hands clasped together and buried in her lap. It was all her fault, she told herself guiltily. She had promised she'd get them both safely away from the pimp. He'd stalked them for days, trying countless times to force them into joining the group of young prostitutes who worked for him.

She'd calmed her friend's growing fears, promising her it would be all right.

They'd arrived in New York just days apart, runaways like so many other teenagers who filled the city streets. Only on those desperate streets could their paths have ever crossed, for they were from opposite ends of the social spectrum. Their backgrounds were as different as the rigid divisions of class could make them. Christina Grant Fortune, heiress to a San Francisco shipping empire, had been raised amid the wealth and privilege of Pacific Heights. Ellie Dobbs grew up in the poverty and squalor of a trailer court outside Memphis, Tennessee.

Initially they noticed each other because of their remarkable resemblance. But they shared more than a striking like-

ness to one another. They shared the nightmare of the same
traumatic experience that had forced both to run away from
home. That, along with their reliance on each other for survival, created a powerful bond between them. It was a bond
of love and trust in a time and place when both were rare.

Now the girl heard the sound of footsteps on the drab linoleum floor. Her eyes were moist with desperate hope as she
looked up. The young emergency room physician, who had
only recently completed his internship, slowly approached.

"Is she your sister?" he asked gently.

She shook her head. "No . . . my friend."

"You look so much alike . . . I thought maybe . . ." He
cleared his throat and asked, "What about her family?"

She ignored his question. "Is she gonna be okay?"

He hesitated, then slowly shook his head. His eyes
searched hers, as if trying to assess whether she was strong
enough to hear the truth. "I'm sorry."

He laid a hand on her shoulder and went on, "She lost a lot
of blood before they brought her in. There's nothing more we
can do. You can see her if you like."

He took her upstairs to the Intensive Care Unit. She hesitated at the doorway. Her friend lay pale and still in the white
bed, her ashen face starkly pretty. Dark hair lay limp against
the white pillowcase. Tubes ran into her body like strings
holding a puppet. Machines surrounded the bed, filling the
room with faint beeping, pulsing sounds.

"I'll leave you alone," the doctor said in a lowered voice.
The door closed gently behind him.

As the girl stood there, staring down at her friend, she
fought back the sharp sting of tears. Guilt welled up inside
her. "It's all my fault," she whispered.

Her friend's eyelids fluttered, then opened. She tried to
smile past the breathing tube. Through dry lips she whispered,
"It isn't your fault."

"I'm so sorry." The girl clasped her friend's hand, holding
on to her as tightly as she'd held on to her in that alley.

"You have nothing . . . to feel sorry about. You're my
friend. You risked your life for me."

"You're the best friend I ever had. I should have gotten us

out of there." She swallowed back the tears that choked her throat and stared down at their clasped hands.

"There wasn't . . . anything you could do." Her friend breathed with great difficulty. "He would have just kept after us. You know that."

The girl felt the hard squeeze of her friend's hand. The strength of it surprised her.

"I want you to do something for me," her friend said. "You have to promise me you'll do it."

She nodded quickly. "Anything."

The girl on the bed lay completely still except for her short, shallow breathing, as if she were gathering the last of her strength to speak. "Promise you'll get off the streets. I know you can't go home, but there has to be another way. You can't end up like this." She paused, her dark eyes searching her friend's face, the pressure of her fingers almost painful. "You have to live for both of us now."

Her voice trailed off, and her eyelids closed, all the strength seeming suddenly to have drained from her. "Promise me . . ."

The girl clung fiercely to her friend's suddenly slack hand, as if she could give her some of her strength, as if she could will her to live.

"I promise," she said, the words lost amid the rhythmic, electric sounds of the machines. "And someday I'll make them pay for what they did to both of us."

Her friend lay completely still, her lips parted slightly, her eyelids blue-veined and almost transparent over her closed eyes. There was a new sound now, the incessant, single tone of a machine, the glare of that solid line of green light perfectly straight across the monitor.

When the doctor and nurse rushed in, pushing her aside, she left the room in a daze. Now she felt more lost and alone than ever.

A priest waited near the nurse's station. She recognized him. He ran House of Hope, a refuge for kids who lived on the streets of New York. She'd seen him often, talking to some of the other girls and boys, but she hadn't been able to bring herself to trust him. He might be a priest, but he was still a man, and she didn't trust any man.

He came toward her, holding out a hand, compassion etched in every deep line of his face. "The doctor told me about your friend. I'm sorry, child. I'd like to help, if you'll let me."

"You can't help her!" she exploded at him. "No one can help her! It's too late!"

"I can help you," he insisted in a gentle voice. Then, sensing her mistrust, he added quietly, "That's all I want, just to help."

Consumed with guilt that she hadn't been able to save her friend, she turned her back on the priest and started to walk away.

"Do you want to live?"

She stopped and whirled around. "What?"

"Do you want to live? Or do you want to die, like your friend?" The words were meant to be hard. "Those are the choices. You can come with me and let me help you make a new life for yourself. Or you can go back to the streets. You know as well as I do what's waiting for you there. Is that what you want?"

The brutal honesty of his words stopped her. As the two stood there staring at one another, she remembered her promise. Yes, she knew what waited for her on the streets. If she went back, she would very likely end up dead, like her friend. She had promised she would live . . . for both of them. At that moment her promise to her friend mattered more to her than her own life.

Sensing his advantage, the priest went on, "I won't notify your family, if you don't want me to. I hope that one day you might decide to contact them yourself."

Never! she thought, but didn't say it aloud.

"All right," she gave in grudgingly.

There was no hint of smugness in his smile, merely relief softened with kindness. "Good. Now then, perhaps you'll tell me your name. It'll make it easier for us to get to know one another."

She hesitated. How much could she trust him? Her fingers

closed around the forgotten necklace at the bottom of her pocket. The gold felt cool against her fingers, the jade smooth. She remembered a time—it seemed so long ago—when she'd been able to trust.

Slowly she came to a decision. Looking directly at the priest, she said, "My name is Christina . . ."

# Chapter 4

Christina stood before the steamy mirror in the bathroom, wrapped in a thick towel. Her wet hair streamed across her shoulders. As she made a wide arc across the glass with her hand, she suddenly stopped. Her muted reflection on the smudged surface of the mirror looked much younger, obscuring the fine lines at the corners of her eyes. She saw a young woman with long, dark hair . . .

*"Is she your sister? . . . You look so much alike . . ."*

For just a moment she was back in that hospital emergency room. The sharp antiseptic smell swept back over her, bringing with it the old fear and a faint roll of nausea in her stomach. She saw again those cold, sterile walls; felt the cracked, peeling vinyl upholstery of the straight-back chair as she frantically dug her fingers in; heard the muted, swishing sound of soft-soled shoes on linoleum as the doctor came toward her down that long hallway.

Her throat tightened.

*"You have to live for both of us . . ."*

The steam slowly retreated to the center of the mirror, then disappeared completely, taking the illusion and the memories with it. Now the face that stared back at her was that of a mature woman, her cheeks pale in spite of the heat in the bathroom, her eyes filled with tears.

"Oh, God . . ." She leaned against the tiled bathroom counter, suddenly weak.

She'd known it wouldn't be easy to come here, but she'd reassured herself that a certain amount of emotional insulation came with the passage of twenty years. Yet it was as if it hadn't been twenty years at all, as if it had all happened only yesterday.

Because she hadn't expected it, she wasn't prepared to deal with the fear she only now admitted to herself—a fear that came from the reality that she *was* vulnerable. Twenty years ago she'd vowed she'd never be vulnerable again. Vulnerability had made her a victim, and there was no honor in that. Being a victim meant losing an essential part of yourself—innocence. Once lost, it could never be found again.

She grabbed the hair dryer and switched it on high. The blast of hot air dissolved the memories, shoving them back into the past.

As she finished drying her hair, the newscaster began his final story of the broadcast. "Just this evening Channel Six News has learned that the announcement of major changes within Fortune International, the San Francisco–based shipping company, has been delayed for at least several days. Those changes within the power structure of the international shipping firm were anticipated immediately following distribution of stock from the trust of heiress Christina Fortune, who disappeared twenty years ago and is presumed dead."

Moving into the sitting room, Christina saw an old photograph of a young girl flash on the screen. She stared at it as he went on with the story.

"Over the past twenty years Fortune International has been at the center of a bitter power struggle between Katherine Fortune, widow of shipping magnate Alexander Fortune, and her son, Richard. There have been continued rumors over the past several months of problems within the privately owned shipping company, prompting financial experts to predict a public stock offering to help stabilize the troubled company."

The newscast ended, and the station immediately aired several local commercials, but in her mind's eye she could still see the photograph of a smiling fifteen-year-old girl with long, dark hair and dark eyes.

The buzzer sounded at the outside door to the suite. Room service. Her stomach grumbled, a reminder that she hadn't eaten since breakfast. Hurrying back into the bathroom, she took a satin robe patterned in a dark blue paisley print off the hook on the door and slipped it on.

"I'll be right there," she called out as she hastily finger-combed her hair. She grabbed a couple of one-dollar bills out of her purse to tip room service, then went to the door.

"I'm sorry. I was in the bathroom . . ." she explained breathlessly as she pulled the door open. She stopped midsentence and stared in surprise at Ross McKenna.

Ross was equally surprised. She looked so different from the woman who'd walked into the boardroom that morning and coolly announced she was Christina Fortune. She was as casual now as she had been formal that morning. He'd caught her just out of the bath, and she wore no makeup at all. She didn't need it. Her flawless skin was gently flushed. The glow extended down her slender neck to that V where the silk robe closed. Her long chestnut hair was loose about her shoulders and slightly damp.

He'd spent part of the afternoon looking at old photos of the young Christina Fortune, and now he looked for similarities between that girl and the woman who stood before him. Allowing for changes over the passage of twenty years, there was a remarkable resemblance between the girl in the photos and this woman, with her patrician, fine-boned features—the straight nose, high cheekbones, round chin, sensual curve of mouth, and dark, expressive eyes, like clear amber beneath the brush of delicate brows.

Forcing his attention back to the purpose of his visit, he said, "We've got to talk."

She stood behind the half open door, using it as a shield. "I've already ordered dinner from room service." Her voice was a mixture of honey and smoke, deep and throaty, something else he hadn't noticed that morning.

"I took the liberty of canceling your dinner," he said.

Her hand came up at the edge of the door, as if she were

prepared to slam it in his face. "You had no right to do that. I didn't agree to meet with you. I tried to leave a message with your service, but you were conveniently unavailable."

The barest flicker of a smile tugged at the corners of his mouth. "I had no intention of giving you the opportunity to refuse my invitation." Then he added, "Either then or now." Before she could respond, he hurried on, "We'll need to have this conversation sooner or later. I think sooner will be better."

"I'm really very tired. And I've already been threatened once today. That's enough."

He reached the logical conclusion. "Richard."

She nodded.

He felt a flicker of anger at Richard for resorting to threats. Even if this woman was an imposter, that was uncalled for. He resented being lumped together with Richard. "I'm not Richard Fortune. I don't resort to threats. We'll have to talk sometime. Why not get it over with?"

"Look, I'm not dressed to go out."

"I'll wait." Then he added, "And please don't tell me you have to wash your hair tonight." He reached out and lifted a strand of still-damp hair from her shoulder. "You've already done that."

She gave him a long look. "I don't suppose it would do any good simply to refuse."

"No, it wouldn't."

She sighed in frustration. "All right. I'll need a few minutes. Help yourself to the bar." And with that she disappeared into the adjoining bedroom.

"I would have thought you would have gone out on the town tonight, to celebrate," he remarked from the sitting room.

"It's been a long day," she called through the partially open door.

"Yes, I suppose your schedule was quite full. First the board meeting, then a meeting with the local press." He glanced up as she reappeared in the doorway.

"I didn't leak information to the press about problems at the company."

He quirked a dark brow. "Really? I thought the press was part of your strategy."

"I'd prefer to keep everything as private as possible," she replied, then disappeared back into the bedroom.

As he waited for her, he inspected the sitting room, the half-empty bottle of wine, the suede jacket carelessly thrown across the back of the sofa. Picking up the jacket, he examined it quickly. He wasn't certain what he was looking for. Perhaps something more personal, a revealing note left in the pocket, a garment tag that would indicate it was part of a newly purchased wardrobe, anything that might tell him something more about this woman who claimed to be Christina Fortune.

The jacket had been purchased from a small, exclusive clothier in Boston. Obviously expensive, it was as elegant as the woman who wore it. It carried the faint, lingering essence of perfume. There was something at once familiar and seductive about the scent that made his senses stir, but it was too subtle to identify.

He put down the jacket just as she walked through the door. He'd half expected her to wear something sexy. After all, he was one of the enemy, and if she could win him over, that would help her cause. But she surprised him. She wore a short, forest green skirt and a jacket of the same forest green with black pin stripes. The unmistakable cut of an exclusive designer was apparent in the simple yet elegant design. The blouse underneath was black silk. For jewelry she'd added simple pearl ear studs to the ring and watch he'd noticed earlier. Her hair was parted in the center and pulled back with a mother-of-pearl and gold clip at the back of her neck.

Understated elegance. Just the sort of style one would expect of a woman like Christina Fortune, who'd been raised amid wealth and sophistication.

He picked up the scent of the same perfume he'd smelled on the suede jacket. It was soft and musky, yet at the same time hinted at something darkly exotic, like a seductive whisper. It was even more familiar now, but he still couldn't quite place it.

Was she Christina Fortune?

The face, the hair, the eyes were right. But hundreds of women in San Francisco alone could have fit Christina's general description.

He knew very little about the real Christina, except that over twenty years ago, at the age of fifteen, only months after the tragic deaths of her parents, she had suddenly and inexplicably disappeared. Aside from a few personal belongings, including some family photos, that could easily have fit in a purse, she apparently had taken nothing with her. For weeks the police, and then private investigators at the cost of hundreds of thousands of dollars, followed every clue, investigated every report of a runaway girl who matched her description.

Finally they found her clothes and a student identification card, in a remote roadside motel just outside Tucson, Arizona. Foul play was suspected. It was common, too common. Kids ran away, connected with the wrong people, and ended up getting killed.

The police closed the case. The private detectives kept at it, occasionally turning up new information. The body of a girl, dark-haired and dark-eyed, would be found, and a member of the family would be sent to identify her. But it was never Christina. She had simply vanished, as if she'd never existed at all.

For years Katherine Fortune refused to accept that her granddaughter was dead. She always believed that Christina would be found. She brought Ross into the company purely as a temporary measure, to help her run it until Christina would return and take her rightful place as the primary stockholder.

But time was running out. The terms of Michael Fortune's will were clear—Christina was to receive her inheritance on her thirty-fifth birthday, an age when he felt she would be mature enough to handle the responsibility. Until then Katherine was to act as executor of the estate. If for any reason Christina didn't claim the shares, then they were to be divided between Richard and Diana. This morning, at the last possible moment, this young woman walked in and made her claim.

He watched her as she walked toward him. With those

long, slender legs, she could get away with wearing such a short skirt. The sheer black stockings had the sheen of real silk. She wore delicate black leather strap heels that emphasized her height. In those heels she was nearly as tall as he was.

She stopped just inches from him and said, "Since you canceled my first dinner, you can buy this one."

He had to give her credit, she was cool under fire. "Of course."

They left the suite and walked down the hallway to the bank of elevators. The first one to open on their floor was practically full.

"There's a convention going on downstairs," Ross explained. "We'd better squeeze into this one."

He pressed his hand against the middle of her back to urge her forward. As he did so, he felt her hesitate.

"I don't mind waiting," she insisted.

"You won't get out of having dinner with me that easily." He stepped into the elevator, bringing her with him. It was crowded, and everyone shifted slightly to accommodate them.

The doors closed behind her. There was that faint sensation that had her stomach dropping as the elevator lifted. Looking around her, she saw a sea of faces, their expressions bored. She clenched her fists and prayed they reached the restaurant quickly.

The overcrowded elevator was unbearably hot. She heard the soft rustle of an evening gown. Someone cleared his throat. From somewhere at the back came the low murmur of conversation. Bodies pressed against bodies. The elevator stopped at another floor, and everyone shifted once more. She moved to the side against the wall, her hand locking over the brass handrail.

It seemed to take forever. Each time the elevator stopped for people to get off at their floor, or others to get on, there was the pressure of bodies pressing against her.

She thought she'd overcome it. She'd ridden in elevators before and felt nothing. Just that afternoon she'd ridden up and not given it another thought. But this was different. It brought back a flood of unwanted memories . . . *the heat, the clammy press of flesh, the stale breath against her face.*

Finally the elevator gently bumped to a stop on the top floor and the doors slid open onto the entrance of the restaurant. She faced the wall of the elevator, her eyes closed and her hands clutching the handrail.

"Are you all right?"

Slowly Ross's concerned voice pulled her back to the present. She opened her eyes. His hand cradled her elbow, partially supporting her. The elevator was empty, the other guests had already stepped out. She felt their curious stares as they glanced back at her.

She pulled her arm from his grasp. "I'm just a bit lightheaded. I haven't eaten all day." As she stepped out of the elevator, she took several deep breaths. The feeling of helpless terror slowly receded.

The maître d' led them across the deep blue carpet to a table by the window. Only after they'd been sitting there for a few minutes did Christina realize that the restaurant was slowly revolving, giving a panoramic view of the city, the Northern California coastline, and the Pacific Ocean.

Dinner was exceptional—endive salad, salmon quenelles in dill sauce, and grilled antipasto. She was starved and would have thoroughly enjoyed it if she hadn't been aware of the constant scrutiny from across the table.

Ross didn't waste time on polite small talk. He began, "Assuming you are Christina, why did you stay away so long?"

The way he phrased the question, qualifying it rather than insisting she couldn't possibly be genuine, emphasized the difference between he and Richard. She was surprised—and dismayed—to find herself liking him, just a little.

She chose her words carefully. "I came back when I had to." Before he could question that, she went on, "I gave you all the background information in the portfolio. You can check it out."

"I already did."

Once again she was reminded of power. The kind of power that came with knowing the right people in the right places, being able to verify information by just picking up a phone or accessing computer files. If Ross had found even the slightest inconsistency in the information she'd provided, he would have given it to the Fortune attorneys to discredit her claim. He was *here* because he hadn't yet been able to find a flaw in what she'd told him.

The waiter brought a gleaming silver coffee carafe, poured the aromatic brew, then left the carafe at their table. She took a bracing sip of the strong hazelnut-flavored coffee.

Ross continued persistently, "Why *did* you leave?"

She hesitated, knowing he wanted more than the bare facts contained in her portfolio. But she had no intention of letting him get to know her that intimately. She explained slowly, "After my parents died in the sailing accident, things were very . . . difficult. I had no one to turn to. I felt completely alone."

"Christina Fortune lost her parents, but she had other family. And she had a financially secure life. Why would she leave all that?"

"I had my reasons," she snapped, irritated at his persistence. This area was none of his business, and she was determined not to go into it. "I did what I felt I needed to do at the time. Then it seemed the longer I was away, the harder it was to come back." She took a steadying breath. "It was a long time before I was able to come to terms with everything."

He was silent for a long moment. Then he said in a gentler, less combative tone, "Tell me about your parents."

The question was innocuous on the surface. They might have been any two people, lingering over dinner in casual conversation, getting to know each other. But they weren't any two people. They were adversaries, and she couldn't afford to underestimate him.

"I'm certain you know the important details."

"I'd like *you* to tell me. Most of what I know about Michael Fortune comes from the company portfolio."

Aware that he was testing her, she took another slow sip of coffee to steady herself before finally replying. "My mother's family was from Southern California. She met my father in college. They were married after they graduated from

Stanford. I don't think my mother and my grandmother really
cared for each other."

"Why not?"

She knew the answer perfectly well—because Laura Fortune had felt strongly that Katherine was a failure as a
mother, and hadn't hesitated to say so. But she wasn't about
to tell Ross that. After all, he was, in a sense, no more than
an employee, even if he did run the company. He had no right
to know the family's intimate secrets.

She shook her head. "That was between them."

"There were no other children?"

"My mother had one miscarriage before I was born, and
then two more afterward. After that the doctors warned her
against trying to have another child."

He watched her closely as he said, "Katherine mentioned
there were five years between Michael and Richard."

Recognizing the none-too-subtle trap, she corrected him.
"My father was six years older than Richard."

"And you were born and raised here, protected by the privilege and wealth of the Fortune family." His tone suggested
he didn't find sufficient reason in that for a young girl to run
away. He didn't know that wealth hadn't brought protection.

She forced herself to meet his look. "I was born in Hong
Kong," she corrected him.

"Ah, yes, dual citizenship for those born of foreign parents
in the Crown Colony."

Once again he was trying to catch her in a mistake. "Hong
Kong is referred to as the Territory by those who live there,"
she reminded him. "I'm certain you're aware of that, Mr.
McKenna, since you were born and raised there, as well."

"You seem to know a great deal about me."

"I've done my homework."

"Where did you go to live after your parents died?"

"At my grandmother's house, Fortune Hill, in Pacific
Heights. Richard and his wife, Alicia, lived there, too. He and
my grandmother got along better in those days."

"What happened the night you ran away?"

It came out of nowhere, that sudden direct question that
sliced through to the heart of everything. She hesitated, know-

ing he was waiting for her to make just one mistake. In a halting voice she began, "My grandmother was having a party. The first one since my parents' deaths months earlier. The whole family was there. It was a Halloween costume party."

"Why did you run away?"

The direct question elicited a sudden flash of memory. A heavy body pressing against hers. Hot breath on her face. Pain and terror.

Something of what she was feeling must have shown in her face, for Ross's expression softened slightly with concern. "Are you all right?"

No, she wasn't all right, but she refused to let him see how vulnerable that one simple question had made her feel. "I had my reasons for leaving," she said quickly. "And they're none of your business."

"I think that whatever reason you gave me would be a lie, even if you *are* Christina."

"I don't have to explain why I left. I only have to prove that I *am* who I say I am."

He leaned back in his chair and studied her for a long moment. She was smart and tough and sexy as hell in a carefully controlled way. He wondered what it would take to shake that rigid control. But it would do absolutely no good to pursue that intriguing line of thought, he told himself.

Instead he said, "You realize that Richard will do whatever it takes to get rid of you."

"Yes, I know. He's already offered me fifty thousand dollars to leave. When I refused, he threatened to destroy me. So you see, I've already had this discussion once today. I don't see any reason to have it again."

Ross was intrigued. He wouldn't have expected even the greediest of imposters to turn down that kind of payoff. "What did you tell him when he offered you the money?"

"The same thing I'll tell you. I can't be bought. And I won't be threatened."

Ross's lips curved slightly. "That conversation must have just about topped off Richard's day. He prides himself on being able to control everyone."

Of all the things she expected him to say, that wasn't one

of them. "I don't think he was very happy about it," she admitted with a trace of humor.

"I suspect that is a monumental understatement."

She liked the sound of his voice, the deep timbre made elegant by the refined English accent. At least he hadn't threatened her, or tried to buy her off . . . yet.

She had to be very careful with Ross McKenna. He was the most dangerous adversary of all because he could be charming and unpredictable. She recalled what she'd learned about him in a profile in *Forbes* magazine. He was thirty-seven, born and raised in Hong Kong. Very little was known about his family background, and he seemed almost to have come from nowhere. He had paid his way through a small Canadian university by working for an investment banking firm.

After graduation he returned to Hong Kong, where he went to work for a large international bank. He proved to be both shrewd and fiercely ambitious, and soon was recruited by Katherine Fortune. Over the years he'd acquired a sizable financial stake in the company. He had nearly as much to lose as the members of the Fortune family. She couldn't imagine that he would let it all slip through his fingers because of a power struggle between Richard and Katherine Fortune. He had connections in the highest levels of the international business community. It wouldn't be the first time a chief executive officer of a large corporation mounted a leveraged buyout with private funds. She wondered if he had considered such an option.

Twice he'd tried to catch her in a lie, and both times she had passed the test. She reminded herself he was as dangerous as Richard, but in more subtle ways.

He said with grudging admiration, "You're quite good, you know. Better than the others."

She was surprised by the unexpected compliment. "Does that mean I pass your inspection?"

He gave her a steady look. "I said *better* than the others, not *absolutely convincing*. At any rate, my opinion isn't the one that matters. There is someone far more qualified than I am to judge you. Someone who knew Christina Fortune her entire life, until she disappeared. I've arranged a meeting to-morrow morning."

Who could it be? she wondered. He could be referring to any one of a number of people, but she had no way of know-ing which. She knew it would do no good to ask him. Clearly he was counting on the element of surprise to catch her off guard.

He laid his napkin down on the table and called for the din-ner check. When it arrived, he signed for the amount.

This time the elevator was mercifully empty. They rode down to her floor in silence—a silence that seemed to scream at her by the time they finally reached her door. She felt as if they were playing a psychological game of chess, trying to anticipate each other's next move.

As he took her key-card and opened the door for her, he said, "My secretary will call you first thing in the morning with the time and place."

Even now, as he handed the key-card back to her, she was aware, as she had been earlier in the evening, that he deliber-ately refrained from calling her Christina. It was a reminder that, like Richard Fortune, he considered her an impostor.

She said, "Look, if I'm not Christina Fortune, how do I know so much about the family?"

"That's easy. It's a well-known family, there've been a lot of newspaper articles written about them. You must have done a great deal of research."

"But I know personal information that never appeared in any newspaper," she insisted.

His blue eyes appraised her thoughtfully. "Yes, you do. I suspect you hired a private detective to get that information."

She *had* hired a detective to bring her up to date on the family and the business, but she wasn't about to admit as much to Ross. Instead she said, "Even a private detective couldn't have found out the kind of personal knowledge I have. My memory of the sailing accident . . . and everything else I know. Only Christina Fortune could know those things."

He didn't argue. He was silent for a long moment before fi-nally responding reluctantly, "I admit, that puzzles me. If you're an impostor, you must have gotten that information from some source, but so far I haven't been able to figure out what that source could be. No one in the family would have any reason to help you. Quite the contrary, in fact."

"Then I must be the real Christina."

He shook his head. "Not necessarily. At any rate we'll see what happens at the meeting tomorrow." He finished abruptly, "I assure you, if you're an impostor, I'll find out exactly how you're doing it."

And without saying another word, he turned and left abruptly.

She went into her suite, closing the door firmly behind her. She stood just inside the doorway for a moment, thinking hard, then went into the bedroom and took her attaché case out of the closet. Opening it, she took out a small, worn, leather-bound book. Stenciled on the cover in gold letters was the word *Diary*. She flipped it open to a random page . . .

*September 1, 1968: Jason kissed me tonight!!! It was so wonderful but so sad, because we have to leave for different schools tomorrow and we won't see each other for weeks. Our family's being so cruel about this, tearing us apart . . .*

The words were so familiar. She'd read and reread them many times. Closing the book, she looked around the room, trying to decide on a safe hiding place. Finally she shoved the thin book between the mattress and the box spring of the bed, pushing it far in so that the maid wouldn't feel it when she changed the sheets.

# *Chapter 5*

*S*he rose early the next morning and chose her attire with care—a chemise dress with a high, rounded neckline. The simple design was enhanced by the elegant pale blue linen fabric. Over it she wore a matching, full-length black coat. The sweeping collar and folded-back cuffs revealed a soft silk lining of that same blue. The color was striking on her, but she hadn't chosen it simply because it complimented her. She'd chosen it because it was the same shade of blue as the trademark color of the Fortune Shipping line.

Ross McKenna's secretary called at eight-thirty to tell her that a limousine would pick her up at nine o'clock for a meeting with Mr. Phillip Lo. Christina frowned as she hung up the phone. So that was the person Ross had referred to the night before—the person who had known the young Christina so well. Phillip Lo had been the attorney for the Fortune family for nearly forty years. He was Katherine's most trusted personal adviser. And Christina's godfather. If anyone could recognize her, he could.

Or could he? she wondered. After all, it had been twenty years. Lo was past seventy and might not be as sharp mentally as he had once been. To think that her claim rested in the hands of an elderly man who might, or might not, be able to remember clearly back over twenty years was unsettling.

Christina felt nearly as nervous about confronting Lo as she'd felt the day before when she'd faced everyone at the board meeting.

At exactly nine o'clock the hotel concierge called to say that a limousine was waiting in front of the hotel's main entrance. When Christina walked up to the car, a uniformed chauffeur held open the door. Stepping inside, she saw that the backseat was empty. Ross had chosen not to accompany her. Once again he was deliberately unavailable.

Her nerves were drawn taut by the time she arrived at Lo's office in a four-story Victorian building located in the area where the financial district bordered Chinatown. The area was an odd mix of the old and new as several grand old Victorian ladies of nineteenth-century San Francisco shared with multistory skyscrapers of the modern city some of the most expensive real estate in the world.

The receptionist told her that Mr. Lo was waiting for her on the third floor, and motioned toward the elevator. It was authentic Victorian, a simple brass cage that rose very slowly. When it reached the third floor, Christina pushed open the grille and was greeted by a young Chinese woman. "Good morning. Please come this way." She led Christina across the carpeted hallway to a set of old-fashioned mahogany double doors.

Christina mentally prepared herself for whatever lay beyond those doors. Everything she had done over the last twenty years, every choice she'd made, every goal she'd set had been intended to prepare her for this. Ross's interrogation of her over dinner had been a piece of cake compared with what was to come. Confronting a complete stranger who knew very little about Christina Fortune was one thing. Confronting someone who'd known her extremely well was completely different.

The secretary knocked softly, then opened the doors.

They waited for her as she walked in: Richard, Steven Chandler, Ross, and a small, elderly Chinese gentleman—Phillip Lo.

She looked at Ross, whose glance gave only the briefest acknowledgment. Richard refused to meet her gaze. Steven dismissed her with a mocking smile. Phillip Lo scrutinized her carefully. At that moment she felt as if she knew exactly how it must have been to face the grand inquisitors during the Spanish Inquisition.

He stood up to greet her, leaning forward slightly, bracing his fragile weight upon spread fingers on the desktop. "Good morning," he said in a voice that was studiously polite without being at all warm or welcoming.

The expression in his eyes was impassive behind rimless glasses. His sparse hair was pure white, but his skin was unlined. He didn't extend his hand to her as he introduced himself, "I am . . ."

"Hello, Mr. Lo," she said softly. Then she offered the traditional Chinese greeting of old and honored friends. "I hope you are well, I hope your children are well, and that fortune smiles upon your honored name."

"Christ! Do we have to continue this game any further!" Steven exploded, his voice filled with impatience. "Let's get this over with."

She saw the expressions that passed across Richard's and Steven's faces. One was restrained, with the experience of countless confrontations; the other, volatile and immature.

"Yes, let's get on with it. We all have more important matters to see to," Richard agreed.

Lo turned to Richard, impassively polite. "You will please allow me to conduct this meeting."

"Just do it quickly. I have other meetings today." He sat down impatiently on the edge of a chair, refusing to allow himself to get comfortable. Clearly he didn't intend to be there very long.

Steven walked over to the large window behind Lo's desk, leaned against the sill, and stared out.

Ross sat down in a chair as far as possible from Richard.

So, she thought, he's to be the observer, sitting quietly in the corner, watching for the slightest hesitation, the smallest flaw.

Pointedly turning her back on Ross, she focused on Lo and tried to remember everything she knew about him. His grandfather had been born and raised in mainland China, and had emigrated to the United States. Lo respected and honored the dual cultures that had formed his life. China, with its ten thousand years of history and traditions, had given him a strong sense of family heritage. America had given him opportunity.

The duality of his life was reflected in the location of his offices, where he had practiced law for more than fifty years. The Victorian building represented his strong ties to his adopted American tradition, while its location, only steps away from Chinatown, represented the unbreakable blood heritage.

He and Christina's grandfather had built their lives in the cross-cultures of Hong Kong, Hawaii, and San Francisco. When his lifelong friend died, Lo assumed the responsibilities of unofficial uncle, guiding Alexander's oldest son, Michael, as he took his place at the head of Fortune International. When Michael died, he provided counsel to Katherine as she inherited the awesome task of running the company. He had known Christina from the time she was born until she was fifteen years old. He had drawn up Michael's will and arranged the trust for Christina's inheritance.

Responding to her greeting, he said, "You have some knowledge of the old ways."

"Yes. It isn't something I would forget."

For a moment he studied her in silence. Then, gesturing to a chair directly facing his desk, he said, "Please sit down."

He waited until she had done so before sitting in the tall leather chair behind the desk. "I have been informed of your most dramatic appearance at the board meeting."

"I wasn't sure the board would admit me to the meeting if I made a formal request. So I chose simply to show up."

He nodded. "You are probably right about their disinclination to meet with you." He shifted in his chair. "You are aware there have been several claimants in the past?"

"Yes, I've read about them from time to time."

"And you've read a great many other things about the company and the Fortune family." It was a statement, not a question.

"I've read very little. For the most part I've been in Boston the last several years. The newspaper there rarely runs articles about the family."

"But of course, subscriptions to our local newspapers, which often mention the Fortune family and business, are available worldwide."

"I'm not a subscriber. You can check that."

"We already have." He pressed the intercom button to the outer office, summoning his secretary, who sat in a chair just behind Christina. "I would like to ask you some questions that might perhaps help us in this matter. And if you do not object, I would like to keep a record of your answers."

She clasped her hands tightly in her lap, determined not to show her tension. "Ask me whatever you like."

He began, "Do you remember when you first visited Hong Kong?"

She smiled at him. "You are aware that I was born in Hong Kong and lived there for almost two years. Then my parents returned to San Francisco." Her face assumed a thoughtful expression. "Let's see, the next time I recall returning to Hong Kong was when I was six. That year my father allowed me to attend the Queen's Cup races at the Jockey Club."

Lo nodded. "I remember." And then he added, "I also attended those races."

"Yes, that's right, I remember now. You were there with us."

Lo's impassive expression suddenly hardened. "That's enough. You may go now."

"Is that all you wanted to ask me?"

"It is enough."

"But . . ." She hesitated, unsure what to say or do. Had he accepted her or not?

In the same completely unemotional voice she was sure he used with clients, he said, "I commend you. The resemblance is remarkable. If we were to meet on the street, I would have been quite taken with the similarity of features."

Dismay washed over her. "You don't believe me."

"You have been instructed most admirably. But your answer to my last question was incorrect. Of course, it was such a trivial matter that only the immediate family would have

known. I did *not* attend the races that day at the Jockey
Club."

She frowned. "But you *were* there, Mr. Lo. You arrived
late, just in time for the final race. The son of a cousin was
very ill, and you were at the hospital with your family until
the danger passed. I remember, because he was only a year
older than I was, and we had played together. I was frightened
for him."

She looked directly at him. "You took a picture when the
jockey put me astride the winning horse."

Lo's shrewd eyes narrowed. "It was a bay colt, with four
white stockings."

"No, it was a black filly. She caused quite a stir. Everyone
bet against her because she was a filly. But my father bet on
her, and told me that females should never be underestimated."

Lo was clearly shaken. "Can it be?" he whispered.

Christina leaned forward. "I *am* Christina, Mr. Lo."

For one long moment, fraught with tension, he said nothing. Then he went on slowly, "If, in fact, you are Christina
Fortune, there is one overriding question. *Why* did you
leave?"

Her throat tightened. "It was a long time ago. The reason
I left is important only to me."

Steven's face contorted in anger as he came across the office. "And now, after twenty years, you come here and expect
us simply to accept that you are Christina, and turn over the
company to you? Forget it! You're a fraud!"

Lo said in a polite but firm voice, "Perhaps you'd better
wait outside, Steven."

Before Steven could argue, Richard said, "Go back to the
office. I need you to prepare the information for our meeting
this afternoon." At Steven's look of defiance, he finished, "I
can take care of this. We'll discuss everything when I get
back."

Without another word Steven stormed out of the office,
slamming the door behind him.

Lo turned back to Christina. "I am afraid that in spite of
your persuasive information about the family, there is still no

concrete proof that you are Christina Fortune. And without such proof . . ."

His voice trailed off. She realized that as far as he was concerned, the meeting was at an end. She had answered his questions, and even related information that no one but the real Christina could have known. But it wasn't enough.

It was time to play her last card.

She rose, but instead of turning to leave, she opened her purse. Carefully, she took out an antique gold chain and a jade pendant with a hand-carved dragon, rampant and fierce-looking. She laid it on the desk in front of Lo.

"This is called Tai-sing. It depicts one of the nine dragons that, according to legend, are the ancient guardians of Hong Kong harbor. I'm sure you recognize it." Her clear dark gaze met his. "My father gave it to me for my fourteenth birthday."

For the first time Lo allowed naked emotion to show in his face. "If this is real, it is nearly priceless," he whispered.

"My grandfather gave it to my grandmother. At my father's request she reluctantly gave it to my mother on their wedding day. It has been passed down to the women of the Fortune family through six generations, since Hamish Fortune first sailed the China Sea."

Richard came out of his chair. "That can't be real!"

Lo gestured to him to sit down. He was clearly trying hard to maintain his composure, but his fingers trembled as he tenderly ran his fingers over the jade pendant, lightly tracing the outline of the dragon.

"There have been reproductions," he said slowly. "Fakes."

His meaning wasn't lost on her. Fakes—like all the young women who had claimed to be Christina Fortune.

"You know the history of the Tai-sing in my family," she reminded him. "It was given to Hamish Fortune as a symbol of a blood bond to the family of Wang Tsi, a merchant, over one hundred and forty years ago, when my great-great-great-grandfather first sailed with a cargo from China to Hawaii. Hamish Fortune saved the life of Wang Tsi's firstborn son."

"You have studied your history well," Lo commented. But his eyes glittered with excitement as he turned the medallion over and over in his fingers.

"It is my family's history," she said softly.

He laid the medallion down carefully on the desktop. The likeness of the ancient Chinese ruler was an eerie reflection of his enigmatic expression. "There are people who can authenticate the medallion," he said. "I have someone in particular in mind. It would require leaving the medallion with me for a few hours, if you're willing to entrust it to me."

She looked down at the medallion. It represented so much, both her past and her future. Looking up at Lo, she nodded reluctantly.

He assured her, "I will have it back to you at your hotel no later than five o'clock this afternoon."

It was obvious that the meeting was at an end. She said, "Very well. Thank you for seeing me." As she rose to leave, her gaze met Ross McKenna's briefly. His expression was as impassive as Richard Fortune's. She was reminded that no matter how different from Richard he seemed last night, he, too, had a great deal at stake.

"Is it real?" Ross asked after she left the office.

Lo slowly shook his head. "I am not the best authority to make that decision. I will have a friend of mine, the curator at the Chinese cultural exhibit at the museum, look at it."

"Of course it's not real!" Richard came out of his chair. "The real necklace was a priceless artifact. Christina wouldn't have been walking around with it."

Lo gave him an enigmatic look. "Your mother let Christina keep it in the safe at Fortune Hill, instead of in a safety deposit box in the bank."

"What? She never told me that!"

"She knew you wouldn't approve. She realized it was dangerous to keep such a valuable piece of jewelry at home, but Christina begged her. It was the last thing Michael gave Christina before he and Laura were killed. It meant a great deal to the girl."

He finished meaningfully, "The necklace disappeared from the safe the same night that Christina disappeared. The logical assumption is that she took it with her."

Richard was silent for one long, drawn-out moment. Then

he said tightly, "I still don't believe it's real." He rose. "Call me as soon as this expert looks at it."

He strode across the room, but as he reached the door, Ross stopped him. "I wasn't informed about any meeting this afternoon. What is this all about?"

Richard said in a dismissive tone, "It's nothing important, not worth your trouble. I'm going over the shipping agreements with the Pacific Rim Cartel."

Ross was immediately suspicious. Any meeting that Richard didn't want him to attend was one that he knew he'd better not miss. "Then you won't mind my sitting in," he said smoothly. "We need to go over the details with Steven before he returns to Hong Kong. That agreement has a direct bearing on our business in the Far East. We can't afford for anything to go wrong this time."

Richard barely masked the fury behind a polite response. "The meeting is at four o'clock in my office."

"I'll be there."

Richard turned and left the office. The heavy mahogany door snapped shut behind him.

"You are like a cat who must walk the earth that shifts beneath your feet," Lo observed, quoting an old Chinese proverb.

"That's what Katherine's paying me for," Ross answered with a wry smile. "I've gotten used to it." Then his expression sobered. "Do you think the medallion is real?"

Lo picked up the pendant and carefully inspected it. "The workmanship is excellent. The gold is very old, but I cannot say whether the medallion is real or not. The Tai-sing is of special interest to my friend at the museum. He authenticated the original medallion for insurance purposes when Michael gave it to Christina. My friend was devastated when it disappeared twenty years ago. He has photographs and very detailed notes documenting the medallion. But more than that, he is Chinese and he is an expert on ancient artifacts. He will know if it is real or not."

Ross said, "I'll be meeting with the port authority and the engineers for the final inspections aboard the new tanker before we on-load cargo. Call me as soon as you know."

Lo inclined his head slightly. "You will be the first person I will call."

The call came through as Ross stood in the engine room with the engineers going over the last of the safety inspections for the *Fortune Star,* the newest ship of the line. Taking the phone from the chief engineer, he frowned as Lo shouted to make himself heard over the echo of voices inside the steel-walled engine room.

Ross was stunned. "You're absolutely certain? There's no possibility of a mistake?"

"None whatsoever," Lo responded. "The medallion is authentic. Do you want me to call Richard?"

"No. I'll be meeting with him shortly. I'll tell him." He paused, then added, "Katherine will have to know."

"I've already put through a call to her."

Ross said slowly, "This changes everything."

Lo agreed. "We must be very careful. There is a great deal at stake. Not just the company, but the emotional well-being of an old and fragile woman who has already borne more than her share of tragedy."

Two hours later, following an abbreviated meeting, four men representing a consortium of Pacific Rim financial resources left the conference room of Fortune International. The men, three Asians and an Australian, had been surprised to learn that the board had abruptly adjourned its previous day's meeting without settling any business. Before they could press the matter, Ross had assured them that everything was fine. Richard had no choice but to agree with Ross. Neither of them wanted these men to know about the young woman who had walked into the board meeting the day before, claiming to be Christina Fortune. The last thing they needed was renewed speculation about the financial security of the company.

Richard explained that the distribution of the trust had been delayed because of some last-minute paperwork that would soon be completed.

As soon as the door closed behind the men, Ross said. "I talked to Phillip Lo earlier. The medallion *is* real."

Richard's voice was tight. "He's certain?"

"There's no question."

"We'll get a second opinion from another expert."

"There is no other expert on this side of the world who knows as much about the Tai-sing. And I'm certain the government of mainland China would be less than cooperative in assisting in the authentication of a medallion that is one of their ancient artifacts. They look upon it as stolen."

"It doesn't mean that young woman is Christina," Richard insisted. "If it *is* real, then she probably stole it."

"Maybe. Maybe not. But one thing's clear—we'll have to deal with her, whether you like it or not."

And with that, Ross strode out of the room. As he headed toward his office, his mind raced. The possibility that this woman might actually be Christina complicated everything. Until yesterday he'd had to worry only about Richard. In spite of the fact that he knew Richard wanted to get rid of him, he was confident that he could ultimately win. Now he had to worry about a mysterious woman who might soon be in charge of a company that Ross was determined to continue running.

As soon as he was alone, Richard unlocked his desk drawer and took out the small book that contained the private numbers his secretary didn't have in her Rolodex. He found the number he wanted and picked up the telephone. The call was answered on the second ring.

"Yes?"

"I have a job for you."

"What is it?"

"I want you to find out some information for me."

"What kind of information?"

"Not the usual facts that anyone can get through the DMV. This is different. I want a *full* investigation," Richard emphasized.

"It will cost you."

Richard frowned. "It always does."

"Who do you want me to check out?"

"I have a portfolio. The information in it will get you started."

"Is there a name?"

"Yes," Richard answered. "Christina Grant Fortune."

There was a moment's silence on the other end of the telephone, then, "You had me investigate her disappearance twenty years ago. Far as I could tell, all the evidence showed she was probably dead."

"A woman just showed up claiming to be Christina. I want you to dig into her background, find out everything there is to know about her, especially the things she doesn't want people to know."

The man on the other end of the line chuckled. "I get it. You want me to dig deep, so you can bury her."

"Exactly," Richard replied, then hung up.

He smoothed back the hair at his temple and straightened the collar of his silk shirt. He wasn't about to let this woman, whoever she might be, disrupt his carefully laid plans.

Even if she turned out to be the real Christina.

Ross stepped into the foyer off the main lobby of the Hyatt Regency. At five o'clock, after a lengthy conversation with Katherine, Ross had called Christina and invited her to have a drink. She had refused at first, and agreed only when Ross explained that this would give him an opportunity to return the pendant. She hadn't asked the results of the examination. At first it surprised him, and then he realized that if she truly was Christina Fortune, she would be certain that the medallion would pass the closest scrutiny. If she was an impostor, she was demonstrating remarkable nerve.

She was to meet him here in the lobby, and he settled down in a chair to wait for her. A few minutes later he watched her step out of an elevator and walk toward him. Only two people came off the elevator with her. There was none of the paleness or anxiety in her face that he'd seen on that crowded elevator the night before.

She looked cool and elegant in a long-sleeved, high-necked black silk dress that would have been positively demure if not for the fact that it hugged every curve. Ross noticed a couple of men turn to stare at her in appreciation and realized that he was looking at her in exactly the same way.

She might try very hard to appear cool and self-contained, but he sensed that was merely a carefully calculated shield to protect a vulnerable, passionate nature. What would it take, he wondered, to get past that shield? To touch the fire beneath the ice?

She said politely, "Good evening."

"Thank you for agreeing to meet with me."

"I didn't really have much choice, did I? After all, you have my medallion."

He smiled. "Are you accusing me of blackmail?"

She angled her head as she looked at him, her dark hair sweeping low over her shoulder, and Ross found himself wondering what it would feel like to bury his hands in it.

"Are you aware that you hardly ever give me a direct answer? You usually answer my questions with another question."

He slipped his hand beneath her elbow as they left the lobby and waited for the driver to bring the limousine around. "Isn't that the preferred method for keeping someone guessing?" he quipped.

"You're doing it again," she pointed out.

"Forgive me. Force of habit."

"It must come from working with my uncle."

It was the first time she'd referred to Richard as her uncle. It also suggested that she was well aware of the conflict between Richard and Ross in running the company.

As the limousine pulled away from the curb, Ross handed her a small, hand-carved cherrywood box. "Your pendant. Safe and sound."

"Thank you," she murmured, opening the box.

She fumbled as she tried to unclasp it.

"Allow me," Ross offered.

She pulled her hair back and leaned forward as he fastened the clasp. His fingers lightly brushed the soft skin of her neck, and he felt something he didn't want to feel—the heat of sudden sexual attraction.

He could tell by her sharply indrawn breath and abrupt movement away from him that she felt it, too.

Clearly trying to put the mood back on an impersonal level, she asked, "Where are we going?"

Their driver carefully negotiated heavy evening traffic through the Embarcadero area to Market Street, then slipped onto the highway interchange, and took Highway 101 south, leaving the city behind.

"Are you concerned that I might be abducting you?"

"Are you?" she asked with a faint smile.

"The place I have in mind is uncrowded, and the view is incomparable."

They drove in silence for almost a half hour. The quiet luxury of the limousine insulated them from the rush of traffic and the glare of lights as the sky darkened. When they left the highway and headed toward the airport, she looked at him in surprise but said nothing.

They skirted the main terminal, then drove down a secured road that passed behind the commercial airline hangars. The limousine slowed when it reached a row of smaller hangars perched almost at the water's edge along the runways that jutted out like a giant arm extending into San Francisco Bay. Just three days earlier she had flown in over that bay.

The driver guided the limousine down a one-lane service road between two unmarked hangars. He continued out across the short access tarmac, then stopped the car, got out, and came around to open the door for them. Ross held out his hand to her.

As she stepped from the limousine, she looked first at Ross, then at the gleaming blue and white jet with the Fortune insignia on the tail section.

A young steward came down the steps to greet them. "Good evening, Mr. McKenna. We have our clearance and are ready for takeoff."

"Good. Then let's get under way immediately."

Christina turned to Ross. "Where are you taking me?" she demanded.

His hand was firm as he clasped her arm and guided her up the stairs. "We're flying to Hawaii. Katherine wants to meet you."

# Chapter 6

*I*t was almost midnight when the Fortune jet touched down at Keahole Airport. The small airport, a cluster of thatch-roofed, open-air buildings, was nearly deserted at this late hour.

The five-hour flight had been made in nearly total silence, aside from the polite chatter of the steward as he served dinner. Ross had expected Christina to be angry at being shang-haied like this. But her cold silence made him feel uncomfortably guilty. He could have dealt with open anger far more easily. He told himself he had no choice, this trip had to be made, whether she was the real Christina or an impostor. But a tiny nagging voice that sounded suspiciously like his conscience pointed out that he could have shown a little more consideration and a little less *droit du seigneur* arrogance.

He was immensely relieved when they finally touched down on the island. As they made their way to the limousine waiting at the curb, Ross watched Christina, trying to analyze her reaction. But she remained as closed as she'd been on the plane, and he couldn't tell how she felt about being here, in this place where the real Christina had spent so much of her childhood.

He felt the gentle caress of the breeze blowing in off the ocean and tasted the hint of salt in the air. It was different here than in either San Francisco or Hong Kong, even though both were by the ocean. Here the air was thick with the scent of exotic flowers. Palm trees swayed in dark silhouette against a night sky. In the distance, he knew, was the rough black surface of ancient lava flows that reached down to the sea.

This part of Hawaii was different from other parts of the islands, where the exotic, lush tropical splendor gave way to hotel strips and overcrowded beaches. Every year people poured into Honolulu and thought it was paradise with its high-rise hotels crowding each other for space, while tourists crowded each other for a patch of sand and surf.

Those same tourists thronged the open-air markets and dropped money for "authentic" island trinkets that had been imported from the Philippines or Taiwan the week before. They mingled with sailors down on "Shit Street," overrun with seedy bars and overeager young women wrapped in sarongs, and were certain they'd found paradise.

But this was true paradise. When the jet engine whined down to silence, there was only the sound of the night breeze rustling through palm fronds, and the occasional murmur of voices from the maintenance crew who'd waited for their arrival. Each time Ross came here to meet with Katherine, he felt the seductive lure of the place, potent and hypnotic.

*Paradise.*

There was a sexual energy about it, subtle and sultry, and it affected him profoundly, turning his thoughts to the physical rather than the cerebral.

This time he didn't respond as he usually did, relaxing his guard and looking forward to a brief respite from the stress of a high-powered job. This time there was a stranger in paradise. A stranger who might very well change everything.

The chauffeur, a middle-aged native Hawaiian, held the door open for them. Ross nodded at him. "How have you been, Kane?"

"Very well, thank you, Mr. McKenna."

Kane smiled politely at Christina, but said nothing. He had come to work for Katherine after Christina's disappearance, and therefore never knew her. He had the quiet reserve of a well-trained servant; nevertheless, Ross saw intense curiosity in Kane's dark brown eyes.

So, he knows why she's here, Ross thought, marveling at the amazing efficiency of the servants' grapevine. Unfortunately, none of the small staff of servants at Fortune Ranch had known Christina. There would be no one to recognize—or disclaim—this mysterious woman sitting beside him in the comfort and luxury of the limousine.

No one . . . except Katherine.

As the limo sped up the highway that followed the curve of the Kohala Coast, Ross thought about his telephone conversation with Katherine. Phillip Lo had called her earlier that afternoon and broken the news to her of another claimant to her granddaughter's inheritance. When Ross talked to her afterward, she wasn't upset or angry. As always, she was completely controlled.

"Someone else wants a piece of the pie," she said tersely.

"This woman seems much better prepared than the others," Ross responded.

"So I've been told. Phillip seems to think I'd better see her in person. He worries too much."

"There is the matter of the pendant," Ross reminded her.

There was silence at the other end of the phone. When she spoke again, her voice was strained, the only outward sign of emotion. "I suppose Phillip is right."

She paused, then made a quick decision. "Very well. Bring her here tonight. Don't give her a chance to think about it, or prepare any more than she already has. It will be late when you arrive. I'll see her first thing in the morning. It won't take long." Her voice grew stronger. "I'm certain I'll send her packing after five minutes." And with that she hung up.

Ross often marveled at Katherine's iron discipline and self-control. She never revealed emotion, never betrayed weakness. That amazing strength of will had enabled her to endure the deaths of her husband and older son, within the same year. And the disappearance, and presumed death, of her granddaughter the following year.

Since then she had run Fortune International with all the autocratic rule of Catherine the Great. Only when she was

well into her seventies, and ill health had forced her to retire
to the ranch that had been the beginning of the Fortune empire, had she allowed herself to rely more and more on Ross.

He had the energy and mobility she herself now lacked. He
carried out her ambitious plans for the company, but was far
from being her lackey. He was blunt when he disagreed with
her, and insisted on doing things his way when he felt it was
an improvement over her ideas. She didn't take his imperti-
nence well, but she tolerated it because he had made it clear
to her that he would leave rather than follow orders that he
disagreed with.

Over the years since she had first brought him into the
company, they had developed a grudging respect for each
other. He wasn't sure he liked her, but he admired her
strength of character.

Now he glanced at the woman sitting beside him. It was
disconcerting to realize she seemed to have that same strength
of character. Did it come from Katherine? Or was it merely
the stock in trade of a clever impostor?

Her face was averted from his as she stared out into the
darkness toward the hills on the right. For the first time since
she had burst into that board meeting, upsetting everyone's
plans, he had an opportunity to observe her without distraction.

He recalled the photographs he'd seen of Christina
Fortune—a pretty, dark-haired teenager with a poignant expression in her almond-shaped brown eyes. She had looked
like a girl who would grow up to be a real beauty.

Was this what she would have looked like? he wondered,
scrutinizing her face in the dim shadows of the car. It was
possible. The resemblance wasn't exact, but then twenty years
changed everyone.

This woman had the same classic features as the girl in the
photos, though her face was fuller than the youthful
Christina's had been. Christina had worn her hair long and
straight, in the popular style of the late sixties. This woman
wore hers with a hint of a wave, cut so that it barely brushed
her shoulders.

Her face was softly lit and shadowed by the moonlight

pouring in through the window. Even in the comfortable confines of the car, she held herself erect, perfectly poised, unwilling to relax. She had presence, he had to admit reluctantly.

Once again he picked up the subtle fragrance of her perfume, pleasurably aware that it was neither too sweet nor cloying, as perfume so often was. There was that hint of familiarity.

Suddenly, with a rush of feeling so strong it was almost physical, he remembered where he'd encountered that scent before. The woman who'd been his first lover had worn that same exotic fragrance.

He was nineteen. He had no idea what he wanted to do with his life, and had gone to work right out of school, driving a delivery truck. Anna Chin was Eurasian, that mixture of European and Chinese often found in Hong Kong.

They were the hidden people, frequently born of an illicit relationship, part of both cultures yet recognized by neither in a classist society where the restrictions were unbending. They were shunned by society and given only the most menial of work.

The young men worked the docks or stowed away as sailors on an outgoing vessel—anything to escape from Hong Kong. If possible, they emigrated to the United States or Canada, where class restrictions were less rigid. The women had fewer options. Uneducated and impoverished, they were often abandoned by their mothers. Many were sold by their families, or became prostitutes. For a select few there was opportunity, if they were fortunate enough to become the mistress of a foreign diplomat or businessman.

Anna was the mistress of a Swedish businessman. She was older than Ross, although she never revealed her exact age. And in the timeless tradition of the experienced, sophisticated older woman and the inexperienced, younger man, she initiated him to the art of love.

He lived with her for almost four months while the Swedish businessman was in Europe. She taught him the erotic power of the senses: sight, sound, touch, taste, and scent. He learned to appreciate the allure of a woman who is confident

in her sexuality, the feel of a woman's skin when it goes from
cool to restless heat, the soft sounds of a woman's breath
when the coolness becomes passion, the taste of a woman's
mouth, her skin, and all the dark, sensual places, and the scent
of a woman—that particular essence that is hers alone, that
will identify her from all others.

"A real lady wears only the best, and most subtle, of
scents," she once said. "And when she leaves, the memory of
her scent should linger, barely discernible yet still enticing."

*White Ginger.* That was the name of the perfume she wore.
It was as *exotic* and *mysterious* as the woman who first taught
him the sensual meaning of those two words. The woman sitting beside him wore that same understated yet provocative
fragrance. It was exactly the type of perfume a well-bred
woman like Christina Grant Fortune would choose.

Suddenly she turned to look out the opposite window, and
caught him staring at her. He could tell that she knew exactly
what he'd been thinking only a moment earlier—was she the
real Christina or a fraud? Surprisingly, her full mouth—a
mouth meant for deep, lingering kisses—curved almost imperceptibly in the barest hint of a smile. Instead of becoming
nervous at his scrutiny, she seemed amused.

"You'll never be able to tell simply by looking at me."

She was right. And it angered him.

"Katherine will be able to tell," he shot back. She was so
confident, so self-assured. He wanted to break through that
perfect facade. "That should worry you just a little."

Her brown eyes widened, and for an instant her air of cool
self-possession and reserve wavered. She looked more than
nervous—she looked scared. Surprisingly, he discovered he
wanted to hurt her, yet was unaccountably irritated with himself when he realized that he'd succeeded.

But in an instant the mask was back, hiding her emotions.
She said evenly, "If she doesn't recognize me, it will be because she rarely spent any time with me. She never had time
for anyone, not even her own children. My grandfather—and
later the business—were all that mattered to her."

Then she added, "When he died, she became obsessed with
the company. She never had time for any of her grandchil-

dren. Her secretary always chose the gifts we received. And when we visited the house in San Francisco, the servants always made certain we never bothered her. After grandfather died, she was too busy making sure the company survived as a monument to him to do any of the usual grandmotherly things."

Ross was startled to realize that sounded completely like Katherine. On the other hand, he told himself, it was precisely the kind of glib excuse an impostor would use to set up a defense in case Katherine didn't recognize her.

They rode in silence for a few minutes longer, then Christina asked, "What are all those lights?"

Following her gaze, he saw that she was looking at the brightly lit outline of the recently built hotel and condominium developments along the beach. "This area's growing rapidly," he explained.

"Grandmother must hate it. She was always opposed to any kind of new development. Did she sell off this land?"

"Richard and Diana controlled title to this property. It's all part of Richard's new development program, a joint venture with Japanese investors to build a resort here and bring more capital into Fortune International."

Her question was logical, since the real Christina would have been surprised at the massive changes that this part of the island had undergone since she had last been here. But she *wasn't* the real Christina, he told himself. She was nothing more than a clever fake, and Katherine would quickly see through her. Then she would be sent packing, lucky to get off without being prosecuted for somehow having stolen Christina Fortune's necklace.

"I'm certain you know all about the property and the development with the extensive research you've done." He watched her for a reaction, but she turned back to the window. They rode the rest of the way in silence.

When they reached the northernmost tip of the island, the car slowed and turned onto a private road. A black wrought-iron sign, hung between twin pillars made of lava rock, proudly proclaimed the name, "Fortune Ranch."

The road meandered uphill toward the lush, green highlands that were in vivid contrast to the starkness of the ancient lava flows and the pristine white beaches.

They passed white-fenced pastures. The headlights glanced over dozing horses and cattle. The land around them, to the far horizon and beyond, belonged to Katherine Fortune—over two hundred thousand acres, the largest privately owned cattle ranch in the U.S.

After a few minutes Kane brought the car to a halt in front of the main entrance to the Fortune ranch house. It was one of the few remaining historical plantation estates in Hawaii, built at the turn of the century by Christina's great-grandfather. Set amid towering palms, lush ferns, and ohia trees, the house was large yet comfortable-looking, with wide balconies and verandas, whitewashed walls, and panoramic windows.

Kane held the car door open for Ross and Christina, and they stepped out onto the graveled drive. Ross noticed that her hands were clenched at her sides. If she was the real Christina, she was looking at the place where she had spent many summers as a child with her parents. If she was an impostor, she was about to be exposed.

They followed Kane through the giant double doors and across polished teak floors. The house was silent, except for the whisper of the tropical breeze through windows that had been left open. Lights were left on in the entry, and illuminated the hallway. When they reached the bedrooms at the rear of the first floor, Kane stopped in front of an open door and said, "Your room, miss."

Ross noticed that he didn't say, *"Miss Christina."*

Kane crossed the room, turned on the light at the dressing table, and opened the double doors out onto the veranda.

"The staff has provided everything that you will need." He gestured to the cosmetics and toilet articles set out on the table. "There are clothes in the closet." He turned to Ross, who said, "Thank you, Kane, that will be all."

Christina turned briefly just inside the room. Her fingers were wrapped around the small jade pendant, her eyes shadowed by fatigue and carefully guarded emotions. "It seems the staff has thought of everything." There was accusation in her voice. "You could have told me you were bringing me here tonight."

"Katherine thought it would be more effective not to warn you."

She nodded. "It's so like her, of course." Then she added, "And you always do exactly as Katherine asks."

"Not always. But in this case I agreed with her." He didn't add that he'd come to regret it during the long flight over.

As she stood in the doorway, weariness shadowing her dark eyes, she looked quite fragile. He said in a gentle voice, "You'd better get some rest. You'll be meeting with Katherine early in the morning."

Her dark eyes met his. "And then we'll take an early flight back to San Francisco?" she asked with obvious meaning.

"I'll be staying on for a few days," he answered. "Katherine and I have some business to discuss."

"I see. Then you've already decided that I'm not Christina Fortune."

"It really doesn't matter what I think," Ross replied evenly. But they both knew it was a lie.

"Good-night, then," she said tersely.

"Good-night," he responded as she closed the door firmly.

The dream was always the same—the other children staring at him, their expressions cruel and taunting. Then one older boy shouting, "You're a bastard, you don't belong here." The other children took up the singsong chant, repeating, "You don't belong here . . . don't belong . . ."

He ran away, searching desperately for his mother. She would comfort and reassure him; she would protect him from the other children and their jeering taunts.

He ran out of the school yard, passed the ornate iron gates and stone walls onto the crowded streets filled with carts and bicycles, and vendors with ancient Chinese women squawking through toothless gums as they bargained for a scrawny chicken that hung trussed by its feet.

He ran down one street and then another. He fell and scraped his knees. The white shirt of his school uniform was torn and stained. He picked himself up and kept running. He had to find his mother. She would make everything all right. She would make the other children stop laughing.

He cut across an alley where laundry hung between the buildings high above the street, and knew this was the part of town his mother always warned him about. He cut down another street, and another, until he found the familiar road that led along the quay and then cut back up a hill lined with small, modest houses. They looked so shabby and worn, but he kept running until he found the one with the mimosa tree in the small yard.

Running up the steps, he opened the door. To his surprise, he heard voices. Then he remembered. His mother had said that his father was coming for a visit today. But when he'd begged to be allowed to stay home and see his father, her expression had grown sad and she had said that wasn't possible. His heart leapt at the thought that he would be able to see his father after all. That happened so rarely.

He hurried into the small living room and saw his father, familiar from a worn photograph. His clothes were expensive—a silk suit, immaculate white shirt, polished gold watch. He was an imposing figure, and Ross was in awe of him.

"What is he doing here?" Ross heard anger in his father's voice.

"I don't know," his mother said, concerned. "He's supposed to be at school." She came to him across the small living room and knelt in front of him. Her fingers were cool and soothing on his warm forehead.

"What is it, darling? What's happened? Look at your clothes." She didn't scold. She never scolded him. Her voice was as soothing as her hands, but he saw the frown in her eyes and knew he had done something wrong.

He couldn't get the words out to explain, because suddenly he'd started crying again and couldn't seem to stop. All the while his father stood there, looking at him with that same expression of rejection he'd seen on the faces of the children in the play yard.

"Send him away, Barbara. I want to discuss this with you alone."

He saw anger glint in his mother's eyes. Her face was very pale as she wiped the tears from his eyes. Then she slowly stood and faced his father.

"I won't send him away. He's my son." Her voice was low but clear. "He's your son, too."

"We've discussed this before, Barbara. This situation is very difficult."

"Difficult?" His mother's voice shook with anger. "Is that all this is to you—a difficult situation? For God's sake, we're talking about a little boy."

She stopped, took a moment to compose herself, then turned back to Ross, smiling down at him reassuringly. "I want you to go to your room, darling. But first get yourself some cookies from the jar. And then we'll talk about what happened at school."

He looked from his mother to the father he barely knew. Their expressions were so different. His mother's face was filled with love and tenderness. His father's expression was cold and impassive as he looked away. In that moment when his father refused to look at him, he *knew* . . . his father wanted nothing to do with him.

He pulled back from his mother and ran down the small hallway to the room at the back of the house. Slamming the door, he ran to his bed, burying himself beneath the covers. But still he could hear the voices . . . *You don't belong*. And he knew it was because his father didn't live with them . . . didn't want him . . .

Ross awoke in a sweat, his bare chest damp and his black hair plastered against his head. For a moment he felt the sharp stab of the old, familiar pain as he lay in the darkness of the unfamiliar surroundings—the pain that little boy found in the darkness of his room in that small house so many years ago. Then he remembered where he was, and the pain receded along with the faces of the children and their jeering taunts. It took longer for his father's face to recede.

When he felt in control once more, he flung off the sheet and got up from the bed and strode naked to the open French doors. He stepped out onto the balcony and breathed the cool night air, feeling the welcome sensation of the night breeze against his bare skin.

He had no idea what time it was, but it was obviously very late. In the distance there was a streak of silver on the horizon, suggesting that dawn would come soon.

As always, he told himself it was ridiculous to let himself be bothered by childish dreams. He was a man now, not a little boy. He had learned how to bury the pain of his illegitimacy. He'd learned to stand his ground, he'd learned to confront, and he'd learned to win, as his opponents invariably discovered. But in the dark of night, when he was alone, the dreams came to remind him the pain was still there—from a time and place where social class was everything, and a bastard child could never be accepted.

Hearing a sound, he looked down at the veranda below. Someone else couldn't sleep, either. He saw the young woman who called herself Christina Fortune leaning over the wooden railing that surrounded the veranda. She looked out at the night, oblivious to the fact that he stood only a few feet above her.

Her hair was disheveled around her shoulders, as if she, too, had slept restlessly. She wore a white silk nightgown that fell to her ankles. Full breasts were evident in the low-cut bodice.

She was breathtakingly beautiful, in a way she hadn't appeared to be before, in her tailored suits and careful makeup. He felt desire stir, sharper, more urgent now than it had when he'd watched her in the car. If the situation were different, he would have gone to her and quickly, effortlessly, seduced her. At this point in his life, after many relationships, he was confident of his appeal to women.

He imagined pulling down the thin straps of her gown, slowly, carefully, savoring the pleasure of undressing her. Then kissing her, at first gently, then more roughly.

But this situation didn't allow for desire, seduction, satiation. This was business. Critical business. And it would be over in the morning when Katherine sent this intriguing impostor packing.

He started to turn back to his room when he heard a sound

drift up from below—a tiny sob, filled with heartbreaking sadness. And then whispered words that seemed to hold a world of feeling . . . *"Oh, God, I shouldn't have come here."*

Suddenly she turned from the railing at the veranda, her arms wrapped about her as if she were cold. He watched as she disappeared beneath the balcony where he stood.

What had she meant? Was she an impostor, filled with the knowledge that she could never pull this off? Or was she the real Christina, overcome by despair at the knowledge that Katherine might never accept her, just as that little boy had felt such aching pain at knowing his father would never accept him?

He hadn't wanted to believe that she might actually be Christina Fortune. But he understood pain and loss all too well, and now he wasn't at all certain what he believed.

At nine o'clock the next morning, Ross joined Katherine in the formal study. She rarely used this room anymore, and he realized that she meant to confront her would-be granddaughter against the most imposing of backdrops.

There was nothing casually Hawaiian about this room. In here the teak floor was covered by priceless Aubusson carpets in vivid shades of deep burgundy and gold. Burgundy leather furniture dotted the large room. Three of the walls were covered with floor-to-ceiling bookcases filled with leather-bound editions. On the fourth wall were hung stunning works by Renoir, Degas, Monet.

And in the center, holding pride of place, was a portrait of Hamish Fortune, the sea captain who had come to this island one hundred and fifty years earlier, married a granddaughter of King Kamehameha the Great, and created the Fortune dynasty.

Hamish was a rugged-looking man with bright red hair and deep blue eyes, who looked as if he would have preferred to be on the deck of a ship instead of sitting in the very chair Katherine Fortune was sitting in now. He had come to these islands, sailing the China route to San Francisco, with a cargo hold full of priceless sandalwood, a small pouch of equally priceless pearls, and a single jade medallion.

He sold the sandalwood for an exorbitant profit, presented the pearls to King Kamehameha in exchange for the hand of his granddaughter in marriage, and gave his bride the ancient jade medallion. She, in turn, brought him a huge land dowry that was the beginning of Fortune Ranch.

Hamish continued sailing the China route, starting the first intra-island steamship company, and then extending steamship service to San Francisco. He was a shrewd man who never forgot his humble beginnings but never looked back. He imported cattle from California and Texas and transplanted them to the vast, lush wilderness of Hawaii. He diversified, planting sugarcane and pineapple. All of his valuable cargoes were transported on Fortune clippers, schooners, steamships, and eventually trawlers and tankers.

Beside the portrait of Hamish Fortune was a portrait of his wife, Leah. The ancient Hawaiians were beautiful and physically free-spirited. Ross wondered if Hamish had appreciated his wife for her own charms and not just for the massive dowry she'd brought to the marriage.

Following Ross's look, Katherine said pointedly, "He wasn't an easy man. The islanders loved him because he respected their ways and didn't look down on them as heathens. The haoles hated him, though. He knew how to drive a hard bargain when he wanted something. But I don't suppose you achieve what he did without making a few enemies."

Her voice was low and dusky, with a hint of her Southern upbringing. Ross imagined it must have been her most attractive quality as a young woman, for she wasn't particularly beautiful. She was, however, a woman who would always stand out because she had real presence, and that was far more compelling than mere beauty. Even now, when she was old and frail, her hair gray and her face deeply lined from a lifetime spent outdoors, he could see what Alexander Fortune had found so irresistible in her.

She continued, "I told Kane to bring her here. We'll get this over with, then he can take her straight to the airport. There's a commercial flight leaving in a couple of hours. I see no reason to send her back on the company jet. Besides, I want you to stay for a day or two. We have business to discuss."

He knew what business she referred to—the aborted board meeting, and the new one that would quickly be scheduled to pick up where the old one left off.

"Richard has the upper hand," Ross said bluntly. "Once your granddaughter's estate goes through probate, he'll have enough shares to override you. He'll be in full control, unless we can persuade Diana and the others to side with us."

"They won't do that."

"Even when they realize that Richard isn't the right person to run the company?"

Katherine's smile held no real humor. "You don't understand my family. None of them cares about the company. They just want to get as much money as possible out of it."

"Then we're finished, because that's our only chance to retain control."

"There's always something we can do—if we have the guts. Somehow I have to stop Richard. He will sell the company to the highest bidder, because all he wants from it is cold, hard cash. That isn't what Alexander would have wanted. I won't let it happen. I won't!"

He admired her tenacity, but this time he felt it was pointless. He had assumed he could persuade Diana and her sons to side with him, once they realized that Richard couldn't run the company as effectively as he could. But if Katherine was right, and they were interested only in draining it financially, then it was hopeless. Katherine would lose. And Ross would be forced to proceed with his alternative plan of a leveraged buyout.

He said slowly, "Richard had a meeting yesterday afternoon with a group of foreign investors."

Her sharp-eyed gaze fastened on him. "Who were they?"

"Businessmen from Taiwan, South Korea, the Philippines, and Australia."

Her gaze narrowed. "Four of the most powerful governments in the Pacific Rim. What was the meeting about?"

"Nothing terribly important. But I got the distinct impression that if I hadn't been there, the agenda would have been very different."

"How do you mean?"

"I think Richard wants to bring in outside investors."

"He can't do that!" Fury leapt into Katherine Fortune's light blue eyes. Her voice shook with emotion.

"He can do it if he controls the stock from the trust. He'll sell off just enough to bring in capital to pay the interest to the lenders for those six new tankers."

"Outsiders owning part of Fortune International." She shook her head in dismay, and her grip tightened on the crown of the cane she was now forced to use. Her pale, delicate skin had become translucent with age, exposing the network of blue veins.

"I promised my husband I would never allow that to happen." Her voice shook. "If Michael had lived . . ."

Ross watched as she fought the tide of emotion that threatened to overwhelm her at the memory of her beloved firstborn son. The body might be frail, but the indomitable will that had gotten her through so much tragedy was more defiant than ever.

She insisted, "No matter what I must do, I will not allow my . . ." she hesitated for a moment, then went on, "my *son* to sell off this company, piece by piece, simply to feed his own greed."

At that moment there came a deferential knock at the door. For one split second Katherine's self-assurance wavered. Then she composed her emotions behind that imperious facade and said in a voice that faltered only slightly, "Come in."

Kane entered and said, "Your guest is here, Mrs. Fortune."

He stepped aside, and the woman who claimed to be Katherine's granddaughter came in. She stood just inside the doorway, as if hesitant to enter all the way. Her dark eyes met Katherine's, and while there was nervousness in them, there was also strength and determination.

Ross was impressed. He'd seen the strongest men wilt under Katherine's piercing gaze, but this young woman stood her ground. Glancing from Christina to Katherine, he was surprised to see a flicker of doubt in Katherine's eyes.

Christina greeted the woman she claimed as her grandmother, by saying simply, *"Grandmère."*

Ross saw the doubt deepen in Katherine's eyes.

It *can't* be, he thought. She can't be Christina Fortune. Or can she?

# Chapter 7

*K*atherine drew in her breath sharply. Her voice trembled as she asked, "What did you say?"

*"Grandmère,"* Christina repeated. "It's what you asked us to call you when we were children." Her eyes locked with Katherine's. She didn't look away as most people usually did when confronted by Katherine Fortune.

Christina continued in an even voice, "You said that it sounded more elegant than grandmother. It was what you called your grandmother when you were growing up in Louisiana."

Katherine thought of her childhood in the poorest part of the French Quarter in New Orleans ... walking beside her grandmother down the narrow streets of the Vieux Carré, hearing the syncopated clop of the carriage horses mingled with the sounds of street musicians, climbing to the top of the levee and looking out over the mud-colored Mississippi River. And listening as her beloved *grandmère* said, "Someday, Katherine, you will have everything that you don't have now. I promise you, child. You will have love and happiness and wealth beyond your wildest dreams."

It was nothing more than the romantic dreams of a woman whose own life had been hard and filled with disappointments, who wanted something more for her only grandchild.

Ironically her grandmother was proved right. In spite of the fact that she was poor and not especially pretty, Katherine had achieved all those things. Unfortunately, she achieved them too late to share them with her beloved *grandmère*.

She was overwhelmed by a profound sense of loss for the illiterate woman who had worked as a cleaning lady and raised her when her mother died and her father abandoned her. That same sense of loss was something she'd had to deal with many more times—the loss of the husband she adored, her favorite son, and . . . her granddaughter.

Her attention fastened on the young woman who stood before her. She demanded, "Who told you this? Who gave you such personal information about my granddaughter?"

"No one told me. I *am* Christina. How else would I know these things?"

How else, indeed, Katherine thought. Pulling herself together, she turned to Ross, who stood silently beside the desk. He hadn't said a word, but she knew nothing escaped him. He was as sharp as they came, which was why she'd hired him in the first place. And why she relied on him. But she couldn't rely on him in this situation. She had to do this alone.

"Leave us. I want to talk to her alone."

She could tell by the set of his mouth that he didn't think it was wise, but at the moment she didn't care what he thought. Later he could give her his opinion, and she would listen. But not now. Now she needed a little more time with this young woman who claimed to be her granddaughter.

"Very well," Ross agreed reluctantly. "But call if you should need me." The glance he gave the young woman spoke volumes. He didn't believe she was telling the truth. Neither did Katherine. But she had to find out how this young woman had obtained information that only the Fortune family would have known.

When the door closed behind Ross, the two women stared at each other. Finally Katherine said, "You may as well sit down. Apparently this is going to take a bit longer than I expected."

The younger woman sat on the sofa and faced the desk. Katherine began, "First, I must decide what to call you."

"My name is Christina."

Katherine was unconvinced. "So you say."

The young woman raised her chin in a defiant gesture. "You'll have to call me something. It might as well be Christina."

Katherine was silent for a long moment before finally relenting. "Very well. I will call you Christina." Then she added pointedly, "For the time being. But I don't recall my granddaughter's being so disrespectful."

"I was fifteen the last time you saw me. It's been twenty years. I've changed a great deal."

"That brings us to the critical point, doesn't it? If you are Christina, why did you leave?"

This was a question that an impostor would find almost impossible to answer satisfactorily. Katherine expected her to hesitate, to make excuses, and finally to come out with some vague explanation that wouldn't hold water. Then Katherine could dismiss her, and put the whole distasteful episode behind her.

When Christina looked down, breaking eye contact, Katherine was certain she was finding it impossible to come up with a convincing answer. When Christina finally looked up, her face was pale, her eyed wide and dark with emotion. Her voice was hardly more than a whisper. "I was desperately unhappy and lonely. I had no one to turn to. There was nothing—no one—here for me after my parents died."

Both the response and the naked emotion were unexpected. So, Katherine thought, she was an accomplished actress as well as a liar. "*I* was there for my granddaughter," she shot back.

Christina's eyes darkened in anger. "You were never there for anyone, except Grandfather, and later the company. All you cared about was the company, and Grandfather's dreams for it."

The guilt that Katherine had buried deep all these years clawed its ugly way to the surface. Every word this young woman spoke was true, and the truth was more painful than Katherine could have imagined after all these years. She took refuge in defensiveness. "My granddaughter had a great deal more than I did at her age. She was well provided for."

"Provided for?" Christina was on her feet. She paced across the room, then whirled back to face Katherine. "A child needs love more than money. Where was that love when I needed it?"

Katherine came up out of the antique captain's chair behind the desk. She leaned forward, her hands spread on the desktop. "I loved my granddaughter!"

Christina's voice trembled. "How can you say that when you turned me away? You don't even know the meaning of the word."

"I didn't turn you away!"

"You turned me over to Richard and Alicia. They didn't want the responsibility of raising me, but you didn't care. You simply didn't want to be bothered with me."

Katherine stared at her, trying to see beyond the changed appearance, beyond the past twenty years, to the girl this young woman had once been. Dear God, she thought, was it possible that she *was* Christina?

All her strength seemed to seep out of her as she sat down heavily in the chair. Her voice wavered. "It seemed the best thing to do at the time. After your father . . ." She caught herself. "After *my son* died, it was necessary for me to take over the operation of the company. Richard and Alicia lived with me at Fortune Hill, and it made sense that they raise Christina."

"Richard hated me." Christina's voice quivered. "Just as he always hated my father."

"That's not true!" Katherine's voice rose. Then she stopped as she realized that this young woman had caught her in her own lie. Richard *had* always hated Michael, from the time they were small children.

Her sons were always fiercely competitive, and so very different. Both had the same aggressive spirit inherited from their father. Alexander taught them that there was no acceptable alternative to winning. Winning was everything, nothing else mattered. But the critical difference between her two sons lay in their manner of winning.

Michael was a fierce competitor who enjoyed the competition itself as much as he liked winning. He was a gracious loser, who never seemed to feel that losing in any way diminished him. For Richard, winning was a matter of life and death, and he did whatever he had to do to achieve it. When he lost, he could be violently angry and resentful.

She was grateful that it was Michael who was older and would one day take his place as head of Fortune International.

Then Alexander died in 1968, and Michael took over as President and Chairman of the Board. In less than a year, he, too, was dead, drowned along with Christina's mother, in a sailing accident. Richard had assumed he would take control, but Katherine didn't trust him to run the company with the same sense of honor and integrity that Alexander and Michael had possessed. Since then, she and Richard had been locked in bitter combat.

Now watching the young woman who restlessly paced the room, Katherine knew that whether or not she actually *was* her granddaughter, she was right. Katherine should never have put Christina in Richard's hands.

This conversation wasn't going at all the way Katherine had planned. She wasn't prepared for such emotional bloodletting. Where had this young woman obtained such personal information about the family? Katherine believed she was a fake, but she was a fake with a good source of information.

"Who put you up to this?" she asked angrily. "Is it my daughter, or perhaps one of my grandsons?"

"Do you really think any of them would have anything to gain by helping me?"

No, Katherine thought, of course not. They would have nothing to gain and everything to lose. They needed control of the stocks held in trust, in order to control the company.

Katherine went on, "Phillip told me that you're well informed about the family. There's no point in asking the same questions he asked. You obviously won't be caught that way. But I have a few questions of my own."

Christina sat down once again. "Ask whatever you like." Her voice was calm and steady, although Katherine sensed wariness in her. This young woman wasn't quite as confident as she tried to appear.

"Where did you get the pendant?"

Christina's hand instinctively went to the small medallion that hung about her neck. Then her hand dropped to her lap. "My father gave it to me for my fourteenth birthday. It's a family heirloom."

Her gaze fastened on the table and the double portraits. "Hamish Fortune gave it to his Hawaiian bride when he came to the island. It's been passed down to the firstborn son in each generation. Grandfather Alex gave it to you on your wedding day, and you gave it to my mother when she married my father."

Katherine told herself this was information anyone could have gotten by reading frequent publicity about the family, or perhaps old newspaper accounts from when her granddaughter disappeared. The question was, Where did this young woman get the pendant if she wasn't Christina?

Katherine went on, "What did your mother call you when you were little?"

"Kiki. That was how I pronounced Christina, and she used it because she thought it was cute. I was twelve when I asked her to stop because it sounded babyish."

That, too, was something she might have learned from the newspapers, Katherine thought. There had been countless articles about Michael Fortune and his family. Katherine had to find some other way to expose this young woman for the liar that she was. Her expression remained carefully neutral as she asked, "What happened to the pony you had as a child?"

As she'd expected, this question unsettled Christina in a way that others hadn't. She appeared flustered and confused, and repeated blankly, "Pony?"

Katherine allowed the awkward silence to stretch out between them. Then she smiled slowly, certain she had finally caught her.

"You didn't have a pony," she explained. "You wanted one, as all children do, but your father told you that you must be satisfied with the horses here at the ranch."

"I know that I didn't have a pony," the young woman shot

back angrily. "I was confused by the question. I thought you must be referring to one of the horses I rode here."

Katherine leaned back in the chair and collected her thoughts. She obviously couldn't intimidate this young woman. It would take hours, perhaps even days, of intense questioning to prove anything beyond a shadow of a doubt.

"Very well," she finally said, "tell me where you went when you left and what you've been doing for the past twenty years."

"I took a bus to New York. I had some money—about two hundred dollars. For a while I lived on the streets with some other kids. When my money ran out, I went to a shelter that was run by the Catholic church. They helped me finish my education. I went to college in Boston. I've worked for an investment banking firm for the past fifteen years."

Katherine considered all of this. Since it would be easy to verify this information, she assumed the young woman was telling the truth. If that was the case, she was rather impressive. Whatever she might be, it was clear she was neither stupid nor ill prepared. "It sounds as if you've made a successful life for yourself. Why come back now?"

"You know why. If I hadn't returned, the inheritance would have gone to the rest of the family."

"So you admit that you're here solely because of the money," Katherine responded with grim satisfaction. "I suspect that's the first entirely honest answer you've given me this morning."

"You know as well as I do that any money I might inherit is tied up in shares of the company, a company my father cared about very deeply. I want to be part of it."

"You want a great deal."

"It's my inheritance," Christina insisted, "All that I have left of my parents. And I've waited a long time for it."

To Katherine, it seemed those words held far more meaning than merely the obvious. The young woman was an impostor, she was convinced of it. Still, there was *something* about her.

The sweet, gentle young girl she remembered would never have spoken to her the way this young woman had, or looked at her as if she felt nothing but contempt. The granddaughter she *thought* she knew would never have run away. But Christina *had* run away. This young woman had mentioned living on the streets. Katherine could well imagine what she had endured there.

Katherine had grown up in poverty. She understood it. She knew the kind of determination and resilience it took to survive it. But her granddaughter had grown up in a sheltered, privileged environment. The only adversity Christina had to face was the death of her parents. While that was devastating, she didn't have to go through it alone. She had a family to care for her. Would she have had what it took to survive on her own? And if she had survived, would she have grown into this strong, determined woman fighting for her inheritance?

Katherine finally spoke, in an uncharacteristically wistful voice. "My granddaughter was very special to me. I wanted the best for her. And I loved her deeply."

Christina considered her for a long moment before finally responding, "Perhaps you did, in your own way. But you never showed it."

No, Katherine was finally forced to admit to herself, I never did. She reached a hand to her forehead. This meeting had brought profound and unresolved feelings sharply to the surface. She suddenly felt too old and too tired to deal with it any longer.

She closed her eyes and sighed heavily. Then she slowly opened them and looked at the young woman before her. *"Who are you?"* she demanded.

"I've already told you."

Katherine slowly shook her head. Her voice trembled with fatigue as she said, "My granddaughter died twenty years ago. The police were convinced of it."

"They were wrong," Christina answered simply.

Katherine gestured weakly with her hand. "Leave me."

Christina stood slowly. So, it was over. She had no idea where she was supposed to go from here. Did Katherine want her to leave immediately? Or had Christina persuaded her, just a little?

Katherine's voice stopped her at the door. "You will remain here for a few days. I need time to think about this." It was not a request or an invitation, but a command that she assumed would be obeyed without question. Then she added, "Kane will be waiting outside the door. Send him in."

Watching her go, Katherine felt a tiny surge of hope that she was terrified to acknowledge after all these years.

Christina sat on the veranda, looking out at the lush green pastures and, in the distance, the ocean. The water sparkled with silver pinpoints of light on this crystal clear, sunny morning. Sailboats with boldly colored sails skimmed across the water. Every so often, she could make out the telltale spout and gently rounded hump of a migrating whale. The whales were early this year. Normally they didn't come until December or January.

It had rained earlier that morning, the kind of brief, soft rain that came and went so frequently in the islands. It had left everything glistening with moisture. A rainbow arced across the sky in the distance over the mountains.

As a child she had believed that rainbows were magical. That was before life became so terrifying that even a rainbow's beauty couldn't dispel its ugliness. She had stopped believing in rainbows. She couldn't imagine ever believing in them again.

She sat there, sipping the tea the young Hawaiian maid had brought her. The warmth of the strong, dark liquid was calming after the emotionally draining confrontation with Katherine. Even more than Richard or Ross, Katherine was the key to her success or failure. When Christina had walked through the door of the study and come face-to-face with Katherine, she realized that this deceptively frail-looking woman—and not Richard or Ross—was her strongest adversary.

Richard was ruthless and determined. She didn't take his threats lightly. After long, frustrating years he finally had something within his grasp that he had wanted very badly. He would go to almost any length to stop her from taking it away from him.

Ross was dangerous for entirely different reasons. From the moment she first saw him in the boardroom, he affected her in ways she didn't want to admit, eliciting feelings within her that she couldn't allow herself to feel. He was a disturbingly attractive man, who didn't fit the mold of any other man she'd known. He was polished and sophisticated. Yet she suspected that when the polish and sophistication were stripped away, he could be as ruthless as Richard when he wanted something. He wanted to continue running Fortune International. He wouldn't simply hand his power over to her.

Katherine was different. The company was her lifeblood. She'd devoted herself to it and for years had fought Richard over control of it. She wasn't about to hand the company over to someone she knew must be an impostor.

But the events of the morning had been far more difficult than Christina had expected them to be. She hadn't anticipated the depth of emotions she now felt. They were frightening in their intensity.

She'd had to fight to keep them carefully in check. If she fell apart, Katherine would simply send her away, and she would lose the chance to accomplish her *real* purpose in coming here.

She told Katherine that she came to claim her inheritance. That was certainly the obvious motive, one that Katherine, and everyone else, might easily believe. The truth was far more complex—and terrifying.

If Katherine denied her claim, then it would probably be almost impossible to prove that claim in a court battle.

She sensed that Katherine didn't want to believe her. Because if she *was* Christina, that would force Katherine to confront the painful truth that she had somehow failed her granddaughter and was at least partially to blame for Christina's disappearance twenty years earlier.

She had seen a glimmer of the pain that Katherine tried so hard to hide earlier that morning. It wasn't expected, and it had surprised her. For those few moments, she sensed Katherine almost believed her . . . or wanted to believe her. Everything she knew about Katherine, everything she'd read about her activities over the past twenty years hadn't prepared her for that glimpse of emotional vulnerability.

"Mind if I join you?"

She jerked around at the sound of Ross's voice. She was so

deeply submerged in her own thoughts that she hadn't heard him come out onto the veranda.

"Please do," she murmured, trying to sound casual. In the two days she'd known this man she'd found it impossible to feel completely at ease in his presence.

He was, she noticed, perfectly relaxed, or at least he appeared to be, as he sat down at the table and poured himself a cup of tea. He prepared it the English way—with a little milk. It shouldn't have surprised her, she thought. After all, he'd grown up in Hong Kong with its predominate English influence.

As always, he looked polished and sophisticated. But his well-publicized reputation for taking a tough, street-wise approach to business didn't fit the sophisticated image. None of the articles she'd read about him in business journals had revealed anything of his family background. Whatever his background was, she sensed that it wasn't one of breeding and privilege.

One important thing all those articles had revealed—he was capable of playing hardball. But then, she reminded herself, so was she.

She said pointedly, "You're surprised I'm still here. You expected Katherine to pack me off on the next available flight to anywhere, didn't you?"

His smile was unexpected and disarming. She felt something stir within her, and had to remind herself not to trust that smile, no matter what disturbing physical responses it evoked. She leaned back against the railing of the veranda, her hands braced at either side.

"Yes," he answered. "Apparently I underestimated you."

"Apparently." She watched as he sipped the tea, his long fingers lazily entwined about the exquisite Limoges china cup. His expression was contemplative.

"Why do you refer to her as Katherine, and not as your grandmother?"

"She was never what you would call the typical grandmother. Our relationship was very . . . distant."

"But you did spend a great deal of time here each summer," he reminded her.

"Oh, yes." She smiled, angling her face away from him to stare out at the ocean. "My cousins and I came here for several weeks each summer, but we rarely saw Katherine. She was always busy with the company or the ranch, leaving us in the care of servants who didn't bother to watch us too closely. We had the time of our lives—the four of us, the servants, and the ranch hands. Frankly, it was better when she was gone."

"You don't like your family very much, do you?"

Her gaze snapped around and fastened on him. "I like some of them very much. How do you feel about them?"

"They're not *my* family. It doesn't matter whether I like them or not." Then his expression shifted to wry amusement. "They don't exactly seem the ideal, all-American family— love, apple pie, and all that sort of thing, as the saying goes."

"They're tremendously wealthy and powerful. That doesn't always bring out the best in people."

"I suppose I'm fortunate that I only have to work with them."

"If I hadn't shown up, and the inheritance had been divided between them, you wouldn't be working with them."

His blue eyes narrowed. "What makes you think that?"

"It's no secret that you and Richard have been at odds from the very beginning. You represent Katherine, and she wants to preserve the company as it was when Alexander Fortune was running it. Richard wants to sell off a portion to foreign investors to bring in more capital. If that fails, he'll take the company public. You're the only one who stands in his way. All he needs are enough shares to override Katherine, and then he'll get rid of you, and undoubtedly make Steven his new CEO."

"You seem to know a great deal about the company."

"I made it my business to find out everything about it. After all, it *is* my company, too."

"That remains to be seen. Katherine hasn't accepted that you are her granddaughter."

Christina had turned back to her view of rolling pastures that surrounded the ranch, and the expanse of ocean that seemed to go on forever. "She will," she said in a quiet voice.

"You seem very confident."

"I have to be. I have promises to keep . . ." There was a wistfulness that hadn't been there before, that same wistfulness he'd heard the night before when he'd eavesdropped on her.

Ross's eyes narrowed. "What did you promise?" For just a fraction of a second her guard was down, and he saw the vulnerability beneath the facade of detachment.

Then she had herself under careful control again, and she explained simply, "I promised myself that I would do this."

He knew she wasn't about to explain further. He said, "Katherine asked me to inform you that she'll see you at dinner. She's not as strong as she likes everyone to think she is, and your meeting tired her considerably. She's going to rest for the remainder of the day. She's asked me to show you around the island."

She wasn't fooled for a minute. "What you really mean is that she's asked you to keep an eye on me, ask me more questions, check my responses, and see if you can catch me in a lie."

Once more that smile curved the corners of his mouth. "Exactly."

"Do I have a choice?"

"No."

She gave in gracefully. "Very well. What are your plans?"

"I thought we'd visit some of Christina's favorite places."

"And see if I remember them?"

He ignored the pointed question. "You might change into a bathing suit and pull some shorts over it." Then he looked out across the vast expanse of emerald green pastures that rolled away from the main house. "It's going to be hot today, you might want do some swimming. You should enjoy that. Katherine tells me that Christina was an excellent swimmer."

"I wish you would stop referring to me in the third person like that. I'm Christina."

His smile was enigmatic. "We'll see."

She found shorts, a tank top, and a bathing suit in the wardrobe of the guest room, and wondered whom the clothes belonged to. She asked a maid, who explained in a half-embarrassed manner that Steven Chandler often entertained female "friends" at the ranch. The shorts, and other assorted clothing, including the nightgown she'd worn the night before, made her feel like one of those "friends"—a transient guest, invited for a weekend or holiday, and then expected to leave.

Ross lowered the top of the white Mustang convertible before they left the ranch. They drove down Queen Kaahumanu Highway, past Anaehoomalu Bay and the airport.

The liquid heat of the sun beat down on them as they followed the gray ribbon of coastal highway. Christina had pulled her hair back in a ponytail and tied it with a scarf. The wind drowned out any possible conversation. She laid her head back against the headrest and simply let herself absorb the sun, wind, and salt air.

The Hawaiian sun glaring off the water could be intense. And it had been a long time since she'd been out in the sun like this. Still, as a child, she rarely burned. She had the kind of dark gold skin that went with her dark hair and eyes.

Ross wore white cotton shorts and a deep blue T-shirt that matched the deep blue of his eyes. With his dark skin, he certainly didn't need to worry about sunburn. She found herself wondering if he was naturally dark or if he took time from the pressure of business to enjoy the outdoors.

A picnic hamper, along with a small ice chest filled with drinks, sat in the backseat. Ross obviously intended to keep her out all day. She understood his motive all too well. He had undoubtedly been instructed by Katherine to take her to every spot that Christina Fortune had known as a child. If she failed to recognize something, or react appropriately, that would be ammunition Katherine could use to discredit her claim.

*Everything* was on the line. This was the ultimate test, and she simply must not fail. But the tension that drummed along her nerve endings didn't come entirely from the need to win Katherine's approval. It also came from the fact that she was alone with Ross, and despite all her efforts, she couldn't help being aware of him as a man.

She studied him as he kept his gaze fastened on the winding road. The T-shirt molded him, outlining the contour of muscles across his chest and shoulders. The shorts revealed a lean waist and long, sinewy legs. She realized this was not the body of a man who spent all his time in corporate jets or behind a desk in an artificially lit office high above the skyline of San Francisco or Hong Kong. It was the body of a man who was accustomed to hard physical exercise.

She thought of tennis, or racquetball, then quickly dismissed both. She was only just beginning to get to know Ross McKenna, but she sensed he would have little patience for either. There wouldn't be enough challenge in smashing a ball across a court, or against a concrete wall.

She took in the solid, angular bones of his face. His British ancestry was evident in his aquiline nose, high cheekbones, and firm chin.

He flicked a quick glance at her, and in that moment, when their eyes briefly locked, the air seemed charged with a sexual tension that was as powerful and reckless as it was sudden and unexpected.

She held herself absolutely still, barely breathing, wondering if he felt it, too. There was a subtle change in his expression. Then he abruptly turned his gaze back to the road.

The sensation of intense sexual attraction vanished instantly, as if it had never happened.

But it *had* been there. She couldn't pretend it hadn't.

Ross was dangerous in ways she had just come to understand. She realized there was far more at risk here than an inheritance and old promises to be kept. Her heart was at risk, as well.

# Chapter 8

$C$hristina looked around her at the lush coconut palm grove that dotted the crescent-shaped, white sand beach; the small, shallow lagoon; the massive stone wall formed from lava that once flowed here; and a tall, narrow, thatched building.

"Pu'uhonua," she whispered. Then, looking at Ross, she translated, "It means *'place of refuge.'*"

"Do you remember it?" Ross asked, watching her carefully.

She knew perfectly well what he meant. "My parents used to bring me here on picnics, when I was little. I thought it was a wonderful place to swim. It was only when I was older that I understood the significance of it."

"And what is that?"

She was sure that he knew as much about this place as she did. "It's a sacred refuge, the ancient home of an *ali'i*, a ruling chief. Defeated warriors could take refuge here, and their enemies couldn't harm them. People who had broken the *kapu* came here. The Hawaiians believed that breaking the sacred *kapu* offended the gods and the gods would react by causing lava flows, tidal waves, or earthquakes. So if someone broke the *kapu*, he would be pursued and killed, unless he could reach this place."

Ross knew about the ancient legend, but he found himself

drawn to the way she explained it with almost childlike wonder. "And if he made it here?" he prompted.

"A ceremony of absolution was performed by the *kahuna pule,* the priest, and all was forgiven. This was a place of life, where someone could find a second chance." Once again there was that faint wistfulness in her voice, which hinted at more than she wanted to reveal.

"Second chances," Ross repeated thoughtfully. He stood near the water's edge, his back to the small lagoon, the breeze lifting his hair from his forehead. He almost looked like an *ali'i* himself, with his black hair, dark skin, and air of command. Christina could easily imagine him presiding over a kingdom like this, just as he presided over the kingdom that was Fortune International.

At that moment she understood perfectly why Katherine had chosen him over everyone else to run the company. He had the steely determination, confidence, and strength that was needed to run a multinational company like Fortune International, and to fight Richard Fortune and anyone else who attempted to take it away from Katherine. She knew he would fight her with equal determination. Suddenly she was frightened of him, and it was all she could do not to tremble before his relentless, probing gaze.

He asked, "If you really are Christina Fortune, is that why you came back? For a second chance?"

She was caught off guard by the question. It was far more perceptive than Ross could possibly imagine, and for once her defenses weren't strong enough to hide the turbulent emotions beneath the carefully controlled surface.

"I . . ." She stopped, then looked away, focusing on the *ki'i*—a stone carving standing on a rock in the shallow end of the lagoon, then the Great Wall that had once separated the palace grounds from the commoners' huts, the temple itself, *anything* other than Ross.

He persisted, "Did you come to San Francisco looking for some kind of sanctuary?"

Her thoughts went back twenty years, to that terrifying night when two young girls had tried desperately to find a safe place, not only from the man who chased them but from the shared nightmare experience that had driven them to the dangerous streets of New York.

"I don't believe that sanctuary exists anywhere," she whispered. "Not even here at *Pu'uhonua*."

"What about forgiveness?"

Still not meeting his look, she said in a small voice, "That seems to be the most elusive thing of all."

She forced herself to look at him. There was a poignant expression in his eyes that revealed a vulnerability she never would have suspected he possessed. She was surprised to see that his own defenses were a bit shaky at that moment.

"How do *you* feel about forgiveness?" she asked. She was uncertain exactly why the question had occurred to her, but as soon as she asked it, she knew she'd touched a nerve.

Anger glinted in those deep blue eyes. "As a virtue, I think it's highly overrated. Revenge makes a lot more sense to me than forgiveness."

"Then we have something in common."

Before he could question her further, she said, "I've had enough of interrogations for a while. I'm going swimming."

Turning her back on him, she pulled off the shorts and tank top, letting them fall on the sand, and kicked off her sandals. She was aware that he watched her as she raced into the water, splashing in the shallows, then throwing herself into the deeper part. The water was placid in the sheltered cove, with no breaking waves to impede her progress. With quick, sure strokes, she headed away from the beach, away from Ross and his disturbing questions and his even more disturbing presence.

She was careful not to swim out too far. She knew the current beyond the cove could be treacherous, and could easily carry her out to sea if she went too far. Gradually she felt her body relax as the tension of their confrontation left her. The water was warm and clear. Beneath her she could see schools of brightly colored tropical fish swimming amid multicolored coral. Turning around to face the beach, she treaded water and looked at the magnificent setting. Despite what she'd told Ross about sanctuarys not existing anywhere, she felt drawn to this place. If there were such a thing as sanctuary, it would be here, in this lovely, serene setting.

Perhaps someday, if she accomplished what she'd set out to do, she could return here and try to find the forgiveness that had eluded her for twenty years, that had kept her heartsick in a way that nothing could alleviate.

Perhaps.

She saw Ross sitting on the beach, watching her. Her arms and legs were tired now, and she decided to return to the beach. But as she swam toward Ross, who stood there, waiting for her, she wasn't at all certain if she was swimming toward sanctuary—or danger.

When she walked out onto the sand, she saw that he'd spread out a blanket and opened the picnic hamper and ice chest. Instead of the usual paper plates and Styrofoam cups that most people used on picnics, there were gold-rimmed china plates, real silverware, and crystal wineglasses. There was a bottle of white wine, cold chicken and ham, foie gras spread on thin crackers, and a luscious assortment of fresh Hawaiian fruit—guava, apples, mango, and papaya, all sliced and ready to eat.

Picking up a beach towel that lay folded at one end of the blanket, she dried her face. Then she wrapped the towel around her shoulders and sat down cross-legged on the blanket. Ross watched her without saying a word. She was intensely aware of their nearness to each other . . . the scant coverage the bathing suit provided . . . their isolation on the deserted beach. And Ross, watching her, always scrutinizing, searching for some inconsistency, a flaw, anything that would give her away.

Determined not to let him win in this war of nerves, she forced herself to look directly at him with an unwavering gaze. He was almost, but not quite, too handsome to be taken seriously. In Christina's experience, men who were this handsome were usually shallow. But not this man. He was compelling in a way that she couldn't dismiss.

She noticed the fine weave of his T-shirt, with its designer logo, the musky sandalwood fragrance of his cologne, and his hands—surprisingly rough-looking for someone so sophisticated. Her pulse quickened, and there was a slight tremor in her hand as she reached for a piece of fruit. As she bit into the soft, sweet, white pulp of the apple, she realized she was absolutely ravenous. She hadn't eaten breakfast, and she tried to convince herself the lack of food and the unaccustomed swim were entirely responsible for her suddenly sharp appetite.

"I hope you like the lunch Katherine had them prepare for us. She said these are all your favorites."

"It's delicious," she responded, taking a bite of the crisp, cold fried chicken.

"Try some of the ham. It's excellent," he said, offering her a slice.

She smiled and shook her head. "I don't eat pork. Katherine knows that."

He didn't say anything, but she caught the subtle change in his expression. He'd tried and failed to catch her at something trivial, yet significant. She'd passed one more hurdle.

They ate in silence, watching the water lap gently against the beach, listening to the breeze murmuring through the giant fronds of the palm trees, and feeling the warm sun on their backs. When they finished, she helped him pack up the hamper, then they sat there, sipping the last of the wine. She breathed in the clean, fresh air, thinking how different it was from the pollution of Boston. But then everything about this island was different from Boston. Different and better. She found herself wishing she could stay here forever, and never have to face the terrible dilemmas that awaited her back in the real world.

She smiled inwardly. She wasn't the first person to be seduced by paradise. She wondered if Ross felt the same, if he ever let himself relax and come out from behind that wall of reserve. Looking at him now, she felt instinctively that the image he presented to the world wasn't an accurate portrait of the real man. There was too much of the street fighter about him, in the way he handled himself.

Whatever his background was, he was far too tough to have been born with a silver spoon in his mouth. He was a highly successful executive, in charge of one of the biggest privately held corporations in the country. He'd fought his way to the top. She knew he'd fight to stay there.

As she watched him, she was uncomfortably aware of the shift of hard muscles beneath his shirt, recalling an earlier impression that he would always demand more—of himself, his work, and any woman who was willing to risk falling in love with him.

"You're analyzing me," he said suddenly, breaking the silence between them.

She hid her thoughts behind a smile. "Why not? You've been analyzing me from the first moment I walked into that board meeting."

"That's part of my job. To prove you're the impostor I'm convinced you are. There's nothing personal in it."

"Isn't there?" she couldn't resist asking.

She felt pleased, somehow, to see that her question unnerved him slightly. But he instantly turned the tables by asking, "Is there anything personal in your scrutiny of me?"

"Of course not!" she insisted. But it was a lie, and not a very good one. No matter how hard she tried to convince herself that she shouldn't be physically aware of him as a man, the truth was she was intensely aware of him. With each breath she inhaled the musky fragrance of his cologne. With each look she noticed more details about his appearance—a small white scar under his eye, the way his perfect mouth narrowed into a hard line when he was angry, or softened appealingly when he was pleased about something.

She forced herself to break off the dangerous thoughts, furious with herself for the uneven beat of her pulse. Control was something she'd worked hard at the past twenty years; control over situations and her emotions. The past two days she had felt constantly on the verge of losing that control. She'd known this wouldn't be easy, and she'd prepared herself for it. But there was another side to this situation that she hadn't anticipated—Ross McKenna.

She decided it was safer to ignore him and enjoy the peace and quiet and solitude. This exquisitely lovely place might very well be the quintessence of paradise, and she wanted to drink it in, if only for a little while. She put away all thoughts of Katherine and Fortune Shipping and the huge inheritance that was at stake, and focused on the here and now. She felt almost at peace, and that was a feeling she hadn't known in a long, long time.

Forgetting for a moment that Ross wasn't merely a friendly companion in this lovely place, she turned to say something to him. He leaned toward her, and her shoulder brushed his.

As she jerked back abruptly, his hand steadied her. For one long, delicious moment his glance focused on her face, then traveled down to her throat and finally her breasts, outlined clearly under the tight, wet bathing suit. His eyes lingered for only a split second, before returning to her face, but that was long enough to make her wonder what it would be like to kiss him.

She quickly pushed the thought aside. Remember who he is, she warned herself.

She pulled back from his touch, aware of a faint sensation of heat across her skin, and said, "Sorry."

"It's all right," he replied in a voice that had become gruff. "We'd better be going," he continued without looking at her. "We have several other places to visit."

While Ross folded the blanket, Christina slipped on the shorts and tank top, slid her feet into the sandals, then pulled a comb from her purse and combed through the wet, tangled strands of her hair. They walked in rather awkward silence back toward the car in the small parking lot near the beach.

For a little while there on the beach, she and Ross had set aside their psychological warfare. For a few minutes they were nothing more nor less than a man and a woman enjoying a beautiful place together. She was relieved to be leaving a place that was far too isolated and seductive for her good. Yet she longed to stay in this safe haven, where she'd been able to escape both the memories of the past and the uncertainty of the future.

Ross was clearly determined to take her to every location on the island that Christina Fortune had ever visited. Magnificent Kealakekua Bay, where Michael Fortune had often anchored his sailboat so he and Christina could go snorkeling . . . The Little Blue Church, built on the foundation of an old Hawaiian pagan temple, where Christina's parents were married in a simple, private ceremony that had surprised San Francisco society . . . And magnificent Akaka Falls, where the family went on picnics.

At each stop Christina dutifully recited the importance of that particular place in her personal history. Ross listened in silence, rarely asking questions.

They drove north along Highway 11, traversing the slopes of Mauna Loa along the lush Kona coffee belt. Christina, used to the noise and tension of life in a big city, was enchanted by the quiet, laid-back rural flavor of the area. As the road snaked to lofty heights, the air cooled and a panoramic ocean vista opened before them.

Late in the afternoon they stopped for coffee at a ram- shackle roadside cafe perched precariously on a steep hillside. They sat on the veranda, taking in one of the most magnifi- cent views Christina had ever seen. In the foreground were emerald green pastures dotted with cattle and horses, sloping down to the deep blue ocean in the distance. The entire sweep of the Kona coast was visible here, and Christina relaxed in her chair, taking in the incredible sight with a feeling of amazement.

For a moment she forgot why she was there and who she was with and, lowering her defenses, allowed herself to sim- ply drink in all this natural beauty.

"It's incredible," she murmured, more to herself than to Ross.

He replied, "Yes. For now. But if we haoles have our way, it shall all be resorts and condominiums one day."

She looked at him in surprise. "As a businessman, I should think you'd support development."

"Just because I'm a businessman, that doesn't make me a despoiler. This place truly was paradise before the missionar- ies came. They made the native Hawaiians wear clothes and replaced their natural openness with the burden of original sin."

"You're quite a heretic, Ross McKenna," Christina said with a slow smile.

"I'm an Englishman raised in a British territory. That

means I understand colonialism and what it does to a native population. Even now there are still places on this island where haoles can't go without being in danger of being beaten up by native Hawaiians."

"Why?"

Ross frowned. "Because they're justifiably bitter about what's been done to them and what they've lost."

"But can't they fight back, through the courts or the political system?" Christina asked.

Ross shook his head. "You don't understand how corrupt it is here. Power rests in the hands of the big landowners, the corporations that own the resorts, and the giant ranchers. The native population is powerless."

*Power.* Even here, in this magnificent paradise, Christina realized that she couldn't escape its effect.

Ross finished, "We must be going. There's one more stop to make."

As they walked back to the car, Christina looked at him quizzically. He had surprised her in the cafe, revealing an attitude that she never would have expected him to have. Did his attitude toward power and the abuse of it have a personal connotation? she wondered. If so, she was certain he would never admit it. But she couldn't help wondering what other surprises his personality might contain.

By the time they reached Waikoloa Beach, their final stop before returning to the ranch house, Christina was physically and emotionally exhausted. She wracked her brain, trying to recall some significant personal history relating to Waikoloa, but she couldn't think of anything. Nervousness made her clench and unclench her hands as she waited for Ross to question her. This time she didn't have any answers.

To her surprise and relief, he didn't say a word. He simply sat beside her on the sand and watched the sky turn breathtaking shades of red-orange, lavender, and gold while the setting sun cast a golden path across the water. When she realized that he wasn't going to say anything, she relaxed and drew in deep breaths of the cool, salty air. It was lovely and peaceful here, nearly as wonderful as it had been at *Pu'uhonua.* She didn't want to go back to the ranch and face

Katherine, who'd had an entire day to think about their meeting that morning and to plan her next strategy. But she had to. As she had told Ross, she had promises to keep.

"It's time we were getting back," Ross said quietly.

For a moment Christina almost thought that he, too, sounded reluctant to go back.

They drove in silence back to the ranch house. By the time they arrived, it was dark and the house was brightly lit. The limousine was parked in the wide circular driveway near the main entrance. She wondered briefly if it had been brought around for her return trip to the airport. She gave Ross a questioning look.

"We have visitors," he remarked without much surprise, almost as if he had anticipated it. At least it relieved her first thoughts that Katherine meant to send her away tonight.

All the downstairs windows were alight, and as Ross and Christina entered the foyer, she heard the sound of voices from some distant part of the house. Kane met them as soon as they entered the house.

"We have guests from the mainland," he announced.

"Is Katherine all right?" Ross asked.

Kane smiled. "Everything is under control. She asked me to inform you both that dinner will be in one hour. She suggested that you might want to dress for dinner. It's to be in the formal dining room."

"Did she say anything more?"

Christina knew that Ross was hoping for some indication of whether Katherine had arrived at any decision about her. But Kane's expression was impassive. "She said only that you were to join her at eight o'clock."

Ross turned and slipped a hand beneath Christina's elbow as he guided her down the hallway to her room. "I expected this," he said thoughtfully.

"What is it? What's happened?"

They'd reached the door to her room, and Ross leaned a shoulder against the door frame, his hands thrust casually into the pockets of his shorts. But the expression in his eyes was anything but casual. "Richard and Diana will be joining us for dinner."

"Richard?" The uneasy response was instinctive after her last encounter with him. She tried to cover it. "I just wasn't expecting . . ."

"You'll find that where Richard is concerned, it's wisest to anticipate the unexpected. It eliminates a lot of surprises."

"You sound as if you're speaking from experience."

He smiled. "Absolutely. It's the first thing I learned from Katherine. It was a valuable lesson."

"You realize, of course, that the same could be said of you," Christina pointed out.

"Or you, for that matter," he countered. "From the moment you walked into that boardroom."

She shifted the conversation away from herself. "Did you know he was coming here?"

His mouth curved in a half smile. "Let's just say that it's no surprise. Actually I thought he'd be here first thing this morning. One of his people must have slipped up."

"Slipped up?"

His gaze came back up to hers. "One of his spies." He explained, "He has several of them in the company. They're paid very well to keep him abreast of all information that doesn't flow through normal channels. And then there are the people outside the company that he keeps on his private payroll."

She was stunned. "My God. It sounds like some sort of covert operation."

"Yes, and a very serious one. Richard plays for keeps, in everything. You'd do well to remember that. This little game you're playing may be more dangerous than you realize."

They'd had such a lovely day together, she'd almost allowed herself to forget they were on opposite sides. But the underlying threat of his last statement reminded her precisely who they were and what was at stake here.

"You're certain that Katherine is going to deny my claim, aren't you?"

"I know her as well as anyone. As difficult as it was for her to accept the fact that her granddaughter was dead, Katherine is a realist. For twenty years she has run this company the way Alexander Fortune would have if he were alive. Whether that is right or wrong is beside the point. She would never turn it over to a complete stranger."

Her expression hardened. "I won't give up without a fight."

"You can't fight both Richard and Katherine," he pointed out. "And ultimately that is what it would come down to."

"You can't be certain that I'm *not* Christina Fortune."

His hand came up. She reacted instinctively, jerking away from the contact. The expression in her eyes was wary.

Her reaction took him by surprise. "I wasn't going to strike you," he assured her gently. He didn't know what to make of her reaction, except that it gave him a sudden, unexpected insight that no investigator's report had contained. He brought his hand up once more, and slowly stroked the back of his fingers against her cheek, much as he would have a frightened animal.

"I was going to say that your hair and eyes are the right color. You seem to remember most of the important things . . ."

It took all of her control not to jerk away from his touch. She always reacted instinctively when a man moved abruptly like that. Some scars never healed, the nightmare of some memories never disappeared completely. But the unexpected gentleness of his touch was even more unnerving than her initial fear.

"Then what will you tell Katherine?" she asked, her voice shaky.

He leaned toward her, and for a moment, like that moment on the beach, she wondered what it would be like to kiss him. In two days she'd learned enough about the man to imagine what it would be like. There would be enormous control and a great deal of experience. But she suspected there would be another side to him that could easily slip out of control. It frightened her and . . . intrigued her.

He extended his finger, tracing the fullness of her lower lip. "I won't have to tell her anything. I know Katherine. She's already made up her mind."

Her heart sank. "I see. You knew what her answer would be all along, didn't you?"

"I was fairly certain. After all, you're not the first young woman who's claimed to be Christina Fortune. But you are the most convincing."

His hand dropped away, and he finished, "I'll see you at eight."

Entering her room, she told herself Ross might be wrong. Katherine might not have reached a decision yet. Then all hope died as she turned on the lamp at the dressing table. The light shone into the open wardrobe, revealing that the clothes she'd worn on the flight from San Francisco had been cleaned, neatly pressed, and hung in a lightweight garment bag prepared for travel.

The meaning was clear—she would be leaving the island shortly, perhaps even that night if a flight could be arranged.

She slumped down on the bed. So, Ross was right after all. Katherine had made her decision. No other conversation or further questions had been necessary.

She felt her heart constrict. How could she have come this far, how could she have planned so carefully all these years, only to end in failure?

She felt numb as she stripped off the shorts, the tank top, and the swimming suit underneath. In the adjoining bathroom she turned the shower on hard and hot. Liquid heat pummeled her body, driving back the cold fear that slipped under her skin. Thoughts churned over and over in her head under the frantic rhythm of the water streaming out of the jets.

The heat made her feel like a rag doll. All the tension seeped out of her. For the longest time she simply stood under the pouring stream and let her thoughts drift aimlessly. It reminded her of the languid heat on the beach earlier that day, and the even more drugging heat of Ross's nearness.

She knew just how dangerous those thoughts could be. Especially now. She jammed on the cold water, letting it sluice over her body in icy rivulets, jarring her back to awareness.

Twenty minutes later she'd dried her hair and let it fall simple and loose about her shoulders. The closet provided an ample wardrobe, as she'd discovered earlier that day. She'd been after something sporty and practical then. Now she needed something sophisticated enough for the formal dinner Kane had mentioned.

She found a sleeveless dress of teal blue silk with a halter neckline and full skirt, perfect for the warm, sultry evening, yet formal enough for this dinner.

Precisely one hour after they had parted, she stepped into the hallway outside her room and found Ross waiting for her, leaning against the newel post at the stairway. He wore a white linen suit with a midnight blue shirt underneath, left open at the throat. His dark hair, still damp from his shower, was combed straight back off his face. His dark tan had deepened from their afternoon at the beach. The color of the shirt picked up the mesmerizing blue of his eyes. And there was the faint scent of masculine cologne. It was subtle, faintly spicy, teasing at her senses as he slowly walked toward her. Casual elegance. There was no other way to describe how he looked.

"White Ginger," he said as he stopped only a few inches away from her, an odd expression on his face.

"I beg your pardon?"

"Your perfume," he explained. "You always wear White Ginger." Then he leaned toward her ever so slightly.

Once again her natural instinct was to pull back, to keep a safe distance between them. But she knew it was unwise to withdraw when confronting a man like Ross. He was bold and decisive, just as she'd been when she walked into that boardroom. Now was not the time for hasty retreats. It would only convince him that her wariness concealed deceit. And she was determined to prove to him and everyone else that she wasn't afraid, nor was she an impostor.

She smiled faintly as she turned her head and gave him a sideways glance, praying it concealed the turmoil of emotions that his closeness evoked. But all that was shattered in the next moment as he reached up, his fingers grazing her skin as he gently lifted the jade pendant from where it lay just above the exposed swell of her breasts.

Only a half hour earlier she had thought herself fortunate to find a gown that was both formal and cool in the tropical heat. Now she felt a different sort of heat—the heat of those long, lean fingers.

"It might not be wise to wear this pendant," he said, his gaze traveling from the jade medallion to fasten on hers.

"It means a great deal to me," she murmured thickly.

His fingers tightened over the pendant, his knuckles grazing her flesh, reminding her of that earlier impression of the raw energy and power that lay just beneath the surface.

"It belongs to the Fortune family," he reminded her.

Her fingers closed over his, prying them loose from the pendant. "It belongs to *me*."

"We'll see," he said, reaching out and stroking her cheek, giving her no warning of the physical contact before it happened.

As her hand came up in a defensive gesture, he seized it in his and tucked it through his arm. "I'll escort you into the lion's den. Katherine is waiting."

Katherine *was* waiting, along with her *guests*. As Kane opened the sliding double doors onto the formal living room, Christina saw Richard first. His gaze fastened on her the moment she walked in, then it slid away with cool self-assurance. Diana Chandler was seated near her mother, looking slender and elegant, her pale hair piled on top of her head in an intricate twist and secured with tortoiseshell combs. Brian stood in the background.

Diana's gaze was accusatory. "Really, Ross, you are the one for sly maneuvers, whisking this impostor off for a sudden meeting with Mother, without letting any of the rest of us know about it. It would almost make one think you were up to something."

"There was nothing sly or sudden about it, Diana," Ross smoothly informed her as he stepped around Christina and went to the bar for a drink.

"I insisted on the meeting," Katherine said, glancing briefly at Christina, then looking away.

"Still," Diana went on, "Ross could have informed someone that he was taking the company jet."

"I did." Ross casually dropped two ice cubes into a tumbler, then splashed it over with Chivas Regal. "I informed the captain and the copilot."

Richard said irritably, "Let's get on with this. We all have a great many things to do, and a meeting to reschedule." His meaning wasn't lost on anyone.

Kane broke the awkward silence in the room by announcing that dinner was ready.

"Thank God," Diana announced. "Then we can finally get this business over with." She crossed the room and linked her arm through her husband's. Richard escorted Katherine into the adjoining dining room. That left Ross to accompany Christina.

He took her hand in his. When she resisted, he gently but firmly tucked her arm through his, as he'd done earlier, and smoothed her fingers over his coat sleeve. It was an almost mocking gesture, considering the fact that he was convinced Katherine was about to deny her claim.

The table was a reminder of the vast wealth and history of the Fortune dynasty. The china was delicate Limoges with a gilt border. Christina recognized the elegant enamel pattern as very rare and very old. As she well knew, it and many other treasures in the house had first come to the island on a Fortune clipper ship.

By contrast, the baroque silver pattern was Reed and Barton, and the crystal was Baccarat, its hidden facets set off like precious jewels set aglow by the heat of the deep burgundy wine that Kane poured.

The air hung thick, warm, and fragrant from wild hibiscus that grew in profusion in the gardens. The conversation at the table was stilted as Diana tried to draw her mother into their discussion as if she were a senile old woman who needed to be entertained. Brian sat in silence across the table, as always somehow not quite part of things. Christina was seated at the opposite end of the table from Katherine, with Ross on her right.

Christina was only dimly aware of the food that Kane served, and barely tasted it. She felt like a convicted felon awaiting the executioner, and wondered when Katherine would bring the agony of waiting to an end.

Suddenly there was the authoritative ring of sterling silver against priceless crystal as Katherine demanded their collective attention. Everyone grew silent. Diana wore an expres-

sion of faint boredom. Brian outlined patterns in the linen
tablecloth with his dinner knife. Richard sat back with the
ease of someone who knows exactly what is about to take
place and simply waits for it to happen.

Beside her, Ross sat staring thoughtfully into his wineglass.

Christina's fingers twisted around the dinner napkin that
lay in her lap as she watched Katherine slowly stand at the
head of the table.

Looking at Katherine's grim expression, Christina knew
that she'd failed. In a moment Katherine would denounce her
as a fraud and deny her claim as Christina Fortune.

It can't end here! she told herself. I won't let it! I *promised*.
Her nerves twisted along with the linen in her hands as she
listened to Katherine.

"It has been a long time since so many members of the
Fortune family have been assembled at this table," she began
with an enigmatic expression, looking down the length of the
table.

Her eyes rested briefly on Christina, then traveled to Diana,
Brian, and finally Richard, her keen gaze appraising as it lingered on each person.

Ross watched her intently.

"And therefore I wish to make a toast," Katherine announced. Picking up her wineglass, she held it aloft. Her eyes
focused on Christina. "A toast to my *granddaughter*,
Christina. Welcome home, my dear."

# Chapter 9

*T*he shouting had long since died down, and the house was eerily quiet. Christina wandered out onto the veranda outside her bedroom.

After making her startling and completely unexpected announcement, Katherine had asked Christina to leave them, insisting that it would be best if she dealt with the others alone. As Christina left the study, she saw a look of utter disbelief on Ross's face. For once his careful reserve failed him, and his expression revealed exactly what he was thinking. Like the others, he was completely stunned by Katherine's announcement. He hadn't expected it and didn't understand it.

Neither did Christina. Katherine's about-face made no sense at all. Christina had been trying to figure it out for the past hour and hadn't come up with any answers.

What was Katherine up to? Did she mean what she'd said?

Christina couldn't believe Katherine was sincere, not after the way things had gone between them earlier that morning. It was especially puzzling that Katherine hadn't waited to get a report from Ross on the events of the day. She had made up her mind while Christina was out with him.

The evening breeze was restless, matching her mood. It stirred the leaves of the fragrant hibiscus growing at the edge of the veranda. Christina was so deep in thought that she jumped at the sound of a knock at the door. Stepping back into the room, she called out, "Come in."

Katherine entered, looking exhausted. "I'll take only a moment of your time," she began in a tired voice. "There's a great deal to discuss, legal matters to go over, but most of it can wait until tomorrow. All you need to know tonight is this—despite what I told Richard and Diana, I don't for one instant believe that you are my granddaughter."

Christina wasn't surprised. It had all been too easy, Katherine's acceptance too quick. *This* is what she had expected. She didn't have a clue what game the elderly woman was playing, but she knew it was a deadly serious one.

Katherine eased herself down into a high-backed occasional chair. She sat there, her back stiff, her bearing regal. The lines about her mouth seemed more deeply etched, her skin like finely webbed and fragile parchment. Her hand shook visibly from strain and fatigue, and she rested it atop the head of her cane. Her voice wasn't as strong as it had been earlier, revealing the heavy emotional and physical toll the evening had taken. But her eyes, light blue and piercing in their scrutiny, were absolutely clear and unwavering as she fastened them on Christina.

Sensing Christina's unspoken questions, Katherine went on, "There is something you must understand about families of great inherited wealth and power. Most of the time the women in those families have no real control of the money or the family business. They've been trained to be passive and ornamental."

Her voice changed subtly, thickening with the emotions of old memories. "I came from a very poor background, but I married well. I've learned a great deal over the past fifty-five years by very carefully observing the class I married into. And I've come to realize that it often works in reverse for women. They are treated like children and are not given an opportunity to seize control."

Christina was bewildered. "What does this have to do with me?"

"I'm coming to that. You must understand that very wealthy families are patriarchies. *Men* have the power, not the women. Even if a daughter is an only child, she very rarely inherits any family wealth. Quite the opposite. The expectation is that she will do everything necessary to make a brilliant marriage. Then the true power in the family is passed on to her husband."

"But *you* run Fortune International," Christina pointed out.

"Only for the last twenty years. When my husband died, he left me a significant number of shares in the company, and he left a *few* shares to our daughter. The largest numbers of shares were left to our two sons, with Michael inheriting controlling interest. My husband assumed a man should run the company, and that man should be his first born son."

Her voice trembled. "He had no way of knowing that Michael would die young. Or that Richard would turn out to be selfish and disloyal. While I controlled my granddaughter's shares, I controlled the company and was able to keep it going as Alexander would have wished. But if those shares are divided up among Richard, Diana, and Diana's children, I will lose control. Diana will throw in with Richard, because she is as greedy as he is, and he will control the company."

Christina was beginning to understand. In spite of herself, she couldn't help feeling a grudging respect for Katherine's determination and cunning.

Katherine repeated, "I don't for one moment believe you are my granddaughter. But I am willing to make a bargain with the devil to retain control of Fortune International and ensure its survival."

"And you consider me to be the devil," Christina said flatly.

"I consider you to be rather a convincing impostor who can serve me very well!"

Christina swallowed back her anger. "What exactly do you expect me to do?"

"I expect you to live at Fortune Hill, where my staff can keep an eye on you. And I expect you to do as I tell you. You'll be the nominal head of the company, but you'll take orders from me and run things as I see fit. According to the portfolio that you gave them at the board meeting, you have an impressive amount of business expertise. You shouldn't find it difficult to carry out my plans for the company."

"In other words," Christina said bluntly, "I'm to be your puppet, exactly as Ross McKenna has been all these years."

To her surprise Katherine laughed softly. "You could never call Ross McKenna a puppet. You'll learn that quickly enough." Her voice hardened. "The important thing is that you do exactly as I say."

Christina was strongly tempted to say, "No, I won't do it. That isn't what I came back for." She forced herself to control her resentment toward Katherine's domineering attitude and instead asked, "Where does Ross fit in with all this?"

"Where he always has. You will work for him, and will report all pertinent information to him, while you're acting out the role of my granddaughter."

"And if I refuse?"

Katherine smiled briefly. "You won't. Whatever else you may be, you're obviously not stupid. If you don't accept my offer, I'll denounce you as an impostor. And that will be the end of it. Then your only recourse would be through a costly, long, drawn-out court battle that I promise you would be extremely bloody. You must know you couldn't possibly win such a battle."

Christina met her gaze evenly. "I think I could."

"Are you prepared to spend a number of years and a great deal of money trying to prove it?"

She hesitated. She knew Katherine was right. A court battle would be expensive and time-consuming. There was no guarantee she would win. She knew all too well that in the real world, justice didn't necessarily always triumph. More often than not, the person with the greater financial resources won. And even if Christina did win, by then the company might have failed or been sold off by Richard. It could end up being a hollow victory.

There was an even more critical consideration. If she didn't accept the deal Katherine offered, then she would be cut off from the family. She'd come here for a far more important reason than claiming an inheritance. To accomplish that, she needed access to the family.

As she met Katherine's look, she knew she really had no choice at all. "All right."

Katherine seemed surprised at her quick capitulation. "You understand the terms of our deal?" she asked.

Christina nodded. "Yes, I understand."

"Then understand this, as well. I can change my mind at any moment. I have only to say you fooled me, an easy enough thing to do, since I'm a frail old woman. I would undoubtedly have the full support of my . . . loving family."

Christina's mouth curved in a wry half smile. "You're not nearly as frail as you would like everyone to believe."

Katherine looked at her with real interest. "Perhaps you and I have something in common, after all. We're both willing to do whatever it takes to get what we want. I'm glad we understand each other."

She rose then, leaning heavily on the cane. "There's one last thing—you must call me *Grandmère* in public in order to complete the charade, but in private you're not to use that expression. My granddaughter called me that, and you are *not* my granddaughter."

Christina said slowly, "Have you ever considered the possibility that you're wrong?"

"I am *not* wrong," Katherine answered with finality.

But it wasn't final as far as Christina was concerned. Anger roiled inside her—anger at what she'd endured, all the years of loneliness and longing for some semblance of family. And more important, anger at the terrifying event that had driven a fifteen-year-old girl away from her family.

"You don't *want* me to be your granddaughter, do you?" she accused.

"What do you mean?" Katherine snapped.

"If I *am* Christina, then it means I left because you failed me when I needed you most."

For a split second Katherine's iron-willed composure faltered, and the expression in her eyes was so bleak and stricken that Christina thought she might have pushed her too far. Perhaps because they were so much alike, and had both lost so much, she felt an unexpected compassion for Katherine, and a sharp stab of guilt for hurting her. Whatever Katherine's failings, she didn't deserve that.

"I'm sorry," she whispered, extending a hand toward her.

But Katherine had her emotions under control once more. Her expression was aloof, her tone cool as she said, "You'll return to San Francisco tomorrow. I expect you to move into Fortune Hill tomorrow evening. There will be a dinner party to formally reinstate my . . ." She paused, then finished dryly, "*Granddaughter,* within the family circle." Her tone was now almost mocking, as if she knew better than anyone precisely how shallow the term *family* was when applied to the Fortune family.

"Will you be there?"

Katherine shook her head. "I rarely travel anywhere. You'll have to deal with everyone on your own. But from what I've seen of you, I'm sure you can handle it. Call me as soon as you're settled. I have some instructions for you regarding company business, now that the matter of the trust will be settled. We must act quickly, before Richard moves against us."

"Then you still expect him to try to block my claim, even with your public acknowledgment?"

Katherine hesitated at the door. "There is a great deal at stake, my dear. Richard expected to achieve full control of the company. Now he's seen that taken from him. Make no mistake about it, he will do everything in his power to stop me."

She walked out of the room slowly, closing the door behind her.

For a long moment Christina simply stood there, absorbing what had just happened. She had *won.*

Now she could focus her energy on the real reason she'd come here. Somehow she found that hard to do just yet. The confrontation with Katherine had shaken her deeply. She had expected to dislike Katherine, and had been prepared to fight her ruthlessly for the vast inheritance that was at stake.

Instead, she found herself feeling sorry for Katherine. Beneath the autocratic, even hard exterior, Christina sensed profound unhappiness and loneliness. Here was a woman who had lost the people who mattered most to her. The most poignant aspect of it all was the fact that she herself was at least partially responsible for the loss of one of those people.

Her unanticipated feelings for Katherine made this less than a total victory, but it was, nevertheless, a victory.

Katherine found Ross pacing the study. He was furious. "What the bloody hell do you think you're doing?" he demanded.

She slowly crossed the study to the bar and poured herself a glass of wine. Her hand shook slightly as she returned the stopper to the crystal wine decanter. She took a sip of wine, feeling the reassuring warmth as it slid down her throat. When she felt steadier, she said, "I'm saving the company. And your position in it."

She sat down heavily in a chair, exhaustion etched in every deep line of her pale face.

"If you turn over control of the company to that woman, do you seriously believe she'll allow me to run it as I've been doing?"

"I am not turning control over to her. She isn't my grand-daughter."

"But you just acknowledged her . . ."

"I had my reasons for that. I can just as easily denounce her. And that's exactly what I've told her I will do if she doesn't follow my instructions. Nothing has changed, Ross," she assured him. "She'll report to you, and you will continue to run the company as I see fit. It will buy us time—time to make certain Richard will never have control of Fortune International. This opportunity will give us the freedom to accomplish what we need to do to strengthen the company the way we could have done if we hadn't been absorbed in this hopeless infighting."

He paced around the room. "Richard won't take this lying down."

"I realize that. You forget, Ross, I know my son."

His gaze came up as he turned back to her. "He's probably got a private detective checking out her background as we speak."

"Probably. And that is precisely why I want you to hire one

as well. We have to be prepared for whatever Richard may uncover." She passed a hand across her forehead as if to physically clear away the weariness. "It might be best to hire someone in Boston, since that is where she claims she is from. But don't leave it up to him alone. I want you to go back there and oversee the investigation. It's imperative that we know everything about her *before* Richard does."

Ross gave her a long, searching look. "You're willing to live a lie, to retain control of the company?"

"I'm willing to do it to *save* the company. We both know Richard will destroy it. I would be failing my husband and everything this company represents if I let that happen."

"I know you've said you're convinced she's not your granddaughter, but how can you be absolutely positive? There must be records that could either prove or disprove her claim—birth certificates, hospital and dental records," he suggested.

"Christina was born in Hong Kong. She was delivered prematurely, by a Chinese physician in a Chinese hospital. Her birth certificate, if you want to call it that, stated only that a female child was born on a specific date to my son and his wife. Christina traveled under her parents' passports and visas. And she was too young to have a driver's license when she disappeared."

"What about other records either here or in California?"

"There were none here. There were physician records and dental records in California, but they no longer exist."

Ross frowned. "I don't understand."

Katherine sighed heavily. "A few years after Christina disappeared, all of her medical records were sent to me at Fortune Hill. By that time there had been a couple of claimants, but they were both proved to be impostors. Shortly after the second claim, there was a fire at the house."

"Let me take a wild guess—the records were destroyed."

Katherine nodded. "It was very sudden. Supposedly some cinders from the fireplace started a fire on the carpet. It spread to the desk. The entire study was a loss."

"And the alarm system?" Ross asked, referring to the elaborate one at the Pacific Heights estate.

"It was conveniently turned off. Apparently there were problems with it and the household staff shut it off until it could be repaired."

Ross's gaze met hers evenly. "Richard," he concluded.

Katherine smiled faintly. "He had everything to gain if Christina remained missing. With those records destroyed, there was no way to absolutely prove that a claimant *was* my granddaughter."

Ross had to laugh at the irony. "And without those very same records, he can't prove that this young woman is *not* Christina."

Katherine's smile met his. "Precisely."

Ross's expression became serious once more. "There's something I've never asked you. It was none of my affair. But now the situation has changed, and I'm getting involved in your internecine family relationships, whether I want to be or not."

Katherine's tone was wary. "What is it?"

"Why have you and Richard always been at odds?"

"You're right—it's none of your business."

"I think it is now," he persisted.

She didn't answer at first. From the time Michael and Richard were children, Katherine had realized there was something dangerous, even ruthless, about Richard. Her thoughts went back to Michael's twenty-first birthday. He had invited several of his friends to a party at Fortune Hill. Even though the party was off-limits, Richard sneaked in, and joined the older people in their drinking. Somehow a simple joke made by one of Michael's friends escalated into an angry confrontation. Richard refused to back down. It ended in a bloody fight. Michael and three of his friends had to pull the combatants apart.

Then Richard turned on his brother, eager to continue the fight. Michael blocked Richard's punch, saying good-naturedly, "Hey, Rich, back off."

"I won't back off!" Richard had screamed at Michael. "You're not gonna make a fool of me in front of everybody!"

Other boys had to step in to hold Richard back. Michael simply walked away. For the first time Katherine, who had watched the confrontation, was forced to acknowledge the frightening difference between her two sons. She never forgot the look of bitter hatred she saw on Richard's face as he watched his brother walk away.

Now she said in a voice that quivered ever so slightly, "A mother is supposed to love her children. *All* her children. Equally. But mothers are only human. And so are children. And sometimes . . ."

She paused, then finished in a voice that was utterly exhausted and filled with a great deal of sadness and pain, "Sometimes we see the best of ourselves in our children. But sometimes . . . we see the worst."

She looked away. "That's all I intend to tell you. I'm rather tired; I think I'll go to bed now. It's been a long day."

As she rose on unsteady legs, he reached out to help her. But she pushed his hand away. "I may be old, but I don't yet need to lean on anyone else."

And with that she walked out of the room, head upright, shoulders straight. He heard the tap, tap, tapping sound of her cane as she moved across the entry hall.

Alone, Ross thought about what she'd said of Christina. He knew this young woman who called herself Christina Fortune a little better than Katherine did, and he wasn't at all certain she would allow herself to be controlled. Even if she did, the truth was that Katherine was old, and might not live much longer. Christina could find herself, in the near future, in sole control of the company. He doubted very much that she would allow him to continue running it. Ross would lose everything he'd worked so hard for.

A look of determination hardened his expression. He hadn't spent all these years fighting Richard simply to turn things over to a clever impostor.

# Chapter 10

Christina stared out the small round window of the jet. Below, a plateau of white clouds stretched with endless grace like a white magic carpet, creating the illusion that if she chose, she could walk on it. Then the clouds broke, exposing the Pacific Ocean, glistening silver blue on this clear, sunny day.

There was a faint rumble, and the jet began a slow banking turn toward the coastline. The clouds transformed into a veil of vaporous mist as the jet descended through the cloud bank. Rivulets of moisture formed on the window from the sudden change in atmosphere.

Christina leaned forward in her seat, like an expectant child, nose pressed against the glass for that first breathtaking view of the coastline. The pale hues of a rainbow shimmered off the moisture beaded across the wing of the jet.

*"You'll have to deal with everyone on your own. But from what I've seen of you, I'm sure you can handle it."*

Katherine's words, spoken only hours earlier, echoed over and over in her thoughts as the flight attendant reminded the passengers to fasten their seatbelts for the final approach to San Francisco International Airport.

Christina wasn't at all certain she liked Katherine, but she respected her. In spite of Katherine's advanced age and the ill health that had forced her to retire to the ranch on Hawaii, she was determined to keep control of Fortune International out of Richard's hands.

Richard, Diana, and Brian had returned to San Francisco on a commercial flight late the night before, without seeing Christina again.

The next morning Katherine bade Ross and Christina farewell at the airport. She assured Christina that everyone, including Richard and Diana, would be in attendance at the formal dinner that night at Fortune Hill.

"Richard wouldn't dare defy me in this. After all, I'm not a well woman. There is a great deal more he might lose by crossing me."

Despite Katherine's strong words, Christina was struck by the elderly woman's air of frailty. She had seemed especially tired as she accompanied them to the airport. Her features were drawn and haggard, but her hand, as she laid it on Christina's before she got out of the car, was rock-steady.

*"Make no mistake, Richard won't give up. He will do everything in his power to take control of Fortune International,"* she warned.

Now, watching the ground rise up to meet them, Christina wondered if Katherine was up to the battle that lay ahead. But her doubts dissolved when the jet rolled to a stop and she saw the press waiting for them.

"Katherine's been busy," Ross remarked dryly, but with little surprise. Christina was stunned to see a camera crew from one of the network affiliates push past the maintenance crew who had come out of the hangar and had now taken on the role of security guards, trying to keep the press at bay.

"I had no idea . . ."

"Katherine believes in the power of the media, and she knows how to use it," Ross explained. "She's known the owners of the *Chronicle* for years. The appearance of a long-lost heiress is a hot item, especially after all the speculation that Richard was about to take over the company. I hope you're not shy in front of cameras."

As the plane rolled to a stop, there was an immediate rush of newspaper reporters, camera crews, and newscasters descending on it. Christina gave Ross a murderous glare as a newscaster equipped with a live remote elbowed his way to the front of the pack.

"What am I supposed to say to them?" she asked in a tight voice, angry at this unexpected confrontation.

"I'm sure you'll think of something. You're quite good at making surprise announcements."

She was about to retort that he was pretty adept at making unexpected moves himself, when their copilot came back to the cabin and announced, "We have immediate clearance if you're ready, Mr. McKenna."

Christina stared at him in dismay. "You're leaving?"

"I've been called away on business," he answered evasively.

She smothered back the panic that rose in her throat at the thought of facing the press alone. "Aren't you going to help me with this?"

There was the flash of a quick smile. "If you can handle the board of Fortune International, I'm certain you can handle the press."

"What about tonight?" she asked, trying to keep her voice calm. Without realizing it, she had been counting on his presence to help her face the family that night at the dinner party. The thought of facing them alone made her feel more than a little like Daniel walking into the lions' den.

Instinctively she reached out to touch him. She felt the sudden shift of muscles beneath his coat sleeve as he reacted to her touch. Embarrassed, she jerked her hand away.

An odd expression crossed his face. She almost believed the regret in his voice was sincere as he said, "I'm sorry that I have to go."

"I see." She wondered what business forced him to leave so quickly, without even putting in an appearance at the office. With a tone of cool self-possession that she didn't really feel, she said, "So, Katherine is throwing me to the wolves."

"Not the wolves—your family," he corrected. Then he added, "Phillip Lo will be there to smooth the waters. He'll be handling the legal aspects as far as the inheritance is concerned. I'm certain Katherine has already contacted him. She never makes a move without Phillip. I'll be gone only a few days. It'll give you time to get settled in at Fortune Hill."

She hated the thought of moving into the family mansion. She had no intention of staying there for long, no matter what Katherine wanted.

Determined to erase that momentary electric connection she'd felt with him, she made a point of putting things back on a business footing. "I had hoped to go into the office tomorrow. I want to start familiarizing myself with the business right away."

Ross pulled out a business card with the Fortune logo embossed on the front and flipped it over. He scrawled a name and handed it to her.

"My assistant is Bill Thomason. He's already been briefed, and he can help you with whatever you need."

She knew without a doubt that Thomason would help her only to the extent that Ross had approved. Jamming the card into her shoulder bag, she said, "Very well. Good-bye."

As she rose, Ross's fingers closed gently around her upper arm. "I'll be back soon," he repeated, as if he suddenly felt the need to reassure her. Or perhaps sensed her need to hear it.

She gave him a cool look. "I think I can survive until then."

"Until then . . ." he called, as she left the cabin.

As she descended the steps, she heard the young blond reporter with Channel Six news complete the lead-in to her story. ". . . We are at San Francisco International Airport, where the Fortune International corporate jet has just landed, opening a new chapter in the twenty-year-old mystery of the disappearance of shipping heiress Christina Fortune . . ."

As Christina walked away from the plane, the ground crew helping her make her way through the crowd of reporters, her thoughts raced. What was the urgent business that required Ross to leave again as soon as they arrived? Where was he going? Why had he refused to discuss it with her?

But she had no time to dwell on these questions. No sooner had she walked a few yards from the private jet, and had it taxied away, than she was surrounded by the press, who shouted questions and shoved microphones in her face. The company limousine was waiting, and after a succinct "No comment," she slipped inside. The driver quickly sped away.

A half hour later he pulled up before one of the side entrances to the hotel. "I thought this might be better, Miss Fortune," he explained as he came around to open the door for her. "There's probably a crowd of reporters out front, just like at the airport."

She smiled her appreciation. She wouldn't have been up to repeating the scene from the airport. Surely it wouldn't be like this every time she went someplace, she reassured herself. But a nagging little voice deep inside warned her that, like Richard Fortune and Ross McKenna, the press was determined to know more about her.

The chauffeur, a handsome young man with close-cropped black hair and shrewd brown eyes, tipped his cap as he opened the hotel door for her. "I've been instructed to pick you up at seven this evening, Miss Fortune."

"That will be fine . . ." She hesitated as she realized she didn't know his name.

"My name is James, Miss Fortune. I'll be your driver whenever you need to go anywhere."

"Thank you, James. I'll be ready at seven."

There were countless messages at the front desk, and flowers from the staff at Fortune International waiting in her room. Her phone rang constantly, until she asked the front desk to hold all calls.

A stack of telegrams had arrived throughout the day, including several from friends and business associates in Boston who had known her only as Christina Grant.

It was obvious who was behind it all. As Ross had said, Katherine believed in the power of the press, and she was determined to use it to her advantage. When she set things in motion, it didn't take long for the entire country to learn that Christina Grant Fortune was alive and had returned to claim her inheritance.

At seven o'clock that evening the weather was cool and clear across the city as James guided the limousine through midtown traffic. Christina found the telephone and pressed the button for the intercom.

"Would you please take Broadway?" she asked. "There's a place I want to see." James nodded, and turned west off Van Ness onto Broadway. The circuitous route would eventually take them to Pacific Heights. As they approached the corner of Baker Street and Broadway, she asked him to slow down. A moment later she said, "Please, stop here."

The large, three-story red brick mansion filled the corner of Broadway and Baker Street. It had mullioned windows, flower-draped terraces, and a breathtaking view of the Bay. The garages and servants' quarters were on the ground floor. The front entrance opened onto pockets of gardens on different levels filled with primroses, and draping bougainvillea glimpsed through a heavy ornate wrought-iron gate with security locks.

The gate stood between brick pillars with a span of wrought-iron decoration over the gate. The letter *F*, for the Fortune name, was gone, creating a sad anonymity to the house. Christina had no idea who lived here now—perhaps a wealthy investment banker, physician, or philanthropist. But she knew who had lived there twenty years earlier—Michael Fortune, his wife, and their daughter, Christina.

Silently she lowered the smoked-glass window of the limousine. It was like opening a window onto the past . . .

"You live in a mansion?" fifteen-year-old Ellie Dobbs whispered in awe.

"Lived." Christina emphasized the past tense as they huddled together in a futile effort to keep warm in the rundown, abandoned New York tenement. They could hear the faint scratching sounds of rats scurrying along the darkened floor. "My grandmother lives in the big house now with my aunt and uncle. It's called Fortune Hill."

"God! A whole, entire hill named after your family!" Ellie was incredulous. She shivered as she nibbled on a piece of discarded fruit they'd rummaged from the garbage behind a restaurant earlier that night. She said in disbelief, "I can't imagine anythin' like that." Her Southern twang punctuated her words. "With servants and everythin'?"

Christina laughed, but it was a bitter sound. Her own voice was cultured, articulate, emphasizing the glaring difference in their backgrounds—a difference of money and class. That difference between them, which would have seemed so important back in San Francisco, disappeared here on the cold, dark streets of New York.

"Yes," she answered quietly. "With servants."

"I didn't think anybody ever really lived that way." Ellie breathed in awe. "It must have been like a fairy tale."

Only on the outside, Christina thought. Underneath, it was ugly and terrifying. Just like the masks everyone had worn for the Halloween party that last night.

Ellie's teeth chattered against the biting cold in the drafty building as they snuggled together under layers of discarded newspapers and a flattened cardboard box. "Tell me about it. Tell me *everything*. Maybe then I can forget this awful place."

Christina smiled at Ellie's almost childish curiosity. "Do you want to know about my house or Fortune Hill?"

"Both. I want to be able to see it all in my mind, just the way I used to do when my momma read bedtime stories to me about castles and knights and princesses."

Christina rubbed her hands together, then shoved them under her arms—as Ellie had shown her—beneath the ragged coat she'd taken from a box left in front of a thrift store. She began, "There were terraces and gardens at different levels all around my parents' house."

Ellie interrupted her. "Did you have your own room?"

"Yes, I had my own bedroom and bathroom."

"Your very own bathroom? I don't believe it! How many rooms were there in the house?"

Christina stopped to think. "There were fourteen, not including the maids' quarters."

"Fourteen! *Wow.*"

"There was a tennis court. I used to play with my cousins."

"You never said nothin' about cousins," Ellie interrupted. "How many you got?"

"Three." Talking of her cousins reminded Christina of Jason and the ugly quarrel they'd had that last night. She shivered, wishing she could banish the memories of that last night in the almost fairy-tale description of what her life had been like.

"I've got pictures of them," Christina went on. "Want to see?"

"Sure."

From a cardboard box in the corner, where Christina kept her meager possessions, she pulled out a slim, leather-bound book. Inside were a handful of snapshots.

"What's that?" Ellie asked.

"My diary," Christina admitted with a sheepish grin. "My mother gave it to me for my twelfth birthday, and I wrote in it every day until . . ."

She stopped.

Ellie didn't press her to explain. She knew when and why Christina had stopped writing in her diary. Taking the snapshots from Christina, she said, "So tell me who's who."

"That's Steven," Christina said, pointing to a tall young man with a cocky grin.

"Boy, he's sure cute," Ellie exclaimed. "Too bad he's your cousin."

"He's cute, all right, but he knows it."

"Who're these guys?" Ellie asked, pointing to two teenage boys with an unmistakable resemblance that strongly suggested they were brothers.

"That's Andrew and Jason." Christina hesitated, then went on awkwardly, "Jase and I, well . . ."

"You liked him," Ellie said with a grin.

Christina blushed. "Well, yeah. He's so sweet. After my parents died, he was the only one who really cared about me."

"Is that your house they're standing in front of?"

"Uh-huh. That's the back of it, on the terrace, by the steps that lead down to the swimming pool."

"Boy, it's really somethin'. When did you move in to it?" Ellie asked.

"My father bought it for my mother when they were married."

Ellie's dark eyes glittered with excitement. "Like a prince takin' the princess away to his castle." Then she frowned. "The closest I ever came to a castle was the Mother Goose

Miniature Golf Course back home in Memphis. But that wasn't real. *You* lived in a real castle."

"It wasn't a castle. It was just a big house."

"Go on," Ellie urged her. "Tell me more."

Ellie didn't say it out loud, but Christina knew she wanted to hear more about the house because it helped her to forget, at least for a short time, that they sat in a cold, dark hellhole, alone and frightened and hungry.

"We had a Chinese cook," Christina went on.

"Christ! A cook, too?" Ellie pretended to faint back against the wall.

Christina laughed at Ellie's reaction. "He was always preparing these fancy meals for my parents' dinner parties. They entertained a lot."

"I'll bet they was big society bashes, with everyone in fancy gowns and jewels," Ellie murmured dreamily.

"Sometimes." Christina thought back with the wistfulness of a child. All she had now were the memories—and her diary, along with the photos she'd shoved inside it as she hurried away late that last night.

She went on, "There were always the best smells down in the kitchen. Our cook's name was Thomas Wing. He would make these elaborate French desserts, then I would ask him to make me chocolate chip cookies. He said they were disgustingly unimaginative." Christina mimicked Thomas's crisp, disapproving tone.

"Tell me what else he cooked. I know it'll make me hungry, but maybe I can imagine these two rotten apples are some fancy French dessert."

"At Christmas he always fixed cherries jubilee. You should see it, Ellie. It's made of vanilla ice cream topped with cherries and brandy. Just before it's served, you light the cherries and brandy with a match. It bursts into flame, and then it's poured over the ice cream. It's all hot, syrupy, and sweet. It's wonderful."

"Cherries jubilee," Ellie murmured, her mouth watering. She made a joke of it, complete with an exaggerated accent. "My dahling, we really must dine at the Plaza on New Year's Eve. And of course, we'll order cherries jubilee!" She made an elegant gesture, as if she were waving a cigarette holder through the air. Then she dissolved in laughter.

"Ellie, you're such a good mimic. You should be an actress."

"You know, I always wanted to be an actress, like Mia Farrow in *Peyton Place* or maybe even Raquel Welch in the movies."

"You could do it," Christina responded eagerly, "you really could. Remember when you mimicked Arnie the other day? You did his Brooklyn accent just perfectly. You're so good at pretending to be other people."

Ellie's look of self-conscious pleasure at Christina's encouragement was transformed by an expression of sadness that crossed her face. "Sometimes it's easier to pretend to be someone else than to be me."

Both girls were silent for a moment. Outside, the typical city noises of sirens screaming and horns honking reminded them that they were in a densely crowded city. But inside the building it was just the two of them, alone and clinging to each other for reassurance and protection.

Forcing a smile, Ellie said, "I always wondered what it would be like to be a rich bitch. And now here I am, huddling in this damn tenement building, freezin' my ass off with one."

"We're really a pair, aren't we?" Christina found herself laughing, too, in spite of their miserable surroundings. "Oh, Ellie, you do make me feel better."

"Tell me more," Ellie insisted.

"Well, the table was always set with my mother's finest crystal and china. The china came all the way from England. It was over a hundred years old. My great-great-grandfather brought it to San Francisco on one of his clipper ships. Sometimes my grandmother was invited for dinner, but not very often, because she and my mother didn't really like each other. I'll never forget the time she arrived early. I was in the dining room. The table was set for this party. The mayor was invited. My grandmother walked in and caught me sitting at the head of the table, eating pizza and drinking Pepsi, using my mother's finest china and crystal."

"What did she say?"

Christina giggled as she lifted her small nose ever so slightly, fixed a disapproving expression on her face, and lowered her voice in imitation of Katherine Fortune. "My dear, what on earth do you think you are doing?"

"What did you say to her?" Ellie asked in mock horror.

Christina gave her a look of wide-eyed innocence. "I told her I was eating pizza and asked her if she wanted a piece."

They both laughed.

"Tell me more," Ellie whispered hungrily. "Tell me everything. The way things looked and tasted and sounded, and the people and everything you did."

Christina became thoughtful. "I remember the sound my mother's evening gowns used to make—a faint rustling sound. And she used to wear high heels that made clicking sounds across the marble floors downstairs."

Her voice grew sadder as she continued pensively, "And I remember the perfume she always wore. It was called White Ginger. She kept it in a crystal decanter on her dressing table. Sometimes I would watch while she got dressed. When she put on the perfume, she let me wear just a little. She would dab just a little behind my ears and on each wrist. I remember how it used to tickle, and it smelled so good." She added wistfully. "It made me feel so grown-up."

Ellie sensed the sadness those memories brought. "And I'll bet you went to private school, too," she said, changing the subject.

For a long moment Christina was silent. Then she said, "After my parents were killed, my aunt sent me away to boarding school. The Elizabeth Barrett Browning School for Girls in Pebble Beach. It was supposed to be the best in the country, and there were daughters of famous movie stars and politicians. But all I wanted was to go home." She ached with remembered loneliness.

Ellie sighed. "God, it *does* sound like a fairy tale. Why the hell did you ever leave?" But even as she asked, she knew. "I'm sorry. Lord, I'm stupid! Forget that I asked."

Christina pulled tighter within herself, trying to drive away the cold that seemed to penetrate so deep, no amount of heat could reach it. "It wasn't a fairy tale."

She looked at Ellie, and she knew they both understood how the fairy tale had become a nightmare. Underneath the newspapers and cardboard box, she grabbed hold of Ellie's hand. "I can't ever go back there," she whispered.

Ellie wrapped her arm around Christina's shoulders. "I know. And you don't ever have to go back. Neither one of us is goin' back. We'll make it here. Just the two of us."

Christina looked up at her with wide dark eyes. "We'll be okay, won't we?"

"Sure we will. We'll take care of each other. Just you and me."

"I don't know what I would have done if you hadn't helped me, Ellie."

"Hey, you helped me a lot more. That cop who caught me shopliftin' would've taken me in if you hadn't distracted him so that I could get away."

Christina smiled. "I *was* pretty clever, wasn't I?"

"You sure were. You saved my hide, kiddo."

"I never had to be clever before."

"Bein' on the streets makes you learn all kinds of stuff," Ellie said, trying hard to sound tough and streetwise and confident. But Christina knew that behind the words, Ellie was every bit as scared as she was.

Ellie asked tentatively, "Would you mind maybe readin' a little bit out of your diary about the time when your parents was alive and everythin' was nice?"

Christina replied softly, "No, I wouldn't mind."

Opening the diary, she skimmed through the pages quickly, then stopped. "This is a good part. I remember when I wrote this; it was one of the best days of my whole life. Listen." And she began reading haltingly, the words illuminated by the bright moonlight coming through a broken window.

"June 15, 1967: My mother took me shopping at Magnin's today for a dress for their anniversary party. We found the most beautiful dress, all in white lace with little pink rosebuds around the neckline. She said I looked so grown-up in it, and then she hugged me and she had tears in her eyes. I don't know why she seemed sad that I'm getting older. I can't wait to grow up . . ."

# *Chapter 11*

*M*iss Fortune?" James's insistent voice pulled Christina from her reverie. "They'll be expecting us, Miss Fortune."

"Yes, of course," she said, blinking back tears. She took one long last look, then pressed the button to close the window.

Fortune Hill was only a few minutes' drive from the house at Broadway and Baker. It sprawled over half a city block, on the largest privately owned property in the middle of San Francisco. The twenty-five-room mansion made of white limestone sat atop a hill and resembled a park. The French baroque style was the hallmark of an era of wealth and opulence in San Francisco, when the fortunes of a sea trader had established the upstart family in San Francisco society. From the street at the bottom of the hill, with the setting sun bathing the facade, it looked like an elaborate confectioned ornament set on a cake.

James pulled up to the wrought-iron security gate. Picking up the telephone, he entered the security code, and the gate slowly opened. They drove up the long circular driveway to the porte cochere. James got out and came around to open the door for her.

There were several other cars parked ahead of them, down

the wide curve of driveway set with paving stones. It appeared that everyone else had already arrived.

James took her hand, helping her out of the limousine. She turned briefly, taking in the panoramic view of San Francisco Bay, the Golden Gate Bridge aflame with the light of the setting sun, the golden Marin hills, and infamous Alcatraz Island. According to countless magazine articles on lifestyles of the rich and famous, this was the most spectacular view of the entire Bay area. She smiled faintly as she imagined old Hamish Fortune standing where she stood at that moment, probably swelling with pride at the thought that he had become wealthy enough to buy the best damn view in the city.

His grandson, Alex, had actually built this house, tearing down a smaller one built by Hamish. Alex was a shrewd young man. In 1909 he predicted there would be a world war and there would be a great need for ships. He built up his fleet, and when war came, he was ready. With every available ship afloat commissioned for the war effort to transport troops, supplies, and armaments, Fortune vessels picked up valuable contracts for domestic shipping.

After the war the honored ties to the Orient gave him the opportunity to expand shipping in the Pacific. Over the next twenty years, until the outbreak of World War II, Fortune International dominated the East Asia trade routes, and Alexander Fortune became a very wealthy man.

He spent ten years building this imposing mansion. When it was finished, he felt the pressing need for a wife and family to continue the Fortune dynasty. There was no shortage of wealthy young San Francisco socialites. Early in 1930 Alex was engaged to the daughter of one of the most prominent families on the West Coast. It was a brilliant match of prominent families. Then, on a business trip to New Orleans, Alex met the young secretary of an associate. Her name was Katherine Marie Rawlins.

She was no great beauty. But beneath the carefully cultivated genteel manners and speech was the steely determination of a young woman who'd grown up in an impoverished family and put herself through business school. Her intriguing air of independence, and a smoky voice that got under his

skin, attracted him to her. He made a pass at young Katherine
Rawlins. Instead of falling into a delicate swoon, or bursting
into genteel tears, she responded with a passion to equal his.
And Alexander fell immediately and hopelessly in love with
the young woman who matched him in spirit and ambition.

He returned to San Francisco, broke off his engagement,
and promptly sent for Katherine. They were married two
weeks after they met. Fortune Hill had a mistress, and Alexander Fortune had a wife who complemented him in every
way. One year after they were married, Michael Alexander
Fortune was born; Richard and Diana followed. The Fortune
dynasty would continue into the next century.

Standing there, staring at the house, Christina realized that
finally, after twenty years, she once more had a family. And
it was time to meet them, whether she wanted to or not.

As she climbed the wide, shallow steps to the front entrance, the door opened.

"Good evening, Parker," Christina greeted the butler who
had been at Fortune Hill for forty years.

The elderly man's pale, hazel eyes widened behind the rimless glasses he wore. His hair was thinner and grayer, but the
way he stared at her down the length of his patrician nose was
unchanged.

He was torn between joy and shock. "Miss Christina!"

"Yes, Parker, I've come home." She laughed softly, remembering how many times he'd been the object of practical jokes
by all the Fortune cousins. It was a wonder he'd survived.

"Miss Christina!" he repeated, unable to say anything else.

"How are you, Parker?"

"Very well, thank you. Oh, this *is* a wonderful surprise.
Mrs. Fortune called, but I couldn't quite believe . . ." He
cleared his throat, struggling to regain his normally rigid de-
portment. "It is very good to see you again, miss. It's been a
long time."

For the first time Christina heard the unmistakable sound of
sincere joy at her homecoming, and it touched her deeply.

She laid a hand on his arm. "Yes, it has been a long time.
It's good to see you again, too. Is Mr. Lo here yet?"

"Yes, he arrived just a few minutes ago."

She allowed herself a small sigh of relief. "Then I suppose I shouldn't keep everyone waiting."

He continued to stare at her. When he realized she'd caught him at it, he cleared his throat uncomfortably and tried to speak, but no words came.

"It's all right, Parker. I know it's quite a shock."

His wrinkled face softened in a warm smile. "Yes, but it's a very pleasant shock, Miss Fortune. Now then, if you will follow me, everyone is waiting in the drawing room."

They had dressed in their impressive best for the occasion, the men in black tie and the women in formal gowns. Richard Fortune glanced up, a drink poised in his hand, as Christina stepped into the doorway of the formal drawing room.

She was tall and elegant, in a brilliant blue full-length sheath dress. Over it she wore a matching blue bolero with wide white satin lapels turned back to accentuate the bare column of her throat. Her long, dark hair with deep red highlights glinting in the subdued glow of the recessed lights in the ceiling was pulled back in a sleek chignon. The severe style emphasized the features that bore such striking resemblance to the young girl in the photograph that sat atop the black ebony grand piano across the room.

For just a brief moment there was a stunned silence as everyone stared at the woman whom Katherine had formally accepted as her granddaughter.

The brandy Richard had been drinking wasn't enough to take the edge off the fury he'd been nursing since the night before. Once again he felt that sharp sense of betrayal, and once again it had come from his mother.

He'd devoted his life to the company. He'd spent the last twenty years fighting his mother for control of it. It was rightfully his, and would have been if the woman across the room hadn't shown up and claimed to be his long-lost niece. Katherine had accepted her far too easily. It didn't make sense. Uneasily, he wondered what his mother was up to now.

Phillip Lo started across the room first, to greet the young woman who called herself Christina Fortune.

Tossing back the remnants of his drink in one swallow,

Richard abruptly set down his glass, then moved to cut Phillip off. Holding out his hand to Christina, he said in a smooth voice, "Let me be the first to welcome you . . . back to Fortune Hill."

It wasn't a handshake, but a firm, almost painful clasp of her right hand. Christina looked up in surprise as Richard bent forward and kissed her briefly on the right cheek. Then he pulled her arm through his, and turned toward the other members of the family.

"Here she is, everyone," he announced. "Our Christina has come home."

There was a momentary hesitation, as if everyone were standing back to allow someone else to be the first to greet her. Finally someone spoke.

"Welcome home, my dear."

Christina turned to Alicia Fortune, resplendent in a breathtaking emerald necklace and satin gown of emerald and black stripes. Aunt Alicia. Mentally Christina reviewed Alicia's impressive social resume. She was chairman of the Children's Hospital Foundation, president of the Opera League, and involved in at least a dozen other charities and society organizations. She organized benefits, charity balls, luncheons, and yachting parties. A member of one of the oldest and most influential San Francisco families, she had married into an equally influential one. She was mainline San Francisco society. And Christina disliked her immediately.

"Well, I suppose you know everyone . . ." Alicia continued, gesturing vaguely toward the other family members.

Richard interrupted her. "Of course she knows everyone." He glanced down at Christina. "After all, we're her family. We haven't changed that much over the past twenty years. Christina had no trouble recognizing everyone at the board meeting on Tuesday."

"Oh, yes, of course, the board meeting." Alicia turned to Steven, who had positioned himself at the bar. "Perhaps Christina would like a drink."

"White wine would be fine, thank you," Christina said as the other members of the family came forward to greet her. A circle of piercing eyes scrutinized her, the expressions behind them carefully guarded.

Her cousin Andrew was the first to break the odd, tension-filled silence. "Isn't it wonderful to be back in the loving bosom of your family." His breath was thick with several drinks, his voice laced with cynicism. His expression was pained. But she sensed real warmth as he kissed her cheek. "Welcome home, Christina." Then he added in an undertone, "I hope you know what you're doing by coming back here. Frankly, I would have stayed away if I were you."

"I've been away long enough, Andrew," she said, feeling pity for the sadness that she knew lay beneath the cynicism.

He saluted her with his drink. "Just call if you need me. I mean that."

As he stepped back, she found her cousin Jason staring at her from across the room. He stood apart from the others, watching her with an intense expression. What was he thinking? she wondered. Was he remembering that last night, when they'd quarreled? Did he remember all the hurtful things he'd said to her?

For a moment their eyes locked, and she sensed how torn he was between wanting to believe her and not wanting to believe her. With a rush of anguish she realized the passage of time hadn't diminished his feelings for her. All the sweet, sad, yearning helplessness of first love still lay between them, and somehow, sometime she would have to resolve it.

"My dear, it's so good to have you with us again," Brian Chandler said with a shy smile.

She forced her attention away from Jason and focused on his father. "Thank you, Uncle Brian."

"This is quite a surprise. You certainly took everyone by storm. You're a lot like Katherine that way." He squeezed her arm with a reassuring gesture. He was so like Andrew, but in place of the cynicism, she sensed a profound weariness. Brian, she remembered, had never been a happy man. He'd had the misfortune to get what he thought he wanted—marriage to the boss's daughter—and had lived to regret it.

"Yes, isn't she though." Diana joined them. Her beaded silver sheath hugged the aerobicized contours of her firm, slim body. Looking at her, most people would think Brian a lucky man to have such a stunning wife. But Christina knew differently.

The two women faced each other. Diana's expression was cool, appraising. She gently swirled the drink she held in her hand. "This must seem to you a victory dinner of sorts."

Christina looked at her evenly. "I didn't know there was a war."

"Oh, didn't you?" Before Christina could respond, she went on, "Katherine loves this sort of thing. Changing the rules of the game at the last minute. You're precisely what she was hoping for. But then I'm certain she explained all of that to you. Tell me, how long have the two of you been planning this?"

Brian shook his head. "Diana, please. This is supposed to be a pleasant evening."

"Yes, of course, darling." Diana lifted her drink in mock salute. "And all of us are so glad to see Christina again." She moved away, leaving them in awkward silence.

Brian said with some embarrassment, "I'm afraid that sometimes Diana drinks a little too much."

Christina laughed softly, trying to ease her taut nerves. "I could use a drink myself."

Awareness dawned on his face. "I suppose this is difficult for you, too."

"Yes, it is."

"Here we are," Steven announced, appearing at Christina's side. He handed her a glass of wine. "Thank you."

Watching him, Christina was aware of how much he resembled his mother. He'd been good-looking as a teenager. Now, in his late thirties, he was movie-star handsome, with a charm that was no less lethal for being distinctly devilish. From the information the private detective had given her, Christina knew that Steven had never married. That was hardly surprising. He probably couldn't bear the thought of confining himself to one woman for the rest of his life. He'd always been devastatingly attractive to women and had gone through them with an energy and enthusiasm that left his two younger brothers sick with envy.

He proposed a toast, much as Katherine had made the evening before. "To the prodigal's return." There was just a hint of mockery in his smile.

Christina was determined not to let any of this get to her. Taking several careful sips of wine, she waited for the false courage to take hold. When dinner was finally announced, she breathed a sigh of relief. The moment dinner was over, she intended to make her excuses and leave.

Brian escorted her in to dinner. As they left the drawing room together, a woman who appeared to be the housekeeper came in to remove the dirty glasses that had been left on various tables. Dressed in a plain black dress, she had gray hair pulled back in a bun.

She stopped Christina. "Welcome home, Miss Christina," she said in a quiet, deferential voice. Beneath the impassive facade of the well-bred servant lay a hint of intense curiosity.

Christina stared at her in confusion. She had no idea who this woman was. But it was clear that the woman knew her, and expected to be recognized.

The other members of the family had paused in the doorway of the dining room, and looked back at Christina questioningly. She could tell what they were thinking—the real Christina would have recognized this woman. She struggled to remember, but it was no use. Panic engulfed her, and she fought to hide it.

"Why . . . thank you," she murmured, finally responding to the housekeeper. But everyone was aware she didn't use the woman's name. She couldn't. She didn't know it.

Richard started to speak, but before he could challenge her, as Christina was sure he intended to do, the housekeeper said, "Of course you wouldn't remember me after all these years. I'm Rose Maitland, the housekeeper now. But when you were here, I was just the parlor maid."

*Of course,* Christina thought in a rush of memory. Rose Maitland had come to Fortune Hill shortly before Christina left. "Hello, Mrs. Maitland," Christina said with a smile. "I promise not to leave any peanut butter smudges on the woodwork."

The remark startled the housekeeper. "Peanut butter? Good

heavens! I'd forgotten all about the peanut butter on the grand staircase."

"You never told Grandmother. You said it worked almost as well as lemon oil, as long as the whole house didn't end up smelling of peanuts," Christina reminded her.

Tears appeared in the woman's eyes. She seized Christina's hands in both of hers. "That was *our* little secret. I promised I wouldn't tell a soul, and you promised . . ."

". . . to keep the peanut butter between slices of bread," Christina finished for her.

"My God," Mrs. Maitland breathed. "I hadn't thought it was possible after all these years."

A slight pressure on her arm told Christina that Brian was discreetly indicating it was time to go. "I'll see you later, Mrs. Maitland," she said.

Looking at Richard, she saw him frowning. For a moment he thought he'd caught her in a telltale slip, but to his intense disappointment she'd turned the near-fatal situation into a triumph. Inwardly she breathed a sigh of relief. It was all right now. But she'd come close—too close—to giving Richard what he wanted—proof that she wasn't Christina.

As they moved on, she looked up at Brian to say something and was surprised to see an expression of amazement on his face. Despite his politeness, he, too, had doubted she was really Christina. The exchange with Mrs. Maitland had clearly caught him off guard.

Dinner was delicious, but Christina barely ate anything as she answered the none-too-subtle questions from her family.

"So," Steven cut through the polite conversation that Alicia struggled to keep going. "Where have you been keeping yourself for the past twenty years, *cousin*?"

She picked at the white endive salad, aware that all other conversation ceased as everyone waited expectantly for her answer. "The portfolio that I gave you clearly states that I've lived in Boston the past several years. I went to school there, and for the last fifteen years I worked for Goldman, Sachs, an international investment banking firm. I started out part-time during college and went to work there full-time after graduation."

"You work?" Alicia was amazed. The women of the Fortune family had never worked outside the home. Which was one of the reasons Katherine's behavior in taking control of the company had antagonized everyone. She laughed faintly. "I can't imagine."

Steven asked, "What exactly did you do there?"

"I was an investment analyst and adviser on foreign trade. I made recommendations to clients."

Brian said with real interest, "Didn't I hear somewhere that the federal government has worked with Goldman, Sachs regarding the East European market now that the Eastern bloc countries are opening up to free enterprise?"

"Yes," she answered eagerly. "I attended meetings in Geneva on that subject."

Steven said, "Geneva? Well, it seems that *our* little Christina is one of those high-powered businesswomen. The next thing we know, she'll want to take over Fortune International. Grandmother better watch out." Then he added with a dangerous smile, "Maybe we'd better all watch out."

"Maybe you'd better," Christina replied with spirit.

To her surprise Steven laughed and responded, "*Touché,* cousin."

After that the conversation was stilted, barely polite. Christina was grateful that Brian sat next to her. From time to time she felt the comforting pressure of his hand against hers. Phillip Lo sat across the table. Occasionally her gaze met his, and he gave her a reassuring nod.

By the time dessert was served, Christina's stomach was twisted in knots from the emotionally charged atmosphere.

Surprisingly, it was Richard who'd kept the flow of conversation going. Andrew was silent, making her wonder about his earlier warning. Periodically she looked up and found Jason watching her intently. But as soon as their eyes met, he would look away. More than anything, she wanted to know what he was thinking, and remembering.

Christina was relieved when Alicia announced that coffee would be served in the drawing room. She needed to escape the close confines of the dining room.

"The family can be a bit wearing," Brian said with a world

of meaning as he escorted her to the formal parlor. "Are you all right?"

"Yes. I think I'll just get a breath of fresh air."

"Would you like me to join you?"

"I just need a minute alone," she explained. She had to sort out her confused emotions. The French doors were open onto the terrace that led into the gardens. She stepped through them and crossed the terrace.

Out across the Bay the lights of the Golden Gate Bridge arced across the water. She descended flagstone steps leading into the gardens. The night air cooled her heat-flushed skin as a thousand memories pulled her into the past. She followed the flagstone steps, knowing where they led.

It looked just as she knew it would—the summerhouse at the end of the garden. Twenty years ago a distraught fifteen-year-old girl had run down those same steps. And Jason had followed her . . .

"Oh, Jase!" Christina flung herself into his arms. "I slipped away from the party as soon as I could. I'm so glad to see you again. I've missed you so much."

He grabbed her roughly by the arms and pushed her away from him. She was stunned. Jason had never been anything but tender and gentle with her.

"I'll just bet you did," he answered angrily. "Two months, and you missed me so much that you didn't even bother to write or call." He paced away from her.

She stared at him, trying to understand the anger. "I *did* call, and I wrote to you. I wrote you every day. What are you talking about?"

Jason whirled on her. "I thought we meant something to each other!"

"We do," Christina answered. "You know how much you mean to me. You're the only one I can talk to, the only one who understands how awful it's been since Mom and Dad . . ." Her voice quivered and broke. "I wrote you about how much I hated the new school. I waited for your letters. But they never came."

"I sent you letters," he flung at her angrily, "and cards, and a book—that book of poems by Shelley that you wanted. You sent them all back."

She stared at him in dismay and confusion. "I didn't send them back. I never received them. Jason, you *must* believe me." She went to him then, slipping her hand in his, twining their fingers, reaching out for some small caring gesture.

He jerked away from her. "She told me it was wrong. She said you were only using me." His words were tight with pain.

"Who?" Then she suddenly knew. "Aunt Diana?"

He nodded. "You lied to me."

"I *didn't* lie to you." She reached out to him, but he pushed her away again and stormed out of the summerhouse.

The door slammed behind him.

"Jason! Don't leave me! Please, Jason." She collapsed in tears against the wall of the summerhouse, letting the darkness absorb her.

Eventually, when she was utterly exhausted and had no more tears to shed, she stopped crying. She felt empty, except for a dull ache deep inside. She had no idea how long she'd been there alone. She knew only that if Jason turned away from her, she had no one . . . no one she could confide in, no one who cared.

Then she heard steps on the flagstones outside the summerhouse. He's come back! she thought with a surge of hope.

The door opened. She saw a dark figure slip inside the summerhouse, but the moon was hidden behind a cloud, and it was pitch black now.

"Jason? Where are you? I can't see you." She smiled faintly. "I'm sorry. Please, let's not fight. You're all I have."

She heard the faint tread of footsteps as the figure moved around inside the summerhouse, then the scrape of a chair, and a curse. Suddenly she felt uneasy.

"Jason?" She slowly backed away. It wasn't like Jason to tease her like this. Still, he'd been so angry when he left.

"Jason?" she called out again. Before she could say another word, a hand clamped down over her mouth. Another hand twisted around her wrist and jerked it hard behind her.

"Christina . . ." It was a hoarse whisper, unidentifiable and frightening.

She cried out against the pressure of that hand at her mouth. Terror clawed into her throat at the hot breath that burned against her cheek, and the cruel fingers that tore at her Halloween costume. She'd dressed as a fairy princess . . .

Now, twenty years later, Christina heard the unmistakable sound of steps on the flagstones. The door creaked open, and a dim, gray figure was vaguely outlined in the darkness. Her breath caught in her throat, and her skin went cold as ice as a hand reached through the shadows and clamped over her wrist.

# *Chapter 12*

Ross often traveled to the East Coast on business, but he hadn't seen much more of Boston than the inside of offices, hotels, restaurants, and cabs. Still, he had seen enough of it at different times of the year to understand why people loved it. The dramatic change of seasons made it especially appealing to someone who had grown used to the sameness of San Francisco weather.

The lingering warmth of summer felt ephemeral. There was a sense of expectancy in the air. The chilly breath of fall was only weeks away. Winter came hard and fast this far north. But no matter the time of year, sailboats filled the harbor, inlets, and small coves. Ross felt the familiar longing to get out on the water, to experience the roll of a deck beneath his feet, the changes in the wind that could be seen out across the water, the unpredictability of both that could test a man and boat to the last of their endurance.

It had been weeks since he'd been able to get out on his boat. The way things were now, it would probably be several more weeks before he'd get another chance. He needed it. He needed to lose himself in the physical demands of the wind and water. But it would have to wait. Everything would have to wait until the matter of Christina Grant Fortune was resolved.

Now, sitting in James Buchanan's office in one of the charming old office buildings in downtown Boston, Ross thought Buchanan looked more like an accountant than a private detective. Short and slender, with neat blond hair and large, round glasses, he seemed as if he would be more comfortable carrying a calculator than a gun. But he was one of the top detectives in Boston, with nearly two dozen operatives working for him.

When Ross had called from Hawaii, he had told Buchanan he wanted Buchanan himself to handle this. Cost was not a consideration. Speed and accuracy of information were.

Now Buchanan flipped through a dossier that lay open on his immaculate desk.

"The information that she gave you in her portfolio is accurate. She graduated from Boston U., worked for the companies listed, and lived at the addresses she gave. She doesn't have a criminal record, and in fact seems to have lived an exemplary life. A real rags-to-riches story, working her way through college, starting at the bottom at Goldman, Sachs, and eventually becoming one of their most valued employees."

He smiled at Ross, "You know, Mr. McKenna, we do most of our investigating via computers nowadays. They can tell us almost anything we want to know about a person. You just have to know how to access the proper systems. The computers told us that Christina Fortune *is* who she says she is. She used the name Grant, but as you told us, that *is* a family name. It's not unusual for people to use other names, especially if they don't want to be found."

"You found *nothing* out of the ordinary?" Ross asked skeptically.

"We did find something rather interesting. You'll find it in the copies of her bank records. There are several checks written out to one individual."

Ross leafed through the pages until he found it.

Buchanan went on to explain, "The payments go back over the last six months. They're to a private investigator."

"Who is it?"

Buchanan tossed a business card across the desk. "I know

the guy. He works right here in Boston. He has a small office, just he and another fellow. He's reputable." He held up a hand as Ross started to ask if he'd questioned him.

"I already asked. But this sort of thing falls into the area of confidentiality. He wouldn't give us any information, and there is no way to find out why she hired him."

Ross pocketed the business card, then continued looking through his copy of the report.

It had to mean something. Christina Grant Fortune had used a private investigator. For what purpose? The list of checks written to the private investigator indicated the last one was dated six days ago, just before she left for San Francisco. She must have hired him to get information on the Fortune family. But that in itself wasn't enough to prove she was a fraud. She had information no private investigator could possibly obtain, and she had the pendant.

Buchanan continued, "There's another thing that's kind of intriguing that you should know about. Someone else has been checking her out, too."

"Who?"

"I don't know. It doesn't sound like any of the local investigators, so I'd say it's probably an outsider. All I know is that he's after the same information we're after. Do you know of anyone else who might be interested in her?"

*Richard.* It had to be.

Ross felt a renewed sense of urgency. He had to learn the truth about Christina before Richard did. There was no telling what Richard might do with such information.

Ross read on through the report, then looked up at Buchanan. "This tells me only what happened to her after she went to House of Hope. What about before that?"

For the first time, Buchanan looked less than confident. "We couldn't find out anything about her life before that. Believe me, I tried, but it's a blank. There are no records of her before that, and without records . . ." He shrugged.

He went on, "You told me that she lived on the streets. Hundreds of runaways live on the streets. There's no documentation unless they seek help, and then only if they allow it."

"This says that the priest who ran House of Hope picked her up at the emergency room of New York Memorial Hospital. Did you speak with him?"

Buchanan nodded. "I flew to New York and talked to him myself. A nice old guy, the closest thing I've ever seen to a real saint. But he had absolutely no information that was helpful to us. The only thing he knew about her was her name—Christina Grant. She refused to talk about her past or tell him anything about her family or where she came from. She stayed there for a couple of years, until she graduated from high school, then left to go away to college. His name, address, and phone number are at the end of the report."

Ross turned to the end and saw the name—Father Paul Munro. He reached a quick decision. "I want to talk to him myself."

Buchanan had expected as much, even though he was irritated that Ross didn't trust his competence. "I'll call him right away and set up an appointment as soon as possible."

Ross stood to leave. "I'll be at my hotel. Let me know as soon as you've made the appointment."

As Ross turned to the door, Buchanan said, "If she really is Christina Fortune, she inherits a lot of money, doesn't she?" Ross nodded.

Buchanan said thoughtfully. "Yeah, I can see there's a lot at stake. Well, for what it's worth, Mr. McKenna, I've checked out a lot of phonies in my time, and I think she's for real."

The next afternoon Ross stood on a New York street, looking at the unimpressive facade of House of Hope. The derelict building, in a downtown Manhattan enclave that hadn't yet been made fashionable, had been donated by a slumlord who was interested only in unloading it before the authorities decided to prosecute him for an endless list of violations.

Ross noticed that an unusual number of teenagers, most of them underfed and uncared for, loitered outside the building. Inside he found that it was surprisingly bright, immaculate, and cheerful. Posters with upbeat slogans or uplifting, life-affirming pictures covered the white walls. In a large living room, several youths sprawled in chairs, watching television, and in the adjoining dining room, a young man was setting a long trestle table for dinner.

The teenagers in here all looked well fed and clean—in every way.

"Can I help you?"

The young woman who addressed Ross was casually dressed in jeans and an oversize white shirt. But there was an air of quiet authority about her. He gave her his name, and she said with a warm smile, "Of course, Mr. McKenna, we were expecting you. This way, please."

She led him upstairs to an office on the second floor. The door was open—somehow Ross had the feeling it would always be open—and inside sat Father Paul Munro, the founder of House of Hope.

He was a tall, thin, elderly man, dressed in black, except for the sliver of white collar that circled his neck. He had wispy white hair and stooped slightly. His expression was benevolent, and Ross thought he had the kindest eyes he'd ever seen . . . eyes that would offer hope and compassion.

Father Paul stood up and extended his hand to Ross as the young woman introduced them. He gestured to Ross to sit down in the tattered leather chair facing his desk. House of Hope had been refurbished with a great deal of love and care and donations. But it was clearly a shoestring operation where money was in perpetual short supply.

"I understand why you've come," Father Paul began in a gentle yet firm voice. "I'm afraid there's nothing I can add to the information I already gave the private investigator."

"I appreciate that, Father. But I hoped that by speaking to you myself, I might learn something, *anything,* more. You see, this matter is extremely important. A great deal is at stake."

"Yes, I understand. The investigator explained about the inheritance." The priest's tone was polite, but it left no doubt as to how much importance he placed on money.

"It isn't just the money," Ross insisted. "This woman claims to be my employer's granddaughter. If that's true, it will mean a great deal to my employer. If not, it's a cruel trick that could break an elderly woman's heart."

The priest's expression sobered. "Believe me, I am sensitive to the ramifications of this situation. That's why I agreed to give the investigator the information at my disposal. Normally we protect the privacy of our kids with a vengeance. It's the only way we can earn their trust. They deserve that much."

Ross nodded. "I am grateful to you for your cooperation."

"What would you like to know?"

"I read Mr. Buchanan's report. I won't waste your time going over information you've already given us. But I would like to know a little more about how you met Christina."

The priest frowned. "In my work I tend to spend a great deal of time in emergency rooms, for one reason or another. Too many street kids end up there, either as the victims of violence or as a result of drug abuse. I had gone there that night to give the last rites to a boy of fourteen."

He paused, still shaken by the memory after all these years. "I tried so hard to get him off the streets," he whispered in a voice that was infinitely sad. "Unfortunately, he was one of my failures."

"You saw Christina come in?" Ross prompted.

"No, the young emergency room physician sought me out and told me about her. She had come in with a friend who was the victim of a knife attack."

"What happened to the friend?"

"She died, poor thing. I try to be with them, even those who don't believe, but this happened so quickly that I couldn't get to her in time."

Ross wanted to know more about this friend, whom Buchanan hadn't mentioned in his report.

"Did Christina tell you anything about her friend?"

Father Paul shook his head. "She refused to talk about her. She was clearly devastated by her death. I remember she asked me to pray for her friend. She insisted that she herself wasn't a believer, but her friend had been."

"Did the doctor say anything about the other girl . . . something she might have said before she died?"

"No, nothing." He added as an afterthought, "But I do remember that he said they looked remarkably alike."

Ross was suddenly alert. "How much alike?"

"He thought they were sisters at first. But Christina said they weren't."

"Do you know anything else about this girl?"

"I'm afraid not. As harsh as it may sound, I had to put her out of my mind. Christina was the priority. She was alive, and there was a chance I could help her and get her off the streets."

Ross asked, trying to control his excitement at this information, "Do you by any chance remember that doctor's name?"

Father Paul smiled. "Actually, I know Adam Bradford well. In a sense we're in the same line of work. We both try to save lives. I've kept in touch with him through the years." Taking out a pen and paper from a desk drawer, he scribbled a name, address, and phone number. "I'm not sure he can help you any more than I have. But I know he'll speak with you."

As Ross accepted the paper, he said, "Thank you. I appreciate your time." He rose to leave, then hesitated. "Would it be possible for me to make a donation to House of Hope?"

"Of course. We are not so unworldly as to try to exist without money. In fact, we rely on donations to survive."

He didn't understand why he felt an irresistible urge to make a sudden donation, except that in some small way he understood what it was like to be abandoned and forgotten. He took out his personal checkbook, wrote out a five-figure check, and handed it to the priest. Once he was back in his office, he would see to it that the Fortune Foundation put House of Hope at the top of the list of charities it supported.

Adam Bradford's office wasn't what Ross had expected. He assumed Bradford would be a prosperous, middle-aged doctor with a practice in uptown Manhattan. Instead, his office was in an old, renovated building in a marginal area near New York University. The short street was lined with other shabby buildings that had been turned into apartment buildings and small struggling businesses. For years it had been an area dominated by street people.

On the walls of the dilapidated houses, graffiti was scrawled in multicolored paint. On a pillar at the entrance to the street was a proclamation of gay liberation pasted over an old poster for a rock concert starring The Who.

Bradford's office turned out to be a free clinic for street people. The small waiting room was filled with people, mainly teenagers and young adults, who looked poor and uncared for. Considering that most doctors opted for lucrative private practices, Ross was impressed. Now he understood Father Paul's enigmatic comment that he and Bradford were in the same line of work. Like Father Paul, Bradford was obviously an exceptional man.

Ross gave his name to the receptionist, who looked as if she was no more than eighteen or nineteen. She said, "Oh, yeah. Doc's expecting you. This way."

She led him down a narrow hallway lined with cupboards, then knocked on a door marked Private. A voice called out, "Come in," and she opened the door for Ross to enter.

Bradford was short and thin, with unkempt hair and a pale, tired-looking face. Ross realized that running this clinic must be an exhausting and financially unrewarding job. Yet there was something about Bradford—in his quick and easy smile and relaxed air—that suggested he was a man at peace with himself and who had no regrets.

"Sit down," he said immediately. "Mr. McKenna, is it?"

"Yes. I appreciate your time. I'm sure you're very busy."

"Yeah, afraid so. There's always something to deal with here. That's why I live on the second floor. It makes it easy for me to get to emergencies in the middle of the night."

"Do you mind if I ask why you do this, instead of—" Ross stopped, unsure how to express his thought.

Bradford smiled. "You mean, instead of driving a BMW and living in a river-view condo?"

Ross nodded. "Yes. I suppose I did expect something like that."

Bradford laughed. "I know it seems like an old-fashioned notion, but I became a doctor because I wanted to help people—people who really need it, not just some society matron looking to have her crow's feet smoothed away, or her thighs remodeled. There are enough plastic surgeons; I went to school with some of the best in the country. I decided a long time ago that if I was going to have only one chance at life, I wanted to make it count. Here, I feel that maybe in some small way I can make a difference."

Before Ross could respond, Bradford went on, "Look, I don't mean to rush you, but I've got a lot of patients waiting."

"I understand. I'll get right to the point. Did Father Paul explain why I'm here?"

"Yeah. But I don't think I can tell you any more than he did. The girl I met that night was like hundreds of kids off the streets, both then and now. Unfortunately, things haven't changed. She was obviously a runaway, deeply troubled, probably abused at home, but determined to be on her own. I never saw her again. I always wondered what happened to her. Father Paul said that according to you, she turned out pretty well."

"It seems so. But at the moment it's her friend I'm interested in."

Bradford sat back in his worn leather chair and thought hard for a moment, trying to think back over so many years. "At the time, I was amazed at how much they resembled one another. I thought they were sisters, but she said they weren't."

"Is there anything else you can remember about the friend?"

"She was obviously a runaway, too. They were both underfed, skinny, but clean. I didn't find any trace of drug abuse. She was a pretty girl. With the same dark hair and eyes, and about the same age."

Ross said, "You seem to remember a lot about these girls. It's been a long time, and obviously you see a lot of young people. Why do you remember so much about these two?"

Bradford ran his hand over his chin. "First of all there was the resemblance. It was uncanny. They say we've all got a twin somewhere, and that was sure the case with those two. Still, you're right, it has been a long time. I see so many come through those doors. Normally I would have forgotten all about them. But the girl who died that night was the first."

"The first?"

Bradford got up from behind the desk. There was a poignant expression on his face as he picked up a stack of files. He started for the door and the patients who waited, gesturing to Ross to accompany him. As they headed toward the waiting room, he explained, "I had just started my residency at the hospital. It was my first rotation in the ER—emergency room," he translated for Ross. "It can be a real horror show. You see everything come in. Some nights the ambulances can't even back out after dropping someone off because of the congestion. It's always a shock, but it was worse because that was the night I lost my first patient."

Ross stared at him. "The girl who was knifed?"

Bradford nodded. "By the time you're finished with medical school, you think you're immune to death, in a way. Then it happens—*your* patient, someone whose eyes you've looked into, someone you've tried desperately to save, and you never forget. The first one stays with you forever, and reminds you that no matter how many you save, you're not God."

He added, "I suppose maybe that was the first time I really considered the kind of doctor I wanted to be. As I said, you never forget."

He hesitated, then finished, "I'm sorry, but I've got patients to see."

Ross thanked him and made his way out of the clinic. Outside he stood on the sidewalk for a long time. Then he walked to the nearest public telephone and called Buchanan.

When the private investigator came on the line, Ross said crisply, "I want you to check out the girl who was with Christina that night, the girl who died."

"That isn't going to be easy."

"Just do it."

He hung up the phone and returned to his car. But as he headed toward the airport, his thoughts weren't on Christina or the volatile situation at Fortune International. They were on a young girl who had died twenty years earlier.

Who was she?

# *Chapter 13*

*I*n the summerhouse Christina's heart leapt in a spasm of terror. *It was happening again.* She fell back against a support post and looked wildly about for some escape. But there was only the one door, and he was blocking it. Her legs were shaking, and her heart beat frantically against the wall of her chest. Her lips parted to scream for help, but the only sound that emerged was a faint, trembling gasp.

"Christina? My God! What's wrong?"

Through her terror she saw a hand outstretched toward her, but there was no attempt to grab her again. The voice, filled with concern, reassured her, calming her fear.

"Jason?" she whispered, a small, desperate sound that caught in her throat.

"Yes, it's me. Who did you think it was?"

He started to come toward her through the shadows. Her hand came up instinctively to stop him.

"I'm sorry," she breathed as she tried to hold on to what little control she had. "I thought you were . . ."

"Who, for Christ's sake?"

He was close enough now to be illuminated in the shaft of light from the main house that spilled through the opaque panes of glass.

"I don't know . . ." she murmured helplessly. "I don't

know." Tears filled her eyes. She *didn't* know who had been in the summerhouse that night twenty years ago. Therefore, she didn't know which of the Fortune men she could trust. Which one of them saw Jason storm out of the summer-house, leaving Christina alone and vulnerable?

It had been dark that night, and Christina couldn't see her attacker clearly. Whoever it was, he had worn a Halloween costume, and the only people who attended the Halloween party had been members of the Fortune family.

"Are you all right now?" Jason asked.

She nodded. "It's just that I wasn't expecting anyone. You . . . startled me."

"I saw you come in here," he explained. "I needed to talk to you."

But she didn't want to talk to him, not here, not now. She started to walk past him, determined to get to the safety of the main house. When he reached out to stop her, she cringed. Seeing her reaction, he frowned, then let his hand drop to his side.

"It's just so incredible that you're alive . . . you're here. I *had* to see you, to talk to you . . . alone."

He hesitated, then went on, "I couldn't believe it when you disappeared. I kept thinking you'd just show up in a couple of days. But you didn't . . ." He made a helpless gesture with his hand. "God! I was so angry at you!"

His expression reflected his misery. "I thought you didn't care anymore. It was as if everything we'd said to each other, everything we'd meant to each other, was nothing but a lie. I didn't mean those awful things I said to you. I was just so hurt. Oh, Chris, I never meant to drive you away."

He looked so unhappy and vulnerable at that moment that she could almost see the lonely, insecure teenage boy he had once been. She wanted to reassure him that he hadn't driven her away, but she couldn't be sure that was true.

Without saying another word, she left, leaving Jason alone in the summerhouse with the memory of an intense young love that had gone very wrong.

•    •    •

Christina reluctantly moved from the Hyatt Regency to the house at Fortune Hill the next day. She was immediately plunged into a hectic social schedule. Alicia had already accepted several social invitations on her behalf. It seemed all of San Francisco wanted to know about her. The local papers were filled with the latest installment of the Fortune family saga.

Phillip Lo sent over endless paperwork for her signature: affidavits, transfers of stock, bank signature cards, and other forms. Once Katherine set out to do something, she wasted no time.

That same day Christina also went into the corporate offices. Ross's assistant, Bill Thomason, gave her the grand tour, ending up at her small office far from both Ross's and Richard's offices. So, they thought they could simply shut her away from the center of operations. Well, they thought wrong.

"I'll need a different office," she informed Bill.

"But Ross said . . ."

"I don't care what Ross said." She knew she needed to take a firm stand from the very beginning, or she would get nowhere. "I'll choose my own office, and it won't be in Timbuktu, like this one."

Bill was obviously unsure how to react to her demand. He worked for Ross. But Christina was the majority stockholder in the company. She could see indecision written all over his face. Her refusal to accept Ross's decision had placed him in a very difficult situation.

She smiled and said, "Don't worry. I'll take the heat for this decision."

Bill sighed, then returned her smile. "That's going to be some heat, Miss Fortune."

"I think that is an understatement. And, please, call me Christina." Then she added, "I can handle Ross."

He grinned. "If you can, you'll be the first."

Bill was about her age, with close-cropped, curly, reddish brown hair and soft brown eyes. He and Ross had known each other for years, since attending college together in Canada. It didn't take her long to find out he was staunchly loyal to that friendship.

Bill gave her copies of the two previous year-end reports on the company. They were both more than three inches thick, and he obviously thought that would keep her occupied for several days. She had no doubt that he was following Ross's specific instructions to keep her busy on unimportant matters until Ross could return and deal with her.

By the next morning she had moved into the office adjoining Ross's and had gone through the reports thoroughly. She was about to buzz Bill and ask for more information, when Steven ambled in without bothering to announce himself to her new secretary.

"Well, well," he began, "looks like you've made yourself at home." Glancing at the pile of work on her desk, he went on, "I really wouldn't bother with all that if I were you."

"Oh? And why not?"

"Because despite the fact that Katherine likes to issue orders from on high, women have never taken an active role in running this company."

"Then it's about time we did."

He perched on the edge of her desk and smiled down at her. "A beautiful woman like you should have much better things to do with her time than bother with boring reports."

"Oh, really?"

"Yes, really. For instance, you could spend the day shopping for something wonderfully sexy to wear out to dinner with me tonight."

As he spoke, he leaned forward and cupped her chin in one hand. His face was only inches from hers, and she was taken aback at her elemental response to him. Steven was far too attractive for his own good.

Pulling away, she snapped, "You seem to be forgetting that we're blood cousins."

"Are we?" he responded with a teasing smile.

"Yes, we are. So stop trying to seduce me, Steven. It would be tacky as well as pointless."

At that moment Bill Thomason came into her office with some files that she had requested. Bill clearly wasn't intimidated by Steven. "Isn't this your day at the Yacht Club?" he asked with thinly disguised sarcasm.

Steven remained unperturbed as he slowly turned to leave. He stopped at the door. "Don't think that anything is going to change around here. As I said, women just aren't competent to run a business." His tone was chauvinistic in the extreme. "They should stick to what they do best."

When he was gone, Christina allowed her anger to show. "Is he always like this?"

Bill grinned. "An unbelievable number of women seem to like that kind of treatment."

"He needs to realize this is the nineties, not the fifties," Christina retorted.

"It wouldn't help. He's doing just fine being the spoiled, self-centered bastard he is. I'm sure he's always gotten his way, and he probably always will. That combination of money and good looks seems to be irresistible to most women."

"Yes," Christina reluctantly agreed, remembering how even she had felt a momentary response to Steven's seductive charm. Why is it, she wondered, that bad boys were always so much more intriguing than nice guys like Bill?

She was impressed with Bill's frankness, but also more than a little surprised by it. "You obviously aren't intimidated by Steven."

"I don't work for Steven. I work for Ross, and he's the only one who can fire me."

"And if Ross himself is fired?" she asked, referring to the conflict between Ross and Richard.

Bill shrugged. "Then I'd leave, anyway. I wouldn't work for Richard."

Changing the subject, he said, "Here are the previous ten years' reports."

She glanced at the stack of files. It was time, Christina decided, to come to an understanding with Bill. "This isn't what I asked for," she pointed out. "These reports are public knowledge. They're available to anyone who walks in off the street and asks for them. I want to see the *private* financial reports. And I want the up-to-date status of all liquid and encumbered assets, copies of all outstanding loan portfolios, plus the prospectus for profit and loss projections over the next five to ten years."

It took Bill a moment to recover. His expression behind his glasses was stunned. "That's a great deal of information. It might take me a while to put it all together."

She smiled at him. "Or you could let me into Ross's office. I'm certain he has precisely the information I'm looking for."

"I can't do that. He can give you that information when he gets back."

"From his trip to Boston?" she speculated.

A startled look crossed his face, and she knew she'd guessed correctly. Ross was digging into her past. It didn't surprise her. She'd known him only a few days, but already she knew enough to realize he would do everything he could to find out the truth about her identity.

She'd anticipated that every aspect of her past would be investigated. Still, it left her with an uneasy feeling to know that Ross was personally checking up on her. He wasn't the type who would be satisfied with dry facts. He would dig deeper than that—deep into her heart and mind.

"All right," she said evenly, not pressing Bill about the trip. He wouldn't tell her anything more, anyway. "If you won't let me into his office, then I'll need copies of all that information."

Bill groaned. It was a mountainous amount of paperwork. But he nodded and said with a sigh, "I'll see that you have it."

"Good." In spite of the fact that Bill Thomason was clearly loyal to Ross, she liked him. He was sharp, almost as sharp as Ross. He had a quick mind and an even quicker wit. But he didn't take her interest in the company seriously. Like Ross, and even Steven, for that matter, he tried to put her on the same level as Diana or Alicia—who had no working knowledge of what it took to run a company of the magnitude and scope of Fortune International.

It reminded her of something Katherine had told her before she left the islands—that women born to wealth were never given the power that went along with it.

But Christina wasn't about to sit back and accept the pa-

tronizing little tidbits of information that were thrown her
way even though she was absolutely certain that Richard,
Ross, and even Katherine would prefer it that way. She'd
risked a lot to come here and stake her claim to the inheritance. She wasn't about to take a passive role.

She smiled at Bill and said in a disarmingly sweet voice,
"By the way, I'd really appreciate it if you could get that information to me by tomorrow morning."

"Tomorrow's Saturday," he pointed out.

She met his gaze evenly and knew he was stalling for time,
until Ross got back. "I'm aware of that." Then as he turned
to leave with a shake of his head, she added, "I'd like to see
the new ship. Can you take me down to the Embarcadero?"

His expression of relief suggested this, at least, was a fairly
innocent request. "Sure. We can go now. I'll have the company limo brought around to the front."

A few minutes later, as they sat together in the limo, she
said, "You've known Ross for a long time, haven't you?"

Bill looked a bit wary. ". . . Yes."

"I suspect that your loyalty has nothing to do with your salary or position in the company. It must be friendship," she
added, understanding completely just how binding those ties
could be.

He nodded. "Yeah, we go back a long way. Back to our
university days up north. We shared an apartment before I got
married. I got him a job at the bank where I worked. I guess
you could say we made our way in the business together."

"And he never forgot the favor?" she interjected.

Bill laughed. "Yeah, I guess. You see, when we met, we
both were a long way from home and didn't know anyone.
Neither one of us had anyone else we could depend on. We
both came from lower-class backgrounds. We felt isolated
from the richer, more sophisticated students. We made a pact
that we would sort of look out for each other."

*"Look out for each other,"* she repeated, suddenly lost in her
own thoughts, as those words echoed out of the past.

"I beg your pardon?" he asked.

"I was just thinking that friendship is a very special thing."

"It's sure meant a great deal to me over the years," Bill admitted. "When Ross came on here, the first thing he did was bring me into the business."

"That doesn't fit the public image of Ross McKenna—ruthless, cunning, completely without scruples or conscience when it comes to business," she pointed out.

"Don't get the wrong impression. He can be all of those and more. I've seen him in action."

"And he'll be equally ruthless protecting his interest in the company," she concluded.

Bill nodded. "He has a great deal at stake. And he doesn't like to lose."

"I'll remember that. By the way, I want to see him the minute he returns."

Clearly anxious to change a conversation that had strayed into uncertain territory, Bill said, "Okay. You might need a secretary for all these messages you're passing along."

"I've already got one. She started yesterday. I have her working on another project."

Bill laughed as he shook his head. "Good. I was beginning to have a strange itching sensation in my fingertips—that vague feeling that I was about to be recruited to the typewriter, with an irrepressible urge for the smell of Wite-Out."

She grinned. "Sorry, you're not right for the job."

He feigned a wounded expression. "I have a feeling that may be a sexist remark. I'll have you know that we have several male secretaries with the company."

He went on conversationally, "Is the family keeping you busy?"

She groaned. "Of course, with the requisite number of luncheons, afternoon teas, and appearances at both the theater and the opera. Alicia is determined that I attend everything, to make a statement about family unity."

"That sounds a bit like Katherine," he suggested.

She agreed. "It sounds *exactly* like Katherine. I suspect that Alicia is only carrying out Katherine's orders. So far I've been able to dodge most of the afternoon teas, and I begged off lunch today. That sort of thing isn't my style. And then there's the press to deal with."

"It's only natural that there's going to be a great deal of cu-

riosity and speculation in the press. The Fortune family has
been a part of San Francisco history for over one hundred
years. With all the publicity about the disappearance, you've
caused quite a stir."

She frowned. "It's a nuisance. I finally had to rent an in-
conspicuous Toyota to avoid being followed around by reporters. I park in the general parking area along with all the other
employees."

Bill raised an eyebrow. "That doesn't allow for very good
security."

"Why do I need security?"

"You're an heiress, remember? You could be mugged, or
even kidnapped."

"This isn't Italy," she said, dismissing the melodramatic
suggestion. Yet thinking of the unresolved question of the rapist, she realized that Bill might not be so very wrong. There
*was* potential danger in throwing herself into the middle of a
volatile situation.

The limousine pulled up beside the pier. Nearby she saw
the newest addition to the shipping line, the *Fortune Star*.
Like all the ships of the fleet, the gleaming white cargo ship
was registered out of Hong Kong. It was several stories tall
and emblazoned across the stern was the blue Fortune logo.

Tilting her head back as her gaze swept the massive ship,
Christina felt a surge of pride. So must every member of the
Fortune family have felt over the generations, she thought.
From the era of multisailed clipper ships sailing the China
Sea, through the intra-island steamship line started by Hamish
Fortune, down to this steel behemoth, Fortune ships had carried an aura of adventure. In spite of her determination to
remain businesslike and unemotional, Christina couldn't sup-
press a thrill of excitement. Fortune International was more
than a ledger sheet, or a year-end report. It was more than a
source of staggering amounts of money. It had a bold and
proud history.

At that moment Christina understood why it meant so
much to Katherine, why she fought so hard to maintain its integrity . . . and to hold on to it.

She was caught completely off guard by her own reaction,

and she found herself sharing Katherine's sense of pride and concern.

Bill smiled at her. "It's pretty impressive, huh?"

She nodded, returning his smile.

"Would you like to go aboard?" he asked.

"Another time. I need to get back to the office and catch up on some things."

As they returned to the limousine, Bill cleared his throat, then suggested with a hint of nervousness, "Uh, it's lunchtime, you know. There are some marvelous places down here at the Embarcadero."

She was touched that he felt awkward about offering to take her out to lunch. "I'd love to have lunch. But not at a fancy place. You know what I'd really like?"

Bill grinned. "I have no idea."

"A hot dog. With onions and cheese and chili. Washed down with a Coke. How does that sound?"

"Great! I know this terrific little place—best hot dogs on the Coast. My treat."

She laughed. "It's a deal."

A half hour later they had finished a couple of delicious hot dogs purchased from a hole-in-the-wall stand near Washington Square. They sat on a bench in the small square. Wiping her mouth with a white paper napkin, Christina said, "That was great. A really primo hot dog."

"I'm surprised you're into hot dogs, considering your background and all," Bill responded.

"I developed a taste for hot dogs at Rooney's on Fifty-seventh Street in New York. They are *the* hot dog for aficionados. I go there whenever I'm in the city."

"A habit from your misspent youth," he joked good-naturedly. Then his expression sobered. "I'm sorry. I didn't mean to pry."

"Yes, you did." Her recovery was quicker than his, and there was no resentment in her voice as she said, "Ross gave you specific instructions to find out whatever you could about me."

He didn't bother to deny it.

"It's all right." Then she added with a mock-serious expression, "Did you know that a really good hot dog is one of the three best ways to bribe someone for information?"

"Is that right?"

"Of course."

Bill laughed. "And what are the other two?"

"Double fudge ripple chocolate ice cream with chocolate chips, smothered with hot fudge and marshmallow cream."

"Good God!" Bill exclaimed. "No one could survive that. I'm almost afraid to ask what the third method is."

She winked at him. "You're right, don't ask. Just stick to hot dogs and chocolate."

Then in a more thoughtful mood, she said, "Tell me about yourself."

He shrugged. "I've told you just about everything. Basically I've spent the past fifteen years working with Ross, in one way or another."

"I'm not talking about business. I mean, tell me about yourself personally."

He looked suddenly shy. Clearly he didn't feel comfortable talking about his private life. But Christina was curious about him. So far, he was the first person she'd met in San Francisco who might actually turn out to be a friend, and friendship was something she needed rather badly at the moment.

Bill cleared his throat and began hesitantly, "I was an only child . . ."

"Like me," Christina responded encouragingly.

"Yeah. I grew up on a small farm outside Calgary, Canada. All I ever wanted to do was get out, and to my surprise I actually managed to do it."

"Why were you surprised? You're very bright and capable."

He was embarrassed by the compliment. "Thanks."

"There must have been more to your life than your career. You said you were married."

He smiled awkwardly. "You come right to the point, don't you?"

She smiled. "It saves time."

"Yeah, I guess so. The fact is, I was married for a couple

of years. Her name's Bonnie, and she's a kindergarten teacher. But ..." He stopped, then finished slowly, "It didn't work out."

"I'm sorry," Christina said with real feeling. "That must have been very hard on you."

He couldn't meet her look now. "Yeah," he whispered.

"Look, if I'm out of line, just say so. But if you'd like to talk about it, I'm a good listener."

He looked over at her, his eyes moist with remembered pain and loss. "You're not out of line. I appreciate your concern. It's just, well, it wouldn't do any good to talk about it. There's nothing anyone can do."

"But you still seem to care about her."

He nodded miserably. "I think I always will."

"Does she still care for you?"

"The last time I talked to her, a few weeks ago, she said she did."

"Then maybe you can work things out."

Bill shook his head. "We're too different. She wants kids, and she wants a father who'll be around to raise those kids. I've got a job that demands my full attention eighteen— sometimes twenty-four—hours a day."

"Why not cut back on your commitment to your work?" Christina suggested. "You job is simply what you do, it isn't who you are."

"You don't understand," Bill said in a voice filled with frustration. "I'd be letting Ross down."

"I think he could handle it," Christina said dryly.

"I'm not sure I could handle it. I've worked too hard, come too far, to risk losing my success because I wasn't willing to give it my all."

"Instead you've lost someone who means a great deal to you," Christina pointed out.

Bill was silent for a long moment. Then he spoke in a tone that clearly indicated he'd had enough of this conversation. "You don't understand what it means to grow up with nothing and want so much."

"Oh, but I do," Christina said with feeling.

Bill looked at her in surprise, but didn't question her. She was relieved that for once someone didn't probe too deep.

They walked back to the limousine in silence. Finally he said, "There's something I've got to say. You're absolutely right about my loyalty to Ross. But that doesn't mean I do everything he says without questioning it. From here on out, you don't have to worry about me spying on you for him."

She was touched by his honesty. "Thanks. I appreciate that; I don't have too many allies."

"Well, you've got one now."

She flashed him a warm smile of gratitude. "Thanks. Look, I have to go to the theater tonight with Brian and Diana and Alicia and Richard. Would you like to come?"

The invitation caught Bill off guard. "You mean . . . like a date?"

"Well, we'd both have to get dressed up and you'd come to the house to pick me up, and I'd probably kiss you goodnight. So, yeah, I guess you could call it a date."

Bill grinned. "I'd love to."

Ross sat at his desk, flipping through the more critical messages waiting for him. It was Sunday evening, and the office was closed for the weekend, but typically it was the first place he'd gone on his return from Boston. Bill had met him there.

"What else did she ask for?" Ross queried.

"You name it," Bill answered as he sat on the corner of the desk. "She wanted everything that has anything to do with the company. She knew exactly what to ask for, and she went through it fast. Also, she's taken an office." He cocked his head in the direction of the one next door to Ross's.

Ross frowned. "Why did you let her do that?"

"Just how would you suggest I stop her? She's no fool, Ross. She's already got a good grasp of the business. She went over information on shipping tonnage, trade agreements, and new shipping data for our competition. And she understands it all."

Ross said irritably, "You sound as if you're beginning to like her."

"It's a little difficult not to like her. She isn't at all what I expected."

"What is that supposed to mean?"

"She's got an impressive business background. She's intelligent, knowledgeable, warm. And frankly, she's a knockout in an evening gown."

A frown deepened the lines of fatigue on Ross's face. He pinched back the ache at the bridge of his nose that he'd been carrying around for days. "How do you know what she looks like in an evening gown?"

"I escorted her to the theater Friday evening. Alicia's trying to get her involved in the San Francisco social scene. You know how she likes to be in the limelight, and the sudden reappearance of the missing heiress to the Fortune inheritance has definitely created quite a stir." He added, "By the way, she likes hot dogs."

Ross looked up. "Hot dogs?"

"I took her to this great little place—"

Ross cut him off. "Were you able to find out anything besides what she gave us in that portfolio?"

"Only what she wanted me to know."

"Meaning?"

"Meaning that whatever she chooses to keep personal stays personal. I couldn't get anything out of her. And from now on I'm not going to try. I don't feel comfortable spying on her for you."

Ross was completely taken aback by Bill's vehemence. "You think she may be telling the truth." It was a statement, not a question.

"Have you considered the possibility that she *is* Christina Fortune?" Bill responded.

Christina had asked him the same thing in Hawaii. Until yesterday, he had almost begun to believe it might be possible.

Then Bill added, "She wanted you to call her as soon as you got back. By the way, what did you find out in Boston?"

"The private investigator located the priest who found her in New York and took her to House of Hope."

"Was he able to tell you anything else about her?"

Bill's interest was stronger than Ross would have liked. He answered slowly, "He gave me some very interesting information she chose to leave out of that portfolio."

"I see." Bill was clearly disappointed. "What does it mean?"

"That is precisely what I'm going to ask her."

Christina found Ross waiting in her office first thing Monday morning.

"I didn't know you were back," she said with just a hint of unease in her voice.

He looked up from the pile of files and portfolios neatly stacked on the credenza. She had several more tucked under her arm, and laid them on the desk.

"I got in last night. Bill told me you've been going over some information about the company." He closed one of the files and met her gaze directly.

She'd forgotten just how unsettling Ross McKenna was, how handsome, and . . . intense. She felt uncomfortable under the scrutiny of those penetrating blue eyes.

She put her shoulder bag in the bottom drawer of the large mahogany desk that she'd requisitioned from storage. It was old, massive, with deep drawers, clearly a relic from the earlier days of the company. It resembled the desk she'd seen in one of the portraits of Alexander Fortune at the ranch in Hawaii, though she doubted it was the same one. Still, it had a solid, traditional feel to it that she preferred to the stark coldness of the modern furnishings that dominated the Fortune offices.

She wanted to ask him about his trip to Boston, but she had a feeling she'd find out about it soon enough. Clearly Ross had something he wanted to discuss with her. She was cautious as she came around the desk.

"Would you like some tea?" she suggested. "I thought I'd get myself some."

"Marie can do that," he said of the secretary who occupied the desk outside her office. Christina was aware of a hard edge in his voice that hadn't been there before he went to Boston. He'd questioned her relentlessly, probing for flaws from the moment they'd met. But he had done so with a certain objectivity that convinced her it was all just business to him.

Yet she sensed that this trip had changed things. He'd found out something.

She felt a slight frisson of apprehension as she buzzed Marie on the intercom and asked her to bring in a pot of tea and two cups. A moment later the middle-aged secretary brought in a silver tray and set it on the credenza.

Christina had hired Marie over several much younger applicants because she sensed Marie really needed the job. Already Marie had shown her gratitude through a touching loyalty.

Marie started to pour, but Ross stopped her. "I'll get it." He nodded curtly. "Thank you."

"Your secretary asked me to tell you that there have already been several calls for you this morning, Mr. McKenna," she reminded him.

"Please tell her to hold all my calls, and do the same for Miss . . . Fortune."

The hesitation was just enough to be noticeable. So, Christina thought, they were back to that again. As she sat behind her desk, she clasped her suddenly icy hands in her lap.

Ross added, "And please close the door on your way out. I don't want to be disturbed."

Marie left, and he poured tea for both himself and Christina. "Sugar? Cream?"

She nodded yes to both, then accepted the cup he handed to her. He took a while to prepare his own tea, slowly adding sugar, then carefully stirring in cream, and drawing out the tension. He took a sip of tea, looking about the office and the antique furnishings.

"You didn't waste any time settling in." It was an offhand comment, yet the meaning behind it was anything but offhand.

She set her cup down and stood up. "I have a great deal of work to take care of. If you don't mind . . ." She crossed the office to the credenza and picked up a file.

"Who is Ellie Dobbs?"

For a long moment she simply stood there, her back to him,

leaning forward on her spread fingertips, staring down at the open file.

She took a deep breath, and her voice was calm as she finally answered, "She was someone I knew a long time ago, in New York City."

"Tell me about her."

Slowly Christina turned around. She leaned back on the credenza, her hands braced at either side as she met his gaze. How much did he know? she wondered desperately. She began slowly, marshaling her defense. "We met on the streets right after I first got to New York. We had a lot in common."

"For instance?"

She tried to appear calm, but her stomach twisted in knots. "We were both fifteen, both of us had recently run away from our homes . . ."

"And you both had chestnut hair and brown eyes. In fact you looked so much alike that people mistook you for sisters."

She admitted reluctantly, "I suppose some people thought so."

"The physician I found in New York specifically remembered the resemblance."

So, that was how he'd found out about them—through the emergency room physician. She clasped her hands in front of her in an unconscious gesture of self-protection. Her voice trembled. "That was a horrible night. I've tried to forget it."

"I'll just bet you have," Ross accused.

Christina's eyes darkened as she met his gaze. "I said I've tried. I didn't say that I've succeeded. Somehow you don't ever forget the death of a friend. Especially the way it happened."

"How *did* it happen?"

She hesitated. She had no idea how much he'd learned, and that made it difficult to lie to him and get away with it.

"Ellie had been in New York for a couple of weeks before I got there. We met when I helped her out of a jam. Then we went to one of the places where kids hung out then. Safety in numbers, I suppose. She seemed confident, stronger than I was. We had something in common—we both felt that no matter how bad it was on the streets, it was better than going home."

"Where was her home?" Ross probed, determined to know more about Ellie Dobbs.

"She didn't say."

He didn't believe her for a moment, and she knew it.

"Why did she run away?"

Christina was pale, her voice tremulous. "She told me there were problems at home. Her father had died, and her mother had remarried. She didn't get along with her stepfather."

Ross leaned back in the chair, his fingers propped thoughtfully against his chin. He knew better than most the loneliness and pain that come from an unhappy home life.

The question now was what had happened in Christina Fortune's life that had left her no other choice but to run away.

"Why did you leave?" he asked, and there was a steely determination in his voice that said this time he would demand an answer.

She didn't meet his gaze. "I was in danger here."

"What danger?" he persisted.

Her eyes were stark and troubled as they finally met his. "I was in danger of being killed."

# Chapter 14

$R$ichard sat in his study at Fortune Hill. The wood-paneled room was decorated with valuable English sporting prints, bronze sculptures, and heavy, burgundy leather furniture. Richard had overseen the decoration himself, determined not to let Alicia pretty it up with chintz and spindly Louis XIV furniture as she'd done in the rest of the house. This was his retreat. The entire household knew that he was not to be disturbed when he was in here, save in the gravest emergency.

Normally he enjoyed his privacy here, and the comfortable, masculine aura of the room. But tonight he was filled with a bitter frustration that ruined the peaceful, private atmosphere. As he finished the final page of the private detective's report, he slammed it down on his desk and swore under his breath. The report was worse than useless. The man had found out nothing that Richard could use against Christina.

Disappointed and angry as he was, he knew it would do no good to hire another detective. This one was one of the best, and he wasn't shackled by qualms about breaking the law to get information. If he couldn't find out anything about Christina, then no one could.

Still, Richard wasn't about to accept defeat. Picking up the phone, he dialed the detective's number. When the detective came on the line, Richard berated him viciously for a couple of long, tense minutes. He finished by saying, "There's got to be something, some evidence you can find, that will prove who she is, because she damn sure isn't Christina! Now get out there and find it!"

When he hung up, he felt slightly better for having vented his fury, but it wasn't enough. Frustration ate away at him. There had to be *something* he personally could do . . .

In her bedroom Christina sat propped against her pillows, reading the diary.

*July 3, 1975: I almost drowned today because of Steven's ego. We were out on the Bay, and he insisted on being in charge as usual . . .*

Christina stopped. She didn't want to read about that. Instead she turned to another entry that described a picnic at Akaka Falls in Hawaii. It had been a wonderful day, just Christina and her parents and the magnificent falls. She smiled gently as she read the description. What a special time that had been, full of love and innocence. The adolescent girl who had written about it couldn't possibly know what a tragic turn her life would take.

Christina's eyes misted with tears, and she closed the diary. Without getting up, she reached down and pushed the slim, worn volume between the mattress and box spring, as she had done in the hotel.

She went into the office every day, going over records, reports, and countless stacks of information about the company going back over the past twenty years—since the death of Michael Fortune. Both she and Ross often worked long after the other staff had already gone home for the day.

He repeatedly questioned her about her reason for running away from home and about Ellie Dobbs. In the face of her stubborn refusal to explain any further, he finally gave up in frustration. But she knew that his silence didn't mean that he would quit trying to learn the full truth. It meant simply that he realized he wouldn't get it from her.

At first he refused to give her access to highly confidential information about the company. She immediately turned to

Katherine, threatening to leave if she wasn't allowed to participate fully in running the company. To Ross's surprise, Katherine agreed with Christina. Katherine refused to explain or defend her decision, but Christina suspected it had to do with her own resentment over the way women had been excluded from positions of power in the company.

After that, Ross gave Christina access to the information she requested, and on more than one occasion she managed to surprise him with her astute comments.

They worked together on charts, projections, and development proposals. Ross included her in meetings with financial advisers, clients who transported their goods on Fortune ships, and prospective clients he was trying to woo away from the competition. She knew she was included in these meetings only because Katherine wanted her to be familiar enough with the business to implement her own plans for it without delay or confusion.

On the evenings they both worked late, Ross stopped by her office and reminded her that the work would still be there tomorrow. He saw her safely to her car, then they disappeared in separate directions—she to Fortune Hill and the social events that Alicia insisted she participate in, and Ross to his condominium in the Marina district.

Their paths crossed socially one evening, at a gala charity fund-raiser at a starkly modern, gray and white Nob Hill penthouse. Christina was with Bill, who had become her steady escort at these affairs. They were laughing together over one of Bill's corny but cute jokes when Christina glanced across the packed living room and saw Ross descending the low flight of gray marble steps that led down from the foyer into the sunken living room. On his arm was a stunning blond. She wore a black silk dress that would have been positively conservative if it weren't for the slit that revealed all of one long, slim leg. In comparison, Christina's simple white satin sheath looked almost dowdy.

Following the direction of her look, Bill said, "This is a surprise. Marianne must've used every persuasive tactic she knows to drag Ross here. He hates these things."

Trying not to sound too curious, Christina asked, "Mari-anne?"

"Marianne Schaeffer—Ross's long-standing significant other."

"Are they engaged?"

Bill's grin was rueful. "Ross is allergic to commitment. Actually he and Marianne are perfect for each other. He travels on business so much, he couldn't handle a woman who wanted a real relationship. And Marianne is equally dedicated to her work, and isn't interested in playing Donna Reed for anyone. They're both perfectly satisfied to see each other when they're in town at the same time."

"What does she do?"

"What most women do who come from old-line, filthy rich families. She plays with her money." He paused, then went on, "That really isn't fair. The truth is, her billionaire grandfather established an endowment for the arts, and Marianne runs it. She studied at Berkeley and the Sorbonne, and really knows what she's doing. Although I've always kind of suspected that her dedication to the arts tends to focus on hand-some young artists."

Christina smiled. "And they say women are catty."

"All right, I admit it. That was a bruised ego talking. I met her first, and she turned me down flat for Ross."

Christina said gently, "That must've hurt."

"Frankly, he did me a favor. The woman's a barracuda. She would've eaten me alive."

Watching Marianne gazing adoringly at Ross as they chat-ted with the host and hostess, Christina commented dryly, "Ross seems to handle her pretty well."

"Ross is better at swimming with sharks than I am," Bill said with an easy laugh.

Marianne flashed a brilliant, seductive smile at Ross, who responded by slipping an arm around her shoulder. Christina told herself the fact that they were a couple was none of her business and shouldn't bother her at all.

But it did.

Suddenly she sensed Bill watching her intently.

"What's wrong?" she asked.

"Nothing, I suppose. It's just that I had the funny feeling that history might be about to repeat itself."

"I have no idea what you're talking about," Christina lied.

Just then Ross looked up and saw them. He said something to Marianne, and they made their way through the crowd to join them. Ross made the introductions. As Christina murmured a polite hello, she surveyed Marianne critically. Bill was right—this was no mere pretty socialite. This was a smart, tough woman who probably always got her way.

"I've heard all about you, of course," Marianne said in a direct, straightforward manner."

"Oh?"

"What a sensation you've caused. And so much secrecy. I've tried everything to get Ross to tell me the inside story."

"I'm sure you have."

Bill looked immensely amused at the thinly disguised cattiness, but Ross frowned in irritation. "We'd better find our way to the buffet," he said tersely. "You did say you were starving."

Marianne again flashed that wide smile that Christina knew must look captivating on the society page of the *Chronicle*. "Lovely meeting you. I'm sure we'll run into each other again. After all, we're in the same social circle."

"Yes," Christina said without enthusiasm. As Ross and Marianne walked away, she added under her breath, "But not for long."

"What do you mean?" Bill asked.

"I just realized how much I detest all of this. No matter what Alicia says about putting up a united front, I'm through being a social butterfly. She can hold up the Fortune family banner on her own from now on. I quit."

"She won't like it," Bill warned with an amused expression. "She'll say you're letting down the family."

"The family let me down a long time ago. I don't owe them anything."

Before Bill could question her last remark, she took his arm and said, "How about if we forget the cracked crab and mini quiche buffet, and have a fat, juicy hot dog?"

"With onions and cheese and chili?"

"Of course."

Bill grinned. "All right. But don't expect me to kiss you good-night."

Christina considered her decision to be a declaration of independence from the control of the Fortune family. She told a stunned Alicia that she had far too much work to waste time on frivolous social events that she didn't enjoy. That may have been the way the Fortune women occupied their time in the past, but this was the nineties, and times had changed.

She was equally determined to set her own course at the office, as well, but she knew she would have to be careful. The arrangement she'd made with Katherine gave her entrée to the company. But she wasn't fooled that her suggestions about the business would carry any weight if those suggestions went contrary to Katherine's wishes. She simply had to wait until she had a strong enough proposal to enlist Ross's support.

Ross was polite to her, in the same way he was polite to all employees. There was absolutely nothing personal in his treatment of her. Still, more than once she felt him watching her and looked up to find that intense blue gaze fastened on her thoughtfully.

Always there lay between them the question of her identity—who was she? Ellie or Christina?

She knew he must have told Katherine what he discovered in New York and Boston. After all, he kept nothing from her. Still, when Christina spoke to Katherine, the subject never came up. She remembered what Katherine had said on her visit to the ranch in Hawaii—that she didn't believe she was Christina. All that mattered was that the rest of the world believe it.

No matter what Ross or Katherine or Richard believed, Christina was determined to make a place for herself in the company. The more she learned about it, the more she cared about whether it survived. Fortune International had a proud heritage. Christina felt a rush of emotion at the thought of being part of that heritage.

She had accomplished her first goal—as far as the world was concerned, she *was* Christina Fortune. But there was another, far more important reason that she had come back—she had to find out who had come to the summerhouse that night twenty years ago. And she had to make him pay.

Bill persuaded Christina to leave the office early enough one evening to take in a movie and dinner. She was exhausted, and her eyes ached from poring over columns of figures, copies of manifests, and contracts with clients. The last thing she wanted to do was go out. But when she told Bill that she intended to go home and go to bed early, he insisted. "You know what they say about all work and no play. Come on, it will do you good. And I won't take no for an answer."

She let him hustle her out of the building before it was dark outside. They barely made it to the theater in time for the opening credits of the movie. The theater was showing a retrospective of Jimmy Stewart films, and on this night the feature was *Harvey*. It was one of Christina's favorites, and she happily settled in with a Coke and popcorn.

By the time they left the theater an hour and a half later, with Bill doing a remarkably clever imitation of Jimmy Stewart talking to the invisible rabbit, Christina felt happier and more relaxed than she'd felt at any time since arriving in the city.

"You should have been an actor," she said between giggles.

"Is that a comment on my financial acumen?" Bill asked with a grin.

She squeezed his arm affectionately. "Of course not. I don't know what the company would do without you."

Suddenly his grin dissolved and his demeanor turned serious. "And what about *you*?" He stopped and took her hands in his. Ignoring the people who frowned as they detoured around them, he said, "I know this isn't the time or place to say this. I was going to wait till we got to the restaurant. It's small and candlelit and has just the right ambience to sweep a girl off her feet. But all of a sudden I can't wait any longer. Christina, I have to know—do I stand a chance with you, or not?"

Looking at the helplessly infatuated, vulnerable look on his boyish face, Christina felt all her lightheartedness dissolve in an instant. She seemed to melt inside, but it was with compassion, not desire.

"Oh, Bill, I would give anything to be able to say yes. But I . . ." She stopped, completely at a loss for words. Forcing herself to go on, she said, "I care for you very much. You're the only real friend I have here."

*"Friend."*

The word lay between them, separating them rather than bringing them together.

"I'm so sorry," she whispered.

He pulled himself together and managed a smile that was a brave but pale imitation of his usual cocky grin. "No, don't apologize." Raising one hand, he tenderly brushed aside a strand of hair that had blown across her cheek. "You don't have anything to apologize for. I knew it probably wasn't gonna work, but I had to give it a shot."

She tried to smile, but found it impossible.

"For heaven's sake, don't look as if someone just drowned your kitten. I'm okay. Honest." Then, more convincingly, "I still want to be your friend, Christina."

"Oh, Bill, you're my *best* friend."

"Good. Now, let's get to that restaurant before I faint from hunger."

"How can you possibly be hungry? You had Milk Duds, a large Coke, and a giant bucket of popcorn."

"Hey, I'm a growing boy."

They continued bantering good-naturedly as they walked down the street. But inside Christina felt far from lighthearted. She knew she had hurt him. She also knew there was absolutely nothing she could do about it.

Back at Fortune Hill she was about to tiredly climb the stairs to her room when Alicia stopped her.

"Oh, Christina, you're finally back." There was a faint air of reproach in her voice, as if Christina were a teenager who'd stayed out past her curfew.

Christina bit back a tart response and forced herself to respond politely, "Bill took me to a movie."

"Oh . . . well, I just wanted to let you know that Ross came by, looking for you."

Christina was surprised. Ross never came to Fortune Hill. "What did he want?"

"I'm afraid I don't know. I was out, you see. When I got back, Parker said he had been here. Richard was home, but Ross didn't ask to see him."

Of course not, Christina thought.

Alicia went on, "Apparently Parker put him in the library, then went about his duties. When he came back later to see if Ross needed anything, he was gone. So we have no way of knowing how long he waited."

Christina couldn't begin to imagine why Ross would come looking for her. Murmuring good-night to Alicia, she went up the broad, sweeping staircase, her thoughts confused.

In her room she kicked off her shoes and slipped out of her dress, wondering all the while if she should call Ross. Then she realized that she didn't have his home number. Whatever he wanted to discuss with her would have to wait until she saw him at the office.

She had just taken off her earrings and set them down on her vanity when she noticed something was amiss. The top drawer, the one she kept her jewelry box in, was slightly ajar. Pulling it open, she found everything in order. Her little cherrywood jewelry box was there, and a quick search reassured her that nothing was missing. But instead of being at the front of the drawer, where she always kept it, the box was shoved to the back, as if someone had taken it out, then put it back again hastily.

With a sick feeling of apprehension, she quickly scanned her other drawers. They were all the same. Nothing was missing, yet there were subtle indications that someone had looked through them.

Her apprehension growing, she crossed the large bedroom quickly and shoved her hand under the mattress, feeling for the diary.

It was gone.

# Chapter 15

*H*ad Ross taken it? Was that why Bill had insisted she go out with him that night, so that Ross could search her room? She didn't want to believe it of Bill, but she knew the depth of his loyalty to Ross.

It would do no good to confront Ross. If he had done it, he wouldn't admit it. At least not yet, before he had a chance to go through the diary and see if it contained any information he could use to discredit her. And if he hadn't done it, she didn't want him to know of the existence of the diary.

There was always the possibility that Richard had taken it. He was there that night, one of the rare nights when he wasn't out with Alicia. Christina found it easy to believe that it could have been Richard. It would be just like him.

But she couldn't rule out the possibility that it had been one of her cousins, or even Uncle Brian. They all went in and out of the house with casual frequency, rarely bothering to announce themselves to Parker.

At the moment it didn't much matter who had taken it. What mattered was that it was in the hands of someone who almost certainly would try to use it against her. That wouldn't be difficult to do. It was a logical explanation of Christina's knowledge about the family.

She felt sick inside and rushed to the adjoining bathroom.

Leaning over the sink, she splashed cool water on her face, but it didn't help. Her position had been precarious from the beginning. Now it was even more so. And there was absolutely nothing she could do about it. Except wait for the ax to fall.

When she awoke in the morning, after a miserable, sleepless night, she was filled with a desperate resolve. Since there was nothing she could do about the loss of her diary, she would simply have to go on, as if it had never existed. Whoever had stolen it would do what he was going to do in his own good time. Maybe by the time he confronted her with it, she could have accomplished her goal of identifying the rapist.

Difficult as it would be to face everyone as if nothing had happened, that was precisely what she had to do.

She did ask Ross why he had come to the house. His response, "I needed a file you apparently took with you in your briefcase," sounded plausible but rather thin. Yet she didn't press him. She couldn't.

Late one afternoon Christina called a meeting in the boardroom. When he arrived, Ross was surprised to see that the only other person there was Bill.

"This isn't an official meeting," Christina explained, "so there was no need to include Richard, Diana, and my cousins."

Ross sat down at the head of the table, with Bill sitting to his left. Bill's face was alight with curiosity and excitement. He knew something was up and couldn't wait to find out what it might be.

"You have our full, undivided attention, Miss Fortune," Ross said with just a faint suggestion of impatience.

She took a deep breath and jumped in. "I've analyzed all the information on the company over the past several years. The only information I couldn't get involved several joint venture proposals that Richard has put together. He hasn't been very cooperative."

Ross gave her a measured look. "It's no secret that Richard

had been trying to put together outside financial resources prior to your miraculous reappearance. I have copies of those proposals."

So he had the information but had chosen not to share it with her. She bit back an angry comment. She was determined to maintain her composure. "This is only a preliminary analysis, but this is what I've come up with." She took a deep breath. "The company is in far more serious trouble than has been previously speculated."

She saw the wary look that passed between Ross and Bill.

"I suppose you have information to back up that statement," Ross said after a lengthy pause.

"Yes, I do." She rose from her chair and crossed the conference room, stopping at the presentation boards that swung open on the far wall. An intricate array of graphs, flow charts, and diagrams were displayed.

"The Mediterranean market is the weak link. Fortune has a total of forty-six ships of the line in that area. Twenty of them were in service when my grandfather was still alive and running the company. Of those, fourteen are single-hulled tankers. The balance of the fleet is composed of newer tankers and undersize cargo ships that have incurred exorbitant expenses for repairs because of age and retrofitting for the cargoes carried today. They're also obsolete in terms of fuel consumption."

Bill pointed out, "We have the four new ships that Ross commissioned. We've just taken delivery on the newest one, the *Fortune Star*."

"Four ships out of forty-six in the Mediterranean fleet," she remarked. "It doesn't make for a very strong profile."

"We lost three ships in the Med last year," Bill added. "Insurance has just come through on those."

"But according to these reports, it won't be enough to replace all three ships. The insurance was for value only, not replacement cost," she pointed out. "And insurance for our ships has become so exorbitant in that area because of the volatile Mideast situation. You're in direct competition with other companies based in the area. They can afford to absorb their losses. Fortune can't. It's become almost prohibitive to maintain a fleet in that region."

Ross spoke up for the first time. "You're not telling us anything we don't already know. We've got problems. We're trying to deal with them."

She referred to the three-page summary she'd drawn up. A copy lay before each of them on the table. "Fortune International is suffering a severe cash-flow shortage. With the exception of the four new ships that Ross has currently brought into the line, the assets of the company are composed of aging vessels. The entire line is spread precariously thin over several global markets, some of which are shaky at best. In addition, many of the company's assets, including several prime dock and warehouse properties, have been heavily mortgaged to finance the development of the Hawaii resorts."

She looked directly at Ross as she finished bluntly, "In short, without an infusion of cash, or the promise of very lucrative shipping contracts, the company will be without enough ships and financial resources to meet its current contracts."

The boardroom was silent. Ross didn't bother to look at the graphs or charts. He simply stared at her.

She turned to Bill. "Well?" she asked, knowing she'd made an accurate analysis.

Bill glanced at Ross. "I think . . ." he began, then stopped as Ross cut him off.

"With a few minor discrepancies due to lack of up-to-date information, you're basically correct," he said. "This company is on the verge of bankruptcy, at worst, and a forced sale, at best."

Christina was amazed at his matter-of-fact acceptance of the situation. She'd expected an argument, criticism of her conclusions, probably a flat denial of her doomsday prophecy. Instead, he agreed with her.

"All right," she said slowly. "Then the question is, What are we going to do about it?" Again she caught the look that passed between Ross and Bill, only this time she was at a loss to interpret its meaning.

"How long have you been working on this?" Ross asked.

"Since I got back from Hawaii."

"Have you come up with a solution for the problem?"

"I have several ideas that I'd like to discuss with you."

Ross frowned. "You're aware that Katherine has already made a decision?"

"I know that you and Bill have been working on it the past few weeks. I also know it has to do with the Mediterranean fleet, but I don't know the details."

"You sound as if you don't agree with that."

"No, I don't agree with it. I've just told you my reasons. Concentrating on an area as unstable as the Mediterranean and Gulf could be a fatal mistake."

Ross looked at his watch. "I'm late for another meeting. It's going to last at least until seven or eight. I'll come by your office when it's over, and we'll discuss this further over dinner."

When she started to protest that she didn't want to relegate this to just another business dinner, he said, "I think it would be best to have a little privacy while we discuss your ideas."

She knew exactly what he meant. Richard had an extremely efficient information network operating throughout the company. "All right," she agreed.

When he walked out of the boardroom, she turned to Bill. "Do you think he meant it? Does he really want to hear my ideas?"

"Ross always means what he says. I'm impressed with how thorough you were. I could tell that Ross was impressed, too. You got through to him. He just has a hard time admitting it."

Alone, back in her office a few minutes later, she stood by the window and gazed out at the breathtaking view. On this crisp, clear autumn day, the buildings seemed to thrust toward the cloudless, pale blue sky. But Christina's thoughts weren't on the towering skyscrapers, the bronze-colored Golden Gate Bridge in the distance, or the glistening, deep blue bay. They were on Ross. Tonight would be the first time they had been alone together since the flight back from Hawaii. For some reason the prospect made her even more nervous than she'd been before the meeting. That was business. This was supposed to be business, too. But dining in a chic restaurant somewhere, just the two of them, didn't sound like an entirely businesslike situation.

He took her to Chinatown.

They left the Toyota parked in the lower-level garage at Fortune Tower and took Ross's sleek black Jaguar. As soon as he got behind the wheel, he relaxed visibly. He loosened his tie, and the collar of his tailored shirt lay casually open against the tanned skin at his throat. The windows were open, and the cool air caught at his hair, spilling it down onto his forehead. He guided the car with agility through the dense, early Friday evening traffic.

He parked in a side alley in the heart of Chinatown. He didn't seem at all concerned about leaving such an expensive car in a dimly lit, poor area.

"I know the owner of the shop," he explained as they got out. Someone called out from overhead. Christina looked up to find an elderly Chinese woman smiling down at them from the second-story window above the rear entrance to the store. She called down again in Chinese, and Ross answered fluently and with a wave of his hand.

He apologized for the instinctive lapse into Cantonese. "Sorry, I didn't mean to make you feel excluded. Force of habit. Most people who grow up in the Territory are bilingual."

She smiled. "My father spoke Cantonese. I understand enough to know that she acted as if she knew you."

Ross shrugged as he guided her up the alley to Sacramento Street, his fingers lightly wrapped around her wrist, cradling her arm in his. "I did her a small favor once. I sponsored her nephew when he wanted to come over from Hong Kong to attend Stanford several years back."

She looked at him in surprise. "That's a rather large favor."

"It's hard enough getting a start in this world. I just gave him a chance."

They stopped in front of the old St. Mary's Center, a red brick structure with arched, leaded windows and large double doors left open for any who felt the need to seek sanctuary. It was a shelter for street people.

"Just a minute," she murmured, then stepped inside.

After a moment Ross followed.

The traditional architecture was typical for a Catholic church, but this church was atypical in that it welcomed people of all faiths. Pews stretched away to the altar, aglow with candles. A side door led to the adjacent center for the homeless. Beside the door was an offering box with a sign above. All donations were for the homeless, the lost. Christina slipped in a hundred-dollar bill.

"Repaying old favors?" he asked, reminding her that he knew a great deal more about her now.

"It really isn't much, in the scheme of things, but if it helps someone, in some small way, then it's enough," she said. Then she stepped back outside into the fading warmth of the early evening.

They walked in silence for several minutes, past typical tourist shops and fresh food markets with fish, poultry, and vegetables displayed in a teeming profusion of scents and aromas. Ross had revealed so little about himself during the time she'd known him, and she was curious to learn more. She decided to seize this opening in the conversation.

"Was it hard for you when you were young?"

"It was just my mother and myself. She worked with the English foreign affairs department in Hong Kong. That doesn't make for the kind of wages to accommodate a university education. So I went to work at seventeen when I finished my A levels." He recited it all so casually that he almost convinced her that he had no secrets of his own.

"Then you were educated in an English school."

He nodded. "One of the fringe benefits of being attached to the foreign office. It was provided for senior staff and their assistants.

They had stopped in front of a sidewalk restaurant with small grills aflame with chicken wings, strips of savory pork, and spicy beef skewered on sticks. Ross bought two wings and handed one to her. She nibbled at the chicken wing covered with a mixture of brown sugar, soy sauce, and sesame seeds. It was delicious.

After a moment she asked, "Who taught you Cantonese?"

"I picked it up here and there."

She shook her head. "You speak it fluently with perfect intonation and dialect. You don't pick that up on the street."

He smiled at her, for the second time in less than an hour. The boyish quality of the smile made her want to reach up and brush the strands of dark hair back from his forehead.

"You mean you don't buy that, Miss Fortune?"

"No, I don't, and please stop calling me that."

"All right . . . *Christina*," he agreed, and then asked, "Can you keep a secret?"

"Yes," she answered, intrigued.

"There is a rather dark, unsavory period in my life that few people know about," he revealed in a conspiratorial voice.

"Dark and unsavory?" Somehow she didn't find that difficult to believe.

"Before I came over here, I worked for two years on the Hong Kong docks. You learn quickly how to survive in a place like that."

At first she thought he was joking; then she realized he was perfectly serious. She'd heard stories about the infamous Hong Kong harbor and docks, the myriad boat people who lived on the fringes of society, a place where anything could be bought or sold if a person had the price—whether it was stolen artifacts, drugs out of the Golden Triangle, or a human being.

She couldn't imagine Ross in that environment. Then again he hadn't learned his particular brand of ruthlessness in business affairs at an elite English university or the Jockey Club.

"And you learned to speak Cantonese on the docks?"

"I already had a respectable knowledge of the language. I perfected it there, along with a few other talents necessary for survival." The way he said it sent a frisson of something—fear, excitement—down her spine, reminding her that she had sensed from the very beginning that there was something innately dangerous about the man. Dangerous—and fascinating.

She was discovering intriguing contradictions about him—bits and pieces that didn't fit in with his carefully cultivated image of polished sophistication. He would have been far less interesting, and easier to resist, if he were merely sophisticated.

"And after your apprenticeship on the docks of Hong Kong?"

He shrugged, as if the rest were all very boring. "University up in British Columbia. After graduation I worked for several companies. Then I met Katherine. What about you?"

He slipped the question in so easily. She smiled, going along with the easy conversation as they slowly ambled down the sidewalk, past the ornate pagoda facade of a Chinese meeting hall, garish red-framed store windows with intricately carved wooden dragons in all shapes and sizes, boxes of incense, hand-painted, folded paper fans, and carved sandalwood.

"I went to school in Boston, where I majored in economics and business administration. I went to work for Goldman, Sachs, and remained with them until coming here."

"Word-for-word out of your portfolio," he observed with a challenging look.

She finished the chicken wing, then wiped her fingers and face on a napkin. "You know everything there is to know about me."

"Do I?" he asked, his voice soft and dark with unasked questions. "I wonder." He reached out, grazing her chin with the curve of his finger. "You missed a place." He didn't withdraw his hand immediately, but traced the curve of her mouth.

Her lower lip trembled at his touch.

He whispered, "This time you didn't pull away."

The caress of his finger was unbearably light—lingering on her skin—long after his hand fell away. His face was near hers as he bent close, the blue of his eyes darkening as they held hers.

This was the man she'd glimpsed in Hawaii, with his defenses stripped away, the barriers down. Somewhere on that flight over the Pacific he'd disappeared, slipping once more behind the cool, impersonal facade that had earned him that ruthless reputation.

She felt her skin heat, and knew this man was even more of a threat to her than the cool executive she worked with, who was so determined to learn her true identity. The threat had nothing to do with his hand near her face and the old fear of powerlessness, and had everything to do with the sensations he stirred deep inside her. She forced herself to pull away.

He said slowly, "Once before, you pulled away as if you were frightened. What are you afraid of?"

She looked away from him. "I'm not afraid of anything."

"You, my dear, are a liar," he accused. "You reacted as if you thought I might strike you."

Her gaze snapped back to his. "You're wrong."

He ignored the lie. "I assure you, that's not my way," he said gently, yet with such sincerity that she knew it was true.

"What *is* your way?" she asked, because it was obvious he wanted her to ask, and because she wanted very much to know.

He smiled, the tanned skin crinkling at the corners of his eyes. "Usually exotic flowers, extravagant food, and an equally extravagant wine do the trick every time."

"I see." She held up the remnants of the chicken wing that she'd devoured. Because she needed the safety for her sensitized emotions, she retreated behind a teasing smile. "If this is what you call extravagant, I think you'd better change your ways."

"Actually," he said, taking the chicken wing and tossing it into a nearby trash can, "I had something more like this in mind." He gestured to the building they stood in front of. It was a white plaster, one-story structure with a dark green tile roof and bright red doors. It was set back from the street behind an ornate wrought-iron fence with ancient Chinese symbols worked into the design. She recognized the symbols. They represented each of the levels necessary to attain spiritual life according to the ancient religion. There were Chinese letters over the door, but otherwise there was nothing to identify this as a restaurant. The windows facing the street glowed with faint, shimmering lights.

"What is this place?"

"This is where we will find extravagant food and wine."

"It looks like a private residence."

"It is. Only those who are very good friends of the honored master are invited."

At her perplexed expression, he smiled and confessed, "It's owned by Phillip Lo's cousin. He serves the finest cuisine this side of Hong Kong. And dinner is by special invitation only."

Inside she discovered the shimmering light came from traditional lanterns decorating the tables. She also discovered the food was as extravagant as Ross had promised—Peking duck with fresh oysters, served in a rice wine sauce with fresh mushrooms and capers. The wine, too, was extravagant—light, fruity, and served warm so that it slipped around the senses and made everything glow in the soft light from the lanterns. They lingered over their wine long after their dinner plates were cleared away.

They had made casual small talk as they ate, but now the conversation was strictly business. Ross was genuinely interested in her ideas about the crisis the company faced. He asked several questions and made suggestions she hadn't considered, or expanded on her ideas. He made her think, and he made her feel as if her ideas had merit. She was stunned to realize that he'd actually taken the time to go over some data and financial projections she'd submitted earlier in the week. He'd given no indication of it in their brief meeting that afternoon. No wonder he had a reputation for being cunning in business. He had a complete grasp of everything she discussed and the ability to slice through to the heart of the problem, and the possible solutions available to the company.

"All right," Ross said thoughtfully as he studied her over the rim of his wineglass, "let's speak hypothetically. If you had unrestricted control of the company, what changes would you make?"

That caught her off guard. True, it was only hypothetical—*what if* time. What if the company were hers to control? Most people had moments when they dreamed of such unlimited possibilities. Still, she was amazed that Ross would ask her such a question, much less that he was interested in knowing the answer.

"My first move would be to scrap the Mediterranean fleet."

Ross reclined in his chair, his elbows propped on the arms,

fingers wrapped around the bowl of the wineglass he held before him. His expression remained impassive. Still, she caught the faint flicker of reaction in the arch of a dark brow.

"The Med fleet is the heart and soul of Katherine's expansion plan," he reminded her.

"I know," she answered bluntly. Then even more bluntly, "And she's wrong."

His eyes narrowed. "Why?"

"It's not cost-effective. It will cost the company millions of dollars that it doesn't have to bring the fleet up to standards over the next five years just so it can pass new safety and environmental inspections that are going to be enacted. And that doesn't take into account the additional millions of dollars to put several of our oil tankers into port for retrofitting for double hulls. You know as well as I do the government is going to require those changes on all vessels, in the wake of the Exxon *Valdez* disaster."

He caught her subtle possessive use of the word *our* as she talked about the fleet. He smiled faintly at the resemblance to Katherine. There were so many things about her that were exactly like Katherine. "So what do we do with all those ships? Simply open the ports and scuttle them?"

She gave him a look that suggested they were both more intelligent than that. "Sell them," she stated simply. "To the highest bidder, for scrap if necessary, but get rid of them. It shouldn't be too difficult to get top dollar. It would be a feeding frenzy among our competitors, especially if they thought it was part of a massive liquidation. It's no secret that Fortune is experiencing financial difficulties."

Ross looked at her with new appreciation. "Make them think we're getting out of the business."

"Exactly."

"And then what? I suppose there *is* more to this plan."

She took a slow, deep breath, trying to control the heady effect of the wine and the excitement of being able to express her ideas. "There are a combination of possibilities. Could we discuss them tomorrow? I have all the information, but not with me."

"Where?"

She smiled as she lifted her glass of wine. "Actually, the prospectus I put together is at Phillip Lo's office. I didn't want . . . to clutter up my desk."

She didn't elaborate. They both understood that anything that needed to be kept secret wasn't safe at the Fortune office, where Richard had access to everything.

"All right. Let's go over it first thing tomorrow."

Ross started to pour them both more wine. She held up her hand as he splashed the golden warm rice wine into her glass. "I don't think I'd better have any more. This wine is lethal. A person could lose control."

"I'd like to see you lose just a little of that perfect control," he said quietly.

She studied him through the soft golden glow from the lanterns, aware of the unexpected, almost forgotten sensation of heat spiraling through her body. The atmosphere, the wine, and the long-forgotten feeling of physical desire made her think of the distant past—and David Chen.

# Chapter 16

Christina first met David Chen in a World Economics class at Boston University. He was a senior, she was a freshman. He was from mainland China, one of a small contingent of students allowed to study in the United States under a special exchange program set up by the Nixon administration.

The other Chinese students banded together, a closed community within the university student body. They lived, worked, and studied together, having little social contact with other students except in the classroom or lecture hall. But David was different. He was determined to interact with the diverse student community at Boston University. For that reason, he took an American name, in place of his Chinese name of Chen Li. It also helped that he spoke fluent English, learned when he spent the summer with relatives who had left China during the communist revolution in the late forties.

He was as tall as Christina, thin, yet with a wiry strength. There was an elegance, a refinement, about his features, that hinted at generations of Mandarin ancestors. At twenty-four he had already graduated from the university in Canton, and he had an air of maturity, a clear-cut sense of purpose.

Christina's first encounter with him was a lengthy debate in class over emerging world economic powers. David challenged the professor on a question about the possibility of Pacific nations' becoming a strong economic force. The professor argued against it, giving examples of the current political upheaval and unrest in the wake of the Vietnam war, which had created economic chaos in Southeast Asia.

Christina jumped in on David's side, pointing out the escalating domestic labor costs in the U.S. She reminded the professor that Hong Kong already provided a source of competitive inexpensive labor, thereby undercutting many foreign manufacturers. When she finished, she saw David smiling at her in gratitude for her support.

He sought her out after class. They continued their discussion while he walked her to her next class. To her surprise she found him waiting for her when the class ended, and they continued their discussion of future world economics over hamburgers at a local campus hangout.

They were worlds apart in culture and upbringing, but as their friendship grew, they discovered they were kindred souls. They were both separated from their homes and families—though for very different reasons. Their shared loneliness, and their common interest in world economics, drew them together. They began to study together, then to attend campus lectures and films.

David's outspokenness and his adoption of many Western customs set him apart from his fellow Chinese students. Unlike the powers that be in his country, he felt it was necessary to learn about the world community that lay beyond the boundaries of China. He was convinced that it was the only way his country could move into the future.

"We've closed our eyes and our minds for too long," he told Christina. "The older generation believe we can live within our borders, clinging to the old ways, under communist rule. We must become part of the world, if we are to survive. Eventually communism will crumble under the weight of its own failures. My father and many men like him believe it. I believe it, too."

"Maybe you shouldn't talk so freely," Christina responded, concerned that he would face repercussions from his repressive government.

Once more he flashed that rare, sweet smile. "I know better

than to speak to just anyone about such things. But I can trust you. You are my friend."

*My friend.* It had been almost three years since that horrible night in New York when she had lost her best friend. Since then she had been polite but rather reserved with the people she met. She was afraid that if people got too close, they might ask questions—questions that it would be awkward for her to answer. And though she wasn't consciously aware of it, she was afraid of getting close to people, counting on them, then losing them. She couldn't bear ever again to feel that terrible pain of loss.

Her hectic schedule contributed to her social isolation. She had almost no free time, making her way through the university on a combination of student loans and working. Her days were totally taken up with classes, two part-time jobs, and homework. While the other students got together after concerts or college sports events at the local Italian restaurant, she waited tables at that restaurant.

Now, with David, Christina found herself lowering her defenses and opening herself to the possibility of having a close friend whom she could trust and confide in. Through that fall and early winter, their friendship grew.

The semester break was only days away, and the other students, including Christina's roommate, were busy making preparations to return home for the Christmas holidays. David was supposed to spend the vacation with his American relatives who lived near Boston. Friday came, and the campus became a ghost town as dormitories and apartments emptied and the last Volkswagen Beetle chugged off through the new snow.

The campus bookstore where Christina worked was to be closed during the holidays, so she took all the extra hours she could get at the restaurant. She didn't buy a Christmas tree. There didn't seem much point. It had been a long time since Christmas had meant anything. Even during the years at House of Hope, where the counselors and Father Paul tried their best to make Christmas meaningful for the runaways and outcasts who'd found refuge there, she'd come to feel that the holiday was something to be gotten through, not something to enjoy.

She tried not to remember long-ago Christmases when her family was intact, when there was a reassuring aura of love and joy, and all she had to worry about was whether or not that gaily wrapped box under the tree held the Tiny Tears doll she wanted so desperately. She couldn't bear those memories. They made the emotional emptiness of the present too hard to face. So she simply tried to ignore the Christmas holidays, politely turning down her roommate's invitation to go home with her.

At Thanksgiving she had awkwardly accepted an invitation from her roommate to go home with her for the weekend. She discovered that no matter how welcome other people tried to make you feel, borrowing someone else's family for a temporary period just didn't work out. So this Christmas Eve Christina worked late at the restaurant.

It amazed her how many people ate out on this particular evening. The ones who were alone were the saddest to watch. Even though she was extremely busy, she tried to take time to chat with them briefly, especially the elderly, who seemed so transparently grateful to speak with her.

Mr. Pastorini closed the restaurant early on Christmas Eve. He spent Christmas Day with his large, extended family, which included aunts, uncles, cousins, and Grandma Pastorini, who was over ninety years old. He planned to reopen the day after Christmas.

"Are you certain you won't come home with us?" Mr. Pastorini asked once again as he closed the red-checkered curtains at the windows. His sister, Antonia, who also worked in the restaurant, shut off the lights to the kitchen. The restaurant was quiet, with the last customers gone home for the night, the last take-out order of lasagne picked up for Christmas Eve dinner.

Christina shook her head. "I appreciate the invitation, but I can't." She gave the best excuse she could think of. "I'm expecting a telephone call later. I wouldn't want to miss it. And I am very tired." At least that much was true. The other waitress had taken the day off to be with her family, and Christina had taken her shift. Her feet ached and her head throbbed.

Mr. Pastorini shook his head. "It's not good to be alone on Christmas."

"Please, don't worry about me." His concern touched her deeply, but somehow it emphasized her loneliness. It was all she could do to force a smile. "I'm fine, really. What time do you want me here on Thursday?"

"Not early. We'll open at six, in time for the dinner crowd." Then he suggested, "I could get Debbie in that day."

Again Christina shook her head, as she slipped on her worn coat and long woolen scarf. "Give her another day with her family. The bookstore is closed until school opens after the holidays. I need all the hours I can get."

"You work too hard, you study too hard." Mr. Pastorini frowned at her affectionately. "When do you have time to have fun? To be young? You are much too pretty to be so serious."

"Life *is* pretty serious."

"Yes. But it should also be fun."

Just then Antonia crossed the small restaurant and handed Christina a brown grocery bag. It was heavy, and an enticing aroma wafted up from it.

"For your Christmas dinner," Antonia announced when Christina looked at her questioningly. "Lasagne, some fettuccine, salad, and bread. You're too skinny."

Christina swallowed a lump that suddenly filled her throat and murmured thank you in an unsteady voice.

They walked out together. Mr. Pastorini locked the door, then he and Antonia turned toward the side street where he parked his car.

"Merry Christmas!" Antonia called out, the warmth of her greeting sending a misty vapor into the chilled night air.

"I'll see you the day after tomorrow," Christina called back, unable to return the holiday greeting that was echoed thousands of times during this season. Then she turned and walked in the opposite direction, toward the campus, past rows of old brick houses that lined the bordering streets.

A light snow had begun to fall. She trudged home, her thin-

soled boots making squeaking noises in the newly fallen
snow. The old brick houses down the street took on a make-
believe quality as lights glowed through decorated windows.
She heard a door open, a sudden burst of excited conversation
as a couple left a house. They huddled together and laughed
as they ran to a car parked at the curb. Doors slammed, and
then the engine roared to life, drowning their voices. They
raced away, the small sports car fishtailing slightly on the ice-
slickened street. The taillights glowed brightly, then vanished
as the car slid around the corner.

Another door opened briefly across the street. She heard a
child's laughter as a large dog bounded out into the snow. It
sauntered off on its rounds down the street, stopping at its favorite trees and shrubs.

Then all was quiet again, with an eerie sense of solitude
that is found when snow falls thick and quiet, blanketing everything in wintry silence. Christina pulled her coat collar
higher around her neck and wished it were any other night of
the year.

At her apartment building she stamped the snow off her
boots in the downstairs entry. Checking for mail, she found
the usual bills—from the university library, for overdue book
fines, and from the power company. As she started upstairs,
her landlady poked her head out of her first-floor apartment.

"I thought you might have gone home with one of the other
girls," Mrs. O'Connell remarked with a kind smile.

Christina returned the smile. "I have a lot of studying to
do, and I can make good money if I work double shifts at the
restaurant during vacation."

Mrs. O'Connell shook her head. "It's not good to be by
yourself at Christmas. Why don't you come in and spend the
evening with us?"

Christina knew that *us* referred to Mrs. O'Connell and the
odd assortment of cats she kept. They were like wandering
children who strayed in and out of the old woman's life, and
Mrs. O'Connell loved them all.

"That's very nice of you, but I'm really tired." And then
because she couldn't stand to hurt Mrs. O'Connell's feelings,
she lied for the second time that evening. "I'm expecting a

telephone call. I wouldn't want to miss it. But I appreciate the invitation."

Mrs. O'Connell smiled in spite of her disappointment. "At least take one of the Christmas boxes I prepared." She turned back into the apartment and returned a moment later with a gaily wrapped and ribboned box.

Christina knew it contained an assortment of homemade cookies and candies. Mrs. O'Connell had given everyone in the building the same gift.

"Thank you," Christina said with heartfelt sincerity. "I have a little something for you, too. It's not much, but . . ."

Self-consciously she took a small package from her coat pocket and handed it to Mrs. O'Connell. She saw the elderly woman's lined face break into an even broader smile.

"You shouldn't have spent your hard-earned money on me, Christina. This is so sweet of you, my dear. I'll just put it under the tree with all my other presents. Oh, I can't wait to open it bright and early tomorrow morning!"

Christina had been in Mrs. O'Connell's apartment only the day before and knew that she was exaggerating when she talked of "all my other presents." There were only two or three, all of them from tenants who appreciated what a kind and caring landlady she was. Mrs. O'Connell had no family. Her husband had died in Korea, six weeks after their wedding. They'd had no time to start the big Irish-American family that they'd planned.

Mrs. O'Connell went on, "Merry Christmas, dear. And come on down later if you like."

As Christina climbed the two flights of stairs to her apartment, she hoped Mrs. O'Connell would like the present she'd selected. It wasn't much, just a book of plays by Mrs. O'Connell's favorite playwright, George Bernard Shaw. Christina had found it in a secondhand bookstore, but it was in remarkably good condition.

Rounding the landing, Christina was about to climb the second flight, when something made her stop suddenly. She stared up the flight of stairs, where David sat on the very top step, smiling down at her.

"David! What on earth are you doing here?"

He had obviously been there for quite a while. He'd taken off his gloves, and his jacket was dry. As he came to his feet, he said, "I wanted to celebrate Christmas with a friend."

She was so glad to see him that tears mingled with laughter as she said, "Since when is Christmas a Chinese holiday?"

"I've borrowed Western language and knowledge. I thought I should also borrow a Western tradition." He held out his hand to her and led her up the last steps. Pushing open the door to her apartment, he said, "I also borrowed your roommate's key."

In the center of the tiny apartment stood a small, sparsely branched Christmas tree. On it were a few cheap blue glass balls, a few strands of tinsel, and a string of multicolored lights. Seeing it, Christina came to an abrupt halt.

Gesturing toward the pathetic little tree, David explained, "The man at the campus tree lot gave it to me for nothing. I suppose no one was willing to pay money for such a poor specimen."

The look Christina gave David was filled with joy. "It's beautiful," she breathed, and she meant it.

Their eyes met, and for one timeless moment the atmosphere between them was electric. David colored slightly with embarrassment, and to cover it he gestured toward some plastic containers sitting on the small kitchen table. "My cousin's wife prepared some Cantonese dishes for us, and there is rice wine."

With a grin Christina set her brown bag down on the table next to the containers. "How do you think that will go with lasagne and garlic bread?"

"I think it will be a feast," he answered.

Later they sat on the floor, in the glow of the colored lights from the tree. The remnants of a picnic of Chinese and Italian food was spread across a red and white checkered cloth in the middle of the worn braided rug that covered much of the hardwood floor.

Christina leaned back against the side of a threadbare overstuffed chair, and closed her eyes. The warm rice wine chased away the inner chill she'd carried with her for days. It was the same every year—as everyone prepared to go home for the holidays, she realized all over again that she could never go home.

But David had made this Christmas different. She smiled at him across the rim of the cheap wineglass she'd gotten at a supermarket. The way she felt tonight, it might have been the finest crystal.

She watched quietly as David tried to string popcorn with a needle and thread the way she'd shown him. "You could have been with your family," she said softly.

He looked up, and the smile he gave her warmed her in a way that even the wine couldn't do. "You are my best friend, Christina. I wanted to be with you"

*His best friend* ... and yet he never asked questions about her background, never pushed to know more about her. Perhaps that was the reason she found it so easy to talk to him. Perhaps it was why she had told him more about her past than she had told anyone in a very long time. He knew she'd run away from her family and had been on her own for a long time. Eventually she had even told him about New York and her friend's death.

He said nothing, merely listening intently, and when she finished, he took her in his arms and held her as she cried in a way that she hadn't done in years.

Now she watched with amusement as he tried to string more popcorn on the chain. It crumbled and fell off. Frowning, he said in frustration, "I think this is a very foolish custom. It is better to eat popcorn than to decorate trees with it." And he popped several pieces into his mouth.

Christina laughed. It was all so silly and so wonderful.

"Thank you, David."

He smiled shyly. "For what? A sad little tree and moo goo gai pan?"

Reaching out, she took his hand in hers. "Thank you for a magical night."

"Ah, but there is more." Reaching into the pocket of his jacket that lay across the back of a nearby chair, he took a small package and handed it to her. "Giving gifts is a Chinese tradition, as well. Merry Christmas, Christina."

She took the package with trembling hands. When she was

at House of Hope, there were gifts for all the kids—charitable handouts that were usually woolen gloves, thick socks and sweaters, occasionally some candy, *practical* gifts donated to assuage the guilt of those who had far more in life.

But this present was different. It was rather awkwardly wrapped in plain green paper and tied with a red satin ribbon. And it seemed to hold all the mystery and excitement of the gifts that had lain under the tree in her childhood Christmases.

She didn't open it immediately. Instead she went to the bookcase and took a gift off the top shelf. "I was going to give this to you when you got back," she explained, and handed it to him.

David turned the package over in his hands. It was thin and lightweight. She watched as he ran his hands over the silver foil wrapping paper, and she held her breath, hoping he would be pleased.

He looked up at her. "This is too kind of you. Thank you, Christina."

"You haven't opened it yet."

"I will cherish it, whatever it is. Because you have given it to me. Because you have accepted me as your friend." Before she could respond, he said, "Open your gift first."

"Let's open them together," she suggested.

They tore away ribbons and paper. For a long moment David sat very quietly, staring down at his gift. Then he read the title of the slender hardcover book—*Sonnets from the Portuguese* by Elizabeth Barrett Browning.

"Are you familiar with this?" Christina asked.

David shook his head.

"It's one of my favorite books. I had a copy when I was younger. My mother gave it to me. I read it over and over. Elizabeth Barrett and Robert Browning were poets in nineteenth-century England. He fell in love with her through her poetry, and he took her away from her cruel, domineering father. They married, had a child, and lived happily together until she died. He called her his little Portuguese because she was so dark-skinned. She wrote these love sonnets to him."

Suddenly, intense embarrassment washed over her. "This

copy isn't new," she stammered in apology. "But the leather is in good condition."

David had opened the book and was scanning its pages. He stopped at one particular poem, read it silently, then finished aloud, ". . . and if God choose, I shall but love thee better after death . . ."

He looked up at Christina. "Thank you. I will treasure it always."

Somehow the silence that stretched between them wasn't awkward. It was . . . special.

Turning back to her gift, Christina finished unwrapping it. Inside were two hand-carved gleaming wood hair combs, decorated with ancient Chinese characters.

"They're made of sandalwood," David explained. "It is highly prized in my country. And the symbols carved into them are for good fortune. They are very old. They once belonged to my grandmother. She gave them to my mother. When she died, they came to me, for she had no daughters. They are passed down to each generation and worn only on special occasions."

Taking Christina's hands in his, David said soberly, "May you always have good fortune, my special friend."

Christina's eyes filled with tears. He had no way of knowing the bittersweet symbolism of his gift.

"Thank you, David. I will treasure them and wear them only on very special occasions. Like tonight."

Taking them from the box, she pulled back her shoulder-length hair and inserted the combs. But she handled them awkwardly, and David reached over to help her. His hands brushed lightly against hers. Before she could even think to pull back from the contact, he was kissing her, the gentlest, most tentative of kisses.

Her first instinct was to pull back. In all the years since she had run away from the horror of that last night at home, she had never allowed any man to touch her. She was terrified that if she let down her guard, then what happened that night might happen again.

Her trust and innocence had been shattered in one violent act. Even now, years later, she vividly remembered the fear, guilt, and shame. And the pain—the agonizing blows of fists beating her into submission.

Now, with David, there was no fear or shame. He didn't grab her. He simply pressed his lips against hers as gently as if she were made of fragile porcelain and might break under the slightest pressure.

To her amazement she felt a slow, breathless awakening. A deep, inner trembling—from pleasure, not fear. She was filled with a sense of wonder at the realization that she wanted the kiss to go on forever, she wanted David's warmth to melt the cold that always seemed to lie deep within her.

But because she'd lived with fear for so long, these new, uncertain feelings confused her, and she pulled back from him.

"I can't," she whispered in a broken voice.

"I'm sorry," David apologized. "I shouldn't have . . ."

"No, please, it's nothing to do with you," she said hurriedly, desperate to reassure him. "It's me. I . . . I just can't."

David looked profoundly ashamed. "I shouldn't have been so forward. I understand how difficult it is for you. It's only that I wanted to express the depth of my feelings for you."

Christina was deeply moved. She realized it must have taken a great deal of courage for him to kiss her. She reached out and touched his hand.

"It's the first time anyone has kissed me, since . . . before . . ." She bit at her lower lip, emotions warring within her. "I'm glad you kissed me," she finally said, and when he looked up at her in surprise, she said with determination in her voice, "Would you kiss me again, please?"

Her heart beat frantically, from fear and all those unknown emotions she'd so carefully guarded against all these years. As David leaned toward her once more, her breath caught in her throat and fear tightened in her stomach. It took all her strength to remain completely still and not pull back. Then she felt that feather-soft contact, sending warmth coursing through her trembling body.

When the kiss finally ended, she looked up at David and knew that with him she could conquer the fear.

He brought both his hands up slowly. Her wide-eyed gaze

fastened on his as he slowly cupped her face. His touch was almost reverent as he slowly bent to kiss her again. This time he drew the kiss out, leaving her with a profound sense of loss when it finally ended . . .

David didn't return to his cousin's house that entire semester break. He stayed with Christina in her apartment. When they finally made love, it was slow, tender, compassionate, with a shared sense of caring and wonder. It was the first time for David. And in a very real sense, Christina felt that it was the first time for her, as well.

It was a time of sharing, and for Christina, a time of healing.

They spent as much time together as possible the following spring term. Though they were in a crowded university, in a crowded city, they felt almost as if they were the only two people in the world.

Before Christina realized how it happened, somehow it was June. David was graduating, and it was time for him to return to China.

There had never been any question about David's future. He was expected to return to his home in China. His family eagerly awaited him. And his government expected him to put what he had learned to use in helping the country. From the beginning he'd been completely honest with Christina. She even knew about the young woman chosen for him to marry.

On graduation night he took her out to dinner. Then they walked along the promenade at old Boston Harbor. It had always been a very special place for David. He was fascinated by the events that had taken place there over two hundred years before, when the people of the American colonies had taken critical steps toward changing the destiny of their country. He and Christina talked of many things, but neither acknowledged the fact that this was good-bye.

It was very late when he drove her back to her apartment. They said good-night at her door. He kissed her with a passion that had grown stronger during the months of their love affair, and he whispered, ". . . and if God choose, I shall but love thee better after death . . ."

And then he was gone.

The following morning David's cousin came to see her. David had taken a late flight home the night before. His cousin gave her a letter David had written and asked him to deliver:

Dear Christina,
It is difficult for me to express how much you mean to me. When I said good-bye to my family in China, it was painful. But it was even more painful leaving you last night. I could not bring myself to say good-bye to you. Our life paths are very different. We have always known this. We were given only a small space in time to be together. But we were more fortunate than many people who never know even the fleeting joy that we shared. You will always hold a very special place in my heart.

Chen Li.

# Chapter 17

*D*avid ...

Thinking about him now, seventeen years later, brought a bittersweet smile to Christina's lips.

Watching her, Ross was struck by the change in her expression. For one unguarded moment he saw past the defenses she'd so carefully erected. What he saw made his breath catch in his throat. There was such vulnerability that he instinctively wanted to encircle her in the safety of his arms and murmur words of endearment and reassurance.

Up to that moment she'd elicited two strong responses from him—curiosity and anger. Now, to his chagrin, he felt something even stronger—a desire to protect her, though he had no idea what threatened her. He hadn't felt this way since he was a little boy and had wished with a helpless desperation that he could protect his mother from the sorrow that his father brought to her.

The feeling pierced his heart and left him shaken. He wasn't used to this. He was used to being in control, of himself and the people around him.

Irritated with himself, he said more harshly than he should have, "I wonder what it would take to make you lose control."

Her expression changed in an instant, the vulnerability gone, replaced by defensiveness. "I don't lose control."

Ross was once more sure of himself. "We'll see about that."

When they finally left the restaurant, Christina thought they might have stepped out onto any street in Hong Kong. Street lamps shaped like ancient lanterns hung suspended in the mist, down the length of Sacramento Street. The sidewalk vendors with their charcoal braziers and spicy sweet foods had retreated for the evening. The front of one store was garishly lit by strings of tiny white lights. The owner stood out front, potbellied in his white Mandarin-style shirt worn over black pants, with black slippers and a trailing stream of fragrant smoke from a long cigarette spiraling through the crisp night air.

A sleek sports car passed by, with several Chinese teenagers inside, the CD player blaring a relentless beat of rap music in stark contrast to the ancient culture that dominated this city within a city. It reminded Christina that this wasn't Hong Kong, but a close cousin who observed some of the traditions.

The Jaguar was exactly where they had left it, gleaming faintly in the soft pool of light from the second-story window above. The fog had started to roll in, slipping silently through the darkness, wrapping around lampposts, coating the streets. Christina shivered and huddled deeper inside the lightweight coat she'd thought to grab out of her car at the last minute before they left the Fortune building.

Ross walked her around to the passenger side of the car. She shivered again. He reached for her and gathered the lapels of her coat beneath her chin, at the same time pulling her closer. Her hands came up in that instinctive reaction, her fingers locking around his wrists to stop him. For several seconds they simply stood there, each with particular thoughts, doubts, and needs.

Then his fingers were gliding along her jaw, twining through the long silken hair that draped her neck. He tilted her head back, forcing her to look up at him. He studied the strong, pure lines of her face, the play of shadows in her eyes, the sudden quiver of her lower lip on her indrawn breath.

"Who are you?" he whispered.

"Who do you think I am?" she asked.

He searched her face, as if he could find the answer in the angled features, or unravel her secrets in the depths of her dark eyes. His breath was warm against her cheek, then the corner of her mouth. Then he kissed her, long and slow, with a relentless, building intensity that gradually took possession of them both.

She had told him she never lost control, but that was a lie. She felt it slipping away, disappearing in the mist that closed around them. As control vanished, instinct took over. Her fingers tightened around his wrists, her nails biting into the starched cuffs of his shirt, holding on, rather than pushing away. Her lips parted under the stroke of his tongue—hot and moist, tasting of wine and some other intoxicating flavor that was uniquely his.

She shivered, not from the cold but from heat and the chaotic frenzy of sensations and emotions that built inside her. She felt a powerful warning go off in her head, reminding her that this was dangerous—that he was dangerous.

She pulled back first, staring up at him through the soft glow of mist and wine, as she struggled to hold on to the tattered remnants of her self-control. "I think we had better go." Now she *was* pushing away. She stepped back, shoving her hand nervously back through her hair, reaching for the door handle, stepping into the car. Ross said nothing as he closed the door, then walked around the car.

He slid behind the wheel and put the key into the ignition. The Jaguar purred to life. They rode in silence back to the Fortune building to pick up her car. Neither said a word as she left the Jaguar. But both knew damn well that a line had been crossed tonight, and from now on neither would be able to pretend this was strictly business.

She arrived at the office later than usual the next morning. The late evening, the wine, and her unsettled emotions kept her tossing and turning all night, and she overslept. Remembering the previous evening and Ross, and a kiss that had shattered her defenses, she felt confused and wary.

Could she trust him? She had asked herself that question over and over again all night long. By the time she finally fell into a restless sleep just before dawn, the answer was still the same—she just didn't know.

On her way to work she stopped by Phillip Lo's office and picked up the portfolio she'd left for him to go over. It was almost nine-thirty when she arrived at Fortune Tower. Marie greeted her with a bright "Good morning."

"Has Mr. McKenna come in yet?" Christina asked.

"He came in early, before anyone else."

"Where is he now?"

"I think he went down to the conference room. He said he wanted to go over some material there."

"Thanks." Christina gathered the files and headed down the hall.

The conference room doors were slightly ajar. She was about to push them open when the sound of familiar voices made her hesitate. It was Ross and Richard.

"Whatever our differences in the past," Richard was saying, "you know I'm right about this. Katherine can't possibly come up with some magic formula to keep the company private. We desperately need investment capital."

"A situation that you created," Ross reminded him with sharp disapproval. "That resort development was an ego trip for you, and not in the company's best interests. You were trying to compete with Hyatt, Hilton, and the others. It was a stupid move that sent this company into a serious cash-flow problem. If I had controlled that property, I would never have allowed you to go forward with it."

"Well, you didn't control that property. I did. And I still say that development will come around."

"You'll be forced to sell it."

"I'm *not* selling," Richard insisted.

"You can't meet the debt payment any other way. If you're lucky, the Japanese will give you ten cents on the dollar."

"You'd better hope it doesn't come to that. I secured that note with my shares in Fortune. How do you think Katherine would like being partners with the Japanese?"

Impatience edged Ross's voice. "Why are we discussing this?"

"Because I think there is a way to solve all our problems." Richard moved across the office, his voice sounding much closer now.

"I'm listening," Ross said.

"A deal."

"What kind of deal?" Ross asked warily.

"Katherine is old, and we both know that she's in poor health. She might live another two or three years, and then what? She's accepted this young woman as Christina. I don't believe it, and I know you don't believe it, either." There was a pause, and then he went on, "She's using this woman to retain control of the company. But what happens in two or three years when Katherine dies?"

The silence once more stretched out in the room. With a jolt Christina realized that Ross was considering what Richard was saying.

"Go on," he said.

Something inside Christina coiled tight with apprehension.

"This young woman might be allowed to sign documents, but you and I both know who is making all the decisions. If she chooses to make different decisions, execute different documents, who is there to stop her? Especially after Katherine is gone."

"I could mount a leveraged buyout of the company,' Ross shot back.

"You could try," Richard said. "There's no guarantee you'd succeed."

"Get to the point."

"You're in a precarious position, McKenna. You have nothing if Katherine dies and this imposter runs the company. But if you and I work together, the arrangement could be very lucrative for you."

"In other words, a partnership," Ross concluded.

Christina couldn't believe what she was hearing, couldn't believe that Ross would actually consider betraying Katherine.

Richard responded evenly, "Yes."

"What's in this for me?"

"A great deal more than you'll get if that woman takes over."

"You actually believe you can stop her?"

Richard sounded utterly confident. "With your help I know I can. I haven't been taking this lying down. I'm working on some angles. There are ways to get her out of the picture."

Christina felt physically ill, with a mixture of bitter disappointment and painful betrayal. She spun away from the door. She couldn't bear to listen any longer. The truth was that Ross, who had a reputation for being cunning and ruthless, was making plans with Richard to take over Fortune International.

And Christina was now a threat to his plans—a threat that had to be removed.

Christina spent the rest of the morning locked away in her office, after telling Marie she didn't want to be disturbed. By *anyone*. She needed time to think about the conversation she'd overheard. Clearly Richard was trying to make a deal with Ross to gain control of Fortune International. Even more disturbing was the fact that Ross seemed to be considering it.

Ruthless and cunning. Those two words came back to her over and over, reminding her that Ross's reputation in the world of business was that of a rebel who would do anything to succeed. He'd come far from the docks of Hong Kong, where he'd worked as a roustabout. A man who'd reached his position, and achieved such power, wouldn't give it up easily.

She swung around hard in her chair to stare out the wall of windows in her office. The charts, diagrams, prospectus, and proposals were temporarily forgotten. It would all mean very little if Ross was mounting some kind of takeover of his own with Richard's help. Was it really possible? Had Richard found some way to take control of the company from Katherine?

As far as Christina knew, the shares held in trust, *her* shares now, controlled the stock vote on any major transactions. That meant that whatever Richard planned, he would need her to go along with it. Or he would need to eliminate her.

She'd developed a raging headache, and she winced as Marie buzzed her on the telephone intercom. The telephone buzzed a second time before she swung around and picked it up.

"Yes, Marie?"

"Mr. McKenna just called again about your meeting. What do you want me to tell him?"

She hesitated, then said, "Tell him I've already gone to lunch, and you don't know when I'll be back."

"But, Miss Fortune . . ."

"Thank you, Marie. That will be all." She set the phone back on the cradle. For several seconds she sat staring at the stack of papers spread across her desk and overflowing onto the credenza. She certainly couldn't discuss her ideas for salvaging Fortune International with Ross if he might be on the verge of betraying both her and Katherine.

Absentmindedly she flipped through the countless letters, cards, and invitations that had been arriving on a daily basis for her, both at Fortune Hill and here at the office. She paused at an elegant piece of parchment, embossed with the initials JF on the outside, and a rude hand-sketched caricature on the inside. It was from Julie Francetti, formerly of Boston and now living in Sonoma.

She'd met Julie six years ago at Goldman, Sachs. Julie was on the fast track, determined to make it big as an investment banker. Julie was in her Alan Roberts phase—her then current boyfriend. Until that time the rapidly changing phases in Julie's life had involved an amazingly diverse group of young-executives-on-the-rise, starving artists, and university professors. Unlike Christina, who rarely dated and never became seriously involved with any man, Julie threw herself wholeheartedly into each relationship, convinced that *this* one was the real thing. For some reason all her relationships ended badly, leaving Julie depressed for weeks afterward until the next boyfriend came along.

Alan had seemed the most promising, but then, like the others, he decided he wasn't ready for commitment. He left Julie for an upscale condo on West 57th Street in New York and a gorgeous female roommate who was a highly successful ad agency executive. Julie was devastated. And pregnant.

Without asking questions or giving lectures, Christina provided emotional support through the weeks of panic and depression, culminating in Julie's difficult decision to have the baby and raise it on her own. Then, in her fourth month, Julie miscarried. The terrible sense of loss was even more devastating than Alan's abandonment had been.

Through it all, Christina was there for her, lending a shoulder to cry on whenever necessary, encouraging Julie to return to work when all she wanted to do was give in to debilitating depression, and eventually helping her understand that maybe, just maybe, life was worth living after all.

And then one day a charming new client, Giancarlo Francetti III, who owned the renowned Francetti Vineyards in California, entered Julie's life. Christina gave Julie one piece of advice—go for it! After a whirlwind three-month bicoastal courtship, Julie traded in her corner office with a window and dress-for-success suits for marriage and the quiet life in the country.

A beaming Julie told Christina, "I'm not going to turn into a couch potato, watching *Oprah* and *Santa Barbara*. I'll still be managing investments. But this time they'll be mine and Giancarlo's."

Christina hadn't told Julie anything about her plans for coming to San Francisco. But when her picture and the story hit the West Coast newspapers, Julie was one of the first to contact her—with flowers and that vaguely obscene little caricature that had been a trademark of their interoffice memos to each other at Goldman, Sachs.

*Talk about fortune seekers??? (No pun intended). Why didn't you tell me you were an heiress???? Anyway, when the furor dies down (if it does), you've got to call me. We'll get together, and you can tell me all about it. Or better yet, don't call, just come up to Sonoma. You can't miss it. Just ask for Francetti Vineyards. We've got so much to catch up on. Love, Julie.*

The timing of the invitation was perfect. Christina needed to get away, she needed time to think. Making a sudden decision, she tucked her more important papers in her briefcase, then buzzed Marie.

"Did you give Mr. McKenna my message?"

"Yes. He was on his away to a luncheon meeting. He said he would get together with you this afternoon. He insisted that I schedule a block of uninterrupted time. I hope that's all right."

Christina frowned as she held the phone. She wondered who the luncheon meeting was with. Richard?

No doubt, Ross was *very* eager to have a meeting with her to find out what her specific ideas were. Undoubtedly, he intended to pass them on to Richard at the first opportunity.

She said, "I won't be able to see Mr. McKenna this afternoon. I'll be out of the office for the next couple of days. If anyone asks, say you don't know where I've gone."

"But, Miss Fortune . . ."

"I'm sorry, Marie. I can't explain further. I'll be in touch." And she hung up.

Marie had gone to lunch by the time Christina left her office a half hour later. Ross's office was dark, the door closed. She felt a surge of relief. She wasn't ready to face him yet.

A few minutes later she drove down to Marina Boulevard, skirted the Marina district with its yacht clubs and slips occupied by gleaming sailboats, and the familiar tree-lined entrance to the Presidio. Then she took the Golden Gate Bridge over to Marin and caught Highway 101 north.

It was a mild, clear day typical of early October. Christina had taken off her taupe linen suit jacket and unbuttoned the first two buttons of her silk blouse. The car windows were down, and the wind blew through her hair, sending her smooth coiffure into disarray. She didn't care. She needed the mindless oblivion of the drive and the freedom of the wind.

She passed rolling brown countryside covered with a green patchwork of vineyards. All the grapes were in, except for the varieties that vintners exposed to just the first few brisk cool nights of fall to capture a particular essence of flavor. Then those special varieties were stripped from the vines and rushed to the winery, where they were crushed, processed, and set up to ferment.

Sonoma was a special blend of pastoral beauty, with its hillsides that were dry and brown at this time of year, before the winter rains set in, contrasting with the lush vines that still hung full and verdant. In a few weeks, when fall set in for good, the leaves would wither and turn brown, and the vines would be cut back to nothing more than wood stalks, to lay dormant until the next season.

As Julie had promised, the Francetti Vineyards were easy to find. Carved wood signs marked the entire route along 101, all the way to the cutoff road. The vineyards lined the highway for mile after mile, extending far back into the rolling hills.

In the distance Christina could see the large redwood and cream-colored stucco main residence. The winery, with huge steel holding vats nestled against the hillside, was a surprisingly ultramodern facility for processing the traditionally ancient varieties of wines.

Christina had called Julie from Santa Rosa to prepare her for the visit. Now she swung into the main drive and stopped in front of the imposing entrance to the sprawling house. One of the massive carved oak double doors opened immediately, and Julie came running down the steps to greet her.

Julie looked reassuringly the same. Her flaxen hair was pulled back in a casual ponytail tied with a white ribbon, and her hazel eyes sparkled mischievously. The only difference was the golden tan that darkened her normally fair complexion.

"I can't believe it!" Julie exclaimed, throwing her arms around Christina. "I thought maybe the mountain was going to have to go to Mohammed."

Christina grinned as she and Julie stood back to look at each other. "As you can see, Mohammed decided to come to the mountain."

Julie draped an arm around her shoulders. "Well, it's about time. I thought maybe all this heiress stuff had gone to your head."

"I thought maybe all this wine had gone to yours," Christina reproached her. "You promised you'd get back to Boston for a visit."

Julie grimaced. "I know. *Mea culpa*. But the business requires constant supervision, and Carlo is strictly a hands-on person. He insists on overseeing every part of the operation. He makes me handle the money, though. He says I have a better head for it than he does."

She gave Christina a sheepish grin. "The truth is, I *love* it! We get up at dawn every morning and ride out to the vineyards, just the two of us. It's amazing, but we seem to love each other more every day."

Christina hugged her tightly. "Oh, Julie, I'm so happy for you. You deserve all the happiness in the world."

Julie's expression turned sober. "The only drawback was missing you. We were such good friends, we went to hell and back together. I always knew I could turn to you. I've met some nice people here, but there's no one to take your place." Her face brightened as she finished, "I'm so glad you're out here, too. Carlo's wonderful, but there are times I really need a friend to turn to."

"I know. I feel the same way. I feel very isolated."

"Isolated? But you have a family now."

Christina didn't want to go into some of the hard realities of the Fortune family just yet. She said vaguely, "It's hard to feel close to them after being on my own for so long . . ." Her voice trailed off.

"Yeah, I guess so," Julie responded awkwardly. Clearly she was dying to ask why Christina had left her family and lived under a different identity for so long, but she restrained her raging curiosity. Instead she asked, "Where are your bags?"

Christina held up her briefcase. "It was a last-minute decision. This is all I brought."

Julie grinned. "Never mind. I've got plenty of things you can wear, and unless all the pasta I've been eating has snuck up on me, I think we're still about the same size. I think that's really why we became roommates in the first place. So we could wear each other's clothes."

Christina smiled warmly. "Hey, it doubled our wardrobes."

Looping her arm through Christina's, Julie led her into the house, "Carlo is away for a couple of days. I'm dying for you to see him again, but in a way I'm glad he's gone. We can have a slumber party, stay up all night gossiping and eating mocha almond fudge ice cream. You can tell me what it's like to be a long-lost heiress, and I'll tell you about the passionate and exotic wine business."

Christina felt herself relax inside, as all the pressure she'd been feeling seemed to melt away. Julie was just what she needed. Aside from being more relaxed than she'd been at Goldman, Sachs, she was still the same, down-to-earth, sweet-natured, a joy to be around. Everything about her life seemed perfect. She adored her husband, and together they lived an idyllic life. Christina was genuinely happy for her, but she couldn't help feeling a twinge of envy. Julie's life was so complete. And her own was so unsettled.

Thinking of David Chen had reminded her of the emotional emptiness and loneliness of her life. Now, seeing how happy Julie was reinforced that sense of loneliness. She hoped fervently that it wouldn't always be this way. Someday soon she wanted finally to be able to put the past behind her, and begin to build a life that involved more than just a career.

They sat up until the early hours of the morning, gossiping like a couple of teenagers, catching up on everything that had happened over the past three years. Julie tactfully avoided questioning Christina about her background, and instead happily discussed her own life.

Just before they finally turned in, Julie confided that she was four months pregnant. Christina let out a whoop of delight and congratulated her enthusiastically.

"I thought you looked as if you were getting a bit of a tummy, but I didn't want to say anything. Oh, Julie, I'm so happy for you. I know how much this means to you."

"I was terrified at first," Julie admitted. "I was so afraid I would miscarry again. But my doctor thinks that was probably brought on by stress, and he says this time there should be no reason to worry. I'm healthy as a horse, and Carlo makes me take it easy. He treats me as if I were made of glass. I have to confess, it's kind of nice being pampered like this."

"What do you want, a boy or a girl?"

"I know it's a cliché to say so, but I honestly don't care. I'll be thrilled no matter what it is. My life with Carlo is so wonderful, having a child will make it absolutely perfect."

She stopped and gazed thoughtfully at Christina. "Oh, Chris, I want so much for you to have this kind of happiness, too."

Christina swallowed past the sudden knot in her throat and smiled. "Maybe I will. Someday."

"You know, it's strange, considering everything you went through with me, but I don't think I ever asked if you want to have children."

"Of course I do. I can't imagine spending the rest of my life focusing on a career, no matter how successful or fulfilling it is. I want something *more*. But I don't necessarily want to have my own child. I'd like to adopt."

"Why?"

Christina frowned, unsure how to put her thoughts into words. "When I was living on the streets, I discovered just how many unwanted kids there are out there. Throwaways, like everything else in our throwaway society. People talk about the shortage of kids for adoption, but that's not true. There are plenty of kids, but they're older or they're a minority or they have a problem. And no one wants them. That's the worst feeling in the world, to know that no one really wants you."

She stopped, embarrassed at having suddenly become so serious. "I'm sorry, Julie. I should be celebrating your good news, not getting up on a soapbox."

Julie reached out to squeeze her hand. "Hey, it's okay." She added softly, "I always knew you were a good person, Chris. That's all that matters. Not who your family is."

Christina knew that Julie was saying she accepted Christina for herself, that her background didn't affect their friendship. Christina was deeply moved. Here, at least, was one person who didn't care if she was Christina Fortune or Ellie Dobbs.

When Christina awoke a little after nine o'clock that morning, she discovered that Julie was already up, padding around the huge, blue-tiled kitchen in an oversize flannel shirt and knee socks. Fall was in the air, and it was chilly in the big house.

Julie shoved a mug of rich, dark coffee into Christina's hands as she walked sleepily into the kitchen. Gesturing toward a stool at the long breakfast bar, she said, "Sit. I'm making breakfast."

"You cook now?" There was a distinct note of amazement in Christina's voice. "The last time you attempted it, we had to disconnect the smoke alarm because you burned dinner and filled our apartment with smoke."

"Yeah." Julie grinned in remembrance. "That was the time I tried to impress Carlo with my cooking. I gave a whole new definition to the term blackened fish."

With both hands wrapped around the cup, Christina closed her eyes and sipped some of the nut-flavored brew. "You make good coffee."

"Mr. Coffee and premeasured packets make good coffee. But I am a whiz at French toast. It's the one thing I can make that is guaranteed edible. Other than that, we have Louisa. She's about ninety years old and has been the cook here since Carlo's grandfather ran the place. She's practically blind with cataracts, but she can still cook like crazy. She refuses to retire. Carlo says she'll probably fall facedown into the marinara sauce one day, and we'll have to wheel her out."

Christina choked with laughter.

Julie went on, "Actually I think marinara sauce is a lousy way to go. I'd rather drown in a wine vat—being perfectly preserved in a Special Reserve Chardonnay doesn't sound so bad."

Christina smiled at her friend over the rim of her cup. "I really needed this."

"That bad, huh? So lifestyles of the exceedingly rich and famous aren't what they're cracked up to be."

"You don't have it so bad," Christina remarked, glancing about the ultramodern kitchen with huge glass windows that looked out onto the vineyards. For what she'd seen of the rest of the house the night before, Julie had married not only happily, but exceedingly well.

The lighthearted banter continued through breakfast preparation. Then, as Julie set down two platters heaped with sausage and French toast made from sourdough bread, she casually said, "So, why didn't you ever say anything about your family all that time we worked together? I've had to read about it in the *Chronicle*, like the latest installment in a soap opera."

Christina stopped, butter knife poised in midair. Then she slowly resumed buttering her French toast. She had been closer to Julie than anyone else during her years at Goldman, Sachs. They had shared a great deal. But as far as family was concerned, she had simply let Julie assume that she had none. Now was a time for at least partial truths.

"Things were very difficult when I was young. There were a lot of . . . problems."

Julie listened intently. "What sort of problems?"

Christina shrugged in an attempt to make light of it. She couldn't tell the whole truth, not yet. "The usual thing that I suppose most teenagers go through. It was especially hard after my parents died. Anyway, I ran away to New York."

"And your family never knew where you were?"

"No. I lived on the streets for a while, and found out just how dangerous that can be." She heard the tightness in her voice and struggled to lighten it. "Eventually, I connected with House of Hope, got my high school equivalency, and went on to college in Boston. You know the rest."

"Except for the fact that your family just happens to be one of the wealthiest in the country," Julie pointed out. She started to say something else and then clamped her mouth shut as she crossed the kitchen for the coffee carafe to refill their cups.

"You were going to ask me something," Christina prompted, watching her friend's face carefully.

"I changed my mind."

"Let me guess," Christina went on. "Something like 'Why didn't you get in touch with them before now?' "

"All right." Julie set the carafe down. "Why not?"

"For a long time I couldn't bring myself to go back or even contact them. The memories were too painful, but I always knew that I would do it someday. *Someday* finally came."

"The inheritance," Julie concluded.

Christina was just as honest with her as she had been with Ross. "That's part of it, but only a small part. The money was never really important to me."

"I guess not, if you ran away from it in the first place," Julie concluded. "But if the money doesn't matter, and you have serious problems with your family, then why did you come back?"

She saw concern and compassion in Julie's expression. She knew she could trust her implicitly, in a way that she couldn't trust anyone else in her life at that moment. She came as close to telling Julie the whole truth as she had ever come to telling anyone. But she couldn't. Not yet. Not until it was over.

"There's something I have to do," she said slowly. "I made a promise to someone."

"And you don't want to tell me what that is."

"I can't right now. Maybe someday. I hope ... well, I hope you'll understand. I know that's asking a lot ..."

"Hey, what are friends for? When you feel that you can tell me, if that day ever comes, you will. Until then I accept your decision." She reached for Christina's hand across the counter and squeezed it affectionately. "God knows you accepted a lot of things about me, no questions asked, when we were in Boston. It's the least I can do."

Then Julie gave her familiar, quirky smile. "I think it comes under the classification of 'unconditional friendship.' "

Christina knew that Julie didn't feel as blasé as she tried to sound. But she deeply appreciated Julie's patience and understanding. She felt a rush of emotion as she contrasted

Julie's loyalty with the lack of trust she felt toward almost everyone she was involved with in San Francisco.

"So, how about some croissants?" Julie went on. "They're my weakness. If I go on eating like this, I'll be a fat pregnant woman, and Carlo will fall out of love with me."

"I don't think he'll ever do that," Christina assured her.

Julie's expression softened. "You know what? I don't think he will, either. But enough about me. I want to hear all about you."

Over breakfast Christina confided in Julie about the deal with Katherine, the analysis she had made of the company's problems, her ideas for restructuring, her dinner with Ross in Chinatown, and the conversation she had overheard between Ross and Richard.

"Jeez!" Julie said through a mouthful of croissant. "When you do it, you do it up big."

"That isn't exactly what I was expecting for advice," Christina pointed out.

Julie shook her head. "I'm afraid I don't have any easy answers for you, kiddo. This is a real complicated situation."

"Yes, I know."

"How do you *feel* about all this?"

Christina summed it up in one word. "Scared."

Julie was thoughtful. "You've come up against tougher problems than this at Goldman, Sachs. It's usually just a matter of finding the key that fits the lock." Before Christina could answer, Julie went on carefully, "How do you feel about Ross McKenna?"

Christina had been waiting for that. Julie had a way of slicing straight through to the heart of the matter.

"I'm not sure. It's . . . complicated."

"Complicated in a business way, or in a personal way?" Julie asked astutely.

Christina gave her a long look. "Well, he has quite a reputation."

"Yeah, in the bedroom and the boardroom. I understand

there's a long-standing thing between him and some San Francisco socialite."

"Marianne Schaeffer—beautiful, blond, willowy, and connected to all the right people. Her father's in investment banking."

Understanding dawned in Julie's hazel eyes. "Which might come in very handy if Mr. McKenna wanted to put together a buyout package."

"Yes," Christina said slowly. *Of course.* It all made sense—Ross's relationship with Marianne gave him access to one of the top investment banking firms in the country. And he had admitted to Richard that he would consider attempting a leveraged buyout if all else failed and Katherine was no longer around to demand his loyalty.

She went on thoughtfully, "The point is, I don't know if I can trust him. Especially now."

"Have you asked him point-blank what the hell is going on?"

Christina shook her head. "No. I decided to come here instead. I needed some time away from the pressure of performing like a trained seal."

"But this is your grandmother you're talking about," Julie replied. "Surely she doesn't see you that way."

Without replying, Christina got up and cleared away their dishes. She rinsed them off in the sink, then turned back to Julie. Her brow was wrinkled in concentration. "There is *one* thing I am absolutely certain of."

"What's that?"

"I'm going to make this work—I'm not going to let anyone break up the company and sell it off piecemeal to the highest bidder."

Julie said, "Well, for today at least, why don't you forget about business and try to relax? How about riding out into the vineyards with me? It's beautiful this time of day. It'll take your mind off your problems."

Christina groaned. "I haven't ridden since that disastrous weekend we went to the Lundy estate in West Virginia to celebrate that merger."

Julie laughed. "I remember. You fell off the horse as you were trying to mount it. You didn't ride at all."

"I know you seemed to find it very funny, but I had to sit on a pillow for a week afterward," Christina responded ruefully.

Julie took hold of her arm and dragged her out of the kitchen. "Come on. It's about time you used those slack executive muscles. It'll be good for you."

Two hours later Christina knew Julie was right. The morning air was crisp and cool. Everything smelled of earth, sun, and wide-open countryside. They rode the perimeter of the last vineyard yet to be harvested. Workers were bent over in the rows, cutting the purplish red clusters with grape knives, then piling them high in wooden lug crates and carrying them to the end of each row. A flatbed truck drove slowly down the dirt service road that bordered the rows, and the crates were loaded onto the back of the truck.

"Those are the last of the Pinot Noir. We left them out late this year to bring up the sweetness just a little," Julie explained. "Carlo is experimenting with a new variety for a special reserve we hope to put up. I promised him I'd see these were brought in today."

"It's beautiful," Christina murmured appreciatively. "All of it. The vineyards, the hills, the sky. And not a skyscraper around. This place is paradise."

"It really is," Julie enthusiastically agreed. "Who would've thought that I would get off the fast track and end up growing grapes?" She turned around in the saddle as the driver called her from the truck. A call had come in for her over the mobile phone. Watching her ride over to the truck, Christina was amazed at Julie's air of quiet self-assurance. It was a happy contrast to the nervousness and stress that had plagued her at Goldman, Sachs.

A moment later Julie rejoined her, explaining, "That was from the main plant. They've got some problem. I need to get back."

"I'll come with you." Christina couldn't disguise the unmistakable note of disappointment that crept into her voice at the thought of cutting short this pleasant ride.

"Not necessary. This could take a couple of hours, and it's b-o-r-i-n-g. Stay out here as long as you want. You know the way back."

"Are you sure? I feel as if I'm deserting you."

"I'm sure." Julie wheeled her horse around. "I'll see you back at the main house."

Christina waved, then turned her horse down one of the rows. Julie had mentioned a creek in a stand of trees off in the distance. That would be a great place to take a brief respite from the hard saddle. The day had begun to grow hot. When Christina reached the shallow creek that meandered through the oak trees, she dismounted, dipped her handkerchief in the water, and wiped her face and neck while she let her horse drink. Here, in the stand of oaks, it was shady, cool, and peaceful. The water was the only sound as it murmured restlessly over the rocks and around exposed tree roots.

Her horse snorted restlessly. Glancing at her watch, she saw that it was getting late. It was time to start back to the house.

Gathering the reins, she slipped the toe of the boot she'd borrowed from Julie into the stirrup, pulling herself atop the saddle. She could already feel a tightness in muscles that by tomorrow morning would probably ache. But it had been worth it. She hadn't felt this relaxed in a long time, and her talk with Julie had helped her resolve some of the questions in her mind. The one big unsettled issue was Ross and his involvement with Richard. She would simply have to face it head-on.

She swung her horse toward the vineyard, moving out of the stand of trees just south of the last rows of grapevines. The workers were gone. They had moved on to an adjacent section. She could see a cloud of dust in the distance, churned up by the truck as it moved along the end of the rows.

The sun beat down, warm through the chambray shirt and jeans that Julie had loaned her. She'd gotten only about four hours' sleep after she and Julie finally said good-night. Fatigue, the heat, and the slow, rocking gait of the horse combined to make her less alert than she should have been.

Suddenly the sharp crack of a gunshot exploded in the air.

There was no time to react as her horse reared violently. She clutched at the reins too late, felt a bone-jarring lurch, then a sick feeling in the pit of her stomach as she was thrown from the saddle. Her immediate instinct was to hold on to something, anything—the reins, a tuft of mane, the saddle. But part of her mind was still thinking clearly enough to realize she'd better throw herself away from the terrified, out-of-control animal.

When she hit the ground, there was a brief, brilliant flash of light behind her eyes, excruciating pain, and then complete darkness.

# Chapter 18

*S*enorita? Senorita! Are you all right?"

The urgent words, spoken in a frantic mixture of English and Spanish, slowly pierced through the pain and the gray fog that wrapped around her brain.

Christina blinked uncertainly. There was something familiar about the anxious young Hispanic who bent over her. As the fog receded, replaced by the solid feel of the ground under her and the sun beating down on her, she recognized him—the driver of the flatbed truck.

She sat up slowly. The young man smiled hesitantly as he helped her. "Be very careful, senorita. There may be broken bones."

Her laugh was shaky. "I don't think so. I'm afraid my pride is the only casualty. I'd like to try standing now."

His arm went around her waist, his other hand gripping hers firmly as he helped her to her feet.

As soon as her head quit spinning and settled into one place, she gave him a hesitant smile. "Everything seems to work okay."

"You have a very big bump on the head, senorita. I will take you back to the house."

He walked with her to the truck. She crawled slowly into

the cab, reclining against the worn and cracked vinyl seat. She closed her eyes briefly as the dizziness returned.

By the time they reached the main house, she was fairly certain nothing serious was wrong. The dizziness was gone, but her head felt as if it were twice its normal size. As the driver steered the truck into the driveway, Julie came running from the house.

"My God! What happened? They called up from the barn to tell me that your horse came back by itself. Are you all right?"

Christina fumbled for the door handle, then got out. "I'm okay, I just took a fall. One minute I was in the saddle, and the next I was on the ground."

Julie frowned. "I don't understand it. That horse is gentle as a lamb. I specifically chose him because I knew you'd be safe on him."

The driver came around to help, and they both put an arm around Christina.

Christina looked up as she leaned on her friend. "I heard a gunshot. That must've frightened the horse."

Julie frowned. "In the vineyards?"

"Si, senora," the driver confirmed. "We heard it, too."

"What I don't understand," Christina asked, "is why someone would be hunting in an area where people are working."

"Not hunting," Julie explained. "Occasionally we have problems with crows getting at the grapes during the harvest. We send the workers out to frighten them off. Enrique, do we have anyone out there today?"

He shook his head. "There isn't supposed to be anyone out today, senora."

"Could you check that out for me and make certain no one is out there? And thank you, very much, Enrique, for helping Miss Fortune." With a firm arm around Christina's waist, she started to walk with her to the front entrance.

Christina's gaze fastened on the sleek, black Jaguar that sat parked in the driveway.

*Ross.*

She glanced at Julie in surprise and dismay.

"He just got here," Julie explained. "I told him you were out riding. He insisted on seeing you."

"Where is he?"

"In the study."

As they stepped into the foyer, Ross came out of the study. "Good God! What happened?"

"Her horse was spooked by someone with a gun out in the vineyards. She was thrown."

"Are you okay?"

She wanted to believe the tone of genuine concern in his voice. She longed to relax against the gentle pressure of his hands as he put his arm around her. But was it the truth? Or was it simply a very good act?

In spite of her protests, Ross picked her up. When he looked questioningly at Julie, she said, "Take her into the study. There's a sofa in there."

"I'm fine," Christina protested. She flattened her hand against Ross's chest to push him away and immediately regretted the contact. His warmth, through the thin cotton shirt, sent her pulse racing. She was intensely relieved when he put her down on the sofa. Julie put a cushion behind her back while Ross pulled a lap rug across her legs.

"I'm fine," she repeated stubbornly. "Really. I just have one hell of a headache, that's all."

Julie wasn't convinced. "You could have a concussion. I'm going to call the Emergicenter in Healdsburg and tell them we're coming in."

She looked at Ross, who nodded agreement. "I'll keep her quiet."

They were talking around her as if she were a child. "This really isn't necessary."

Ignoring her, Julie went on, "I'll have Enrique bring the Wagoneer around."

Christina didn't quite meet Ross's curious look as Julie disappeared into the main hall. She could sense the unasked questions as Ross sat with her, his fingers resting lightly against her wrist as it lay across her lap. His touch was disconcerting, but when she tried to pull away, he simply held on to her wrist.

"Be quiet and quit moving around."

She forced herself to look directly into those deep blue eyes. "What are you doing here?"

"At the moment I'm feeling your pulse."

"You're not a doctor."

"No. But it doesn't take an expert to know a good strong pulse from one that's weak or erratic."

"I told you, I'm fine," she repeated, not bothering to disguise the edge of anger in her voice. She jerked her wrist away. "How did you find me?"

"It wasn't too difficult. From what I've been able to learn about you, you have only one friend in the Bay area. When you left that message with Marie, it was easy enough to conclude that you might have come here. The question is, Why?"

Julie saved her from having to answer as she returned to the office and announced, "The Jeep is around front, and they're expecting us at the Emergicenter."

At the small emergency center the physician on call confirmed that Christina had no concussion, just an impressive bump on the head. Other than a few bruises and sore muscles, she was okay. They drove back to Julie's house in silence.

"I'll see what Louisa has scheduled for lunch," Julie said, excusing herself. She left them alone in the living room.

Ross stood before the leaded glass windows that looked out onto the front landscape of lawn bordered by driveway, a stand of tall pine trees, and then vineyards. His hands were thrust into his pockets. His expression was thoughtful as he turned to look at Christina on the sofa. "I rather like Julie. She's quite straightforward."

Christina looked up, wondering what he and Julie had discussed in the waiting room while she was in the examining room at the clinic.

Sensing the question, Ross answered, "She's protective of you."

Christina stared down at her folded hands. "Julie and I go back a ways. But of course you know all about that."

He met her look. "I'd still like to know why you came up here, without a word to anyone."

She concentrated on her folded hands. It was easier than

meeting that direct blue gaze, and her head was beginning to pound again. "I needed some time to think things through."

"Does this have anything to do with your ideas about the company?"

She was reminded of something Julie had said just that morning—that she had to face things head-on. She didn't want to do it now, with her head feeling as if it were splitting in two. On the other hand, she realized, this was a good place for such a confrontation. This wasn't the office, or Fortune Hill, places where others were in control. This place was safe because it was neutral territory and Julie was there. That was why Christina had come the day before—because she needed a safe haven. Just as she'd needed to reach a safe haven when she'd left home twenty years earlier.

Meeting Ross's gaze squarely, she said, "It has to do with a conversation I overheard between you and Richard yesterday." She watched him for a reaction, reminding herself that he would never let anything show that he didn't intend.

He immediately looked concerned. "How much did you hear?"

"Enough to hear Richard's very tempting offer!"

To her surprise his look of concern dissolved into relief. "Then you didn't hear quite everything."

"What is that supposed to mean?"

"It means that I turned him down."

She looked at him incredulously. "Just like that?"

"Yes, just like that." He leaned back on the edge of the table beneath the window, his hands braced on either side.

His eyes never left hers as he continued, "Over the years he's made me some very attractive offers to join him against Katherine. I've turned them all down."

He added tightly, "You can ask Bill if you like. You seem to trust him more than you trust me."

She knew there was no point in wasting her time responding to that. She trusted Bill up to a point, but she knew that he was loyal to Ross and would simply agree with anything Ross said. But there were others she could ask, and he knew it.

"Does Katherine know about the offers?"

"Yes. I told her about each one. And I'll tell her about this one, as well."

"I see," she said stiffly. She was surprised at how badly she wanted to believe him. "Why *did* you turn him down?"

The penetrating blue gaze fastened on her gave away absolutely nothing of the emotions behind the patrician features. Then his expression shifted, and he smiled. But it wasn't the boyish smile she had found so endearing the evening they were in Chinatown. It was cold, self-contained.

"Richard will destroy the company if he controls it. I haven't given ten years of my life building it up to see him take it apart ship by ship."

Suddenly she felt a sense of urgency to get at the core of the man. She wanted more than a glib explanation. She wanted the whole truth about him. "I don't buy that. Loyalty is bought and sold every day, and for a lot less than Richard was offering you. You haven't gotten where you are because you're a nice guy who believes in company loyalty."

"You're right," he admitted without the slightest hesitation. "Nevertheless it is a quality that I value highly." His expression softened almost imperceptibly. "When all is said and done, I suppose there really is no way to convince you that I'm telling the truth. You're simply going to have to trust me."

"Why should I trust you? You don't trust me!" she flung back at him. "You've had an investigator checking into every aspect of my background."

He made no attempt to deny it. "That's right, and he'll continue to check into your background until he can give me the answers to some questions."

"Why? What difference does it make? Katherine doesn't care who I am, as long as I play her little game so she can keep control of Fortune International."

"*I* want to know who you *really* are."

The words were spoken in a cool, almost detached tone. But underneath she sensed a fierce determination to get at the truth. The intensity of it caught her off guard.

He went on carefully, "Who you are, your identity, is important. It's the most important thing about you."

From the first she'd found him intriguing. Now she found him compelling. She had to remind herself forcefully that she couldn't allow herself to be beguiled by him.

They were at an impasse, and she knew it. She'd confronted him about the meeting, and he'd responded with what seemed to be honesty. There was nothing more to be said. At the bottom of all this was the undeniable fact that they needed one another. He needed her cooperation as Christina Fortune, heiress to those stock shares, and she needed him to help her make this work. But there was no way she could bring herself to trust him.

Just then Julie walked into the living room. "Lunch will be in a half hour," she announced. Looking at Ross, she asked, "Can you stay?"

Before he could reply, Christina said apologetically, "I have to get back to San Francisco."

Julie was astonished. "But you just got here, and you shouldn't even be thinking about going back so soon after that accident. You need to rest."

Christina took hold of her friend's hand. "I have to get back, Julie. Please understand."

Julie glanced from one to the other, then sighed in frustration. "All right." She squeezed Christina's hand affectionately. "But you had better call me, and I expect another visit, soon."

"I'll call," Christina promised. "Maybe you can come into the city and we'll have dinner."

"Just let me know when." Then looking at Ross, she said meaningfully, "Don't let anything happen to my friend."

"Don't worry. I'll watch her very carefully."

Julie wasn't aware of the double meaning in his words, but Christina knew exactly what he meant.

She wasn't up to driving her own car back, so she reluctantly agreed to go with Ross. She left her car with Julie, who said she would drive it into San Francisco the following week.

During most of the two-hour drive back, Christina rested quietly with her eyes closed. She was uncomfortably aware of Ross's nearness in the close confines of the car. Why had he come after her? she wondered. Was he afraid she was running away? But it shouldn't matter to him if she left. He'd probably say, "Good riddance!"

She'd gotten so used to the silence that stretched between them over the long miles back to the city that she was startled when he spoke abruptly. "This won't do. We're on the same side, and we've got to work together."

She gave him a sideways look. "Are you suggesting that we should actually trust each other?"

His gaze was fixed on the road ahead. "I'm willing to give it a try if you are."

She couldn't believe it. Her first thought was that it must be a trap of some kind. Was he trying to disarm her, only to turn on her later? She didn't know what to believe. She knew only that she was tired of keeping her defenses up, and longed to be able to let down her guard, at least a little.

"I'm not some clever con out for the inheritance," she insisted. "Do you believe me?"

"Do you want the truth?"

She nodded, and found herself holding her breath, waiting for his response.

"I don't know what the devil to make of you anymore. In the beginning I was absolutely convinced you were just another impostor."

"And now?" she prompted.

"Now . . ." he paused, then finished in a husky voice, "Now I don't know who you are. But I'm willing to trust you."

"Completely?"

"I don't trust anyone completely."

She was silent for a long moment. Then she said, "All right."

He glanced at her briefly, before concentrating once more on the road. In that brief moment when their eyes met, she felt the barriers between them begin to dissolve, just a little.

Ross offered to drive her to Fortune Hill, but she asked him to take her straight to the office.

She'd made a decision on the drive in from Sonoma. She

couldn't trust Ross completely, but she would have to rely on him.

The rest had helped some, but her muscles were already starting to complain. Marie gave her a concerned look as they stepped off the elevator and Ross headed toward his office.

"Welcome back, Miss Fortune." Seeing Christina's pale, drawn expression, she asked, "Are you all right?"

"Yes, I'm fine, Marie. I just stopped in to check for my messages. I'm expecting some information from the engineering department. Has it come in yet?"

"Yes. Brian Chandler brought it up this morning. He said to tell you he was sorry he missed you, but they'll see you for dinner Friday evening."

Christina had forgotten she was supposed to have supper with Diana and Brian this coming Friday, before opening night for the opera. This was to be her last social engagement, now that she refused to play the role of social butterfly, and she wasn't looking forward to it.

Ross had just returned from his office, where he'd checked his messages, and stood waiting to drive her home.

"Oh, Miss Fortune," Marie called out to her as she turned to leave. "I nearly forgot. Richard Fortune said if you came in, he wanted to see you in his office."

Christina exchanged a puzzled look with Ross. Since she'd returned from Hawaii and moved to Fortune Hill, Richard had maintained a polite distance.

"I wonder what he wants," she commented as Ross walked with her to Richard's massive office at the end of the hall.

Richard's secretary greeted them. "Go on in, Miss Fortune. I already informed Mr. Fortune that you had arrived. He's expecting you."

Ross started to open the door for her, and Richard's secretary spoke up. "He wants to meet with Miss Fortune *alone,* Mr. McKenna."

His smile was perfectly polite. "I'm sure he does, Mrs. Fleming." Then he pushed Richard's door open for Christina and followed her into the large office.

Richard looked up. His eyes narrowed in irritation as he saw Ross come in with Christina.

"This doesn't concern you, Ross."

"Anything that concerns this company concerns me. Now, what did you want to talk to Christina about?"

Richard was furious at Ross's stubborn insistence on remaining, but there was nothing he could do. Ross clearly wasn't about to leave.

"Very well," he gave in grudgingly.

Turning to Christina, he gave her a look of such cold contempt, mingled with triumph, that she shivered inside. Instinctively she sensed that she was in danger.

He began carefully, "From the beginning your success in impersonating my niece rested on inside information that only Christina could have possessed."

"I'm not impersonating anyone," Christina shot back.

"Oh, but I think you are. And more important, I know how you've done it."

Taking a key from his pocket, he opened a locked drawer in his desk. He took out a slim book and placed it in the middle of the desk where both Ross and Christina could see it clearly.

The diary.

*Oh, no,* Christina thought.

"What is that?" Ross asked in confusion.

Christina wanted to run, as far and as fast as she could. Instead she mustered every last ounce of courage that she possessed and went on the offensive. "That's my diary from my childhood. Richard stole it."

"You're the one who stole it!" Richard snapped. "Somehow you stole this diary and the necklace. And used them both to persuade a sick old woman that you were her long-lost granddaughter."

Ross stared at Christina. She saw doubt flicker across his face before he managed to assume a blank expression. "What's in the diary?" he asked.

Before Christina could answer, Richard jumped in. "Everything an impostor would need to know to pass herself off as Christina Fortune. And something more—something from her days in New York that explains who this impostor really is."

He buzzed his secretary. "Would you please have the gentleman come into my office, Mrs. Fleming?" Turning back to Christina, who stood rooted to the spot in front of his desk, he said, "There's someone I want you to meet. Someone I think you'll remember."

Mrs. Fleming opened the door and stepped inside. She was followed by a portly man dressed in an ill-fitting summer-weight white linen suit that was completely out of place in San Francisco in the fall. The suit was so wrinkled, it looked as if it had been slept in. The man's unfashionably wide tie had been loosened from his thick neck and was slightly askew. He wore a narrow-brimmed straw hat with a dark brown hatband.

He mumbled "Thanks" to Mrs. Fleming for showing him in, then turned to Richard. Sweeping off the hat, he exposed a balding head and florid features. He said in a thick Southern accent, "Hello, Mr. Fortune. Nice to see you again."

Then his gaze fastened on Christina. He stared at her, his pale gray, lashless eyes boring into her. A confident smile slowly spread across his thin lips. "Hello, Ellie, darlin'. Remember me, your ol' stepdaddy?"

# Chapter 19

Christina turned to Ross. For once his vaunted self-possession was shaken. The stunned expression in his eyes revealed all too clearly what he felt. Only an hour earlier he had offered to trust her. Now ...

"Ellie, aren't you going to say hello to your stepfather?" Richard's tone was triumphant. "After all, you haven't seen each other in over twenty years."

He said to Ross, "I'd like you to meet Cal Loomis, from Memphis, Tennessee. Cal is Ellie Dobbs's stepfather."

"Afternoon," Loomis said with a nod to Ross. Then, shifting his hat in his thick hands, he turned back to Christina. "I know this is a surprise, darlin'. It was a surprise for us, too, when this gentleman contacted yer momma an' me, an' said he knew where you were. After all these years we'd given up hope of ever seein' you again."

All she could do was stare in stunned horror at Loomis. *After all these years* ... She had never expected ... But then she should have known, if Ross dug deep into her past, Richard would dig even deeper. And he had the diary to help him.

All the blood had drained from her face. Her hands were clenched into rigid, cold fists. In her mouth was the strong metallic taste of an old, deeply ingrained fear, mixed with revulsion. She knew Loomis all right—knew what he had done to a fifteen-year-old girl twenty years ago. Now he was about to wreak devastation again.

She stared at him in fury and loathing. "How much is Richard paying you?"

Taken aback by the unexpected question, Loomis blinked in confusion. "I, ah . . ." He fumbled for words. "Ah, c'mon now, Ellie. That's no way to talk to yer stepdaddy. Yer momma would'a come, but she hasn't been any too well lately, an' she didn't feel up to the trip."

Her throat was thick with bile at the thought of being in the same room with this man. She forced herself to go on. "I asked how much he's paying you to discredit me."

"Now, Ellie . . ." he cajoled, "you know that's no way to talk, even though we aren't rightly kin, 'cept for marriage. Ain't ya got nothin' kind to say to me after all these years? We were so worried about you, never sendin' no word about where you was and all."

Despite the bluster in his voice, she sensed he was losing his initial confidence. He kept glancing at Richard, as if looking for reassurance that he was saying all the right things.

The uncertainty in Loomis's gray eyes gave her courage. She clung to the loathing and rage that built inside her, needing both to confront this man who had caused such pain and terror.

She said slowly, distinctly, with great dignity, "My name is Christina Grant Fortune. *Not* Ellie Dobbs."

She didn't look at Ross, but she knew he was watching her intently, searching for any hint of confusion within her. But she didn't feel confused now. She felt determined—to stand up to Loomis, and in doing so, to resolve a fear that had crippled her for twenty years. She wanted to make him suffer as he had made a helpless, innocent young girl suffer.

"How much is he paying you?" she demanded again, her voice rising.

He twisted his hat as he glanced uncertainly at Richard. "I believe . . . ten thousand was mentioned," he said hopefully, and then quickly added, "plus my expenses for comin' here. But that's only fair. After all, things ain't been easy for yer momma an' me."

"So you're being well paid to say that I am Ellie."

Loomis hesitated, then answered, "Wait a damn minute, here. I wouldn't lie. Yer Ellie, all right. You think I wouldn't know my own stepdaughter?"

The pain from the fall, the fatigue, and the old, impotent rage made her feel as if her knees might buckle at any moment. But she forced herself to stand there, even though she couldn't tolerate the sight of him. There was no safe refuge from this man; the only safety lay in confronting him.

She couldn't give way to her feelings. Not now. At this moment she had as much at stake as she'd had that first day in the boardroom of Fortune International.

"Do you still live in Beecham's Landing, outside Memphis?" she asked in a steely voice.

He nodded. "Yup. Same little town. Same house, for that matter."

"Do you still run a Bible house there?"

"Yup." He explained to Richard and Ross, "I sell religious books and records and such."

"And of course you're an upstanding pillar of the community," Christina went on in a voice colored with sarcasm.

He responded proudly, "That's right. I'm deacon of the Redemption Baptist Church."

"This is a waste of time!" Richard snapped at Christina. "It's time for you to stop this charade and leave before I have you arrested."

Ignoring him, Christina continued to focus on Loomis. Her voice was strong and sure as she said, "Are the good citizens of Beecham's Landing aware that twenty years ago you savagely beat and *raped* your fifteen-year-old stepdaughter?"

A sudden silence descended on the room. Richard flashed a quick, surprised look at Loomis. Ross stared at Christina, as if seeing her for the first time.

The accusation shattered Loomis's composure. Whatever he had expected from this meeting, this wasn't it. He went rigid, his expression filled with a fury that he was clearly having a hard time controlling.

"That's a damn lie!" he shouted. Beads of sweat broke out across his forehead. He wiped his forehead with a wrinkled, stained handkerchief, then drew it across his mouth. His face was ashen.

Christina faced Richard. "You wanted the truth! Well, now you have it! Twenty years ago this sick, twisted man viciously raped his stepdaughter! *That's* why she ran away."

Turning back to Loomis, she finished coldly, "Now the only question, Mr. Loomis, is how much you're willing to risk for ten thousand dollars, plus expenses. Your good reputation? Your position as deacon? Your business? I promise you, if you swear that I am Ellie Dobbs, then I will go to the sheriff in Beecham's Landing and charge you with rape."

"You cain't do that!" Loomis shouted. "I know about the statute of limitations. You cain't charge me with a crime that old."

Christina didn't back down. "Maybe not. But I can file a civil suit for damages. I'm sure the local newspaper would run the story. Everyone in town will know what you did. I've heard that people in small Southern towns are very righteous. Think what will happen when the good folks of Beecham's Landing find out the truth. What will happen to your business? How many people will buy Bibles from a rapist?"

She finished determinedly, "I'll make you suffer just as you made Ellie suffer, and I won't stop until you're left with nothing."

Loomis looked wildly from Christina to Richard. "You said this would be easy!"

Richard glared at him. "That's enough! Those are empty threats. She can't prove anything."

Christina didn't bother to acknowledge Richard. Her dark eyes fixed on Loomis, she whispered, "I can prove it."

Loomis wiped at his thin lips again, then stammered hoarsely, "It *has* been over twenty years . . . I could be wrong about her bein' Ellie. Her face sorta looks the same, an' she has the same color eyes, but . . ." He laughed, a nervous, trapped sound. "Truth is, I cain't be absolutely certain."

"You were certain enough when you first saw her!" Richard shouted.

Loomis shifted uneasily. "Well, I *ain't* certain!" he blurted out. "Fact is, the more I listen to her an' look at her, the more

I'm certain that she *ain't* Ellie." He crumpled his hat in his thick hands as he started to back toward the door. As he was about to let himself out, he hesitated, "I don't suppose there's much chance of you seein' yer way clear to givin' me part of that money?" he asked Richard. "After all, I come here, like you asked me to."

Before Richard could answer, Ross said in a voice heavy with disgust, "Get out of here, Loomis."

Loomis grabbed the door handle. "Yessir!" Then he added as a quick afterthought, "Good day, Miss Fortune."

The door slammed behind him.

She was shaking so badly, Christina was certain she'd collapse if she tried to walk. Ross seemed to sense it. Crossing to her, he slipped a strong arm beneath hers. As he led her out of the office, he said to Richard, who stood in mute rage, "See to it that Christina gets her diary back. Or I'll make sure you're charged with theft."

Inside Ross's office a moment later, he poured Christina a shot of brandy. When she shook her head, he insisted. "After what you've been through today, you need it."

She drank it slowly. Ross watched her, trying to see beyond the rigid control that was now firmly back in place. From the first moment she'd walked into the boardroom, he'd been surprised at the sense of empathy he felt toward her. He'd fought and struggled all his life, and he'd sensed that she'd done the same.

Since that first meeting in the boardroom, he'd watched her react to myriad situations. He'd seen her strong. He'd seen her cool under fire. He'd seen her confident, poised, and as polished as they came. He'd seen her angry. Only once or twice had he seen her vulnerable, as she'd appeared when she first saw Loomis. That vulnerability had been almost heartbreaking to see.

But she'd quickly masked the vulnerability and refused to be intimidated by either Loomis's claim or Richard's tactics. In that explosive confrontation she had been willing to lay everything on the line and go for broke in order to defend herself. At that moment she reminded him so much of himself that for the first time he began to feel it really didn't matter whether she was Christina Fortune or Ellie Dobbs. Whoever she was, she was one hell of a woman.

She stood with her forehead pressed against the window, staring out across the city. The drink was cradled in both hands. Those hands trembled as she reluctantly took another sip.

He knew that she needed him to believe in her . . . and to his amazement he found that he wanted that more than anything. "How did you know what happened to Ellie?" he asked in a quiet voice.

She didn't answer at first. The office was silent, eighteen stories above the frantic heartbeat of the city. She stared out the window, remembering. It was several moments before she answered. Her voice was almost a whisper. "When you go through hell with someone and survive, you become very close . . .

Christina and Ellie walked along the path in Central Park. It was late morning in the middle of winter. They'd bought hot pretzels from a sidewalk vendor with money Ellie had stolen from a table at a sidewalk restaurant.

They were both still breathless from their mad dash, a young waiter hot on their heels, in pursuit of his tip money. When they could run no longer, they stopped at the first place that sold food. They hadn't eaten for two days.

"I told you I'd get somethin' for us." Ellie smiled as she stuffed the soft, warm pretzel into her mouth. "Lord, I never knew anythin' could taste so good."

"I can't believe you stole that money," Christina said between mouthfuls.

"Yer stomach can believe it," Ellie pointed out with a huge grin. Then she became more serious. "I don't like doin' it. But yer money ran out days ago, and we got to survive. It's only until we can find work."

Christina looked at her with somber eyes. "What kind of work are we going to find? Who's going to hire two fifteen-year-old girls?" There was a catch in her voice, and her eyes filled with tears. Ellie wrapped her arm around her shoulders.

"Cheer up. We'll find somethin'. And not what that low-life slime Jackson has been offerin', either," Ellie said with grim determination. "I'm not gonna be no whore like those other girls we seen."

They walked on together through the park. It was early December, one of those rare, warm days that surprised everyone in New York City once in a while. It hadn't snowed in days, the sun shone brightly, and the park was crowded. There were business-suited executives, secretaries in miniskirts and knee-high boots, young mothers with toddlers bundled in snowsuits against the cold.

"I like walkin' through here," Ellie was saying. "It's pretty and peaceful, almost like back home, and people seem so happy—when they aren't havin' demonstrations against the war or somethin'. I like seein' the families—mommas with their kids, young couples, happy folks." Her tone was wistful.

"Do you miss your family?" Christina asked. At times she felt a peculiar sense of loss and loneliness that had nothing to do with the people she had left behind, but more for the way things might have been if her mother and father had lived.

Ellie shook her head. "Nah! Nobody gave a shit when I was there. I'm sure they're glad to be rid of me." They were hard words, spoken in a hard voice, but her face was averted as she stared across the park to the playground where young kids rode back and forth on the swings, their laughter shrill in the crisp air.

"Why *did* you leave your family?" Christina asked in a quiet voice as she stopped to share the last of her pretzel with the squirrels. Ellie didn't stop, but kept on walking in silence.

"Ellie? Wait up!" Christina ran to catch up with her. She was breathless when she finally fell into step with her again. "Ellie . . ." she pulled at her friend's arm, unaccustomed to the silence between them. Ellie was usually the chatterbox; she never seemed to shut up.

"Ellie, I'm sorry. I didn't mean to pry . . ."

Suddenly Ellie whirled around. Her eyes were glassy with tears. She wasn't smiling anymore. Her mouth twisted with emotion. "My stepfather took a likin' to me," she blurted out. Once she started, everything came out in a flood. "He and my momma were only married a few years. It was after my real daddy took off. She and Cal got married, and then she had my brother and sister real quick. She felt poorly after my sister was born. I guess she couldn't . . ." Her voice broke, and she rubbed at her eyes with the back of her sleeve. "That's when he started comin' into my room at night."

"Oh, God!" Christina whispered, her eyes full of tears, and pain welling into her throat. "You don't have to go on."

"Yes, I do!" Ellie cried. "I gotta tell someone, or I'll die from keepin' it inside!"

She took several deep breaths to steady herself, then went on. "At first he just came in and sat on the edge of my bed. I didn't understand. He was always drunk. He'd ramble on about his work, about how hard it was trying to make a livin' with a wife and, three kids. Then he held my hand. I thought it was what daddies were supposed to do."

She sobbed and hiccupped. Then she went on. "Before I knew what was happenin', he was touchin' me in other places. When I told him I was scared and didn't want him to do that anymore, he said it was my duty now that Momma was so sick."

"Ellie, don't!" Christina pleaded with her, but Ellie went on.

"One day after church he said he wouldn't do that no more. But the next night he come home drunk again. Momma and the babies were asleep. He came to my room. I could smell the liquor on him." She dragged the back of her hand across her nose and wiped at the tears. Her voice was only a whisper. "He wanted more than just touchin'." She looked up at Christina, all the misery and shame in the world reflected in her eyes. "I tried to fight him off, but he kept hittin' me, harder and harder. And he . . . he raped me."

Once she said it, the worst seemed over. She sniffled hard, but she was already composed, her eyes dry. "I left that night, and I stole his liquor money to help get away. I never phoned or wrote any letters. And I never will. I blame him, but I blame Momma, too. I tried to tell her, but she called me a lyin' little troublemaker. She just didn't want to know what was goin' on."

Then she mustered a pathetic little laugh, as if to make light of it all. "Some story, huh?"

"I had no idea," Christina said softly, her eyes warm with compassion.

"What the hell! Onward and upward, to bigger and better things." Then Ellie asked jokingly, "Why did *you* run away? Did yer rich uncle threaten to cut off yer allowance?" She hooted at that thought.

Christina stared down at her hands, clasped together in an effort to keep warm. She hadn't felt the cold before, but now she did. "No," she said in a small voice. "Nothing like that."

Ellie gave her an elbow in the ribs. "C'mon. Here I tell you everythin', and you won't even tell me nothin'. That's not fair. If we're gonna look out for each other and share everything, then we have to be straight with one another."

When Christina looked up at her new friend, she realized Ellie was right. All they had in the world was each other. "I guess we're more alike than you thought," she told Ellie, her eyes glistening with sudden tears.

"Oh, Lord!" Ellie breathed. "You mean . . . Damn, I'm stupid, makin' fun of you like that. I'm sorry. I thought things like that didn't happen to rich people."

"It doesn't have anything to do with money."

Ellie took hold of Christina's hands. "I guess we are alike, in too many ways. But you know somethin', Chris, we'll make it. I promise."

Christina held on to Ellie tightly. "Do you really think so?"

"I really think so." Then Ellie finished fiercely, "And we'll make them pay for what they did to us. Someday we'll make them all pay."


In the office Christina took another sip of brandy and slowly swallowed as she stared out the windows. She took a deep, shuddering breath, resting her forehead against the cool glass. "We told each other things we couldn't tell another living soul. I knew her as well as I know myself."

Ross said nothing. But his thoughts raced. My God, so *that* was what she'd meant when she told him she left home because she feared for her life. Watching her as she was suddenly and unexpectedly confronted by Loomis, he'd decided she was Ellie, after all. Her emotions about Loomis, and what he'd done, were so raw, so deep, it seemed that she must be Ellie.

Now he wasn't so sure. But whether she was Ellie or Christina, one thing was certain—she'd gone through hell and somehow found the strength and courage to survive.

She had no idea how long they'd been in Ross's office until she noticed the traffic in the street below had slowed. Rush hour was over. Those who worked past six o'clock to avoid the traffic now trickled out of their offices. An occasional car appeared from the underground parking garage. The crowds of commuters who rushed frantically to make connections to the ferries, rapid transit, or buses that would take them across to the East Bay, or over to Marin, had all but disappeared.

Only those who lived in the city, or those who chose to linger in upscale taverns, trendy restaurants, or gay bars because it was Friday night, the start of the weekend, remained.

The offices of Fortune International were completely silent. Christina snapped out of her reverie. "I didn't realize it was so late." She turned to find Ross sitting in the thick, over-stuffed leather chair behind his desk, watching her. "You probably have someplace you're supposed to be."

He shook his head. "I make my own plans and my own schedule. Both are flexible. Are you ready?"

She nodded. "I'd like to get out of here."

They rode the elevator down to the parking garage in silence. Ross turned the key, and backed the Jaguar out of his space. He swung out of the garage, and started to turn left toward Pacific Heights.

Christina stopped him with a hand on his arm. "I'm not going back to Fortune Hill," she said resolutely. "I would appreciate a lift to the Hyatt."

Ross frowned. "I understand that you can't bear the thought of living under the same roof with Richard any longer, but I can think of a better place than the hotel." At her questioning look his mouth softened with one of those rare smiles. "Trust me."

Then he cut the wheel to the right and moved into the traffic that streamed steadily along the Embarcadero.

Emotionally exhausted, she laid her head back against the headrest and closed her eyes. It seemed only a few seconds before Ross was gently rousing her.

"Open your eyes, sleepyhead. We're here." He swung out of the car.

Sitting up, she looked out at the line of pleasure craft, yachts, and sailboats that lined the dock.

Ross came around and opened her door. The cool evening breeze and the tangy salt-sea air off the water focused her senses. They were at the yacht club just down from the Marina district. She had driven past it on her way over to Marin the day before. God, had it been only twenty-four hours? she thought. A lot had happened since then.

"You might want to slip on your jacket," Ross suggested. "It gets a bit cool down here." He reached inside the back of the Jag, where she had hung her suit jacket. When she returned to the city, she had worn the jeans and sneakers Julie loaned her along with her silk blouse. Her skirt and jacket hung in back of the car.

Ross slipped the jacket around her shoulders, and then, as if it were the most natural thing in the world, his fingers wrapped around hers. "I want to show you something."

They walked along the dock lined with private slips. Several contained motor launches of various sizes or large cabin cruisers. Most were empty and covered, hatches closed and locked. Several more slips contained sailboats of differing lengths. The largest slips were at the far end of the dock.

The dock under their feet rolled as the changing tide rose and fell restlessly. They stopped at the last slip.

A huge sailboat was moored to the dock, rolling gently on the swell of the water. The others they passed were mostly white, fiberglass-hulled, with slashes of brilliant blue or green stripes, and fancy, elaborate names stenciled on their fantails like *Midnight Magic, Fandango, Bodacious,* or *Makin' Waves.* They were lean, low, and sleek, undoubtedly with the latest state-of-the-art, computerized navigational equipment aboard.

This sailboat wasn't like the others. At least fifty feet long, it had a deep draft and decks made entirely of hand-rubbed mahogany. Instead of aluminum, all fixtures were gleaming brass, with two masts thrusting sixty feet into the air. The name *Resolute* was lettered across the fantail, along with the registry, out of Hong Kong.

All the sails were neatly wrapped, and the empty lines moved restlessly in the breeze. Below decks were completely sealed off behind locked cabin doors, and the wheel moved lazily back and forth with the rocking motion of the boat, as if it only waited to return to the open sea.

"It's beautiful," Christina breathed in awe.

"She was built in thirty-two," Ross said. "She was a rum-runner off Cape Hatteras, then a fishing boat, then a tour boat in the Bahamas. She was sunk in fifty-eight and scuttled onto a sandbar off the coast of Bimini. She's been around the world three times and sailed across every ocean and sea." He turned and looked at Christina. "We both almost went to the bottom of the sea one time off the coast of Africa."

"This is yours?"

Ross nodded, gazing lovingly at the boat. Clearly it meant a great deal to him, and he was almost childishly proud of it. "I bought her fifteen years ago with the first money I made after college. I fixed her up, then took off for two years and sailed her around the world. She's not the fastest—I leave the America's Cup racing to your cousin Steven. But she has incredible balance, and deep draft. The man who built her knew the sea."

"How many people sailed with you?" she asked, intrigued by this new side of Ross.

"No one. I went by myself. Bill thought it was the last he'd seen of me. More than once I thought he might have been right."

When he turned back to her, the smile on his face was completely relaxed and genuine, like that of a little boy proudly showing off a favorite toy. He held out his hand. "Would you like to go aboard?"

She nodded and slipped her fingers through his. As they stepped up onto the deck, Ross turned and said, "This is the alternative I had in mind. It won't cost you a thing, there isn't a problem with reservations, and the best hotel in the city can't compete with the view." He walked past her to the cabin, unlocked the cabin doors, and disappeared below deck. She followed him down the steps.

He flicked on a cabin light that illuminated the luster of finely polished wood and brass in the cabin. It was larger than she had expected. There was a narrow companionway, then the main cabin lined with chairs, a table, and bench seats. The companionway disappeared forward.

At her glance Ross said, "The galley and private quarters are all forward. Boat house and all navigation are topside."

He turned on other lights, illuminating a very masculine but comfortable domain. There were no feminine touches at all, and she wondered if Marianne Schaeffer had ever been here. Somehow she thought not.

She started to say, "I can't stay here . . ." but Ross cut her off.

"You need a place completely removed from the events of the last couple of days. There's plenty of room here, and it's cozier than a hotel."

She had to admit that it was undeniably better than a hotel. She wanted to say yes, but still she hesitated, wondering what strings might be attached.

"It wouldn't be . . ." she hesitated, unsure how to express her reservations without coming off sounding like some sort of prude.

Ross interjected with amusement, "What? Wouldn't be proper or appropriate?" Then he said more seriously, "There's no one here to pass judgment, Chris. You're the only person who has to decide what is right for you."

It was the first time he'd called her that, and it caught her by surprise. She liked the sound of it.

She smiled. "Then I'll stay. Where is the bathroom . . . I mean, the head?"

"Straight forward, past the galley, second door to starboard."

She held up a hand before he could translate. "I know my starboard from my port."

"That's right, you've done a bit of sailing, haven't you?"

For the first time she felt that he'd made an innocent comment, one that wasn't weighed down by innuendo. She nodded. "Yes, but it's been a while."

She found the bathroom. It was complete with basin, chain-pull flush toilet, and narrow shower—all the conveniences of home. She carefully brushed through her hair, wincing at the tenderness of the bump on her head, and washed her tear-stained face.

All the cabin lights were on as she returned. Ross was just hanging up a telephone. "Ship-to-shore," he explained. "I ordered up some food. I keep the basics for myself, but it's nothing I would serve to guests."

"The requisite can of beans and canned peaches for scurvy?" Christina asked with a smile.

"Don't laugh," Ross responded. "When I was at sea for months at a time, I lived off canned peaches, sardines, and beans."

Christina made a face. "Maybe I should reconsider the Hyatt."

"Don't worry," he quipped, "I won't make you eat the beans."

"That's reassuring."

Christina inspected the cabin. She found charts, a sextant, a compass, daily logs, and the small library that lined one wall. There were several classics: Dickens, Robert Louis Stevenson, Poe, Sir Arthur Conan Doyle.

"I wouldn't have thought you were the literary type," she remarked.

"You become the literary type or go mad when you're becalmed at sea. I've read each of those at least six times and discovered every typographic error, plot inconsistency, and cliché. I made a list."

"Were you becalmed often?"

"Often enough for me to install a motor in this thing. There are some modern conveniences that are absolutely necessary."

She was reminded again of the contrasts in him—those subtle blends of the cultured man and the rebel, the Renaissance man and the bold entrepreneur. Light and dark. Good and evil? she wondered. There was a soft thumping up on deck, and a voice called out.

"Food delivery," Ross announced as he went topside. He quickly returned with a bagful of food clutched in each arm, followed by a young man carrying two more bags.

"Where do you want these, Mr. McKenna?"

"In the galley. Tommy, this is Miss Fortune. She'll be staying aboard tonight."

The young man nodded. He wore a pair of jeans with holes at the knees, worn deck shoes, and a clean shirt with the marina logo on the front. "We have security twenty-four hours a day, Miss Fortune. If you need anything, you just give a call on the ship-to-shore. There's someone up in the office at all times."

She smiled. "Thank you."

Tommy turned to leave. "Will there be anything else, Mr. McKenna?"

Ross handed him a generous tip. "That will be all for tonight, Tommy."

"Good-night, Miss Fortune."

"Good-night."

"Why don't you go up on deck?" Ross suggested to her after Tommy left. "I'll fix something to eat. You must be hungry."

She gave him a look of mock horror. "Promise me it won't be sardines. Anything but that."

"I promise." Then, as she was climbing the steps to the deck, he called after her, "You should be warned, however, that sailors always lie. Comes from having so many girls in so many ports."

She grinned. "I'll remember that."

Dinner was marvelous. They had green salad, hot garlic dinner rolls, and prawns in marinara sauce over angel hair pasta.

"You couldn't have cooked this in that small amount of time," she accused as they set the table on deck.

Ross grinned. "I know this fantastic little Italian place. Joe's in North Beach."

She'd heard of Joe's. It was one of those small, tucked-

away places that catered to a very exclusive clientele. All the
food was authentic, old-world cuisine. Joe had come to the
United States from Italy in the twenties. All the locals ate
there. Dinner was by reservation only for the twelve tables
that filled the tiny restaurant, and a two-month waiting list
wasn't unusual.

"I didn't know Joe does take-out meals," she said as she
stole a mushroom from the salad and popped it into her
mouth.

Ross held up the wine for her approval. "He doesn't." It
gave her another insight to him, that he had managed to con-
fiscate this exclusive dinner for their desktop dinner. She held
out her glass as he poured.

"Francetti Vineyards!" she exclaimed with surprise, as she
saw the label.

Ross then filled his own glass. "I gave Tommy specific instructions about the wine. I was curious about it after meeting
your friend."

"I would've thought you'd already know everything about
her," Christina retorted as she dished up the salad. "I'm certain it's in that thick file you've compiled on me."

Ross put a second bottle of Francetti wine to chill in the
small tin bucket that sat on the deck at their feet. He frowned
slightly. "That file doesn't begin to tell me what I really want
to know about you."

Something in his tone made her catch her breath. She
wanted to respond, but she didn't know what to say. Instead
she forced herself to concentrate on the delicious food, studiously avoiding the penetrating look in his eyes.

They finished the second bottle of wine as they watched
the Pacific sky turn to liquid gold, then soft amber, and finally
inky purple. Lights illuminated the marina and the city beyond like first stars that had just come out. The faint breeze
off the water carried the occasional murmur of voices from
other boats nearby. When the sun had set, it abruptly grew
colder, and Ross brought out a blanket for her as they sat on
deck, enjoying the evening.

"Do you take her out often?" Christina asked about the
sailboat.

Ross sat across from her on one of the bench seats that lined the fantail, his feet kicking up, a wineglass in his hand. "As often as I can, which isn't as often as I'd like. I had decided that if Richard was successful in taking control of the company, I was going to take off for a while."

"Sail off into the sunset?" she suggested over the rim of her glass.

"Something like that perhaps."

She studied him thoughtfully, "Somehow running away doesn't seem like your style."

His dark blue gaze fastened on her. His mouth quirked in a faint smile. "I never run away. But tell me, Miss Fortune, just what is my style?"

She laid her head back against the thick wood railing and closed her eyes while she thought about an answer for that. It had been a long, exhausting day. The wine made her more than mellow. Her thoughts were a little slow and fuzzy, and she felt less guarded than was probably wise.

When she opened her eyes again, she found him watching her. She looked about the large open deck of the sailboat, and smiled as her gaze came back to him. "You remind me of a pirate."

"A pirate?" There was a low rumble of laughter in his voice.

"Yes," she said with conviction. "Definitely a pirate. You sail into places, you raid and pillage, and you take whatever you want." She laughed softly at the mental images it created. "And I suspect that if I pried open some of those compartments below deck, I might find a treasure chest."

Ross watched her with a lazy grin as he reclined against the opposite railing. "You forgot to include the seduction of lovely ladies in your description."

Even through the haze of the wine, she was aware he'd deliberately changed the word from *rape*—which was the usual description of pirate activities—to *seduction*. Whether it was the fatigue or the wine, or a mesmerizing combination of both, her eyes became misty with gratitude for this *pirate* who was so surprisingly sensitive to her emotions.

"I suspect you've seduced your fair share of women," she commented.

"Never aboard the *Resolute*." He set his wineglass aside and crossed the deck to her. Taking her empty glass from her fingers, he set it aside, too. Then he gently pulled her to her feet. Their bodies brushed together lightly, tantalizingly.

Each waited for the other to step back, to move aside, or to pull away. But for once neither of them did. They simply stood there, their thighs touching, the only barrier between their bodies the thin fabric of their clothing.

His fingers curled into the collar of her blouse, recalling that night in Chinatown. And as he had that night, he pulled her closer, until she felt the heat of his breath on her face. The breeze lifted the strands of his dark hair from his forehead, and the burning look in his eyes was very much that of a pirate—a man who took what he wanted.

The cool night air seemed to grow warmer as his mouth moved over hers. And as on that night in Chinatown, she felt the danger, sensed it, tasted it. But tonight she pulled him closer, the heat driving the long-awakening hunger deep inside her. Her hands clasped his waist. No alarm went off inside her, warning her against the danger. There was only the warm glow of the wine and a growing awareness that she liked whatever danger he represented.

Then, to her surprise and dismay, Ross pulled away from her. The cool night air jolted her back to reality. His arms didn't leave her, though. They held her firm against the length of his body, reminding her of the heat, and of the powerful needs within both of them.

She was breathless, fragile, her emotions exposed. At that moment she couldn't have hidden her feelings from him if her life depended on it.

Ross tenderly brushed his mouth against hers. "You take the main cabin below deck."

Christina looked up at him in confusion. "But . . . where will you sleep?"

"Up here. I've done it before at sea. I can make it very comfortable."

His rejection hit her like a fist. She felt awkward and embarrassed, and couldn't bear to meet his look. She started to pull away, but he stopped her.

Taking her chin in his hand, he forced her to look up at him. "It will happen, I promise you. But not tonight." He brushed his fingers against her cheek. "You're too vulnerable, and there are still too many secrets between us. When we make love, Christina, there will be no more secrets."

# *Chapter 20*

When Christina awoke, there was none of the confusion or sudden, engulfing fear that she usually felt in a strange place. Instead there was a gentle rocking motion, and the muted sound of water lapping against the hull of the boat. She lay there for a moment, and as her senses cleared, she became aware of other things: the brisk coolness of the air in the cabin, and the permeating aroma of fresh-brewed coffee. She felt secure and at peace in a way that she hadn't felt in a long, long time.

Then she remembered the night before. As Ross had promised, he had left her alone. She lay by herself on the bunk. Yet no matter how hard she tried to tell herself that it was definitely for the best, and she'd been rash and unwise even to consider giving in to the desire she felt for him, the thought was far from reassuring.

The chilly air might have driven her deeper under the covers and the downy mattress, but the mouth-watering smell of coffee made it impossible. Clad only in a white T-shirt of Ross's that she had found in one of the built-in drawers, she slipped from the bunk. The mahogany floor beneath her bare feet was cold. She glanced out the starboard porthole glass. It was still gray outside; dawn had only barely begun to lighten the night sky. Pulling one of the blankets around her, she walked through to the galley.

All the comforts of home, she thought, admiring the small but efficiently constructed galley. A briskly bubbling coffee-pot sat on a propane burner. Looking for a coffee mug, she acquainted herself with the cupboards and cabinets especially built to accommodate the roll of a ship on the open sea. She smiled at the thought of a rain-slickered captain shouting to his first mate to "batten the hatches and lash down the yard-arm."

When she found the brown porcelain mugs, she filled one with steaming hot coffee, pulled the blanket around her more tightly, then precariously made her way up the low flight of steps. As she stepped out onto the deck, she was illuminated in the glow of light from the cabin below.

Ross stood behind the wheel, just past middeck. He smiled. "Good morning."

"Good morning," she answered hesitantly as she took a slow look around. The lights of the marina and the city glowed in the distance. A good breeze had come up, filling the jib sail and moving them steadily out into the Bay. After a moment she found her balance and walked toward the stern and Ross. "Where are we bound, captain?" she asked, slipping into a seafaring mood.

"I thought I'd take you out onto the Bay. The sunrise is spectacular out on the water."

She curled up among the cushions on the bench seat. Except for the soft glow of cabin lights and one cruising light out on the bow to enable other boats to see them, they were surrounded by darkness.

"Isn't it a bit dangerous in the dark?" she asked as she sipped her coffee.

Once more he smiled, in a warm, relaxed way that contrasted sharply with his usual air of toughness and cynicism. "Only if you don't know what you're doing. I was practically born on the water. I started sailing when I was five with a friend of my mother's who was something of an old reprobate but a magnificent sailor. Old Ned taught me well. I could sail this Bay blindfolded."

There was none of the wariness or tension that seemed such an innate part of him when he was at the office. He was different out here, completely relaxed, his expression almost boyishly happy as he looked at the mizzen and the billowing jib.

"Blindfolded?" she asked skeptically.

He laughed. "An exaggeration, perhaps. But it's really just a matter of feeling the wind and the water, and reading the stars. An accomplished sailor knows how to navigate by them. You should know." he added. "You used to sail with your cousins."

She shook her head. "I left most of the actual sailing to Steven. Then, after that disastrous episode when the Coast Guard had to rescue us, I was reluctant to sail."

"You haven't sailed since?"

She gave him a wary look, wondering if they were back to the same old questions concerning her identity again. She said carefully, "I had friends back east who sailed. I went out with them a couple of times. But the Atlantic is different from the Pacific."

"Yes, it is," he agreed. Then, as if to reassure her that they were still on a casual, less guarded footing, he asked, "How about some of that coffee?"

She rose and walked over to him, handing him the cup. His fingers brushed hers when he took the cup from her, and it was all she could do not to visibly react to the feel of his skin against hers.

"Would you like to try your hand at the wheel?" he asked.

"I don't know ... It's been a long time, and I've never handled a boat this size."

"I'll stay right here. I won't let you get in over your head."

She laughed. "That just might happen to both of us if you let me take over."

But she took the wheel, with Ross close behind her. Even through the thick blanket, she could feel the warmth of his body. His hands rested on hers until she became familiar with the weight and pull of the wheel.

"Hold her on course, due east into the sunrise," Ross instructed as he moved forward.

Panic tightened her fingers on the wheel. Then she watched as the mainsail rose high above the deck on the center mast, billowed loosely, then snapped and filled with air as Ross cranked the lines taut. When he was satisfied with the trim of the sail, he rejoined her. As his hands slid over hers once more, she felt her panic subside.

"I thought you said you could sail this thing by yourself?" she asked. "How would you manage a maneuver like that without a first mate?"

"Out on the open sea I rig the lines so that I can adjust them from the wheel. In port the maneuvering gets a little trickier. Usually I just fly the jib. It gives me enough power but doesn't make her unwieldy in a crowded harbor."

Christina turned her head to make herself heard over the rising wind. "I can't imagine spending months alone at sea."

Ross bent low to explain, his breath warming her ear and the side of her neck, making her tingle with remembered wants and needs. He said, "You get used to it. Civilization drives you crazy when you get back."

Desperate to put some distance between them, she stepped out of the circle of his arms. "I'll leave the navigation to you, and I'll keep to the galley. More coffee?"

"Yes, thanks. But you know, somehow you don't fit my image of a typical galley slave."

He caught a trace of her smile in the light from the cabin as she turned slightly to call back to him. "I could handle the job, all right. Just so long as there are places like Joe's in every port."

Then she disappeared through the hatch.

She made more coffee and dressed in the jeans she'd worn the night before. When she returned to the top deck, the sky was a softer, pearlescent gray, then gradually shifted to soft blue as dawn light spread across the Marin hills. They had tacked a steady course with the wind, cutting far out into the Bay, past Alcatraz Island, then turning into the wind on a far reach that took them past Angel Island. The spinnaker now ballooned out into the wind.

With all sails full, the *Resolute* was like a majestic bird, wings spread wide, gliding across the water. The water was choppy with the morning wind, but there was no pitch and shudder. Instead there was only a slow forward roll alternating with a gentle, upward thrust as the bow sliced through the waves with Ross's sure, experienced hands at the wheel.

Christina handed him a fresh cup of coffee. She had donned a windbreaker she found in the locker below, but it was still cold, and she hugged herself against the early dawn chill. Ross pulled her into the curve of his body, and she leaned against him, feeling warm and safe.

Standing there with the deck rolling gently, rhythmically beneath their feet, Christina sensed something akin to a strong, vibrant heartbeat, as if the *Resolute* were alive. She leaned back, savoring the warmth of Ross's body, and the exhilaration of the contrast of a chill wind at her face. She felt liberated, set free from the restrictions and problems of her normal life.

They sailed a steady course toward the Marin shoreline, watching the hills turn gray, then gold, then aflame with the rising sun. It was no longer dark. Now they had daylight to guide their course.

Christina held the wheel, as Ross lowered the jib and the mainsail. The *Resolute* slowed in the water, almost reluctantly. The water slapped sharply against the hull as the billowing spinnaker pulled them forward into the marina at Sausalito. Then the wind died, and they slipped slowly through the water.

Ross started the engine briefly, guiding them through the water to a bright orange and yellow buoy that bobbed just off the port bow. He gave Christina instructions to cut the engine on his signal, and then went forward while she guided the *Resolute* closer into the marina.

When the signal came, she shut down the engine and then cut the wheel hard to starboard. He quickly reappeared, released a lever, and lowered anchor. "That will keep us from drifting. Now, how about another cup of coffee?"

When she returned to the top deck several minutes later, two mugs in hand, the rich mahogany of the deck gleamed in the golden light of the sun as it rose over the distant hills. It was just after six o'clock. Ross was on the forward deck, tying down the sails and stowing lines, as meticulous and precise as he was in everything else.

She handed him the mug of coffee. They sat together on top of the forward hatch. Ross reclined, one leg thrust forward, the other bent at the knee, his arms loosely draped around her.

"You can feel the sunrise," he said with quiet appreciation.

She turned to look at him. "*Feel* it?"

"Of course. According to the ancient Chinese, we can feel everything around us."

"Is that anything like the 'Force'?" she joked.

He assumed a wounded expression. "You don't believe me."

"Well, let's just say that I'm not familiar with your theory. My appreciation of sunrises is limited to the purely visual."

As he pushed to his feet beside her, Ross said, "But sight is only one of our senses. Here, give me your hand." Extending his, he pulled her to her feet beside him."

"Close your eyes," he ordered. When she started to protest, he laid a finger gently against her lips. "Ssh. Close them."

She did as he asked. Then she felt the light pressure of his hands at her shoulders as he turned her around, so that she was facing him.

"Now tell me what you feel," he instructed.

She smiled, playing along with the game. "I feel the breeze off the water, and I feel the warmth of the sun."

"Very good. But that's only the surface of your feelings. You're capable of a great deal more."

She opened her eyes and gave him a suggestive look. "Is there supposed to be some hidden meaning in there somewhere?"

"Only what you want there to be, Chris." His voice was husky, intimate, beguiling.

Her lips parted slightly as she stared at him.

Then he took hold of her wrists. "Hold up your hands and press your palms against mine. Now close your eyes again."

She did as he asked. They stood on the deck of the *Resolute* in the early dawn, hands held before them, palms lightly touching. Then Ross drew his hands away. "Keep your hands where they are. See if you can sense when I bring my hands close to yours."

At first she failed miserably. When she thought Ross was close, she found nothing but air as she pushed with her hands. Opening her eyes, she shrugged. "I guess the 'Force' just isn't with me today."

"Let's try again," he urged. "This time, instead of trying to *guess* when my hands are close, I want you to *feel* it. Clear your senses of everything else, and concentrate on what you feel when we are touching. Then see if you can feel those same sensations just before they actually occur."

She smiled self-consciously. "I think you're trying to make a fool of me."

*"Never,"* he said in a voice that was unexpectedly tender. "Now try again. Remember, you must feel my energy. Sense when I am close."

This time she actually managed somehow to sense his closeness. Twice she pushed her hands out, her palms flattening against his.

Ross grinned. "That's a big improvement. You're learning to rely on senses other than sight. Now I'm going to move away from you. Keep your eyes closed. Let's see if you can sense when I come closer. Remember, it might be from any direction—either side, or even behind you."

"All right, Christina agreed, even though she felt a faint tremor of uneasiness as she closed her eyes. She took a deep breath and let her senses open up—touch, hearing, smell, even taste.

The sense of anticipation drew out until it was almost unbearable, and she was convinced he was playing games with her. She heard the water as it lapped against the hull of the boat, the cry of the birds overhead, the feel of the wind, and the taste of the moist salt air on her tongue. But nothing else.

Then she felt it, something so subtle she could describe it only as a barely perceptible change in the air around her. Eyes tightly closed, she turned around suddenly, arms outstretched. Her hand brushed his arm.

"Very good," Ross complimented her as he steadied her on the rolling deck. "How did you know I was there?"

"I don't now. I kept feeling for a change in the wind to indicate if you were coming from a certain direction. But the wind didn't change. It was something else." She finished hesitantly, "Perhaps feminine intuition."

He laughed. "It has nothing to do with intuition. Once you opened up your senses to the physical world around you, you were able to sense my presence. It's called *zanshin*."

She repeated thoughtfully, *"Zanshin."*

"Do you know anything about t'ai chi?" Ross asked.

"Only that it's one of the oriental martial arts."

He explained, "It's actually a physical exercise, in which you use *zanshin*. Here, I'll show you."

She shook her head. "I don't think I'd be very good at it. I've never been into karate or judo or that sort of thing."

"Just try it. Place your palms against mine." When she did so reluctantly, he explained, "In Chinese philosophy, t'ai chi is the union of two opposing forces of nature—the yang, which is the active aspect of nature, and the yin, which is the passive aspect. The tension between the active and the passive is what you feel in *zanshin*. There must be a balance between those two forces."

He pressed his palms against hers ever so lightly. "Two forces coming together and reaching a harmony that is stable but filled with energy."

She was acutely aware of the heat of his skin against hers.

He continued softly, "You feel that energy now. As I pull my hands away, the energy decreases. If I push more firmly," he demonstrated, "the energy increases. In both cases the balance is disrupted. It can be maintained in perfect harmony only if both forces of energy are equal."

His dark blue gaze was fastened intently on hers as he went on, "You must use *zanshin*, the awareness of *everything* that surrounds you, to sense when the balance is about to change—if I am about to pull my hands away . . ." He did so. "Or if I am about to apply more pressure." He pressed his hands more firmly against hers. "When you're ready to try it, simply push against my hands."

She pushed hard, and he said quickly, "Gently. This isn't a test of strength or power or control over another person. The purpose is to work together with your partner to keep your hands steady and in constant contact, while continuing to push and maintain the balance of energy. You anticipate and compensate for your partner's movements."

It had become a challenge. Christina took several deep breaths and tried to relax. She discovered she had a better sense of Ross's energy with her eyes closed. She began to anticipate changes in the pressure as he pushed, then withdrew.

Ross drew her into a series of hand movements, and gradually they began to move as one. Their hands touched lightly and moved together in a wide arc, then returned and moved into an arc in the opposite direction. She felt the energy, anticipated the changes, and moved at precisely the same time he did.

Then she opened her eyes and watched Ross as they made the perfectly matched movements, as if they were choreographed. It was an experience unlike anything she had ever known. Touching Ross, looking deep into his midnight blue eyes, saying nothing, yet feeling the energy that built inexorably between them.

Now the energy that only minutes earlier had seemed impossible to sense was transformed into something profoundly moving. Only their hands touched, yet it seemed as if the energy invaded every part of her, transformed into an intense heat that built with each movement into a heightened sensuality.

Suddenly Ross stopped and said in a husky voice, "You see, Chris, you can feel the energy—the perfect balance we create."

She looked at him and had a premonition of what could be between them—a coming together so complete, so intimate, that it would be unlike anything she had ever known before.

# Chapter 21

*S*he had never experienced anything even remotely like this with any man. It was frightening in its possibilities. Suddenly afraid, she withdrew her hands.

Ross sensed her fear and didn't press her. Instead he asked casually, "Hungry?"

She was absolutely starving. She laughed, feeling a powerful energy still humming along her nerve endings, searching for release. "I think I could even eat sardines this morning."

He grinned at her, with that engaging boyish expression that slipped under her defenses so easily. "I had something a little better than that in mind. Get ready. We're going ashore."

Christina quickly disappeared below desk. She pulled her hair into a ponytail, brushed her teeth, and applied fresh makeup. When she returned topside, Ross was lowering a small skiff into the water at the stern. They stepped down into the shallow boat, and he expertly rowed the short distance to the marina.

It wasn't even seven o'clock yet, but the marina office was already open. The attendant waved a greeting to Ross. They circled the office and found at least a dozen mopeds in several bright colors lined up against the back of the building. Ross swung a leg over a bright red one and held out his hand to her. Christina climbed on back, and the small engine sput-

tered to life. They turned out onto Bridgeway Boulevard.
Christina held on, her arms wrapped around Ross's waist as
they sped through the tiny, hilly oceanside community.

Her ponytail streamed back in the wind. The feeling of the
wind rushing at her recalled the same sensation she'd felt
aboard the *Resolute*—a sense of freedom, without a responsibility or a care in the world. The other sensation was even
more potent. *Ross*—the feel of his lean body beneath her
arms, the faint spiciness of his cologne that mingled with the
salty air and wind in a heady mixture.

She told herself she clung tightly to him only for safety's
sake. But she knew she held on to far more than that . . . For
the first time in a long while she felt wild, free, and breathless
with abandon.

They skirted Richardson's Bay, past the Sausalito Yacht
Club and the ferry terminal, then took a side street up a hill
away from the water. Below them Sausalito lay spread out in
the peace and quiet of early morning. Set among the tree-
studded hills of the Marin coastline, Sausalito was originally
a fishing community. Later, around the turn of the century, it
was transformed into a community of summerhouses in the
main village. By midcentury it was invaded by artists and
craftspeople seeking a suitable site for their bohemian life-
style. Small arts and crafts shops sprung up in the village, and
eventually it became fashionably eclectic. Christina loved the
laid-back, creative ambience.

Ross turned up a sharply winding driveway and then
stopped before a sprawling Spanish-style villa. He cut the motor to the moped. His hand covered hers as it rested on his
waist. Then he twined their fingers as he swung off the back
of the moped and pulled her with him. "Welcome to the Alta
Mira."

The Alta Mira hotel wrapped around the hillside, a mixture
of pale pink stucco walls and ornate red tile. Overhead, at the
second-story, a large terrace with an ornate wrought-iron railing jutted out from the building. Christina could just see the
rims of dozens of table umbrellas, their fringed borders ruffled by the breeze.

Ross said with a smile, "I promise, no sardines, unless you specifically request them."

They walked up the red tiled steps to the ornate entry, decorated with a magnificent sunburst made of hundreds of bright pink tiles that radiated from the center. Inside the lobby they were greeted by the front desk manager, who showed them through to the restaurant. Walls of glass opened out onto the terrace, with the Bay and San Francisco beyond. The view was breathtaking.

The head waiter seated them at a table out on the terrace. Christina let Ross order, reclining in the chair and turning her face to the rising sun to enjoy its warmth.

"What do you think?" Ross asked, as the waiter left with their breakfast order.

"I think this is absolute heaven," she murmured, eyes closed. "I could stay here forever and not move an inch. It's so peaceful." Then she opened her eyes and gazed out across the Bay to San Francisco. "Everything seems so far away— the city, all the problems."

"Do you regret your decision to come back to San Francisco?" he asked quietly.

The directness of the question startled her. Her gaze came back to his and held for several moments. "No," she finally answered. "It had to be done. I never thought it would be easy."

"But you didn't realize it would be this difficult?"

The waiter brought champagne, poured it for them, and then left.

"It's difficult in ways I hadn't expected," she said as she lifted her glass.

"In what ways?"

"You," she answered with complete honesty.

His mouth curved in a slow smile. "I've been called difficult before."

"I'm sure you have. Would you prefer I used another word?"

"You already have," he reminded her. "You referred to me as a pirate."

"My opinion about that hasn't changed," she teased.

"Well," he said, "I can see I'm going to have to work very hard to change your opinion of me, starting now." He raised his glass. "I propose a toast. To infinite possibilities."

She raised her glass. "Possibilities," she murmured. After taking a sip, she set her glass down and stared out at the Bay. Sailboats dotted the water, and the first Grayline ferry of the morning churned away from the terminal toward San Francisco.

Ross said, "This is probably as good a time as any for you to tell me your ideas for Fortune International."

Over breakfast she outlined the current status of the company, reemphasizing the need to withdraw the newer ships of the line from the Mediterranean and Persian Gulf areas.

"All right," Ross conceded. "That *is* a possibility. But as you well know, Katherine wants to expand the Mediterranean fleet. She's had me working on a specific plan for that."

Christina shook her head. "She isn't making the best decision for the future of the company. You know how volatile that area is."

Their discussion was all business now as Ross pointed out, "Merely cutting back on the Mediterranean operation may reduce the operating expenses for the older ships, but you have to confront the loss of revenues, as well, when you reduce your shipping capabilities."

"You don't reduce it, you merely change the focus," she explained. "Fortune International has a global network. That was my grandfather's goal after each of the two world wars, and he made it work." She turned over one of the elegant gold-embossed paper placemats and drew a layout of the entire world with all the Fortune markets.

"In the late sixties my father expanded those markets into the Mediterranean and Persian Gulf areas, which were rich in oil potential. Katherine supported the move, and it proved to be very lucrative. It is no longer lucrative."

She took a deep breath and went on. "I understand Katherine's reasons, but her thinking is shortsighted. It might be profitable to expand the Med fleet in the short term. But I'm convinced the high risk factor, because of the instability of the entire region, along with the rising costs of liability insurance just to protect our vessels, doesn't make sense or add up to long-term profits. The figures aren't there to support that sort of plan."

Ross was silent for a long time. When he spoke, she expected an argument.

"You're right, of course," he admitted without the slightest hesitation.

She was stunned. "You agree with me?"

"I concluded the very same thing a long time ago."

"Then why go forward with something that isn't feasible?" But she knew the answer even as she asked the question. "Katherine," she said quietly.

"She's determined to preserve the company as it was when Alexander, then Michael, ran it."

"Even though the markets and the world have changed, and it may mean financial ruin for the company?"

"Don't get me wrong. Katherine is a very strong, intelligent, astute woman. But the fact is, she has become isolated from the realities of what it's like to do business in a volatile atmosphere worldwide. She's never dealt with changing governments or shifting world markets. Neither has Richard. Your father was the only one who might possibly have had the experience to deal with the global changes taking place now."

"*I* could deal with it," Christina insisted, meeting his gaze squarely. "*I* control Fortune International now."

"Whatever you have in mind would mean going against Katherine."

"What is Katherine's goal?" she asked, already knowing the answer to that, as well.

"To preserve the company. You know that's why she was willing to acknowledge you as her granddaughter, to keep Richard from selling the company off."

"That's *my* goal, too. I'm simply proposing a different way of going about it."

"What exactly are you proposing?"

She took a slightly worn newspaper clipping from her purse and smoothed out the folds in it. She stared for several long moments at the image in the photograph, then handed it to Ross. As he read the article, she said just one word, "China."

He looked at her, then his eyes narrowed thoughtfully. Scanning the article, he asked, "Who is this Chen Li?"

The article was several months old. Christina had clipped it from the Boston paper in January. It profiled the newly appointed Minister of Economics of the People's Republic of China. "I knew him in college," Christina explained vaguely. "Except then I knew him as David Chen. He had family in the United States, and he was allowed to study in this country as part of a cultural exchange program. It was an offshoot of the strong diplomatic ties the Nixon administration established with the government of mainland China."

"And you think David Chen—Chen Li—might be a connection for Fortune International?"

She could tell that while Ross was skeptical, he was also intrigued by the possibilities of the plan. She explained, "His family is very well established within the Beijing government. I've been following the news that has trickled out since the Tiananmen student revolt."

Ross looked up. "How well did you know him?"

She chose her words carefully. "We had several classes together." She could see by the expression on his face, he wasn't satisfied with that answer. She went on, "In many ways we had a great deal in common. We were both on our own. We were both strangers in Boston. He was a good friend, when I needed one. He helped me through some very difficult times."

With a flash of remembered pain, Christina thought of the disapproval she and David had faced because of their interracial romance. His American relatives' anger when he told them of his relationship with Christina had torn him apart. But he cared for her too deeply, needed her too much, just as she needed him, to give way to the prejudice against them. Only David understood her alienation from other people; only she understood his loneliness so far from his roots. His love and gentleness had brought her back into the world of feelings, after years of being numb. He had taught her to trust again, and for that he would forever hold a special place in

her heart. Just as he had told her in that final letter that she
would always hold a special place in his.

"All right," Ross conceded. "Even if you were able to es-
tablish contact with Chen Li, what sort of a trade agreement
are you proposing?"

Over the next half hour she described what she had come
up with, explaining her theories about the emerging government in Beijing and recent government decisions regarding
the promotion of limited expansion of the free-enterprise system.

She said eagerly, "You know as well as I do that once they
open the door to free enterprise, it will be like opening the
floodgates. There is no way they can turn it back. The farmer
will want the best price for his crops, the factory worker will
want a fair wage. Mainland China is a market on the brink of
a trade explosion. The survival of its economy demands it."

He continued to listen intently as she explained, "The Ko-
reans and the Taiwanese have already changed the entire
scope of cheap labor. The Chinese leaders aren't naive. They
know they can have those revenues from labor to stimulate
their own economy. Remember, the Chinese are the original
economists."

"And in conclusion?" he prompted with an ironic smile
that suggested he already knew the answer.

She took a deep breath as she focused on the final point of
her argument. "There will be a massive movement of raw materials and piecework to factories for manufacture and assem-
bly, and then those finished goods must be transported to
market."

"And the company with shipping contracts in place when
that happens will become very wealthy," he finished for her.

She smiled. "Hamish Fortune did the very same thing one
hundred and fifty years ago. He built a fabulously successful
company on that foundation."

Without further comment Ross asked the waiter for their
check. He said to Christina, "Let's go for a ride."

He hadn't said one word of either approval or disapproval.
Doubt ate at her. She'd laid all her cards on the table, holding
back nothing. He'd said, "Trust me," and she had. But what

if he went against her and sided with Katherine? Could she possibly fight them both?

They walked down to the parking area. As they waited for the parking attendant to bring the moped around, Ross said, "We need to talk more about your ideas. Do you have a formal proposal drawn up for me to take a look at?"

She turned to him in surprise. Relief flooded through her. "I've got everything in my notes. Give me a day, and a good assistant, and I can put it together for you."

"All right," he agreed. "I'll have Bill help with whatever you need. He's the only person at the company who can be trusted. Then we can go over it."

He kept his tone neutral, as if this were no more important than any other business discussion they might have. But the truth was that Ross was dangerously close to crossing a Rubicon. He had a great deal to lose in siding with Christina. And not just in terms of his career.

As he swung astride the moped, he said, "You realize that if you're wrong, you could lose Katherine's support, the company—*everything.*"

It was a somber warning. He'd left the rest unsaid—that *he* might also lose everything if he sided with her.

"We can put this together," she responded confidently. As soon as she said the words, she realized it was the first time she'd talked in terms of "we" with him.

They left the Alta Mira, drove back down to the boulevard, and returned the way they had come in. Instead of turning off at the marina, however, Ross continued on around the small harbor. He pulled into Kappas Marina, a secluded inlet lined by slips on one side and houseboats tied up to pilings that jutted out from the water at intervals. It was an odd little community of water dwellers. One houseboat was shaped like an alpine A-frame, another was all redwood siding with a pitched roofline. Still another looked as if it had once been a paddle wheeler off the Sacramento Delta. A huge smokestack stood behind the wheelhouse, with the paddle wheel housed midship.

They were all moored securely. Some had window boxes spilling over with flowers, others had patio tables and chairs

and elaborate barbecues. All had small rowboats tied at the
docks for those occasional trips to the local market. It was
like a small floating city and seemed like a vagabond existence until Ross informed her of the prices of some of the
houseboats.

"It's not unusual for one of these places to cost several
hundred thousand dollars," he explained. "And then you have
all your amenities—mooring fees, water, and sewage treatment. That is unless, of course, you live like my friend Jack."
He pointed out into the harbor at what appeared to be a small
island composed of junk.

"Who is Jack?"

"You might say he was once my landlord," Ross's mouth
quirked into a smile. "I didn't have much money when I first
came to the area. Jack was working the commercial fishing
trade then. He'd sailed in and out of Hong Kong for years. He
reminded me of Old Ned, and we struck up an acquaintance.
He let me live with him for a while, and helped me restore
the *Resolute* after that world voyage. I returned the favor
when the local commission tried to pass restrictions against
houseboat owners."

"I wouldn't call that a houseboat," she remarked dryly.

"No? You haven't seen the inside yet," he quipped. "Come
on."

Christina considered the few people Ross had allowed close
to him—a college buddy whom he'd carried with him up the
corporate ladder, an old fisherman. She was seeing sides to
his personality that only a few short days earlier she would
never have dreamed existed. Did it mean he was beginning to
trust her?

Leaving the moped on the dock, they took a small dinghy
out to Jack's houseboat. Stepping onto the deck that surrounded it, Ross called out, "Ahoy, Jack!"

A moment later a deep, almost guttural voice boomed from
within, "Who the hell's botherin' me this early in the
mornin'!"

The man who flung open the door and stepped outside
seemed as big as a mountain. He was at least six and a half
feet tall, and close to three hundred pounds, with sparse gray

hair and a face baked by the sun for so many years that it looked like leather. His size and his fierce scowl were intimidating, to say the least, and Christina felt herself shrink back against Ross.

But the scowl turned to a broad grin the moment Jack saw Ross. "Ross, you young devil, where the hell you been keepin' yourself? I s'pose you've become such a high-muck-a-muck, you don't have time for your less fancy friends."

He gave Ross an affectionate bear hug that belied the tone of his words. To Christina's amazement Ross responded with equal affection. For a moment his air of cool reserve was gone, and she saw the human being he could be when he allowed himself.

Before Ross could speak, Jack turned to Christina. "And who's this pretty little lady?"

"Christina Fortune," Ross introduced, omitting any explanation of their relationship.

Clearly explanations weren't necessary, for Jack's eyes narrowed thoughtfully, and he said in a quieter voice, "I see. Well, now, come on inside, and I'll make some coffee."

As Christina stepped inside the houseboat, she was amazed to discover that it was much nicer than the exterior. So this was what Ross had meant when he'd said, "You haven't seen the inside yet." It was small, but compact, with built-in oak shelves and cupboards lining all four walls of the combination living room/kitchen/bedroom. Two brown and beige striped sleeper sofas faced each other on opposite sides of the room, with bolsters built in to the walls.

Noticing Christina's look of surprise, Jack chuckled. "It looks kinda spiffy compared to the outside, don't it?" He glanced at Ross. "This fella did it all himself, with his own hands."

Christina turned to Ross. "You did all this?"

Ross shrugged. "It wasn't that hard. I got a book on carpentry and simply followed the directions."

Jack grinned. "He told me we needed to fix up the place a bit. The next thing I know'd, it looked like somethin' out of one of them house magazines. Now then, I'll just get that coffee. You two make yourselves t'home."

They sat down together on one of the sofas. Behind it a large window faced the Bay.

"People pay millions of dollars for a view like this," Christina commented wryly.

"Jack has it for almost nothing. What do you suppose that means?"

"That money isn't important?"

"Oh, it's important. But it can't necessarily buy the most important things in life."

"That's a heretical attitude for the CEO of a powerful company."

"In some ways being a heretic has gotten me where I am."

Christina eyed him thoughtfully. "I'll bet it has."

Just then Jack returned with a scarred, stained wooden tray that looked as if it had seen service on many a voyage. On it were three white mugs, two of them slightly chipped, along with sugar and cream. The coffee looked and smelled delicious, rich and dark and steaming hot. It tasted just as good, and Christina sat there quietly, enjoying its taste and the stunning view.

She listened as Jack and Ross caught up with each other. Jack told of a long voyage he'd just made to the Mediterranean and back, and Ross described improvements he'd made to his boat. Watching them, the easy way they responded to each other despite their differences in age and financial position, their special camaraderie, reminded Christina of something, but she couldn't quite remember what.

Then it came to her. They treated each other as father and son. Jack beamed at Ross, with a father's special pride, as Ross described the work he'd done to the boat. Ross literally looked up to Jack, listening intently as Jack explained how to perform a particularly dangerous sailing maneuver. Father and son. What did it mean, Christina wondered, that Ross had this kind of relationship with Jack? What about Ross's real father? Once more she was reminded of how little she knew about him personally.

An hour later they all stood outside on the deck as Ross and Christina prepared to leave. Suddenly Ross remembered a book on ships that he'd meant to borrow from Jack. While he was inside, getting it, Jack said to Christina, "I'm glad he brought you here to meet me."

"I'm glad, too," she said sincerely.

"You're the first woman he's brought here." The look Jack gave her spoke volumes.

Taken aback, Christina had no idea how to respond.

Then Ross returned, and there was no opportunity to say anything more. As they got in the dinghy and rowed back to the dock, Christina watched Jack standing there, his gaze never leaving them.

Christina turned to Ross. "He's really something."

Ross smiled. "Yes. There's no one else like him."

"He obviously means a great deal to you."

Ross didn't quite meet her look. "Yes."

She thought of her own father, and how long it had been since she'd felt that bond. "It must be wonderful to have someone who's like a father to you, even if he isn't your real father."

Ross's expression hardened. "I learned a long time ago that blood relationships don't necessarily mean a bloody thing."

They dropped the moped back at the marina office. While Ross went inside, Christina stood on the dock, admiring the different sailboats.

Ross returned quickly. "We'll be driving back," he told her, an edge of urgency in his voice.

"Is something wrong?"

"There's been a bit of trouble at the office."

Christina walked back to the marina office with him, and waited as he made arrangements to leave the *Resolute* moored there until he could get back.

"What kind of trouble?" she asked as they got into the rental car Ross picked up at an agency down the street.

He frowned as he started the car and pulled out of the parking lot. "Bill didn't say, but he suggested we get back right away."

She thought first of Katherine—that something might have happened to her. A knot of apprehension tightened in her stomach, in spite of the fact that she'd told herself she didn't like Katherine very much. "Whatever it is, it must be serious," she said worriedly. "It's not like Bill to overreact."

Ross looked at her briefly as he swung the rental car out onto the highway interchange and caught Highway 101 to take them to the Golden Gate Bridge and back into the city. "No, it's not," he agreed.

It had taken them over two hours to sail from the city to Sausalito. The traffic was light this time of day going back into San Francisco. In less than half an hour they were pulling into the underground parking garage of Fortune Tower. They rode up the private elevator in silence.

As they stepped off on the eighteenth floor, where the corporate offices were, Christina knew why Bill hadn't elaborated about the trouble at the office. There was no way to describe what they found without making it sound like a major disaster.

The reception area looked normal, except for the presence of a uniformed policeman and two men in rumpled suits who were obviously plainclothes detectives. But a quick glance in the opposite direction toward the private offices down the hallway revealed the damage. It looked as if a madman had run amok, demolishing everything in sight. Papers were strewn all over, file cabinets overturned. And there was the vague smell of smoke. As they stepped out of the elevator and into the reception area, the carpet squished beneath their feet. There had obviously been a fire of some kind, although the damage in the offices didn't appear to be from fire. It had been enough however, to activate the overhead sprinkler system.

The door to Ross's office was open. The desk was strewn with papers. Several file drawers, recessed into the opposite wall, gaped open, and their contents were strewn across the carpet.

Christina hurried to her office next door. Stepping inside, she saw Bill, who looked exhausted and frazzled. "I'm glad you're back. Where's Ross?"

"Next door. What happened?"

He shook his head. "That's what the police are trying to figure out. The internal alarm system went off just after eleven o'clock last night. I didn't know about it until I stepped off the elevator this morning. No one bothered to call."

She frowned. "Didn't the alarm company notify the police and someone with the company?"

"They notified Richard. He just didn't bother to contact me, which is usually the case when Ross is away. It's a hell of a mess."

"Do they have any idea what set off the alarm system?"

"Obviously smoke." He cut past her on his way to find Ross.

Christina stepped aside as two policemen came into her office. Her office was an even bigger mess than Ross's. Drawers had been pulled from the desk, the contents dumped across the top. The telephone had been knocked off the corner. Everything was soaked with water.

Stepping out of her office to let the police do their work, she heard one of the officers say, "The way every drawer was ransacked, it was probably somebody looking for petty cash. The funny thing is, there was no sign of forced entry downstairs. Better have one of the guys check with the maintenance company that takes care of the building. Find out who was working last night."

Somehow Christina didn't believe this was the work of a thief. Aside from a small petty cash fund that the receptionist kept to pay for the pastries that was delivered each morning, there was no money in any of the offices. There were a few art objects in the main reception area, the conference room, and the executive offices, but nothing of great value. Most of the truly priceless artwork was either at Fortune Hill or at the ranch in Hawaii.

Still there were a few pieces of original artifacts that Hamish Fortune had brought from the Orient, but artifacts were often difficult to get rid of. They could easily be traced. And from what she could tell, none had been touched.

She'd once read that there was a hot underground market for office equipment, and there was a bounty of it on this floor: fax machines, telephones, several copy machines, and computer equipment, including the latest in laser printers in practically every office. Several pieces of office equipment had been vandalized, but as far as anyone could discern, nothing was missing. Whoever had vandalized the Fortune offices obviously wasn't after artwork or office equipment.

What were they after? she wondered.

She found Marie at her desk. The police had already finished checking out her workstation. She was blotting water from the top of her file cabinet.

"It'll take days to get this mess cleaned up," Marie moaned. "There's water in *everything*." For emphasis she held up a stack of soggy pink "While You Were Out" telephone messages. "At least the ink didn't run."

She handed them, along with some paper towels, to Christina. "You've got several messages. Someone by the name of Julie called a couple of times."

Christina looked up. "Did she say what she wanted?"

"No. Just that she needed to talk to you as soon as you got back. She said it was important."

"Are any of the phones working?"

"Use my phone," Marie offered. "It works. Good old Ma Bell. We could do an ad for television."

Christina slid behind the desk while Marie went in search of more paper towels. She quickly put through a call to Sonoma.

"Hi," Julie greeted her. "I understand you took the rest of the day and night off yesterday. Good for you. That was a pretty bad fall you took. I hope there weren't any lasting bruises."

"I'm fine." Christina decided not to tell Julie about the mess at the office. "When can you come into the city?"

"Well, actually that's part of the reason I called," Julie explained slowly. "I'm going to have to take a rain check until maybe the week after next. But I didn't want to wait until then to tell you." There was a slight hesitancy in Julie's voice.

"Tell me what?"

"The thing is, Chris, a couple of our workers found the gun that was fired yesterday in the vineyards."

"I hope you gave the owner a piece of your mind for me."

"That's just it—we don't know who it belongs to. The

sheriff's department is running some tests on it now. I don't
know much about guns, but one of my workers said the serial
numbers had been removed."

"Removed?"

"One of the sheriff's deputies explained that the numbers
are usually removed when a gun is stolen, or . . ." her voice
trailed off.

"Or what, Julie? Tell me."

"Or in a case where someone doesn't want the gun traced
back." There was an odd silence on the phone line. Then Julie
asked, "Has anything else unusual happened since you came
back to San Francisco?"

Christina felt a sick feeling of fear churn in her stomach.
"Why do you ask?" she managed to say.

"Well, you are an heiress now. There's a lot of baggage that
comes with that sort of thing. Believe me, I know. I've had to
adjust a little myself since Carlo and I got married."

Christina looked through the open door into her office. And
suddenly it was all crystal clear. Someone had torn up the
whole place, had even started a fire to set off the sprinkler
system, to try to cover up a search through her office. *She*
was the target.

When Christina didn't respond, Julie went on, "All right. It
was just a suggestion. I'm probably being melodramatic. I'll
give you a call when I know when I can get into the city.
Sooner, if I hear something from the sheriff's office on that
gun."

"Take care, Julie. I'll talk to you soon." As she hung up the
phone, she continued to stare into her office. The police were
removing their equipment.

"Can I go in there now?" she asked one of the detectives.

"Sure. We're finished." He shook his head. "It's a real
mess, huh? It's terrible what vandals can do."

Christina didn't reply. She was absolutely certain this
wasn't the work of vandals.

Just then Steven came into her office. She said coolly,
"Hello."

He looked around her office and laughed. "I don't suppose
there was much of a loss in here."

She ignored his deprecating remark. "What about your office?"

He shrugged. "It's a mess down there, too."

She looked up in surprise, and realized that for a moment she'd entertained the idea that Steven might be behind this. But surely he wouldn't have torn up his own office, as well. Unless he wanted to throw off suspicion.

He picked at a stack of soggy papers. "There's water everywhere in my office, too. Whoever it was, was real thorough." Letting the stack of papers plop back down onto her desk, he went on, "I sure hope you didn't have anything important in here, cousin."

She wondered what he meant by that remark. She glanced briefly at the computer terminal, then said, "No, nothing important."

Richard and Brian came into her office. Richard frowned when he saw Christina, but he didn't say a word to her.

Brian attempted to fill the sudden, awkward silence. "Christina, isn't this awful? I'm just glad you weren't working late last night. Whoever did this might have harmed you."

Before Christina could thank Brian for his concern, Richard said to Steven, "In spite of the mess, we need to meet this morning to go over the details of your Hong Kong trip."

Steven nodded. "I think they're through in the conference room. There didn't seem to be as much water damage in there." As he followed Richard and his father out of the office, he stopped and turned back to Christina. "Aunt Alicia will want to redecorate the entire floor now that she has a good excuse. You can help. It'll give you something useful to do."

She didn't bother responding to the put-down. She hadn't been aware Steven was returning to the Orient so soon. She wondered if Ross knew. Then her gaze came back to the computer on her desk.

She had remembered to cover it before she left to go up to Julie's place two days earlier. Water was puddled on top of the cover, but when she removed it, everything appeared to be dry underneath.

On an impulse she switched it on and accessed the base

program. The usual information came up on the screen, reassuring her there had been no damage. There was a quick scroll of the program ID numbers and licensing credits, and another quick flash of entries as the program scrolled to the current date and time. Something caught her attention, but was gone before she could read it.

She punched in the information to access the base program again, and watched carefully as it repeated all the opening data. As it approached the area of information she wanted, she keyed in a stop-screen command so that she could read the information slowly as it came up, like individual frames of film. When she found the information that had caught her attention, she read through it slowly. The last activity on the computer was logged on with yesterday's date, at 10:47 in the evening.

Someone had used her computer.

She'd been given a personal code key from the data processing department, and had been assured that all code keys were confidential. She had changed hers, anyway, to one that no one else could possibly know.

Now she entered that special code key and waited anxiously as the program she had been working on was brought up. The last date and time of activity were logged on within the opening frame of the program. She let out a slow sigh of relief—it was identical to the last time she had accessed the program herself. Whoever had used her computer hadn't been able to access any information.

She quickly made a backup of the program on a floppy disk, then erased the original program from the computer data base.

"What are you doing?"

She looked up to find Ross standing in the doorway of her office.

"I was just checking out the computer to see if it was damaged."

Somehow he sensed she wasn't telling the full truth, and he frowned.

Putting the disk in her purse, she looked around at the mess. Who would do this? *Who* had gone to all this trouble to mask what she was sure was the real objective—accessing her private computer files.

What had one of the police said? There was no sign of forced entry, and the main alarm system for the building hadn't gone off. Only the fire alarm system, activated by the sprinklers, had alerted authorities that something was wrong at Fortune Tower.

The police would question the maintenance crew that came in during the night. But Christina knew from the evenings she had worked late that the cleaning people were usually gone from the eighteenth floor by nine-thirty. That meant that who-ever had caused the damage had come in after the cleaning people, and had easy access to the building.

An ugly thought surfaced—it *might* very well have been Richard. He'd been furious at her for ruining his ploy with Loomis. Katherine's warning came back to her: *"Richard will do everything in his power to take control of the company."*

Did that include stealing if he thought she had come up with a feasible plan to stabilize the financially troubled com-pany?

If Richard had been behind this, what was Ross's role? To get her away and keep her occupied while Richard ransacked her files? Ross was the only one who would have been certain that she wouldn't be in the office late the night before. It would have been easy enough for her to let Richard know the coast was clear, so Richard could use his key to get into the building and try to access her computer files.

*No,* she told herself, unwilling to believe it. Surely every-thing that had happened between them over the last twelve hours couldn't have been a lie. And besides, she'd told him what her plans were for the company. He knew everything.

But what if he didn't believe she'd told him everything? She knew that, despite everything, he still didn't entirely trust her. Just as she didn't entirely trust him.

*"Being a heretic got me where I am,"* he had told her. Part of being a heretic was putting your own convictions ahead of all other considerations.

And that wasn't all. Julie's question about problems nagged at her. Surely there was no connection between the burglary and her accident at the Francetti Vineyards. Or had it been an accident? Would Richard actually try to kill her? And would Ross go along with him?

Then an even uglier possibility pushed its way into her thoughts—Ross had shown up at the Francetti Vineyards immediately after her accident.

"I'll take you back to Fortune Hill," Ross was saying impatiently. "Then I need to get back to Sausalito to get the boat."

She gathered up her purse and pushed past him as she hastily left the office. "It won't be necessary to take me to Fortune Hill. I won't be staying there. I've decided to take a place of my own."

She didn't look back as she headed for the elevators.

The one thing she had been determined to resist had happened. She had let down her guard and allowed herself to begin to care for Ross. Caring for him made her vulnerable.

# Chapter 22

Christina sat curled up in a corner of a plain white sofa, the only piece of furniture in the living room of her new apartment. Things had been so unsettled at the office the day before that she'd left early, and with Marie's help had found this apartment and a furniture rental company that would deliver immediately. After arranging for the bare necessities, she'd spent the night in Marie's spare bedroom, then moved in this morning.

From the moment she'd discovered that Richard had stolen her diary, she'd known she couldn't go back to Fortune Hill. She needed to put as much distance as possible between herself and him, as well as the rest of the family. And she needed her own space, where she didn't feel that she was constantly being watched.

Now she sat staring at the list she'd made in a notebook. The names were possible suspects in the vandalism.

*Richard—a strong probability.*

*Steven—he might very well have been in on it with Richard.*

*Andrew—he doesn't seem at all interested in the business. But it is his source of livelihood. Like all the members of the family, he has a great deal to lose financially because of me.*

*Jason—the same motive as Andrew. And perhaps an even*

*stronger one. He's barely acknowledged me, and clearly still has a tremendous amount of lingering anger about the past.*

*Diana—I can't see her sneaking into the building and doing such damage. But she might have forced Brian to do it. I don't think he would have wanted to, but he clearly has a hard time standing up to her.*

Christina hesitated, her pen poised in midair, then reluctantly added a final name:

*Ross—if he thought I was withholding information from him, he might very well have joined forces with Richard to get that information. I have no proof that he was being honest when he said he turned down Richard's offer to run the company together.*

She stopped, her expression grim. She didn't want to believe it could be Ross. Because that might very well mean that he was also responsible for what she now felt was an attempt on her life. Surely she couldn't feel toward him as she did if he was capable of such acts. But then, she realized unhappily, there were probably a great many women who were battered, even killed, by men they loved and trusted.

*Loved.* She'd never used that word in connection with Ross, even in her own most private thoughts. The possibility that she might be falling in love with him was staggering.

No, she couldn't think of that now. She had to concentrate on the crucial question—who might be trying to kill her?

She knew it would do no good to question Richard or Steven. They probably wouldn't even talk to her, let alone answer questions regarding their whereabouts at two critical times—the morning of her horseback ride at Julie's and last night, when someone broke into the office and tried to access her computer.

The same thing applied to Ross. He was far too careful, and too clever, to betray himself.

However, she could at least try to narrow down the list of suspects by checking on Diana, Brian, Andrew, and Jason. She thought hard for a moment, trying to come up with just the right approach. Then she picked up the phone and dialed Diana and Brian's number. When their housekeeper answered,

Christina asked for Brian. He would be easier to talk to than Diana, and, she hoped, less on his guard.

When he came on the phone, she said, "Uncle Brian, I'm sorry to take so long to get back to you, but I just learned that you left a message for me the other day—when I left the office early."

There was a pause, then Brian said hesitantly, "I don't recall trying to reach you. What day was that again?"

She told him, and he said, "No, I couldn't have called you that day. I was playing golf."

Christina made a mental note to check with the country club where Brian played, but she didn't expect anything to come of it. They wouldn't have paid particular attention to one member out of the hundreds who played there. But just because he might have an alibi, that didn't mean Diana did.

Christina replied in a tone of what she hoped sounded like genuine confusion, "Maybe Marie made a mistake, and meant to say Aunt Diana called."

"No . . . no, I doubt it. That's the day Diana's bridge club meets. They make a day of it, playing bridge, having lunch, and, I suspect, gossiping a lot."

"Well, I guess I'll just have to question Marie on Monday. Sorry to bother you."

"No bother. Are you all right, Christina?"

"Yes," she lied. "I'm fine."

When she hung up, she sat there, lost in thought for a long moment. While this information didn't automatically remove Diana and Brian from the list of suspects, it certainly made them seem unlikely. That left Andrew and Jason. Since neither of them ever called her, she couldn't use the same excuse with them.

Then she thought of something—the last time she'd talked to Andrew, at one of the social events Alicia had dragged her to, he'd invited her to come down to the shelter sometime and see what they were doing there. She could go down there now, and try somehow to turn the conversation to those two critical times.

•   •   •

An old three-story Victorian town house in the Mission district was the home of the Sansome Street Shelter. The buildings surrounding it were dilapidated, many of their windows broken and boarded up, the paint peeling. But the shelter was bright with new white paint, the clean, unbroken windows trimmed in soft yellow. A hand-lettered sign over the front door said simply, All Are Welcome.

Inside, Christina found a day-care center set up off to the right of the central hall and a rudimentary medical clinic on the left. While several children and a handful of adults waited to be treated at the clinic, a large group of children ranging in age from toddlers to adolescents played in the center under the watchful eye of a young volunteer. Through an open doorway Christina could hear the sounds of more children playing in the small yard behind the house.

The sound of the children's laughter was like that of any group of exuberant youngsters. But when Christina looked at them closely, she saw wary expressions in their eyes. They had learned a harsh lesson about life's insecurity far too early. It brought back painful memories.

Christina's heart ached for them. No matter what the outcome of her conversation with Andrew, she told herself, she would come back here someday and do whatever she could to help give these kids the kind of hope that a priest had once given her, a long time ago.

She asked a passing volunteer to direct her to Andrew, and was told he was upstairs in the general meeting room.

On the second floor she passed several doors, looking for one labeled Meeting Room. Most of the doors were closed, but a few were open. The rooms were all bedrooms, and most had at least one bunk bed set, along with a twin bed. Every room clearly was occupied. Sansome Street Shelter was, unfortunately, doing booming business.

At the end of the hall Christina looked through an open doorway and saw Andrew standing in front of a group of a half dozen men and women. Christina soon realized this was an initiation meeting.

Andrew was saying, ". . . and there are classes on health and nutrition and family relations. Alcoholics Anonymous and Narcotics Anonymous conduct meetings in this room every night at seven and nine, respectively."

He'd been glancing at a list in his hand. Now he looked up, smiled at the group, and finished, "For right now, this is your home. But we're going to help you find jobs or get job training and then get jobs. As soon as possible you'll be in homes of your own. Now lunch is about ready to be served, so why don't you all go down to the dining room."

As the group filed out, passing Christina, she saw expressions of tenuous hope on their faces. None of them wanted to be at the shelter. But for now it was a big improvement over where they'd been—living on the streets. It was a feeling she understood all too well.

Turning to follow them out, Andrew stopped when he saw her. She smiled tentatively. "I decided to take you up on your invitation. I hope this isn't a bad time."

He returned her smile. "No. This is fine. I'm free for a while."

He looked relaxed and happy in a way he hadn't been on the rare occasions when she'd seen him up till now. On those occasions he'd been surrounded by family—a family where he just didn't fit in.

She went back over what she knew of Andrew. He always kept his emotions locked up tightly inside. Only once had those emotions broken through. They were at their grandmother's estate at Fortune Hill, in Pacific Heights. Steven teased Andrew unmercifully all day about his shyness and a certain girl Andrew apparently liked. Steven goaded him, making cruel remarks that he wasn't capable of liking a girl, that perhaps he preferred boys.

He went on and on until suddenly the quiet, meek Andrew exploded in rage. He attacked Steven, giving him a bloody nose, busting his lip, trying to choke him. Christina thought he might actually have killed Steven if Jason hadn't pulled him off.

Afterward, to Andrew's frustration and humiliation, *he* was forced to apologize to Steven. It was the only time Christina had ever seen him like that, but it made her aware there was another side to her cousin—a violent, explosive side.

When he was still an altar boy, he became serious about attending seminary and training for the priesthood. But his mother adamantly refused to consider it. Now, twenty years later, he wore no neck-cloth or crucifix. He had obviously tried to find some meaning to his life by helping others here at this shelter. But Christina wondered if he had found true fulfillment.

She said slowly, "I think I can understand why this means so much more to you than the company does."

"Can you? The rest of the family can't."

"They probably never will. Does it matter?"

He hesitated, then said, "You're right, of course. It shouldn't matter. But they're capable of applying a great deal of pressure when they choose to."

"Is that why you didn't become a priest, as you wanted?"

He was startled. "You remember that?"

"Of course. I remember an argument you had with your mother over dinner on some holiday. I think it was Thanksgiving. We were all at Fortune Hill, and you ended up being sent home for being disrespectful."

He shook his head. "I can't believe it. You know, up until this moment I really didn't believe you were Christina."

"And now?"

He was honest with her. "Now . . . I'm not sure."

"Do you care whether or not I'm Christina?" she asked frankly.

He was silent for a moment, then he said, "No, I don't think I do. All I really care about is getting enough money out of the Fortune Foundation to keep this place going. Nothing else matters." He finished, "You know, people assume I'm trying to be some kind of saint or something. They talk about the sacrifices I'm making to spend my life here, with these people. They don't understand that I need this work as much as these people need to be helped. For years I was miserably unhappy and felt I had nothing to live for. Now . . . well, I get far more from the people here than I give."

Looking at him, with his expression of utter and complete frankness, Christina reached a sudden decision. "Andrew, I'll be honest with you. I came here for a reason."

He lifted an eyebrow quizzically. "Oh?"

"Will you tell me what you were doing last Tuesday morning?"

"Why?"

"Because I think someone tried to kill me then."

His expression of surprise and dismay seemed so genuine that she wanted desperately to believe he'd had nothing to do with it.

"I can't believe it," he began, then stopped. When he went on, his voice trembled, "My God, are you sure?"

She nodded.

"I know how furious everyone has been about all of this, but surely they wouldn't . . ." He shook his head. "I never would have thought any one of them would go that far."

"Who might go that far, Andrew?"

He stared at her. "I honestly don't know who it could have been. I can only hope you're wrong."

"I wish I were," she said heavily.

*"Christina."*

She whirled around at the sound of Jason's voice. The surprise in his voice was nothing compared to the vulnerable expression that caught at her heart. He was completely unprepared for running into her unexpectedly like this, and his feelings were all too transparent.

"Jase," she began, instinctively reaching out toward him.

"What are you doing here?" he demanded angrily.

Andrew interceded. "I invited her. She's just told me the most horrible news. Someone may have tried to kill her!"

For an instant Jason's anger was replaced by amazement, and an automatic concern for her. "What? Were you hurt?"

"I'm all right," she assured him. "Just a few scrapes and bruises from the fall. But I'm convinced that someone made an attempt on my life."

Jason had himself in hand now. "I don't believe you."

"Why not?"

"Why would anyone want to kill you?" he demanded.

She said carefully, "Perhaps someone doesn't believe I'm Christina."

He didn't respond. He knew perfectly well that she hadn't really been accepted by the other family members.

She went on, "I know my return has upset everyone. Including you, Jase. I'm so sorry. I never meant to hurt you."

His lips quivered, but he was a man now, not a sensitive teenager overwhelmed by raging emotions, and he didn't give way to tears. "If you never meant to hurt me, then why did you leave?"

Though her eyes were locked with Jason's, she felt Andrew watching her, waiting for her answer. "It had nothing to do with you," she began.

Jason interrupted her. "That isn't good enough! Maybe they're right, maybe you're not Christina!"

And with that he turned and ran from the room. She heard the sound of his feet racing down the stairs.

She started to go after him, but Andrew stopped her. "No, let him go, Chris. It nearly killed him when you left twenty years ago. Now that you're back, it's just as bad. He'll have to come to terms with it eventually, but it will take time."

She asked slowly, "Andrew . . . do you believe I'm Christina?"

He didn't answer for a long moment. Finally he said, "I don't know. The truth is, I'm not really sure it matters."

On Monday morning Ross charged into Christina's office. "Where the hell have you been for the past two days?" he demanded.

Marie rushed in just behind him and stood inside the doorway, glancing uncertainly from one to the other.

Momentarily ignoring him, Christina asked Marie, "Did you put through that call to Mr. Lo's office? It's important that I meet with him as soon as possible."

"I'll try again, Miss Fortune." She glanced hesitantly at Ross.

"It's all right, Marie. Thank you."

When Marie left, closing the door behind her, Christina braced herself for the confrontation she knew was coming.

"Well?" he demanded. "Where were you all weekend?"

She thought of several acerbic remarks, including, "It's

none of your damn business," but checked the impulse. "I needed some time to myself."

"Is that right?" Ross said, his voice sharp with disapproval. "Are you aware that Richard immediately informed Katherine that you had moved from Fortune Hill? My phone hasn't stopped ringing. She's been burning up the telephone lines between here and Hawaii for two days. She isn't happy about this."

"I didn't expect her to be." But Christina didn't want to argue with him about Katherine's standing order that she was to live at Fortune Hill. She went straight to the heart of the matter. "Have you discussed my proposal with her?"

"It's your plan; I thought I'd let you tell her," he said tightly. But he wasn't about to be deterred. "You weren't at the Hyatt."

"No, I wasn't."

He glared at her. "Damn it, I have a right to know where you were!"

Her head snapped up, her dark eyes blazing. "I stayed with Marie the first night. The next day I moved into an apartment. Now, is there anything else?"

"It wasn't necessary to find an apartment on your own. The company has several investment properties here in the city. I'm sure we could have found something for you."

"I wanted a place that was safe and secure, and not controlled by the company or the family," she informed him in an icy tone.

"What is that supposed to mean?"

"I think it's obvious. Katherine wanted me at Fortune Hill because it was easier to keep an eye on me there. Richard and I were both pawns, keeping each other in check in this little game she's playing. But I'm not playing by her rules any longer. From now on I play by my own rules."

The intercom buzzed, and she picked up the phone. It was Marie. "Mr. Lo says he can meet with you at ten o'clock."

Christina glanced at her watch. That gave her just a little less than half an hour to get to his office. "Tell him I'll be there." She hung up the phone and began putting files into her attaché case.

"Do you mind telling me what this is all about?"

"I've got a meeting with Phillip. You're welcome to come along." She snapped the case shut and started to walk past him.

He grabbed her arm. "I want some answers."

She yanked her arm away. "You'll get them at the meeting. And not before."

It was only a few blocks to Phillip Lo's office, but at this time of the morning the traffic was heavy, and it took the better part of twenty minutes to get there. She could sense Ross's anger and impatience as he guided the Jaguar through the heavy traffic.

The doubts she'd wrestled with since Friday afternoon resurfaced. She needed Ross to make her plans for the company succeed, but could she trust him? She *had* to know. She decided the best way to find out was to confront him head-on.

"The damage at the office was no simple burglary," she began.

He kept his eyes on the road, but she saw him tense.

"Do you have some sort of inside information the police aren't divulging to the rest of us?" he asked in a faintly mocking tone.

"No," she answered as he stopped for the next light. "But I found something the police didn't find."

"Such as?"

The light changed, and they shot across the intersection, darting through traffic. "My computer was tampered with," she said bluntly.

They reached the next intersection and were forced to stop as an approaching cable car made a left turn across traffic. While they waited, she glanced at Ross. He didn't meet her gaze. Instead he stared straight ahead. Finally he said in a low voice, "I think you'd better explain that."

Was it necessary? she wondered. Or was he aware of it, and simply wanting to find out how much *she* knew?

The cable car turned down the hill, and traffic cleared. Ross turned in the opposite direction and headed up Montgomery to Sacramento Street.

"When we got back into the office on Friday, I checked my

computer. Before I left, I had been working on the data we discussed. It was easier to update the information by computer with the overseas information as it came in."

"Some of the computers *were* damaged by water from the sprinkler system," he pointed out.

"Not mine. When I checked it, I discovered that someone had tried to access my files the night before."

A car pulled out of a curbside parking space just down the street from Phillip Lo's offices. Ross swung sharply into the space and turned off the engine.

She looked briefly at him before getting out. "The time logged onto the computer was just prior to the time the fire department was notified that the sprinkler system had been activated."

Ross got out and locked the car. "Go on," he snapped.

As they walked to Lo's office, she continued, "There was no burglary. The offices weren't broken into, someone simply walked in and bypassed the security system—someone who had a key."

"You think the vandalism and that small fire in your office were meant to cover up what they were really after—your plans to solve the company's financial crisis."

She nodded.

"Did they get it?"

She turned and confronted him on the sidewalk in front of Lo's office. "*You* tell me."

His eyes were completely void of all emotion as he met her gaze. "Is that an accusation?"

"I need to know the truth."

"I wasn't in the office Thursday night. I was aboard the *Resolute* with you."

"Yes, you were aboard. But we both know how easy it is to get something done. All you have to do is pick up a telephone and tell someone—perhaps Richard—that I'm safely out of the way."

Ross grabbed her by the arm and pulled her out of the stream of sidewalk traffic. His face was very near hers, his voice hard with barely controlled fury.

"I don't operate that way," he spat out. "If I want something, I go after it myself—aboveboard, everything out in the open. I don't play games, and I don't screw up. I'm perfectly aware that burglary was a farce. *Somebody* screwed up, but it wasn't me."

He let go of her arm. "If I were going to fight you for control of Fortune International, I wouldn't try to hide it. But I wouldn't do it, because it would mean going against Katherine."

Her anger was laced with sarcasm. "That's right, and as we both know, you're completely loyal to her."

"That's right!" he said without hesitation. "And my first and only goal is the survival of this company."

*So you can take it over eventually?* she wondered. Aloud, she said, "I find that kind of loyalty just a little difficult to understand."

"I'm sure you do have a difficult time understanding loyalty," he said, "since you ran away from your family twenty years ago."

"I had my reasons!" she responded in a voice choked with emotion.

"And I have mine," he replied. "And for now you're going to have to trust me, because the bottom line, Miss Fortune, is that you need me to help you pull this off. You don't have any other choice but to trust me." He walked past her to the entrance of Phillip Lo's law offices, grabbed the door and flung it open. "Now let's find out what is so urgent that you have to meet with Phillip this morning."

She sensed instinctively that everything he said was true. Ross wouldn't have screwed up. If he thought she had stored secret information in her computer, he would have found a way to get it, instead of walking away empty-handed.

She'd spent an entire weekend torn with indecision, wondering if she could trust him. Now she reluctantly faced the terrible truth—she might never be certain. Reaching inside the attaché case, she pulled out a fax memo and handed it to him.

He read it as they stepped into the office entry.

When the downstairs receptionist had greeted them and sent them on their way in the elevator, Ross looked up at Christina. "How did you get hold of this?"

"It came in from London last night. You didn't know about it?"

He shook his head. "I was busy trying to find you." He reread it, then shoved it back at her, his expression grim.

"This trouble in the Persian Gulf makes my proposal all the more imperative," she pointed out.

Ross agreed. "Katherine will have to be informed. But even with this information, we're going to have our hands full convincing her we're right."

She was stunned. "Then you agree we should do it?"

"These new hostilities in the Gulf put everything in a different light. But once a decision is made, we'll have to act fast. At best it will take us several days to get all our ships out of the area."

She agreed. "Bill assured me we can do it within forty-eight hours."

"I see you've already been checking out the possibilities." His expression softened, and for a moment she was reminded of their time alone aboard the *Resolute* in Sausalito. He went on, "I take it this meeting with Phillip has something to do with your plan."

"I'd like to do this *with* Katherine's support, instead of fighting her all the way. If we can convince Phillip that the plan has merit, he may be able to persuade her to go along with it."

"He could just as easily refuse," Ross pointed out as they arrived at the second floor. "What are you prepared to do if he can't be persuaded?"

Her expression was fiercely determined. "I'm prepared to do whatever is necessary."

They stepped into the reception area and were quickly shown into Phillip's private office. She caught a glimpse of her cousin Jason through the door of one of the adjacent offices. She'd forgotten that Jason worked for Phillip.

Phillip greeted them in his quiet, impassive manner. "Katherine is very upset," he said as his secretary brought them tea. "She is concerned about this decision of yours to move from Fortune Hill."

Christina faced Phillip. "It was necessary. I don't feel comfortable there. It's not my home, it never was. But I came to speak to you about another matter that's far more urgent."

For the next hour Christina explained all the information she had put together, and the threat to the company because of the latest crisis in the Middle East.

"It's an extremely volatile situation," she concluded. "If we act quickly, we can remove most of our ships from potential danger. It may be weeks or months before that political situation stabilizes."

"And what do you propose to do with all those tankers?" he asked.

"The newer ones with double hulls will be transferred to domestic service. Ever since the Exxon *Valdez* disaster, the government has been pressing for tighter controls and double-hull construction for all domestic oil tankers. We already have a tentative commitment from two independent companies to haul their oil."

"And what do you propose to do with the proceeds from the sale of the older tankers as scrap metal?"

"Half the proceeds will go toward reducing the company's overall debt structure. The estimated figures are in the proposal."

She hesitated. This next part was where she would undoubtedly encounter opposition. "And I propose the other half be funneled into expansion."

His expression revealed nothing of the deep reservations he must be feeling about such a risky proposal. He said quietly, "The company is in the difficult position it is in today because of speculative expansion."

"There is nothing speculative about my proposal."

His dark eyes measured her carefully. "Please explain."

"I propose that we expand Fortune Shipping in the market where the company began—mainland China. I've outlined a proposal. It's also included in the report."

Phillip stared at her thoughtfully. It was a long time before he finally spoke. "Does Katherine know of this plan?"

Christina glanced at Ross. He stood at the window, listening quietly. It was reminiscent of that day when she had first come here with the jade pendant. He smiled encouragingly, and she turned back to Phillip. "No, I haven't spoken to her yet. I wanted to discuss it with you first."

A knowing smile spread across Phillip's face, deepening the lines. "I see. And you thought perhaps to convince me of the wisdom of your plan with the hope that I might be able to persuade Katherine to agree to it."

Christina knew he was testing her, just as he had weeks earlier. Leaning toward him, she said in an urgent tone, "The bottom line is that the company is in financial trouble. It's loaded down with a heavy debt structure, and a portion of the fleet is in excess of thirty years old. Ten years ago Katherine's plan to expand in the Middle East had great merit, but the fact is that she has isolated herself from the current world situation."

She went on, "We have also received notice that Lloyd's of London is increasing insurance costs by seven percent to underwrite our ships as long as we sail in the Persian Gulf area. We need to think of other possibilities. I would like to have Katherine's approval, but I will move ahead without it. The company's survival depends on it."

He nodded with complete understanding. "So, you now wish to exercise the full extent of the power of your inheritance."

"I've made an accurate analysis of the situation. Ross concurs with it."

Phillip's gaze briefly shifted to Ross, before returning to Christina. "It's not a new concept," he admitted. "The Mediterranean and Persian Gulf fleets have accounted for our highest costs and biggest losses over the past ten years. In spite of the higher prices for crude oil, we continue to lose money. I've been arguing with Katherine over it for years."

Christina was stunned. So Phillip had been trying to do the very same thing himself.

"Do you have up-to-the-minute information about the crisis in the Gulf?" Phillip asked.

She handed him the fax and several newspaper clippings. "This came in from the London shipping office overnight, and these articles are from today's paper. By this afternoon the State Department will make the announcement that several Persian Gulf ports have already been closed off. Any ships caught in areas close to the hostilities are in danger of being sunk."

Phillip rose and walked to the windows that faced out onto Chinatown and the street below. He stood near Ross, his hands clasped behind his back and his expression thoughtful as he stared out the windows.

"Your plan is not without precedent," he said without looking at her. "Alexander Fortune was the first to resume shipping to the Chinese mainland after the two world wars. Michael Fortune also envisioned such an expansion." He sighed. "But the times were not right politically. The government of mainland China was not amenable to opening its doors to the Western world." He finished, "But then, everything changes over time."

He turned toward Ross. "I would like to know your feelings on this."

She held her breath. This was the moment of truth. She needed Ross to pull this off. Without his support she would never be able to convince Phillip of her plan. As she watched him now, silence filled the room.

Ross faced Phillip, his expression sober, his hands shoved into his trouser pockets. Finally he said, "It could work."

"I sense some hesitation," Phillip Lo commented.

Ross looked briefly at Christina, then back at Phillip. "There are several key elements that must come into play. Christina already has a tentative commitment for the purchase of fourteen of the oldest ships out of that fleet. We would have to notify London immediately to get the rest of the fleet out of the area. Depending on whether they've off-loaded cargo or not, it could take several days. It won't be easy. And then there is the matter of establishing contact with the right people within the Beijing government. That entire situation is unstable."

"No more unstable than the Middle East," Christina interjected. "And the Chinese government is extremely motivated to consider our proposal in view of the latest trade agreements with our country. Economically they need this."

Phillip nodded. "Everything you say is true. But the wheels

of progress turn very slowly in the Far East. Ross knows this. It is not like doing business in the Western world."

"I'm aware of that," Christina argued. "I know someone who may be able to help us. A man named Chen Li. We knew each other well when we were students together in Boston."

Ross gave her a sharply inquisitive look, but she ignored him.

We knew each other very well, indeed, she thought with a feeling of both love and loss that was bittersweet.

*"There is nothing I wouldn't do for you,"* he had said as they walked the quiet path along the Charles River for the last time. *"If ever you need me—even though I'm on the other side of the world . . ."* The rest of his words were lost in their last kiss.

Now she did need him, halfway around the world, and she had no doubt that he would answer.

"I have heard of him," Lo said. "He is very powerful within the government."

He paused, then turned back to Ross. "You understand what it will mean to defy Katherine in this way. Christina is willing to risk a great deal. Are you?"

Ross looked at Christina. Keeping his gaze on hers, he said in a quiet but confident voice, "Yes, I am."

Again there was a lengthy silence. Finally Phillip said, "I will need time to consider your plan."

She started to protest that they didn't have a great deal of time, then stopped. It wouldn't do any good to pressure him. Thanking him for his time, she left the portfolio of information on his desk, and she and Ross turned to leave.

"Are you aware that Richard has been meeting for some time with several members of the Pacific Rim Cartel?" Phillip asked.

"Yes, I'm aware of it," she told him. "I'm also aware he hasn't been able to put anything together."

Phillip smiled knowingly. "In the Orient honor is everything. Alexander Fortune understood this. Michael Fortune also understood it. It is the reason they were able to expand the business into Hong Kong and the Pacific Rim. There is no place for a man who has no honor."

He left the obvious implication about Richard unspoken.

She said slowly, "Thank you, Mr. Lo. I will remember that."

Over the next two days Christina and Ross had several more meetings with Phillip. Twice she ran into Jason. He was a junior partner in the law firm, specializing in corporate law. They exchanged polite but cool greetings. More than once it seemed that he wanted to say something to her, then decided against it.

Apparently Phillip trusted Jason completely, for he asked Jason to sit in on the meetings. But Christina's own feelings were still shadowed by the past.

A pretty young Chinese woman also sat in on the meetings. She had joined the firm three years ago as the first female associate, and specialized in international law. Her name was Leann Shiu, and Christina liked her immediately. Born in mainland China, Leann had an excellent grasp of the political realities of the country.

Christina and Ross were leaving Phillip's office Wednesday morning when he returned to discuss something briefly with Phillip. Leann stopped Christina in the outer office. "Your plan has a great deal of merit, Miss Fortune."

Christina was a little surprised that Leann was so outspoken when her boss, Phillip, still refused to commit himself. She smiled. "Thank you."

"You're very serious about this, aren't you?" Leann asked.

"Yes, I am."

Leann spoke frankly. "There are many who still have their doubts that you are Christina Fortune."

"I'm aware of that."

"I didn't want to believe it," Leann confessed.

"I don't understand. Why should it matter to you?"

"I know I shouldn't say this. I have no right." Again Leann hesitated. "It's completely unprofessional, but . . ."

"What is it?"

"Jason," she finally said. The expression on her face conveyed her feelings all too clearly. "Your coming back has affected him very deeply."

"I see." Looking back on it, Christina realized she should have noticed the special feeling that existed between Leann and Jason. She'd caught an occasional glimpse of an intimate smile, the touch of a hand. It was obvious their relationship was far more than merely a professional one.

She wondered how much Jason had told Leann about what had happened twenty years ago. Leann looked as uncomfortable as Christina felt. "Would it be possible for us to meet and talk?" Leann asked.

"I don't think that would be right . . ."

*"Please,"* Leann begged. "I know there's no reason why you should, but it would mean a great deal to me . . . and to Jason."

Christina saw Leann's eyes fill with sudden tears. She wondered what it must have cost Leann's pride to come to her like this.

"All right," she agreed reluctantly, wondering if she was making a big mistake. Ross had returned and was waiting for her. "How about meeting for a drink soon?" she suggested to Leann. "Perhaps at the Washington Street Bar and Grill."

Leann took her hand. "Thank you."

"What was that all about?" Ross asked later, after they'd left Phillip's office.

"Oh, just the girls getting together for a drink," she said casually as they got in his car. Changing the subject, she asked, "Did Phillip give you an indication when he would let us know if he'll support our proposal?"

"No. But remember, the philosophy of the Far East is very different from Western philosophy. They believe in taking their time."

"Time is the one thing we don't have," she pointed out impatiently. "And besides, Phillip *is* an American."

Ross smiled dryly. "But first and most important, he's Chinese. Remember that."

Richard was waiting for them when they returned to her office. She was surprised to see him. He'd barely acknowledged her since the scene with Loomis. But he had done as Ross ordered and returned the diary to her.

She wondered again if Richard had anything to do with the

"burglary." There had been no arrests, and at this point the
police admitted that none were likely. He'd fired the maintenance company, anyway, leaving everyone to assume he considered it to be the maintenance crew's fault. His manner as
they went into her office together was relaxed and amiable.
She was immediately wary.

"You two have certainly been busy the past few days," he
remarked smoothly. "Tell me, how is Phillip?"

Christina looked at Ross. His expression betrayed nothing.
"He's very busy," Ross said. "There's a great deal of
paperwork to take care of with the inheritance."

"Ah, yes, the inheritance," Richard said absently. Then he
added almost as an afterthought, "By the way, I've put together a meeting on Monday with the Pacific Rim group. You
did say you wanted to be included in all meetings. They want
a firm commitment from us on the new contracts."

Ross didn't look at Christina or give even so much as the
slightest indication that there was anything amiss. "Don't you
think that is a bit premature? We have some time left on the
old contracts, and Christina will need time to acquaint herself
with them."

Richard turned to Christina. His tone was condescending.
"Of course you might like to participate in the meeting."

"I intend to be present at *all* meetings that have anything to
do with this company." She met Richard's gaze evenly. "And
in the future, as acting President and majority stockholder, I
want all meetings cleared through me first."

Richard's expression changed subtly. His eyes were cool as
he regarded her with thinly disguised disdain. "I am still
Chairman of the Board, and I've always set these meetings."

"From now on I'm taking an active role. I appreciate your
position, but in the future I want to know about every contact,
meeting, or negotiation made on behalf of this company."

Richard's expression remained calm, almost amused, as he
commented, "That sounds almost like a threat, Christina."

Inwardly her stomach tightened. Outwardly she remained
calm, perfectly controlled, aware that anything else would be
perceived as weakness. "This company has suffered the last

ten years because of a battle for control. That stops *now*. Legally I'm in control, and I intend to exercise that control."

Richard's smile remained in place. "You might find it's a bit more than you're prepared to take on."

She arched a delicate brow. "Is *that* a threat?"

His smile deepened as he crossed the office to leave. He stopped at the door, his hand resting on the doorknob. "I never make threats." Then he added, "Oh, and I'm certain you'll let me know about all the meetings *you* schedule, as well."

After he left, Christina looked at Ross. "Do you think he knows about the proposal we submitted to Phillip?"

"Richard always makes it his business to know everything that has anything to do with the company. Don't underestimate him, Chris. He's managed to thwart many of Katherine's efforts in the past, in spite of the fact that she was in charge."

Looking at Ross, she realized that he was the only person on her side. *If* he really was on her side. Again she wondered if she could trust him. But there was no way of knowing.

# Chapter 23

She got the call a little after three o'clock in the morning. Her voice was slightly husky from sleep, and it took a moment for her thoughts to collect. She'd been up half the night going over all the information she'd put together to make certain she had considered all aspects of the proposal she'd given to Phillip. She didn't want any flaws to mar it. Too much was at stake.

"Are you awake?"

It was Ross. His voice was deep, with that hint of an English accent that slipped around her sleep-dulled senses.

She answered his question irritably. "I'm awake now."

"One of our ships has been fired on in the Persian Gulf."

She sat up in bed—it was one of only two pieces of furniture in the otherwise empty apartment. She forced back the mind-numbing fatigue. "What happened?"

"She was dry, just putting into Bubiyan Island in the Gulf to take on oil. The first reports we have say she took several rounds of shells from a gunboat patrol."

Christina shoved her fingers back through her disheveled hair. She squeezed her eyes shut. "Oh, God," she whispered. Then, urgently, "What about the crew?"

"We don't know. There were other vessels nearby, but our reports are real thin at this point."

She said in a determined voice, "We have to move fast. I'm going down to the office."

She left the bed and went in search of clothes, with the portable phone propped on her shoulder.

Ross said, "I'll pick you up; it's on my way."

Before she could object or think to give him the address, he had clicked off. Then she realized it probably wasn't necessary. By now he undoubtedly knew her address, the way he knew just about everything else about her.

Twenty minutes later his call came through from the security entrance downstairs. She buzzed him through and was just opening the door as he came up the single flight of stairs. He glanced past her into the apartment.

"Your taste in interior furnishings is rather Spartan."

"It's called Easy Maintenance—a sofa and a bed." Then she was serious once more. "Are there any new reports?"

He shook his head. "I sent Bill to the office straightaway. He's monitoring all overseas reports. He should have something more for us when we get there."

The streets were nearly deserted at that time of the morning, slicked down by the thick mist that clung to everything. Unencumbered by traffic Ross made the ten-minute drive in less than five. He pulled into the first-level garage and parked beside the private elevator that bypassed all the lower floors. Bill's white Fiat convertible was parked nearby.

Bill greeted them as they stepped out onto the eighteenth floor. His expression was grim. "We lost the *Fortune Crest*. We don't have anything accurate on the crew yet, but it appears most of them got off and were picked up by other ships in the area. It could be days before we know for certain about casualties."

*"Most of them?"* Christina repeated, her throat tightening with a mixture of sadness and anger.

"What else?" Ross asked as they quickly walked to the telex room. The overseas telex was transmitting another message. Several more had come through on the fax.

Bill explained, "As far as anyone can discern, the attack was unprovoked. The captain had received his clearance to on-load crude oil at Bubiyan Island. Things have been tense over there, but everyone had been assured there would be no intereference in port activities."

"Tell that to the families of the men on that ship," Christina said grimly. "What were the statistics on the *Fortune Crest*?"

Bill answered, "She was eighteen years old, single-hulled, registry out of Hong Kong, with a standard crew of fifty-five men."

"How soon can we contact the captains of each of the ships in the area?"

Before Bill could answer, Ross added, "How many do we have at sea? How many in port? And where?"

Bill looked exhausted and harried. "They're spread all over. I have the docking schedules in my office."

Ross said, "Get them." Then he turned to Christina. "Even in the age of satellite communications and computers, it could take several hours to notify all of them to get the hell out of there."

"Then we'd better get started now."

Later, in her office, Christina went over a printout that contained the ports of call for all Fortune ships in the Persian Gulf area. She looked at Ross. There was no time to consult Phillip Lo, or Katherine. A decision had to be made now. The Persian Gulf was half a world away. They had to act quickly before there were any more losses.

Without hesitation she told Bill, "We're pulling all Fortune ships out of the Persian Gulf. We need to send the necessary orders to each of the captains of those ships right away, and get clearances for alternative ports of call."

Bill stared at Christina and Ross in dismay. "Who's giving the authority on this?"

Before Ross could respond, Christina said defiantly, "*I* am. It's my company."

"That's the last telex to London," Bill announced as he came out of Ross's office.

There was a series of faint beeps, then the solid tone from the satellite linkup of the overseas phone connection. The operator came back on and asked if their transmission was completed. Bill looked at Ross, who nodded.

"That will be all," Bill said into the speakerphone, and then disconnected the call line.

The office was silent. It was almost noon, and the three of them had been on the telex for hours, sending overseas messages to every Fortune ship in the Persian Gulf and the Mediterranean. Christina stood at the bank of windows at the back of Ross's office, considering the full impact of the decision she'd made, and the action she'd taken. There was no going back.

Until now she'd followed Katherine's orders and hadn't put her claim to the inheritance, and control of Fortune International, on the line. For the most part she'd behaved as the figurehead Katherine intended her to be. But she was unable to go blindly along with Katherine's decisions when she knew those decisions might well mean the loss of life and the ruin of the company.

Her fierce sense of loyalty toward the company, the depth of her concern for its welfare, surprised her. She'd come here for one main purpose—to fulfill a promise, finally to see justice done for a twenty-year-old act of violence. Neither the money nor control of the company had mattered anywhere near as much. She felt little sense of loyalty to the current members of the Fortune family. Part of her felt that it would serve them right if the company that was their source of wealth and power and social position came crashing down around their well-heeled feet. But Fortune International carried her name, too.

Now, thinking of Katherine and the desperate bargain she had made to save the company, Christina felt a new commitment. She couldn't bear to see Katherine's life end with the destruction of the company that meant so much to her grandmother—that was coming to mean so much to her.

Ross came to stand beside her. He said quietly, "You've taken a tremendous risk. Katherine will be furious. She'll almost certainly retract her recognition of you as Christina."

She nodded. "I know."

Curiosity glinted in those midnight blue eyes. "It would have been far simpler to take the money and do as you were told."

Her smile held a hint of irony. "I've never been very good

at doing what I'm told." She looked at him intently. "I suspect you have the same problem. Why else would you be in this with me?"

He simply stared at her for a long moment. Finally he answered, "I'm not entirely certain."

The admission was wrung from him unwillingly. Christina could tell that he was a man who always needed to be sure of himself and his motivation. Self-interest would always guide that motivation. Or at least it had until now. He was taking every bit as big a risk as she was. And she didn't think it was entirely out of concern for the survival of Fortune International.

The thought that he might actually be taking her side out of concern for her seemed impossible to believe.

Suddenly she felt a need to lighten the atmosphere between them. "Well, someone has to stop Richard."

Ross frowned. "Yes. But when he realizes you're effectively taking control of the company, he'll do everything in his power to undermine you. He'll stop at nothing."

Christina's voice was tight as she responded, "I've had some experience as a street fighter myself." She sighed heavily. "At any rate there's no turning back now."

"No," Ross repeated, "there's no turning back."

She faced both Bill and Ross. "Phillip Lo will have to be told immediately."

Ross nodded agreement. He said to Bill, "Put in the call to his office yourself. Use your private line, and emphasize to his secretary that it can't wait."

"What if he wants to know what it's about?" Bill asked.

"Tell him we'll explain everything when we get to his office."

When Bill had left, Ross said, "It appears we'll be taking the company in a new direction a bit sooner than expected."

"Yes. We have no choice now but to pursue the China route."

The nervous tension Christina had felt during the last few hours dissolved, replaced by an almost childlike enthusiasm. She went on, "It'll be the way it was in the beginning, when Hamish Fortune sailed with his first cargoes of sandalwood one hundred and fifty years ago. We *can* make this work. Oh,

Ross, we have to make it work, or there may be no Fortune International."

He gave her a long, penetrating look. "You care deeply about this company, don't you?"

She hesitated, then said, "Yes. I do."

"Why?"

"I suppose because . . . I finally feel connected to it, in a way I didn't before."

Bill burst into the office, shattering the silence that had followed her words. "The meeting is all set," he announced. "Mr. Lo said he would wait for both of you in his office." When neither one of them responded immediately, he looked from one to the other. "That's all right, isn't it?"

"Yes, of course," Ross responded. "Thanks, Bill. And remember, not a word of this to anyone. We have to choose just the right time to make the announcement."

"I understand." Then Bill asked, "Do you want me to stay here and monitor any incoming messages until you get back?"

Christina answered, "Yes. That's a good idea. If anything critical comes in, you know where to reach us."

Bill nodded. "You got it. I'll just order lunch in and sit tight until you get back."

She grabbed her purse and attaché case with the telex they'd received in the middle of the night, along with several others on the status of the *Fortune Crest*. She squeezed Bill's hand. "Thanks for all your help."

He gave her a big smile. "Actually I wouldn't miss this for the world. When the lid blows off everything around here, it's gonna get pretty exciting. Besides, I'd like to see you pull this off."

Ross picked up his jacket from where it lay across the back of a chair, hooked one finger in the collar, and swung it over his shoulder. "Call us if any news comes over from London, especially news about the crew of that ship."

When they arrived at Phillip Lo's office a half hour later, they discovered that he had arranged for lunch to be catered by a nearby restaurant. A buffet of fresh crab, salmon, and shrimp, with several Chinese side dishes, had been set up against the far wall of his office. He rose from behind his desk as they were announced.

He smiled congenially. "There is no reason to starve oneself simply because we decide to work through luncheon." He nodded to his secretary. "Thank you for staying. You may go now." She bowed in the traditional Chinese manner, then left the office.

Phillip explained, "I thought it would be more private if we were alone, with no interruptions."

"Thank you for seeing us so quickly," Christina said.

He spread a hand expansively toward the buffet. "We can eat while we talk."

Christina took a few pieces of shrimp and dim sum, more out of courtesy than with any real appetite. Her stomach was too tightly knotted to enjoy any of it. She followed Phillip and Ross into what had once been an adjoining sitting room in the old Victorian mansion and now served as a comfortable private suite. The furnishings were period pieces, clustered before a Victorian fireplace and mantle. The three of them sat in high-backed upholstered chairs with small side tables.

"Mr. Thomason said it was a matter of some urgency," Phillip began.

Christina set down her plate and reached for her briefcase. She took out the telex Ross had received in the middle of the night and handed it to Phillip. "We received this from the London office."

He wiped his mouth with a linen napkin, then read the telex. His expression betrayed nothing as he set it aside. "The fate of the ship and the crew?" he asked.

Christina again reached for her case, but he waved it aside. "Tell me in your own words."

She explained everything they knew about the fate of the *Fortune Crest* and her crew, ending with a brief explanation of the number of Fortune ships in the Persian Gulf area, and their concern about the current political situation.

Phillip nodded. "I am aware of the increased tensions in the Persian Gulf area. I assume you have taken appropriate actions to ensure the safety of the other ships."

Christina looked briefly to Ross. He nodded, but made no

attempt to enter the conversation. He was going to let her handle this by herself. She took a deep breath. "Yes, I have," she answered quietly but firmly.

She went on to explain. "We conferred with the London office and also our contacts in several Middle Eastern ports. "*I* gave the authorization to withdraw the entire fleet from the Persian Gulf area, with instructions for alternative ports of call."

Phillip looked up sharply. For once his normally impassive expression showed emotion. He looked at Ross. "You concurred with that decision?"

Ross nodded. "Completely."

Phillip said nothing for a long moment. He slowly nodded. "It was a necessary decision."

Relief flooded through Christina. So far, so good. But she wasn't at all certain how her next news would be received. "In view of the Mideast situation, it's clear that the company must pursue an alternative market." She kept her voice even and steady, in order not to reveal the profound nervousness she felt about what was to come. "I've decided to pursue the proposal I gave you. I want to contact Beijing and make a formal proposal to the government there as soon as possible."

Phillip set down his plate on a side table and folded his hands in his lap. He didn't respond for a very long time. Finally he said, "The Middle East crisis has presented a unique situation, and admittedly there are many who consider mainland China a viable market. I have studied your proposal. It has intriguing potential. But that potential is not without risk."

"I'm aware of the risk," Christina informed him. "I hope to eliminate a great deal of it through Chen Li, if he'll agree to meet with me." She sat forward in her chair, her hands clasped, her expression earnest. "You once told me that honor is everything. Alexander Fortune was an honorable man. So was my father. I want the opportunity to bring honor back to the Fortune name. I believe my plan can work. I want the chance to *make* it work."

Phillip rose from the high-backed Victorian chair and walked to the windows that looked down on the street and Chinatown beyond. His hands were folded behind his back.

He was a study in contrasts. With his short stature and a benign smile that could have meant anything or nothing at all,
he looked as if he lacked only the long, braided pigtail snak-
ing down his back and a black silk tunic worn over black pa-
jama pants and slippers to complete the appearance of the
stereotypical wise old Chinaman.

In contrast to that cliché, he wore an expensive wool and
silk blend Bond Street suit, gleaming gold Cartier watch, and
custom-made shoes. Everything taken together was symbolic
of the blend of cultures that had shaped his life—the traditional Chinese mannerisms that affected every word and gesture, and the Western appreciation for innovation and success.

For several moments he simply stared out the windows, his
expression contemplative, his gaze distant. Christina began to
think that perhaps their meeting was at an end. She started
to rise, but Ross shook his head, and she sat down again.

When Phillip finally turned to face them and began to
speak, he took Christina completely by surprise by telling a
story. "In the first year of this century, two brothers left their
home in Canton, what is now called Guangzhou. They made
their way downriver to the sea and were smuggled aboard a
boat to Hong Kong. The older brother chose to remain in
Hong Kong, where he was certain he would make his fortune.
The younger brother was determined to go to America. His
name was Lai Kwok-lee.

"It was not difficult to get aboard a ship if one had the
price of passage. The difficult part lay in obtaining the necessary papers to enter America. Lai had no such papers, nor was
he likely to acquire any. Still he was determined to make the
voyage, and the two brothers bade each other farewell.

"The journey was hard, the conditions wretched. Hundreds
of immigrants were crowded into the hold of a ship meant
only to carry cattle. There was very little food or water, and
no ventilation below deck. Lai slept on a thin blanket in the
steel-hulled belly of the ship. Those who survived did so by
hoarding their food and rationing it. Lai befriended an old
man who had no family. They were much alike, each hoping
to fulfill a dream in America.

"There was much sickness on the ship. By the time the ship

came within sight of the California coastline, over one third of the passengers had died. It was dangerous to keep the bodies aboard ship, because of the risk of spreading more disease. Therefore the bodies were simply thrown into the sea. The old man lay dying. He knew he wouldn't live long enough to set foot in America."

Christina glanced at Ross, wondering what significance the story held. His expression was just as confused as hers, but it clearly said, "Hear him out."

Phillip continued, "Lai had shared the precious hoard of his food and water with the old man. The old man had nothing to give Lai in return for the act of friendship, except for a packet of papers he kept in the pocket of his tunic. These were his official entry papers, which were required of all immigrants who wished to enter the United States.

"Before he died, the old man gave his papers to Lai Kwok-lee. It was the gift of a new life in a new country for the young man. And when his friend's body was thrown into the sea, Lai took his name and made a sacred promise always to honor it."

Phillip's reserved expression was unchanged, but his words had become filled with a profound emotion barely held in check. "Lai Kwok-lee, who took the name of Lo Sha Tsui, was my father. I carry the Lo name with pride, and honor it as my father honored it."

Christina looked up at him, stunned. He smiled at her gently. "My father was determined to make the Lo name an honorable one. He worked very hard. He took great pride in the fact that I attended university and became a lawyer, but even greater pride in the honor I brought to our name." He looked directly at her. "You see, it wasn't the name that mattered, it was how we honored it. The Fortune name once held a place of great honor. It is possible that it will once again."

Without saying it in so many words, she realized, Phillip Lo had given his approval to her plan. And, more important, to her. She was filled with a rush of emotion so profound, it was all she could do to keep from bursting into tears. For the first time since she came to San Francisco, someone was saying to her, "I accept you as you are."

She cleared her throat and started to thank him, but he held up his hand.

"What you are attempting will not be easy. In many ways it will be more difficult for you than it was for either Michael or Alexander Fortune. There are those who will try to stop you."

She knew he referred to Richard, and possibly Katherine.

"The key to your plan lies with Chen Li. I know people who may be able to make contact with him."

It was the one part of her plan she and Ross hadn't discussed, although she had hoped that with his connections in Hong Kong, he might be able to help. Phillip now offered a potential solution to the problem.

Their luncheon was over. Christina stood as Phillip crossed the room to them. She understood now that he didn't want her to embarrass either of them with an outward sign of emotion for the gratitude she felt. "You honor both the names of Lo Sha Tsui and Lai Kwok-lee," she said with deep sincerity. "Thank you, *my friend*."

He smiled warmly. Taking both her hands in his, he said, "This is what Michael Fortune would have wanted had he lived. Perhaps it is *your* destiny to fulfill the dream of Hamish Fortune."

"Assuming Phillip is able to make that contact for us, there's going to be a lot of work ahead," Ross pointed out as they walked to the car after their meeting. He came around the car to open the door for her. For a moment he stood there, looking at her. He reached out and brushed a tendril of chestnut hair back from her cheek. His fingers grazed her skin. "It won't be easy. We could lose this fight."

She thought of other things she had lost along the way, and still others she wanted desperately to hold on to. Meeting Ross's look, she responded, "I never thought it would be easy."

They worked until well after midnight, when Ross finally called a halt. "That's it for tonight," he announced. "We're all starting to run on at the mouth."

"I could make more coffee," Bill volunteered, although his tone suggested he was hoping someone would object.

Christina looked up from the spread sheets she had been

trying to focus on through exhausted eyes for the past hour. She found both men looking at her expectantly. "If I was asked to give blood right now, I know they'd find nothing but pure caffeine. All right," she agreed, "let's call it a night."

She stood up and stretched, then looked at Ross. "I don't want to leave this information in the office."

He agreed. "You take it to your place." Then he added with a wry smile. "You certainly have enough empty space for storage."

She made a face at him as she began putting the spread sheets and files into her attaché case. Bill had gone to check on the telex machine for any overseas transmissions on the latest developments in the Persian Gulf situation.

Suddenly overwhelmed by exhaustion, she asked tentatively, "Do you really think we can pull this off?"

"It's your idea. And it's a damn good one. You should be the well of confidence."

"I do have confidence in the concept. But there's a lot to be done in a relatively short period of time. And we still don't know if the Beijing government will agree to meet with us."

"We'll let your friend David Chen worry about that once we've made contact." His gaze was thoughtful. "Or are you having second thoughts?"

"No, not second thoughts about the plan. I've been through it six different ways. I know it will work."

"Then what is it? Uncertainty about David Chen?"

"Not exactly," she answered evasively. "It's just that it's been several years since I last heard from him."

Ross was intensely curious. There were so many unanswered questions about Christina. David Chen's role in her life was one of them. "What exactly was your relationship with him?"

She looked up, then glanced back down at the table as she closed the attaché case. "I already explained, we were very close friends."

Lack of sleep and all that coffee consumed over several hours made him less subtle than he should have been. "Were you lovers?" he asked bluntly.

Her head came up, the fall of her chestnut hair swinging

forward to frame her finely sculpted features. There were smudges of fatigue beneath her eyes. "That's none of your business."

"I think it is. I want to know exactly what I'm dealing with, and whom."

"My personal relationship with David has nothing to do with the proposal."

"It has a great deal to do with it, because you're relying on the basis of that relationship to get access to him."

When she started to turn toward the door to leave, he reached out and caught her by the wrist. "I want the truth."

She whirled back around. Her anger had turned hard as ice. "We were friends and lovers. It *is* possible to be both."

He caught a glimpse of the wounded expression behind her eyes, and knew he'd peeled back one more layer of the carefully constructed facade she kept securely wrapped around her emotions. David Chen had clearly been extremely important to her, and it was obvious that her feelings for him weren't entirely forgotten or resolved.

He had learned that she was fragile. The contrast of her strength and that fragility drew him in. The secrets that kept him at a distance also drew him in. He wanted—*needed*—to know who she really was. Not merely in the sense of whether or not she was Christina Fortune, but the person she had become over the last twenty years, since a fifteen-year-old girl had died in a New York hospital. He wanted to know about all the events, both good and bad, that had shaped her life and made her a survivor. But she didn't trust him enough to reveal those things. Perhaps she never would.

"All right," he gave in for the moment. It bothered him terribly to know that he was the one who had caused the pain he saw in her eyes. "I'm sorry. You're absolutely right. I had no right to ask that question."

An apology wasn't at all what she expected from him. She suspected he rarely apologized.

"Apology accepted." She smiled faintly. His smile in return had a devastating effect on her already weakened defenses. "Do I have to try to find a taxi this late at night, or can I persuade you to give me a lift to my apartment?"

Ross's smile turned wicked. He reached out and lifted a tendril of hair from her shoulder, stroking it between his thumb and forefinger. "I have a feeling, Miss Fortune, that you might persuade me to do almost anything."

Her laughter was faintly uneasy. "Just a lift will do."

"Are you two children ready?" Bill called in from the front office.

As they joined him, Bill said, "There's another telex from London. The first of our ships reached its new destination, and the captain and all the crew of the *Fortune Crest* have been found. They're aboard a Japanese freighter."

"Thank God," Christina said with a long sigh of relief as they got into the elevator.

Ten minutes later Ross was escorting her to the door of her apartment. She found her key, and he took it from her, opening the door. As he stepped back from the doorway, she said, "I would invite you in, but . . ." the excuse dangled unfinished between them.

She brushed her hair back from her forehead, in a gesture he had come to recognize as uneasiness. Ross liked the fact that he made her uneasy. He reached out and brushed back a strand of hair that she had missed. His fingers grazed her forehead.

She remembered a promise he had made . . . *We will make love.*

"I understand," he said softly as his fingers brushed her cheek and then traced the curve of her chin. "It's still too soon."

He smiled at her, then his lips brushed her mouth just long enough to make her long for more. He stepped back. "Goodnight."

And then he was gone.

She heard the door close behind him in the foyer downstairs. A moment later the Jaguar purred to life. She touched her fingers to her mouth, where she could still feel the heat of his lips. And the heat of that promise . . . *We will make love.*

# Chapter 24

$A$t eight-thirty the next morning Christina stepped off the elevator at the Fortune offices. They were nearly deserted at this early hour, since the work day didn't officially begin until nine o'clock. But the light was on in Ross's office. He was already hard at work.

"Good morning," she said with a smile, sitting down in a chair facing his desk.

He looked up from the latest telex and returned the smile. "We have good news. Six more of our ships made port without incident."

She breathed a genuine sigh of relief. Despite her determination to appear outwardly confident, there had been a hard knot of apprehension deep within her ever since she'd heard about the loss of the *Fortune Crest*. She no longer tried to understand why any of this had become so important to her. She only knew that those ships and their crews mattered a great deal.

She replied, "That's great news. Any word yet on the other seventeen ships?"

"Not yet. We'll start to get regular reports now that they've had time to readjust their courses for alternate ports. The next twenty-four to thirty-six hours will be critical. By the way, did you see the morning papers?"

He shoved the morning edition of the *Chronicle* across the desk toward her. The headlines were filled with the news of the latest crisis in the Persian Gulf. Three other ships had been either badly damaged or sunk. Shipping companies worldwide were scrambling to pull their ships from the area. Ross and Christina were fortunate they'd received word of the crisis as early as they had. It enabled them to minimize their losses.

"We made a good decision," Christina said.

"No," he corrected her. "*You* made a good decision. A difficult one."

She smiled wryly. "I have ulterior motives."

"Speaking of those motives," he reminded her, "we'll have to notify Katherine. It's better she learn about the decision to withdraw those ships directly from us, rather than from Richard."

Christina agreed. "It was my decision. I'll call her, just as soon as we have confirmation that all the ships have reached their alternative ports. I don't want to worry her unnessarily."

"We'll both call her," Ross insisted. "And there's no need to say anything about your proposal until everything looks a bit more definite about our meeting with the People's Republic of China."

Suddenly Richard burst into the office. He was furious, his hands balled into tight fists, as if he were ready to hit someone. He threw down a piece of paper onto Ross's desk. "Have you seen this?"

Christina recognized the familiar numbers printed out at the top. This was a telex from overseas. Without bothering to pick it up and read it, Ross said simply, "Yes, we've seen it."

"The schedules and ports of call for all our ships in the Mediterranean and Persian Gulf have been changed!" Ignoring Christina, Richard focused his rage on Ross. "What the hell is the meaning of this?"

Ross rose to face Richard across the desk. "One look at the newspaper should be explanation enough. The entire region is practically in a state of war."

"We have shipping commitments!" Richard shot back.

"How am I supposed to justify the delayed schedules to our clients expecting oil deliveries?"

"It would be more difficult to explain the loss of those cargoes, not to mention the loss of our ships." Picking up one of the telexes received late the night before from London, he thrust it at Richard. "The *Fortune Crest* was sunk yesterday."

Clearly Richard hadn't known about this. Instead of showing dismay at the news, he seemed only to grow more angry. "Why wasn't I told immediately?"

"You were gone. Your secretary didn't know where to reach you."

Christina knew that Ross hadn't tried very hard to reach Richard. Richard knew that, as well. "You took advantage of my absence to recall the entire line. That was a damn stupid thing to do!"

"Every other line is recalling its ships. The only ships currently sailing the Persian Gulf are aircraft carriers and battleships."

Christina saw the rapid pulsing of blood in the thickened vein that stood out on Richard's neck as he fought for control. "That is beside the point." He wasn't about to back down. "A decision of this magnitude requires board approval. I want to know who gave you the authority in the middle of the night to make these changes! You've overstepped your authority here, McKenna. I'll have your ass for this."

Christina spoke with a quiet authority. "I don't think so."

Richard turned on Christina. "What is that supposed to mean?

"*I* authorized the changes."

"Who the hell gave you the authority to do that? Katherine wouldn't have agreed to it. What is going on here?"

Christina said, "No one gave me the authority, Richard. I don't need it. I control the majority of stock in this company."

Richard was thunderstruck. "You can't make a decision like that! It has to go before the board of directors."

"It was a crisis situation. There was no time to call a meeting. I chose to expedite the matter to minimize the risk of losing more of our ships."

"The by-laws specifically state . . ."

She knew exactly what he was going to say and cut him off. "They provide for emergency action. This was an emergency, and I took the appropriate action. It's done."

"Does Katherine know about this?"

"I'll call her as soon as the crisis has passed and advise her of the action we took. I'm certain I'll have her approval on this."

"Well, you don't have mine!" he snapped. "You're a fraud, and everyone, including Katherine, knows it! There's no way you're going to have any part of my company!"

He stormed out, slamming the door behind him.

Christina let out a long, shaky breath. She had seen Richard angry before, but not like this. He looked as though he wanted to kill.

She turned to Ross. "What do you think he'll do?"

"He'll try to find some way to discredit you. He may even try legal action to reopen the matter of the inheritance. All of that will take a great deal of time. But if he tries that, he'll be taking on Katherine and every lawyer her money can buy. That is a confrontation Richard hasn't been willing to make in the past."

"Then you don't think there's anything to worry about?"

"I didn't say that. Richard is dangerous because he's unpredictable. So far he hasn't been able to get information on your Beijing proposal. But we won't be able to keep it secret for long. Once we leave for Hong Kong, he'll be able to make a shrewd guess as to what's up."

"We'll deal with that when it happens," she said with renewed determination. She wasn't about to let Richard intimidate her into backing off from what she knew was the right thing to do.

The lunch hour came and went unnoticed as Ross and Christina worked feverishly to fine-tune the proposal. Bill interrupted them around one-thirty. "Lunch break," he announced.

"We don't have time," Christina answered without looking up from the stack of papers that she and Ross were poring through.

"Yes, you do," Bill said with a grin. Looking up, they saw

that he was juggling several paper food cartons. He set them down on the credenza across from the desk.

The food was Italian, from a little deli that made office deliveries, and smelled wonderful. They ate while they worked, and Bill gave them the latest figures on mainland Chinese manufacturing. The phone rang constantly as Christina's phone calls were put through on Ross's line. Late in the afternoon a call came for Christina.

It was from Phillip Lo.

Christina looked at Ross, mentally said a little prayer, and picked up the phone. When Phillip asked if Ross was there, she switched on the speakerphone.

"I made the contact we spoke of," he began. "The gentleman is an old friend with very strong business ties within mainland China. He knows of Chen Li, and he has promised to make immediate inquiries on your behalf. He will contact us as soon as he has any information."

They spoke briefly about the progress they had made with the proposal that day. She told him of her confrontation with Richard.

"I have known him all his life," Phillip said quietly. "He has always harbored a profound sense of outrage at being denied what he feels is his rightful due. Do not underestimate him. He has lost a great deal with your return. Both in terms of money and power. But most important, he has lost face." There was a pause, then he went on, "You must go to Hong Kong immediately. But as soon as you do, Richard will know that something is going on."

"Ross and I are aware of that. We'll simply explain that it's a routine trip for me to acquaint myself with the Pacific Rim operation of the business."

"What about Katherine?" Phillip asked. "She must know of this."

"I know," Christina finally answered. "I fully intend to tell her. But I wanted to wait until we had everything in place in Hong Kong. There's no point in telling her about all this until I know whether or not we'll be able to make it work."

There was silence on the other end of the phone for several long moments. Phillip Lo had always been completely loyal to Katherine. She knew he wasn't in complete agreement with her on this part of it.

"Very well," he finally said. "Call me as soon as you arrive in Hong Kong. If all goes well, I will have heard from my friend and will be able to tell you when the meeting will take place. And if the meeting goes well, then Katherine must be told."

"I understand. Thank you, Mr. Lo. For everything," Christina said with heartfelt gratitude.

Bill left to make arrangements for their trip, and Christina and Ross continued to work for two more hours. At that point she had a raging headache from staring at reports all day. Ross offered to get her some aspirin, and she waited alone in the office, massaging the pulsing pain at her temples in between jotting down some final notes. She didn't turn around at the sound of her door opening.

"I've just about got this all done," she said without looking up.

"I'd say you've already done enough."

The words were hard, edged with anger. She spun around in her chair and came face-to-face with Steven.

"Hello, Steven," she said curtly.

He sat perched on the edge of her desk with that air of superiority and arrogance he wore as if it had been tailored for him. He smiled, but there was no warmth or humor there. It was more like the expression of a predatory animal contemplating its next prey.

She had no intention of being that prey. "I thought you were already on your way to Hong Kong," she remarked.

"I'm on my way to the airport now. There was some sort of mechanical glitch with the jet. They've finally fixed it."

He went on, "I heard about your little power play. Rather impetuous of you, wasn't it, taking over like that without consulting the rest of us?"

She refused to be intimidated or badgered. She'd known men like Steven: handsome, smoothly charming when they got what they wanted, vicious when they didn't. She'd learned long ago, out of necessity, how to handle herself around men like him. Still she couldn't help feeling nervous.

She stood up. "What can I do for you?" she asked, trying hard to keep her voice strong and confident.

He came up off the corner of the desk, lithe and lean, with the body of an athlete. He glanced around the spartan, uncluttered office with its traditional antique furnishings that were a stark contrast to the expensive, elegant leather and marble furnishings that filled his own office. His gaze flicked to her desk, but she had closed the file she was working on the moment she saw him come into the office.

He idly picked up the bronze letter opener that lay beside a stack of correspondence. It was the standard issue from the supply department. He slid it back and forth between his fingers, pressing the point into his thumb. Somehow the idle gesture seemed fraught with a subtle menace, and she found herself holding her breath.

"You made a mistake today, *Christina,*" he said quietly, bringing his gaze slowly up to hers. "A very big mistake."

"I don't think so." She put more distance between them with a half step back toward the credenza behind her desk.

He reached out, his fingers trapping her wrist as he jerked her toward him. The letter opener was still in his other hand. He increased the pressure at her wrist until it hurt.

Christina was terrified, but she refused to give him the pleasure of knowing he could intimidate her. She reminded herself that she had confronted worse than this and survived.

"A very big mistake," he repeated. "Katherine will never support your decision. And without her support . . ." He let the thought trail off, unspoken. They both knew what he meant.

She met his gaze without blinking, instinctively understanding that any sign of weakness on her part would only feed his ego. But in spite of her determination not to betray her fear, an old memory slipped through her defenses, reminding her of another time and place when someone had held her just like this. Then she had been vulnerable. A victim. She had no intention of ever being one again.

When she spoke again, her voice was void of all emotion except one—grim determination. "Let go of my wrist, Steven."

"Is there a problem?"

Ross stood in the open doorway of her office.

For a moment longer Christina met the unspoken challenge in Steven's eyes. Then he said, "No problem at all."

The bruising pressure around her wrist eased abruptly as Steven released her. Before Steven left, he took a parting shot. "Be careful of the decisions you make, cousin. Think about the consequences." Then he smiled at them both. "I have a plane to catch." And he was gone.

"What was that all about?" Ross demanded.

She could barely control the sudden shaking of her hands, and her legs felt as if they'd turned to water. She laughed weakly. "I don't think Steven likes women who stand up to him."

Ross gently took hold of her wrist and held it up. Red marks from the pressure of Steven's fingers were plainly visible. Ross's expression hardened in a way that Christina had never seen before. "If he ever touches you again, he'll regret it."

Christina knew that he meant exactly what he said. Despite her anger at Steven, she hoped, for his sake, he wouldn't repeat his mistake. Pulling her hand away, she said, "I'm all right. Steven's all bluster." But her tone lacked conviction.

Ross didn't argue with her, but it was clear he totally disagreed. After a moment he said, "This is enough work for one day. We've done as much as we can until we hear from Phillip's friend. Come on. I'm taking you out to dinner."

"I can't," she said with real regret. "I promised to meet Leann Shiu at the Washington Street Bar and Grill for a drink after work."

Before he could insist, she said, "I'll be all right there. And afterward I'll go straight home. The truth is, I'm exhausted and I want to turn in early."

He gave in reluctantly. "All right. But I'm driving you over there myself, and I'll wait in the car until you're through."

"Ross, I don't need a bodyguard." She tried to make light of the situation, but the hard truth was that she might very well need one. She didn't want to admit it, even to herself, but his protective attitude made her feel infinitely better. She had worked hard over the years to become independent and self-sufficient, not to need anyone. At that moment she desperately needed Ross, but she was determined not to show it.

"Steven's on his way to Hong Kong. I'm perfectly safe."

For a moment he looked as if he might argue. Finally he conceded. "All right. But if you're the least bit worried about anything, call me."

She smiled in gratitude. "All right." Glancing at her watch, she went on, "We'd better go. I'll be late."

"I didn't realize you two had gotten to be such friends," he said as they walked toward the elevator.

"I like her. She's nice, and she's smart. And I think she's involved with my cousin."

"Steven?" he asked in surprise.

"No. Jason."

A half hour later she met Leann at the Washington Street Bar and Grill, a cozy little restaurant at the edge of Washington Square. It was one of those unpretentious little places that long-time San Francisco residents favored. San Francisco *Chronicle* columnist Herb Caen often had lunch there, along with the mayor, and any visiting politicians.

There was room for only a dozen tables, all draped with white linen. The carpet was deep forest green, and the walls beneath the wainscoting were painted a dark burgundy. The windows looked out onto the park. There were only a few people at the tables: two couples enjoying hors d'oeuvres and glasses of white wine, a couple of businessmen stopping for a drink at the end of the day.

Leann waved to Christina as she came in.

"I thought you might have changed your mind," she said hesitantly.

"I'm sorry. I got hung up at the office," Christina explained.

"You seem to be very busy with your proposal."

"It will take a lot of work, and there's definitely some risk, but I'm convinced it's worth it." Christina eyed Leann thoughtfully for a moment, then went on, "But you didn't ask me here to talk about Fortune International."

The waiter came to their table, and the two women ordered drinks. Leann didn't say anything while they waited for the waiter to return. When he did so, then left them alone, she nervously stirred her mixed drink. "I don't know how to begin."

"I generally just jump right in the middle," Christina said with a smile, trying to break the ice. "Everything usually falls into place."

Leann's expression became wistful. "Jason and I have been seeing a great deal of each other the past several months."

"Is your relationship serious?"

"Jason is a very special person. I care for him very much. He's sweet and sensitive. And he's a good listener. We hit it off right away. Everything was going along so well until . . ." She stopped, and Christina knew what came next.

"Until I came back to San Francisco," she interjected.

Leann nodded. "I knew about you, of course. Working with Mr. Lo, I'm well acquainted with the Fortune family. It was a very big surprise for everyone when you returned."

Christina smiled. "I think that's an understatement." She said nothing more, but waited for Leann to continue.

Leann nervously twisted the stirrer in her fingers as she went on, "In many ways, I think your coming back was perhaps more difficult for Jason than for anyone else."

Christina didn't quite know what to say. So many of her own feelings about Jason were confused. She said carefully, "It's been difficult for everyone."

"But worse for Jason because of his feelings for you," Leann explained. Her dark eyes were filled with uncertainty as she looked up at Christina. "He told me how it was between the two of you when you were teenagers. And he's always felt responsible that you left, because of what happened that last night."

Suddenly Christina went absolutely still. How much had Jason told Leann? Could he have been the rapist, after all?

She felt ill at the thought. She had never believed it was Jason. Her fingers tightened on the stem of her wineglass. She said slowly, "What exactly did he tell you?"

"He told me that you quarreled. He said terrible things.
Then you disappeared."

Christina felt relief wash over her. It wasn't Jason.

"He always blamed himself for your disappearance," Leann
was saying. "He's certain it was because of the argument, the
things he said to you, turning away from you just when you
needed him most." There was anguish in her voice. "Ever
since you returned, he's wanted to talk to you about it, but he
can't quite bring himself to do it." She added uncertainly. "I
just don't think anything will ever be resolved until he does."

Looking at Leann, Christina saw a reflection of her own
lost hopes and dreams reflected in the girl's dark eyes. As she
well knew, real happiness, in terms of a true and lasting romantic relationship, was rare and elusive. For one brief moment she had thought she might have it with David. But that,
too, ended.

Since then she'd been involved in a couple of short-term
affairs that ended because she couldn't seem to give enough
of herself. She was too consumed by the past to allow herself
to have hopes and dreams for the future. She had begun to accept that it simply wasn't going to happen for her. But Leann
was young enough and optimistic enough to think about the
future—a future with Jason.

"It was a long time ago," Christina began, choosing her
words carefully. "We were both very young. I had just lost
my parents, there was a lot of turmoil in my life. Jason was
my cousin, my friend, my safe-person." She laughed softly. "I
suppose I thought I was a little in love with him, but it was
an adolescent love."

She took Leann's hand in hers. "There was a misunderstanding, we quarreled the way teenagers do. But I swear to
you, it had nothing to do with the reason I left San Francisco.
It wasn't Jason's fault, and I'll do everything I can to make
him believe that."

Because she knew Leann needed to hear it, she added, "I
resolved everything about the quarrel and my feelings for Jason a long time ago. It was a schoolgirl infatuation on my
part. And I honestly believe his feelings for me were just as
immature."

Leann squeezed her hand. "Oh, Christina, thank you. I was so worried. At least now I know that Jason wasn't the reason you came back. Perhaps in time Jason will be able to resolve his own feelings. And . . . and learn to care for someone else."

"I think there's a very good chance of that," Christina answered. She finished her drink and then begged off from dinner. "I'm going home and straight to bed. But I'm glad we talked."

Leann said warmly, "So am I." Gathering up her purse and coat, she finished, "Thank you for coming tonight."

They parted outside the restaurant. It was almost dark, and Christina decided to walk the few short blocks over to Powell Street to catch the cable car that would drop her off near her apartment. The night air was brisk, reminding her that it was October. There were other pedestrians on the street, on their way home from work or to meet someone for drinks or dinner. The usual crowd of tourists that filled the streets at all times of the year stood out with their "I Love SF" T-shirts, windbreakers, and Giants baseball caps pulled down snuggly around their ears.

The cable cars—a favorite of tourists and a necessity to commuters—were always crowded. Passengers were scrambling aboard as she reached the corner at Powell and Jackson. She waited for the next one making the return trip up Powell.

It arrived a few minutes later, and before all the passengers had disembarked, Christina quickly slipped aboard. She moved toward the back as other passengers crowded on. The conductor called for fares, and then the cable car lurched as they got under way. They stopped briefly at the next two intersections. With each stop Christina moved further toward the outside platform at the back of the car.

The wind had come up. It was brisk, and she gathered the collar of her coat more tightly about her neck. At the next intersection she moved to the outside. Her stop was next. She had pulled on her gloves for warmth and clasped her hands around a pole. The cable car lurched uphill. A woman passenger on the bench beside her stood up in anticipation of the next stop. Christina squeezed forward to give her room, readjusting her grasp. As she held on with one hand, several passengers jostled behind her. She reached to steady herself with her other hand just as the cable car lurched up the next hill.

It happened in a split second. One moment she was standing on the edge of the platform holding on to the pole, the next she felt a hand, pressed hard against the middle of her back. One thought focused with startling clarity—she was being pushed. Then she was reaching ... grasping desperately to try to hold on to something, anything that would prevent her fall into the street as the cable car gathered speed ...

# Chapter 25

O h, my God!"

"Miss? Are you all right?"

Dazed, Christina looked up into the circle of faces that peered down at her. Her head began to clear, and she realized she was lying in the middle of the street. She felt like a fool, lying there, and tried to sit up, but several hands restrained her.

"Don't try to get up. You may be injured," someone said.

The hands pressing down on her, mixed with the panic and fear that came instinctively, brought an eerie flashback—darkness, the distorted shadow of a man standing over her, his large, strong hands groping for her . . .

Terrified, she fought off the restraining hands and pulled herself to her feet. "I'm all right!" she insisted.

She was aware of an arm gently supporting her as she was helped to stand on shaky legs. A wave of dizziness washed over her, and she had to close her eyes for a moment to steady herself. When she opened them, she looked into the face of the cable car conductor. "Are you sure you're all right, miss?" he asked worriedly.

She nodded, "I'm fine. Just give me a minute." She shoved her disheveled hair back from her face. Then her gaze scanned the faces of the people who stared at her, and a flash of memory came back hard and certain—*she had been pushed!* But who would have done such a thing? It had to be someone who knew her, yet she saw only strangers surrounding her as the crowd slowly began to disperse.

"I think I'd better call this in and get you to an emergency room," the conductor insisted.

"No, please. I'm not hurt badly. Just a few scrapes and bruises."

He looked at her skeptically. "At least let me call someone to come and get you."

Again she shook her head. "No, thank you. My apartment's close by. I can walk there."

He shook his head, undoubtedly concerned that this would result in a lawsuit. She laid a hand on his arm. "I'm fine, honestly." Then, recalling her fall from Julie's horse, she added, "I've taken worse spills than this."

"At least let me get a taxi for you. I won't take no for an answer."

He waved to a taxi driver stopped in the line of traffic jammed behind the cable car. After escorting her to the taxi and closing the door after her, he leaned through the open window of the taxi. "We'll need you to come down to the main office and make a report to the supervisor. It's regulations."

"All right," she agreed impatiently. She was grateful for his kindness, but anxious to get out of there and back to the safety of her apartment.

"That was some accident. You sure you're all right?" the taxi driver asked, glancing back at her in his rearview mirror.

"I'm sure," she answered wearily. She had begun to feel the aftereffects of the fall. Her entire body felt bruised and sore, and her cheek hurt where her head had hit the pavement.

Inside her apartment she slumped on the new sofa. Marie had proved to be more than a secretary. She had taken it upon herself to add some homey touches to the barren apartment—a couple of plants and some inexpensive but bright mounted posters. She had also helped Christina get a television, and a minimal supply of dishes, utensils, pots and pans, towels, and sheets. She seemed to think Christina needed taking care of, at least as far as her domestic life was concerned. Looking down at the torn and stained hem of her coat, Christina was inclined to agree with her.

She took off the coat, then lifted the hem of her wool skirt. Her stockings were a mass of runs, and red, raw skin showed through at both knees. Carefully peeling off the stockings, she tossed them in a nearby wastebasket. She hadn't had skinned knees since she was a kid and fell off her bicycle when she was first learning to ride.

Her hands had escaped injury because of the leather gloves she wore, but there was an ugly scrape at her wrist where she'd tried to break her fall. Her cheek throbbed. She winced as she probed it and decided it was time to have a better look.

Checking out her face in the bathroom mirror, she was relieved to see that it didn't look as awful as she'd feared. Her cheekbone was tender, the skin already purpling with a bad bruise beneath a scrape the size of a half-dollar. But a thick foundation could cover up the discoloration and allow her to show a presentable facade to the world.

Makeup, however, couldn't disguise the most disturbing aspect of the situation. Here, alone in her apartment, she had to confront the truth. This had been no accident. Neither was the shot that had spooked her horse in the vineyard. She shivered and held herself tightly. The terrifying truth was that someone had tried to kill her—twice. And whoever it was had come damn close to succeeding.

In the darkened bedroom she sat down on the edge of the bed and stared into the pool of light from the bathroom.

*Who?*

Who was behind it all?

Richard? Steven? *Both?*

Or someone else?

That was the really scary part. It could be almost anyone. All of the members of the Fortune family had reasons to want her out of the way.

She told herself she couldn't just sit there, letting panic overwhelm her. Forcing herself to stand up, she undressed, then slipped on a thick terry robe, wrapping it snugly about her like a security blanket.

Her gaze fastened on the bedside telephone, and she thought of Julie. She'd been intending to call her for days. Their plans to get together, and to get Christina's car back to her, had been postponed indefinitely. The last time Christina had talked to Julie, the local authorities still hadn't learned anything about the gun that was found in the vineyard.

She checked the time on the clock radio. It wasn't late, only a little after seven o'clock. She picked up the phone and dialed Julie's number in Sonoma.

"Hello?" the male voice was vaguely familiar, remembered from brief phone conversations years earlier, when she and Julie were still in Boston.

"Hello, Carlo? This is Chris Fortune . . . Chris Grant," she corrected, recalling that he had known her only by that name. They exchanged friendly greetings, and he apologized for missing her visit. Then he put Julie on.

"Hi!" Julie's greeting was exuberant. "I've been reading all about you in the newspapers. It seems you're really asserting yourself in the shipping business, Miss Fortune," she teased.

She realized Julie must have read about the withdrawal of all Fortune ships from the Persian Gulf. It seemed impossible to make a move that wasn't in the next day's headlines.

"Oh, I'm keeping busy," she answered evasively. "I'm going over to Hong Kong soon, so don't worry about returning my car yet. I wanted to let you know I'm no longer among the dispossessed. I found an apartment: two bedrooms, two baths, spectacular view, great neighborhood." Her voice sounded almost too cheerful, even to her.

"Hey, that sounds great. At least I won't have to sleep on the sofa when I visit," Julie quipped.

"Say, Julie," she tried to make her voice sound casual, "did you ever hear anything more about that gun that was found in the vineyard?"

"They're still working on it. Sometimes the wheels of justice move a little slow up here. We just have the county sheriff to look into these things, and he never has to deal with anything more serious than some guy who's drunk and disorderly. But I'll give him another call in the morning. Maybe they have something by now."

"Great," Christina said with false brightness. "Let me know what you hear."

There was a moment of silence, then Julie asked, "What's wrong?"

Christina laughed shakily. "Why would you ask that?"

"I don't know. You just sound a little strange. Has something happened?"

"No," Christina rushed to assure her, determined not to worry Julie. "I'm just a little tired, that's all. Look, I'll call you when I know for sure what my schedule will be over the next few weeks. Then we can get together."

"Are you sure everything's all right?" Julie sounded skeptical.

"Absolutely," Christina assured her. She looked up as the door buzzer sounded from the living rom. "I've got to go, Julie. Someone's at the door. I'll call you later."

She frowned as she hung up. The buzzer sounded again. A sudden frisson of apprehension skittered along her nerve endings. She wasn't expecting anyone. It buzzed insistently, a third time, and she pressed the button to the downstairs intercom.

It was Ross. "Can I come up for a few minutes?"

Somehow she was reluctant to face him. "I'm really tired. I was just on my way to bed." She realized how ridiculous that sounded this early in the evening, in spite of the hours they'd put in lately.

"This will take just a few minutes. It's important. Buzz me through, Chris."

She could have refused, but the simple truth was he would find out sooner or later about the accident . . . unless, of course, he already knew. The sudden suspicion hit her like a blow to the stomach. It couldn't be! Ross wouldn't do such a thing! And then she remembered how he'd turned up at Julie's immediately after someone had shot at her. Now he was here, immediately following a second "accident." Had he come to see how badly hurt she was?

She felt sick inside. *NO*. Not Ross.

He'd asked her to trust him. And she'd actually begun to

do so. Had she been a fool? "My God, how can I even think such a thing?" she murmured to herself.

"Chris?" His voice came over the intercom.

"Come on up," she finally said, pressing the release button for the door downstairs.

She was in the bathroom when she heard a light knocking at the door a moment later. She'd tried applying makeup to her cheek so that it wouldn't look as bad as it really was. But it didn't quite work.

Ross knocked a second time before she got to the door. There was only one lamp on, beside the sofa. Christina remained in the shadows at the side of the door as she opened it. "Come in."

Ross entered her apartment, and his gaze took in the terry robe. "I'm sorry," he apologized. "I didn't realize you'd be going to bed this early."

"I . . . was tired. What did you want to talk about?" She kept the bruised side of her face turned away from him.

"I worked late and came up with some new figures for the joint venture financing to present to Phillip. With the profit potentials we came up with I think we have a strong package to offer the Chinese government." He opened the large envelope he'd brought with him and pulled out several typed pages. Then, glancing around at the meager lighting, he stepped to the wall switch and flicked on the overhead lights.

When he turned to face her again, he exclaimed, "My God, Chris! What the devil happened?"

The fear and anger she'd kept carefully controlled until that moment, welled up inside her. "I had a slight accident," she said tightly.

"I'd say it was more than just an accident." She winced as his fingers clamped over her injured wrist. He loosened his grasp but still didn't release her. Instead he turned her wrist over.

"Is there more?" he asked, his tone low, barely controlled.

"Just a few scrapes and bruises." She pulled away from him and went over to sit on the sofa. She pulled her robe tighter about her.

He wasn't about to let her off that easily. "Tell me what happened."

Without looking up, she said, "You mean you don't already know?"

"What is that supposed to mean?" he demanded, staring down at her.

She heard the anger in his voice, and felt her own at the breaking point. She wanted desperately to trust him, but she knew she shouldn't—she couldn't. Not now. Her anger, and a fear that gnawed away at her, drove her to her feet. She glared at him. "It means that my little *accident* was no accident. I was pushed off a cable car this evening. The thought occurred to me that you already knew about it. After all, you knew where I was going to be tonight."

His dark blue eyes glinted with anger. "Is that an accusation?"

"Should it be?" she flung back at him.

He slowly shook his head. His voice was low, carefully controlled, yet edged with a fury that was more intimidating than she cared to admit. "We've been through all this before. I didn't push you from that cable car. I don't know who did. But I intend to find out."

"So you can see that it's done right next time?" She was on the verge of hysteria, and she knew it, but she couldn't seem to control her turbulent emotions. She pushed her hair back from her forehead with a shaking hand. "You asked me to trust you, and I did."

"You *can* trust me." He saw the naked fear in her eyes, and his tone softened. "Think about it, Chris. If I wanted to hurt you, I've had a dozen opportunities."

His argument made sense. She'd used that same argument. But she was beyond reason. "Maybe you prefer to let someone else do your dirty work!"

He seized her by the shoulders. "Think of how many times we've been alone together—on the way back from Sonoma; that night in Chinatown; aboard the *Resolute;* any one of a dozen other times. What you're saying doesn't make any bloody sense!"

She knew he was right. Suddenly she was crying, and that

made her all the angrier. "Damn!" she cursed. "I hate crying!"

Ross pulled her into his arms. When she resisted, he held on even tighter.

"Go ahead and cry. Considering what you've been through, you're entitled to a few tears." One arm was wrapped around her waist, holding her against his chest. His other hand stroked her back, calming her, much as he would a frightened child. Except that the woman in his arms was no child.

He was acutely aware of that. His senses were assaulted by her—the subtle scent of her perfume, the silkiness of her hair, the softness of her skin as it trembled beneath his touch. For weeks now it had been all he could do to keep his hands off her. It had been nearly impossible. Restraint wasn't his style. When he wanted something, he took it. When he wanted a particular woman, he went after her with the same single-minded determination he showed in business.

But Christina wasn't just another woman whose body he wanted to explore and enjoy. He was intrigued by her, and drawn to her in a way that wasn't merely physical. He felt toward her as he hadn't felt toward any woman in a long, long while. He wanted to unravel the mysteries of her mind and heart, as well as the tantalizing mysteries of her body.

But at that moment he was also acutely aware that she was intensely vulnerable. So he simply stood there, holding her, letting her cry out all her pent-up emotions.

After a long while she pulled back from him, releasing her hold on the front of his shirt. "I got you all wet," she whispered thickly.

"I think I'll survive." He pushed back some strands of hair from her bruised cheek. "Any other injuries?"

She gave him a watery smile. "I skinned my knees when I fell." She opened her robe just enough to give him a glimpse of her scraped knees.

He grinned at her, trying to lighten the mood, sensing that she needed it. "You look like you've been in a street fight."

She sniffled. "Yeah, well, you should've seen the other guy."

They both laughed. Then he said, "This report will keep

until tomorrow, but I thought you'd like to know that Phillip Lo called." She was instantly alert as he went on, "Contact has been made with David Chen." Then his expression shifted. "You must have meant a great deal to him. He's willing to meet with us."

"Oh, Ross, this is wonderful! It means there really is a chance we can put this together."

"You had your doubts?"

She smiled. "You've had yours."

"Only a few. But doubts add to the stimulation of the challenge."

"Did Phillip say when David would be willing to meet with us?"

"He'll contact us in Hong Kong through diplomatic connections. That means we need to go over as soon as we have everything put together here. There will still be a lot more to do over there."

She nodded. "We could've gone over with Steven, if we'd known about this earlier."

He shook his head. "The longer we can keep this to ourselves, the better chance we have for success."

"Yes, of course. But Katherine will have to know eventually. I don't want her finding out about this from Richard."

His expression sobered. "This is important, but it isn't nearly as important as what happened to you tonight. Did you see anyone you recognized?"

"I saw only strangers."

He ran his hands down her arms and took her hands in his. "Chris, you know that fall in Sonoma probably wasn't an accident, either."

"I thought about that, and I called Julie." At his questioning look, she said, "The sheriff didn't have anything new on the gun that was found."

"You'll have to be very careful from here on out."

Her expression turned stubborn. "I won't give whoever is doing this the satisfaction of seeing me running scared. I refuse to sleep with a gun under my pillow."

"I think I could suggest an alternative to that plan," Ross

said with a deepening smile that sent her pulse racing. "But tonight you need your rest. Have you eaten yet?"

She shook her head. "Just a drink with Leann."

"Do you have anything in your fridge?"

She shook her head.

"All right," he said. "You head for the bath. A long soak will do wonders. I'll arrange dinner. Take it from someone who knows, a street fight can really work up an appetite."

"I suppose your experience was on the docks of Hong Kong?"

He grinned at her. "Working for Katherine."

She laughed, realizing how true that statement was.

Then she grew silent. They simply looked at each other for a long moment. His smile faded, and he looked deeply concerned. While she was still badly shaken, somehow she didn't feel nearly so scared. She said softly, "Thank you."

His fingers tightened at her shoulders, and for just a moment she thought he might pull her close again and kiss her. Instead he brought his hand up and stroked her bruised cheek with amazing tenderness. "You have nothing to thank me for."

She didn't say everything she was thinking. She wasn't quite ready to do that yet. But she insisted, "Yes, I have. I have a great deal to thank you for."

She must have dozed. When she looked at the small gold clock on the bathroom counter, she realized she'd been lying in the tub almost an hour. She drained the now-tepid water and dried off, slipping back into the terry robe. She towel-dried her hair, thought about applying makeup, then decided against it. When she didn't hear any sounds coming from the living room, she assumed Ross must have gone home.

In the living room she found a fire crackling in the fireplace. Two brandy snifters sat on the coffee table, the amber liquid catching the golden light from the fire. Delicious aromas drifted out from the small kitchen.

"I was about to check on you. I thought you might have drowned," Ross said as he came out of the kitchen. He'd taken off his suit jacket. His tie was gone, his shirt was open at the throat, and his sleeves were rolled up, exposing his tanned forearms.

"I must have fallen asleep. I think I'm all pruny from being in the water so long."

"You don't look all pruny," he said, stopping at the coffee table just long enough to pick up the two brandy snifters. He handed one to her.

It went down warm and smooth, dulling the last traces of anxiety.

"Sit," he ordered. "Dinner's almost ready."

"It smells wonderful. Need any help?"

"How are you at salads?"

She padded into the kitchen. "I can handle salads, and anything that can be nuked in the microwave." At his horrified expression she explained, "I was always too busy to learn how to cook. Where did you learn?"

"Oh, I picked up a little here, a little there," he answered evasively.

"I see," she nodded with understanding. "An old friend?"

He gave her a sly smile. "She wasn't so old at the time, and she was one hell of a cook. We experimented a lot."

The twinge of jealousy at a past lover surprised her. "I'll just bet you did."

He looked up at her, an odd expression in his eyes. He reached out, seizing her by her uninjured wrist. Then he kissed her . . . slowly, thoroughly, hotly, reminding them both of a promise yet to be kept.

"God, you're beautiful," he whispered huskily against her mouth. He lingered just long enough to trace the curve of her upper lip with the tip of his tongue. Then he pulled back from her and thrust a set of salad tongs into her hands. "If you want to eat around here, you have to earn it."

Dinner was broiled butterfly scampi smothered in butter thick with garlic and parmesan cheese, wild rice with mushrooms and scallions, spinach salad with wine dressing and grated hard-boiled egg sprinkled over the top, and a crisp gray Riesling wine.

"They didn't carry Francetti wines at the corner market," Ross apologized as he refilled her glass.

"I'll have to speak to them about that. They'll have to mend their ways if they expect to have my business," she said lazily as she pushed aside her empty plate. She felt thoroughly content, safe, and sleepy. She yawned in spite of her best efforts not to.

"All right, Miss Fortune. I can take a hint."

He got up, came around the small table, and pulled her out of the chair. Then he led her to the couch before the fire and said, "Sit."

She rested her head against the arm of the couch, watching his easy familiarity in the kitchen. "Why aren't you married?" The question popped out almost before she realized she'd asked it.

He looked at her across the pass-through counter that served double function as a bar. After drying his hands, he came out of the kitchen and sat down beside her on the sofa. "Are you always so direct?"

"I find it's usually the best way to get an answer."

He gently traced her fingers with his. "I haven't exactly had the time. And I haven't lived the sort of life that's fair to a wife and family. I've made my work the most important thing in my life, and sacrificed certain things along the way." It almost sounded as if he regretted it. She understood that feeling. It was something she'd had to confront in her own life.

She yawned again and tried to hide it behind her hand. "I guess I'm just surprised that no one's caught you yet." She thought of Marianne Schaeffer and felt another sharp stab of jealousy.

"I don't believe in being caught," he said in a low voice as he studied her hand and fingers, twining them with his. "When a man and woman make a commitment to each other, it should be because they both want each other more than anyone else in the world. Anything less only causes pain and heartache, and no one has the right to hurt anyone that way." His voice was low, almost a whisper.

Then he looked up and smiled. "I don't usually put my dinner-companions to sleep."

Her eyes were closed, her lashes lying in thick crescents

against her pale cheek. Her breathing was slow and deep with sleep. He slipped an arm beneath her shoulders and another beneath her legs and gently lifted her. He carried her to the bedroom and laid her on the bed, pulling the covers over her as she curled onto her right side. She was already asleep.

He bent over her, kissed the corner of her mouth, then whispered, "Good night, Christina . . . or Ellie."

As he left the bedroom, he gently closed the door behind him.

In the living room he picked up the phone and dialed. When it was picked up on the other end, he asked in a hard voice, "What the bloody hell happened tonight?"

He listened briefly, then cut in, "I don't want excuses, I want results." Then he firmly put down the phone and let himself out of the apartment.

# Chapter 26

Morning sunlight streamed into the apartment. Christina awoke slowly, immediately feeling the pain from the bruises she'd received in her fall from the cable car. Sitting up carefully, she saw a note from Ross on her bedside table. She realized, with a mixture of surprise and disappointment, that he hadn't spent the night.

She remembered the wonderful dinner he'd prepared, the wine, and the brandy. Everything after that was a little vague. The last thing she remembered was Ross's lifting her up and carrying her into the bedroom. She picked up the piece of paper torn from the pad she left by the telephone. The note read simply:

Take the day off and rest. I'll call you later. Ross.

Not likely, she thought, as she slipped out of bed and slowly made her way to the bathroom. Every muscle in her body complained, and she groaned as she saw her reflection in the mirror over the counter. To quote Ross, she looked as if she'd been in a street fight.

Her cheek was scraped and slightly swollen. A purplish-blue bruise spread across her cheekbone. She tenderly probed the skin. "This is going to need more than cover-stick," she groaned. Then she inspected her knees. Fortunately dark stockings would camouflage most of the damage.

"Learning to ride a bicycle is definitely easier," she remarked as she went to the shower and turned on the tap full.

An hour later, freshly showered and dressed, she inspected her appearance in the full-length bedroom mirror. She wore a winter-white wool skirt and silk blouse with a jacket in a warm shade of caramel with accents of burgundy and gold threads running through the weave. The colors were rich and striking. It was a deliberate choice that drew attention to the elegant designer style, and away from her face, where too close a scrutiny would reveal the bruises on her cheek.

As a further camouflage, she wore her shoulder-length hair loosely styled. It swept against each cheek in a soft curve that concealed a great deal.

She was about to call for a taxi to take her to the office when the intercom buzzer sounded from the main entrance downstairs. Pressing the button, she said, "Hello?"

There was a moment's hesitation that sounded almost like surprise, and then, "Christina?"

She heard the surprise in her own voice. "Uncle Brian! Good morning."

There was another pause, as if he might have forgotten what to say next, and then, "May I come up?"

It seemed that Ross wasn't the only one who had discovered where she was now living. She hesitated, wondering what could have brought Brian by the apartment without calling first.

She thought of her fall the evening before and felt a frisson of apprehension. Then she mentally shook herself. She certainly had nothing to fear from Brian. Of all the members of the family, he was the one who had made her feel welcome from the very beginning.

Christina realized that they had a great deal in common. She was an outsider—the heiress everyone wished had never returned. Brian was also an outsider—the man who married a Fortune daughter and worked in the company, but had no power or authority within that company . . . or within his own family.

"I was just on my way into the office," Christina explained as she buzzed him on through. "Come on up."

When he arrived, she said, "There's coffee in the kitchen. Help yourself."

She went into the bedrom and returned a moment later with her purse and attaché case. Brian sat at the edge of the counter with a cup in his hand.

"You make good coffee."

"It's one of the few things I can make," she confessed.

"I see you decided to move from Fortune Hill."

"I needed a place of my own."

He nodded in that quiet, introspective way of his. "I can understand that."

"How did you find me?" Christina asked.

"I didn't. Richard managed to get your address, somehow."

Of course, Christina thought.

Brian looked distinctly uncomfortable as he went on, "I'm afraid this isn't a social call. Richard asked me to bring you to the office."

"Why?"

He set the coffee mug down. "Katherine is in San Francisco. She arrived early this morning from Hawaii."

As they drove in Brian's car to the office, he explained, "Richard must have called her as soon as he found out about your orders to withdraw all our ships from the Gulf."

She stared out the car window, her thoughts racing, trying to guess what Katherine's mood would be and how to approach her. There was no question what Richard's motive was. He'd been furious when he found out and had left no doubt that he would do whatever was necessary to stop her.

Damn! she thought. She needed more time. For that reason she'd put off contacting Katherine about the changes, stalling for every possible day to give her a margin of time to set the rest of her plan in motion.

"Does Ross know?"

"Katherine rarely makes a move that he isn't aware of. But in this case . . ." Brian left the rest unsaid.

"There's more." Brian's expression was grim, his voice

filled with regret at having to be the one to tell her. "Richard has called an emergency meeting of the board."

Christina let out the breath she'd been holding. "When?"

"This morning at ten o'clock."

"Katherine warned me that Richard would do everything in his power to stop me," she mused out loud. "It seems he has. He'll no doubt try to discredit me with this."

There was a long, thoughtful silence between them as Brian moved through midmorning traffic toward Fortune Tower. Finally he said, "Richard has been fighting Katherine for control of the company ever since Michael's death."

"He was fighting for something that was never rightfully his," Christina insisted.

"As far as Richard is concerned, Fortune International belongs to him, and he'll do anything to hold on to it."

*"Anything,"* Christina murmured thoughtfully, lightly rubbing her fingers across the scrape on her wrist concealed by the cuff of her blouse.

They pulled into the parking garage on the basement level of the Fortune building. Brian wheeled his black Volvo into his parking space. Beside them was Diana's distinctive gleaming red Mercedes 580 SL. She obviously intended to be on time for the meeting. All the other spaces were filled. All the members of the board were present and waiting—like sharks closing in on the kill.

Brian didn't get out of the car. He turned, his hand covering Christina's on the seat between them, in a comforting gesture. "There's something you need to understand. As far as Richard is concerned, it doesn't matter whether or not you are Christina," he explained.

For the first time she understood the cold reality. It *didn't* matter whether or not she really was Christina. What did matter was the threat that she represented ever since Katherine accepted her.

She squeezed Brian's hand, grateful for his kindness—the only real kindness anyone in the family had shown her since she had come to San Francisco. She sensed that in his own way, he was looking out for her. His kindness touched her deeply. And it filled her with a sense of longing so sharp that it was almost painful—a longing for the father she lost so many years ago.

She leaned over and kissed him on the cheek. "Thank you."

"For what?"

"For caring. It means a lot."

When they stepped out of the elevator onto the eighteenth floor a few minutes later, Christina found the atmosphere charged with tension.

The receptionist greeted her hesitantly and didn't quite meet her look. "Good morning, Miss Fortune."

"Good morning, Miss Bennett." Then in a calm, perfectly controlled voice, as if there were nothing unusual about this particular morning, she asked, "Is everyone here?"

"Uh . . . yes, Miss Fortune," Miss Bennett responded nervously.

"Good."

"Chris." Ross came out of his office and crossed the reception area in quick strides. "I tried to call you."

"Brian told me about Katherine. And the board meeting," Christina explained.

Brian murmured something about leaving them alone to talk, and walked away.

Christina said, "Richard didn't waste any time."

Ross slipped his arm through hers as they walked to his office. "No, he didn't. I learned about all this only when I arrived a few minutes ago." He frowned. "It isn't like Katherine to make a move like this without talking to me. That isn't a good sign."

She set down her purse and attaché case on Ross's desk. "What can we expect?"

"Richard is no fool. Even though Katherine made that announcement in Hawaii, he's perfectly aware that she's been making the decisions through you. His strongest weapon against you is the fact that you made vital company decisions without first consulting her."

Christina knew he was right. Katherine must be furious. And if she made the long, tiring trip from Hawaii, then she clearly was determined to do something.

"What can I do?" she asked Ross.

"Katherine made you the acting President. Use your position. Don't let anything go to a board vote."

"How can I stop it?"

"You have to speak with Katherine alone, without the rest of the board. It's your only chance. Demand it."

"Do you think Katherine will agree to speak to me?"

Ross frowned. "I honestly don't know. But it's your only hope."

Bill poked his head in the doorway. "Richard is calling the meeting to order."

As Christina and Ross walked into the boardroom, she thought of that other morning, only a few short weeks earlier, when she had first stepped into this room and faced these people. There had been so much at stake that morning. There was even more at stake now.

In one quick, sweeping glance, she saw that everyone was present, including Brian. He sat beside Diana, staring down at the table. Her cousins were all present, occupying the same chairs as they had that first morning. The only difference this morning was that Richard sat in the first chair on the left side of the table. Katherine sat at the head of the table, in the chair reserved for the Chairman of the Board.

Conversation stopped at her entrance. Diana's expression was smug as their gazes met briefly. Then Diana looked across the table to Richard. He was coolly efficient, arranging a stack of papers—proof, no doubt, of Christina's betrayal of Katherine, in the form of telegrams and overseas telexes.

Jason looked at Christina, all the old questions so evident in his expression. Then he looked away.

But Katherine was the one who mattered, and Katherine refused to meet her look. Instead she stared grimly ahead, clearly determined to get this over with as quickly as possible.

Before anyone spoke, before Richard could officially open the meeting, Christina announced, "I demand that this meeting be postponed."

Richard said, "You don't have the authority to make that demand."

Christina sensed Ross's silent support as he stood beside

her, and took strength from it. This time, at least, she wasn't alone in facing these people. "As acting President I have the authority," she announced flatly. Then her gaze fastened on Katherine, and she said, "I need to meet with you privately."

"This is ridiculous!" Diana spat out. "For God's sake, Mother, surely you aren't going to listen to her! She's an impostor. We've known it from the very beginning. You trusted her, and now she's betrayed you. It's that simple."

"I fully agree," Steven added his support to his mother. "You can't allow this to go on, Grandmother. The company is in jeopardy."

Richard slammed his hand down hard on the conference table. "This meeting will come to order now, without further delay or interruption." He glanced coldly at Christina. "You have no place here."

"Yes, I do!" she shot back. "As long as this company has existed, the women of this family have been told they had no place in it. Well, that isn't true any longer. This is my company, as well as yours. Everything I've done has been to ensure its survival. And I won't give up my position just because you think a woman has no right to be here!"

She looked at Katherine, searching desperately for some sign that her words had made a dent in Katherine's cold fury. But there was no softening of the implacable lines in her face.

I've lost, Christina thought miserably. There was nothing more she could say or do. Except, perhaps, for one thing.

Looking at Katherine she said pleadingly, "Please, *Grand-mère*."

It was a calculated risk. Katherine had ordered her never to use that term of endearment, and Christina knew she might very well react with even stronger anger.

For one tense moment Katherine stared at her, and it was impossible for Christina to read her response. Then, to Christina's surprise, Katherine slowly stood up. "We shall delay this meeting for five minutes while I speak alone to . . . to the acting President."

"Mother!" Diana stood abruptly and reached out to grab Katherine's arm, as if to physically restrain her. Katherine stopped her with a steely expression.

"Damn it, Mother!" Richard shouted as he rose to stand beside her. "You can't do this! She's betrayed you."

He towered over Katherine's frail height. But she had stood her ground with him in the past, and refused to back down now. She ordered, "Clear the boardroom. Ross, you may stay."

The others angrily complied, but as they filed past Christina, she knew they would be back in exactly five minutes, ready to finish what they'd started.

Five minutes. Very little time to save herself.

Christina turned to Katherine, who had sat down again, exhaustion etched in the deep lines of her face. She began quickly, "I'm sure you're aware that two days ago we lost one of our ships in the Persian Gulf . . ."

"I know all about that," Katherine snapped.

"It happened quickly. Time was important. Many lives, as well as the future welfare of this company, were at stake. *I* made the decision to withdraw our ships in order to save lives and to protect the welfare of this company."

Christina took a deep breath and went on, "There's more. I've made several other decisions. I've come up with a plan to expand Fortune International into a new, safer market. The withdrawal of our ships from the Persian Gulf gives us the prime opportunity to set this in motion. The survival of the company depends on it."

"What new market?" Katherine asked disdainfully.

"Actually it's an old market," Ross responded, speaking to Katherine for the first time. "The market that created Hamish Fortune's wealth and made it possible for him to found a dynasty. *China.*"

Quickly Christina outlined in broad strokes the plan she and Ross had been discussing with Phillip Lo. When Katherine heard that Phillip was aware of all this, she frowned in displeasure. "How dare he go behind my back!"

"He wasn't being disloyal," Christina insisted. "We had to assure him that we would present the plan to you for your approval the instant it was complete."

"Who gave you the authority to make these decisions?" Katherine demanded.

Christina retorted, "*You* did. When you made a bargain with the devil, and told everyone you accepted me as your granddaughter."

Katherine seemed taken aback. Then she looked at Ross. "Did you know about this?"

"Yes. Christina made these decisions with my full support. This is the only way Fortune International will survive."

Katherine's gaze fastened once more on the young woman who claimed to be her granddaughter—the young woman she had accepted so that she could use her to hold on to control of the company.

*"Who gave you authority to do this?"*

*"You did."*

Those words echoed back at Katherine from across the span of years. The memory was brief and startling in its intensity.

She was a young woman again and her husband, Alexander, had lovingly rebuked her after they gave a lavish private dinner at Fortune Hill for several congressmen . . .

He pulled Katherine into his arms. "You neglected our other guests tonight, my dear, in favor of Senator Stanton. Not to mention that you also neglected me. Who gave you permission to behave that way?"

"You did," she reminded him as she laid her hands against the front of his stiff white shirt. "You told me to see what I could do about persuading him to vote in favor of that new trade expansion bill."

"And did you?"

She smiled at Alexander. "He understands that it will be extremely beneficial to many people if Fortune International is allowed to expand into the Asian market. I think Senator Stanton can be relied upon . . ."

Reluctantly pulled back from her memories, Katherine faced the disturbing fact that this young woman reminded her of herself. Christina also reminded her of someone else—old Hamish Fortune.

Katherine had accepted Christina in order to use her for her own purposes—to save the company. Perhaps Christina had done precisely that. It was exactly what Alexander would have done—and old Hamish Fortune before him.

All the emotions that Katherine had kept so carefully hidden away for the past twenty years welled to the surface, and it was all she could do to fight back tears. This young woman was intelligent, strong-willed, and unafraid. More than that, she was a fighter and a gambler, willing to risk everything to succeed. She possessed all the qualities Katherine would have wanted in her granddaughter.

"Very well," Katherine said in a voice fragile with physical and emotional exhaustion.

Christina was stunned at the abrupt capitulation. "Then I have your approval?"

Katherine nodded. "You have my approval." Then she added, "Keep Richard out of this as long as you can. He'll fight you. Make this work, my dear. I'm getting too old for these battles. Everything depends on you. The entire future of Fortune International is in your hands."

# *Chapter 27*

Christina and Ellie raced into the dark alley . . .

The stench of rotting garbage filled the air, and trash caught at their feet . . .

He was close behind them now. They could hear the sound of his feet pounding the wet pavement behind them, coming closer, closer . . .

They cut down another alley. A dead end. Whirling around, they saw him standing there, blocking their way. He came at them, a knife held in one hand . . .

Then there was a scream of pain, mixed with the chilling wail of a siren . . .

One girl sat alone in the emergency waiting room . . .

"I'm sorry." The words echoed away from her . . .

She held on to the slender hand that clung to hers. "You have to live for both of us now." The words were a ragged whisper. "Promise me . . ."

She clung fiercely to her friend's hand. "I promise."

Then that hand lay cool and lifeless in hers.

Hot tears streamed down her cheeks as she whispered, "Someday I'll make them pay for what they did to us. I promise . . . I'll make them all pay . . ."

"Chris?"

She jerked awake, and the nightmare dissolved.

Beside her, Ross said, "We're here. Hong Kong."

She blinked in momentary confusion at the sleek compact surroundings of the first-class compartment. After all the hard work and countless meetings, everything had finally come together. They had to move quickly, before Richard found out what they were trying to do and could come up with a countermaneuver. Phillip Lo had made contact with government officials in Beijing and was busy trying to arrange for Christina and Ross to meet with other businessmen in Hong Kong.

Now, two days after the aborted board meeting, they were here. It was just past one o'clock in the morning. The jet banked low over the rooftops of Lai Chi Kok industrial center—the legendary sweatshops that existed even today, where a fine silk suit could be bought for one fourth the price it would bring overseas.

The plane leveled out over the pattern of lights on that distinctive finger of land that provided the single landing strip of Kai Tak Airport.

October in Hong Kong was cool, the steamy summer season washed away by the last of the monsoons, with only a whisper of exotic sultriness that slipped across the senses with provocative sensuality.

This was the Territory, the Pearl of the Orient, a blend of old-world China and a dozen European cultures. It was seductive and sensational, a mixture of Suzie Wong and James Clavell. It was five thousand years of Chinese history and a century and a half of Western control. The contrast between old world and new, East and West, was vivid. And it was big business. It was a world unto itself, where wealth meant power.

Here in Hong Kong, the Fragrant Harbor, over a century earlier Hamish Fortune had made his fortune on a cargo of sandalwood and founded a dynasty. This was a far different city than he had known, but it still held the same promise for Christina.

Bill Thomason had come in the day before. In spite of the late hour, he met them as they deplaned. He whisked them past the usual immigration area and Customs Hall, where a

dozen lines of weary, anxious travelers waited in front of an
equal number of small desks with slack-faced uniformed immigration officers.

An immigration official recognized Bill and Ross, and
waved them through a gate. There they were stopped briefly,
their passports inspected and stamped. Then Bill guided them
past the immigration cordon, up a small corridor, past the VIP
lounge to the taxi queue and the congestion of automobiles.

They threaded their way through waiting red and gray
Toyota taxis, to the limousine. Bill gave their driver instructions to go directly to the Regent Hotel.

As the driver pulled away from the curb, Bill told Ross,
"Phillip Lo called. He's set up a meeting for you tomorrow
with his cousin. It seems he has connections to the Triad boss
you'll be dealing with. And your first meeting with the Cartel
is scheduled for the following day."

"The Triad?" Christina looked up in surprise. "I hadn't realized we'd be meeting with them."

Ross picked up the faint notes of disapproval in her voice.
"It's a necessary part of doing business here. We deal with
them regularly. They control most of the transportation within
the Crown colony, as well as the ports."

"But they're the Chinese mafia," she insisted.

"They're also involved in legitimate business. Look upon it
as dealing with a necessary middleman. You won't be able to
pull off this expansion without them. They've been in Hong
Kong for centuries. I'd be willing to bet old Hamish Fortune
did more than a little business with them. Remember," he
said, "this is Asia. Things are different here."

"You're saying we can't change the Eastern culture, so
we'd better accept it," she replied as the lights of the airport
concourse disappeared behind them.

"Alexander Fortune, and Michael after him, understood
how to deal with these people. They moved within Hong
Kong with far more ease and respect than most *gweilos*."

She was aware that *gweilos* were any "foreign, blue-eyed
devil," usually the English who had first opened this part of
the world to clipper trade. However, the term also applied to
Europeans and Americans.

"It will be difficult enough for you in other ways," Ross added.

"Because I'm a woman."

He smiled ruefully. "Yes. But you're still Michael Fortune's daughter. And that will count for a great deal with the men you'll meet. The trick is, you must not approach them as a woman."

She was deeply grateful that he referred to her as Michael Fortune's daughter. Maybe they'd finally left behind the questions and suspicions. *Maybe.* "Short of cutting my hair and wearing three-piece pinstripe suits, what do you suggest?"

"Be professional," he told her flatly. "Exactly the way you were when you walked into the boardroom of Fortune International. In many ways this is no different. You'll be staking your claim to the right to do business here. And that's a little dangerous, because you're going against the status quo—a woman doing business in a man's domain."

She saw a look pass between Ross and Bill. "Why do I get the feeling I haven't been told everything?" she asked.

Bill continued to look at Ross. "You should tell her, before she walks into the meeting with the Cartel."

She turned to Ross. "What is it you should tell me?"

He was thoughtful for several moments. "I was concerned that if they knew who they were meeting with, they might refuse. Business in Hong Kong is a very closed fraternity."

"Just who do they think they'll be meeting with?" she asked.

Bill had a slightly amused expression. "They think they're meeting with Richard. They've met with him in the past over other proposals."

"Richard never understood the meaning of the words *trust* and *honor*," Ross added. "Even among the Triads, those are the most important elements to any deal."

"Honor among thieves," Christina said dryly.

They drove along the western end of Victorian Harbor, and Bill pointed out several Fortune ships waiting to off-load at Kwai Chung's well-lit container terminals, the busiest in the world. Then they turned onto Salisbury Road.

The Green Dragon, symbol of the Territory, fluttered over the red granite and glass facade of the Regent Hotel.

There was no sign, no marquee with the hotel name. It was distinctive by its location, set back from the busier shopping district of Tsim Sha Tsui on pilings reaching out into the harbor. It was one of the most prestigious addresses in the entire colony.

Ross pointed to the two-story windows that looked out onto the harbor. "Those windows allow the nine dragons easy access to the harbor and guarantee the hotel a favored place with the gods."

Christina knew that the nine dragons referred to Kowloon itself—and the legend that the peninsula was actually made of nine resting dragons who awoke each day at sunrise and bathed in the harbor. They were mythical guardians against any outsider who ventured to the Orient.

Even before their car came to a full stop, a uniformed concierge immediately stepped to the curb to open the door for them. Ross stepped out first and held out his hand to Christina.

The doorman held the door open for them. As they stepped inside the lobby, Bill left, saying, "I've got some calls to make to the States. I'll see you later this morning, when the offices open. We can go over everything then."

Ross and Christina were greeted by a Chinese man dressed in an elegant suit. He looked like any other successful businessman. But he wasn't just any businessman. He was the manager of the Regent, a position of prestige and privilege.

"Good evening, Mr. McKenna. It is good to have you back with us at the Regent."

"Kwang, this is Miss Fortune."

Kwang bowed his head. "Welcome to the Regent, Miss Fortune. This is indeed a very great pleasure. I have already checked you in at the desk. I will escort you to your rooms."

Their rooms were located on the fifteenth floor, directly across the hall from one another. Kwang opened the door to her suite and preceded them inside.

The suite was elegant, with mahogany furnishings upholstered in pale peach, plush peach carpeting, and white damask drapes. A set of double doors opened onto the adjoining bedroom and bath. A second set of doors opened out onto a landscaped terrace.

Kwang went about the suite, wiping at a nonexistent speck of dust, straightening the fold of a drape, rearranging the exotic bird-of-paradise floral arrangement on the marble-top table. Nothing escaped his critical eye. Christina was certain that if he found anything amiss, heads would roll.

Obviously satisfied with what he found, Kwang stepped to the phone, spoke several words in Cantonese, then returned the phone to its cradle.

"May-may is first house girl," he informed Christina. "She has been told of your arrival and will see to all your needs. Is there anything you wish at this time?"

"Our luggage is still at the airport," she reminded Ross.

"It will be brought up as soon as it arrives," Kwang informed her. "May-may will see to it."

Ross thanked Kwang. "There's no need to show me to my suite." Kwang bowed and silently left the suite. Ross turned to her. "How about eight-thirty for breakfast in the morning?"

"All right."

He reached up and gently caressed her cheek, still bruised from the fall she'd taken off the cable car. "Till then," he said softly.

A long, hot bath was wonderfully refreshing after twenty-four hours on a plane in the same clothes. She wrapped herself in the thick monogrammed terry robe provided by the hotel and brushed her hair as she came out of the bathroom.

The clothes she'd carelessly thrown across the bed were gone. She walked past the walk-in closet and noticed that her luggage had arrived. Her clothes hung in the closet on padded hangers. Her shoes were lined up neatly in the bottom of the closet, and her undergarments had been folded and put away in the lined drawers of the dresser. This was obviously the handiwork of first house girl, May-may, who was quiet as well as efficient. Christina hadn't heard a sound in the bathroom.

Seeing this neatness and order, she couldn't help smiling at the thought of the way she behaved at home, leaving a trail of clothes from just inside the front door of her apartment all the way across the living room and into the bedroom. Almost obsessively meticulous in her professional habits, she deliberately abandoned that obsession in her personal life. As Julie had told her once when they were roommates, "You're so on top of things at work, and so laid-back at home. I guess that creates an odd sort of balance in a way."

She'd often thought how great it would be to have someone to pick up after her so that she didn't have to worry about it. This, she decided, would take very little getting used to.

She restlessly stalked the suite. She'd been keyed up when they arrived at the hotel, and was certain she'd never be able to get to sleep. Leaping time zones always played havoc with her internal clock. And there were so many things to think about.

Would the members of the Cartel listen to her proposal?

*If* they listened, would they even consider it? Or would they simply dismiss her, as a woman and therefore as unworthy of doing business with, and send her on her way?

She knew the proposal was sound. With the participation percentages she'd outlined, there was the potential for all to make back their investment and show a profit of over two hundred percent within three years.

There had never been a trade agreement like this with mainland China. Now was the time to move forward with it. But would the members of the Cartel even listen?

And then there was the fact that they had been led to believe they would be meeting with Richard.

Ross had called the Cartel an exclusive fraternity. Had he ever been part of that fraternity?

She lay down on the bed. The satin was cool beneath her bruised cheek. Ross had said that what they were doing could be dangerous. She thought of other dangers . . . the very real possibility that someone wanted her dead. *Who?*

She fell asleep without finding an answer to that question.

A soft, pleasant tone awakened her. She lay there while her senses adjusted past the momentary confusion, the muted light in the room, the coolness of the satin coverlet against her bare shoulder. The tone sounded again and she reached for the bedside phone.

"Are you awake?" The masculine voice reminded her of another morning, aboard the *Resolute*.

"Hmmmm. What time is it?"

"Seven-thirty."

She groaned.

"I've ordered up breakfast. You have exactly one hour."

She curled on her side and snuggled lower into the satiny coverlet. "What did you order? I might not approve."

He chuckled softly. "If you'd been here, you could have ordered. As it is, you take your chances. See you in an hour."

She lay there for a few minutes longer thinking of what he'd said. *". . . if you'd been here . . ."*

At precisely eight-thirty she rang the door chimes to his suite. Ross opened the door. He was immaculately dressed in charcoal gray silk slacks, pale blue shirt with white collar and cuffs, and a charcoal and burgundy chevron-design tie. The elegant cut of the clothes was in sharp contrast to the rugged handsomeness of the man. "Good morning," he said, stepping aside to let her in.

Through open French doors, she saw that breakfast had been set out on the veranda. At the table she found hot croissants with orange marmalade, fresh tropical fruit, and scrambled eggs with herbs. Suddenly she felt as if she hadn't eaten in days. She didn't know if her appetite was sharpened by the brisk breeze coming in from the bay, the long trip . . . or the entirely too stimulating effect of Ross's presence.

Whatever the cause, she ate much more than she normally would have done, and enjoyed every bite. Afterward Christina sipped a cup of fragrant tea as she stood at the railing and looked at the sweeping view of Hong Kong Harbor.

"What are you thinking?" Ross said quietly as he came up beside her and leaned his hip against the railing. He watched her, instead of the captivating view.

She hugged her arms about herself in the cool morning air. "I'm trying to imagine how it must have looked when Hamish Fortune first sailed into Hong Kong Harbor."

Ross's gaze followed hers. "Block out the skyscrapers, put clippers in place of all the steel-hulled container ships, and it's probably not very different."

"It must have been exciting," she murmured, giving way to her imagination.

"And dangerous," Ross put in. "Ships from all over the world, every man a law unto himself, immigrants, warlords. Many a man found himself shanghaied aboard a ship bound here and never found his way back home."

"Were there pirates?" she asked.

"Undoubtedly. In fact, I'd be willing to bet old Hamish Fortune did more than his share of pirating. Those were different times. It wasn't considered breaking the law unless you got caught."

"He must have been an enterprising businessman to have succeeded so well in that kind of cutthroat environment."

Ross choked with laughter. "He was enterprising, all right. He swindled a merchant out of his sandalwood, for a nonexistent cargo of opium that he managed to convince the old weasel he'd taken off a scuttled Dutchman bound for Amsterdam."

She'd heard the colorful story before, and was aware that the family insisted it had never been proved. "But he never dealt in opium," she insisted.

"As I said, he swindled that old merchant. The cargo of opium never even existed. But the merchant didn't know that when he bought the cargo."

She laughed. "Now there was a true salesman."

His amused expression changed, turning serious. "You'll have to be the same kind of salesman. I think you can do it, Chris."

She thought, *He believes in me.* Another thought quickly followed—*I could love this man.*

He had turned to stare out at the panorama of the busy harbor. He seemed energized, less guarded than she'd ever seen him before, even aboard the *Resolute.*

"You love all of this, don't you?" she said with an expansive sweep of her hand, indicating Hong Kong.

"It's more exciting than any other place I've ever been.

And dangerous. And temporal. Although it's thousands of years old, it's constantly new. Now it's in the midst of perhaps the greatest transition of all."

"You mean when China takes over in 1997."

"Yes. You can see it everywhere—for instance, in the helipads atop all the professional buildings."

She looked at him quizzically. "The perfect toy for busy executives?"

Ross's expression was grave. "A quick escape if things heat up after the Chinese take back control of the island. It's a relatively short flight to the safety of Taiwan."

She looked out on the city that he obviously loved with an intensity that only those who'd been born and bred there could possibly understand.

"There's an almost frantic air to it now," Ross went on, as if he were talking to himself. "Everyone rushing to do things yesterday, as if tomorrow may not come."

"A contradiction of the Asian way of doing things," she said thoughtfully.

"A reminder that everything here is very fragile, on the edge, no matter how much money everyone *believes* flows through the Hong Kong and Victoria banks."

"Believes?" she asked, picking up on the word.

He nodded. "There are no longer any large amounts of liquid assets in Hong Kong. Everyone with influence and power has gradually and quietly transferred all his money to banks in Taiwan, or Europe. Since the agreement was signed, there's been a bloody rash of new Swiss bank accounts."

"Do you think the British should have signed that agreement?"

He was thoughtful. "They had no choice. The days of colonialism and Empire rule are over. This is Chinese territory; it doesn't belong to Britain."

"But European trade made Hong Kong what it is today. There are some who believe that handing it all back to the Chinese will be like turning back the clock two hundred years. And that equates into thousands of years of development."

"That's a risk everyone will have to take. The taipans have

ruled here long enough." There was an edge to his voice that bordered on bitter anger. He finished, "It's time to let the Chinese control their own destiny."

She was surprised at his attitude, so at odds with how most businessmen, especially English businessmen, felt. She had considered him to be a pragmatist, guided by ambition. Now she realized that he was actually a passionate idealist. Where had that attitude come from? she wondered.

He went on, "Of course, the transition will be difficult and painful. And there are those who believe it won't work. That's why they crowd the immigration offices daily, hoping desperately they can be among the few allowed to emigrate to England or Canada."

"Will you still come to Hong Kong?" she asked.

"Yes. I'll always come back. This is my home."

Home. A sense of family. They were things she understood with a sharp awareness of the great void in her own life over the past twenty years.

"I always thought that home was anywhere I happened to live," she said slowly. "But lately I've come to feel that it has to mean more than that—roots, stability, a sense of belonging."

"A sense of belonging . . ." he repeated thoughtfully. "Yes. That's important. Without it you have nothing."

She looked at him with a heightened curiosity. From the moment they'd touched down in Hong Kong, she'd sensed a change in Ross, a lowering of his defenses. She felt that, in a very real sense, she was seeing the man beneath the tough facade for the first time. She longed to know more about him. How did he feel? What did he think? What did he want and need? How much could he give?

And most of all, could he love her as she was only now beginning to understand that she needed to be loved?

That question couldn't be answered yet. There were other priorities at the moment. But Christina knew it would have to be answered. And soon.

Ross kept a Range Rover permanently garaged at the Regent. They left the hotel and took Canton Road, cutting past

the ferry terminal to the cross-channel tunnel. Within minutes
they emerged on the other side—Hong Kong Island.

Central, the business district of Hong Kong, was ultramodern and sleek, and could have been any modern city in any
one of a dozen countries with its jungle of skyscrapers thrusting into the clear blue sky. The streets were filled with taxis,
Mercedes automobiles, and countless suited executives scurrying about with briefcases and cellular phones.

They passed the Admiralty suburb, and the government and
legal buildings, then turned onto bank row.

The architecture was fascinating, a mixture of steel and
concrete perched beside the sea. It almost looked like San
Francisco's financial district, except for the huge ornate me-
dallions, embossed with ancient characters set into the granite
and stone facades of the Hong Kong Bank, the Shanghai
Bank, and the Bank of China across from the Chater Garden
park. They drove around the park onto Queensway and pulled
to a stop before an older brick building of the style of the old
Empire. Ross came around to help Christina out of the car.

The garden was beautiful, but Christina's attention focused
on the six-story building that bordered it. A simple bronze
plaque affixed to the brick facade contained the crooked characters that proclaimed it to be the Fortune offices. But she
would have known it anywhere by the sculptured anchor that
flanked the main entrance. It was an exact duplicate of the
one outside Fortune Tower in San Francisco.

The building was much older than the others, flanked by
huge, modern skyscrapers.

"It all began here," she murmured to herself as she stepped
out onto the sidewalk and stared at the building with a feeling
of awe mingled with pride.

She knew that the original shipping office was nothing
more than a desk in a warehouse over in Kowloon. Hamish
Fortune built on this site after establishing his shipping line
between Hawaii and San Francisco. That first building burned
down and was replaced by this one at the turn of the century.

Stepping inside the lobby, Christina experienced that same
feeling she'd encountered so many times in some of Boston's
older buildings, a sense of history and permanence. The lobby

was high-ceilinged with gleaming wood floors, wainscoting, and tall mullioned windows. The doorman was dressed in a uniform of the old Empire and opened the door for her with military formality. Paintings of dozens of Fortune ships lined the walls.

A young woman sat at a desk behind a curved teak counter set with marble and brass. The wood smelled rich and old, and gleamed with care and fine oils. It was like stepping back in time, except for the sophisticated, well-dressed Chinese woman at the desk. "Good morning, Mr. McKenna, Miss Fortune," she greeted them.

The familiarity was unexpected and surprised her. "Good morning," Christina replied.

Noting her surprise, the young woman smiled and explained, "Mr. Thomason said you would be coming in this morning." Then she turned to include Ross. "He and Miss Jeung are waiting for you upstairs."

"Who is Miss Jeung?" Christina asked as the elevator doors closed on them.

"My personal secretary. She and Adam Quon virtually run the office in my absence. You'll be meeting both of them, along with the Fortune staff, if Lisa is up to her usual efficiency. I hired her away from another company ten years ago. Quon has been with the company for over thirty-five years. It's a family position, but he's earned it every step of the way. He worked for your father. His father and grandfather also worked for the company."

"I thought Steven ran this office."

Ross smiled. "He thinks he does."

When the elevator doors opened, Ross and Christina were greeted by an attractive Eurasian woman. "Good morning, Mr. McKenna," she said with a warm smile. "It's good to have you back." Then she turned to Christina, and her greeting was studiously polite, but with a faint reserve. "Welcome to Hong Kong, Miss Fortune."

"Thank you."

Christina was unaccustomed to such professional formalities, and had to remind herself that while Hong Kong was an international city with a reputation for being one of the most modern and sophisticated cities in the world, it was still inherently Asian by influence. As Bill and Ross had reminded her, honor and respect were everything. And it was obvious that the honor and respect shown to Ross resulted from more than mere courtesy. He'd earned them. She saw it in the warmth behind the formal greeting. It was there when the receptionist greeted them as they came in. It was there now, as his secretary spoke with them.

"Lisa is my right and left hand," Ross explained as they crossed the reception area. He went on, "When you have a chance, you might want to take a look at your father's old office. Katherine used it in the past, but it's been closed in recent years since she's been unable to travel."

"I'm surprised Richard hasn't taken it for his office," she remarked.

Ross shook his head. "He took the set of offices your grandfather used when he was alive." He pointed out the office as they passed down the hall, then pointed to the one directly across the hall from it. Both were closed, behind frosted glass doors. Michael Fortune's name remained stenciled on one, while Alexander Fortune's name had been replaced with Richard's.

"Your father and grandfather worked here together for many years. Your grandfather would shout across the hall whenever he wanted him. Your father tried to get him to use the phones, but he refused."

They turned down another hall. Ross was giving Lisa instructions. "Miss Fortune and I will be working together. Make arrangements to have an extra desk and chair brought up from the basement and put in my office."

The doors that lined both sides of the hallway were open. A man or woman stood in the doorway of each and watched as they approached. Christina looked questioningly at Ross.

"I thought that Miss Fortune would like to meet our office staff," Lisa explained.

The entire staff had obviously been informed of her arrival. By tradition, it was expected that she meet each one. It was another subtle reminder of the Asian influence that dominated Hong Kong.

"Yes," Christina replied. "I would like that very much."

As they slowly walked down the hallway, she was introduced to each employee. They all greeted her with stiff formality, their expressions closed, their manner polite but reserved. They clearly didn't know what to make of her.

First impressions were critical. Christina knew that her future relationship with these people would be determined now. And so she instinctively chose to greet them with a slight bow, in the traditional Chinese manner, rather than shaking hands, surprising them even more when she greeted them in Cantonese.

The last man she met was small and reed-thin, his black hair streaked with silver. "My name is Quon," he introduced himself. "I have served your grandfather and your father. I am honored to serve you."

"Thank you, Mr. Quon," she spoke carefully, "I am privileged that you honor me in this way."

His head was bowed slightly. When he looked up, he beamed at her, obviously pleased by her response.

When the introductions were completed, she turned and said to them all in Cantonese, "It is my wish to take my place in this house that my honored ancestors built. Thank you for making me feel welcome."

Ross watched her with a contemplative expression. He knew these people, and behind their implacable expressions, he sensed their surprise. Unlike Richard, who chose an aloof, authoritarian position, or Steven, who was callous and inconsiderate of the people who worked for them, Christina was completely unpretentious. Her choice to greet them in their own language was a subtle reminder that while she was the boss, she respected them.

When had he quit thinking of her as the young woman who claimed to be Christina Fortune, and simply begun thinking of her as Christina?

There was something intensely compelling about her that made him want to believe. It was more than just the physical attraction—the curve of her cheek, the softness of her mouth, a look in her eyes. It was the real person deep inside—vulnerable, tough, smart, a survivor, not a victim. A person who curled on her right side when she slept, and whose dreams were filled with dark shadows that caused her to cry out in her sleep.

He had his own secrets and had always respected the secrets other people had. But with this woman he wanted to learn her secrets, to take them apart one by one, until there were no more shadows in her dreams.

He looked up as a single round of applause cut through the soft murmur of greetings. Steven Chandler stepped out of his office at the end of the hallway. "Very good, cousin," he said as he slowly walked toward her. "I heard that you got in last night."

Ross saw her quick flash of anger. Just as quickly it was hidden behind a cool expression.

"Hello, Steven. I thought it was time for me to come over and find out about our Pacific Rim operation. Bill and Ross were coming over, and they were kind enough to offer to show me around."

Steven eyed her with a blatantly sexual expression as the employees all went back to their offices. "Why don't you let me show you around? There are some intriguing places in this city. I guarantee, you won't be bored."

Before she could respond, Ross said tightly, "Right now I need to discuss something with Christina in my office," and he shepherded her past Steven into his own office, closing the door behind them.

"He's up to something," Ross said bluntly.

"He's just being his usual oversexed self."

Ross shook his head. "It's more than that. He didn't for one moment believe your excuse for being here."

As easily as he shifted from one problem to the next, he shifted the conversation. "I wasn't aware you spoke Cantonese."

"As someone once said, I picked up a little here, a little there." She gave him a conspiratorial smile. "I know only a few greetings, and I'm always afraid I'm asking someone where the bathroom is rather than saying hello."

"You did very well," he assured her. "And you didn't ask where the bathroom was."

She glanced around his office. It was decorated simply, with black lacquer furnishings, an expensive Oriental rug on the teak floor, and several glass tables with Chinese artifacts.

The collection represented a blend of several dynasties: a shallow Ming water bowl, a vase from the Sung dynasty, and several small carved soldiers and war horses set in columns as they marched across a black jade table. They appeared to be excellent reproductions of the magnificent life-size army that had been excavated a few years earlier.

"These are beautiful," Christina said. "I saw several pieces of the original army when they were on loan to the museum in New York. Where did you get these reproduced to such perfect detail?"

"I didn't get them reproduced," Ross said as he came around the desk.

She looked up, stunned. "They're originals?"

"The life-size army drew worldwide attention. These tiny figures were found at the same site but were almost ignored. They're an exact duplicate, hand-carved as a game set for the emperor. The game is very similar to chess."

"And you just happened to acquire them?"

"I know certain people." His smile was disarming. "At any rate, the life-size ones were too large for this office."

"It's about time you got here," Bill greeted them as he poked his head into the office. "I hear you caused quite a stir among the employees. And what did you say to Steven? I saw him on his way out. He practically bit my head off."

"What's he been up to since you got back?" Ross asked.

Bill shrugged as he came into the office and sat in one of the cane chairs before the desk. "I heard he lost heavily at the tables in Macau. He's been staying over in Wanchai since he got in."

At Christina's questioning look, Ross explained. "Wanchai has undergone a great deal of new construction lately— apartments, condos. Most of the young executives keep a place there. It's very upscale, as they say."

"Does Steven have a place there?" she asked.

Bill shrugged. "He has a particular friend he keeps over there. He visits her whenever he's in Hong Kong."

"Quon said he's been spending a lot of time down at the terminal when we have a new ship coming in. Have you heard anything about it?"

"He mentioned it to me, too." Bill was thoughtful. "We haven't made any big changes with our clients. I can't put my finger on it, but something's going on."

Ross nodded. "Check it out, and let me know what you come up with."

"All right. By the way, Lisa mentioned that she discovered some discrepancies in the cargo manifest for one of our ships."

Ross's dark blue gaze narrowed. "What sort of discrepancies?"

Bill shrugged. "Something about some missing containers that got held up in port because they hadn't been cleared by customs inspectors. Anyway Steven took it upon himself to solve the problem."

Ross frowned. "It isn't like Steven to take on a responsibility that he can turn over to someone else. He's always been more interested in the yacht club regattas and bedding every woman he meets than he's been in the operations of the company." He finished, "Have Quon keep an eye on him."

They worked on Christina's proposal for the Cartel throughout the morning and well past lunch. They went over every possible question the Cartel might raise about investment participation, risk factors, and profit margins.

They worked side by side, as equals, updating the proposal, exchanging ideas, drawing on each other's expertise to make the proposal absolutely solid.

Christina had no misgivings about their professional collaboration. She knew Ross was shrewd and cunning. He proved it a dozen ways that morning as he improved on her suggestions. And when she surprised him by suggesting a percentage buy-back option as part of the joint venture, he simply sat back in his chair and let her run with it.

He didn't patronize her or minimize her participation, and he obviously didn't feel threatened by her. He asked her opinion of every detail. If he agreed, he told her so. If not, he was frank in his criticism.

They were good together, she realized, with a surge of excitement. It made her wonder how good they might be together in other ways.

They were just finishing when Bill walked in. "In Hong Kong, as opposed to the United States, lunch is a ritual. It's unheard of for people to work through lunch."

Christina grinned. "Is that a hint?"

"Hey, I don't know about you two, but I'm starving." He looked over at Ross. "Do you have plans?"

Ross nodded. "I thought I'd take Chris up to Victoria Peak," he said as he put everything away in his private safe.

"Then you won't need me along to keep you out of trouble," Bill quipped. Leaning across the desk, he said just loud enough for Ross to hear, "Watch this guy. He's on his own turf now. He knows a lot of shady characters from his youth."

She looked over at Ross speculatively, thinking there just might be a great deal of truth behind the joke. She smiled. "I'll remember that."

Bill swung away from the desk. "I'm off to the docks. Oh, by the way," he added, stopping at the door, "Katherine called on the private line. Richard will be coming over soon. Steven must have notified him of your arrival."

"Thanks," Ross said, then added. "Be careful."

Bill's expression shifted. "I'm always careful." He looked at Christina. "You be careful, too."

"We'll see you later this afternoon, back here," Ross said by way of a none-too-subtle hint to Bill to get going. Ignoring him, Bill said to Christina, "He may be my friend, but watch out for the guy. He has no scruples."

"So I've heard."

"Bye, kids," Bill said, closing the door behind him.

"So," Christina said, "Where are we going for lunch?"

"There's this place I know—spectacular views, incomparable food, excellent company . . ."

Sensing that what he had in mind was a private tête-à-tête, she said, "And exclusive?"

"Very exclusive," Ross assured her.

# Chapter 28

Christina had driven the crowded streets of Boston and New York. She'd learned to maneuver through downtown San Francisco's maze of one-way streets and steep hills, all the while evading the cable cars and electric buses. But nothing prepared her for the frantic stop and go pace of the Central district during the height of rush-hour traffic. Cars were either blocked behind tour buses, taxis, and limousines, or whipping through intersections at top speed to the peril of anyone who stepped off the curb. An amazing number of people did, somehow miraculously escape unscathed.

Ross negotiated the narrow streets and alleys with ease, cutting across Queen's Road Central, Wellington, and something known as the Loop. Then they climbed out of Central on Old Peak Road up into the hills above the Harbor district. The air was cooler and clearer here, and the traffic smoothed out on the two-lane road that steadily wound up into the green, lush hills.

It was as if someone had magically drawn a curtain. One moment they were staring at concrete and steel walls, the next they were surrounded by stands of pine, eucalyptus, and banyan trees. The trees' pungent fragrance filled the air. Christina rolled down her window and let the wind blow through her loose hair. As they wound through the hills, she caught glimpses of the harbor spread below, and was reminded that Victoria Peak claimed the most beautiful views of the island from all directions.

She sat back in the passenger seat, closed her eyes, and let her other senses take over. *Zanshin*, Ross had called it. She felt, tasted, and smelled the exotic essence that was Hong Kong Island, letting the awareness of it fill and surround her.

The past, present, and future . . . memories, reality, dreams. They were all here. This strange, fascinating island held the key to a promise made twenty years ago. But even as she made that promise, she'd had no idea how far it would bring her.

"A penny," Ross said as he reached for her hand on the seat and enfolded it in his.

She turned to stare at his strong profile—the chiseled features that seemed almost too handsome to make him a man to be taken seriously. Then he turned and gave her a brief glance, and a raw, fierce intensity lit his eyes. The power of it might have intimidated, even frightened, someone else. Perhaps it accounted in part for his ruthless reputation. But she was no longer frightened by him. Now she understood him, for in his expression she saw somthing of herself and what had driven her the past twenty years.

Then a surprisingly tender smile curved the corner of his mouth, stirring feelings deep within her. And the reassuring touch of Ross's fingers twining through hers, reminding her of his promise—*"We will make love. But it will be when there are no more secrets between us."*

What are your secrets, Ross McKenna?

Am I ready to reveal mine? Am I strong enough? Can I trust you that completely? Can I risk losing myself in you?

Finally she answered his question. "I was thinking of promises."

"What about them?"

"A long time ago I made one that I have to keep."

He looked at her again briefly, his expression contemplative.

"Can I help you keep it?" he asked.

"I hope so."

He turned the next corner, into a residential district where huge estates rivaled any of those in fashionable Long Island, Beacon Hill, or Pacific Heights in San Francisco.

He turned another corner, and the homes were comparatively modest—although the word *modest* was hardly an accurate description for the sprawling bungalows and two-story houses set back from the road. He pulled into a driveway, stopped, and turned to her, taking her hand once more.

"I made a promise to you, Chris. One I intend to keep." He stroked small circular motions across the palm of her hand with his thumb, his eyes never leaving hers. Then he slipped his left hand behind her neck and pulled her toward him.

His gaze never left hers as he slowly kneaded the taut cords at the back of her neck. Her skin was like warm velvet. He wound her shoulder-length hair about his hand and slowly drew her toward him, reminding them of shared needs and desires as his mouth caressed hers. She could taste the sweetness of his breath as it mingled with hers.

When they finally pulled apart, she couldn't speak. His voice was shaky as he said, "There's someone I want you to meet."

Christina combed her fingers back through her disheveled hair as they walked up the short driveway hand in hand.

The house was a blend of architectures—stone masonry and wood, with a slate roof that gave the impression of an English country home. That first impression from the cobbled drive was enhanced by the leaded paned windows on the ground floor, the steeply gabled roof, and the surrounding garden.

Ross unlatched the wooden gate, and they walked through.

Christina felt as though she'd stepped into a fairy woodland. Any moment she expected gnomes to poke their faces from behind trees, so perfect was the setting. Primroses bordered the garden, then gave way to a wild profusion of hibiscus, cyneraria, begonias, hollyhocks, and loubelia. Bougainvillea draped a low stone fence. She tried to imagine how many hours of work it must take to maintain an enormous garden like this. Then she thought of the hours she'd spent in a futile attempt to coax life into the single houseplant she'd kept in Boston.

The front steps were red brick and worn, the door heavy and solid. Ross rang the bell, and as they waited for an answer, he turned and gazed out at the garden.

"It's quite something, isn't it? I always dreamed of a garden like this when I was a child, a private forest of my own to hide in."

What did he need to hide from? she wondered. But she knew she couldn't ask him such an intimate question. Yet.

"It *is* beautiful," she agreed. "I can't imagine anyone having a green thumb like this. Inside of a week I'd kill everything with too much watering, or not enough."

"It's hard to kill plants here. Everything is always so green and lush."

Then the door was opened by an exquisitely lovely, middle-aged Eurasian woman. Her eyes widened, and she clapped her hands to her cheeks when she saw Ross. "Aiyeeee! Ross McKenna, you blackhearted devil!" she squealed. "You didn't tell us you were coming!"

Before she had a chance to recover, Ross scooped her up in his arms and whirled her around.

"Put me down!" she cried indignantly. When he refused, she began yelling at him in Cantonese.

Christina understood a few of the words. The ones she didn't understand she decided probably weren't worth repeating.

As she stood in the doorway, she remembered what he'd said about a woman who had initiated him as a young man. Could this possibly be her? she wondered with a sinking sensation.

From the height of his extended arms, the woman ordered, "Put me down. You have the manners of a *gweilo*!" Then she looked past Ross to Christina, and an expression of dismay crossed her face at the realization that she'd used that kind of language in front of another *gweilo*.

"See what you have done!" she rebuked him. "You have dishonored me in front of your friend."

Smiling broadly, Ross finally put her down.

"What is it, Lin? Did I hear someone at the door?"

A tall, extremely attractive Englishwoman came into the foyer. "Ross!"

He crossed the entry hall in long strides and embraced her, holding her for a very long time.

When he finally let her go, she said in amazement, "What are you doing here? You didn't write, you didn't call. The least you could have done was let me know you were coming. When did you get in?"

"Last night, love. It was very late," Ross said as he stepped back, still holding the woman's hand.

"And you've brought a guest," she said, smiling politely at Christina. "Don't you think you should introduce us?"

Ross grinned sheepishly. "Why do you always make me feel as if I've forgotten all my manners?"

"Because you usually do." There was laughter in her eyes as she teased him. The laughter transformed her mature, striking beauty with its flawless complexion framed by softly waving, dark hair, giving her a surprisingly youthful air.

"Then I suppose I should make introductions before you throw me out," he quipped.

"If she doesn't throw you out, I will," Lin announced from her guardian position beside the still open door. Her expression suggested she would do just that.

Ross turned back to Christina. "I'd like to present Miss Christina Fortune from San Francisco. Chris, you've already met Lin. She has the temperament of a goat."

Standing beside the door, Lin gave him a disgusted look. She closed the door and then turned on her heel. "May a pox descend on you," she muttered over her shoulder as she disappeared.

Ross was completely unaffected, and Christina could only assume this was a familiar scene between them. He took her hand and drew her beside him.

"And this lovely lady," he said, finishing the introductions, "is Barbara McKenna, my mother."

Christina was completely taken aback.

Barbara McKenna shook her head helplessly. "Forgive my son," she said with a smile that turned up at the corners in an all-too familiar way. "He delights in catching people unaware. You have my permission to call him several well-chosen names when you leave, if you like."

"I might just do that," Christina said, glancing at him.

So, she thought, this was Ross's mother. The resemblance was unmistakable. They had the same dark coloring, aristocratic features, and that same charismatic smile.

"Come in, Christina." Barbara took her hand and led her into the drawing room, deliberately ignoring Ross. "It's so nice to meet you."

The afternoon passed quietly. The four of them—Ross, Christina, Barbara, and Lin—ate lunch in the garden. The roast leg of lamb with plum sauce, fresh garden vegetables with hollandaise, curried rice, and chardonnay wine were wonderful. And the setting was incomparable. Christina couldn't remember when she'd had such a peaceful, pleasant time.

"I know quite a bit about your family, through Ross," Barbara said as he poured more wine for them. "What brings you to Hong Kong?"

Christina glanced at Ross. He didn't look up, didn't convey any message by either word or gesture. Clearly he hadn't told his mother about their plans, and Christina wasn't sure how much to reveal. She said carefully, "There are certain changes that I want to make in the company. The world market is changing, and Fortune International has to change with it."

Ross explained, "Chris wants to take the company into the mainland China market."

Barbara looked at her with new interest. "I was born in mainland China and lived there for several years, in Guangzhou Province. My parents were missionaries there."

Christina was amazed. "Ross didn't tell me."

Barbara laughed. "If you spend much time around him at all, you'll find that he has a tendency to say only what's necessary for his own purposes. I suppose that comes from being an Englishman raised in Hong Kong. It can be very isolating for a child."

"But not for you?" Christina asked.

Barbara said easily, "I love China and the way of life I grew up with. Much of it is gone now, since the communist regime took over."

"Are your parents still there?"

"No," Barbara answered with a sad smile. "They're both dead now. We were forced to leave Guangzhou Province when the Japanese invaded. We returned to England and spent the war years there. My older brother flew with the RAF. His plane went down over the English Channel. After the war I missed living in China dreadfully. I was young and adventurous, and I wanted to come back." She smiled at the memory.

"I got on with the diplomatic department in London through friends of my parents. After the war I was allowed to come back over to Hong Kong. By then, ill health prevented my parents from returning."

"And you never went back to England?"

"I returned for occasional visits. But after my parents were gone, there didn't seem to be much reason. I had Ross by then, and in my own way I created a bit of England in my garden."

"It's beautiful."

"You should have seen the garden at the house on Connaught Road," Ross interjected. "I remember the roses."

Barbara laughed. "Everyone thought I was crazy, including Lin."

Lin picked up the story. "That was when I first came to live with Barbara and Ross. Here was this dotty English-woman trying to grow roses in Hong Kong."

Barbara continued, "And then Ross bought this house for me, and the garden here is ten times the size of the one at the little house."

Christina looked at Ross. She'd just discovered something else about him—he, not his father had bought this house. And by its location, with a sweeping view of the harbor, she knew it hadn't come cheaply. Why, she wondered, hadn't Ross or his mother mentioned his father?

When she'd walked through the living room to get to the French doors that opened onto the garden, she'd seen a collection of family photographs on the piano. There were pho-

tographs of an older couple, who she now realized were
Barbara's parents, and a dashing young man with a cocky grin
in an RAF flight jacket, who bore a striking resemblance to
Ross. There were photographs of Ross and Barbara through
different stages in his life—his graduation from his A levels
in school, and an early one of Ross and Bill obviously taken
when they first met in Canada. But she'd seen no photos of
anyone who might be his father.

Realizing she'd been silent for too long, Christina asked
quickly, "How did your roses do?"

"They won blue ribbons," Ross said, pride evident in his
voice. "She even cultivated a hybrid that is called the Barbara
Blue Rose."

Christina looked at her with amazement. "I'm impressed. I
never knew anyone who had roses named after her."

"My dear," Barbara leaned over and fondly patted her
hand, "you have ships named after you. *I'm* impressed with
that."

Christina shook her head. "Building a ship requires merely
technical expertise. Cultivating a rose is creating beauty. You
have a wonderful talent. It must be very time-consuming."

"Not really. I still have time to work for the diplomatic department as a translator. That is, until 1997."

At the mention of the upheaval due to take place in fewer
than six years, both Barbara and Lin grew pensive.

Then, shaking herself out of her reverie, Lin asked, "Would
you like to see the roses, Miss Fortune?"

Christina knew this was a polite way of giving Ross and
his mother some time alone. "I would like it very much," she
replied.

Lin led the way down a cobbled path through a wood gate
into the rose garden at the back of the house.

"She's very beautiful," Barbara remarked.

"Yes, she is," Ross said as he watched them disappear into
the rose garden.

"Are you in love with her?"

The words forced him to confront something he'd tried
very hard to avoid. "It's not that simple."

"It never is," she replied.

Restlessness drove him to his feet, his hands shoved deep into his pockets. "Some people believe she's an impostor."

"I know. I read the newspapers." At his surprised look she smiled. "The Fortune name has quite a history in Hong Kong." Then she asked, "What do you believe?"

He gave her a long look. "I'm not sure it matters who she is."

"Ah, so that's how it is."

They were silent for a long moment, then she asked, "Can this plan of hers succeed?"

Ross looked out across the garden again, as if looking for Christina, though she was out of sight. He didn't answer his mother directly. "I've never known anyone like her before. She's intelligent and warm. And she's one hell of a business-woman." He didn't try to explain the other part of it—that there was a strength in her, and a stubbornness that came only from fighting personal demons. And a certain quality that came from the streets. He knew what it was. God knows he'd confronted it in himself often enough. It was a ruthlessness, a determination to win. The possibility of losing didn't even exist. It was something he understood and empathized with far more than he could ever explain to this beautiful, gentle woman beside him.

"It can work," he went on to explain. "All the elements are there. If she succeeds, Fortune Shipping has the potential to be bigger than even old Hamish Fortune ever dreamed." Finally he looked at her. "But there's a price."

"There always is," Barbara said softly.

At that instant Ross realized that his mother understood exactly how he had felt all these years—why he had been driven to succeed no matter what the cost. He took her hand and held it between both of his. "We're taking her proposal before the Cartel." He felt the slight tremor that passed through her slender hand, then the strength that flowed after as she curled her fingers tight into her palm.

Her voice was low, but firm. "I raised you to be your own person," she told him. "You must do what you think is right."

His expression was troubled. "I don't want to hurt you."

She laughed gently. The tenderness and love in her laughter had comforted him in his childhood. She laid her other hand against his cheek. "You will never hurt me, Ross. It's not in you to do so."

"When I confront him, it could turn ugly. You know how I feel about him."

She shook her head as she recalled an old Chinese saying learned in her youth. "The past is but an image we carry with us. In time the image fades, and the only reality is what we hold in our hands." She held his hand very tightly. "I love you, and I am proud of you. I trust in you. Do what you have to do."

Ross stood, still holding on to her hand. He bent and kissed her cheek.

Christina and Lin were just returning from the garden. Christina held a single long-stemmed blue rose that Lin assured her Barbara would want her to have. She heard Ross and Barbara in deep conversation and was suddenly embarrassed at having walked in on what was obviously a very private moment.

Barbara looked up. "Ah, I see Lin gave you a souvenir of your visit."

"I hope you don't mind," Christina said hesitantly. She'd never seen anything as exquisite as the blue rose.

Barbara stood and reached for Christina's hand. "Not at all. They won't grow if we don't clip them. I have to throw so many away. By the way, I'm working on a new variety. I should have the first bloom in a few weeks. I hope you'll be able to return to see it."

"I'd like that," Christina said sincerely.

"We should be getting back to the office," Ross reminded her. "We have a great deal of material to go over before our meeting tomorrow."

At the mention of the meeting, Barbara gave him an enigmatic look that Christina couldn't quite interpret. "I wish you every success, darling."

At the front door Ross bade his mother good-bye and promised that he would call in the next few days. The look that passed between them was the same one Christina had

seen in the garden. Suddenly she realized what it meant—
profound maternal concern.

Then Ross grabbed Lin by the wrist. He took a small
wrapped package out of his pocket and placed it in her hand.
"You don't deserve it," he told her emphatically. "You have
the tongue of a shrew."

"Shrew?" she asked with a questioning glance at Barbara,
obviously not understanding what the word meant.

"It's a compliment," Barbara lied, giving Christina and
Ross a conspiratorial wink. She accompanied them out the
door and down the walk. "I wish you wouldn't tease her," she
scolded Ross.

"She loves it."

"I'm not at all convinced of that. But she loves you, in
spite of the fact that you are rude and overbearing.

He flashed a grin at Christina. "I seem to recall being
called that before."

He held the car door open for Christina. Before she got in,
Barbara reached for her hand once more. "Make him bring
you back."

Christina was deeply touched by both the words and the
gesture. "Thank you for a lovely afternoon."

Barbara squeezed her hand. "Thank you for coming," she
said. When both Ross and Christina had gotten into the car,
Barbara waved through the open window to her son. "Take
care, my darling."

Christina held the blue rose, carefully wrapped in a damp
cloth and bound with plastic to keep it from dripping on her
clothes, as they rode back down Peak Road in silence. They
were almost to the bottom, and blending into busier traffic,
when Christina finally spoke.

"I like her," she said quietly, thinking of her own mother,
and what might have been if things had been different.

"I knew you would. The two of you are a great deal alike."

She looked at him, wondering how much he guessed—how
much he sensed. She thought of *zanshin* and what it meant
about opening up your senses to everything. Always before,
the thought of letting down her guard made her uneasy, bringing back those old feelings of physical threat all over again,

and instinctively pulling back. But she didn't feel that way with Ross now. She felt safe with him. She realized how ironic it was to feel safe with a man with his reputation. A man whose ambitions might very well be better served without her.

It was after four o'clock when they returned to the office. Bill was in Ross's office. He looked up as they came in. "Is Barbara's cooking still as bad as ever?"

"Probably," Ross laughed. "Fortunately, Lin prepared luncheon."

Bill chuckled. "Did she give you hell, as usual?"

"Of course." Then he explained to Christina, "She considers me to be an unworthy son."

She was stunned. "Unworthy?"

"It goes back a long way," Ross said vaguely, avoiding a more detailed explanation.

Bill grinned. "It has to do with his wayward youth. He was quite a hell-raiser. He left school when he was seventeen to work the docks. He left the colony when he was nineteen. That's when it was my misfortune to hook up with him."

"And you're a better man for it," Ross quipped.

"That's what I tried to explain to my wife, all those nights Ross had me working late on his business ventures. He became successful, and I got divorced."

Christina knew that beneath Bill's bantering tone lay a very real pain. Remembering what Bill had told her of his wife, she wondered if there might not be some way for the two of them to get together. She told herself that at the moment she couldn't do anything about the situation. But when this current crisis was resolved . . .

"What do you have on the report?" Ross asked, changing the subject of the conversation.

"Lisa should be finished with it." He started for the door, but Ross was ahead of him. "Never mind. I'll get it."

When Ross had gone, Bill pointed to the single blue rose Christina had unwrapped and placed in a water pitcher, for lack of an appropriate vase. "Barbara's really something, isn't she?"

Christina nodded. "I like her very much. I can see where

Ross gets his charm. I wonder what he inherited from his father."

Bill said nothing in response to that, and she wondered if he knew anything about Ross's father.

Christina went on, "Her home is lovely, and the garden is magnificent. Lin took me on a guided tour."

"Lin's a crafty old hag. She and Barbara have lived there together for years. Her family is all gone now, so she's on her own. When she was young, being Eurasian was very difficult. They are looked down upon as less than human. Barbara met her through the diplomatic department. They became friends, and Barbara asked Lin to move in with her."

Christina was thoughtful. "That must have been after Ross's father died."

"Died?" Bill looked up at her in surprise. "Did he tell you that?"

"No, I just assumed it. There were no photographs at the house, and no one mentioned him. I assumed it must be a painful subject."

"It's painful, all right. The fact is, he's very much alive."

He hesitated, then said, "Oh, hell, there isn't any reason why you shouldn't know. Hong Kong is a small place. There are no secrets here, and you'll find out soon enough, anyway."

"You mean Ross's father is here, in Hong Kong?" Christina asked in surprise.

"Yes. He's English, part of the old established aristocracy. He was born and raised in the colony. When the war broke out, his family evacuated back to their estate in England. He didn't come back until a couple of years after the war. Barbara met him through the diplomatic office. She fell deeply in love."

"And he didn't," Christina assumed from the tone of his voice.

"Who's to say? I never knew the man." His voice turned hard. "But the fact is, he was engaged to be married to someone else. Someone more socially prominent. Barbara found out about it the day she found out she was pregnant with Ross."

Christina felt ill. "Oh, God."

"According to Lin, he had no intention of canceling his wedding. He wanted Barbara to get an abortion. She refused."

Christina's stomach tightened in a knot as she thought of Ross and how knowing this must have affected him.

Bill went on, "Beneath that gentle exterior, Barbara is a very strong person. She insisted on raising *her* child on her own."

"That must have been very difficult."

"In those days it was almost impossible. Worse if you were part of the diplomatic community. They tend to look down on unmarried pregnant personnel. They don't like scandals. It was all Barbara could do to keep her job, apparently. And she was really ostracized."

"I can't believe that Ross's father simply walked out on them."

"He didn't," Bill said. "He did the right thing, in the sense that he contributed to their support. He even visited occasionally for the first few years. Then he stopped. Ross has very clear memories of his father, mostly unpleasant."

Christina tried to find her way past the anguish she felt for a small child abandoned by his father—a feeling of loss she identified with closely. "Were there other children?" she asked.

"Oh, yes. He had the necessary heirs to the family dynasty. Ross's half brother, Tony, is two years younger. He's a viscount I believe. He races cars on the Grand Prix circuit and is apparently pretty useless. Ross's half sister, Charlotte, is four years younger and lives in England. She cares very much for the titles and the family estate that goes with it. So much so that she's worked very hard to overcome the scandal of her bastard half brother."

"Has Ross tried to contact his father?"

"As far as Ross is concerned, his father is dead."

"But as you said, Hong Kong is a very small island. They must see each other from time to time."

"Yes," he said slowly. "From time to time. But they don't acknowledge each other. Actually Ross will be going up against him with your proposal."

Her gaze snapped to his. "What are you talking about?"

"Ross's father is head of the Cartel. He's also President of the Victoria Bank. He's been trying to put a joint venture like yours together for years, but he lacks the connections within mainland China. Ross would like nothing better than to cut him down to size by convincing the Cartel to vote against him."

"And we could lose everything if the Cartel votes against *us*," Christina said worriedly.

"That's right."

At Kai Tak Airport, a small, sleek jet skimmed to a stop, then slowly turned. The engines were cut, the hatch was opened, the small steps lowered into place. The jet was a private rental, just over on a short hop from Taiwan.

The pilot and copilot deplaned, going through the usual procedures, handing over their flight documents to airport officials. Then a single passenger deplaned and walked the short distance across the tarmac to the immigration gate. He presented his passport and visa. The immigration officer scanned the entries on the passport: London, Lisbon, Athens, Cairo, and several with varying dates for Hong Kong.

"What is your purpose in visiting Hong Kong? Business or pleasure?"

"Business."

"How long will you be staying in Hong Kong?" The officer asked the routine question.

"As long as it takes."

"Sir?" the officer asked.

"A few days, perhaps longer," the man answered irritably.

"Where will you be staying?"

"I have a residence in Hong Kong."

The officer looked at him for several moments, then stamped the visa and handed it back to him. "Enjoy your visit."

He grabbed the visa, jammed it back into his coat pocket, then impatiently pushed his way through the gate. Reaching the taxi queue, he checked his watch. It was just past six o'clock in the evening.

It had been a rough flight over from Taiwan, riding the edge of a late-season, tropical storm. But he dared not risk a commercial flight, where he might be recognized by one of the same group of people who regularly made the trip between San Francisco and Hong Kong.

He waved down a red and gray Toyota, silently cursing as he climbed into the back of the taxi. He gave the driver the address, then sat back in the seat and mentally blocked out the flight, the driver, and the filthy taxi. He concentrated completely on the one reason he had come here—Christina Grant Fortune. Or Ellie Dobbs.

It didn't really matter who she was. All that mattered was that she had to be stopped.

# Chapter 29

*T*hey worked into the evening.

Bill, Lisa Jeung, and Adam Quon stayed after the other employees had gone home for the evening. Steven was conspicuous by his absence.

They all sat around the black jade table in Ross's office and scrutinized the proposal, searching for flaws, loopholes, some last-minute problem that had gone undetected.

Both Lisa and Adam were able to bring a different perspective to the project and made suggestions that were invaluable. After all, they worked every day in the Fortune office in Hong Kong. They knew the Orient.

Adam had a keen understanding of the Hong Kong business market. He was aware of all the subtle changes going on in the politics of the colony, things only people who lived in Hong Kong could possibly know. He made a couple of excellent suggestions about the approach for presenting their proposal.

His insight was especially helpful to Christina. As Ross had pointed out, she was breaking down barriers—boldly going where no woman had ever gone before—into the heart of the closed male bastion of the business community within Hong Kong. She was a woman, but she also was the new acting President and Chairman of the Board of Fortune International, and controlled Fortune Shipping. The powers that be would be forced to deal with her, whether they approved or not.

Adam advised her how to dress, act, and present herself. After all, these were men of power. The fact that she possessed equal power was of no consequence to them.

She chafed at the notion that she would have to alter her behavior to suit these men, but she knew she had no choice. She needed the cooperation of both the Triad and the Cartel to make her plan work.

Throughout the evening Ross made no mention of the fact that his father sat on the Cartel, and Christina chose not to discuss what Bill had revealed.

Later, when the meeting finally broke up, and she and Ross went back to their respective suites to try to get as much rest as possible before the critical events of the following day, she tried to imagine the intensity of his feelings toward his father. She'd lost her own father at a young age, but her memories of him were pleasant ones. She never doubted that he loved her. In those early years she had felt emotionally secure.

It must have been devastating for a small child to realize his father didn't love him—had, in fact, never wanted him, and considered him a social embarrassment.

Bill had said that Ross was driven. Now she understood why. Like so many other people, he was driven by the need for an approval he could never win. If they were successful in putting this joint venture together with the People's Republic of China, his father would finally be forced to acknowledge him, at least in one sense.

But it was more than that, she knew. It also had to do with revenge. Bill had told her that Ross's father, Sir Anthony Adamson, had been trying to put together a joint venture like this for a long time. According to Bill, Adamson didn't have the connections in Beijing to make it work. If she and Ross were able to pull this off, there was more to be won than simply his father's acknowledgment of his success. He would actually accomplish something his father had been unable to achieve with his title, his wealth, and all his connections within the business and financial communities. Ross, the unwanted bastard child, would beat him at his own game.

Sometime after midnight Christina finally fell into a restless sleep, worrying about the next day's meeting, wondering how Ross would handle the confrontation with his father.

She awoke at five o'clock in the morning. After tossing and turning for nearly an hour, she decided it was pointless to try to go back to sleep. She should have been dead tired, but raw, restless energy drove her. She alternated between exhilaration and the certainty that the proposal was flawless, and the nagging doubt that they had somehow forgotten to consider some crucial point.

She got up, showered, turned on the television, and let the world news broadcast in both Cantonese and English fill the silence in the suite while she went over the proposal one more time.

The door buzzer sounded, and she thrust her copy of the proposal down on the coffee table. She had been too tired to eat dinner the night before. Now she was starving and had ordered up a full breakfast.

May-may stood at the door with the room service clerk. She smiled at Christina. "I will serve breakfast," she announced, without any comment about the unusually early hour.

Christina looked back in embarrassment at the cluttered condition of the suite. She liked having everything organized for her, but it made her feel uncomfortable to have someone bustling around always picking up after her. "I'm afraid I've left things in a bit of a mess."

"I will take care of it," May-may assured her as she directed the houseboy to set up breakfast out on the small veranda.

Christina looked at her watch and checked the time—seven A.M. She picked up the phone and dialed the number to Ross's suite. As she expected, he, too, was up early. There was no hint of fatigue in his voice when he answered.

"I thought you might be up. How about breakfast in my suite this morning?"

"All right. What time should I come?"

"Five minutes ago," she informed him cheekily, then hung up.

Neither said much during the meal. They didn't speak of business. It was too late now to make any last-minute changes. Either the plan would work or it wouldn't. But Christina noticed that Ross ate very little, and as they lingered over coffee afterward, his thoughts seemed to be very far away.

Bill called just after nine o'clock to let them know he was on his way. The plan was for him to pick them up at the hotel. From there they would drive together to the designated location for their meeting with the Triad.

Christina closed her portfolio. Inside was the culmination of weeks of hard work, and her hope for the future of the company. The phone rang again. It was the concierge from downstairs, telling her that Bill had arrived.

The ride down in the elevator was slow. They stopped at several floors to take on guests or let others off. Ross kept a watchful eye on her, but there was no replay of the incident at the Hyatt in San Francisco. She was perfectly calm, controlled, as cool as she had been weeks ago, when she first walked into the board meeting and staked her claim to the inheritance.

Outside, the sun was bright, the air clean and cool. A breeze off the harbor brought a taste of salty air. Christina wondered if it had been a day like this when Hamish Fortune sailed into Hong Kong Harbor. Did it seem to hold both promise and danger for him, as it did for her?

So much was riding on the outcome of this meeting. The Triad controlled the shipping terminals of Hong Kong Harbor under the guise of legitimate business operations. As Ross had explained to her, nothing entered or left the port of Hong Kong that didn't at some point in time pass through the control of the Triad.

It was necessary that the Triad approve the increased volume of shipping that would pass through Hong Kong as part of the proposal for the Beijing government. That approval included her proposal for joint ownership with Fortune International of new container terminals that would be needed to handle the increased volume of shipping.

It was a business deal guaranteed to return an exorbitant

profit if all the key elements were in place. The one critical element was the willingness of the Beijing government to do business with her. As she stepped to the limo, Bill got out and handed her an envelope.

"This arrived just before I left the office." His expression was worried as he met her gaze. She looked down at the ancient dragons entwined about the hammer and sickle, symbol of the communist government of China. "It was delivered by an attaché from the Chinese government."

Christina stared at the snarling dragons in the upper lefthand corner and, beneath them, both the Chinese characters and the English translation of the official government office that had issued the letter. Ever since their arrival in Hong Kong they'd been waiting for notification of the time and place where officials of the Chinese government would be willing to meet with them. She'd grown increasingly impatient, certain that the more time that passed without any word, the less their chances for that meeting. More than once Ross had reminded her that everything moved at a different pace in the Orient.

Now, almost two weeks after Phillip Lo made his initial inquiry to the Chinese government through his cousin, they had an official answer. She looked up at Ross.

He met her gaze. "We might as well find out if they've given us a date and time before we meet with the Triad."

Her fingers trembled as she slipped a nail beneath the flap at the corner of the envelope and opened it. She scanned the brief message. It was written in English.

"They've looked over the preliminary proposal Phillip Lo sent." She looked up at Ross, her dark eyes shining. "The meeting is set!" she exclaimed, unable to control her excitement. "In two days in Beijing!"

A second note was enclosed. The message was circumspect, the words chosen with care, in case a government official might read it before it reached its destination. It was a personal note from David Chen.

She tucked both letters inside her attaché case. "Now we have the key—at least we know they're interested in our proposal."

Ross saw the second note, along with the expression that crossed her face. He didn't need to read it to know whom it was from. A flash of jealousy gripped him, surprising him with its intensity. It took all his self-control to hide it. Holding open the door of the limo for her, he said, "It's time to roll the dice, Miss Fortune. We have a meeting to keep."

The location for the meeting wasn't at all what Christina expected. Somehow she envisioned either a long ride north out into the country to some private estate protected by a security gate, dogs, and armed guards, or some dingy, smoke-filled warehouse down at the waterfront with only a single light bulb hanging over a small table.

They drove north along the coast, past the airport, shopping centers, the Tsim Sha Tsui waterfront promenade, and the typhoon shelter at Yau Ma Tei, which had been converted into a floating city. The street names were a blend of English and Chinese, reminding Christina that the two cultures were deeply intertwined. They crisscrossed through concrete-jungle suburbs with block after block of public housing, factories, and business complexes.

It wasn't far in terms of actual distance, less than ten miles, yet the drive took almost a half hour as they crawled through the congested traffic that clogged the streets. They stopped before an office complex beside an industrial park. It was sleek and ultramodern, and might have been found in any city in the United States. Bill waited in the car while Ross and Christina went inside.

In the lobby of the two-story building they were greeted by a receptionist. The foyer was open and spacious with a clerestory stairwell leading to the second floor. Water bubbled and swirled in an indoor pond filled with colorful Koi, and surrounded by lush, green plants. So much for single light bulbs over a small table, she thought.

"What are you looking for?" Ross asked as the receptionist led them upstairs.

"Security guards," she whispered discreetly. "I expected something out of *The Godfather*. You know, black-suited goons with conspicuous bulges under their jackets posted at every door."

His hand was at her elbow as he leaned forward and quietly said, "They're here. You just can't see them." Her startled gaze met his. She expected him to smile and say it was only a joke. But he didn't.

The conference room could have been any boardroom in any office of corporate America. A side table had been set up with coffee and tea. Several telephones and a fax machine sat atop the counter at the far wall. She recognized the Gunlocke chairs that surrounded the long, polished granite conference table.

The business-suited men who occupied those chairs could have been executives with any one of the companies on the *Fortune* 500 list. She was reminded, as Ross had said, that for them this was business—very lucrative business. They controlled the shipping terminals of Hong Kong. She controlled one of the largest shipping companies in the world. They could both profit from the proposal she was about to present to them.

The secretary who had escorted them from the ground floor lobby made the introductions.

An elderly Chinese man stood and crossed the room to greet them. "I am Thomas Lai," he introduced himself first to Ross. Then he turned to Christina. "Phillip Lo has spoken highly of you, Miss Fortune."

She recognized his name from the story Phillip had told them when he finally gave his approval to her plan. This was Phillip's cousin, grandson of the brother whom Lai Kwok Lee left behind in Hong Kong so many years ago. The blood bond connected them still, in spite of the different choices that led two brothers to live their lives half a world away from one another.

His command of the English language was impeccable, hinting at a university education, probably Oxford or Cambridge. There was nothing about him even to hint that he and the other members of this board controlled the very lives of thousands of people, not to mention countless legitimate and not-so-legitimate industries within Hong Kong and the New

Territories. This man and his influence with this board were essential to the success of her plan.

"Good morning, honored cousin of Phillip Lo," she said in polite greeting, knowing that every word, every gesture was being measured, scrutinized against the reputations of Alexander and Michael Fortune, and Richard Fortune.

She had a legacy of honor to fulfill, and another legacy to live down. As with the Cartel meeting, the success of this meeting was absolutely vital. Everything depended on the Triad's participation in the joint venture.

Thomas Lai turned and presented them to the other members of the Triad. Then they were shown to two chairs at the far side of the table.

It was a subtle reminder that they were not in a position of authority here. And a reminder that she, unlike Ross, was looked upon as an outsider. And she was a woman.

Christina carefully restrained both her words and her mannerisms. Something Ross had said to her turned over and over in her thoughts—that East *was* different from West. On the surface it might seem that Hong Kong was a sophisticated, ultramodern, international city. But under that surface the lifeblood of Hong Kong was steeped in ten thousand years of tradition.

She had fought her way up the corporate ladder of Goldman, Sachs, breaking down the stereotypical barriers that so often kept women from reaching high-powered positions. She had learned along the way to play hardball with the boys, and she had succeeded. But that method of achieving success had no place here.

The fact that the men in this room were even willing to allow her presence at such a meeting wasn't because of her reputation for business. It was because of the influence of Phillip Lo, and the honorable legacies of both Alexander and Michael Fortune. But that single courtesy was all that they were willing to extend to her. Success depended on the strength of her proposal, and the way in which it was presented. She would have to earn their acceptance on her own.

Thomas Lai sat down at the head of the table. Then he said to Christina, "We will listen to your proposal now."

She felt the reassuring pressure of Ross's hand on hers as she stood. She greeted them with a gesture of respect as she bowed her head in the traditional sign of obeisance. Then she spoke carefully and precisely in Cantonese, making a speech that Quon had helped her to write. She sensed the surprise of the men she addressed—and she sensed their grudging respect.

At the appropriate time she asked Ross to hand out a copy of the proposal to each board member. His gaze met hers briefly, with an expression that seemed to say, "You're doing great."

The conference room was completely silent when she finished with her presentation. She thanked each member of the board for his time and consideration, then once again bowed her head in a gesture of respect, and sat down.

Silence drew out in the room, like a dying heartbeat, until it became almost interminable. The waiting, she knew, was part of their test of her. After several minutes one of the board members finally asked of Ross, "What precisely is your participation in this joint venture, Mr. McKenna?"

Christina knew that Ross's participation was vital to the success of their meeting with the Triad. He had been born and raised in Hong Kong. He spent the past fifteen years of his life working within the business community as the CEO of Fortune International, and he'd gained an honorable reputation as Katherine Fortune's righthand man.

"My position with the company remains the same, as CEO in charge of overall operations," he explained.

Behind the expressions of polite indifference, Christina sensed them wavering. They knew and trusted Ross. They didn't trust Richard Fortune, and were uncertain of her position within the company.

"Who controls the company?" Thomas Lai asked bluntly.

Christina stood and faced them once more. She said firmly and without the least hesitation, "*I* control Fortune International." And then she added, so that there would be no further misunderstanding, "This is my proposal. I have relied on Mr. McKenna's expertise to put it together, and I will continue to rely on him."

Then she played her trump card. "We received word this morning from government officials in Beijing that they have given tentative approval to the proposal, subject to your participation."

She saw a flicker of reaction on Ross's face. The Beijing government had agreed only to meet with them. But she'd sensed the Triad's hesitation and feared they were about to turn her down. It was a gamble, but she had to take it.

"When will you be meeting with them?" Lai asked.

"It's been set for two days from now."

He nodded, and again silence engulfed the conference room.

Then, without the Triad's even adjourning to consult with one another, the member who had questioned Ross's participation spoke up. "The twenty percent participation that you are offering for our participation is not enough," he said flatly.

Christina felt a small surge of hope. At least they were willing to talk terms. It was a first critical step.

"What would be enough?" she asked, aware that the atmosphere inside the conference room had subtly changed. It was much like an open-air market that could be found on any street in Hong kong, where the vendor and the customer bargained over the price of merchandise. With an inward smile she realized that for all the high-tech gloss of machines and business suits, nothing had changed in the Orient over the past ten thousand years. They might have been haggling over a bowl of rice, or the day's fresh catch laid out on wooden racks.

Now, instead of impassive expressions of indifference, she saw the sharp glint in their eyes that revealed their interest, and she knew they would make a deal.

The same man said, "Twenty-five percent participation." He added firmly, "No less." There wasn't a word of dissent from any of the other men at the table, and she realized they had decided how much they would ask before they came into this meeting.

She sat down in the chair next to Ross. Now *she* let silence draw out in the room as she stared down at her clasped hands, using the silence to her advantage, as they had used it earlier to try to undermine her confidence.

She felt the tension in Ross as he sat beside her, and was reminded of something he had once asked her—*"What are you prepared to do to have what you want?"*

Her answer then was no different from her answer now—*"Whatever it takes."*

She looked up and met the gaze of each man in turn, as they watched her studiously. Once more she spoke in Cantonese. "My final offer is thirty percent participation."

They were stunned that she would increase what they had demanded by another five percent.

She added, "I also propose that a separate holding company be set up for ownership of the new container terminals. My company will have two positions on the seven-member board for that holding company, with two other positions occupied by members of the Cartel."

Out of the corner of her eye, she saw Ross's brief glance and knew that she had surprised him as much as she had any of the members of the Triad.

A separate holding company would give the joint venture legitimacy. With the seven positions on the board divided up between Fortune, the Triad, and the Cartel, power was evenly distributed. The Triad would have three positions on the board. But any decision would require a majority vote of four, which meant a split either between members of the Cartel or in the votes held by Fortune. It was a shrewd balance of power, and the men sitting opposite her knew it. If there was one thing they respected, it was shrewdness when it came to business.

Finally the member of the Triad who made the original counteroffer spoke up. "One more condition before we will consider your plan. Mr. McKenna will occupy one of the positions on the board of the holding company."

She agreed without hesitation.

Then he made his final demand, "The other position will not be occupied by either your uncle, Richard Fortune, or Steven Fortune." It was a clear message that they would not deal with Richard or Steven.

At least they hadn't insisted that she couldn't occupy the position, she thought as relief washed through her. But this last condition would result in a confrontation with Richard that she knew would be cataclysmic.

She said firmly, "Agreed."

"When will you be meeting with the members of the Cartel?" Lai asked.

"With your approval we meet with them tomorrow morning."

He nodded thoughtfully, then looked down the length of the table to the other members of the Triad. There was no indication of either acceptance or dissent.

His gaze came back to Christina. "We will see if you bring honor to your father and grandfather. For your meeting tomorrow with the members of the Cartel, you may consider that we have accepted the terms of your proposal."

It was done. There was no hand-shaking or words of congratulations, which she would normally have expected in an American boardroom. Instead the members of the Triad stood, one by one, and left the conference room. Only Lai remained. He walked around the table and stopped near Ross and Christina.

To her amazement he shook her hand, in the Western tradition. "You are a very shrewd young woman. My friends were not prepared for such bold bargaining."

"I suspect they were completely prepared, Mr. Lai," she countered.

He smiled. "This agreement is unique. No one has been able to put together anything like it before. But it is not yet complete. Your meeting with the Cartel will not be easy." He glanced meaningfully at Ross.

So, she thought, he knows about Ross's father.

"Thank you for your support, Mr. Lai."

He held up a hand. "I have done nothing but make a wise decision that any good businessman would make. Now we will see if you have the power to make all this possible."

He bade them both good-bye.

As Christina and Ross left, she couldn't believe that it was over. The Triad had agreed to her proposal! She felt euphoric.

If she and Ross had been alone, she would have whooped with delight.

Outside, she felt Ross's hands on her arms as he turned her around.

"Thirty percent? Two seats on the board? Where the hell did you come up with that?"

She smiled up at him. "You once asked me what I was prepared to do to have what I wanted. I wanted this very much."

"You realize that by agreeing to their terms, you'll have to confront Richard over this."

"I'm aware of that."

His expression shifted. "You'll have a real battle on your hands."

"I'm aware of that, too. And I intend to win."

On the long ride back into Kowloon, and then over to the offices in the Central district of Hong Kong Island, Ross and Bill went over the changes that would have to be made in the proposal with the new terms and conditions that the Triad had accepted.

Christina rode with them in thoughtful silence. Richard had once threatened to destroy her. At the time, she thought it was an idle threat, made out of anger and frustration. That threat might prove to be anything but idle. Especially if he was the one who'd already made two attempts on her life.

She stared out the tinted windows of the limousine as they passed the typhoon shelter at Yau Ma Tei. The water out on the harbor had gone as still as glass. The sky had been bright blue and crystal clear earlier. Now it hung pale gray. Not a breath of wind stirred the international flags at the ferry terminal as they passed on their way to the cross-channel tunnel.

There was something almost ominous in the damp, warm air as the driver closed the windows, and climate-controlled air poured into the limousine. It was a feeling she'd experienced in the past, on an unusually warm night twenty years ago.

In spite of the sultry warmth that lingered in the limousine, she rubbed her hands down her arms to drive off the sudden chill that came from deep inside.

# Chapter 30

Christina told herself it was just her imagination. Or probably fatigue mixed with the edginess of knowing so much hung in the balance. But as she stepped from the limousine in front of the Fortune building in the Central district, the feeling was even more distinct—a stillness so intense that it left the air electrically charged.

"It looks as if we might be in for a change of weather," Bill remarked as he came around from the other side of the car.

That was it, she thought, just the weather. Surrounded by water, as Hong Kong was, the weather could change in a matter of minutes.

"Do you think we'll get a storm?" she asked, looking up at the darkening sky.

"It's possible," Ross remarked. "The barometer has been falling since early morning. This time of year we often get a late-season squall. It blows things around a bit."

"The calm before the storm," Christina murmured, still feeling uneasy.

But Ross didn't seem concerned, only amused. "I'd say we just weathered our first really big storm and sailed through it with flying colors." He smiled at Bill. "You should have seen her haggling with the members of the Triad over points of the joint venture—she was like a fishwife at market."

Bill grinned. "I would like to have seen that. I'll bet none of them will ever forget. They probably came out of that boardroom swearing each other to secrecy about dealing with a woman. After all, they do have a reputation to uphold."

As they went into the foyer of the building, Ross laughed. "Chris expected to see them packing heat—I believe that's the expression."

"I admit I was surprised to find them so polite and professional," Christina admitted. "It was amazing. They were just like any other board of directors."

Bill almost choked. "You're kidding."

Ross said dryly, "Maybe I should tell you how they take care of clients who step out of line, or try to move in on their business operations."

She gave them both a disdainful look. "You're just trying to get a reaction out of me. There was absolutely nothing about the meeting to suggest that they were anything but legitimate businessmen."

She walked past them both and got onto the elevator.

As they emerged on the sixth floor, Ross said in a much more serious tone. "It was a legitimate business meeting. But I assure you, those are very dangerous men, including Thomas Lai."

They worked through the afternoon on the changes that had to be made to the proposal after the negotiating she'd done with the members of the Triad. The points of her deal with the Triad were separate from her proposal to the Cartel, but the percentages of participation affected the overall profit margins. Then Christina and Lisa closed themselves in Lisa's office to input all the changes into the computer.

Ross was alone in his office when Bill came in. "How are Chris and Lisa doing with those changes?"

"It's coming right along," Bill said in a thoughtful voice. "They'll have them done shortly with a draft of the revisions for us to go over."

Bill sat down in a chair facing Ross's desk, but didn't say anything further. Ross looked at him, and thought once more that Bill was as good as they come. He had a feel for business that meshed with Ross's. Like Ross, he understood the intricacies and nuances of dealing with people, money, and products.

Their personality differences worked to their advantage, as well. Ross was capable of slicing through the unimportant details of complicated deals, negotiations, and paperwork, and finding the least significant factor that could make the most significant difference. He was like a cat, and thought best on his feet, pushing through the emotions and personalities that were involved in deal making. He'd earned a reputation for being shrewd and cunning, but that wasn't enough if it wasn't backed up by solid facts and figures.

That was where Bill came in. He was Ross's alter ego. His was a purely analytical mind. He could look at a spread sheet of facts and figures, analyze it in a matter of seconds, and find the bottom-line profit or loss. Whereas Ross remembered people and names, Bill remembered numbers and percentages with almost demonic accuracy. Ross worked best in chaos, and his desk, covered with stacks of paperwork, reflected it. Bill, on the other hand, was obsessive about order. His desk was absolutely clear at all times, even when he was working on a half dozen projects at the same time.

Ross might forget some small detail of a deal; Bill never forgot anything. It was as if he had a small camera lodged in his forehead, clicking off photos of everything that passed before him. And Ross was absolutely certain all those memory photos were immediately indexed, categorized, and systematically filed for instant recall when needed. The man was absolutely uncanny that way, and it was one of the many reasons he and Ross were so good together.

He knew Bill as well as he knew himself. Something was up. "What is it?"

Bill said slowly, "Remember I said that I had the feeling that something was going on?"

Ross nodded.

Bill thrust a telex at him. It was from their dock manager in Taiwan.

Ross frowned as he read it. "When did this come in?"

"Just a few minutes ago. It may be nothing."

"But you don't think so."

"As I said, I can't put my finger on it. I've checked things out. There's nothing missing. It's just tiny glitches in the shipping manifests." He glanced down at the telex. "I've instructed Donovan to let me know if anything else shows up. As you can see, it's just a couple of containers that somehow aren't on the manifest."

"Where's Steven?" Ross asked abruptly.

"He just got back in from a late lunch."

"What do you think's going on?"

"I don't know what to think. Nothing is ever missing. The containers always show up. This has happened only twice before."

Reaching a quick decision, Ross swung out of his chair. "Can you handle things here until I get back?"

"Of course. Where are you going?"

"I'll tell you later."


He stood in the doorway of Lisa Jeung's office. Lisa had stepped out. Chris sat at her desk, going over the changes in the proposal. She was bent over the proposal, her hair sweeping forward, casting her face in shadows.

He stood there for a moment watching her, wondering about her.

God, she had been magnificent in that meeting with the Triad. She'd been scared. He'd felt it in her, sensed it in a way he'd come to sense her moods and emotions. But it was all carefully controlled when they walked into that boardroom. There had been no misstep that might reveal how nervous she really was. She was a match for anyone, including himself. But instead of feeling intimidated by that, he was intrigued by it.

What was it, he wondered, that drove her? What was it in her past that made her as hungry for success as he was? Whatever it was, they were very much alike. Finally she looked up, and he was aware once again of how beautiful she was.

"I'll have these done shortly. Then we can go over them."

He came all the way into the office and sat down in one of

the client chairs in front of the desk. He leaned back and looked at her thoughtfully. "I have to leave."

"Why?"

"I have to go over to Taiwan."

"You mean this afternoon?"

"Something has come up," he explained evasively. "I want to check it out."

"Can't it wait?"

He shook his head.

He saw the irritation evident in the tight line of her mouth and suddenly rigid set of her shoulders. But it wasn't just anger. He realized that she felt a surge of fear at the thought of being on her own at this point, when there was still so much to do.

"Can't someone else handle it?"

"I'm afraid not."

He watched as she irritably thrust her pencil down on the desk and pushed back in her chair. He came around the desk and sat on the corner beside her, taking her hands in his. "It's a short flight. I promise you, I'll be back in a few hours."

"What's so important that you have to go over tonight?"

"I can't tell you yet."

Anger glinted in her dark eyes. "Damn it, Ross . . ."

He interrupted, "I told you I was with you on this, all the way. *Nothing* has changed. I'll be back in time for the meeting with the Cartel. You'll just have to trust me."

She looked up at him. For a moment everything hung in the balance—their ability to work together to pull off a major coup and, more important, their fragile personal relationship.

She slowly let out the breath she'd been holding. "All right," she said quietly, keeping her voice controlled. But she didn't meet his gaze. "I'll see you when you get back."

Ross lifted her chin, forcing her to look at him. "I'll be back in time. I promise." Then he kissed her quickly, his lips barely brushing hers. Even so, the brief contact was electric, and she was deeply shaken by it.

He flew out of Hong Kong Island on a charter from the helipad. The flight time to Taiwan and back was under two hours. He told himself there was plenty of time to get over, check out the situation, then get back in time for a late dinner. After all, it was probably nothing, anyway. Only his deep mistrust of Steven prompted him to pursue such an apparently minuscule problem.

In Ross's office Christina finished going over the last-minute changes in the proposal with Bill. A dull ache had begun at the back of her head. She glanced at the ship's clock set in the bookcase behind the desk. Ross had been gone several hours and should be starting back any time. He said he would call in before he left.

"The barometer is falling rapidly," Bill said.

She glanced at the antique barometer hanging on the wall, then looked out the window. It was dark now, but she could just make out gathering storm clouds in the distance.

"Do you think it will be bad?" she asked in alarm.

"We could be in for a bit of a blow." He mustered a reassuring smile. "Don't worry. He'll make it back just fine."

At seven-thirty Bill finally snapped the files shut. He glanced at the barometer. It was still falling. They were in for more than a stiff wind.

The building was old, with wood beams and timbers instead of the steel that braced the new skyscrapers. It had its own peculiar noises as the storm grew. Outside it was pitch dark. The heavy clouds added to the darkness, shrouding the lights across the city that twinkled in watery rivulets as rain sluiced down the windows.

Lisa stopped in on her way to the elevators. "They just sounded the warning. One of our people called from down at the terminals. They've hoisted the number five."

At Christina's questioning look, Bill explained. "The storm has been upgraded to a five. That's the squall warning for all outgoing vessels."

"What about incoming flights?"

Bill looked to Lisa for confirmation. "There are still flights going out and coming in. I called over to Taiwan. Ross and his pilot were delayed. They can still get out if they leave within the next half hour."

Bill turned to Christina. "Come on. We're closing down for the night." When she continued to stand there, her expression deeply worried, he wrapped an arm around her shoulders. "He'll be all right. The pilot won't leave if he doesn't think it's safe. I'll take you back to the Regent."

The streets of Hong Kong were practically deserted as everyone battened down for the storm. They passed the ferry terminal and were the last ones back through the tunnel before it was closed down. The flags had been changed. The storm had been upgraded to a number seven.

It was no better when they emerged on the Kowloon side. The wipers were unable to cope with the river of rain that flooded across the glass. An abandoned street stall was ripped off the ground by a strong gust of wind that made the car shudder. The stall whipped across the street, slammed into the side of a building, and disintegrated.

Salisbury Road was almost empty of traffic, a small blessing because they could hardly see the buildings that lined the streets. Tsim Sha Tsui was usually filled with tourists and shoppers this time of the evening. Now no one dared venture out into the storm. There was a strange, eerie emptiness to Kowloon, as if they'd emerged on a foreign planet void of all life.

Then the watery lights of the Regent suddenly loomed before them, and Bill swung into the valet parking area. They stepped from the car under the front canopy. But in spite of the cover, they were immediately soaked to the skin as the rain drove at them horizontally. Bill wrapped his arm around Christina's shoulders, shielding her from the rain as they ran inside the hotel.

They were both drenched. The hotel concierge immediately appeared in the lobby with thick, downy towels.

Neither one of them spoke of the storm as they rode up in the elevator. Finally Bill said, "He'll be all right, Chris."

"Sure," she replied. But her tone lacked conviction.

"Have dinner with me," Bill asked. "We can wait together. I'll leave word at the desk to put your calls through to my room."

The thought of spending the next several hours alone, pacing her room, didn't appeal to her, so she eagerly accepted his invitation. "I'll be over in a little while."

"All right. I'll order up supper. What do you want?"

I want Ross back here, safe, she thought. Aloud, she said, "Whatever you order will be fine."

The shrill ring of the telephone jangled incessantly. Finally after several more rings, the receiver was jerked off its base.

"Hello?" answered a softly feminine voice, thickened with sleep and the lingering aftereffects of a cocaine high. And then, "Just a minute." The dusky-skinned Eurasian woman handed the phone to the man in bed beside her. "It's for you."

The phone was snatched from her hand. "Who the hell is this?" Steven demanded as he swung, naked, to the side of the bed.

He struggled to focus his thoughts, but it wasn't easy as he came down from the last traces of the drug. "When did you get in?" he asked, playing for a few more seconds to clear his head. Then he said, "Yeah. They've been putting in a lot of hours. Supposedly she's here for a few days to take a look around and check things out."

The harsh response that came over the phone grated along his already raw nerve endings. "I'm keeping an eye on her," he replied irritably.

Then Steven's voice rose in surprise. "What meetings?" There was a restless movement from the woman beside him. He carried the phone with him to the window. "Damn it! I told you this sort of thing takes time. It has to be done carefully."

The reply on the other end of the phone was adamant.

"It's too dangerous," he argued. "We shouldn't do anything right now. Someone might get suspicious."

The voice over the phone was insistent.

Steven shoved his fingers through his hair. "All right," he finally said. "I'll take care of it." And then, he added, "Yeah, tonight."

Ross scanned the stack of cargo manifests. Across the desk Mick Donovan sat in expectant silence. Mick was a tough son of a bitch. He'd grown up the hard way, on the docks of Liverpool and aboard an endless string of freighters that sailed nearly every port in the world. He'd been with Fortune International ten years, one of several employees hand-picked by Ross.

Their friendship began with a brawl, when both were rousting cargoes in a Hong Kong terminal. Mick had stood six feet five inches and weighed two hundred forty pounds. Ross was lucky if he topped out at one hundred eighty pounds. It was a ridiculous fight, and afterward neither remembered what had started it.

Ross made the mistake of assuming that a man of that size was probably slow and stupid. He took one of the few thrashings of his life. In the process he learned a healthy respect for the man who weighed as much as a linebacker and stood nearly as tall as a banyan tree. Afterward Mick picked him up off the floor, took him to his place, and patched up his cuts and bruises.

To everyone's surprise they became friends. Ross respected Mick's expertise on the docks, and Mick respected Ross's drive and ambition. Mick stayed in Hong Kong after Ross left—not because he especially loved Hong Kong, but because it was the farthest he could sail from Liverpool. He never spoke of Liverpool, or his past. Ross respected that.

A few years later, when Ross came on at Fortune International, he needed a man he could trust. He immediately looked up Mick and found him scraping the bottom of a gin bottle, in a rat-infested, hellhole apartment. Mick was thirty-five years old and looked fifty.

Ross sobered him up, then made him an offer that turned Mick's life around. He'd been the international cargo manager ever since. He was a troubleshooter, traveling between the ports where their ships sailed, solving problems. He hired and fired all their captains, and kept a hard eye on all dockside activities. He knew how to deal with crews, roustabouts, anxious cargo owners, and port authorities. And he knew how to get a job done. He also knew when something was wrong, which had prompted the telex he sent to Ross in Hong Kong.

Now Ross shook his head as he scanned the computer

printouts of the cargo manifests. "How did you even find these?"

"Perez was down with pneumonia," Mick explained about the dock supervisor for Fortune International in Taipei. "His assistant called me to fill in, since I was due to rotate in soon, anyway. I never would have caught it, except that Perez had the manifests in his truck at his place over on the other side of the island.

"I was on a tight schedule with the extra delay to cover for Perez. I wanted to get the cargoes logged through, but I didn't want to take the time to drive over to Perez's place. Our offices were already closed, so I couldn't get a copy. But I knew the offices for Crown Imperial, where the cargo originated, were open round the clock. I made a call and had them fax me a copy of the printout."

He jabbed a thick, scarred finger at the printout.

"That's when I found the discrepancy—twenty-four full-size containers, and thirty-six down-size in the cargo hold. It was the second number that didn't match up. The manifest onboard out of Hong Kong shows thirty-four down-size."

"You checked it out?"

Mick nodded. He wore a baseball cap pulled down snugly over his head. Ross was one of the few people who knew that Mick's head was covered with artful tattoos and no hair. "You bet I checked it out. My ass is on the line if these printouts don't match up. I called back over to Crown Imperial. They insisted they shipped thirty-four. Okay. I thought maybe they made a mistake. And if they made one mistake, they might've made others. That's when I decided to go back through a few more for the past couple of months."

"You found more?" Ross asked.

Mick nodded. "Three more, over the past six months."

"The shipper?"

"They're all different."

"Any other common factor?" Ross asked. He'd long ago gotten past his amazement that Mick had an uncanny grasp for numbers and computers.

Mick grunted. "The common factor is that there *is* no common factor, except the discrepancy." When Ross looked up at him, he explained. "They were all different cargoes and different holding companies."

"What about destinations?"

"All over the place." Mick had obviously done a great deal of investigating before he contacted Ross.

Ross was thoughtful. An ugly thought that he didn't want to consider kept surfacing. "By any chance, was San Francisco a port of call en route to final destinations?"

Mick flipped back through the printouts, then cross-checked the ship numbers with logs that were accounted for at the end of each month. He looked up. "Each one had a stopover in San Francisco. Two went on to Seattle, one to Long Beach, and the fourth one went on through Panama."

"San Francisco," Ross repeated thoughtfully.

"What do you think it means?"

"I think someone has altered these cargo manifests."

"Why would someone want it to look as if there were more containers than there actually were?"

"Because by the time they were on-loaded, the number of containers matched what was on the changed manifests."

"Smuggling?" Mick said immediately.

"Don't say anything to anyone about this until you hear from me. Absolutely no one."

"Gotcha, boss." Then Mick asked, "You have an idea about this?"

"I need to check out some things. I hope to hell I'm wrong. Because if I'm right, this could explain why the Triad doesn't want to do business with Richard or Steven. And it could be devastating for the company. That's why I want to keep a lid on it. Have you talked to anyone else about this?"

"Just you, boss."

"Good. Let's keep it that way." Ross jammed the printouts into his briefcase and snapped the lid shut.

"Hey, you aren't going back now, are you?"

The wind had come up steadily across the island ever since Ross had gotten in. The bank of clouds had thickened and churned as it rolled in. Ross's plane had flown toward it as it came in off the Pacific coast—a late-season monsoon.

"I've got to get back tonight. Drive me over to the helipad."

It was past midnight. By the time they arrived at the helipad, a stage-seven storm warning had been issued. The wind indicators churned crazily as the wind buffeted the small airstrip. All private craft were tied down, but Ross's pilot was waiting.

"What do you think?" Ross shouted to make himself heard. He knew the pilot. He was Australian and one of the best. He could fly fixed-wing or rotor in just about any conditions, and had, including several stints with the CIA's secret air operations over Thailand and Cambodia a few years back.

The pilot shook his head and gestured toward the small warehouse that also served as a private terminal. When they were inside, and the door was closed against the wind, he explained, "That was a rough flight coming in. We had some rotor damage. Nothing that can't be fixed, but it's going to take a little time. I've got someone on it right now. But the longer it takes, the less likely we are to get out of here tonight. We could get the edge of this typhoon, mate."

"What about using another aircraft?"

The pilot shook his head. "They've grounded everything else. It seems we're the only ones wacked enough to consider going out in this mess." His grin suggested he considered it nothing more than a stimulating challenge.

Ross cursed as he looked at his watch. "How long on that rotor?"

"Maybe another hour. We lost some wiring. It's got to be fixed. I wouldn't take anyone up with it the way it is."

"All right," Ross reluctantly conceded. "An hour. But get that damn rotor fixed." He thought of Chris, and the meeting with the members of the Cartel in the morning. He knew the Cartel well enough to be certain they'd go ahead with the meeting in spite of the storm. Their very British, stiff-upper-lip resolve wouldn't allow them to do anything else.

If he didn't make it back, she would have to take that meeting alone. She'd handled herself admirably in their meeting with the Triad that morning. But Phillip Lo's family carried a great deal of influence. She wouldn't have that advantage with the Cartel. She would also face the distinct disadvantage of offering a proposal in direct conflict with the interests of the Chairman of the Cartel.

He thought of his father, and all of his own reasons for wanting to be there. An impotent rage burned inside him, like the fury of the storm that rattled the building.

The dual glazed windows of Bill's room at the Regent rattled behind the thick drapes. The building, made of reinforced steel and concrete, trembled with each ferocious gust of wind. In the harbor hundreds of ships were moored with anchors out, hatches battened down. All flights had been grounded. And there was still no word from Ross or his pilot.

The barometer fell dramatically. The number-nine storm warning went out across the entire peninsula.

Bill put down the phone. He looked at Christina. "They were given clearance to leave an hour ago. They lost radio contact almost immediately. No one knows where they are."

# Chapter 31

Christina jerked awake. Gusts of rain and wind hit the windows of the sitting room. She'd curled up on one of the couches, forcing herself to stay awake for the latest storm updates, but eventually she'd dozed off.

Now she blinked in momentary confusion at the darkness that filled the suite.

"Bill?"

"Right here," he called out in a weary voice from somewhere to her right. "We must have lost power. These hotels have their own backup source. It should kick in shortly."

The lights came back on, flickered, and then glowed steadily. Christina sat up and pushed back her tangled hair. "What time is it?"

"Just after three o'clock. I called the airport just before the lights went out. Everything is still grounded, and no incoming."

"Is there any word from Ross or his pilot?"

"Nothing."

Her heart sank. *No*, she thought. *Dear God, no.*

At that moment the telephone rang. Bill was immediately across the room, picking up the receiver. "Yes? No, we're all right. Any word? I see. Yes. Thank you, Kwang." He hung up the phone and gave her a tired smile. "Just a call to see if we're surviving the storm. I ordered up some tea a few minutes ago. It should be here soon."

Christina got up and paced nervously back and forth in front of the windows. Water washed the glass.

"Look, if Ross is . . . delayed . . . we'll try to reschedule the meeting," Bill suggested.

She shook her head. "There's no time. I have to fly to Beijing in two days, and everything has to be in place by then." She looked at Bill, remembering what he'd told her about Ross's father. Forcing herself to assume a confidence she didn't feel, she went on, "He'll make it back in time. He has to. This meeting means as much to him as it does to me."

Bill nodded encouragingly. "Of course he'll make it back."

The hot tea arrived, and they drank it quickly, grateful for its soothing warmth. They turned on the television and listened to updates on the storm. The reports weren't encouraging. The entire coastline and all the outlying islands were battered by the tropical storm, which had now been upgraded to a typhoon.

It was past four o'clock when Christina finally decided to return to her own suite. Bill accompanied her. He opened the door for her, then handed her the key. "He'll be all right, you know. He's probably sitting someplace high and dry, waiting this out. He may be reckless, but he's not foolish, and Ross knows these storms better than anyone. He knows when to stay put and batten down the hatches."

"I know. I just wish we would hear from him."

"He'll call if he can. In the meantime you need to get some sleep so that you're ready for that meeting."

She nodded. "I realize it's only a few hours away." She recalled what Ross had said about how short the flight to Taiwan was. There was still time for him to get back if the storm abated.

"Good-night," she said with a tired smile as she tried not to look worried.

"Everything will be all right," Bill repeated. He leaned over and kissed her on the cheek. "Try to get some sleep."

• • •

Christina looked at the clock in the sitting room of her suite for the hundredth time. Ross wasn't going to make it to the meeting. The realization was especially frightening for she knew that he wouldn't have let anything keep him from it. If anything happened to him . . .

But she refused to let herself think of that. Surely he was all right. He had to be. Because she couldn't bear to lose him.

The wind had finally died down, but heavy rain continued to fall. Listening to the morning news on the television, she heard reports of the damage caused by the storm. The airport was still closed.

There were no reports of any downed aircraft. She held on to that tenuous reason for hope as she dressed for her meeting with the Cartel. She chose a cobalt blue Armani suit—a particular shade of blue that reminded her of the Fortune colors.

She drank coffee, strong and black, and nibbled desultorily at a croissant. She had no appetite, and she soon set the breakfast tray aside to go through the proposal once more.

All night she'd waited for the phone to ring. Yet when it finally did ring a little after eight, she jumped with nervousness and apprehension. She grabbed at it, practically knocking it to the floor. "Yes?"

"Good morning," Bill said in greeting.

"Oh . . . Bill." There was no disguising her disappointment.

"I called over to the airport. Still no news of Ross." He hesitated, then suggested, "We could cancel the meeting."

She'd considered it more than once through the long night. The meeting was the last thing she wanted to deal with now. It lost all importance compared with her fear for Ross's welfare. But if they canceled and tried to reschedule, there was no guarantee the Cartel would be willing to meet with them again. It met once a month for two days. If she missed this opportunity, the best she could hope for was to reschedule for a month from now. She didn't think it likely that the Cartel would be willing to grant her a special meeting, but it didn't matter, anyway. It had to be today. Because tomorrow she was supposed to be in Beijing.

She wanted nothing more than to sit tight and wait for word of Ross. But the future of Fortune International was at stake. She'd promised Katherine she would do all she could to make this deal succeed. No matter how difficult it was for her, she had to put her personal feelings aside.

"I'll meet with them as scheduled," she told Bill. She hesitated, then said, "I'd like for you to come to the meeting with me. You're acquainted with the proposal, and I could use some support."

Bill agreed without hesitation. "You got it." Then he reminded her, "We'll need to leave in about ten minutes."

Christina's fingers tightened over the phone. "Okay. I'm almost ready."

Ten minutes later Bill knocked on her door. He gave her a look of approval as she opened it. "They won't know what hit them."

She mustered a nervous smile. "I want them to know what hit them, and then I want them to agree to our proposal." Then she became more serious. "What do you think the chances are they'll go for this?"

Bill didn't pull any punches. "It'll take all you've got, kid, and then some." He smiled, in a way that crinkled his entire face, then added encouragingly, "Ross wouldn't have set this up if he didn't think you could handle it."

She smiled, grateful for his confidence. "I'll try to remember that when they're trying to eat me alive."

The cross-channel tunnel was filled with early-morning traffic, fighting the aftermath of the storm. Debris filled the streets, adding to the havoc. It took twice as long as usual to get across to Hong Kong Island.

Their meeting was scheduled for nine o'clock at the Victoria Bank building. They had only a few minutes to spare as the limo pulled to the curb.

As she stepped from the limousine, she looked up at the Victoria Bank building. It was stately, imposing, a reminder of a bygone era when the sun never set on the British Empire. She realized that today, as then, money ruled this island.

Ross had said very little real wealth remained in Hong Kong. But Victoria Bank and those who controlled it were as powerful as ever. And somewhere inside, in a boardroom where financial decisions had been made for over a century and a half, the members of the Cartel waited.

As she stood there, she had a feeling of déjà vu. Not that long ago she had stood in the plaza of Fortune Tower in San Francisco and fought back the demons of fear. Now, as then, so much was riding on what happened when she went into that building.

"Ready?" Bill asked.

She nodded, though she felt far from ready.

The building was a blend of old world and new. The main floor housed the commercial banking department, with its line of polished brass and etched glass teller windows that might have been found in any bank in London when Victoria was queen. Giant columns filled the foyer. The furnishings, too, were Victorian. Lush green ferns contrasted with warm wood and cool marble. The ceilings were vaulted. Cherrywood wainscoting lined walls that were covered with soft gold and burgundy wallpaper.

But the traditional was interwoven with high-tech. On the opposite side of the commercial banking line, executives sat in imposing offices with computer terminals at their fingertips that could call up the balances of accounts in any city of the world.

Even this early in the morning, there was an almost frenetic atmosphere inside the bank, as customers arrived and meetings were held behind closed doors.

A Chinese man dressed in a butler's black coat and pants with a crisp white shirt and elegant tie came forward to greet them. He directed them to the elevators that would take them to the eighth floor, where their meeting was scheduled to take place.

On the eighth floor they were once more met by a well-dressed Chinese employee, who incongruously reminded Christina of a butler out of an English novel, with his solemn demeanor. He informed them that all the members of the Cartel had arrived, and immediately showed them into the conference room.

She wondered if Hamish Fortune might have once walked

through these same doors. Then the double doors to the conference room opened, and they were announced.

Power. If it had a face, it would look precisely like the nine men who sat around the table before her. Collectively they controlled the major financial interests of the wealthiest nations of the Pacific Rim.

Introductions were made. Christina was aware of the subtle reactions of several of the men on the Cartel as her name was given. Those reactions varied from surprise to guarded curiosity and undisguised resentment.

The one expression she couldn't read was on the face of the man who sat at the head of the table. Sir Anthony Adamson, the head of the Cartel. She was unprepared for his uncanny resemblance to Ross, in the dark hair and deep blue eyes. Even his initial attitude was the same as Ross's had been when she'd first walked into the boardroom at Fortune International—an air of cool detachment.

As she and Bill were shown to chairs at one side of the enormous table, she couldn't help wondering—what sort of man walked out on a woman when she became pregnant with his child? What sort of man abandoned that child and refused to acknowledge him? What sort of man is capable of that kind of cruelty?

The answer came back to her in the form of a question she'd asked herself countless times—what sort of man would rape a fifteen-year-old girl?

As different as the situations were, they were similar in their cruelty, and in the emotional wounds left in the aftermath.

Ross had acquired a reputation for being ruthless and cunning. But that was the hard-edged professional side of him that had nothing to do with the man he was inside. When he opened up his emotions, as he had in Chinatown and aboard the *Resolute,* she'd discovered an intimate, tender side to him.

She doubted that the man who watched her with that detached expression had ever felt such emotions. If he had, she was certain, they were buried so deep that he was unable to find any shred of love for his own son.

She knew that the final vote might well be determined by

this man. She focused on him and wondered what Ross's thoughts must have been, knowing that he was to confront his father. And suddenly she knew—he was seeking revenge, just as she had in going back to San Francisco.

She thought of how much this meeting meant to Ross, how desperately he must have needed to confront his father and finally resolve their relationship. Just as she'd needed to confront the Fortune family.

Then she saw the subtle shift of focus as the members of the Cartel assumed that Bill was presenting the proposal. He saw it, too, and stood briefly. "As acting President of Fortune International, Miss Fortune will be making this presentation," he announced, then distributed copies of the proposal to each of the members of the Cartel.

Her nerves were taut. Everything depended on the success of this meeting. She wanted it as much for Ross as she wanted it for herself.

She was about to begin the presentation when there was a knock at the door. The clerk returned briefly and spoke in whispered tones with Adamson. An expression of surprise, and something more, something not quite definable, crossed his face. Then he slowly nodded to the clerk.

"A moment please, gentlemen . . . and Miss Fortune," he said.

She glanced at Bill. He shook his head. For a moment she thought they had changed their minds and were about to refuse to go on with the meeting. Then the door opened, and the clerk stepped through and announced, "Mr. McKenna has just arrived."

It was all she could do to keep from bursting into tears of joy. A feeling of inexpressible relief swept through her, making her tremble violently. *Thank God*, she whispered under her breath. He was alive! Nothing else—not the meeting, nor the plan to save the company—mattered a damn compared with that.

He was the essence of control as his gaze swept the conference room, resting briefly on each member of the Cartel, and only slightly longer on the man who sat at the head of the table.

For the instant that he looked at his father, Christina held her breath. She understood with perfect empathy the emotional intensity that charged the air between the two men. Then Ross strode to the far side of the table and joined her.

He greeted both Bill and Christina with a circumspect nod. But she knew that had they been alone, he would have swept her into his arms, and she wouldn't have resisted. It was all she could do to return her focus to the meeting. At the moment that was the priority, but later, she told herself . . . later it would be different.

When she'd made the proposal to the Triad the day before, it had been necessary to reestablish trust in the Fortune name. Only Christina herself could do that, so of necessity she'd taken center stage. This was different—it was Ross's meeting, and she felt no resentment at handing it over to him. He was, quite simply, the person best qualified to handle it. He knew these men. He'd met with them in the past over other transactions. He knew what their questions and objections would be. And he knew their weaknesses.

But even more important, he was hungry for this.

She turned briefly back to the members of the Cartel and said, "As CEO of Fortune International, Mr. McKenna will be making this presentation."

He gave a flawless presentation, answering the pointed, sometimes highly critical questions almost before they were asked. He gave them facts, figures, and projections. Then he drew Christina into the presentation, underscoring her importance in the project as the acting President of Fortune International.

As they concluded the presentation, Christina was acutely aware that he had avoided any mention of their meeting the day before with the Triad or her upcoming meeting with David Chen. And she also knew it was deliberate.

She watched Adamson's reaction. Ross might have his father's eyes, but there was none of the warmth that Ross could show in Adamson's gaze. There was only a hard, closed expression.

After a moment Adamson closed the portfolio, a gesture indicating he considered the meeting at an end. His tone was almost contemptuous as he pointed out, "This proposal is not a new concept. It has been attempted in the past. My fellow members of the Cartel are aware of the obvious obstacles." Then his tone became condescending. "The profit potential that you've outlined is very impressive and very imaginative. Unfortunately it is just that—the projections of an *overactive* imagination."

His tone was scathing as he continued to berate the proposal, and Ross. "You've neglected two very critical elements to this proposal. Without them it's a complete waste of valuable time." He looked directly at Ross. "It is, no doubt, due to inexperience in these matters."

Christina's hands balled into tight fists in her lap. She couldn't believe he would talk to anyone that way, much less his own son . . . or did he do so because Ross was his son?

Her throat tightened with loathing and contempt as she realized how Ross must feel, standing there, confronting the man who had abandoned him years ago. But Ross gave no outward sign that the words affected him in the least. Beside her, Bill reached over and squeezed her hand.

"It'll be all right," he whispered. "Ross knows what he's doing."

She watched as the members of the Cartel slowly closed their copies of the proposal. She glanced apprehensively at Ross, but he looked amazingly calm and confident.

"You are no doubt referring to the participation of the Triad," Ross said. "I am well aware that it is a necessary element with any business venture within Hong Kong, along with the commitment of the Chinese government."

"They are two vital elements to your proposal," a gentleman representing South Korea interjected. "Without them you have no possible chance at success."

Christina watched, fascinated, as Ross played out his hand. "You're correct, of course," he said. "The Triad, represented by Mr. Thomas Lai, has agreed to participate in our proposal. The terms were negotiated by Miss Fortune in our meeting with the Triad yesterday." He glanced at Bill, who immediately rose and circulated copies of a formal letter of acceptance they'd received from the Triad.

"In addition," Ross went on to explain, "the Economics Minister of the People's Republic of China has agreed to meet with Miss Fortune." He paused for effect, then added, "That meeting is scheduled for tomorrow, in Beijing."

Bill then circulated a copy of David Chen's letter.

Stunned silence filled the room, followed by the shuffle of paper as the members of the Cartel read the copies of the letters.

Christina felt a thrill of excitement. Ross had known exactly how to present this proposal, exactly what their objections would be, and exactly how to overcome their reservations. He'd taken control of the meeting away from his father and manipulated it so that the members were now asking interested questions: When could Fortune International have additional ships on line? How soon was the Triad willing to begin expansion of the container terminals? What was the projected time frame before goods could be moved from railheads inside China to coastal ports?

They weren't questions about *if*. They were questions about *when*. As if the most important question of all—regarding the Cartel's participation—had already been decided.

Ross's father sat in stony silence at the far end of the table. His expression didn't change until Ross finally put his copy of the proposal inside his briefcase and closed it—a signal that *he* was bringing the meeting to an end.

She glanced at Ross's father, and in that instant she saw something pass across his face that stunned her—it was almost an expression of admiration! Then it was hidden behind that cold, implacable facade.

Ross stepped aside to let her pass in front of him, and they left the conference room.

In the elevator Ross pulled Christina into his arms. "God, you were magnificent," he exclaimed as he slipped his hands through her hair to the back of her neck, and drew her to him. He kissed her, deeply, thoroughly, and with utter abandon. It was glorious, and she wanted it to go on forever.

Neither of them cared that Bill was watching with undisguised curiosity.

When Ross finally pulled away, Christina said breathlessly, "I was so worried!"

"I know," he whispered. "I know, and I'm sorry. There was nothing I could do."

Then a slow, wicked smile softened his mouth. "But think of it—only a typhoon could have kept me from you last night."

"And tonight?" she asked, looking at him directly, without shyness.

"Tonight . . ."

"Ah-hem." Bill's exaggerated cough reminded them that they weren't alone.

As the elevator door opened, and they stepped out into the lobby, Christina asked, "How long do you think it will take for them to get back to us with an answer?"

"They've already made their decision. Of course Adamson will try to change it."

"Then I guess we wait."

"We wait," he agreed. "But not for long. They know how much time they've got."

In the executive conference room on the eighth floor of the Victoria Bank building, Sir Anthony Adamson sat alone as the last member of the Cartel left. The door closed with a jarring finality.

He stared down the length of the enormous conference table, thinking back to that morning, and the brash, confident man who had stood only a few feet away. In the space of an hour, that young man accomplished what Adamson had never been able to accomplish—a proposal for an exclusive trade agreement with the People's Republic of China. Every connection Adamson had, all the years he'd spent in Hong Kong, all the influence he held with other people hadn't been able to acquire that one crowning achievement.

But as he sat there, alone with his thoughts, confronted by the harsh reality that the other members of the Cartel had voted against him, he realized just how much he had lost. For thirty-eight years, he had refused to acknowledge his illegitimate son. Now his son had beaten him at his own game. Except that Ross wasn't really his son. Adamson had destroyed that bond long ago, when he had turned his back on the only woman he had every truly loved because of a misguided, but deeply ingrained sense of family duty and social pressure.

And now—with the cold, haunting reality of facing the end of his life and the consequences of his choices—he realized the loss of that son was the greatest loss of all.

# *Chapter 32*

Christina had insisted that they stay at the office until the call came through. When it finally came in, the conversation was brief. Ross said very little.

When he hung up, Christina asked nervously, "Well? What did they say?"

"We won," he answered simply.

Through her relief she thought, *No. You won, Ross.*

Bill poured champagne for everyone, then held up his glass in a toast. "To pirates," he said to Ross and Christina, amid cheers of approval from Lisa Jeung and Adam Quon. "And the treasures they seek."

Lisa and Adam took final sips of champagne, then excused themselves. It was late, and both had families waiting for them.

When they had gone, Bill said, "I'll be going, too. I've got a call to make."

"Use my phone," Ross said, gesturing to it.

Bill shook his head. "No, thanks. I think I'll make it from my hotel room."

Christina leaned over to kiss his cheek. "Thanks for being there for me last night and this morning. I don't know what I would have done without you."

He smiled shyly. "You would have been just fine."

"I'm not so sure. But even if I would have been, it was still far better having someone on my side, instead of going through it alone."

His expression turned serious. "I know what you mean. I've sort of been thinking along the same lines myself."

"Does this have to do with that call you want to make?"

He nodded.

She felt her heart go out to him. She knew he was about to put his own heart on the line. "Good luck, Bill."

"Thanks. I'll need it."

When he left, Ross asked, "What was that all about?"

"I think Bill is finally getting his priorities straight. If things work out, you'd better be prepared to cut him a little slack at the office."

Ross clearly didn't understand, but he didn't want to get into it at the moment. "Enough of Bill. I have a toast of my own to make." Touching his glass to Christina's, he said, "To a successful partnership."

She hesitated. Did that mean everything she thought it might? Looking into his dark blue eyes, she saw such warmth and tenderness that her heart did a funny little flip-flop. Maybe, she thought. Maybe.

Ross suggested they have dinner together, and there was no question that she would agree. They took his Range Rover, and as he cut through the traffic and took Connaught Road to the cross-channel tunnel, he asked, "Do we go casual tonight, or formal? Hot dogs, or something exotic?"

"Definitely something exotic." Christina laid her head back against the headrest and closed her eyes, enjoying the glow from the champagne. "I can have hot dogs anytime. *This* is a once-in-a-lifetime celebration."

The night air was thick and sultry in the aftermath of the storm. The car windows were down, and the warm air mixed with the scent of glove-soft leather upholstery and Ross's spicy cologne. Christina felt so relaxed and happy, she was almost sorry they made the cross-channel drive so quickly.

In her suite she quickly showered and dressed. She had requested something exotic for dinner, and she dressed accordingly for the dinner, the man, and the celebration. Her black satin dress was street length, with a full skirt that flowed just above her knees, accentuating her long legs. The bodice clung to her slender waist and full breasts. The yoke and long sleeves were sheer black silk with black jet beads that sparkled against the smoky illusion of bare skin. The only jewelry she wore were drop pearl earrings—three perfect white pearls suspending one black teardrop pearl, set in gold filigree.

Ross had said he would call for her at nine o'clock, the usual time for dining out in Hong Kong. She was ready early and decided to meet him at his suite. She stepped across the hall and pressed the doorbell. When Kwang answered the door, she was surprised to see him.

"Good evening, Miss Fortune."

"Good evening, Kwang."

He smiled. "Mr McKenna is almost ready." He showed her into the suite and instructed the houseboy to mix her a drink.

Then Ross came out of the bedroom, dressed formally in a black dinner jacket and slacks, his white shirt crisply pleated in front. Elegant gold and black jade studs gleamed at the cuffs. He looked wonderful, as handsome and elegant as the young Sean Connery in his first James Bond films.

Kwang turned to him and asked, "If that will be all, Mr. McKenna?"

"Yes, thank you, Kwang. As always, everything is perfect."

She wondered what they were talking about. Then Ross gave her a wicked grin, and more than ever she was reminded of her first impression that he was a pirate—an extremely elegant, handsome pirate, with his dark hair waving about his temples and across his forehead.

His gaze fastened on hers, dark and intense, as it was that night in Chinatown, and again aboard the *Resolute*. The night had suddenly become dangerous with promise and possibility. She discovered she wanted to taste the danger, wanted to explore all the possibilities.

She walked toward him, stopping only inches away, her eyes as dark and mysterious as the Orient, where she had come to stake her claim. He reached out and took her hand, lacing their fingers. He saw the amber velvet of her eyes thin to a gold band around inky dark irises as she watched him, heard the expectant intake of breath, sensed the anticipation that tingled across her soft skin.

She thought, if he were a gentleman, instead of a pirate, he would kiss my hand. As if reading her thoughts, he slowly turned her hand, their fingers still entwined. His gaze never left hers as he bent his head, then brushed his lips against the sensitized skin at the inside of her wrist.

But he was a pirate, after all. His lips didn't stop at the back of her hand, they moved to her throat, arousing her to the point that she could hardly breathe.

She wasn't ready for this yet. Pulling back, she retreated to the temporary safety of conversation. "I'm hungry," she whispered, and immediately realized the double meaning behind the words. She collected herself and asked, "Where are we eating tonight?"

He stepped past her to the French doors that led out onto the terrace. He pushed them open, revealing a table set for two with white linens, elegant china, and gleaming silver. Candles glowed in twin crystal candlesticks, and a bottle of champagne chilled in a silver bucket.

"The food is incomparable, and the view unparalleled. And we don't have to wait for our table."

She stepped onto the terrace. It was covered with red tile and landscaped with exotic flowering plants. Their fragrance filled the night air with sultry sweetness. Palms and ferns gave the terrace a discreet privacy. Steps led up to the sunken marble whirlpool spa off the master bedroom. Several more candles set on the rim of the spa reflected off the surface of the water.

Then her gaze was drawn to the view beyond the terrace.

Thousands of lights sparkled like jewels in the crescent crown of Hong Kong Harbor. Night draped the hills like black velvet. It was exotic, beautiful, and mysterious.

Then she turned and looked at the skyline of Kowloon behind them, and she smiled.

"What are you smiling at?" Ross asked as he came to stand beside her.

"The nine dragons," she said, thinking about the old legend. "They didn't chase us away."

"Perhaps they sensed a kindred spirit," he suggested.

"Perhaps." Then she said, "Listen."

They both stood at the edge of the terrace, looking out across the harbor, listening for the sound that caught her attention—the deep tolling of a single bell.

"The vault of heaven," she said, recalling another Chinese legend about the shape of the bell.

"Representing the extremes of good and evil," he added.

She turned and looked at him. "And good always triumphs over evil?"

"They balance one another, like yin and yang."

"Positive and negative forces," she recalled from the lesson aboard the *Resolute*.

"In order to have one, you must have the other."

A young Chinese houseboy suddenly appeared, as if by some silent signal. He stood beside the table, waiting expectantly.

"Dinner is ready, Mr. McKenna," he announced.

"Thank you."

Ross escorted Christina to the table.

The champagne was a Salon eighty-two. It was crisp and dry, and tasted faintly of hazelnuts. The taste lingered long after the bubbles had disappeared. It was different, unusual, and as intriguing as the man who sat across from her.

"This is a very rare vintage, as I recall," she remarked. "A client I used to deal with at Goldman, Sachs drank only Salon champagnes. His favorite was the seventy-nine."

"I tried to get a seventy-nine. There aren't any more to be had, or if there are, someone is hoarding them. Probably some little old lady who likes to tipple on special occasions."

Christina laughed at the mental images that created. That was another thing she liked about him—the way he made her laugh at unexpected moments.

"This has fewer bubbles than most champagnes," she noticed.

"That's because it's turned less frequently, and only by hand. And instead of the usual blend of chardonnay and Pinot grapes that other vintners combine in their champagnes, only the chardonnay is used in Salon champagnes. They're grown in one region, in the village of Le Mesnil-sur-Oger."

She smiled at him teasingly. "So you're an expert on champagne, as well as on t'ai chi and carpentry and sailing, and Lord knows what else?"

His blue eyes glinted mischievously. "The truth is, it's all written on the label."

She laughed, enjoying his unpretentiousness as much as she enjoyed everything else about him.

Silver lids were removed from serving dishes, revealing a tantalizing dinner of Brie bisque, soufflé almondine, and shrimp chinoiserie served with both bourbon-duck sauce and fragrant ginger-soy sauce, and a main course of pheasant with sherried plums. It was the perfect dinner for a victory celebration.

The food, the champagne, and the sultry night air were like an exotic drug to her senses. Later, when the dishes had been cleared and the houseboy was gone, she sat, slowly sipping champagne. Ross sat relaxed in his chair, one leg casually extended before him. He looked like a lean cat—all restrained energy, beneath the formal black dinner clothes.

She didn't want to break the lovely mood, but there was something she had to say. "You wanted this deal because of your father." It was the first time she'd said anything about Anthony Adamson, revealing that she knew he was Ross's father.

He answered without hesitation. "Damn right." And then, as if he thought that might have sounded too harsh, he explained, "My most vivid memory of my father is from when I was seven years old. He visited us occasionally up till then. My mother explained that he didn't live with us because of his work, but my mates at school told me that it was because I was illegitimate."

She tried to imagine how it must have been for him, to hear those horrible taunting words from other children. Her heart ached for him.

"I didn't understand the word," he went on. "But I understood that it set me apart from them. Their parents wouldn't invite me to their parties. They made it clear I wasn't the kind of child they wanted their children to socialize with.

"Then one day I came home from school, and he was at my mother's house, the little one on Connaught Road."

He hesitated, then went on, "He and my mother were talking when I came in. My God, he was the most imposing man I'd ever seen, dressed in his fine suit, with his gold watch. At seven, I knew that a father was supposed to be someone who lived with you, as part of your family. He was my father, but he was a complete stranger.

"He became angry, and I remember staring at him, aware of the difference between him and my mother. She never raised her voice. She was always gentle and loving. I hated him because he was angry with her. Later, after he left, I asked my mother what the word *illegitimate* meant. It's the only time I ever saw her cry, and I knew it was because of him."

Christina reached across the table and slipped her hand around his. "I'm so very sorry. It must have been unbearably painful."

He stared out past the terrace at some invisible point in the distance. "It was more painful for her. She still loved him. But he was married." He looked back at her then. "That afternoon, when I saw her cry, I vowed I would make him pay for every tear."

"And you waited all these years."

"I learned a great deal about him while I was growing up." He gave her a hard smile. "You see, I was the *secret* that everyone in the colony knew about. It was easy to learn everything about him. Hong Kong is a very small place. I always knew what he was doing. When I had the opportunity to go to work for Fortune International, I seized it."

"You knew about his proposals for a joint venture with the PRC," she surmised.

"He's been trying to put it together for years. I discovered long ago that the best way to hurt Anthony Adamson is to take something away from him."

"And now you've done it."

He looked up at her and said without hesitation. "No. You've done it. You've made my revenge possible." Then he added, "I'd say it's worked out for you, too. When this is over, you'll have what you came back for. Your inheritance. Control of a strong, successful company."

She didn't answer him. Instead she rose from the table and walked to the edge of the terrace. She leaned against the railing, staring into the warm, sultry night sky.

Watching her, trying to decipher the enigmatic expression on her face, he had a flash of insight. She'd come back for more than just the inheritance, more than the need to prove she could run the company. He asked, "Why *did* you come back after all these years?"

"As I told you once, I made a promise to someone." But she knew she couldn't let it drop. She had to tell him all of it. They couldn't go on from here until she had.

"Like you, I wanted revenge," she said quietly.

Her hands curled over the railing, and she held on tightly, even though there was no danger of falling. She told him a story, because it was easier that way. "Twenty years ago a fifteen-year-old girl ran away. Her parents had died the year before, and she was sent to live with her grandmother." She paused, took a deep breath, and went on. "That year was very difficult, but she found a friend, someone she became very close to, someone who understood her loneliness and pain."

Ross knew she was speaking of Jason Chandler. He'd heard that Jason and Christina had been exceptionally close as teenagers, perhaps even a little in love with each other. Her eyes glistened with tears as she struggled to go on. He wanted to go to her and hold her, but it was too soon. Instinctively he understood that she needed to tell him everything now, while she had the courage and the moment was right.

"They cared a great deal for each other," she went on. "It was all very innocent. But his mother didn't see it that way."

Diana, he thought, knowing how cruel and manipulative she could be.

"It was arranged for them to attend separate private schools that fall. They promised to write to each other. Weeks passed, and there were no letters. Later she realized that their letters to each other must have been intercepted. The next time they saw each other was at her grandmother's home when they returned for their first weekend visit."

Christina swallowed back the emotions that tightened her throat. "They were both hurt and angry. He followed her out to the summerhouse. They quarreled. They said horrible things to one another."

Her fingers constricted over the railing, her nails biting into the palms of her hands. She squeezed her eyes shut to hold back the tears. "He left. She stayed there alone for a long time. Then someone else came into the summerhouse. There had been a Halloween party that night at the house for the family. The man who came to the summerhouse wore a mask. It was very dark, and she couldn't tell who it was."

Her voice broke. She forced herself to go on. "Then . . . he raped her."

A cold fury churned inside Ross. Who could have done such a thing? Was it Jason? Had he returned to the summerhouse and attacked her in a fit of anger? Or was it someone else? Andrew? Or Steven? Any one of them might be capable of it. What about Brian Chandler? Somehow he doubted it. Yet who knew the mind of a rapist?

There was another possibility. Could it have been Richard? He had the most to lose with Christina's inheritance, an inheritance he had always considered rightfully his. He must have bitterly resented his niece and the power she would one day wield in the company.

Ross went to her then. He stood behind her, wanting to touch her and hold her, but afraid that she was too fragile after what she had revealed, that she might not want to be touched.

"Chris," he said softly, his throat tight with emotion, knowing that the girl she had spoken of was herself. He brought his hands up slowly around her shoulders. She didn't flinch at his touch. Instead she turned and looked up at him.

She went on, "There was another fifteen-year-old girl. Her circumstances were . . . different. Less privileged. Her father was dead, and her mother had remarried. Her stepfather was a drunk."

*Loomis*, Ross thought with distaste.

"He . . . he touched the girl in ways that made her very uncomfortable, but when she tried to tell her mother, she was accused of lying. I think her mother must have been afraid to

believe the truth because then she would have to leave the
man, who'd given her some small measure of financial security. They'd been so poor after the death of her first husband."

Christina took a deep breath, then went on shakily, "One
night the girl's stepfather didn't stop at merely touching her.
He . . . he raped her. Afterward she left. She knew it would
happen again, and she couldn't bear that.

"These two girls met on the streets of New York, and they
became friends. Best friends. They relied on each other to survive. Then one night . . ."

Christina stopped. It was a moment before she could continue. "One of the girls was murdered. And her friend swore
that someday she would get revenge on the men who had bru-
talized them and forced them out into a world on their own."

She'd been staring out at the bay. Now she turned to look
at Ross. "I came back because I had to know who it was . . .
to confront him, and make him pay for what he did."

Ross drew her into his arms. There was no resistance. She
came willingly, softly, her slender body molding against his as
she slipped her arms about his waist.

He held her for a long time, his cheek pressed against her
hair. Then, with his fingers beneath her chin, he tilted her face
up. There were tears in her dark eyes. They spilled down her
cheeks. He kissed away first one tear, then another and another. Her lips were slightly parted as she stared up at him.
Then he bent over her once more, his mouth moving over
hers with aching tenderness.

The kiss lengthened and deepened, slowly rousing both
need and desire. Ross slipped his hands through her silken
hair, cradling her head, as he drew her closer, feeling her skin
heat beneath his fingers. Lifting his head, he looked down at
her—the twin path of tears that streaked her cheeks, the
bruised fullness of her mouth, the pulse that throbbed beneath
his fingers at her neck.

He tried to imagine the strength and courage it had taken
for her to survive what had happened twenty years ago. Rape
was an act of violence that left its victim emotionally scarred,
sometimes for life. But Christina *had* survived. And she had

triumphed over the terrible aftermath of the attack, so that she could now open herself to loving and being loved.

"I need you," she whispered, her breathing shallow and ragged. He sensed her vulnerability, and the courage it took to say those words.

He'd promised they would make love when there were no more secrets between them. There was still one last secret—*Who was she?* But at that moment her emotional hunger was far more important than his need to know the truth about her.

He kissed her again, with a slow heat that began with the taste of her on his tongue. His fingers slipped down her neck and over her shoulders, gently closing over them as he pulled her against him.

There was a ruthless side to him that never allowed anyone else's needs to be more important than his own. Now he wanted only to fulfill *her* needs and *her* desires.

With his hands resting on her shoulders, he brushed his thumbs down over the hollows beneath her collarbone and then across the swell of each breast. The sheer silk of her dress felt soft and smooth.

She brought her arms up and slipped them around his neck, her fingers curling into his black hair. Her mouth opened beneath his, tasting the dark sweetness of his tongue.

He was taking her to a place of pure sensation that she'd only glimpsed before—a place that all the old fears had never allowed her to experience fully without holding back.

Ross curved one arm around her waist and slipped the other beneath her legs as he lifted her. The satin fabric of her dress rustled softly in the sultry night air as he turned and carried her into the bedroom.

The room was bathed in soft shadows. The only light came from the glow of candles out on the terrace. The doors were left open as he carried her to the bed. Beside it he slowly released her. Her legs slipped between his, the curve of her hips slowly settling against his with an unsettling heat.

There had been many other women, other lovers, and those who were with him so briefly they didn't even qualify as lovers. Always he'd made it clear how little he was willing to offer. He wanted to be fair, to avoid misunderstanding and regrets. And he'd always been in control, sure of himself, his feelings, his needs. Now, for the first time in his adult life, he hesitated.

Christina sensed his uncertainty. She saw it in the dark shadows of his eyes as he watched her, in the way he suddenly stood very still, in his hands as they fell away from her. Oh, God, she thought, please don't let him turn away now. I need him so much.

"Chris, if you're not entirely ready, I'll understand," he said tenderly.

She stretched up on her toes and stopped his lips with her own. Then she reached up and slowly pushed the black dinner jacket off his shoulders. When it fell into the darkness at their feet, she untied the silk tie at his neck. She unfastened each button until the white silk shirt lay open across his chest. Smoothing her hands over the hard, flat muscles across his ribs, she kissed him, flicking her tongue across his chest, taking in the special taste of clean skin, spicy cologne, and man.

His fingers closed gently over her wrists. "Chris!" he said in soft warning, staring down at her in the muted light of the bedroom. "If we start this, there's only one way it will end."

"Then don't stop," she murmured. "Show me how it can be." She reached out and flattened the palm of her hand against his, imitating the first t'ai chi movement he'd taught her aboard the *Resolute*. Slowly she pulled her hand away, even as her mouth was only a breath away from his, and an unbearable tension built between them.

"Show me," she whispered.

He slowly undressed her, peeling away layer upon silken layer, until all that remained was a black lace teddy. Then he skimmed the lace down the length of her slender body.

His clothes joined hers on the floor.

They stood before each other, naked, in the pale shadows.

She closed her eyes, held her hands up in front of her, and surrendered to her senses.

He brought their palms together until they were lightly touching. Slowly he began to move his hand in a high, wide arc. She was completely attuned to his movements, making each one in perfect unison with him as he brought his left hand back to the beginning of the arc, and then began a new arc with his right hand.

They completed several more moves together, their bodies within inches of each other, only their hands touching. Then he drew his hands away from hers. Each time he brought his hand close, or moved around her, she sensed his nearness and moved with him as she used *zanshin*. It was like a slow, erotic dance as his hands passed within inches of her waist, her thigh, the taut flatness of her stomach.

Ross watched the sharp change in her breathing, the increased beat of the pulse at her neck, and felt the heat radiate from her skin. Twice as he moved around her, she turned, anticipating him.

She was completely sensitized. Her skin felt as if it were on fire. The more her senses opened, the more acute her awareness of him became, and the more her desire heightened. It built from a languid heat low in her stomach with that first draining kiss, to a raging fire that burned across every nerve ending. As she turned and met his next move, she bit back a startled gasp as his hand brushed her breast.

Making love with David had been sweet and tender. But it never reached the point of unbridled passion. Aboard the *Resolute* she had glimpsed what passion could be. But she had never imagined *this*, never realized that she could desire a man as she desired Ross.

Again he moved, again she anticipated it. The contact was brief and shattering to her senses as the heat of his hand hovered over her bare hip. Eyes closed, she whispered with aching urgency, "Touch me!"

She suddenly felt his nearness behind her, then the startling heat of his hands as they cupped her breasts. She cried out and clasped her hands over his. His body molded her as he pulled her back against him.

Her head rolled back against his shoulder, and he flicked his tongue over the rapidly pulsing vein at her neck. He was aware of the shallow breaths she took as if she struggled up from some deep abyss, and the tremors she no longer tried to hide.

His mouth found hers with new urgency, and they fell onto

the bed together, their legs entwined. Everywhere he touched and tasted there was heat. He moved his hands up the curve of her waist, then further still to the fullness of her breasts. The nipples became taut and hard beneath the circular motions of his thumbs. Then he caressed the flatness of her stomach, spreading his hands over her hips to pull her to him.

She breathed in sharply, deeply, as thigh brushed against thigh, and hip molded to hip. Then she shuddered as her mouth opened under his, a mixture of sweet velvet and dark heat. He shifted, his body poised above hers, desperate to satisfy the needs he'd felt from the very first moment he saw her.

She watched him, her eyes dark and mysterious. He reached for her hands, flattening their palms together in the way they had first touched. Then his fingers laced with hers. He moved his leg, and they slowly came together.

She arched against him, closing her fingers around his hands, giving herself completely and unafraid.

Ross shuddered as he was absorbed into her. He brought his mouth down over hers as their fingers entwined. And *zanshin*—the sensual awareness of the forces around them— became an exquisitely sensual awareness of each other's heart and body and soul as he made love to her slowly, deeply, and completely.

Afterward Ross carried her out to the terrace. Naked, they slipped into the heated, bubbling spa, while the night closed around them. Water glistened on their skin in the moonlight. Their legs entwined, their hands and mouths hungry for each other again, they made love once more, in the shadows of the nine dragons.

Later, as Christina lay beside him in bed, she knew she had finally put the past behind her. In opening herself to Ross completely, without reservation, she'd managed to overcome the old fears that had kept her emotionally imprisoned. She was well now, in a way she hadn't entirely been in twenty years. Whether she ever discovered the identity of the person who'd come back to the summerhouse that night almost didn't matter now. She'd accomplished something far more important than revenge. She'd found peace.

# Chapter 33

The soft tone of the bedside phone beeped insistently. Ross turned and reached for it. Beside him Christina stirred sleepily.

"Yes?"

"I'm sorry to bother you this time of night, boss," Bill's weary voice came over the phone. "I just got a call from Mick Donovan on Taiwan."

Ross's head cleared instantly. He glanced to the clock on the nightstand. It was just after four in the morning. "What is it?"

"We've got some trouble. One of the containers on the *Bountiful Fortune* was damaged. When Mick and his crew went aboard to make a damage report, they found some undocumented cargo."

Ross was immediately alert, a tiny warning bell going off in the back of his head. "What kind of cargo?"

"Pure, uncut heroin. Several hundred kilos of it."

The bell became a full-scale alarm. "Who knows about this?"

"Just Mick and his crew, but there's another problem."

"What is it?"

"The original shipment didn't go aboard in Taiwan. It was

on-loaded four days ago, in a container of manufactured garments, here in Hong Kong."

"That means the trail starts here."

"Right," Bill said.

"Damn!" Ross cursed softly. Beside the obvious legal problems, this could have more far-reaching repercussions. "Keep a lid on this. If word gets out that we're trafficking in heroin, it will cost us the trade agreement with the PRC."

"Mick will do his best to keep this quiet," Bill tried to reassure him. "But you know how things like this get out. We won't be able to keep a lid on it for long."

"Buy me some time," Ross said. He glanced over at Christina. She was awake now and sat up in bed.

"What are you going to do?" Bill asked.

"I've got to find out who's responsible for this, and take care of it. Hopefully before anyone finds out." Ross's thoughts were already racing ahead.

"You don't have much time," Bill repeated. "Maybe twenty-four hours. Then it will be all over the island."

"I know."

When he hung up, Christina asked worriedly, "What is it?"

"Trouble," he said bluntly. "Big trouble."

He looked at her. Her eyes were large and dark in the early morning shadows as she stared back at him. The sheet curled down around their hips as they lay intimately entwined. A frown curved his lips as he reached out and brushed a stray tendril of hair back from her cheek.

He explained, "Mick Donovan and his crew had some damaged cargo aboard the *Bountiful Fortune* in Taiwan."

She recognized the name of one of the newer container ships. "Was the damage extensive?"

"No. But they found heroin in the damaged containers."

"Heroin!"

"Several hundred kilos of it."

"Oh, my God." Even here in Hong Kong, where almost anything could be bought or sold, it was the one commodity that legitimate businessmen stayed away from. "But how did it get there? Why?"

"The *why* is easy enough. That much heroin is worth mil-

lions of dollars. As far as *how,* someone smuggled it aboard
in a shipment of garments."

"Who?" she demanded, her shock giving way to anger.

"We don't know yet. I've got Bill working on it, and Mick
will check it out on his end. But that shipment originated here
in Hong Kong."

"Those containers are already sealed when they're put
aboard," she pointed out, wanting to eliminate any involvement on the part of someone within the company.

"That doesn't help much."

"It means none of our people were involved with it," she
insisted.

"Maybe. Maybe not. It's not uncommon for those containers to sit in warehouses for weeks until they're loaded onto
the ships. It could have happened any time before or after
those containers left the factory, right up until the moment
they were craned aboard our ship."

"Then it's possible our warehouse people *could* be involved."

"Or someone else at Fortune," he interjected. "We can't
overlook the possibility."

Nausea tightened her stomach. Someone in the company,
*her* company, smuggling heroin. "Do you have any idea who
it might be?"

"Not yet, and we have approximately twenty-four hours to
come up with something. So far the authorities know nothing
about this. If they find out, they could shut down Fortune International."

Suddenly she realized the full scope of the problem. "This
could jeopardize our meeting with the PRC."

He nodded. "Yes, if they find out about it. But we have a
more immediate problem." At her questioning look he explained, "The Triad controls all drug traffic out of the Golden
Triangle. It's one of their less legitimate enterprises, and it's
very lucrative."

"What will happen when the Triad finds out about this?"

His expression was grave. "They don't like anyone cutting
them out of their business."

"The joint venture agreement," she concluded.

"It's safe to say that will be the first casualty."

Ross got out of bed and headed toward the shower. "I have twenty-four hours to find out who did this." He twisted the gold faucets, and water spewed overhead. Stepping into the marble and glass enclosure, he felt water pummeling his skin. Steam filled the bathroom. Then Christina came into the bathroom and stepped into the shower beside him.

"*We* have twenty four hours."

"You should stay at the office," Ross told her as they finished dressing a half hour later.

"Bill can handle things there. I'm going with you." She pulled her still-damp hair back into a ponytail. She had gone across the hall for a change of clothes while Ross finished showering and shaving.

"It'll be a long day, and this won't be like taking meetings in executive offices. Besides, you need to prepare for your meeting tomorrow with the PRC." At her surprised look, he added, "We go ahead with the meeting as planned. If we pull out now, they'll know something is wrong."

"All right. But I'm thoroughly prepared for that meeting. I'm going with you. With both of us working on this, maybe we can solve this in half the time."

"Chris . . ." he said in a warning tone.

She shook her head and gave him a look he remembered from the night she assumed full control over Fortune International. She was cool, and completely determined. "I *am* going with you."

"And if I say no?"

"I could always fire you."

"Yes," he gave her a faint smile, "but you don't speak Mandarin, and somehow I don't think you'll be taken very seriously down at the docks when you go down there to ask about that shipment." Then he added. "You need me."

She looked at him, her expression suddenly softening. "I discovered that last night." Then her expression turned serious again. "Come on. Let's find out who smuggled that heroin aboard my ship."

•   •   •

Ross handed her several more bills of lading, written in both English and Chinese characters, then he quietly closed the file cabinet in the office of the Fortune warehouse. They were alone in the huge, cavernous building, and it was eerily dark and quiet.

"That's the last of the shipping invoices for the dates cargo was on-loaded aboard the *Bountiful Fortune*."

She made copies, then they left the office, locking it behind them, and got back into the Range Rover. He drove while she scanned the copies of the bills of lading. "What am I looking for?"

"It won't be anything obvious. Look for discrepancies in numbers of containers, special notations by the warehouse supervisor on a damaged container, maybe a special request from the manufacturer." He stopped at a crowded little restaurant and parked the Rover. They found a table and ordered tea and rice pastries.

She scanned the invoices in between sips of tea and nibbles of pastry. "Who was the manufacturer of the garments in that container?"

"Far East Manufacturing. It's the biggest in Hong Kong. Their factories are over in Lai Chi Kok."

Ross took half the invoices from her and began going through them.

She shook her head in frustration. "Everything seems to be in order. There's no notation about damage or changes in any of the containers. Everything checks out, as far as I can tell."

Ross thought of his trip to Taiwan, and the changed invoices Mick had discovered. There had to be a connection. "We need to see copies of the shipment vouchers from the trucking firm that transported those containers, and the manufacturer's shipping sheets where they originated."

"That's strange," she mumbled around a bite of pastry.

"Did you find something?"

She pushed several bills of lading across the table. "All of these were signed by the same person."

Ross scanned them and nodded. "They're signed by the route supervisor of the trucking company that picked up the shipment at Far East."

Then she shoved another one at him. "But this one is signed by someone else. I can't make out the signature."

It was dated ten days earlier—well within the dates the containers with those garments, and the heroin, had been received at the Fortune warehouses in Hong Kong. Ross folded the copy and put it in the inside pocket of his windbreaker. "Let's find out who this fellow is."

Empress Trucking was a huge company. It was located near the Lai Chi Kok industrial center. The assistant manager was less than cooperative. When Ross asked to speak with the person whose name was on the form, the assistant manager looked at him with a baleful, suspicious expression. He replied in pidgin English that he didn't understand Ross's questions. When Ross switched to Cantonese, the man snapped his mouth shut and stalked off.

He returned a few minutes later with another man—the shipping supervisor. He was the man whose name appeared on all the other documents. Ross asked about the one signature that was different. The supervisor read it, then dismissed it, saying he didn't know anyone by that name.

Frustration gnawed at Ross. As they left the trucking company office, he said, "Let's try Far East Manufacturing. Perhaps they know something about that shipment."

In the business offices of Far East, they were politely asked to wait.

Ross made use of the time to put in a call to Bill at the office. He had several people he wanted him to contact discreetly. A few minutes later they were shown into the office of the assistant manager in charge of overseas contracts.

Christina laid a hand on Ross's arm. "Let me try this one," she whispered.

She introduced herself as the buyer for one of Far East's largest American retailers. She explained that she was in Hong Kong checking out some problems with one of their shipments. Ross sat back with a slightly amused expression as she played the role of an irate customer who was extremely unhappy about millions of dollars worth of inventory languishing in a warehouse in Taiwan. She demanded to speak with the supervisor in charge of shipping.

"Very well, Miss Grant," the assistant manager replied, using the name she'd given him. "I'll check and see if Mr. Hue is available. I'm certain we can straighten this all out." He picked up the telephone, and there was an animated conversation in Chinese. Then he hung up, a deferential expression fixed on his face.

"Mr. Hue would be most pleased to see you. I will direct you to his office."

The Far East plant was enormous, encompassing several acres of industrial complex, overseas shipping departments, business offices, and trucking bays. As they drove over to the shipping offices, Ross said, "That was a very interesting conversation."

Christina shot him a glance. "Did you pick up anything about that shipment?"

"Not specifically, but Mr. Hue was very reluctant to speak with us." Ross parked the Rover, and they went upstairs to the second-floor offices and asked for Mr. Hue.

"I am very sorry," the secretary informed them, "but Mr. Hue was called away from the plant on an emergency. I don't know when he will be back."

Ross angrily questioned the woman in Cantonese, but finally gave up. She insisted she knew nothing about her boss's sudden departure. As they turned to leave, Christina saw a movement at the window of the office behind the woman. The slats of the blinds abruptly snapped shut. She acted on a hunch as she grabbed Ross's arm, then pushed her way past the secretary and headed for the door to the office.

"You cannot go in there!" the secretary screeched.

Christina ignored her as she flung open the door, with Ross right behind her.

It was a large office, with several cubicles down one side and a huge conference table in the middle. At the far end another door was just closing. Hurrying through it, they discovered that it opened to the outside and another set of stairs leading to the employee parking lot. A man—undoubtedly Mr. Hue—ran across the parking lot. Ross whirled around.

"I'll bring the Rover around," he shouted, racing back inside.

A moment later his car squealed to a stop, and Christina hurriedly climbed in.

"Where is he?" Ross demanded.

"He got into a beige Toyota." Christina strained to see the car as they shot down the length of the crowded parking lot. "There he is!" She pointed to the far exit. Ross immediately swerved the Rover in that direction.

They raced out of the parking lot into a narrow alley. Just ahead, the beige Toyota cut around a corner. Ross swerved around industrial garbage dumpsters, then cut around the same corner.

They sped headlong into congested midmorning traffic, weaving in and out of lanes, cutting across intersections, ignoring traffic signals, and skidding down side streets.

Then they were almost on the Toyota's bumper. They jolted across two more intersections in the busy industrial district. Suddenly Ross was forced to brake hard as a delivery truck pulled out from an alley directly in his path. He swore, cut the wheel hard to the left, and scattered pedestrians and factory workers afoot in every direction as he pulled around the truck. Turning sharply, he headed down the street where the Toyota had turned, then braked to a hard stop.

It was an alley, and halfway down the Toyota was stopped, the driver's door standing open. Ross jammed the gear lever into the park position and jumped out of the car.

"Wait!" she shouted, but he was already sprinting down the alley. Grabbing the keys out of the Rover, she took off after him.

The buildings on either side of the alley were tall, the equivalent of tenement apartments occupying the upper floors over stores and traditional sweatshops.

This was the dangerous underbelly of Hong Kong, the side that tourists never saw, with dingy laundry strung overhead and naked, grubby children playing in the gutters. Ross knew it well. He followed a rabbits' warren of alleys, side streets, and passageways that led down to the waterfront, always keeping the man ahead of him in sight. That man was the key to that shipment, and Ross wanted answers.

The walls of the passageways seeped with moisture. He cut

down another, remembering adventures of his youth. Sloe-eyed young women, old before their time, lounged outside of entryways, offering themselves for the price of a needle filled with heroin, or the latest drug fad—ice.

He tripped over a small child, then lunged around a corner. Hue was only a few yards ahead of him. Then Hue turned down the next alley. It opened onto the smaller docks at the end of the terminals, where old women threw morning garbage over the sides of junks, old men huddled in clusters on the pier playing mah-jongg and smoking pipes, and younger men worked in open-air markets lining the wharf. Over all of it was the pervading stench of rotting fish, raw sewage, and the blended scent of smoked drugs, almost like the atmosphere inside a smoke shop.

Hue leapt from the dock onto the bow of a junk, desperately balancing on the side, then jumping to another. Ross followed after him, cat-walking the bobbing bow of one boat to another.

He was chasing the dragon to its lair, venturing where few *gweilos* ever dared. He felt the curious and resentful stares as he negotiated the obstacle course of junks, water taxis, and houseboats. Then he came to an abrupt stop. He'd lost Hue.

He could feel the eyes that watched him as he brought his breathing under control. He knew that somewhere nearby Hue huddled, trying desperately to keep hidden his secrets about that shipment of heroin.

Ross's gaze searched the dock, the congestion of junks and other boats. But there was no sign of Hue.

An old Chinese woman squawked angrily at him for invading her privacy and ordered him to get off her boat. As he was leaving, he caught the movement of several men up on the quay. They weren't dressed like the other men down here.

Then he heard someone calling, and he whirled around. The small but lethal knife he'd taken from his glove compartment earlier flicked open in his hand.

"Ross!" Christina cried out breathlessly. She stopped several feet away on the dock. Her breathing was ragged, her eyes wide as she stared at that gleaming blade in his hand.

"What the hell are you doing here?" Ross shouted as he climbed back onto the dock.

Christina blinked, then recovered enough to say, "I followed you."

He grabbed her arm, his fingers bruising her through the fabric of her jacket as he pushed her ahead of him. He didn't give her a chance to catch her breath until they were back out on the street and headed away from the wharf area.

"Don't you ever do that again!" he shouted at her furiously.

Stunned, she jerked her arm from his grasp. "I wanted to help."

"You had no idea what you were getting yourself into! This is a very dangerous place."

"It's just as dangerous for you," she pointed out, her temper rising.

"You forget, I was born here. I know my way around," he spat out as he pulled her with him down the street. Then he cut across another. One more, and they were just down the alley from where they'd left the Rover.

She had to admit, as she stared at the Rover, that he did know his way around. She would have been hopelessly lost if she'd tried to find her way back alone.

"I was afraid he might get away," she said in a more controlled voice.

Ross got into the Rover. She slid in the other side. He wasn't finished with her. He was furious—at Hue, at her, at whoever was smuggling drugs aboard Fortune ships.

"He can't just disappear," she said in a logical tone as he swerved the Rover about in a tight U-turn.

"People do *just* disappear in Hong Kong all the time. That's precisely why I didn't want you coming after me." He shot her a crude look of assessment. "You'd bring a very high price on the white-slave market."

"That doesn't exist!" she shot back. "That died out with the old Empire, and clandestine meetings at Raffles—another time, another era."

They were back on the main road that led to the cross-channel tunnel. He looked at her again. "Five thousand dollars, Hong Kong," he said crudely. "That's what a pale-skinned woman brings on the open market, more if she's unmarked. That's just about half what it costs to stay one night at the Regent."

She didn't say another word. She simply sat there in stunned silence.

His expression shifted when he glanced briefly at her as they drove through the tunnel. He'd hurt her badly, and he knew the reasons why—when he saw her running toward him across that dock, surrounded by all the filth and ugliness of the worst, most dangerous part of Hong Kong, he was terrified for her safety.

"I'm sorry," he whispered awkwardly, unused to making apologies.

She looked at him in silence for a long moment. Then she said softly, "I know. I'm sorry, too. I just didn't think."

He took her hand in his, keeping his other hand on the wheel. "It's all right."

But she knew it wasn't really all right. They'd lost the man who might have answered all their questions. And Christina knew it would probably be impossible to find him again.

It was early afternoon when they arrived at the office. Ross told Bill what had happened, and Bill brought them up to date on what he'd been able to learn by back-checking all the paperwork for that shipment. Essentially it was very little. They were at a dead end.

Ross thought for a moment, then said, "I'm going to call an old acquaintance who might be able to find Hue."

"One of the unsavory acquaintances out of your past?" Bill asked with a dry smile.

"We can't go to the authorities with this. Not yet."

There was a knock at the door. Lisa Jeung came into the office. She said to Christina, "You have a call from Thomas Lai."

Christina looked at Ross. She desperately hoped this call was a coincidence. But her hopes died as Mr. Lai's voice came over the speakerphone in Ross's office.

"A very grave matter has come to our attention, Miss Fortune. I would like to discuss it with you in private."

Ross looked across the desk at Christina. "Both Miss Fortune and I are free to meet with you at your convenience," he replied.

"Excellent," Mr. Lai said. "Shall we say in one hour in the orchid exhibit at the Botanical Garden?"

"Thank you. We'll be there." Ross switched off the speakerphone.

"He knows," Christina said in a quiet voice.

"At least he's willing to meet with us," Ross pointed out. "That means the Triad would like to save the joint venture. Otherwise they wouldn't have bothered with that call. They would simply have taken care of the matter themselves."

"Do you think they know who's at the bottom of this?"

"I don't know. But they have ways of finding out."

Christina got to her feet. "Let's find out what they want to discuss."

They got to the orchid exhibit a few minutes early and waited for Lai.

"Remember who you're dealing with," Ross cautioned her. "He may be Phillip Lo's cousin, but he's still a high-ranking member of the Triad. That is where his loyalty lies."

"What are you trying to say?" she asked.

"I once asked what you were prepared to do to save the company. In his own way he'll be asking the same question, except that he'll be giving you a choice."

"What sort of choice?"

"A very difficult one. And you must make it with honor. Honor is the most important thing, even among the Triad," Ross reminded her. "It's because he senses that you have honor that he's even willing to discuss this with you."

As they walked into the orchid gardens, she felt that she was walking into a trap. One that might very well close over her, destroying her and Ross and everything they'd tried so hard to achieve.

The orchid exhibit was a lush, tropical paradise filled with green ferns, lantana, banana plants, and exotic displays of growing orchids. After a moment Lai joined them. It was difficult to believe that this man, who was Phillip Lo's cousin— and who had sat with them at a conference table only days ago negotiating a lucrative, legitimate business deal—was also one of the most powerful and feared men in the Orient.

He was only an inch or two taller than Christina. His hair was silver gray at his temples, and there was a pleasant, speculative expression on his face. He looked like a kindly, little old grandfather, not the sort of man who could order another man's death with a single word. She found herself watching the tall, lush plants that surrounded them, looking for his men, who were always close by.

She forced her voice to sound cool and calm as she began, "Thank you for giving us your valuable time, Mr. Lai."

He smiled at her. "And thank you, Miss Fortune, for coming here. We have very grave matters to discuss. Will you walk with me?"

It was clear that he wanted to speak with her alone. She glanced at Ross, who nodded briefly, then replied, "Yes, I'll walk with you."

A few minutes later she and Lai returned. He said, "I knew your father. He was a man of honor. I have come here today because of my respect for him. Now we will learn if you also have honor. Good-bye, Miss Fortune."

Ross stood quietly beside her. When Lai was gone, he asked, "What did he say?"

She turned to him, her eyes wide and dark. Her expression was somber. "You asked what I was willing to do to save the company." Then she explained in a quite voice, "I made a bargain with him. His people have found Mr. Hue. He didn't tell me how, and I didn't ask. The critical thing is that they know who's behind the smuggling operation."

Ross had sensed that they were being followed ever since they left the hotel early that morning. He wondered if Hue was alive now, but he suspected the answer to that question was no.

"Who is it?" he asked in a grim voice.

Her throat was tight. "It's Steven. They've given me until midnight to solve the problem—as a matter of family honor."

"I won't argue with you this time." Ross was adamant as he opened the wall safe behind his desk. "It's gotten too dangerous. Steven may be a fool, but he's not stupid. He knows that shipment was found, and he's hiding out. Bill is checking all the usual places where he might be. I'll find him, but you can't go where I've got to go."

He took out a thick wad of Hong Kong dollars. Then he flipped the safe shut and spun the combination lock. Pushing the painting of a Fortune clipper ship back into place, he shoved the money into his pocket. Then he came to her. He slipped his arms around her. "So far we've been able to keep this quiet. It was inevitable that the Triad would find out. They've got an underground network of people everywhere. I'll wager they knew almost the instant Bill called me this morning. Now we have to keep the authorities out of it. You can do the most good by staying here and helping Bill."

"Why did Steven do it?" she whispered.

"Why does anyone do it? For the money. Greed can be a seductive mistress."

"But it doesn't make any sense. Each of us has a substantial trust, and Steven is well paid by the company, as well. He has more than enough."

"Define *enough*," Ross said cynically. "Steven has very expensive tastes." He tilted her chin up with his fingers. "Look, Chris, Steven made his own choices. If we can find him, we may be able to save his life, but we won't be able to keep him out of prison. At this point prison is the best he can hope for."

She knew Ross was right. And she certainly didn't sympathize with Steven. Drug dealing was horrible. And there was even the possibility that he was responsible for the two attempts on her life. Still she would prefer to see Steven go to prison than to be hunted down and murdered by the Triad.

"What will happen if we can't find him?"

Ross's hands dropped to hers. "Lai will keep his part of the bargain. He won't touch Steven until our time has run out. After that . . ."

He didn't have to explain further.

"We have eleven and a half hours," he said. "We have to find him, for our sake as well as his. God knows how much more damage he could do. Everything is still hanging in the balance."

She shivered. "Be careful. Please."

He stroked his thumb against the curve of her lower lip. "I will."

He looked up as Mick Donovan stepped inside the doorway. In response to an earlier call from Ross, Mick had flown in from Taiwan with a half dozen of his best men. Ross made brief introductions, then turned to leave with Mick. At the door he turned and said to Christina, "I'll call when I can." And then he was gone.

It wasn't as if she and Bill didn't have enough to do. There were telephone calls to make, people who might have had contact with Steven, and might know where he could be found. They split the list in half. She sat down and called the number at the top of her list.

Six hours later she threw her pencil across the desk in mute frustration.

"I take it that means you haven't had very much luck," Bill said as he came into the office.

She shook her head. "He's disappeared, vanished."

"Nothing yet, but I still have a few more possibilities to try. You've been at this all evening. Why don't you let me call the other people on your list? You can go back to the hotel and try to get some sleep," he suggested.

"You've been at it longer than I have," she pointed out.

"Yeah, but I'm used to this sort of thing."

She glanced again at the captain's clock on Ross's desk and rubbed the dull ache that had started at her temples. "I have only two more names on my list."

Bill saw the weary gesture. "That's it. I'm packing you off to the Regent." He picked up the phone and called down to have the limo brought around front.

"Bill. . .!"

"This could go on for hours, and you're dead on your feet. Get some dinner and some rest. There's absolutely nothing else you can do right now."

When she started to protest, he picked up her shoulder bag from the chair where she'd carelessly laid it, and gently thrust it into her arms. "Ross is all right, Chris. He said he would call in, and he will. But it may be a while. I'll hang in here with Lisa and Adam."

She finally agreed. "But I want to know the moment you hear from Ross."

"I promise, I'll call you as soon as I talk to him."

As she got into the limo downstairs, she turned back to Bill and asked, "By the way, how did that call go? The one you made last night." She knew it had been to his ex-wife.

His smile was sheepish. "We talked for over two hours. That phone bill will compare to the national debt."

"Over two hours, huh? Sounds encouraging."

She got into the limo, and he leaned against the opened window. "I thought about what you said—about changing my priorities. Maybe when this mess is cleared up, I'll sit down and have a talk with Ross about cutting back a little."

She laid her hand over his. "He'll listen. I promise."

"I hope so. You see, Bonnie's willing to get together and talk some more when I get back."

"Oh, Bill, I'm so glad."

"There's still a lot to work out, but I think, maybe, we might be able to do it."

"I hope so. Life's too short to go through it alone."

"I know that now."

Bill leaned in and gave the driver instructions. Then he stepped back from the car. "You'll know the moment I hear from Ross," he promised.

Back in her own suite at the hotel, Christina ordered dinner. But she had no appetite, and it went untouched. She turned on the shower, then immediately turned the faucets off, afraid she might miss a call even though there was a phone in the bathroom. She restlessly paced the suite. When the phone finally rang just after eleven, she grabbed it.

"Just checking in," Bill said. "There's still no word from Ross." Before she could voice her fears, he reassured her. "He's all right. Remember, he knows his way around. And he isn't alone. But there isn't a public phone on every corner. And the cellular in the Rover has a limited range."

There was no disguising her intense disappointment. "Thanks for calling, anyway."

Less than a half hour later the phone rang again. Certain that Ross must have contacted Bill, she eagerly picked it up, relief pouring through her.

"Miss Fortune?" a soft, feminine voice asked.

"Yes?"

"Are you alone?"

She was instantly wary. She responded hesitantly, "Yes."

There was a moment's silence, then, "My name is Andrea Santos. I am a friend of Steven's."

The woman's voice was so faint, Christina could barely make out what she was saying. She recognized the name. It was at the top of the list of people she'd called. Andrea Santos—half Portuguese, half Shanghainese—was Steven's mistress! She lived at his place in Wanchai. Christina had called there several times throughout the evening, and there'd been no answer.

"Are you there?" Andrea asked, obviously afraid that Christina had hung up.

"Yes . . . yes, I'm here."

And then, before she could ask, Andrea said, "I'm calling for Steven."

Christina tried to keep her voice level. "We've been trying to find him. Do you know where he is?" For a very long moment there was silence on the other end of the phone.

"He's in trouble," Andrea said in a voice that disappeared in a whisper. "A lot of trouble."

"Yes, we know." Christina was immediately aware that if Andrea knew Steven was in trouble, she also knew where he was. It was obvious he'd been in contact with her.

"He asked me to call you," Andrea went on slowly. "He needs your help."

Christina was stunned. The last thing she expected was for Steven to contact her for help. He must be desperate.

"You have to tell me where he is."

"No one else must know about this . . . he's afraid. You have to promise you won't tell anyone where he is." Andrea was adamant, her voice stronger, and with an edge of something that sounded very near panic.

As Ross had said, Steven might be a fool, but he wasn't

stupid. He knew the Triad was after him. She desperately wished there was some way she could talk to Ross, to let him know what was happening. But she was on her own.

"All right," she agreed. "I'll help him. Where is he?"

Again there was silence, except for a distinct sniffling sound. Then Andrea said, "He's at the China Harbour View Hotel, at Causeway Bay . . . room number two twenty-four. Be there in a half hour. He'll be waiting for you. And please, Miss Fortune, come alone."

Then the line went dead.

Christina replaced the receiver, then immediately picked it up again and dialed the Fortune office. As late as it was— nearly midnight—Bill answered. "I just spoke with Ross . . ."

She cut him off. "I know where Steven is. Andrea Santos just called me."

"Where is he?"

When she gave him the location, Bill said in a tight voice. "Stay right where you are. I'll get hold of Ross."

"I'm going over there."

"Chris. . .!"

"Andrea specifically said I was to come alone. Steven knows the Triad is after him, and he's scared."

"You're not to leave! Do you understand me? Don't leave the Regent!"

"I've got to. If I don't go, he may leave, and God knows how long it would take to find him. We have only two hours to settle this, or the Triad will take matters into their own hands." She took a deep breath. "They'll kill him, and you know it."

"I don't care. I don't want you going over there. It's too dangerous."

"I have to, Bill," she repeated, then hung up the phone before he could object further. She prayed that he could get through to Ross right away.

The China Harbour View Hotel was on Gloucester Road between Wanchai and Causeway Bay. It was typical of dozens of less expensive hotels in Hong Kong that catered primarily to Southeast Asian and Japanese tour groups. In spite of the late hour, three buses were pulled up in front of the main lobby. Passengers disembarked and swarmed to the reception desk. With all the confusion and noise, it was easy to slip inside unnoticed.

There was no doorman or hotel manager to ask her business, and she walked past the crowd of tourists to the elevators. She waited for another fifteen minutes, hoping Ross would get there. And then, afraid that someone might suspect she wasn't a guest, she got into the elevator.

Room 224 was at the end of the hall on the second floor, near the fire exit to the outside of the building. Still she hesitated, stalling for time. But time was running out.

What if Bill wasn't able to find Ross?

Andrea had said that Steven was afraid. Perhaps all he wanted was to turn himself in and get protection from the Triad. She raised her hand and knocked on the door. She knocked again. There was still no answer. Impulsively she tried the door. It opened freely.

"Steven?" she called out, slowly walking into the hotel room. It was typical of low-budget, economy hotels, with laminate wood furnishings, Formica countertops, complimentary coffeepot with coffee doled out for two, and a television bolted down to prevent theft.

A single light glowed at the Parsons table beside the functional brown, beige, and cream-colored couch. A woman's silk jacket in a shade of emerald green was thrown over the back of the couch.

She called out again. A noise came from the adjoining bedroom. She hesitated. Ross's warnings about Steven came back to her. She wished Ross were here, but there hadn't been time to wait any longer for him. Andrea insisted that Christina had to be there in a half hour. No matter what he'd done, she had to get to Steven before the Triad did. She walked to the bedroom door and pushed it open.

She saw a woman lying on the bed. It was late, and thinking that Andrea had perhaps dozed off after their conversation, she approached the side of the bed. She reached out and gently touched the young woman's shoulder to rouse her.

"Andrea?"

She lay on her side, turned away from Christina, facing the shadows at the other side of the bed. She cringed at Christina's touch on her shoulder. Then she slowly turned over, her long ebony hair falling away from her shoulder.

Christina gasped at the sight of her face. It was swollen, and purplish-black bruises darkened both eyes. There was an ugly bruise at the left side of her jaw, and her lip was cut and bleeding. She'd been badly beaten.

"Andrea?"

The young woman answered by nodding her head and trying to shield her face.

There was no sign of Steven. Christina was afraid the men who belonged to the Triad had already been there and taken matters into their own hands.

"What happened?" she asked.

Andrea pushed her away and covered her face. She moaned pitifully.

Christina went into the bathroom and wet a washcloth with cold water. When she returned to the bed, she pulled Andrea's trembling hands away from her face and laid the cloth over the bruised flesh.

"Where's Steven?"

Andrea whimpered pathetically as Christina tried to clean away some of the blood. "Do you know where he's gone?" Her questions met only with soft sobs. Andrea tried to pull away from her again. As she did, her wraparound silk dress rode up over her slender legs, exposing ugly bruises and smears of blood across her thighs.

Christina stared in horror. Andrea had been brutally beaten and . . . *raped.*

"Oh, God!" Christina whispered, as the sight of the blood and bruises jolted through her shocked brain. For a long, horrifying moment she could only stare. Then another nightmarish scene played back through her mind, of another night, twenty years ago . . . *brutal hands grabbing at her . . . her clothes being torn away . . . the oppressive weight of a man's body . . .*

She clawed her way back out of the nightmare memory, dragging cleansing breaths of air deep into her lungs as she forced her frozen brain to jolt forward. She fought the nausea that churned in her stomach, and the paralyzing weakness that seeped into her legs as she drove herself to her feet. She ran back into the bathroom.

For a long moment she leaned against the Formica counter, blocking everything from her mind, willing herself back into some semblance of self-control. Her skin was cold and clammy. A fine sheen of perspiration had broken out across her forehead. She splashed cold water on her face several times. She couldn't give in to this. Not now.

It was several minutes before she felt in control once more. She rinsed the cloth and returned to the bedroom.

Her voice sounded weak and thready as she asked, "Who did this?" Andrea's right eye was swollen shut. She looked at Christina through the painful slit of her left eye. Then she said in a quivering voice, "Steven."

Once more nausea rolled in Christina's stomach. She fought it back. "Why?" she asked, her voice aching in her throat.

Andrea answered pathetically. "It's his way, when he gets angry."

*His way?*

"Hello, Chris."

She whirled around. Steven stood in the doorway of the bedroom. He slowly walked toward her. Behind her, Andrea whimpered pathetically and tried to crawl to the far side of the bed, as far from Steven as possible. But Steven never even noticed her. He was staring at Christina with cold, hard eyes that were filled with an expression of rage.

"I knew you'd come." Then his mouth curved in a horrible smile. "Just as I knew I'd find you in the summerhouse, that night at Fortune Hill."

# Chapter 34

Christina stared at Steven. Her mouth went dry, her heart seemed to stop beating.

*Of course,* she thought. Steven would be capable of that kind of violence. Steven had always been so arrogant and sure of himself, the one who always had to be in control of everyone and every situation. He had a reputation for wildness. Even when he was younger, there were rumors of girls whose parents didn't want him seeing their daughters.

When most teenagers were finding out about sex with steady boyfriends or girlfriends, Steven boasted of making trips into the more dangerous parts of San Francisco to gain *real* experience with the prostitutes who frequented the North Beach bars. There had even been some vague problem with one of the prostitutes.

He'd never been able to accept rejection by a woman, and it must have been particularly galling when Christina rejected him for his shy younger brother.

"You couldn't leave well enough alone, could you?" Steven asked in a low, menacing voice. He slowly came at her. "You had to come back."

He shook his head. "You know, at first I was convinced you were a fake, just like all the others. It's funny—now I'm not so sure. But whether you're for real or not doesn't matter.

You're a problem. And I'm going to deal with you once and for all."

*Move,* her thoughts screamed, but it was as if terror had drained her of all strength. Her feet felt leaden, her hands were ice-cold. He didn't seem at all aware of Andrea on the bed behind her. His entire focus was on Christina.

All the horror and feelings of degradation she'd fought to overcome throughout the years since played back through her broken thoughts like images through a shattered window. From behind her Andrea whimpered in pain and fear.

Those sad, pathetic sounds jolted Christina, as if she were listening to herself, twenty years earlier. And they triggered a profound rage.

*I'll make them pay for what they did to us.*

Her hands clenched into tight fists as Steven came at her. She screamed, catching him by surprise as she lunged at him and threw him off stride. Then she was running past him into the outer sitting room, toward the door.

He caught her there, his hand closing around her hair. With a brutal pull he yanked her back. Momentarily off balance, she reeled from the stinging slap of his hand against her cheek.

"No!" Christina screamed. But this time it wasn't the pathetic whimper of a young girl begging not to be hurt. It was the fury of someone fighting back, someone determined never to be a victim again.

She twisted in his grasp. She was vaguely aware of a stinging sensation at her scalp as he wound her hair around his fist. She blocked out the pain as she grappled to free herself from those hands that were capable of such brutality. For brief seconds she thought of Andrea, and knew if either of them was to survive, Christina had to get away and find help.

He tried to beat her into submission. She twisted and turned, trying to pull away from him. But he was stronger than she was, and driven by a rage of his own. He cursed and grunted as he grabbed viciously at her, his hand poised for another blow.

Then there were shouts and loud pounding at the door. Steven dragged her back toward the bedroom. She clawed at the furniture and the wall, desperately trying to hold on to something . . . anything. She screamed as loudly as she could.

The door to the hotel room crashed open, splintering off its hinges. Steven jerked her into the bedroom and slammed the door behind them. A moment later the thin bedroom door flew open, and Ross ran into the room, with Mick and his men immediately behind him.

Steven had one arm around Christina's throat and another pinning her arms. He cowered against the far wall, like an animal driven to ground.

"Let her go!" Ross ordered, holding out a hand as a signal for Mick and his men to stay back.

Steven shook his head. "Stay back of I'll snap her neck in two! I can do it!"

"You've got just one chance." Ross's voice was low and even. "Take it and let her go. Or you can deal with Thomas Lai."

Christina felt the shudder that passed through Steven's body. But he was desperate. There was no room for reason.

"I'll kill her! I swear I will!" He frantically tightened his grip on her shoulder, his arm choking her throat.

Ross said in a cold, hard voice, "If you hurt her, there won't be anything left for Thomas Lai. I'll kill you myself."

She felt Steven's panic grow as his fingers dug into her shoulder, and in the jerky breath that burned at the back of her neck. Fear and anger welled inside her. She twisted hard in his grasp, and clawed at him over her shoulder. Her nails raked his face, and he screamed in pain.

In the brief instant his hold on her loosened, Ross lunged at Steven and drove him to the floor. They struggled only for a moment. Then Ross jerked Steven to his feet and struck him twice. Steven reeled from the blows, staggered backward, and crumpled against the wall beside the bed.

While Mick and his men grabbed Steven, Ross took a trembling Christina into his arms.

He looked down at her. The red imprint of a hand marred her cheek. But there was no blood, and her eyes were bright and clear. Something behind her eyes told him the worst damage was within her. After a moment he spoke roughly against her hair, "Are you all right?"

Her voice trembled as she said, "It was Steven . . . in the summerhouse twenty years ago . . . *it was Steven.*"

"Dear God," Ross whispered. It was all he could do not to release her and attack Steven as savagely as he deserved. But she needed him too badly. He couldn't have let go of her at that moment if his life depended on it.

He pressed her head against his shoulder as he held her tightly. Turning his face into her dark hair, he whispered, "It's all right. He can't hurt you anymore." Emotion tightened in his chest as he thought of what might have happened had they been just a little later. He would have killed Steven without a second's hesitation or remorse.

He felt her body settle against him as she gave way to the tears. He continued to hold her, wanting desperately to take away all her fear and misery, yet knowing that he couldn't do that for her. Somehow she had to find the strength to take the first step in putting it behind her.

Finally she quit crying. As she let go of the front of his shirt, she choked back her tears. Ross pulled a handkerchief from his pocket. Tilting her face up with his fingers beneath her chin, he tenderly wiped the tears from her bruised cheek.

He lightly brushed his mouth against hers. She tasted of tears and White Ginger, and he knew that for the first time in his life he was truly and irrevocably in love.

In the background Mick cleared his throat, then said awkwardly, "Uh, Ross, what do you want us to do with this piece of garbage?"

"Take him to the warehouse for now. I'll deal with him later.

Mick nodded. He gestured to his men. As Steven was dragged from the room, Christina forced herself to look at him, hanging limply between two brawny men like a drunk or someone strung out on the dope he'd smuggled. "Where are they taking him?" she asked Ross.

"He'll be kept safe, and watched. Lai will keep his word as long as we keep ours that we'll take care of the situation."

"It means that Steven has to be turned over to the authorities."

"Good. I want to see justice done. Finally."

"No matter what it does to the family's reputation?" he asked.

She nodded without hesitation.

Mick had wrapped Andrea in a blanket. "Now then, girl, it's all right. No one's going to hurt you." Carefully picking her up, with more gentleness than Christina would have thought possible of a man so big, he carried her out of the hotel room. Christina started to go after them, but Ross stopped her.

"She'll be all right. She'll have all the care she needs."

"What will happen to her afterwards?"

"That depends on you."

She nodded. "She'll need counseling." She spoke from experience. "Then I'd like to help her start a new life. Maybe away from here, if that's what she wants."

Ross nodded. "Yes . . . what she needs most right now is a friend."

Christina hesitated, then said, "Everyone needs a friend once in a while." Her voice caught at the memory of another friend. But now the memory wasn't quite as painful as it had once been. Now she could remember all the love and support they'd shared, instead of constantly reliving that last tragic night over and over again. Finally it was over. She'd made a promise, and she'd kept it. Steven *would* pay for what he'd done.

She leaned against Ross as they left the hotel. On the ride back to Kowloon, emotional and physical exhaustion overwhelmed her, and her head rolled against his shoulder. When they reached the Regent, she roused sleepily, and it was all she could do to stand during the ride in the elevator up to the fifteenth floor. They paused at the door to her room. Then Ross lifted her in his arms and carried her back across the hall to his suite.

•  •  •

There were faint smudges of fatigue beneath her eyes the next morning, along with some darkening bruises from her encounter with Steven.

Steven had been turned over to the Hong Kong police. So far he refused to say anything about anyone else who might be involved in the smuggling operation. But Christina knew Steven couldn't have run such a complex and, for a while, successful operation by himself. Someone else was in it with him, and she thought it highly likely that someone was Richard.

Bill was expected in a little while. He was driving out to the airport with them for her flight to Beijing. Breakfast had arrived and was set up out on the terrace. It was a perfect morning: clear and cool, with a faint breeze that carried the usual fetid odor of the harbor away from the shoreline.

Ross stood at the railing, staring out over the water. He'd been up since dawn, preoccupied with something that he chose not to share with her. She'd sensed that same preoccupation as they lay together. They hadn't made love. He had simply held her all through the night. She knew something more was on his mind. She saw it in the intense, searching expression behind his eyes when he looked at her. As if there were some question he longed to ask.

Instinctively she sensed that it wasn't the old question about her identity, but something else. But she didn't ask. She would have to wait until he was ready to confront whatever it was that kept him silent and emotionally remote.

She rose from the table, and the breakfast he'd left untouched, and went to him. Slipping her arms around his waist, she leaned against him.

He looked down at her, closing his arms around her and pulling her tight against him.

"You are so very lovely," he whispered. He stroked her cheek, his touch feather-soft and tender. His fingers skimmed along her jaw, slipping to the back of her neck as he pulled her closer. "Until last night I didn't realize how important you are to me."

She tilted her head back to look at him again. He kissed her then, for the first time since his lips had tenderly brushed hers the night before. This kiss stole her breath away, bringing instant arousal. His hands continued a sensual assault as they moved down her back, cupping her bottom through the fabric of her robe. His tongue slipped between her lips, caressing with a primal rhythm as he alternately stroked and then plunged deep inside.

Christina felt the sexual pull, hard and demanding. She sensed how much he wanted her, needed her. And she wanted him as she'd never wanted another man—never believed she was capable of wanting one, even David.

He picked her up and carried her back to the bedroom, where they'd lain quietly beside each other all night. And when they made love and she slipped into a wild oblivion, she felt more safe than she'd ever felt in her entire life.

But when it was over, she still sensed that something was left unsaid.

Later, when they had both dressed and were drinking coffee out on the terrace, the door chime sounded.

Ross said, "That must be Bill."

As he and Bill walked back together, he asked, "Do you have the proposal?"

"Right here," Bill answered hesitantly, glancing at Christina.

"Good," Ross said as he reached for his jacket. "Chris can go over it during the flight."

As they rode to the private airstrip that bordered Kai Tak Airport, Christina and Bill discussed her trip. Ross was conspicuously silent as he stared thoughtfully out the window of the limo. When they arrived, he went into the small terminal to check on the Fortune jet that would take her to Beijing. Bill waited with Christina.

"Is everything all right between you two?" he asked.

"Of course," she said with a too-quick smile of reassurance. "It's just the strain from everything that's happened the past week."

She wished she could believe her own words.

Bill shook his head. "Yeah, it's been one hell of a week." Then he looked past her as Ross came out of the terminal and joined them.

"Your flight is standing by," he said to Christina, indicating a small, sleek white jet that sat a hundred yards away on the tarmac.

"I'll wait in the limo," Bill said, handing Christina the thick portfolio containing the final proposal and giving her a thumbs-up sign.

Ross walked with her to the waiting jet. The jet engines whined as the pilot went through his final preflight check. A single attendant waited at the steps.

Searching for something to say to bridge the gap of silence between them, Christina repeated what they both already knew. "My meeting with the Central Committee is for late this afternoon. They said they'd give me an answer within twenty-four hours, so I should be back tomorrow afternoon."

Ross nodded.

Christina looked at him, waiting for him to say something, but he stared off over her shoulder, his expression and his emotions perfectly controlled.

*What is it?* she asked herself helplessly. But she knew there was no point in asking. He wouldn't tell her until he was ready.

"All right," she said with a tight throat as she turned to walk to the jet. "Till then."

She had nearly reached the plane when she heard him shout "Chris!" He hurried to her, reaching for her, holding her against him. When he finally, reluctantly, let her go, his eyes searched hers deeply, looking for something, but she didn't know what.

The increasing whine of the engines as the jet was readied for takeoff broke them apart. Christina ran for the steps. Then she turned one last time and looked back at him. He simply stood there, watching her.

Ross got into the back of the limo. He said nothing for several moments as they circled back along the harbor road toward the cross-channel tunnel that would take them to Hong Kong Island.

"She'll do all right," Bill said confidently, trying to break the uneasy silence. "I know you're upset that Chen Li asked her to come alone, but don't worry. She can handle herself pretty well now."

Ross had been staring out the window, lost in far different thoughts. Finally he looked back at Bill. "I know. I'm not worried about the meeting."

"Then what's bothering you? I've seen you before when you're about to wrap up a deal. You're usually so up that a cup of tea would be dangerous. The two of you have worked hard to put this together. But right now you act as if you might have just lost instead of won."

"Maybe I have," Ross said quietly, thinking back to that last moment on the tarmac when he'd kissed her—and earlier that morning when they made love. He tried to tell himself there was nothing different about her, nothing had changed between them. Maybe it was only his imagination . . . But he knew it was actually fear that he might be losing her to a man she'd loved deeply eighteen years ago.

He tried to block his doubts about her feelings for David Chen with that perfect, cool control that always worked so well at hiding his emotions. It didn't work this time. By her own admission, she and David Chen had once been lovers, at a critical time in her life. He was the man who'd helped her heal both physically and emotionally. As Ross knew, that created a special bond between two people that couldn't be broken by time or distance. And that bond had opened the door for the meeting that was so critical to the survival of Fortune International.

What were her thoughts now as she flew to keep that meeting with David Chen? Was she thinking of the proposed trade agreement? Or was she thinking of the man, and everything they'd once meant to each other?

David Chen, now Chen Li, had the advantage of a shared history with her. Ross had only the past few weeks. But in those few weeks she had become more important to him than anyone else in his life. Now he was afraid that this deal that was so critical to the future of the company—a deal he had fought to make a reality—might in fact take her away from him.

•   •   •   •

Christina had taken particular care in selecting her clothes for her trip to Beijing. It was extremely important that she fit in, and not look like the stereotypical ugly American, flaunting her wealth and power. In China the favorite attire for men was plain dark pants and a white shirt. The women she saw on the streets of Beijing wore plain dresses, or a skirt and white blouse, with an occasional slash of color in a neck scarf. For that reason she'd chosen a simple black suit with a soft gray silk blouse. The only jewelry she wore was the jade pendant—for luck. Her hair was worn loose about her shoulders, but she'd specifically chosen not to wear earrings or a bracelet. The only other jewelry was her watch, partially concealed by the sleeve of her suit jacket.

Now it was five o'clock. Her meeting with the Central Committee was over. The Chairman thanked her stiffly for presenting her proposal. David Chen—known to his fellow committee members as Chen Li—made the translation, as he had for both parties throughout the entire meeting. It was a signal that the meeting was at an end. She would be given their answer before she returned to Hong Kong the following day.

Christina politely thanked them for their time and careful consideration. Then she returned her copy of the proposal to her attaché case and stood. In a final gesture of respect she bowed her head slightly, then turned and left the conference room. David joined her immediately, and they walked together through the exquisite gardens that surrounded the building.

There had been no opportunity for them to talk when she arrived. A car had met her at the airport and driven her straight to the meeting. For the first time in seventeen years she and David had greeted each other face-to-face. But with the committee members in the background, it was a stiff, formal reunion.

Now, as he escorted her to the waiting taxi that would take her to her hotel, he said with regret, "We have had no chance to talk. There are a great many things I would like to ask you. May I see you this evening?"

She smiled at him. He hadn't changed very much in seventeen years. He was only an inch taller than she was. His features had lost the fullness of youth and were replaced by a handsome leanness. There were faint lines of weariness at his eyes, but the sweet, gentle smile was the one she remembered from so many years ago.

"I would like that very much." She added softly, "I have so much to tell *you*."

"I would like for you to meet my family. Could you have dinner with us this evening?" When she nodded, he gave her the address. "Have the hotel get you a taxi. I would pick you up myself, but it would not look proper. We must be careful."

She had sensed his guarded manner ever since that first telephone conversation. "I understand."

Dinner that evening wasn't strained, as she'd feared it might be. She met David's wife, Soon Li, and his two daughters. His wife was pretty, with delicate features and a quick, sincere smile. Occasionally Christina felt Soon Li watching her, and wondered what David might have told her of their past relationship.

His daughters were twelve and fourteen. They were bright and not much different from teenagers anywhere else. Although they were very respectful of both their parents, Soon Li confided that she had caught them experimenting with lipstick and eyeshadow, which were rarely seen on any Chinese schoolgirl.

Everyone in the family spoke English, as well as Cantonese and Mandarin. The dinner conversation was an animated mixture of all three, as Christina tried to keep up with the girls' chatter. She finally gave up, and the girls dissolved into laughter. Soon Li scolded them severely for their lack of manners toward their guest. They excused themselves and went into their room to finish a sewing project they were working on.

"They're beautiful," Christina complimented Soon Li. "You must be very proud of your children."

She saw a guarded look pass between Soon Li and David. Murmuring, "You are too kind, Miss Fortune," Soon Li excused herself with a shy smile and began clearing the table.

"Come," David said. "We will walk in the garden. It is small, but it is my wife's pride and joy."

Their home was the equivalent of a condominium, joined in a row of other modest houses, with common walls. They were fortunate enough that their small unit was on one end, facing out onto a thick, tree-shrouded garden.

She remembered a favorite story from her childhood—*The Secret Garden*. This had much the same feel to it, with thick, high walls that closed out the other buildings. There was a pear tree rife with fruit and a cherry tree. Fuchsias crowded against azaleas and rhododendrons along the ground. In the spring it would be a mass of cherry and fuchsia blossoms. Now it was a green, lush haven, with lanterns marking the path.

They walked together in silence, each uncertain how to continue the conversation that had begun all those years ago when a young Chinese student far from his family in mainland China had met a shy and lonely girl who'd run away from her family.

David watched her as she walked ahead of him along the path in the garden. He had been stunned to learn of her request for a business meeting. Though it had been a very long time since they had last seen each other, she had never been far from his thoughts. He wondered where she was, what had happened to her, whether or not she had finished college and made a life for herself.

But this was not the Christina Grant he remembered. She was now Christina Fortune—a secret she had kept from him.

When he had gone to the United States to study at the university, his cousin had told him, *"You cannot live within the Western culture and not be changed by it."* He had discovered it was true. Christina had changed him.

Regret was not inherent to the Chinese culture, and yet the part of him that was so deeply changed by having known and loved Christina now felt an ache of regret for what might have been if he had stayed with her. She didn't know how close he had come to remaining with her and turning his back on everything he'd left behind in China—including Soon Li.

David watched as Christina reached out to touch the soft

white petals of an azalea. He remembered that last time they were together before he left Boston. And even as he remembered, he realized that more than her name was changed. She had changed from the quiet, withdrawn young girl, so filled with pain and loneliness, who had such amazing strength. Christina had somehow touched something deep inside him and banished the pain and loneliness within him.

She was a mature woman now, poised, confident, and beautiful. The quiet strength was still there, along with a resiliency and determination he'd only glimpsed in the fragile young woman. And he understood at last that they had shared all that they could. All these years he had remained a little in love with his memory of a lost and lonely girl. That girl no longer existed.

She turned and smiled at him then. And for a brief moment he saw a shadow of that young girl. It was a fleeting image. And then it was gone. Just as the past was gone.

"You've changed," he said. "You're not the Christina I remember. You're stronger, and more confident."

"You taught me how to be strong," she said quietly. "You gave me strength. You helped me heal. I will always be grateful to you for that."

"Are you happy?" he asked.

She thought of Ross and smiled. "Yes. It's taken a long time, but I am very happy."

"You are not married. Is there someone in your life?"

"Yes, there is. He's a very special man. He helped me put the proposal together."

"And what of your future together?"

She laughed at the frankness that was so characteristic of David, as if he had a great many questions to ask and very little time in which to find the answers.

"I don't know about the future," she answered honestly. "But at least now, finally, I'm willing to explore possibilities."

"You are not lonely anymore," he concluded in a tender voice.

"No. I've finally put the past behind me. It was time.

Oddly enough, I had to go back to the past in order to face the future."

"You speak like a wise old Chinaman," he teased her.

"I was taught well by a man who was Chinese, but not very old." She went on, "You have a wonderful family. When you left, I was so hurt and angry, I couldn't even try to understand why you had come back to China. But now I do. Soon Li is very special."

"It's a good marriage. We have similar hopes and ideals for the future of China. We are very well suited to one another." He stopped walking and turned to face her. His voice grew wistful. "But I came so close to staying with you. The choice was very difficult. In the end I knew I had no choice."

"No," she whispered. "I understand that now."

"Even then I knew that someday there would be a great change within China. And I knew that I must be part of that change."

"And I couldn't be part of it," she said with quiet understanding.

"But perhaps, with the approval of the Central Committee, you will be part of it now—you and Fortune International."

"What will you tell them?" she asked. It was a question fraught with meaning.

He was thoughtful. "They know nothing of our relationship. And it must remain that way. Otherwise it might put the agreement in jeopardy."

"And it might be dangerous for you, as well?" she asked in a quiet voice.

His expression was somber. "Change comes very slowly within China." Then his expression shifted. "They might misunderstand my enthusiasm to accept a plan proposed by a woman. But they do not misunderstand a proposal made in the Fortune name. Even here, in mainland China and within the Central Committee, there are those who remember that Alexander Fortune was an honorable man. And they also understand that change is inevitable."

"Our year together was very special to me," she said quietly, needing, after all these years, to tell him what she hadn't been able to tell him then."

"It was very special for me also." He touched her cheek in a familiar, endearing gesture. And then he said something he'd never before revealed to her. "You gave me something very special during that year." He looked at her with dark eyes that were both hopeful and sad. "You taught me about courage and strength. I have never known anyone with as much strength. *Because* of what I learned from you, I was able to make the decision to come back here."

His hand dropped from her cheek, and he walked a few paces past her, staring into the dark night sky.

Then she said something she'd thought about often. "I've wondered what might have happened if we'd stayed together. I loved you, David."

"And I loved you," David said without hesitation. "But it was not possible for us to change our destinies," he added quietly. "They were written long before you and I met. They waited only for us to discover and fulfill them."

"And what are our destinies now?" she asked, standing close to him.

"To be as happy and fulfilled as we can be."

*Of course,* she thought. It was that simple. She needed to open herself completely to the possibility of happiness that Ross offered.

She smiled warmly at David, "You've given me so much, made so many things possible. What can I possibly give you in return, my dear friend?" she asked.

David turned to her then. The flickering light from one of the lanterns reflected in his dark eyes, like a ghost within, and his expression was very somber. At that moment, he looked a great deal older than his forty-one years. He took her hand in his as he whispered, "I must ask a very serious favor."

She held on to his hand. Without hesitation she said, "I'll do whatever you ask."

"Wait until you hear what it is first. There is danger."

"There is nothing I wouldn't do for you, David."

They sat together on the stone bench in the garden while the night sounds of insects buzzed thickly around them.

"I have three children," David explained. "I have a son

who is sixteen. I would have liked very much for him to be here tonight. He is a fine young man. But he is away."

She assumed that he meant away at school. David went on, "To everyone else, except for Soon Li and myself, he is dead."

Christina stared at him, stunned. It was several moments before she could think of anything to say. Then her thoughts focused on part of what he had said. "You said *to everyone else* he is dead. What has happened?"

He whispered now, as if terrified of being overheard, even here in his own private garden. "His name is James. He *was* a student at Beijing University at the time of Tiananmen Square."

Christina had kept close track of the student rebellion as it unfolded in Tiananmen Square, in June 1989. The aftermath, especially the executions of several students, had sent shock waves around the entire world.

David said, "He was part of the student rebellion. He stayed at Tiananmen the entire time. When the arrests began, he managed to escape the city with several others. For weeks afterward the military continued to make arrests. Lists were made. Brother turned against brother. Father turned against son. They betrayed them out of fear.

"His name was on a list of students to be rounded up and taken in for questioning. Others had been taken in and questioned. No one ever heard from them again. Because of my position in the government, I knew what happened to those students."

His voice was carefully controlled. "I knew it was only a matter of time before they would find James. It was for that reason that I decided everyone must believe that he had died. My son was staying with a distant cousin. It was he who arranged the 'accident.' I officially reported my son's death to the Central Committee. Even my daughters do not know the truth. I cannot endanger their lives with that knowledge. He remains in hiding. But he will be found eventually, perhaps soon."

She covered David's hand with hers. "I'm so sorry. How can I help you?"

He turned to her then, his fingers locking almost painfully over hers. "They will kill him if he is found." His voice broke. "I ask you to try to save my son's life. He must leave China. You are our only hope. But, Christina, my dearest friend, it is dangerous for you."

A long time ago she had loved this man. What they'd shared had nothing to do with political ideologies. They had been simply two young people who had come together in a particular place and time. He had been her friend, her lover, in a sense her savior. He had loved her unconditionally and without judgment. His kindness and gentle caring helped heal deep emotional wounds. In a way he had given her life back to her. She could do no less for him now.

She said simply, "Of course I'll do it."

# *Chapter 35*

The Fortune jet taxied down the small runway, then stopped. Christina unfastened her safety belt. She thanked the pilot and the attendant for a smooth flight, then stepped down onto the tarmac.

In her attaché case she carried the formal trade proposal that had been approved and signed by the Central Committee earlier that morning. She also carried a letter with an outline of locations and individuals' names. One of those names was the assumed identity of James Li, David's son. The locations were the small towns and villages within mainland China where he would be over the next four days, staying with friends and distant relatives, constantly moving to avoid being apprehended by the military authorities.

She looked for the limo and instead found the Rover a couple of hundred yards away at the edge of the tarmac. Ross stood beside it. His hands were thrust casually into the pockets of his charcoal gray suit, but she sensed he was anything but casual. There was something tentative about him, and that was utterly unlike his normal demeanor.

He stood there, waiting tensely, as the jet engines whined down, and she slowly walked toward him. That same tentativeness had been there when she left the day before. She hadn't understood what was behind it—the urgency as he said good-bye to her at the airport; the searching look in his eyes, as if there was something he wanted very much to say to her; that final kiss, filled with an almost poignant urgency.

She understood it now. Ross knew what David had meant to her, and he knew that in a way she had clung to her memory of their young love. Seeing David again, reconciling herself to the fact that their love was simply never meant to be, she had finally let go. David was her very dear friend. He always would be. And she would forever treasure the time they shared in the past.

But now she wanted the future, and the man who waited for her at the edge of the tarmac.

She stopped only inches from him and saw the question in his eyes. She answered it as she moved into his arms, slipping hers around his waist, spreading her hands across his back as she kissed him deeply. She held nothing back, conveying everything she felt, everything she wanted him to know.

The fear and uncertainty Ross had felt dissolved in an instant. She was here, in his arms, and he felt her desire in the sweet, hot velvet of her tongue against his. He pulled her against him roughly, deepening the kiss. If he could have pulled her inside himself, he would have, so deep was his desire and need.

Finally, after a long, long time, he drew back.

"I think maybe I should go away more often," she whispered thickly, as she ran the tip of her tongue along the slight bruise at her upper lip.

"Are you all right?" Ross asked.

She understood the full meaning of the question. Caressing his cheek, she responded wholeheartedly, "Yes, I'm all right now. Everything's all right now."

He kissed her again, tenderly this time.

"Aren't you going to ask me about the trade agreement?" she teased.

"All right. What about the trade agreement?"

"The Central Committee approved and signed it this morning."

"And what about David Chen?"

"I couldn't have done it without him," she answered truthfully. "There were several committee members who opposed it. He persuaded them of the merits of the agreement. In the end they voted to go with his recommendation."

"And your feelings for him?"

Honest questions that demanded equally honest answers. She closed her fingers around his, aware how deeply she loved this man. "He's my friend. He always will be. But what we shared *is* in the past. It belongs to the people we once were, not the people we are now."

Ross understood about putting the past to rest. In confronting his father and winning the approval of the Cartel, he had at last put his own past behind him. By letting her go to David Chen, he had allowed her to do the same.

She hesitated, then said carefully. "There's something else. Something I have to do for David . . ."


"There's no doubt about it. Anything of this nature is extremely dangerous," Bill said, sitting across from them in Ross's office.

"But can it be done?" Christina asked.

"It can be done," Bill finally said. "Actually it's done all the time." Then he warned, "But not without a lot of bloodshed. Especially since this young man is already on their lists. It's like a prisoner's trying to escape the posse, with everyone along the way a willing informant."

"Not everyone. David has friends who are hiding him. But they can't go on doing it forever."

Christina got up and paced around the room. "There has to be a way."

Bill shook his head. "The usual means of exit are out. They watch the airports like the Gestapo out of an old movie. It's the same with all checkpoints on the roads between the mainland and the New Territories. Ross and I have been over several times through Macao. They've tightened up security since the rebellion, particularly for anyone who is Chinese."

Ross had been silent through most of the discussion. Now he asked, "What about a boat?"

Bill and Christina both stared at him. Then Bill said skeptically, "I'd say it's crazy. You know as well as I do the number of boats full of refugees that have been apprehended or turned back since the rebellion. They're sitting targets."

"I'm not talking about a motor launch," Ross said speculatively. "I'm talking about a sailboat."

"It would have to be done in daylight, and there would be the risk of being spotted by the shore patrols."

"It could be done after dark."

Again Bill was adamant. "That's impossible. The winds and currents between here and the mainland are treacherous, particularly for sailboats."

"I've sailed these waters all my life."

"No way!" Bill insisted. "You're not going over there by yourself and attempting to sail between here and the mainland."

Christina stared at Ross. "Bill's right. There has to be another way."

Ross took her hand in his, threading their fingers. His expression was sober. "There is no other way, Chris."

When she started to protest, he went on to explain. "If it were simply a matter of getting him out of the country and the repercussions be damned, we could contact the people he's staying with, have them smuggle him to the airport in Shanghai, and simply fly him out aboard the company jet. But it's not that simple. Government officials believe that he's dead. They have to go right on believing it to protect Chen Li and his position within the government. And then there's our involvement. If they knew for a minute that we were trying to get him out, they would cancel that trade agreement, and you could end up losing the company."

"So what you're saying is that we should forget it? I can't do that. I made a promise. And I'm going to keep it."

"I intend for you to keep it," he said, rubbing his thumb along the curve of her hand. "Trust me. Let me do it my way."

"But . . ."

He interrupted stubbornly. "I'll fly into Canton on a commercial flight. I've been there many times on business. Then I'll simply disappear, blend in."

"In a country full of millions of Chinese, a *gweilo* is going to blend in." Bill's tone was derisive.

"There are enough *gweilo*s there so that I shouldn't arouse any suspicion. I'll make arrangements for a boat through people that I know. Then I'll make contact with David's son."

"They'll have to move him again in four days," she reminded him.

Ross nodded. "If all goes well, we could sail from the mainland as soon as three days from now."

"If all goes well," Bill muttered as he rubbed his fingers across his brow. "Except for the military who constantly patrol those waters, except for bullets, and what about the damn unpredictable weather?"

Without giving Ross a chance to answer he went on. "I hate to play devil's advocate here . . ."

Ross cut him off. "Then don't. It's the only way we can pull this off, and you know it."

"But why the hell does it have to be you?"

"Because I know those waters, along with a few places where we can hide out if things go wrong. Besides, I don't plan on encountering any bullets. I plan to stay well away from them. As for the weather, we'll check with the Royal Naval weather station. If we're half lucky, they may be able to give us an accurate prediction of what to expect over the next four days. Other than that, I'll rely on my instincts."

"Christ!" Bill shook his head. "I don't suppose there's anything I can say to talk you out of this."

Ross smiled. "I think you've already tried."

Bill looked helplessly at Christina. "Try to talk some sense into him." Then he stormed out of the office.

"Don't worry about him," Ross said. "He'll be back. He's just gone to check the weather charts."

"He's right," Christina said firmly. "It's too dangerous. I won't let you do this."

He gave her an amused smile as he pulled her down onto his lap. "Won't let me do it?" he asked with a quirk of a dark brow. Then his expression shifted. "A young man's life is in danger. You promised to help him."

"It was *my* promise, not yours. I can't ask you to risk your life for this."

"You haven't asked."

"Then why are you doing this?"

He gazed down at their joined hands for several moments before answering. "I didn't know whether or not you would come back to me. I mean *truly* come back, in spirit as well as body. I was afraid I might have lost you to him." When she started to protest, he silenced her with a finger against her lips.

"But now I understand what it is that you felt for David Chen. And I accept it, because I love you. I've never said that to a woman before. I always felt those words were too easily said and too easily turned into a lie. You've made a promise. Because it's important to you . . . it's important for *us*."

He finished, "You have to trust me not to be an utter fool, and to have the sense to know what I'm doing."

She slipped her arms around his neck and pressed her forehead against his. "I do trust you. I just don't want to lose you."

"Ah, love, you couldn't lose me now if you tried."

"I'm going with you," Bill announced adamantly as he came into Ross's office. It was late evening, the day after Christina got back from the mainland. Communication had been made with one of the people on the list she brought back. They had received a response only a couple of hours earlier. A contact location had been set up and confirmed for Ross to meet up with James Li. Weather charts and tide schedules lay across Ross's desk, along with fake identification papers. Ross looked up.

"And this from a man who turns green on the Sausalito ferry. Face it, you're just not up to a sea voyage, my friend."

"You might need some help. I'll take pills for seasickness. And my Cantonese isn't too bad."

"No, but your Mandarin is lousy, and you have a hard time lying. If push comes to shove, I may be forced to tell a few to get us out."

"What is that for?" Bill motioned to the shaft of metal that gleamed from an open desk drawer. It was a pistol. Ross closed the drawer.

"That's in case I'm not very good at lying."

"Shit! Isn't there anything I can say to change your mind about this?" Bill asked again.

Ross gave him a wicked grin. "If Chris couldn't persuade me—and I assure you, she can be very persuasive—what makes you think that you can?"

"Oh, I don't know," Bill grumbled miserably. "I suppose I was hoping you'd have a moment of sanity and listen to reason."

Ross laughed. "Not bloody likely, my friend." Before Bill could argue further, he said, "I'd best be going. My flight from Kai Tak Airport to Canton leaves in less than two hours."

He had specifically chosen a late-night flight. He would check into a local hotel, where reservations had already been made, ostensibly for a business trip. The trade agreement that had recently been signed gave him a logical reason for visiting the mainland.

In the morning he planned to slip out of the hotel and disappear on the streets of Shanghai. Then he would hire a series of drivers to take him north to Kan-chou, where he was to meet James Li. If all went well, they would make their way to the coast, where a boat was to be waiting for the final part of their journey out of China.

God willing, they would sail uneventfully into Hong Kong Harbor.

An incoming flight roared in over Kai Tak Airport. Ross, accompanied by Bill, was checking in for his flight to Canton. He had one carry-on bag and a thick roll of renminbi, the Chinese currency. Hong Kong dollars would be useless to him on the mainland. Christina waited for him in the passenger lounge area.

As Ross came away from the check-in counter, he drew Bill aside. "Contact Thomas Lai. Tell him what you learned about those records we found that were changed in San

Francisco. We've got to find out who else is involved in the smuggling. Lai may be able to help."

"Okay."

"Tell him he's to do whatever is necessary to stop this."

"You can be a cold son of a bitch sometimes," Bill said under his breath.

Ross gave him a level look. "I don't think Steven was in the smuggling operation alone. I can't take the risk of letting whoever else is involved get near Chris. He tried twice before, and failed. Now that the smuggling operation has been exposed, he has very little left to lose. He may be willing to take whatever risks are necessary to get to her."

He paused, then went on slowly, "If for any reason I don't make it back . . ."

Bill cut him off. "Shut up. Don't even say it."

But Ross went on, "If anything happens . . . I want your promise that you'll take care of her, be her friend."

The two friends looked at each other, surrounded by a sea of milling tourists. Bill's eyes softened. He took Ross's hand as if to shake it, but instead held on hard. "You're the luckiest son of a bitch I know. You'll make it back."

Ross nodded. "Thanks, mate. For everything."

His flight was announced, and he walked over to Christina. Bill didn't join them, but instead walked to the windows that looked out onto the lighted strip of runway as a European-bound flight took off.

Ross touched her cheek with his fingers. "I'll be back the day after tomorrow, before dawn."

"Promise?" she said, fighting back tears.

"Absolutely. After all, you once accused me of being a pirate, and this is what pirates do best."

She tried to laugh past the tears that choked her throat. Then he kissed her with the kind of aching tenderness that she remembered from that very first kiss they'd shared in another city half a world away.

"I love you," he whispered against her mouth. And then he abruptly turned and walked away from her.

"I'll be waiting for you," she called after him as he disappeared through the boarding gate.

It was past one o'clock in the morning as Bill and Christina walked back through the immigration gate together, and out to the parking queue. Bill drove, heading out onto the harbor road and toward Tsim Sha Tsui, to take her back to the Regent.

Sitting in absolute silence in the quiet, dark interior of the car, she thought that the next thirty-six hours were going to be very, very long.

The plain gray rented Toyota pulled away from the parking queue several car-lengths behind them. It held back as they slowed and turned out onto the harbor road, and then followed at a discreet speed, never letting the Rover out of sight.

When they pulled onto Salisbury Road, the Toyota followed. It pulled to the curb across the street as the Rover pulled into the valet parking of the Regent Hotel.

Taut hands curled over the steering wheel as the man watched Christina say good-night to the man in the Rover, and then walk into the lobby. She was greeted by the doorman. Then another Chinese man greeted her inside—probably the manager of the Regent, he realized.

He thought about following her inside, now that McKenna was gone on that flight, but he noticed the uniformed security guard watching him from the unmarked car in front of the hotel. The Regent was one of the most expensive and prestigious hotels in the Territory. Dignitaries and celebrities numbered among the guests. Security was always tight.

His knuckles gleamed white across the steering wheel as his grip tightened. As the security guard started to slowly circle around toward him, he shifted into gear and pulled away from the curb. He couldn't risk the authorities' questioning him. He sped down Salisbury Road and disappeared into the night.

On his arrival in Canton, Ross checked into one of the hotels frequented by businessmen, then he slipped into bed to try to catch a few hours' sleep before getting up at six. He'd paid his hotel bill in advance so there would be no questions when he didn't make an appearance at the usual checkout time.

Four hours later he pressed the button on the compact travel alarm before it went off. Then he showered and dressed. He left the hotel just after seven. He walked, instead of hiring one of the taxis that waited outside the hotel entrance.

The early-morning air was warm and clammy with the sort of oppressiveness that was common this time of year inland. He slipped into the open-air market, where vendors were setting up handcarts and wagons with produce, poultry, and fresh fish. The odors mixed with the blast of diesel fuel from the streets, and the fetid stench of rotting garbage that filled the gutters. Taxis and trucks barreled through traffic jams of bicyclists. And everywhere was the pervading cacophony of jabbering conversations—toothless old women chattering at disobedient grandchildren, uniformed schoolchildren in animated discussion, deliverymen shouting down from their trucks to store owners who stood expectantly on the street.

Ross knew Canton, or Guangzhou as it was now called. to him, it had always been Canton, from the time his mother had taken him inland on his first trip to visit where she was born. It would always be Canton.

On the street between the peddlers' market and the city government offices, he hired a taxi. He paid the driver half his fee in advance, and they drove out of the city.

The four-lane road cut across the countryside through flat fields and sparse woods. Over two hours later they finally arrived at Shao-kuan. Ross paid the driver the balance of the fare, and a bonus. Money could buy a lot of things, including a man's silence—at least for a little while.

Shao-kuan was an agricultural town. Flat fields spread away to the distant hills. Through those hills lay Kan-chou, where he would, he hoped, find James Li.

He visited an old friend of his mother's and inquired where he might purchase a car. He was directed to the garage at the end of town.

The ramshackle tin building was a cluttered workshop full of car parts and tools. The owner, Wah-yim, was the nephew of the woman who'd given Ross directions. He eyed Ross warily, until he saw the thick roll of Chinese bills in his hand. Taking Ross out to the back of his shop, he pulled a tarpaulin off a battered old hulk that had once been a sixties-model Chevrolet.

"Run good!" Wah-yim announced with a grin as he slammed his hand down on the oxidized blue hood of the car.

"It better," Ross informed him in Cantonese as they struck a bargain. "Or I'll come back for my money and not care how I get it."

The threat was sufficient to have Wah-yim bobbing his head and babbling a response in Cantonese that he wouldn't dare cheat a friend of his maiden aunt or she would have a couple of his more private parts with a cleaver.

"We'll see," Ross replied as he slid behind the wheel of the Chevy. Dust rose from the rotting upholstery, and he could barely see out the window. Then the window ran to mud as Wah-yim doused the windshield with water. He grinned at Ross through the glass. Again he slammed his flattened hand down on the hood. "A-one condition."

Ross paid him for the car and a full tank of petrol, along with several more cans filled and stowed in the backseat. Then he threw his bag in the back, backed out onto the road, and headed into the mountains.

Kan-chou was another farming town, like so many others, linked like pearls on a strand of the river that flowed through China. It was after five o'clock in the afternoon when Ross arrived. It was here that the Chevy turned out to be worth every penny of the equivalent of the five thousand dollars that he'd paid for it. With its oxidized paint and dented doors, oil smoke puffing from its rusty tailpipe, it blended with other relics of the American automobile industry.

Ross drove to the edge of town. It was dark when he pulled in behind the small row of workshops and tumbledown huts. He found the third house from the end and knocked at the back door. The light inside was doused, then the door creaked open.

In Cantonese Ross said, "I've come for the son of Chen

Li." A hand reached for him in the darkness and pulled him through the doorway.

A single light was turned on. It was a modest, two-room residence. There were four aluminum-frame chairs with torn vinyl seats sitting around a Formica-topped table. A couch stood against the opposite wall. Heavy drapes blacked out the windows. Two men sat at the table. The man who had pulled him through the door nodded to the slender young man who came in from an adjoining room.

James Li was sixteen, slight of build, with longish hair and clear, dark eyes behind wire-rimmed glasses. He was dressed in jeans, a sweatshirt with the sleeves cut off just above the elbows, and scuffed Adidas. Ross recognized his face from the countless posters that had flooded the streets of Hong Kong after the student rebellion. He was a young man on the run for his life.

Introductions were made, and a meal was served. Then Ross explained to James his plan for their escape.

"How are my parents and sisters?" James asked.

"As far as I know they're fine. A friend of mine met with your father and made these arrangements. She can tell you about them when we get to Hong Kong."

"Her name is Christina." James repeated what he had been told. "I am looking forward to meeting her. My father has spoken of her." There was a knock on the door. The lights were quickly doused once more, then turned back on as their host stepped inside. He had returned from checking the route of their escape.

"It's time. If you leave now, you will have plenty of time on the Chin Chiang road to reach your destination."

Farewells were said. It was a poignant moment that Ross understood well. James was leaving his friends and family far behind. He didn't know if he would make it—and if he would ever be able to return.

"Take good care of our friend," Ross was told. "They will kill him if they find him."

Then they were out on the Chin Chiang road, speeding into the night toward the eastern coast of mainland China, praying they wouldn't be stopped by anyone.

They drove for hours, stopping to empty the extra fuel cans into the Chevy. James spoke excellent English. He was obviously a very bright and curious young man. He talked of the student rebellion in Beijing and about the threads of change that wove through his country.

Then, just after midnight on the road to Shan-t'ou, they encountered a stranded motorist who waved them down. Ross slipped the pistol inside his belt. They slowly drove past and stopped. It was an old man with a load of melons. His ancient truck had run out of petrol. Ross gave him one of their fuel cans.

"Carrying a weapon inside mainland China is very dangerous," James remarked when they were once more on their way.

"It's more dangerous not to have one and find myself looking down the barrel of a Russian-made machine gun."

They arrived in the small fishing village of Shan-t'ou just after two o'clock in the morning. As a young man, Ross had often sailed out of here, and he knew the local waters quite well. They changed into the clothes Ross had brought—black pants, black turtleneck shirts, and black soft-soled shoes. Everything else was packed into his small bag, including their forged identification papers and visitor's visas.

They left the car with the keys in the ignition for whoever was lucky enough to find it. Then they walked the rest of the way into town, keeping off the main road.

They walked down to the small inlet where fishing boats bobbed at moorings. Others were pulled up on the beach. There was a deep-water pier with a small boat house. Ross padded softly across the dock and knocked on the door of the boat house. It squeaked open, words were exchanged, and the old man who ran the pier stepped out into the dark night.

He said to Ross in Cantonese, "I have everything you asked for." He raised his lantern, bringing the pool of light closer to James's face.

Ross stopped his hand. "I'm just taking my friend out for some night sailing," he explained. Then he pressed a fat roll of bills into the old man's hand.

The old man nodded, stuffed the money inside his loose

shirt, and then guided them across the docks to the boat he'd arranged for them.

It was thirty feet long and resembled a ketch, long and low with one center mast and another aft. The sails were tied, the lines moving restlessly in the breeze that came up off the water. Whatever color the hull had originally been, it was now black—a color that would all but disappear on the horizon if they encountered any other vessels.

Ross asked about the supplies. The old man nodded, confirming there was fresh water, an oilskin of food in the half-cabin, life preservers, and lanterns.

The boat had cost Ross ten times what he would have paid for it anywhere else, but it was worth every penny. He checked her over from bow to stern. She was watertight; everything seemed to be in order. There was no time to check the sails. He would have to take the old man's word for it that they were as seaworthy as the rest of the boat.

When everything was stowed, they got under way, slowly slipping away from the dock under the power of the ten-horse motor. As soon as they were beyond the breakwater, Ross went forward, raised the jib, and cut the motor. He smiled faintly at the sight of the sail, which also had been splattered with dark paint. It was barely visible in the night sky.

As the wind pulled them out into the South China Sea, he had James hold the tiller while he hoisted the main sail. Then he returned and sent James to the bow to keep watch for lights out on the water. He didn't want inadvertently to come up on any coastal patrol boats.

The wind held, pulling them out on a steady tack into the open sea. Ross got his bearings. The nine dragons were looking out for them. The storm that had threatened the night before had disappeared. The coast was brightly illuminated. But while that gave Ross a clear course to follow using the stars, it also made them vulnerable to those patrol boats.

"How long will it take?" James asked, pulling on a black windbreaker over his sweatshirt. The wind off the water cut right through their clothes.

Ross readjusted the tiller as the current zigzagged with the coastline. "We should make Hong Kong before dawn if the wind holds."

James became silent as he gazed out across the water, watching for the lights that would warn of an approaching patrol, and Ross readied the pistol in his waistband.

It was just after four o'clock in the morning. Christina jumped as the telephone in her suite rang. She hadn't been able to sleep and answered it immediately. It was Bill.

"I'm sorry if I woke you."

"I couldn't sleep."

"Yeah, I know what you mean. Mick and the others have already left. I'm leaving right now. I'll pick you up in about twenty minutes."

"Has there been any word?" she asked anxiously.

"Ross told us before he left there wouldn't be any contact. We just have to trust that he'll make it all right."

"What about the harbor patrols?"

"That's why we have Mick and the others out on that fishing trawler," Bill explained. "I'll see you in a little while."

She ran out to the Rover when Bill pulled up in front of the Regent. They drove in silence across to Hong Kong Island, then turned along the eastern rim of the island, past Causeway Bay to the smaller docks and piers used by the commercial fishing companies. She didn't ask how Mick and his men had managed to comandeer a fishing trawler. She had a feeling that was one of those little details she would find out about later.

This was the older part of the commercial shipping docks, where the smaller ships coming in from Taiwan and Shanghai usually put to port. The larger container terminals had been built across the harbor at Kowloon to accommodate the larger behemoths of the ocean. But somewhere very near here undoubtedly was the location of the original piers and docks built by the British Empire, and here Hamish Fortune had first sailed into Victoria Harbor.

It was still dark as they pulled out onto one of the long docks. But even this time of the morning, it hummed with activity. One of the dockworkers separated from the others and walked toward them. Christina recognized him as one of Mick's men.

"Mick just called in on the ship-to-shore. They're reached the coordinates, but there's still no sign of 'em. Those swells are whipping up pretty strong out there."

"Think we're in for a blow?" Bill asked, tilting back his head to check the changing night sky.

"Not before late tonight, but it could get a little nasty out there."

"Let us know if you hear anything else," Bill said. The man nodded and returned to listen to the incoming calls in the large boat house.

"It's cold out here," Bill remarked, as the wind came up off the water, reminding them both that it was fall and the weather was changing. "Do you want to go inside and wait?"

She shook her head as she bundled more tightly into Ross's windbreaker. "I want to stay out here. I can see the far end of the harbor better." And so they waited, until it was past six o'clock and streamers of gray lit up the eastern sky.

Christina was practically frozen through from the wind, but she refused to go to the boat house or return to the Rover. Then the call came in, and Mick's man was running toward them.

"They've got 'em! Just picked 'em up. Seems there was a bit of trouble with one of the coastal patrols. A few shots were fired, but they gave 'em the slip." Then he looked at Christina's stricken face. "Sorry, ma'am. I shouldn't have said that. They're both all right. Nobody got hurt. Mick and the boys are bringin' 'em in now. Should be here within the hour."

He went back to monitor any further communications. Christina turned to Bill and threw her arms around his neck. "They're all right!" she cried happily, tears streaming down her cheeks. They hugged each other tight, each letting go of the emotions neither had dared to reveal over the thirty-six hours since Ross had left for Canton.

Christina finally allowed Bill to take her into the boat

house. They sipped steaming hot coffee while they listened to incoming messages from various vessels that operated from the pier. There were occasional routine calls from the skipper of the vessel Ross was on, but no personal messages.

Finally the call came through that they had cleared the harbor entrance. Christina watched out the huge window for sight of the trawler with the wide, red band from bow to stern, denoting it as one of the HK Commercial Fishing vessels.

Then Bill saw it and pointed it out. It churned through the water at what seemed a painstakingly slow pace. But Bill quickly pointed out it was the usual speed for an incoming trawler, and the captain certainly didn't want to alert harbor authorities to his unusual cargo by speeding across the harbor.

It seemed to take forever. The trawler's huge diesel engines slowed as it edged up to the pier, then reversed, becoming almost still in the water. Lines were thrown and secured as Christina and Bill left the boat house and ran across the pier.

Bill had gone forward to help with the lines. Left alone just outside the boat house, Christina waited anxiously, scanning the faces of the men who stood on the deck of the trawler. There were several Chinese crew members, but she saw one who looked especially young. The young man had to be James Li.

She swallowed the knot of emotion in her throat. She had kept her promise to David—no, she corrected herself, Ross had kept the promise for her.

Then she saw Ross. He came up to stand beside James at the railing. She waved at him frantically and thought he had seen her. Then the gangway was lowered. She started to run toward them.

"Christina!"

The sound of her name, and the anger as it was shouted, halted her. She swung around, oblivious to the danger that came with it. But Ross saw it. He saw the reflection of the rising sun as it glinted off the steel barrel of a revolver, and he saw the man who held it pointed straight at Christina.

"Chris!" he shouted to warn her, running down the gangway, pushing men aside in a desperate attempt to get to her in time.

Amid shouts and screams, the loud report of gunfire shattered the cool morning air over the pier.

# Chapter 36

Christina stood, frozen, unable to move. She stared in disbelief. And then the man, who only an instant before had aimed a revolver right at her heart, slowly crumpled on the pier. He lay there with sightless eyes staring up at the sky, a large crimson stain spreading across the front of his shirt.

Brian Chandler lay dead on the dock, his fingers frozen on the trigger of a revolver.

"Chris! Are you all right?" Ross reached her and pulled her into his arms. "Thank God!" he whispered against her face as he held her tight against him, shielding her from the horrible sight.

"Ross!" She clung to him as if she would never let him go. "It's *Brian* . . . Why? . . . What was he doing here? . . . I don't understand."

"It's all right." He held on to her as a crowd gathered. Already the wail of sirens could be heard across the docks.

"But why would Brian want to kill me?" she asked in confusion.

Before he could respond, she saw a man approaching. Thomas Lai bowed his head in a sign of respect. "You have kept *your* promise," he said to Christina, obviously referring to Steven. "You have restored honor to the Fortune name. And now I have kept my promise."

He glanced briefly over his shoulder to Brian Chandler's body. Naturally he hadn't fired the shots himself. One of his men had done so, and then immediately disappeared.

As the wail of sirens drew closer, he bade them farewell. Even though the triad were rumored to control the legal system within Hong Kong, it wouldn't do for the head of one of the most powerful triad to be seen at the site of a shooting.

He smiled faintly as he looked far out across Victoria Harbor and into the glow of dawn on the water. "The nine dragons are once more sleeping peacefully. Good-bye, Miss Fortune."

Late that evening, after a long and exhausting day dealing with Hong Kong police, immigration officials, and the U.S. consulate, Christina and Ross came back to his hotel suite. The day had begun with danger and violence, and finally ended in a morass of paperwork. James Li would be granted political asylum in the United States. His American relatives in Boston, the same relatives who had helped his father when he was a student there, would give him a home.

James told Christina he was certain that one day he would be able to return to China. It was simply a matter of time until the old hard-liners died or lost power and a younger, more flexible generation took control. She hoped he was right.

When James's situation was resolved, Christina and Ross confronted Steven, who'd been taken to jail. Ross told him bluntly that his father was dead, and Steven's only hope of lessening his punishment was to cooperate fully and tell them everything he knew. Alone and terrified, completely intimidated by the atmosphere of the jail, Steven quickly caved in and confessed everything.

The drug smuggling had been Brian's idea. He and Steven had been doing it successfully for several months. They had been certain that Ross and Richard were too busy fighting each other ever to discover their operation. Then Christina had shown up—and begun getting more and more involved in the company. Brian had told Steven they must get rid of her, and they had made the two attempts on her life—first at Julie's ranch, and a second time on the cable car. Brian had planned the attacks, and Steven had carried them out.

Listening to Steven talk unemotionally about the terrible things he and his father had done, Christina realized that he felt no guilt or remorse at all. His only regret was that he got caught. For all his surface charm, he was a classic sociopath, utterly amoral. Whether it was raping his young cousin, dealing in drugs, or attempting to murder someone who threatened his security, it was all the same to him.

When they left Steven, Christina felt physically ill. Only once before had she been in the presence of someone who was so clearly a monster—Cal Loomis.

Now, back in Ross's hotel suite, she collapsed onto the sofa, utterly drained emotionally and physically. Ross had ordered tea, and as she carefully sipped the strong, hot liquid, she said, "Steven's sick. I can see that. He must've always been that way, but no one wanted to face it. But I don't understand Uncle Brian . . . Why would he do all those terrible things?"

Ross answered slowly, "Everyone had a great deal to lose with your claim to the inheritance. But Brian had the most to lose."

"But why get involved in something like smuggling? He had plenty of money from Diana."

"I expect he wanted to leave Diana. Think about it. She constantly berated him. Their marriage was a bitter failure. But if he left her, he would have nothing."

"He always looked so terribly unhappy," Christina said in a hoarse whisper.

Ross went on, "Steven was more than willing to participate in his father's plans. And it went smoothly until you came. You had to be stopped."

Christina admitted guiltily, "For a long while I actually suspected you. You showed up at some questionable times, after all."

To her surprise Ross smiled slyly. "Your instincts weren't that far off. I was keeping an eye on you, all right, through Bill. At first I was simply trying to find out as much as I could about you. Then, when that incident happened at Ju-

lie's, I knew that someone was trying to kill you. I had poor
Bill working overtime after that. The night you were pushed
from the cable car, I raked him over the coals for not keeping
a closer watch on you."

Christina managed a small smile. "And to think I was a little afraid of you, when all the time you were my guardian
angel."

He sat down next to her on the sofa and asked in a searching voice, "Are you all right now?"

For a moment she didn't answer. Then, setting down her
cup, she turned back to him. "Yes. I'm all right now. You
know, I didn't come back for the inheritance. I didn't plan on
getting so involved in the company. I came back to find out
who the rapist was, and to see him punished."

"You've accomplished that," Ross replied soberly. "Steven
will languish in a Hong Kong prison for a long, long time."

She felt a tiny jolt of frustration. "Yes, but he isn't being
punished for the rape. I don't know if you can understand, but
that matters more to me than the drug smuggling—even more
than his attempts on my life."

Ross took her hands in his and held them tightly. "I understand, love. But I learned something about revenge when I
faced my father in that meeting and beat him down. The satisfaction of getting back at him was ephemeral. I realized that
I needed to get beyond my hurt and anger, and leave all that
where it belongs—in the past."

He was absolutely right, she knew. It was time to bury the
past and focus on the present, on the here and now. And Ross.
But before she could do that, there was one more thing that
had to be done.

# Chapter 37

The Hawaiian sun shone down out of a clear blue sky. A cool, salty breeze came in off the nearby ocean, lifting strands of Christina's hair and blowing them across her cheeks. Standing slightly apart from the others, she looked at what remained of the wealthy and powerful and far-from-perfect Fortune family standing by Brian Chandler's grave.

Diana was cold and remote in a severe black dress. Andrew stood by her side, looking utterly overwhelmed. And yet somehow Christina was confident he would survive his father's fall from grace. Andrew was one of the lucky ones, in a sense. He had found a meaning to his life.

Standing next to Andrew, Jason looked terribly young and vulnerable. Christina wasn't nearly so sure of Jason's ability to overcome the harsh reality of his father's betrayal. She worried about him, and was profoundly torn about what to say or do to help him through this tragedy.

Next to Jason stood Richard and Alicia. It had been all Richard could do to control his rage at the events in Hong Kong. Brian's crime was bad enough, but the fact that Christina and Ross had pulled off a deal that put them solidly in charge of the company infuriated him even more.

Christina wondered if he would simply leave the company or stay and do his considerable best to challenge her authority.

She didn't feel intimidated at the thought of his staying. She was confident that together, she and Ross could handle him.

Standing in the center of the group, Katherine leaned heavily on her cane. She had refused the chair that the solicitous minister had procured for her. As always, her expression was unreadable. But Christina knew it must have crushed her sense of family pride and honor to know how her son-in-law had corrupted not only his son, but the company, as well.

It had taken all of the Fortune family's clout to keep Brian's role as a drug smuggler and attempted murderer from the press. The publicity could have been devastating. In keeping with the charade, Diana had insisted he be buried in the family plot on the ranch in Hawaii.

Now, watching Diana standing there, looking white-faced and grim, Christina wondered what must be going through her mind. The realization that her husband had hated her so deeply, that he was so desperate to escape from her control, and had involved their son in a drug smuggling operation, must be shattering.

Oddly enough she found herself feeling sorry for Diana. In a way, she thought, it wasn't really Diana's fault. Like all the Fortune women, and so many other women whose privileged lives were actually velvet cages, she had never been valued as highly as the men in the family were.

It was long past time for that cruel legacy to change, she decided. If she had a daughter, that child would be encouraged to fulfill herself. And might one day find herself running Fortune International.

The minister, an old friend of the family who had agreed to be discreet in his final words about Brian, finished his short, vaguely worded eulogy. The group dispersed silently. Christina's eyes met Jason's, then he dropped his gaze and turned away. Leann, who had come to the ceremony with Phillip Lo, watched in silent misery as Jason walked away alone.

Christina's heart went out to Leann. Murmuring, "I'll be right back," to Ross, who stood beside her, Christina hurried after Jason.

She caught him just as he was getting into his car, alone. "Jase!"

Startled, he looked up. In that unguarded moment, his eyes revealed his deep pain and sense of loss so poignantly that she wanted to take him in her arms and hold him as if he were a child. But he wasn't a child. He wasn't even the sad and lonely young man who'd once turned to his young cousin for the love and reassurance he couldn't find at home. He was a man. It was time he built a new life as a man, with a woman beside him who loved him unequivocally.

"I . . . I have to go," he said haltingly.

"*No.* There's something we have to resolve first. You can't continue running away from me, Jase. Or from the past. I faced it, and I survived. You can do the same."

"I don't know what you mean."

"Yes, you do. Jase, *listen* to me. I didn't leave twenty years ago because of our quarrel. I left because someone else hurt me deeply, and I was afraid. I thought my only chance was to escape. I know now that was wrong. I should have stayed and confronted the situation. But I was so young and so scared."

She hesitated, then went on in a heartfelt voice, "Jase, I loved you. And I know you loved me. But we loved each other as desperately unhappy kids love each other. We're not kids anymore. We both need to make something good and true out of our grown-up lives."

His eyes glistened with unshed tears. "God, Chris, I've been in such hell."

She went to him then and took his trembling body in her arms, murmuring softly, "I know, Jase, I know. But it's over now. You're not guilty of anything, except maybe being my only real friend when I needed one badly."

He stopped shaking and looked at her. "Do you really feel that way?"

Her smile was infinitely gentle. "Yes. I do."

He brushed his arm across his damp eyes, to dry them, then said shakily, "I'm not sure what to do now."

"I am." She glanced meaningfully at Leann, who waited alone, watching them intently.

"Go to her, Jase. She loves you very much. Don't let her slip away."

He hesitated, then slowly walked toward Leann. He stopped once to look back at Christina and give her a grateful smile. Then he turned and moved more purposefully toward Leann. They simply looked at each other for a moment. Then he took her hand in his, and they walked toward the beach together. It would be a good place, Christina thought, for the two of them to have a long, long talk.

Behind her she heard Katherine say, "It's about time those two got together."

Christina turned to her. "So you knew?"

"Of course. Any fool could see it."

Katherine looked even older and more tired than she had the last time Christina had seen her. Christina said in concern, "I'll help you to the car. You should go home and rest."

"Clearly you and Ross can run the company quite competently. I've got the remainder of my days, however long or short they may be, to do nothing but rest," Katherine snapped.

Then her expression softened. She had risked her company and gambled on this young woman. And Christina had triumphed brilliantly. Katherine felt a surge of pride at the thought of all that her granddaughter had achieved.

*Her granddaughter* . . . It stunned her to realize that she actually thought of this young woman as her granddaughter. She looked at Christina thoughtfully.

Meeting her piercing look, Christina steeled herself for the inevitable question—*who are you?*

To her surprise Katherine didn't ask it. Instead she said, "From the moment I first saw you, I was convinced you couldn't be my granddaughter. I told myself that if Christina was alive, she would have come home long ago. Then, as time went by, I saw things in you that reminded me of Christina. I was so torn—were you my granddaughter or an impostor? I began to feel that I had to know for certain, one way or the other."

She sighed deeply, an unutterably weary sound that came from years of struggle and loneliness. "You were right when you said I let down my granddaughter badly. I've suffered with a greater sense of guilt than you could possibly imagine."

Katherine paused. Her next words stunned Christina. "Now, somehow, it no longer seems important whether or not you're Christina."

She smiled tentatively. "There's a tradition among the Hawaiians. A family will take in an orphaned child and raise it as their own in a sort of informal, but very loving, arrangement. They call this child a *hani* child—*a child of the heart.* I'd like to think that your coming here gives me a second chance to be the sort of person I should have been before— the sort of grandmother that I should have been."

She finished, "I accept you as my *hani* child, Christina. I hope you will accept me."

Christina was filled with an overpowering mixture of emotions—love and loss, relief and regret. She whispered, *"Grandmère,"* in a tremulous voice, then hugged Katherine tightly.

Katherine's frail body felt as if it couldn't withstand the force of their embrace. But she refused to let Christina pull away for a long moment. When she finally did so, she inclined her head toward Ross. "You'd better go to him now. He isn't a very patient man, you know."

Christina was amazed. "You know about us?"

"I had the great good luck to love and to be loved deeply in return. It's been a long, long time, but I can still recognize the feeling." She squeezed Christina's hand and repeated, "Go to him."

When Christina reached Ross, he raised one eyebrow quizzically and asked, "Well?"

"I'd rather not talk here," she replied. "Let's go to the sanctuary. I'll tell you everything there."

*Sanctuary.*

How appropriate, she thought. She had finally found sanctuary, after years of running in terror from those merciless pursuers, the ghosts of her past. She had kept her promise, and justice was done, at least as much as it could be after twenty long years. She felt lighter than she could ever remember feeling, as if a terrible burden had been lifted from her shoulders.

Christina remembered a conversation she and Ellie had shortly after they first met. Ellie had asked, "If you could have one wish right now, this minute, what would it be?"

Christina had answered without hesitation, "To have everything the way it used to be. When I was happy."

And Ellie had murmured, "Yeah. Me, too."

Now she accepted that to live was to be in transition, and nothing could be the way it once was. But she also felt that happiness was again within her grasp. It was just a different kind of happiness, with a different person.

She and Ross stood together on the small, crescent-shaped beach, tall palm trees swaying behind them, the blue, blue water of the Pacific glistening in front of them. It was truly paradise, she thought. And it lacked only one thing to be absolutely perfect.

The truth.

She opened her mouth to speak, but he said, "There's something I want to say first." He went on slowly, carefully. "I don't care if you're Christina or Ellie. I only care that you're mine, now and forever."

Her throat tightened with emotion, and tears of happiness welled in her eyes. *I love you so,* she thought. Aloud she said, "I love you more than I ever thought possible."

He kissed her then, tenderly. The kiss held so much love and need and the most tantalizing hint of passion that she felt this sort of joy must be impossible.

When she finally opened her eyes and looked into his, she knew it *was* possible. She said, "I *am* Christina. And I am yours, now and forever."

PAMELA SIMPSON is actually the pen name for the writing team of Pamela Wallace and Carla Simpson.

PAMELA WALLACE, a native Californian with a degree from UCLA, worked as an editor and writer for magazines and newspapers before beginning her career as a novelist and screenwriter. She co-wrote the screenplay for *Witness*, for which she won an Academy Award (the Oscar), a Writer's Guild Award, and the Mystery Writers of America Award (the Edgar).

Three of her novels have been produced as made-for-cable movies for SHOWTIME: *Tears in the Rain, Dreams Lost, Dreams Found,* and *Love With a Perfect Stranger.* She also co-wrote the screenplay for the movie *If The Shoe Fits.*

Her current projects include two television movies for ABC, a pilot for a series for ABC, and a new book for Bantam called SHADOWPLAY. She lives in Fresno, California with her son, Christopher.

CARLA SIMPSON has written nearly a dozen novels, including *Memory and Desire* (a Zebra Special Release), and *Always My Love* (a Pinnacle Super Release). She is the creator of a series of historical mysteries called *California Gold*, coming in 1992 from Zebra. Her next work of mainstream fiction will be SHADOWPLAY, written with Pamela Wallace, for Bantam. Carla lives in Coarsegold, California with her husband and family.

# FANFARE

## Now On Sale
## THE FIREBIRDS
☐ 29613-2 $4.99/5.99 in Canada
### by Beverly Byrne
author of THE MORGAN WOMEN

*The third and final book in Beverly Byrne's remarkable trilogy of passion and revenge. The fortunes of the House of Mendoza are stunningly resolved in this contemporary romance.*

## FORTUNE'S CHILD
☐ 29424-5 $5.99/6.99 in Canada
### by Pamela Simpson

*Twenty years ago, Christina Fortune disappeared. Now she's come home to claim what's rightfully hers. But is she an heiress . . . or an imposter?*

## SEASON OF SHADOWS
☐ 29589-6 $5.99/6.99 in Canada
### by Mary Mackey

*Lucy and Cassandra were polar opposites, but from the first day they met they became the best of friends. Roommates during the turbulent sixties, they stood beside each other through fiery love affairs and heartbreaking loneliness.*

🏷     🏷     🏷